AD 100

100 YEARS OF AVRAM DAVIDSON
100 Unpublished or
Uncollected Stories

Volume II

AVRAM DAVIDSON

COPYRIGHT

OR ALL THE SEAS WITH OYSTERS PUBLISHING

Welcome to *Or All The Seas with Oysters Publishing*, where you are about to embark upon a voyage into *The Avram Davidson Universe*. Within this Universe, you will find the works of Hugo, Edgar, and World Fantasy Award-winning and genre-transcending Avram Davidson, who is considered one of the finest authors of the 20th century, and the works of Grania Davis, Avram's onetime life partner and frequent writing collaborator, a dedicated preservationist of Avram's works, and a talented and acclaimed author in her own right. *Or All The Seas with Oysters Publishing* is dedicated to bringing both the out-of-print and the never-before published writings of both Avram and Grania back to life in print, audio, and e-book formats, and we look forward to making this treasured legacy accessible once again to readers, ranging from longtime fans and scholars to those just beginning this journey.

Avram's Universe is calling—we invite you to step inside: https://avramdavidson.com/join-fan-club/.

DEDICATION

To my Godfather Avram Davidson
To my Mother Grania Davis
To my Brother Ethan Davidson

Also a special thanks to Neil Gaiman, Paul Giamatti,
and Michael Swanwick, your praise of Avram has
inspired me more than you will ever know.

CONTENTS

EDITOR'S NOTE

Much of what makes Avram Davidson's work a joy to read also makes it a challenge to proofread. The flow of his internal and external dialogue, of his exposition, of his prose in general (in addition to his masterful twisty-turny storytelling), is a thing of beauty that as a reader, I feel viscerally. The elements that create the flow–his unconventional punctuation and word choices, vernacular dialogue, uniquely rendered turns of phrase–were also really hard to proofread! Just thinking about the sheer quantity of ellipses and m-dashes makes me anxious. But only the proofreading part of me feels that anxiety–as a reader, those elements work so, so well.

In compiling *AD 100*, Avram's abundance was also a joy and a challenge. This collection of 100 works proved too plentiful to be contained to one volume in a reasonable font. In order to be gentle on your eyes, we present to you *AD 100*, Volumes I and II.

The works included in *AD 100* originate from a variety of sources, from typed manuscripts with Avram Davidson's handwritten notes up and down the margins to impeccably edited book and magazine versions. Typos of all sorts existed in all sources and likely still exist in this *AD 100* version. We fixed what was obviously a mistake; left many things that might have been a mistake; and likely completely missed some mistakes along the way. Countless times I wished I could call up Avram (I feel I know him from these stories) and ask for clarification or suggest a slight edit. Sadly not having that option, I did my best.

—Neva Hickman, April 23, 2023

INTRODUCTION

If you have never read an Avram Davidson story put this book down immediately and buy a copy of *The Avram Davidson Treasury.* Start there. It's a fantastic collection of Avram's stories with introductions from Ursula K. Le Guin, Robert Silverberg, Poul Anderson, Guy Davenport, Alan Dean Foster, Gene Wolfe, Michael Swanwick, and many others. Once you have read *The Treasury* you will have a greater appreciation of *AD 100*. With that said there is no question *AD 100* includes some of Avram's greatest stories.

The *AD 100* collection has taken years of work and generations of love and care (and preservation) to make possible. I believe that Avram Davidson's writing is truly special, and I am confident that readers will find something to appreciate in this collection. There are lighthearted pieces that Avram wrote on a whim, science fiction, fantasy, mystery, Jewish stories and stories that impart valuable historical lessons, and many pieces that can't be characterized by a single genre. The collection includes tales set in Belize which served as the foundation for Avram's *Limekiller!* series, as well as difficult to find "Vergil Magus" and "Adventures in Unhistory" tales.

Avram Davidson is widely considered to be one of the great authors of the 20th century by literary figures such as Ray Bradbury and Neil Gaiman. In honor of his 100th birthday, we present the *AD 100* collection: a compilation of 100 of his previously unpublished and uncollected stories. This collection aims to showcase the breadth and depth of Davidson's work, and introduce his writing to both longtime fans and a new generation of readers. It's also an opportunity to see the evolution of a literary genius.

In terms of organization we decided to list the stories in chronological order *as best as we could*. In many cases the years that the stories were written are our best guesses. Often times the names of stories changed over the years and even notes on manuscripts might have the story listed in the wrong publication. Undoubtedly, we will learn that a story we thought never published was, or was published under a different name or maybe even published in a different magazine. Again we did the best we could. If we made a mistake we apologize in advance.

For some background, Avram Davidson was my godfather. He was a hero to me. He served in the US Navy as a medic from 1942-1945 seeing significant action in the Pacific, and with the Israeli forces in the 1948-1949 Arab-Israeli War. I adored him, but I didn't get to know him as an author until much later in life. He and my mother (Grania Davis) were close, and eventually married. She was entrusted with the rights to his literary works after he passed away in 1993.

She was his biggest fan; you could see how much she loved Avram Davidson, both the person and the author. This love came through in how hard she worked to publish collections of his works, keeping his legacy alive in *The Avram Davidson Treasury, The Investigations of Avram Davidson, The Other Nineteenth Century,* and finishing his novelette *The Boss in the Wall: A Treatise on the House Devil.*

The Irish have long been credited with preserving Western civilization through the efforts of monks who tirelessly copied and safeguarded written treasures. Similarly, Avram Davidson had his own dedicated preservationist in the form of his life partner.

When my mother passed away, the rights to Davidson's work fell onto me, his godchild. It wasn't until the start of the pandemic that I rediscovered my godfather's works in the attic. For the first time in my life, his works resonated with me, and I couldn't put his stories down. As I read through these stories, I experienced a range of emotions, from laughter, to joy, to tears.

Avram Davidson was often referred to as a rebel in the world of writing and known for intentionally breaking some of the most fundamental rules of literature. He would write page-long sentences and make interesting tangents that were ultimately unconnected to the main story.

It's a style that can take some getting used to, but you get unbelievably invested when you do. Yet it was precisely this style that allowed Davidson's depth of personality to come through in each of his pieces. His works are written as though you are sitting with Davidson himself, possibly over a cup of tea, and he is telling you about the stories and worlds he has created. His digressions are unparalleled, but that adds to what makes his stories as charming as they are. How he tells the stories becomes just as engaging as the stories themselves. As the *Encyclopedia of Science Fiction* put it, "Those who love his work, love it deeply."

After falling in love with his works, I learned that Avram Davidson had won multiple awards for his science fiction, fantasy, and mystery stories. He won a Hugo Award, an Edgar Award, three World Fantasy Awards, and dozens of others.

Davidson's work has gained a cult following and is considered to be highly influential in the field of science fiction and fantasy. Yet despite his talent and contributions to the genre, his works are often overlooked by the mainstream literary community. It is our hope that this is rectified.

This is the first Avram Davidson collection to be published in nearly two decades. As the custodian of his literary legacy, I am honored to have played a part in making it a reality. The fact that my son is also helping is a source of great pride and joy for me. I hope that this collection will not only introduce Avram Davidson's work to a new generation of readers, but also help to ensure that his legacy lives on for many years to come.

Whether you're a fan of science fiction and fantasy, or simply a lover of great storytelling, I highly encourage anyone interested in discovering more about Avram Davidson's work to take a look at this collection. I'm confident that you'll find something that resonates with you.

—Seth Davis, April 23, 2023

THE ROADS, THE ROADS, THE BEAUTIFUL ROADS

Originally published in Orbit *5, ed. Damon Knight (Berkley Publishing, 1969).*

The rumor that the already controversial new double-speed thruway would be closed to motorcycles was just that: a rumor: and it had already been officially denied—twice. Craig Burns thought now that perhaps it had been a mistake to deny it at all. Gave the rumor dignity...his mind absently sought a better word as he slipped through the milling crowd (*crowd*? almost a mob) on the steps and in the corridors of the new State Capitol Building. Currency! That was the word.

...gave the rumor currency...

Because, besides the usual knots of little old ladies with their *Trees, Yes! Thruway, No!* buttons, besides the inevitable delegations of hayseeds from Nowhere Flats who were either complaining that the thruway was scheduled to go too near their town or complaining that it wasn't scheduled to go near enough, besides the representatives of the rival guild—the urban planners—with their other ideas and their briefcases and their indoor-pale skins (so different from the ruddy glow or tan of a real out-in-all-weather man; besides all these (and including as always some Hire More Minority protesters), today it seemed as though all the motorcycle freaks in the state were on hand. On hand, and out for blood. Well, well, what the Hell. It added a little color to the scene. And wouldn't make any difference at all, in the end: Gypsy Jokers with long hair, Hell's Angels who were merely shaggy, Brave Bulls in their Viking-horned crash helmets, the Gentlemen of the Road, so super-groomed and—

With the blank face and absent-minded slouch he had learned to be the best thing for slipping through angry crowds, Craig managed to get almost to the door of the Committee Room without being recognized. And even then, with a pleasant smile, he succeeded in getting inside before the reporters and cameramen got to him. With an apologetic gesture. No point in antagonizing Media, generally so helpful in picking out and publicizing the more outstanding of the anti-highways people and thus showing them up for the nuts and oddballs that they really were. But it made little sense to stop in the middle of them just to grant an on-the-spot interview.

In fact, Burns thought, taking one last look, head half-turned, it made no sense at all.

Horns on their crash helmets, for God's sake!

Just as some composers never tire of playing their own music, so Craig Burns never tired of driving over the beautiful highways he...well...he and his Department...had created. It had been a labor of love building them, seeing each one through from the preliminary survey through actual construction to the time he liked best of all. When the roads were ready to go but not yet open to the public. When he could drive along and drive alone for miles...and miles... sometimes for hundreds of miles. Just Highway Chief Craig Burns and his car and his beautiful roads, with their lovely and intricate bypasses and cloverleafs and underpasses, slow and steady when he felt like it, revving it up and gaging the niceties of the straight stretches or the delightfully calculated curves when he felt like it. Over and under and around and across and back and under and—

—nobody on the whole highway but *him*.

It was better than a woman. It was better even than the power of office. It was just about the best thing there was.

Sometimes, smiling to himself, he wondered if he really didn't sometimes push through new road plans just for the sheer pleasure of this, even if the new roads weren't really needed. But the smile was for the joke, the secret, private little joke, for there was really no such thing as a new road which wasn't needed. And as for the things which weren't so nice...the stupid, stupid, jack-ass things which people did with the beautiful roads...crowding and packing and jamming them with their cars and trucks and motorcycles and station wagons...stupid people, stupid jerks, jack-asses! —so that all kinds of things had to be done, afterwards, to the sweet and clean and lovely new roads—

As for that, Craig didn't care to think about that, much. It made him get that hot feeling in the skin of his face, that surging, raging feeling around his heart. That sort of thing, he left mostly to the others in the Department. And everybody else in the Department was the others. He'd created. Let them mar it, since it had to be marred. Changing routes, adding, subtracting, closing down, chopping and changing—let *them* do it. It wasn't his fault.

Probably the hearing had taken more out of him than he'd realized. And so damned unnecessary. Legislative hearings! After all, what did the legislature have to do with it? The very state constitution granted the Highways Department all the authority it needed. It could condemn property and pay what it knew to be right and reasonable. It could say where the roads would go and where they wouldn't go. What shape they'd take. How to design and how to build. The roads, the roads were engineered beautifully. It was the stupid bastard *people* who were engineered wrong. Tiring him out and confusing him with their hearings and demonstrations. No wonder he'd missed the Hadley turnoff. That is, well, yeah, sure, he must have missed it. This cloverleaf was *after* the Hadley turn-off. Well, nothing to do but turn around and go back. The afternoon had yea, you bet, upset him. But what in hell did the rest of the people have to be upset about? All that crap about highways de*hum*anizing, for Christ's sake.—Take this next turn.

No!

Well, had no choice, stupid jerk back there zooming along and forcing him—All that crap about highways exhausting, hypnotizing, confusing…All that crap. Look at this lovely cloverleaf. And this neat tunnel, here. No, but it wasn't the *highway*, for God's sake, it was just that stupid—

Okay, then, he just couldn't remember this tunnel. So what? All the highways in the State—*Okay*, that was that, *out* of the tunnel! Nothing hard about that! And back on the cloverleaf again.

*Clo*verleaf? There wasn't supposed to be—And hadn't he had a clear glimpse, in the shadows and the blinking lights (make mental note: report defective lights) of another tunnel branching off back—Hadley turnoff. Great. Just tired out after that damned hearing, crowd, mob, reporters, motorcycle gangs, what the hell. What the *hell!* Cloverleaf! Tunnel! Tunnel branching off, no he didn't want it, well for God's *sake!* Here he *was.* Lights bad, lights very bad, lights worse. No lights. No traffic, either, for that matter. Must be, yes, certainly: *was:* a discontinued branch tunnel. Vague recollection. Bad drainage. Turned out not to fit in with new, unforeseen traffic pattern subsequently developed. Bad air. Bad smell. Car gone dead! Flip on the radio, signal for the Department's very own high-speed tow-car and ever-ready private Departmental emergency limousine. Radio dead. Of course. Tunnel. Okay. Okay. *Okay.* Get out, walk.

Seemed, it seemed to Craig that it was, must, had to be shorter going ahead than going back. A car. Stopped. He waited for the head to be stuck out of the window, the smashed and dusty window. Motorcycle on its side. Station wagon almost a third of the way up the ramp. What crazy —Of course. Word had gotten around, sure. And those in the know had taken their old hulks and abandoned them here. Oh boy. Thought they'd save money, avoid tickets, ah. Another think coming. *Look* at them all! And what a stink, what—

Definitely, someone, something, was moving up ahead there. Half in the shadows cast by strange, dim light. A man, sure enough. Black leather jacket, filthy jeans, obscene feet, and—

Craig Burns turned and fled, his screams echoing, echoing.

Behind him, unhurried, assured, horns jutting from the helmet on his head, the newest minotaur followed upon his newest victim.

BIG SAM

Originally published in Alchemy and Academe, *ed. Anne McCaffery (Del Rey/Ballantine, 1970).*

Ellen heard Big Sam before she ever saw him—but not much before. He was one of the group of men standing around the aluminum keg of draft at a wedding (Jinny MacKew to Lew Harris) and she, moving around with an air of being less alone than she actually felt, passed by as a deep voice was saying, "No, I don't believe in that. I wouldn't do any asking and I wouldn't do any telling." Something made her give a quick glance around just before the deep voice had finished, and so she saw him. He was big and hulking and he looked just a bit sleepy. But he looked nice. Later on she was to say that she drew a circle around him with an imaginary finger and told herself, *That one is mine.* It was early spring.

The mountain county had a smaller population than it had had a hundred years ago, which hadn't been many even then, but the modern world kept catching up with it at intervals; isolated as it was, still, it couldn't escape that. A new office machine had just lately been installed at the phone company and as nobody already living in the county knew how to operate it, Ellen—who had begun to feel bored and out of things where she was—had been persuaded to accept a transfer, even though it meant giving up her share of the pleasant-enough three-girl apartment and moving two hundred miles north. "Two men to every female up there," the personnel man said, smiling to show he wasn't being offensive, and, "Well, I certainly can't pass up a chance like *that*," Ellen answered, almost without reflecting, but also smiling not seriously.

Afterwards, when her roommates asked her how come, she only said, "It's time for a change." So here she was, in this country hotel, which the wedding party had all to itself, the start of the summer season still a couple of months away.

"Yeah, but suppose there *is*, well, *something*, I don't just mean like, other guys, other women before. But something else," an older fellow, probably the one who'd first asked the question at the beer keg, went on.

"Like what?" the tall and husky one wanted to know. He sipped at his glass.

"Oh…I don't know…maybe a baby…maybe an old trouble with the law…Hasn't the other person got a right—"

"Yeah, how about that, Sam?" asked a third man.

Sam shrugged. "Marriage looks tough enough—from all I *hear*, I mean—" They laughed. "Maybe nobody ever finds out about this premarital whatever-it-was. Maybe by the time they do, they wouldn't care all that much."

Then a fourth man said, "Okay, Sam, you persuaded us: you get married, don't tell her you had a baby." Everyone burst out laughing, Sam with a great big *ha ha*! and Ellen walked calmly on her way to get a ginger ale and a sandwich. This was not a canapé and cocktail kind of wedding party.

By and by Ellen said to the other girl from the office who was at the table, "Who's the guy with the red tie back there? The one who's standing by the beer?"

Mrs. Bartlett, who was a girl by courtesy only, pushed back some gray hair, looked, and said, still chewing, "Who, Sambo? Sam Bock, I call him Sambo, everybody else calls him Big Sam. He's got that gas station out on the South Road. I think he goes to L.A. or somewhere in the winters, just keeps open for the summer trade, hunters, tourists, *you* know. Not enough business, hardly, in the winter, to pay both the stations here in town to stay open. Nice guy. You tried this liver sausage? It's *good*." Mrs. Bartlett was kind of slow, but she always managed to get there, and after a while she introduced them, she called to him—he was off standing by himself by that time—and he shambled over and she introduced him to Ellen. Then she said, "Don't they *feed* you down there in L.A., Sam? You always turn up thin as a rail. Ellen, fix him a sandwich, *I* am going to get some *beer*." Then she went over to the keg herself, leaving the two of them more or less alone.

After a while Sam, who hadn't been very talkative, said, "You like drunk parties?"

"Not very much."

"Didn't think so. This one's about to start." So they went out and went for a ride and he showed her a lot of places she hadn't yet seen out in the country and even the crumbling old joss house from the gold rush days, on the other side of town, when the coolies used to wash the leftovers the American miners wouldn't bother with. Then he drove down the South Road and showed her his gas station and the house behind it.

"I turn up in plenty of time each year to get things ready for the season," he said. "I like to do things slow and easy. But I have to be quick in the summers, you bet."

He already had an arm around her shoulders. Nothing offensive, just friendly in an awkward but nice way. She thought he was moving just fast enough right now. "That's an odd-looking house," she said. "Is it historical too?" He said, well, it was old, but in good shape—roof would hold up a whole winter's snow. He didn't ask her in then, just drove back to town and they had coffee and they made a date for later in the week.

The manager was a little annoyed at first when Ellen quit. "Have to go through that all over again...new girl," he said. But wasn't really angry. "Lots of women keep on working after they're married," he pointed out. Ellen said she didn't believe in that. She believed that a woman's place was with her husband. "Will wonders never cease," the manager said, rubbing his hand over his bald spot. So there was another wedding and another wedding party and once more Sam and Ellen left before it got drunk. They drove down to Sacramento and got on a plane and had a short honeymoon in Mexico, in a place called Rosarito Beach. The nice old lady who ran the motel had a parrot who walked around in the yard like a chicken and there were horses galloping in the sand. Ellen loved it, but she understood that they could stay only a few days, and so back they came.

It surprised her to learn how domestic she could become; in fact, after a while the sight of Sam shambling around made her a bit impatient. "Shoo!" she said. "Scat! You take care of getting the station ready, and the outside of the house. *I'll* manage the inside, all by myself." He laughed but did as she said, and everything worked out fine. She swept and she sewed and she did some painting and she aired the linens and the huge piles of thick blankets and, observing how he liked things, she canned and jarred and preserved a mountain of food. She wondered about a few things, but didn't ask. She trusted Sam.

Gradually Ellen came to pick up the rhythm of the way things went on the long summer days. There was a busy time early in the mornings with hunters and fishermen going farther back into the mountains. The tourists and family vacationing groups would be along later. Now and then she looked out of the window and saw Sam's big form shuffling along from gas pumps to car front windows, then to the cash register in the tiny "office." Kids trotting out to the bathrooms. Sometimes nobody at all, just Sam sitting slouched in a chair. Sometimes horns would blow. And blow. Gradually she learned to ignore that. If it went on *too* long, she might throw up a window and yell, "Closed!" If, as it seldom was, a real emergency, she would sell the people the contents of one of the cans of gasoline Sam had filled. "My husband had to go someplace and I don't know how to work the pump. This will get you into town, anyway."

Once...the first time...she did ask him, "How come you just took off to go hunting and fishing?"

He smiled, stretched hugely. "Felt like it," he said. And gathered her into an enormous hug.

"Stop it," she said. "You'll crack my ribs. *Sam!*" But wasn't angry. Everybody had to have *some* fault or funny way. After all, he put up with her when she chased him outside. "I have *work* to do," she'd say. "Men get in the way."

The summer passed so quickly, and one day the CLOSED sign went up and stayed up. Now Ellen began to wonder about the winter in L.A. or wherever it was. Would Sam expect her to pack and move? What, exactly, or even approximately, *were* they going to do? But he didn't say and she didn't ask, determined not to be one of those suspicious or even nosey wives. Just went on with her work about the house. She cooked. And Sam tucked it away appreciatively, as though he was able now for the first time to sit back and really enjoy it. They had few visitors on the South Road nowadays, few cars even went by. Sometimes Ellen wondered about her husband's background. He never mentioned any family. Never one to talk your ear off, he was talking even less. After supper, dozing by the radio, he might snap awake and ask, "Any more chops left?"

"I'll heat them, they're all greasy by now—"

Down they went, grease and all.

"You're putting on weight, Sam."

He just smiled. She just smiled back. It was very nice, way out alone there, just the two of them. They were both sleeping longer, going to bed earlier, relaxing after the short but busy season. There was a limit, however, to how long Ellen could remain in bed. She had to be up and doing after a while, fixing huge breakfasts of bacon and eggs and steak and pancakes. "Where do you *put* it all?" she asked, curiously. He yawned, held out his plate for more. Lunch had become dinner and supper was immense. "You better take some exercise," she said, just a bit critically. "Look how your belt is digging in." Sam's only answer was to open the belt and lie down on the sofa for a nap. She managed without him, doing the dishes, a million of them though there seemed to be. It was nice being by herself in the kitchen. In fact, afterwards, when she sat down in the living room with one of the piles of magazines which, bought out of habit when in town, she'd had no time to really read till now—in fact, Sam snoring on the sofa seemed a bit...well, more than a bit...in the way.

"Shame on you," she told herself.

It was becoming a nuisance to tug him awake to shamble off to bed. One morning he didn't get up for breakfast. She called him softly a few times. He didn't answer, then he just mumbled, turned over, snored. It was well after dinnertime when, following many peeps into the bedroom, she saw him open his eyes a little way and look at her. "Ellen..."

"Yes, Sam?"

He almost closed his eyes all the way shut again, but he didn't, quite. "You *know*...don't you?"

It was like something from one of the magazines, one of the stories, only different, his asking it like that. She *did* know, and in that minute she realized that she had known for quite a while now. She understood now just what the pile of thick blankets and the well-filled shelves, the stout snow roof and thick walls, were for. She knew there wasn't going to be any L.A. for them, and never had been for Sam. "Yes, Sam," she said.

He gave a deep sigh of contentment. His eyes slipped shut and in another minute he was sound asleep again. She quietly closed the door of the darkened room and went away. After all, there were all kinds of marriages. After all, she had a lot of work to do. She had to get all kinds of stuff ready for the freezer and for the preserving kettle. After all, Sam would be hungry, he would be very hungry, when he awakened in the spring.

RITE OF SPRING

Originally published in Orbit 8, *ed. Damon Knight, (Berkley Medallion Books, 1970).*

"The winter meat is about all *gone*," said Mrs. Robinson.

"So's the winter, for that matter," her husband said. "Al*most*..."

"...*and* the potatoes..."

Mr. Robinson got up rather quickly and looked in the bin. "Guess there's enough, though. I can do without greens with my meat. If I have to. But I sure hate to do without potatoes."

"Yes," she said, drily. "I've noticed."

He looked at her, as though for a moment mildly surprised or puzzled. Then, with a faint smile, he put his arm around her. For a moment she stood there, her head bent and touching his. With a little sound of content, next, she moved away. She gestured toward one of the cabinets. "There'll be all *that* to do."

He nodded. "Not time *yet*, though...Alice..."

"Yes?"

Mr. Robinson coughed. "Boy was trying to get in the girl's room again last night."

She whirled around, quicker than you might have thought. A look of alarm or concern faded from her face. "He didn't, though..."

Mr. Robinson shook his head. "Scuttled off quick enough, he heard me coming." And did quick brief mimicry of himself, bleary-eyed, clutching an imaginary bathrobe, coughing a rheumy, old-man's-nighttime cough, and shuffling along noisily. Abruptly he stopped and straightened up, ceased to be an ill and probably querulous old man, was once again stalwart, thickset, and vigorous, for all his grey hairs. He and his wife chuckled.

"Well," he said, "it's natural enough. Healthy young boy. Pretty young girl."

"*That*," she said, "is beside the point—You speak to him, now, Henry. I'll speak to her."

"Done and done and Bradstreet," said Mr. Robinson. He looked out the tightly closed windows. "Getting to be about that time of the season. Fact, it *is* that time of the season. Oh, I shouldn't be surprised...any day now...Boy out to the shed?"

His wife nodded. As he started getting into his sweater and jacket, she said, "Button up warm now."

Mr. Robinson stepped out the back door and started across the yard. The remnants of last year's vegetable garden lay stark and dead beneath his feet. Looking down, he said, "Well, old friend, we'll put new life into you very soon now." He pushed open the door of a weathered and sturdy old outbuilding. Its smell was cold and faint. Hanging from a beam was a block and tackle and rope and chain. Mr. Robinson pulled, tested, made adjustments, grunted his approval, and went out.

The sound of sawing and chopping ceased as he appeared in the door of the shed. "You doing pretty good, Roger," he said. "Yes, sir, you doing pretty good, Mr. Ames."

Roger picked up an armful of wood and carried it over and stacked it. He wiped his face. He had on it a few freckles and a few pimples and a few hairs. Mr. Robinson put a hand on the boy's biceps and doubled up the boy's arm. "That's good, too," he said. "Better than lifting dumbbells."

A sudden look of cunning came over Roger's stolid face. He swiftly seized the older man in a wrestling hold, heaved. They swayed together for a moment. Then, suddenly, Roger lay on the sawdusty floor and Mr. Robinson was pinning his shoulders to it. "Can't do it yet, can you?" he asked.

"Hey," said Roger. The grip relaxed, the boy started to get up, Mr. Robinson flopped him down again. "Pretty good for an old man with one foot in the grave and another on a banana peel...*Now*...I got something to tell you, young Roger Ames, and you are going to listen to it, too. You were trying to sneak into Betty's room last night. Weren't you. Yes you were." Roger's face, only faintly flushed, still, from the wrestling, now flooded as red as his shirt. "Now you listen. I am not some old prune who doesn't know that females are built different from men. I know all about that. You ever learn as much about that as me, you be doing pretty well. *I* know what's fun and natural between the sects. *But*. And here's the point, you see, boy. There is a *time*. You been *told* that. And when that time comes, why fine. That's what makes the world go round. That's what makes the grasses grow. The flowers bloom. But that time has not yet come for you. You just *wait*, now, till it does. *I* waited. It won't kill you." He got up.

Roger scrambled up as well. He looked embarrassed and, at the same time, respectful. And, for the present moment, just a bit uncertain. Mr. Robinson said, "Well, now. You've cut wood. You've wrestled. So now let's see you practice catching for a while." And for a while there, in the winter-stale garden between the old house and the outbuildings, he watched and instructed Roger as Roger practiced catching. Somewhere in the house a little bell rang.

Mrs. Robinson was putting things on a tray with attention and dispatch at the same time as she was speaking with Betty. "Toast, butter, jam, honey, cocoa," she counted. "Bless me, *how* that woman does eat. It's a pleasure to behold... cookies...is there any piece of crisp bacon, cold, from breakfast? She is *very* fond of that...What was I saying...Oh, there's always so much to think about and to *do* at this time of the year..."

"About Roger and, *you* know," Betty said: a slim young

girl, rather blossomy about the bosom, with a pale-and-pink and shiny face. "Well, I never encouraged him. I don't even... well...oh...I guess I do *like* him okay, but, oh, sort of like a brother, if you know what I mean, Grandma Robinson." The little bell rang and rang.

Grandma Robinson said that she did know what Betty meant. A little smile crinkled the corners of her mouth and eyes. "As for 'a brother,' well, my, many a girl says that, until a certain time comes, and *then* her mind gets changed quick enough." She deftly laid a neatly ironed napkin over the tray and picked it up. Betty went ahead and opened doors. "Oh, I've no reason to complain of you, dear," said the older woman. "You've been as nice as any girl who's ever lived with us. And I'm sure your mother will be pleased, too. Because it's just as she *said*, child, it's just as she *said*. It's hard raising children right, in the city, teaching them the right ways, the old ways, the things to *know*...to *do*...and, for *that* matter, *not* to do..."

Betty said, "And all those things, you know, in the woods, too..."

Mrs. Robinson turned her face, slightly creased with the effort of carrying the tray, and nodded over her shoulder. Betty knocked on the last door. There was a noise from inside, and she opened the door, standing aside for the other to go in.

"Well, Mrs. Machick," said Grandma Robinson, cheerfully, "and here we are, with your half-past ten snack." The room was clean, but it did not smell so.

"Half-past *ten?* You mean more like half-past *twelve*," the woman sitting on the bed said. She was fat. She was very, very fat. Betty deftly pulled up a little table. Mrs. Robinson set the tray down. "No, dear, it's only half-past ten," she said.

"*Sure* it is," said Mrs. Machick, in a low, tight voice. "Oh, sure." She had a small, tight, tiny-tiny mouth, set into the middle of a vast, loose face. Her eyes darted quickly between the lady of the house and the girl, but she didn't meet their own eyes, and then she had eyes only for the tray and what was on it.

"Now. Is that all right?" Mrs. Robinson cocked her head.

"Could you spare it?" the woman on the bed asked. Her brows made quirky little motions. She sighed. She shrugged. All down the front of her nightgown were food stains.

"Now, if there's anything else you'd like, just ring your little bell for it," Mrs. Robinson said, without the slightest trace of annoyance. "If we have it, we'll be glad to bring it to you."

"*Sure* you would," Mrs. Machick said. "*Oh,* yeah." She fluttered her nostrils with the breath of the long-suffering, gave her frowzy head a little shake, and began to feed.

Betty and Grandma closed the door and exchanged faint sighs. They were halfway across the front room when a low whistle was heard from outside. They looked at each other, wide-eyed and open-mouthed, then turned and tiptoed swiftly to the windows, not touching the lace curtains. A bird was on the ground in front of the house, investigating the sere remains of last year's grass. Out from behind an evergreen came Roger. It was a marvel how, body crouched, on the tips of his toes, hands out just so, how swiftly and how silently he sped; for all his size and all.

It was over in a matter of seconds.

Everybody cried out, but not very loudly. Roger, followed by Mr. Robinson, turned toward the house. Grandma and Betty bustled about, taking things from drawers and closets. The men came in, Roger with a wide and surprised-silly grin on his face. "Welcome, welcome, first harbinger of spring," said Mrs. Robinson; and, "Sir, we bid you welcome," her husband said, with a slight bow. She poured wine into a silver goblet. The bird's head peeped out between the boy's fingers. He held them over the goblet, as though he were offering the bird a drink. Mr. Robinson took its head between the thumb and forefinger of his left hand and with his right hand he took the shears Betty gave him and cut off its head.

The bright blood made little swirls in the pale wine, till Mrs. Robinson, with a silver spoon on the handle of which were quaint and curious engravings much more than half-obscured, stirred the goblet. Then the liquid turned pink. She gave everybody a spoonful of it.

For a moment the house was utterly still.

Then Betty gave her lips an absentminded smack. Then she went absolutely pale. Her eyes flew to Roger. From her now white lips came a sound like the rim of a glass being squeaked. His mouth fell open. His eyes bulged. She fled the room in an instant. The door to the hall slammed behind her. Then another door slammed—the back one. But in between the two times, Roger, uttering a noise between a growl and a howl, had begun his pursuit. There was a crash. ("Didn't even try to open *that* one," Mr. Robinson said.) There was a cry, first shrill, then full-throated. There were two noises, quick together, as it might be thud-*thump* or thump-*thud*.

"Well, now," said Mr. Robinson, gently. "He did wait. And it didn't kill him." There were some more noises. A lot more. "Isn't killing *her*, either, presumably," he added.

"It always pays to do things right," his wife said. "You'll get some good greens and potatoes and garden truck *this* year, I shouldn't wonder."

He gave a slow, reflective nod. "You decided what kind of annuals you want out front?" he asked. She started to reply; then, with a tongue click of self-reproof, flung open the front door and emptied the goblet in a wide-scattered toss. Her lips moved. "*There*," she said, after a moment, closing up. The two older people looked at each other in quiet contentment. They sighed. Nodded briskly.

"Plenty to do," he said. "Even before *those* two are ready to help us. Got to get all those knives and cleavers out of the cabinet and sharpen—Oh. *Oh*, yes. Before I forget." He fetched a pad and an envelope, ink bottle and pen, sat. "To the Editor, Dear Sir," he wrote, in his neat, slow hand. "This morning at"—he pursed his lips, consulted his pocket watch, considered—"at about a quarter-to eleven we sighted the first robin of spring in our front yard. Wonder if this is any kind of a record for recent years? Would be glad to hear from any devoted 'robin-watchers' and followers of other good old ways and customs, who may write me directly if they care to."

In her room across the other side of the house, fat Mrs. Machick rang her little bell.

THE CAPTAIN M. CAPER

Originally published in Ellery Queen's Mystery Magazine, *March 1970. Avram's title was "The Man Without a Necktie."*

Abel Serles hurried along Sixth Avenue. Partly he was looking for an answer to the problem of Sally and partly he was looking for a place where he could buy a necktie for not more than a dollar. Without realizing it in his haste, he let the necktie move into first place and then stopped thinking about Sally altogether.

Usually Abel Serles did not wear a necktie, nor did he usually wear a suitcoat.

There had once been a time when he had regularly worn both—both pressed to a fare-thee-well; but then the irresistible force met a movable object: Serles, who had been writing evenings and Sundays for over a year, had in one week sold not just his first story but his first three stories! —and spectacularly failed to meet the quota required of all sales personnel at Banting Brothers. It had been a case of you-can't-fire-me, I-quit—and the firm had let him have it *his* way because old Mr. J. B. Banting didn't approve of unemployment insurance, to which he, Abel Serles, would have been entitled if he'd been discharged.

Old J. B. Banting didn't approve of most of the social changes which had occurred in the U.S.A. since John Quincy Adams had died on the floor of the House with an Abolitionist petition in his pocket and what has been described as "a smile like the Peace of God" on his face.

At the present moment, however, Abel was thinking of a different kind of unemployment insurance. Either Seventh or Eighth Avenue might have been a better bet for what he was seeking—though absolutely not Fifth Avenue or any of the streets farther east—not for a dollar necktie! However, Sixth Avenue was on his way, uptown toward West 44th Street and the lobby of the Algonquin Hotel; and he scanned every store window as he zipped along, not without some rueful recollection of the drunk who searched the north side of the street for the quarter he'd dropped on the south side, because the light on the north side—

The old chestnut ceased abruptly to be applicable as he saw, between a store selling factory-rejected classical phonograph records at $1.50 each and a shop which printed "newspapers" with the customer's own name in the headline of his choice (*Manny Hits Town, Pretty Girls Leave*), a place selling just what he was looking for: NECKTIES! NECKTIES! GOING OUT OF BUSINESS! 99¢ AND UP.

The "and up" he could forego, but the sales tax would cut into his money. Somehow, Serles felt, the Algonquin was not the place where he wanted to go grubbing in his pockets for loose change. He did the grubbing right then and there, finding—thank the Lord!—enough odd pennies to cover the tax and give him four one-dollar bills back for his fiver.

"I'll take this one," he said, not quite snatching the very first cravat he saw, this first one being an imitation plaid in colors gaudy enough to cause another rising of the clans; but the first one he saw which would pass muster. The Algonquin wasn't all that particular—and Godfrey Bland wasn't particular at all. Not about neckties, at least.

"Yessir, very nice, how about some—"

"Don't bother to wrap it up." Serles seized the tie and strode out. It was hot in the street, which was being ripped up again, and the air was thick with asphalt smells and automobile fumes. He adjusted the tie as he continued his rapid pace north. It was 4:15; Godfrey Bland always arrived at 4:00 and would have had at least two drinks by now; he would leave at 5:00 for his home in Great Shores, Long

Island. It was imperative that Serles should meet him after he had somewhat unwound from a hard day at the literary agency—shouting his demands for escalator clauses and movie, TV, stage, radio, ballet, and Punch-and-Judy rights for the United Kingdom, Australasia, and Luxembourg over the transcontinental and transatlantic telephones as if trying out for the finals in a hog-calling contest—and before he started winding up again for the trip back to Great Shores, where dwelt Mrs. Godfrey Bland (who raised show collies) and where whatever he was likely to find cooking on the stove was likelier to be for the collies than for Godfrey Bland.

Yes, between 4:15 and 4:45 was the best time to be in the Algonquin lobby—if you were Abel Serles, that is, and wanting to see Godfrey Bland.

For weeks after his first and tripartite success as an author, Serles had stuck so close to his typewriter all day that when he emerged in the evenings for food and frolic, all the dry-cleaning places were closed; but such was his zeal, his pleasure, and his absorption in his new profession that it was almost a month before he had occasion to discover that they were all closed. His tie and suitcoat, which he'd donned automatically each night, were by then pretty bad. He had flung them in the closet he kept chiefly for flinging things into, kicked off his no longer glossy Thom McCanns, and—shirt-sleeved and stocking-footed—invested in the far, far less formal kind of clothes sold in little stores that never closed, the kind of clothes (he realized with exultation and a sense of infinite release) that he had always wanted to always wear.

And "*Abe!*" she had said. "*You look so* different *tonight!*"

That had been five years ago. Both suitcoat and necktie had been cleaned since then, but not frequently and not recently. Five years..."A lustrum!" as Frederic H. Beard would have said—and did, when opportunity offered. Old Fred Beard, muffled to the eyebrows in unshorn hair and whiskers, cosuitor (so to speak) of Sally—Old Freddie Beard, perpetual student, financing his perpetual studies by writing learned articles about the hilts, tangs, blades, bindings, and what-else-have-you of Japanese swords, on which he was perhaps the nation's leading authority—Old Freddie, how he would snort and how he would scorn if he knew on what purpose his former schoolmate was now hastening.

Stopping just long enough to adjust the necktie, Abel turned into West 44th Street. He hurried on, cursing the erratic memory which had allowed him to remember the necessity for a suitcoat—wrinkled though it was, it would serve—but to forget the equally necessary tie. The lapse was costing him the price of at least one drink, but that couldn't be helped: without coat and tie he could not be served in the Algonquin, and without being served in the Algonquin he could not hope successfully to talk business with Godfrey Bland.

Thirty years past, the Algonquin had been the height of fashion as a literary and theatrical center. Abel Serles had not seen its lobby then. In fact, he had barely been born. Alexander Woollcott was just a name to him, FPA only a set of initials. Unlearned as he was in hotel lobby décor of that period, it nevertheless seemed to him that the place could hardly have changed much, and he liked its small and crowded old-fashioned lobby. He also liked the fact that you could get drinks served to you right there—but he didn't like either a tithe as much as did Godfrey Bland, who was sitting in his usual place at his usual hour: heavy-set, redfaced cherub with curly gray hair, looking into his drink as if it might be a crystal ball and he, crystal-gazer, seeing therein strange things which for all their seeming strangeness yet failed to surprise.

Also, as usual, on the table in front of him was a half-eaten sandwich. A cynic might suppose it was fortification against finding nothing to eat in Great Shores except perhaps a pot of bubbling horse-meat intended for the supper of Great Shores Midlothian Dukie and the latter's current consorts; but Godfrey had another explanation. "It's not the booze that does you in," he said, *"It's the not-eating.* The boys and girls whose livers turn green and kick out on them, it's not because they drank, you know. It's because they forgot to eat! Malnutrition! But not me. No, sir. True enough, when Godfrey Bland eats he always drinks—but when Godfrey Bland drinks he always eats!"

Frederic H. Beard, hearing Abel repeat this once, had raised his eyebrows. "In other words, 'A sandwich a day keeps the A.A. away.' Maybe so, maybe so."

Bland looked up as Abel came to his table, and thrust out his lower jaw in greeting. "Hello, Abe. What are you doing here with this bunch of phonies?"

Abel knew better than to presume on Bland's description of the Algonquin habitués, being well aware that Bland reserved such criticism for himself. "The West Side for morning, the East Side for afternoon, and the Village for evening," Abel said.

Bland cocked his head and moved his mouth reflectively. "Well, as philosophy, it has its faults. But as an aphorism, it'll do. Emil! What are you having, Abe?"

Emil, white-jacketed, hovered over them. Abel had a *shtick* he'd been waiting for the proper occasion to use. It might as well be this one. "A double Demerara," he said.

Emil beamed, Bland stared. "What in the name of Vishnu is even a single Demerara?" he demanded.

"Very fine rum, sir, from British Guiana," Emil said, *"Very* fine rum. No ice, of course, sir."

"Of course not," Abel said virtuously, no sacrifice being too great for his art.

Bland looked impressed, as he was meant to be. "Well, I suppose you might as well drink it while you can still get it," he said. "Look what happened to Cuban cigars...British

Guiana, hey? A government headed by a *dentist*, for crying out loud! You know what's the trouble with dentists, Abe? They've all got inferiority complexes because they're not doctors."

Emil returned with the double Demerara and a drink to replace the one which Bland had by this time finished, which was nominally a martini—although Abel knew that no vermouth was ever allowed to come near it—and Bland drank up, with a gesture to Abel to do likewise.

The rum wasn't bad, although Abel would rather have had it with lots of coke, lots of ice, and half of a lime.

He had paid for this round, allowed Bland to pay for the next. Whether or not he would be able to afford the third, Abel was uneasily unsure. Perhaps it wouldn't come to that. And Bland babbled on.

"I don't know what's the matter with most of you writers," he said, waving a plump hand to a publisher's editor who had just come in. "Think you're a bunch of artists, for crying out loud. Want to know something? You're not. Artists either have patrons or else they go and starve in a garret and are happy about it. Writers don't want to starve, not that I blame 'em, and they don't have patrons, not that they should. Writers are—most of 'em—*small businessmen*—that's what they are. None of you want to admit it, though. Some of you, you can write fine, but you can't meet a deadline to save your lives. Now, what kind o' way is that to run a small business?

"Tom Carp, you take Tom Carp, a *lovely* writer. But—look—I come to him, I call him up, I say 'Tom, I've got an assignment for you. Two sex novels. Good terms, good advance. Six months to write 'em. You can use a pseudonym. What do you say?' 'Swell,' he says, 'swell.' And then I find out he's got three other assignments, he's two months past the deadline on one, a *year*—for crying out loud!—past the deadline on the other, and *two years* past the deadline on the third."

He picked up his glass, moodily set it down again. "So of

course I had to say, 'Sorry, Tom.' Made me feel rotten, because he's a *lovely* writer. Too good for sex novels, but, then, there you are. Now, I've got four or five guys I could get like *that*. Clients of mine, too, which Tom isn't, any more than you are. And they'd meet the deadlines with time to spare. So what's the trouble? The trouble is, they're rotten writers, that's the trouble. Good enough to write one of these crummy little items that pay $500 for all rights. But not good enough for what Clay and Curtain have in mind. They're branching out, had good luck with Crime and Science Fiction; now they want to try Sex. Of course they want something better than ordinary hackwork."

Godfrey Bland brooded a long moment. Then he smiled, somewhat twistedly. Another of his troubles was, he said, that business was too good. All his clients, the topnotch ones, were up to their navels in contracts for books. Meanwhile, he had contracts of his own to supply books for eager publishers.

He had called up or tried to call up other writers, clients of other agents, or acting as their own agents—he wasn't greedy for the measly ten percent—and with what results? Bob Bigelow couldn't take time off from his play, Saunders Pierce (*né* Siegfried Poltz, and who could blame him) was doing a series of biographies of famous women for a hardcover publisher, Nissim Stone was in Spain doing research, and so it went.

"Hmmm, yes, I see your problem," Abel Serles said. He sighed.

"So*phis*ticated sex novels, that's what these have to be."

"Hmm, yes, I see—"

"Not just *love*—love is for animals, only human beings can appreciate lust. But so*phis*ticated lust, you understand."

"Well—"

Abruptly, Godfrey Bland ceased staring into his glass of gin, swung his head around and looked Abel Serles in the face. "What are *you* doing these days, Abe?" he asked.

"I'm working on some short stories, Godfrey."

The literary agent jerked his head back, stared at the younger man reproachfully. "Short *stories*? What a disgusting phrase. Short stories haven't been economical since—since—well, not for years. All right, I grant you" his tone was indulgent, "that short stories are more economical than poems. True. But nobody tries to make a living out of poems. Novels!" He prodded Serles with a fat red knuckle. "*Novels*! That's where the money is!"

Things were beginning to move. Bland almost always had assignments to give out, and when he didn't, he knew who did.

"Sex novels, you mean?" Serles asked, his tone somewhat amused, somewhat scornful—and his mind on his unpaid rent and empty refrigerator.

Bland raised a cautionary finger. "So*phis*ticated sex novels. Otherwise, why would I bother? What are you worrying about? Your reputation? Use a pseudonym. I think we've got a couple of house-names you could choose from, or make up your own. What the hell, fellow, *you're* sophisticated! Anyone who knows a brand of booze *I* never heard of, *has* to be. One thousand on signing the contract and another thousand on delivery of an acceptable manuscript—can you beat those terms? No, of course you can't. What do you say?"

"Well—"

"Come around to the office tomorrow morning. If you need an advance we can arrange for you to have something right away. What time is it?" Abruptly his mood changed. "I've got a train to make. I'll rush like hell, and then it'll stop in Brooklyn for an hour to contemplate its navel or something. Oh, well. See you tomorrow, Abe. *Emil*!" Godfrey Bland paid the tab and plodded out.

It had all gone as Serles had hoped. Not that he hoped, exactly, for two sex novels; but he would have taken anything that came down the pike: juveniles, health fads, Cuban exposés pro or con, the role in the Civil War of the Confederate Bureau of Weights and Measures, or fast-moving novels of crime in which the hardboiled detective hero shoots the erring blonde one inch to the right of her appendectomy scar; such was the urgency of Abel's financial situation.

He sat in a mildly pleasant daze induced not only by success but by two double Demeraras on an almost empty stomach. Authors, editors, agents, publishers, PR men, Girls Friday in a wide variety of shapeliness, actors and actresses and old ladies from Dubuque came and went, gabbling and silent, and off in one corner a man with a beard calmly changed a little baby. Serles was observing, with academic interest only, that it was a little boy baby, when someone gestured to him from halfway across the lobby. Wobbling only in the slightest, he went over.

"I'm Jack Foster," said the gesturer. "We met, briefly, at Bob Bigelow's autographing party when his book came out." It was the publisher's editor to whom Bland had waved earlier.

"Oh, yes, you're with—" The name of the firm failed him.

"Samuel Rice. We're still kind of new. We're young, but we're growing daily. How about a drink?"

Abel shook his head. "I've paid the cocktail hour all the obeisance it's going to get," he said. "But if this is on the expense account I'll have a sandwich."

"All right," Foster said equably. "Let's go in the restaurant. I'm in the mood for a cool green salad myself." He was a thin man in his late thirties, with dusty brown hair.

They talked about Bob Bigelow's book for a while, then Foster asked—almost inevitably—what Abel was working on "these days." And was told. The editor gave a tiny sigh. "Short stories aren't in our line, I'm afraid. We just might bring out a volume of newly discovered tales by Edgar Allan Poe, then again we just might not. Nonfiction is our chief product. When I say product, that's just what I mean— not to underrate the books, you understand; but we sort of specialize in items by people who've got something to say but who aren't professional writers and don't know how to say it. We provide them with professional assistance—"

"Ghosting, you mean?"

"Ghosting, I mean," Foster said, still equably. "The actual writer gets an acknowledgement in the credits somewhere, but none of this *As Told To* stuff, which makes the author of the first instance sound like an illiterate, which he sometimes is. And then we publicize. We publicize very, very much. You may or may not remember, but we are Samuel Rice *Associates*. We've got all kinds of associates in all kinds of media, and when we puff a book, believe me the book *stays* puffed. It sells and sells and sells. Are you interested?"

"Yes."

"You're not doing anything for Godfrey right at the moment?" He ate salad as Abel explained that Bland had made him an attractive proposal to which, however, he had not definitely committed himself. "All right," said Foster, spooning up a dab of dressing. "If you definitely uncommit yourself, and Godfrey isn't sore about it—and he's enough of an old pro himself not to be—you can call me tomorrow for an appointment. I can't tell you now what it is, but I can tell you that it's a lot better than sex novels. There's more money in it, for one thing. And for another thing, you write some piece of paperback tripe, it's dead three months after it hits the stand, and who remembers who wrote it? Whereas a credit like this one, even if you don't get your name on the cover—well, it's a hard cover, not a soft one. And you know what a difference *that* can make."

Abel did. "I'll be in touch," he said.

He heard voices as he came up the stairs of the old three-story red-brick Greenwich Village building he lived in. Sally Stone was in his apartment, and so was Frederic Beard—the latter, on the telephone.

Sally and Fred were often together—had been, in fact, together when Abel first met her. Were they together rather more these days than Abel, now he came to think of it, really liked? He thought they sort of were, then realized it wasn't that so much as that he himself was not so often alone with Sally as he would have liked to be. Their friendship had been casual and comfortable and, at times, very warm indeed: "honest" was the way he had liked to think of it. Was? Had been. Not that it was now *un*comfortable, far from it; but Abel had a while back grown aware that his own *un*willingness to become more deeply involved with her was resulting in her own willingness to become less deeply involved with him; and to this problem he had as yet found no answer.

"...nobody in this country," Old Fred was informing his invisible communicant, who might be anywhere from Point Barrow to Chula Vista, but what difference to Abel?—Fred always paid for his own calls; "and only one man in Japan. He lives in Izo Prefecture, I think, I've got his name and address somewhere at home, and so far as I know he's the only one who still does hilt bindings in the Eighteenth Century Satsuma style. Shall I look him up for you? All right, I'll do that, Dr. Bolzack. And I'll see what dates the polisher has open for your swords, too. Goodbye." He turned around and said, with satisfaction, "We eat."

"Good" said Abel. "But we won't have to wait till Dr. Grulzack or whatever his name is sends you a check—I think I've got a good assignment waiting for me tomorrow."

And Sally said, "We eat. But not because of your assignment tomorrow. I brought a bag of goodies with me *right now*." She was a statuesque brunette, which was just as good as a statuesque blonde any day, with a possible edge in that she was less likely to suffer from sunburn.

"I will now kiss you," Abel said, and did so. It wasn't Sally who had said, that time, "Abe! You look so *different* tonight!"—that one had gone to live in a cave in Guadalajara with three Peace Marchers. Now, from the pride of paper bags on the table, Sally produced two kinds of smoked fish and two of soft cheese, a jar of cold sorrel soup, butter, ice cubes, whiskey, mixer, and Bialystockers—those succulent onion rolls which start out to be doughnuts and then change their minds.

"What is the decision of the caucus?" she asked.

"We eat!" declared Fred and Abel with one voice, Abel adding that he would emit shrill little squeals of delight if he could get his voice up high enough, and Fred wanting to know what the occasion was. The occasion, she informed him, was Quahog State Bank and Trust Company of Boston Check Day. The men gave three cheers for the Quahog State Bank and Trust Company of Boston, then three more for Edward Erastus Leverett XXVth.

Sally, serving out the goodies, acknowledged the cheers on behalf of the absent honored. "I will say—and this is my sincere advice to all poor working girls—if you ever must marry and divorce, by all means let it be to and from a Boston Brahmin with more apartment houses than he knows what to do with. Edward Erastus Leverett XXVth is a *gentleman*, and I'm sure I no longer begrudge him his mother complex in the slightest. The poor man has to have *some* hobby. Dear, dreadful old Mother Leverett, with her diamond dog collar and her spastic colon; oh, well. Dinner is served."

"Any news?" Fred asked presently, his vasty beard flecked with crumbs which he carefully brushed onto his plate.

"Don't ask me," Abel demurred, reaching for another moist, pink, delicious flake of kippered salmon. "I haven't read any periodicals at all lately, except for a copy of the Sam Jones Junior High School Alumni Review, which my sister was kind enough to send me. Ask Sally."

Sally protested that she never read newspapers any more. "Not even the *Village Voice* or *The Realist*. I can stand only so many exposés of Tammany Hall and Organized Religion. However, let me see, I did catch a news program on TV this afternoon. Oh, yes." She nodded, began to tick off her fingers. "Liz has gone ex-communicado again. There was another coup in North Dong Dunc. The U.S. government is either not going to raise taxes or not going to lower them. Somebody else is saying wicked things about the Mafia. And there was a baseball game, but I forget who played, or what the score was."

Abel made himself another drink. "Well, Fred," he said, "so now you know."

But Fred only snorted.

The premises of Samuel Rice Associates occupied two floors over a chi-chi barber shop specializing in blond rinses for aging young men and the showroom of a renegade Zoroastrian who sold imitation *objets d'art* from the Nether Orient. The elevator smelled of shampoo and curried fish, but the publishers' office was air-conditioned and nice. Two men who didn't look at all like writers sat on facing benches in the anteroom and surveyed Abel bleakly as he approached the receptionist's desk, then lost interest when she confirmed his appointment.

Jack Foster, on seeing Abel Serles enter his office, frowned slightly, as if feeling a slight pain somewhere, the location of which momentarily eluded him. Then his face cleared.

"Were you able to satisfy Godfrey?" he asked. Abel assured him that Godfrey had taken it philosophically. "Well, let's go in, then," said Foster. But he did not rise. "I don't remember if I told you or not, but this is all on the q.t., whether you take the job or not. If that isn't agreeable to you—"

Abel said it was perfectly agreeable. Foster nodded, got up, and led the way into another room, which opened off his office. Seated therein was a man, behind the desk, who, was, Abel assumed, Samuel Rice; a man in front of the desk, who had on a flowered sports shirt and gold-rimmed spectacles;

and two men sitting in the corners of the room on the other side of the desk.

"Sam," said Foster, "this is Abe Serles, about whom, et cetera."

Mr. Rice said something affable. The man in front of the desk looked on with interest. "Abe," Foster went on, "this is the gentleman with whom you will be working, if everything figures out satisfactorily. Meet Captain Marryat."

It seemed to Abel that he could scarcely have revealed much surprise, but the man in the flowered sports shirt burst out into a hearty Ha Ha! as they shook hands. "He don't believe it!" he guffawed. "Well, that's okay, why *should* he? One thing I can't stann, I can't stann a dope. Please ta meetcha."

"My pleasure, Captain Marryat." Serles could, with just a little effort, picture him on the poopdeck of a gravel barge.

The "Captain" laughed again. Rice and Foster smiled faintly. The two men in the corners facing the door did not change their expressions, which were expressionless.

"Yer all right, kid," the "Captain" said, taking Abel's arm just below the elbow and giving it a squeeze. "You doe know who I am, do ya? Am I c'reck? One a them writers, all a time in a nyev'ry tar, huh! Well, at's all right, never mine, you'll loin. See, leave me explain the situation to ya. These two gentlemen, Mr. Ice and Mr. Foster, they toll me yer not suppose to know my rill name jus' yet. So *I* figure, what the hell, I'll have some fun witcha. Om gunna be like a writer myself, ain' I? So Om entitle' to a pseudonymph, ain' I? O*kay*. See, when I was a kid I read this book, *Masterman Ready*, by Captain Marryat. Wadda book! *Robinson Crusoe*, you can have it. Dull as a dishwasher. *Swiss Family Robinson*? Kid stuff. But *Masterman Ready*? Great! So I figure, I'll call myself Captain Marryat. Okay?"

Abel said that it was okay with him. "Captain Marryat" hit him a friendly blow on the shoulder, repeated that he was "all right," then turned to the publisher. "Well, does he take the contrack?" he asked.

Rice cleared his throat. "Maybe Mr. Serles should know a few more details before he makes his mind up. Captain, uh, Marryat—how should I put it—has led a very interesting life —"

"*Maron!*" said Captain Marryat.

"—and now he has retired and plans to go abroad for a little while. Now, it seems to us that the story of his life and, uh, professional career would make a very interesting book. He will provide the facts, you—if it'll be you—will write it, and me and my associates will publish and publicize it. That's the general picture."

Captain M., who had been nodding and smiling, suddenly spun around. "I don't wantcha ta think I can't *write*, now, kid. I can write. Gimme a pencil. Anybody got a pencil?"

"Your word is sufficient for me, Captain," Abel assured him.

And so the conference proceeded.

The terms, Ricewise, were not grandiloquent in the extreme, consisting of the same $2000 offered for one of Mr. Godfrey Bland's much-despised sex novels. Bland (or his publishers, Clay and Curtain), it is true, did offer a rising scale of royalties dependent on subsequent editions and their sale, and Rice did not. However, no one ever expected the Bland books to *have* subsequent editions, whereas with Rice—

"You get a straight royalty, it doesn't go up and it doesn't go down. How come?" Rice asked and Rice answered. "Because our books don't sell on account of the writing. They sell because we push them. And a fixed royalty on a book that's pushed the way we push books is a lot better than a paper rise in royalty on a book which is not pushed. That's the picture."

Serles thought that he had seen better pictures, but there was some truth in what the publisher said. And by this time he was rather intrigued. Captain Marryat's "interesting life," whatever it was or had been like, sounded as though it might be much more interesting than confecting even a sophisticated sex novel. Or even two. And then the "Captain" himself had offers to make.

"You'll be woikin wit *me*, kid," he said. "Up in *my* place. It's a pretty classy place, air- condition', private bar, the works. Yull be eatin wit me, yull be eatin what I eat, an', kid—lemme tellya—I eat *good*. An when somebuddy eat wit me, they never even *see* the bill. O*kay*?"

"O*kay*."

Captain Marryat beamed again as Abel dodged his punch. "Drawr up them papers fer the kid to sign," he directed. "I gotta go now. My masewer comes at noon." Suddenly there was no trace of geniality in his face or manner. He leveled his forefinger at Abel Serles. "Ya gotta keep ya mouth shut. Ya know that, dontcha?"

Jack Foster said, smoothly and swiftly, "Mr. Serles is aware that he is contractually obligated to maintain strict secrecy in this whole matter."

For a moment the face of Captain Marryat remained blank. Then he beamed again. "O*kay*!" he said. He snapped his fingers. The two men in the corners rose as one. "Which way the elevator? Left? See yez all again."

Abel did not linger in Foster's office. The latter told him that the contract and a check in advance of the advance would be ready in the morning. Outside, Abel automatically took a left turn. There was an elevator there, all right, but it was not the one he had come up on, and it said *Freight*. For a moment he stood there, thoughtfully. Then he pressed the button. The freight elevator rose slowly, was empty, descended slowly. The cellar was equally empty, and so was the alley—which led to the street behind the one which the building's lobby opened onto.

It was only when he was on the bus that he realized he hadn't seen in the Rice reception office, on leaving, the two men he had seen there on entering. It struck him, in retrospect, how very much in manner and looks they had resembled the two men sitting watchfully in the corners facing the door of the inner office. Had the man who called himself Captain Marryat made a slip of the tongue when saying that the elevator was the one on the left? Perhaps he had meant the one on the right. But, if so, wouldn't either circumspect or circuitous or corrected him?

Captain Marryat, plainly, was either circumspect or circuitous or both—and, equally plainly, he did not move unaccompanied. It was not likely that the hush-hush surrounding the ghost-writing arrangement was the result of an ordinary shyness or delicacy of feeling on the part of the protagonist of the memoirs-to-be.

Abel got off the bus at Washington Arch and walked across the Park. For once its scenes failed to hold his interest—not the playing children, the pretzel and ice-cream vendors, the chess and checker players, the bohemians and beatniks, the old Italian women in their black dresses, the tourists from East Weewaw, Wisconsin, the pipe-smoking artists with canvases under their arms, the girls with their long hair, the fey young men walking their weeny dogs—none of it. And at the kiosk abaft the Sheridan Square subway station he did something he hadn't done in a long time: he bought a newspaper.

It was hours and hours too early for the coffeehouses to be open, so he went into a bar, ordered a beer, took it to an empty booth, and sipped at it while he turned the pages of the *Daily News*. He found what he was looking for, in the center photographic spread. A man was walking down the front steps of a public building and shielding his face with his hat; but enough of the face was exposed for Abel Serles to recognize it as that of Captain Marryat, so-called. The two-line caption convinced him that this not really nautical person had indeed lived "a very interesting life."

And it also informed him who, in Sally ex-Leverett's words, had been saying wicked things about the Mafia.

◆ ◆ ◆

Frederic the Beard was in the apartment again, leafing through a sheaf of photographs of sword-tangs, and comparing them with inscriptions in an old Japanese book printed on soft Chinese paper.

"Did you get the assignment?" he asked.

"I guess so."

Fred scratched his beard, of which there was enough to have supplied a quorum of old-style Mormon Elders. "What's it for?" he asked.

"I am contractually obligated to maintain strict secrecy in this whole matter."

"Oh, come off it! What's it about?"

"I am contractually obligated to—"

"Oh, foosh!" said Frederic Beard. He went back to his inscriptions. "Oh, well," he said, after a moment, "as long as you eat."

Abel did indeed eat, his first meal at Captain Marryat's place being a late breakfast consisting of three kinds of eggs, four of fruit juice, fried flounder, prosciutto ham, Canadian bacon, fresh whipped butter, six kinds of bread, four of pastry, seven of preserves, peanut butter, hot muffins, and Irish, English, Dutch, and American gin—these last to go with the fruit juice.

"Eat up, everybody," directed Captain Marryat, addressing Abel, the bodyguards, and a thin British secratree with white eyelashes and a rabbit nose. "Eat up, everybody—costs me a fawchin."

Everybody ate up.

The place was a penthouse overlooking the East River, with better trees growing on its terrace than Abel had seen at several country estates. He had a room just refurnished for him as a private office, with its own private bathroom; and Captain M. informed him that a bedroom was available for him as well, should he desire to spend his nights there—and informed him, also, that should Abel desire not to spend them alone, he, the host, had Telephone Numbers.

The breakfast having been eaten and its remains cleared away with dispatch by several silent servitors who had presumably been lurking in the woodwork, Captain Marryat said, with a belch and an apology, "Awright, where were we now, doll—I mean, escuse me, Miss Meadowes-Humphrey?"

And Miss Meadowes-Humphrey, after having riffled her steno pad, said, in the voice of one who reads recipes aloud on the Home Program of the BBC, "The icepick murders of the seven Sijjy Brothers in Greenpoint, Mr. Sullivan. Having been lured there under the pretense of discussing the possibilities of heavy investments in the ice-cream and dry-cleaning industries, the brothers—ah, here we are: *'Louis, the fat one, squeal like a pig, so—'*"

This recitative, which might, as far as tone was concerned, have been concerned with novel methods of confecting things from leftover rice pudding, hard-cooked eggs, and anchovy paste, was interrupted by her employer's snapping his fingers in a chagrined fashion. Miss Meadowes-Humphrey stopped as if she had been switched off.

"Did I say Greenpernt?" he addressed one of his samurai.

"'Ats what chew say, Big Smith."

With a sigh and a rueful shake of the head the Captain corrected the location to Red Hook. "I got, like, confused. Greenpernt was where them udder brudders got boined. Sorry, Miss. Change it, please."

Captain Marryat, alias Mr. Sullivan, alias Big Smith, turned to Abel. "The lady, here, she type up a bunch of this stuff that Mr. Ice awready seen. So while we go on, she takin' dictation, why don' you go inna yer office and look it ova? See what it needs, like. In udder woids, kid, get stahted. O*kay*?"

"Very well, Captain," Abel said.

Marryat-Sullivan-Smith snapped his gross fingers again, and the lady at once said, "'—*so we give him a couple more to shut him*—'" The door closed behind Abel and on the sad story of the seven Sijjy brothers.

Neatly arranged on the desk was a wealth of writing materials ranging from an electric-tape typewriter to a battery of gold-pointed fountain pens. There was also an embossed-leather folder of manuscript typed on paper of so good a quality that Abel had never even seen anything like it before. He seated himself in a chair of complex contours which almost adjusted itself to his back and buttocks, and drew the folder of manuscript toward him.

The author's style, at least at first, appeared to have something in common with that of Holden Caulfield. "Where my parents come from and where was they born is nobody's G.D. business and anyway they both die in the influenza epidemict in the First Worlds War and after that I'm on my own"—that was the arresting first sentence. It seemed a shame to have to change it, Abel thought.

What the manuscript possessed in forceful style, however, it lacked in organization. Plunging from the death of the author's parents and his entry into independence, it veered off from his escape from a denominational protectory into an account entitled *Nitty Gerundive Who Place a Tax on All the Cherry Syrup for New York City during Prohibition* to a description of several Syndicate conferences "holden" to consider the opportunities offered by coin-operated television; thence to an interminable apology for the author's rather intimate acquaintance with the world of crime, which was, in effect, a refusal to apologize at all; followed by thumbnail biographies of 137 big and little hoods, alive and dead.

Thereafter was a chapter, on fixing municipal governments and police forces and insuring their staying fixed, a graphic description of several episodes in a Chicago gang war in the early thirties, a patriotic digression on the United States as the land of opportunity, and the "true facts" about Al Capone, Justice Crater, Tammany Hall, Las

Vegas, someone called Little Iggy, Rum Runners' Row, Arnold Rothstein and thirty-odd more persons, places, and things.

Abel leaned back thoughtfully in the form-fitting chair, and it all but clutched at him passionately. As he seized the desk for support, his hand slipped and clawed open a drawer. Regaining his balance, he pulled the drawer farther open, revealing a cedarwood box full of fat brown cigars with Cuban accents. First he lit one, enjoying every rich molecule of its smoke. Then he slowly made a sandwich of two sheets of quasiparchment and a piece of imperial carbon paper, fitted it into the giant typewriter. He switched on the current.

For a moment his fingers brooded above the keys. Then they descended,

In 1932 Al Capone poured two glasses of wine and said to me

There would be lots of places for flashbacks, and lots of flashbacks for those places. He wondered what there would be for lunch.

Abel had not taken advantage of the offer to spend the night at the penthouse, and consequently he was quite surprised the next morning when the doorman of the posh apartment building politely stopped him and said, "Sir, Mr. Sullivan isn't here anymore."

Abel stared at the man in the uniform of a Latvian admiral. "Not—Did he leave any message? My name is Serles. You mean he won't be back at all? Moved out? No message? Well, I'll be darned."

Blankly he moved down the street, with vague notions of calling the Rice office. Would he still collect his money? Not likely. It had been *very* good food, too. A tug rounding the point of Welfare Island hooted mournfully.

As if in echo, a passing car sounded its horn briefly. Then again. He glanced at it. In front were two of Captain Marryat's sideboys. They neither looked at him nor moved at all, that he could see, but the car slowed down and the back door opened. Abel got in.

They drove uptown, crosstown, downtown, uptown again. At one time he almost caught the driver's eyes in the mirror, but the eyes weren't looking at him. At length the other man in front murmured an address. The car slowed down again, Abel got out, the car picked up speed and turned down a side street. He was only a few blocks from the address.

The building was a big old West Side Hotel dating from the architectural era of Stanford White. No name having been mentioned and Abel not having thought to inquire for one, he paused for a moment at the desk, nonplused. The mousy, hollow-chested little clerk, strands of colorless hair swept across his bony skull, looked up at him in silent inquiry. Light glinted on his glasses. An elderly woman with blue hair scanned the pigeonholes for mail, found none, turned and said to Abel, "Go have children," and went away.

Sullivan? Smith?

Probably not. On impulse Abel asked for Captain Marryat. The result would have utterly surprised him, had he never made an intimate purchase from a timid pharmacist. The clerk seemed to melt in upon himself, dropped his eyes, faded rather than moved away from the desk, and furtively consulted a register. He then ebbed back to the desk, still not looking up, and whispered, "Ten-o-three. Use the house phone next to the cigar stand."

No method actor assigned to interpret someone with a guilty secret would have played the role quite like that, but Abel was convinced—convinced, too, that the secret had an earlier origin than the migration of Captain Marryat to the Hotel Bellepaise.

The cigar stand, presided over by a fat man in a grizzled mustache and a stained vest, was just what he appeared to be, making no concessions to the underarm deodorant trade and even having a tiny blue-tipped gas jet in a brass sconce for customers to light their smokes at.

"Still ring-ing," said the operator.

Then, very quickly, "*Yeah?*"

"Abel Serles."

"C'mon up."

Abel went up.

"All new people onna tent' flaw," said the shriveled elevator man.

"Oh, yes?"

"Sure. All re-renovated. Air-conditioned. Ready lass week. But they move in lass night. *Tent'* flaw. Watcha step."

Abel wondered how many other hideyholes were even now in preparation in case another flight of the Tartar Horde should prove indicated. The two men who had driven him from the East Side were already on guard in the corridor; they looked up with their usual sliding, opaque glances. One yawned, another picked at his fingernails. Abel walked on down to Room 1003 and knocked.

The new suite was a mixture of fake French Provincial and midwestern Swedish Modern, as if two rival interior decorators had come to an uneasy truce. The Captain and his staff were once again at meat; he informed Abel that he was just in time, and invited his participation. "Good steaks," the Captain said. "They fly 'em up from Youraguay. Go on. Take. Take."

In a few moments Abel was as greasy about the chops as his host and Miss Meadowes-Humphrey, and then became sticky as well, investigating what was beyond doubt the largest selection of melons he had ever seen in his life. The primest, which fairly swooned away on his tongue in sheer delight, bore on their bosoms roughly printed little tags which might have been Arabic, Persian, or Pushtu. After prawns, mussels, *écrivisses*, wild strawberries, and other goodies, followed by tiny cups of *cawwa* and brandy, Captain Marryat fired his usual salute to the excellence of the meal, then turned to business.

"I read yer stuff, kid, an' it's okay. Ya think it'll sell a lotta books? Bestseller?" Abel said he hoped so, but that it was impossible to predict. Conditions in the book trade, he said, were very fluid. Captain Marryat frowned. "Mr. Ice, he give me his woid, him an' his partners would promote it."

"I'm sure they will."

"Well, *okay*, then. Yer office is over on this side now. Let's see whatcha can do. Miss, where we at?"

Meadowes-Humphrey cleared her throat with a little whinny, peered into her notes. "Assignation of Machine-gun Jack McGurn with a daughter of Senator X, Mr. Sullivan. *'Jack was shacked up with—'*"

The new office was as soundproof as the other. The furniture and equipment were not identical—the typewriter, for example, was pearl-gray instead of lime-green—but it was just as good. The cigars were green instead of brown. Abel looked once at the Hudson, then read over his previous day's work, then turned to the source material. This time he didn't have to put paper into the mill, it was already there. He lit his cigar and gazed at the pseudo-Utrillo on the wall facing him. Then he set to.

When I was setting up slot machines in Louisiana I learned that not every donation to a "parish" has to do with religion, and

Sally had not once been married to a Bostonian for nothing.

"Where do they get off charging prices like that for the drinks in a place like this?"

Abel grunted. "That's the tax for not having to watch old movies. You always pay more in a bar without TV."

She fussed a while more, then sipped her Scotch sour, watching him. "Has your assignment gotten you down?"

"No, why do you say that? It's probably the best

assignment I've ever had."

"Then how come you're so grim?"

He gnawed at a potato chip. "Well, if you must know. I was almost run down by a car on Sixth Avenue today, and besides that it scared the hell out of me, it's made me think about the vanity of human wishes, and what is our life but a dunghill smoke, and all that sort of thing. And if I'm grim, that's why."

She gave a great bosom-swelling sigh—and instantly he became less grim. "Look! There's Fred. *Fred!*"

The moment was gone before it had well arrived, and Fred Beard came towering through the bar, angrily brushing away at the clouds of smoke.

"It's outrageous," he growled, crowding his legs under the table.

"Yes. Pity they don't all chew, or take snuff." Abel was feeling crotchety.

Fred stared at him. "What are you talking about? Oh. Smoke. No. Thesis typists! Idiots! I rupture myself earning the money to pay the cretin—and then she types eleven copies without numbering the pages. Eft. Toad. Gelded sow. And now I've got to number eleven times a hundred twenty-five pages by myself!"

Sally took his hand and patted it. "Never mind, Fred. We'll hold a numbering party, the three of us, and get it done for you in an hour or so. Maybe later tonight. Won't we, Abe?... Poor Abe, he's feeling grim. A car almost ran over him today."

Abel glowered, having had other plans or at least hopes for later that night with Sally, and ignored Fred's clucks of sympathy. Suddenly his drink gave a lurch in his hand. Fred and Sally, having noticed nothing, chattered on together. And the voice in the booth behind him repeated, "Where is Big Smith?"

"Who in the hell is Big Smith?"—a second voice.

"Some crook they're looking for. That's what the headline says. 'Where Is Big Smith?'"

The second voice obviously couldn't care less. "Where is

Bug Stuart, that's what *I* want to know. Why doesn't he get his big fat backside over here? I haven't got all night."

Muttering something about going to the head, Abel got up, observed what newspaper was on the table in the booth behind, and promptly went out to buy a copy.

Where Is Big Smith?

The subject or object of one of the biggest undercover manhunts in recent years, ex-Syndicate stalwart Harold "Big" Smith—alias Jerry Sullivan, alias Popo Bogarty, and many other aliases—was still hiding out in parts unknown today. Earlier this week he sang like a canary to this newspaper's reporters and presumably made many Syndicate ears ring, because he immediately dropped out of sight again. Syndicate hatchetmen would like to know where he is. So would State Senator Elbert Dibbler (Rep., Chenango County), chairman of the Committee on Urban Crime. So would Police Commissioner Brenahan, crusading Congressman Cutler

Abel had just resettled himself at the table, glowered at Sally cuddled up into Fred's beard, and taken his drink in hand again, when it gave another lurch.

"*Where is Big Smith?*" a voice boomed.

"*That is the question which*—click."

"Turn that damn radio down," one bartender directed another, a second after it ceased to be necessary.

Sally separated herself from the country's leading authority on Japanese swords. "Abe," she said, "what you need is a good night's sleep after that awful shock today. Fred and I are going over to his place and we'll do the page numbering all by ourselves, don't you bother. You just drink some hot milk and go to bed."

◆ ◆ ◆

He watched them wordlessly as they went out. Then he paid for his drink and left. On the way home his moody eye was arrested by the blue flicker of a TV screen in an open bar. "—and that's the scene in North Dong Dunc. On the *home* scene the big question of the moment continues to be— Where is Big Smith?"

Abel cursed. And went home to bed.

He dreamed of the squabs they had had for supper at the Bellepaise, a giant pot of them, stuffed with wild rice, and garnished with bacon, peppers, mushrooms, and flaky black bits of truffle. The squabs twittered (do squabs *twitter*? part of his mind wondered) petulantly throughout the dream meal, and then began to scratch at the pot. The scratching became a scraping, grew louder. For some reason everything was dark, and then Abel realized he was wide-awake and in bed and that the scratching and scraping was coming from his rear window.

The pillow hit the floor with a faint noise as he leaped, so to speak, into a sitting position. Someone shouted, *"What's that? Who's there?"* and he recognized the voice as his own. There was a silence, then the slap-slap of feet on the fire escape. He jumped out of bed, tripped, regained his balance, and rushed over, flinging up the window with a bang. *"Police!"* he cried. *"Police! Police!"*

The police, who arrived somewhat later than immediately, consisted of a pair of neat, well-spoken young men. "There you are," said one, pointing. "Jimmy marks. How do you like that? Didn't even tap the joint first, to make sure there was nobody at home. That's what we mean," he said, turning to Serles, "by 'the nerve of a burglar.'"

Something suddenly and belatedly occurred to Abel. "I'll tell you something else they didn't tap first. And that's the window. It wasn't even locked."

Both policemen laughed heartily. "Well, that's the way those addicts are," said one. "They even forget their rudimentary intelligence."

"You're sure it was an addict, officer?"

The officer nodded. "Bound to be. These cheap burglaries —I mean, beg your pardon, but this apartment is no fur loft or jewelry store—they're always the work of an addict. That's what narcotics does to you, undermines the very fabric and basis of society. If I had my way, anybody caught even for a first offense, pushing—the firing squad. Hey?"

"That's where you are *wrong*, Alfred," the second policeman said, softly and earnestly. "That has *never* solved a problem yet and it never *will*. The *only* answer is to make these preparations *legal*, like they do in Siam or wherever it is. Then these unfortunate people would not be obliged to come climbing through this gentleman's window in the hopes of stealing his typewriter at half-past two in the morning."

By the time they concluded their sociological discussion and had left, Abel found he was no longer tired. So he walked across town to the vicinity of Tompkins Square and woke up Fred Beard.

The sword sage peered through his tangled locks and muttered and snorted. "Is Sally here?" Abel asked.

"No, she went home. I thought she advised you to do the same."

"I did, but there was no milk to heat. I thought I'd borrow some of yours."

"Foosh," said the Beard. "Oh, I suppose you might as well come in. Don't sit *there*! Those are my notes on steel analysis of the early Takugawa Era—"

"Did you number the pages?"

"Yes."

"I'll bet you did...What do you think, Fred? Do squabs twitter?"

After a restless several hours on Fred's sofa he returned home to shave, there having been no equipment for such purpose in the Beard's establishment within the memory of man. He found his place in ruins. The chairs had been smashed, the mattress slashed, likewise the pillows and couch, the typewriter was a tangle of broken keys and springs, shattered dishes were everywhere...

"Well, maybe I was wrong, Alfred," one of the policemen said on their second visit. "*This* is not a narcotics-type incident at all. *This* looks like a classical revenge-type bit. Remember that place over on Perry Street? There was this psychology student, female," he explained, turning to Abel, "who had been living with a would-be poet who was under psychoanalysis. That situation finally broke up, then he dropped out of his analysis, and then he decided that it was all her fault, so he went over to her new place of residence and—"

Abel interrupted him. "I'm quite sure," he said bitterly, "that none of my ex-girl friends is responsible for this."

"Ah," said Alfred, gently rebuking him, "but what Patrolman Roberts was just going to explain to you before you got abrupt, see, this nutty kid picked the wrong apartment to wreck. Maybe that's the same case here. Now, the super tells us that the party downstairs is on Fire Island, the party upstairs is in Provincetown, and the party across the hall, *he* was just coming home from having been out all night just as we were coming up the stairs. So there was nobody around to hear anything. *What* a mess!"

Bemused and bewildered, as well as not a little outraged, Abel Serles took the IRT uptown and arrived at the Bellepaise in time for early breakfast, where he was mildly surprised to see Miss Meadowes-Humphrey already on duty, pouring the tea and buttering the scones or shew-bread or whatever they were. A wicked and unworthy thought entered his mind. Could it be? Could they be?—namely, Miss Meadowes-Humphrey and Captain Marryat? No, no, impossible; surely those albino eyelashes, those meagre measurements, could hold no illicit (or even, damn it, *licit*) attractions for one so obviously designed by Nature to seek for depth of chest and breadth of hip.

"How ya comin?" was the Captain's question. Miss Meadowes-Humphrey continued nibbling rapidly. No, no, nothing more than too many years ill-nourished on spotted dog, bubble-and-squeak, jam tarts, thin milk in thick tea, oleaginous chips and cabbage, cabbage, cabbage, were responsible for her early appearance at the Captain's table. Abel decided to keep his troubles to himself, and joined in on the crisp brown trout which had only the previous day been swimming in some cold mountain stream.

"Ya look tie-ed, kid."

"Didn't get much sleep last night."

Captain Marryat gave a lewd chuckle, and they presently parted for the day's work. The noon meal was subsequently served up by a high-class wholesale Rumanian restaurant. Abel partook copiously of the mushk-steak and the jellied calves-foot, but thought there was really more eggplant than he cared to encounter even in such various forms. He wondered if the Captain's gourmet learnings were undermining his own simple writerly tastes, always before so readily satisfied with what was cheapest and to hand. As a background accompaniment to such soul-searching the television demanded: *Where is Big Smith*? And the radio echoed: *Where is Big Smith*?

"Leave 'em fine out," grunted the missing man, stuffing himself with Balkan desserts. Abel left him and his stenographer recapitulating the bloody end of one Fat Dempster, who, as luck would have it, was run to earth at night in a meat-packing plant in East New York, New Jersey. Abel spent the rest of the day trying to organize the memoirs as they related to the non-fashionable suburb of Cicero, Illinois, during the late twenties. And when he opened the door of his apartment that evening, an explosion flung him back against the hall wall and broke several windows.

"Faulty wiring there," said the detective later, chidingly. "Obviously that was meant to go off when you opened the *kitchen* door. Otherwise, why would they have put it in the kitchen?"

Abel felt sickish and aching, but there appeared to be no fractures. "I'll speak to the electricians' union," he muttered.

The detective surveyed him with eyes as bright and alien as a bird's. "This is the third attempt at your apartment in twenty-four hours, isn't it? Come on, you must have *some* idea who or why?"

Abel shook his head. He made a little speech. He had lived in Greenwich Village for six years, in this same house for four, in the apartment for three. In all that time, he said, he had never even so much as been troubled by a friendly drunk; and he had no idea whatsoever.

The detective listened, giving little ornithological nods. As soon as Abel had finished he said, "Come on, you must have *some* idea who or why?"

Feeling bruised and ill, wanting to lie down, Abel, as soon as he could get away from the birdy man, went out. He got a taxi and went up to Sally's place in Chelsea. He was feeling increasingly sick and shaky, and the thought that she might not be in was the greatest fear he could imagine.

But she was in.

He had on numerous other occasions sought her there for a friendly drink or a friendly talk; but he never before had sought her or thought of her as refuge, home, or healing.

As he did now.

She screamed on seeing him, and Frederic H. Beard, who had been joining her for a light supper, leaped up in such alarm that a piece of egg yolk fell onto his ample beard. "Abe, what happened?" they cried, almost together.

"I want to lie down."

Together they helped him into bed, took off his shoes, and then, as he began to shiver, covered him with blankets. Sally got him to drink a shot of brandy, and then she repeated, "But what *happened*?"

"They tried to kill me."

"*Who*?"

"The Mafia."

Fred and Sally stared at him. Then she said, "But, Abe, listen dear, that's only a tiny little outfit over near Bleecker Street. They just get a rakeoff on cigarette machines. I *know* one of them, Patsy Something-or-other, such a nice little man. They don't try to *kill* people."

The shakes had begun to diminish. "I don't mean that Mafia. I mean the real Mafia. The Syndicate. They tried to kill *me*." And he told them of what had been going on in his apartment, and she gave a little scream.

"What about that car that almost ran you down?" Her fingers made a paling over which her large frightened eyes peeped.

"Oh, God! I forgot about that." He wanted to say, Give me some more brandy, but all he got out was "Gick." So he pointed a quivery finger until they poured him another. His friends were patient people: they let him get about half of the second shot down before asking the obvious question, namely, Why did the Syndicate want Abel Serles killed?

Abel pondered. Between bed, blankets, and brandy he was now beginning to feel warmer. And better. "Well, I'm not supposed to say," he said.

"Oh, come *on*! What is this the Code of the Underworld? Sally, talk sense to him—"

"Abe, dear—"

He squirmed in his bed. Was he really bound to keep silence unto the grave? No. Absurd. "Listen: You know all this recent business about Where Is Big Smith?" Sally nodded, Beard blew out of the corner of his mouth a scornful snort which fluttered the end of his piratical mustachio.

"It's everywhere—newspapers, TV, radio. Disgusting. Two hundred ancient and priceless specimens of the Japanese swordsmith's craft are scattered around this country in the houses of people who picked them up as mere souvenirs at the end of the war, and nobody lifts a finger to have their whereabouts so much as identified—and look at all this hullaballoo about a cheap crook who—" He stopped and seized the sides of his vast beard with both hands. "Don't tell me!" he exclaimed. "Don't tell me. *You*?"

Abel nodded. "Me. I know where he is. That's why they're trying to kill me."

Sally sat down on the side of the bed, suddenly and heavily. "Oh, my. Oh, dear. Things like this never happened in Boston. What are we going to *do*?"

Fred was shaking his head. "That doesn't make sense, Abe. Assuming the Syndicate knows that you know where he is, wouldn't they try to get you to *tell*? First by bribery, most likely, then by—well, *force*. But they wouldn't try to *kill* you. Furthermore, how do you know—"

Abel said, "Because I've got the assignment to ghost-write his memoirs, and they don't want the publicity...I wish to hell I'd never taken the job. It seemed like fun until all this started."

But Fred was still shaking his head. "It *still* doesn't figure, Abe. Now, I'm no authority on the Mafia, but from what I've heard and read, they don't operate that way. They seem to keep their killings confined either to their own members or to people they try to victimize who won't hold still for it. After all, you're only one among many, many people who are trying to expose the Syndicate. The cops, Congress, the State Legislature, the newspapers, so on. They're not trying to kill *them*. Why would they want to kill *you*?"

Abel shook his head. For some reason the thought of the many magnificent victuals served up to him at Captain Marryat's table came to his mind. The condemned man had eaten not only a hearty breakfast, but tasty brunch, gourmet dinner, and exotic supper as well...He repeated now, to his friends, what he had said to the detective: all the years he had lived in Greenwich Village without trouble, and now—

"First, someone tries to run me down. Then someone tries to break into my apartment, then someone *does* break into my apartment—and wrecks it—maybe looking for an address, maybe just to warn me. Then somebody plants a bomb in my kitchen. Who else could it be, if not the Syndicate?"

Fred cocked his head, still dubious. Sally was wide-eyed. "But," said Abel, "hey, listen...Wouldn't even gangsters be smart enough to know that killing the man who's writing the exposé would result in *more* publicity, not in less?" It didn't make sense, Abel felt that himself. But what did, in this whole evil-crazy business?

Fred and Sally continued to debate the matter. Abel closed his eyes. He was aware that he was falling asleep, but felt no desire to do otherwise...He awoke with the smell of coffee in the room—plain, good, ordinary supermarket coffee, the kind Sally used; nothing exotic, very much like Sally herself. "Hey, can I have some of that?" he called. It was broad daylight.

"Well, you certainly caught up on your sleep," she said, coming in with two cups. "Which I'm very glad of. Oh, you looked just *terrible* last night. Well. Now we have to decide what you're going to do. Of course you're welcome to hide out here as long as you like. *Or*. Edward Erastus has this eccentric cousin—of course, *I* always got along just fine with her—but anyway, she owns this island off the coast of Maine, and I'm sure if I call her she'll be happy to put you up. She's really very nice."

Abel shook his head. "I'm going to make a phone call, okay?" She nodded, and he dialed the offices of Samuel Rice Associates.

Jack Foster refused to believe he was serious at first, but, convinced at last, was obviously disturbed. "I'll talk to Rice right away. Don't hang up." He was back almost at once. "Rice says to waste no time, but go to the police at once—"

"And tell them everything?"

"Everything."

"Well, fine, then. I guess you'll be hearing from me soon. I hope." He turned to Sally. "The bossman says to tell the police."

She seemed uncertain. "Well...whatever you think Abe; anyway, you can always stay here, or go to Pogunquit Island. But let me know, whatever happens. And if I'm not here I'll probably be at Fred's."

It was another item in his unhappiness that he knew she probably would be.

A dazed-looking woman with a black eye sat on the bench in the precinct house; three young men with shiny black hair and leather jackets to match were slouched in chairs, snickering aimlessly when they caught one another's eye; and an old man scanned a racing sheet. The desk sergeant was engaged in easy discourse with one uniformed and two un-uniformed men, but looked up at Abel's approach and said, "Well, what's your trouble, fellow?"

Now for it. The giant disclosure. "I know where Big Smith is," he said.

All four burst out laughing.

"I mean it," Abel cried, outraged.

"Oh, boy, what a bazzazz," said one of the plainclothesmen. "So you know where Big Smith is. Goody, goody for you. Well, now, you go and tell that palooka that Lieutenant Dick Murphy said, 'Hello' and wants to know who-in-the-hell spread all this talk that the Commissioner wants to see him. Strictly an unofficial in-*quire*-y."

Abel gave a little hiccup of astonishment, at which the four laughed again. "The Commissioner *doesn't* want to see him?"

"Naah. What *for*? That big boob hasn't done nothing illegal since he shot his own big toe in Evanston, Illinoise, thirty years ago. Trying to shake down a candy store or something. And he served his time for that. *I* don't know what all this *Where Is Big Smith*? malarkey is all about. Do you?" He addressed one of his friends, who shook his head.

Lieutenant Murphy proceeded to inform Abel that Big Smith owed his connection with the Syndicate entirely to the fact that he had once been married to the late sister of one Vinny, a middle-upper rank Syndic, who kept him around for laughs.

Abel swallowed. "Then how come he blew the whistle on them? I mean, aren't *they* after him? I mean—"

Murphy shrugged. "Big Smith was strictly a run-out-and-get-me-some-coffee or give-Tommy-a-hotfoot character, until he made a lot of money in the market. He loves to eat and he loves to play these cheap, common practical jokes, and he loves to shoot off his mouth and talk himself up. And that's all there is to Big Smith, and only some dumb apple-knocker like this upstate Senator Whatever-his-name-is would think different. Those dumb apple-knockers are always looking for a way to insult the City and not have to reapportionate the Legislature, anyway. So, if that's all you come to see us about, thanks, and maybe you'll excuse us now, and we'll get on with something important."

As Abel stood in the doorway, poised for the street, he heard one of them repeat, "Where Is Big Smith?" and they all burst out laughing again.

Serles walked slowly along, trying to figure things out. He considered one thing with another, and it seemed to him that a certain configuration was beginning to become dimly visible. Half a block later, he saw a public telephone, and, on a sudden decision, went into the booth.

"Mr. Bland is on the telephone to London," said the girl at the switchboard.

"Let me speak to one of his assistants, then. George or Mary or Sanford."

He wasn't quite certain which one was talking to him a few moments later, but he identified himself and asked, "Do you know who the 'associates' of Samuel Rice Associates are? I'll explain another time." The distant epicene voice of George or Sanford or perhaps Mary named several. Abel thanked him, or her, and hung up.

He then dialed again, rapping impatiently on the tiny shelf, until he heard Jack Foster's voice. Yes, said Abel, he had been to the police. And if Foster, Rice, and Captain Marryat, would like to hear about it they could damn well meet him in the office in an hour.

"Listen," Foster said, "you can't—"

Abel hung up.

◆ ◆ ◆

The Captain greeted him with a wave of his hamlike hand and a large "How ya doin?" Rice expressed instant sympathy, and was about to say more, when Abel overrode him.

"Lieutenant Dick Murphy said to tell you Hello," he addressed Captain Marryat. "He says you're a big palooka and you haven't broken a law since 1939."

"Hoddaya like that fa noive! Listen—"

Abel turned to Rice. "This whole buildup about 'Where Is Big Smith?' is a clever piece of publicity cooked up by your associates in radio, television, and newspapers—that's the gimmick, isn't it?"

Rice nodded. "Coming along very nicely too. Should help get a big price for the movie rights, and maybe a TV and magazine series, too."

Abel said, "And it would have been even more helpful publicity if I'd told the police all about the attempts on my life, wouldn't it?"

Rice stared, frowned. "You mean, you *didn't*? You mean—now just a minute, here. I don't like the tone of your voice at all. You mean you think *we* were behind the violence?"

Foster said, "I can assure you straight out—we had nothing to do with it."

"No, Jack, that you didn't, and maybe your boss didn't. But what about Captain Marryat here? God knows I've given a lot of thought to the whole thing. It *had* to be wrong, my thinking it was the Syndicate doing all that to me, because the Syndicate would be smart enough to know it would only create *more* publicity. Well, who then? Obviously—" His gaze settled on his sometime collaborator.

Captain Marryat bounced to his feet and thrust his hand at Abel, who danced away from it. "Yer awright, kid!" the Captain boomed. "Ya gotta good head on ya! What-the-hell. We're *lookin'* fa publicity, ain't we? We wanna sell lotsa books, don't we? Me an my udder pals, we wooden hoitcha, not fra million dollars! Laugh it up, kid. Laugh it up. I mean—jeest, you musta look funny, dodgin' that cah!" He ha-ha'd happily. "I mean, if we *wanned* a kill ya, we could of. As fa that liddle cherry bomb—"

Abel turned to the bookmen. "I've had the corpuscles scared out of me three times and my apartment wrecked twice. My zeal for my art doesn't include having either happen to me even once. In short—I'm through. You're welcome to what I've already written on your tame hood's life and times."

Foster, in a tired voice, said he was sorry; his employer shrugged. "We won't need what you already wrote. Writers aren't hard to find. Just return your advance and—"

Serles stared at him for a moment. Then he said, "I tell you what, Mr. Ice. We'll compare the damage to my apartment with the amount of the advance, and if there's any difference in your favor, I'll give it to some worthy cause. Gentlemen and Captain Marryat, goodbye."

As the door closed behind him, Abel heard Captain Marryat having the last word, and a mournful one it was. "Kid's got no sense a yuma," said Big Smith.

It was a hot day, and Abel, proceeding north on Fifth Avenue, felt every degree of it. There were several things that badly wanted taking care of.

His apartment was one of them, but he could put the basic repairs in professional hands and leave the rest for later. There would have to be a "later"—for one reason because someone else would be consulted in the restoration, and for another because he felt he both required and deserved an immediate vacation.

If Sally's eccentric-ex-cousin-by-marriage was so sure to have been willing to put him up on Pogunquit Island by himself, it was exceedingly likely that she would put him up accompanied by Sally (Fred, after all, could make do with his swords); and he intended to put this pleasurable prospect before the former Mrs. Edward Erastus Leverett XXV in reasonable hopes that she would not remain so-styled for very much longer. Life, after all, was too short for him to go on keeping one of its most important facets at arm's length forever.

But repairs to and replacements for the apartment, as well as transportation in comfort to the State of Maine, would exhaust what remained of his finances. Certainly he could write while he was there—after a decent interval, that is— but he would have to have something assigned him to write, and an advance against this assignment to finance the rest of his holiday.

His honeymoon...

He looked at his watch. It was 3:43. Without hurrying he could catch Godfrey Bland at just the right moment, over his late afternoon cup in the lobby of the Algonquin Hotel. If he were in luck he might still be able to get those two sophisticated sex novels for himself after all—or possibly— why not?—a better assignment. Hadn't he been settling for second-best and worse long enough?

It was at this moment that another and sudden thought occurred to him. Clasping his hand to the front of his collar, he discovered that he was not wearing a necktie. He also realized that he was not on Sixth Avenue, but on Fifth.

Without a moment's hesitation, and with only the

briefest mental acknowledgment to Captain Marryat, Abel Serles strode into the lavish interior of the nearest swank haberdashery, and made a sizeable donation to a worthy cause.

"Nothing gaudy," he directed. "Just your best plain silk foulard."

THEY LOVED ME IN UTICA

Originally published in New Worlds of Fantasy #2, *ed. Terry Carr, (Ace Books, 1970).*

T he room was dirty and badly lit and it smelled strongly of cheap, greasy food and of something else, which the girl noticed as soon as she came in.

"You're at the wine again, huh? You can't wait till after the performance?"

"And what the hell is the idea, may I ask, of telling everybody you're my daughter? My daughter, for crying out loud! Who do you think is going to believe that?" he wanted to know.

They were at it again.

Nobody was sup*posed* to believe it, she said. It was just a convention. As a matter of fact, it would stand a better chance of being believed if the story was that she was his *grand*-daughter, but she wanted to save his face.

If this meant that he was supposed to look on with fatherly approval while some young punk made a play for her, he said, in that case, he didn't want his face saved, and she could forget the whole idea. Convention! That was a hot one! Since when was she getting so conventional? As if anyone in this burg gave a damn if they were married or not.

"I went over great in Utica," he said. "Capacity house. They loved me in Utica." He drank some more of the sneaky pete. The girl, who had opened her mouth, closed it again. She cocked her head and shook it, half-annoyed, half-pitying. He was apt to go off on tangents like that, more and more every day. The guy was going to pieces fast. But she still thought she'd be able to pull him together again. All he needed was a little success—although, of course, a big one wouldn't hurt, either. Not in a one night stand like this, of course. But if he went over good here, if he just got his self-confidence back, if he'd stay away from the wine, if—

He was still a good-looking guy, with lots of stuff none of these young studs had. His voice was still good, even if he couldn't take the high notes. She noted that he'd cut himself shaving again, and this, for some reason, annoyed her.

"You mean *you* don't care if we're married or not!" she snapped. "All I am to you is a traveling shack-up job." But her heart wasn't in it, and he could tell it wasn't.

"Now, Honey," he said. "Don't pick at me, Sweetie. I'm a sick man. There's nothing the matter with a little light wine. It's like medicine, it's good for you. Have some."

But she said, No, thank you. "How about going over your material some more?" she suggested.

He shrugged. "I don't need to go over it. Once I learn a thing I never forget it. The rhapsodies—"

"Will you for heaven's *sake* please for*get* the rhapsodies?"

"—and the hymns—"

"Forget the hymns *too*! 'All new material' is what you're giving them here, remember?" Yes, he remembered. But he still had his doubts. The ballads were okay; though, boy! what a lie to call them "new"! Maybe they were new here, but, golly, he was singing them before the war—not the last war, the one before it. But he gave them up when the rhapsodies started going over so good.

Then, seeing her frown, he hastily said, "But they're good stuff, the ballads. I had good material, nobody had better. They don't write material like that anymore."

He brooded over his cup. The girl could hear the crowd (if you could call that handful of yokels a crowd!), and this reminded her that the guy's act was supposed to open. "Okay, so you know the stuff. So let's hear it. The strings in tune?" He ran his fingers over them, nodded. He was still in the dumps.

"Hey, you never told me where you picked up the ballads."
Not that she really cared.

The guy shrugged. "Who the hell knows. Here, there. One of them—this one—" He sang the opening line. His voice was a little husky, but it was warm and sweet. "I was knocking it off with this hoofer, see...But you don't want to hear about that...In those days I used to figure, once you're in big-time, you're always in. What did I know? Never figured I'd be singing for cakes in the boondocks again. But that's the way it is. You're only as good as your last season, kid. Gee, this past winter was the toughest I ever remember. I used to go down to the islands every winter. Haven't been able to afford it for years."

He warmed up to his troubles. "...and then the sky-pilots started in on me. 'What's with this guy?' they complain. 'Who needs *his* hymns?' I tell you, Sweetie, once you're down, they all jump on you. It's a great life if you don't weaken." An idea rippled its way across his face. He threw a swift, sly glance in her direction.

How would it be, he said; how would it be if he just threw in one, maybe two, of the rhapsodies? After all, they'd be expecting it. That was what made his rep.

She looked at him and shook her head with a bitter little smile. "Some people never *learn*," she said. "Can't you face up to it that the old material is strictly from Oldsville? Just give the ballads everything you've got. And, oh, say, listen. The M.C. says to throw in a little narration. Some story connecting the songs together."

"Yeah, but doll. I mean, these ballads. Like there *isn't* any story connecting them together. *You* know. There's *war* bits, *love* bits, *trag*edies...but, uh, no *story*."

Then he'd have to vamp one, she said; make it up as he went along. Why, for crying out loud! she complained—he, of all people, shouldn't have any trouble thinking up stories. "Boy!" she said, "when I remember the stories you told *me*! Hey. What's with the tears bit all of a sudden?"

It took a minute, but he got control of himself. Then he said, "My lamps are giving out on me, babe. I can't even shave myself anymore. I can hardly make you out, over there. Don't leave me, kid. What would I do?" She didn't say a word. "Anything you want. A story to hold the songs together? All right. Sure. I can do that. But don't run out on me. Don't—"

The M.C. knocked, and came in without waiting for an answer. There were wine-stains on his clothes, and his sandals were badly scuffed, but he had a measure of coarse handsomeness; a long look passed between him and the girl which the older man didn't see.

"You ready to go on, Grandpa?" he asked.

"Who the hell are you calling 'Grandpa'?" the singer snapped, forgetting his troubles.

The M.C. bowed, exaggeratedly. "Oh, pardon *me*," he said. "Are you ready to go on now, O sweet singer, whose songs deserve the laurels for all times to come?"

"That's better. That's the way to talk to the servant of the Muses...that's what somebody once called me in Utica, you know. They loved me in Utica. Hand me my strings, hon. Sure I'm ready. And, say—listen, pal: Give me a big build-up, will you, huh?"

"Yeah, yeah...sure—Oh, say, listen: Y' got a new name for your new act, so I can announce it?"

The old man gaped and blinked and moved his mouth, started to give his head a shake, No.

But swiftly the girl interposed. "A lot of these songs are about Troy, aren't they? Or what's the other name they used to call it? Ilium? Okay, then: so call your set the Troiad. Or the Iliad. What the hell's the difference?—Here's your lyre, Homer, honey..."

TIMESERVER

Originally published in Galaxy, *May 1970.*

Peter Everett slid his creditcard into the pay slot and dialed the Third *O*, prepared to curse at the blankness of the answer-scan in his office. If this went on, he told himself yet again, he might as well have the damned office turned off, notify T&T before his bill went past Permis and let the circuits stay in the reserve files. However, and to his mingled astonishment and relief, the ashcan was not blank, nor were the number and symbol those of T&T. He hastily dialed *P* and the booth went o-paque—for paranoid, privacy, all the flip, pat jokes.

"Mr. Everett, you called Timeserver Fanwell three hours, eleven minutes and six seconds ago," said the taped receptionist, giving him her taped smile, "but timeserver was occupied at the moment. Timeserver can see you now, if you wish, or the call can be nulled at no cost whatsoever to you."

Everett considered. He had called after intermittent reflection and in a moment of rare optimistic resolution and was perhaps just as glad to have missed connecting.

"Mr. Everett, you called Timeserver Fanwell three hours, eleven minutes and seven seconds ago but—"

Everett sighed, shrugged, dialed acceptance.

Fanwell had the perfect face for his profession, trustworthy and supremely forgettable. They exchanged greetings.

"My time is your time," Fanwell murmured. "I'm here to serve you."

Everett, with a crispness he did not feel, initiated the

minuet of button-pushing whereby the schedule-circuits of both men bowed and curtsied somewhere in the biomagnetic bowels of T&T, compared notes, and agreed upon an appointment.

An insecure over-aged biddy gabble-scowled at Everett as he left the booth.

"You're sure that wasn't P for pornography?"

"F and F, Zerelda, F and F," he said. Not much of a comeback but she made an annoyed noise.

Unlike his office, which had not even position but was dialed into existence, Peter Everett's home actually existed. He was not now one of the poor scons who paid the minifee for dial-a-home service. Having a wife meant he also had just enough points to get and keep an apartment. Otherwise there was not much you could say about it.

Ours is purely a marriage of inconvenience, he had said to his wife one night.

She hadn't even heard him. Sometimes he wondered what it might be like, involvement in a classical-type matrimony. But there was no use in wondering, as most classicals— except for the dwindling handfuls of sectarians—were of an age now when such matters must surely belong strictly to Memory Lane.

Everett's wife for this quarter was named Elissa—they had been married once before, about two years ago, and her name then had been Rosebeam. It didn't much matter. He hadn't even bothered to find out what her current principal lover was named. The CPL wasn't such a bad-o—he sometimes handed Everett a ration and had arranged for him to kip out every third night—which was his, the CPL's, night with Rosebeam—at the home of an affable les named Marchy.

However, she wasn't that affable.

"No, not even hardly ever," she had explained, firmly. Her offer to introduce him to nice—though old—aunties he had declined with a yawn. "It isn't normal for a man your age to go without some kind of sex," she said, concerned at his refusal.

"Then forget about old queans and introduce me to a woman who likes it with men."

She had rather a pleasant laugh.

"Cookie," she said, "the whole zing of it is finding a woman who likes it with men and then persuading her to like it with women instead. Well, make yourself to home, then—but remember: only every third night and subject to discontinuance without notice if I find someone for then."

The other two nights Elissa, ex-Rosebeam, spent away from their apartment with, as nearly as he could reconstruct it, any of a variety of men whom she contacted through a private circuit club she wouldn't turn him on to. He wondered if the CPL knew or cared—or would tell him anything—but had decided finding out was not worth the trouble. At any rate, the other two nights of Elissa were spent elsewhere, so that at least he had a room to himself for two nights out of three and it had taken him long enough to get points for that status. Only now—unlike Elissa or even Marchy—he hardly ever seemed to find anyone to share it with him and even the porno tube was on the blink. Everett looked to see if there was still a ration—the CPL had only Class Three rations, very hoity stuff—and there was. Elissa hadn't munched it herself as she sometimes did. Sim-u-Veg, Braised Meat Flavor, in this one. And a greeny-beny.

No doubt some sort of a sign. Because this gave him a complete set. There were more combos of complete sets than he could keep track of but he knew that two checkerboards, a horned owl, a pink heaven and two greeny-benies made up one complete set. He located his stash and took the works along with the Sim-u-Veg (Braised Meat Flavor) and three measuring cups of water. The appointment with Fanwell wasn't for another three days yet.

◆ ◆ ◆

And by that time Peter Everett was in a conventional condition again and able to read the Timeservers' Oath in its plasti-glow shrine without making a routine phantastick voyage out of it.

I swear by Chronos and by Telex and by all Symbolic Figures that I will not refuse to serve any man or woman of full age and under no legal inhibition or financial embarrassment but will freely relinquish my invaluable Time and of my own volition...

"Timeserver Fanwell will gladly see you now, Mr. Everett," the same receptionist of the taped message informed him in her own full flesh, so real he could hardly stand it. "I am Dr. Farnsworth Penelope, with a Ph.D. and an Sc.D. from the Oxford Consortium in the field of Advanced Receptionism and if you'll just let me have your currently accredited creditcard I'll be glad to see that the Special Low Fee for this non-emergency service is debited to your account without any further effort and attention on your part. Thank you, Mr. Peter Everett, and now just go straight on in through the simulated swinging doors."

Fanwell, clad in the ceremonial robes of a Late Primitive Bartender (Schenleyany-oriented), leaned over the bar—it was either genuine veneer or such a clever simulate that a lay eye could hardly tell the difference.

"What'll it be for yours?" he asked.

The sim-u-scent, Peter E thought sure, was that known as Mom's Apple Pie and he felt vaguely that there was an anachronism involved. But he had no desire to fight Timeservers' Hall.

"The usual," said Pete.

He knew the futility of telling his long, sad tale of woe. Not only would Fanwell know of a longer and sadder one but he would be obliged by his profession's Committee on Infamous Conduct to charge double-time for telling it.

"Straight policy?"

"Straight policy."

Not only had Peter Everett's bio-sire registered the fact

of his paternity—unlike many of PE's contemporaries' bio-sires, who were represented on the record by the crisp words *Mother's Free Choice* and nothing more—but he had also registered his payment of a Timeservers Policy. Both gestures were now generally deemed not merely unnecessary but indicating a desire to implant guilt. However.

"Well, that is just fine, pard," said Fanwell. "Of course it goes without saying that you are fully aware of the shrinkage in credit-power since the days when such policies were accepted by underwriters. I'm not telling you anything you don't know, pal, when I inform you, as I am ethically obliged to do, that the ethics of our profession nevertheless absolutely constrain me to accept service on this policy at a full sixteen-point-seven per cent of the policy's face value. I've heard tell that some timeservers unworthy of the name do their clients the extreme disservice of giving a higher rate than that. But needless to say, such false favors are being rapidly routed out by our Committee on Infamous Conduct."

"Needless to say," said Pete.

Timeserver Fanwell scrutinized the policy form he certainly knew by heart at this stage in his career. He muttered, read in an inaudible mumble, nodded from time to time.

"Uh-huh—uh-huh—hmm—" He looked up. "This entitles you to the full treatment for twenty-seven hours of Ethically Served Time. Last year our Regional Survey for the Study of Policy on the Determination of Infamous Conduct decided that time in excess of twenty-seven hours and less than a hundred hours could not ethically be served without further interpersonal adjustment."

Pete blinked.

After a moment he asked, "You mean—unless I pay more money?"

Fanwell did not blink. His entirely trustworthy, entirely forgettable face did not move except, of course, for the animation required for him to say, "Interpersonal adjustment—" once again.

This meant that not only was PE going to lose all but 16.7% of the face value of his policy, time-wise, to begin with —but that inasmuch as the remaining amount of time came to only ninety-nine hours and ninety-nine seconds, he would also lose the difference between this and twenty-seven hours —whatever that came to. He had, of course, no choice. Not if he wanted any of his time served *at all.*

Long ago it had been learned that the surface personality with all its ruts and grooves and warps and warts and dents could be peeled off for a time, thus liberating whatever other and unrutted, ungrooved, unwarped and unwarty and undented personality lay beneath. The process was compared to skinning the poor surface from a flawed pearl, for sometimes no flaws at all were found underneath. But the only way the outer personality could be detached—and that only temporarily, was for someone else to assume that personality. No one would or could do this forever, of course. And only the highly trained members of the timeservers' profession could do it at all.

Fanwell took down a bottle from the shelf and poured something carefully into a sim-u-glass.

"I serve your time," he said. "For the entire period of served time I am you," he said. "Wherever, whatever, for twenty-seven hours I am the outer surface of Peter Everett. At the conclusion of that period I cease to be him-you. It would be totally unethical for me to refuse to cease to be you or, while serving, to act in any way unbecoming to your usual standards. Should you not appear at the conclusion of the time agreed upon, I, as an ethical timeserver, simply remove myself from your identity. Should you have any complaints about my conduct during this or other periods, simply communicate with our professional Committee on Minor

Matters, which will place your complaint on its waiting list. You or your heirs, if any, will in due course—"

But Pete had quit listening. What tales of adventures were told—obtained when the subsurface personality was for a time released, unvexed, untrammeled, undisfigured, joyous, full and free!

He took up the glass and drained it.

One of those seconds-as-long-as-eternity resulted. He had, it was true, for long years hoped for personal success—it had never really been his. And always there had been the hope of at least possible excitement—escape—side-ego adventure via the liberation from the bonds of situation afforded by having a period of his infinitely unsatisfactory time served by a timeserver...This period of possible time had dwindled without his really being aware of its dwindling and now only a tiny proportion of what he had hoped for was left to him. At any rate he was about to realize on it: it might be good— i.e. as hoped for. It might be bad—i.e. other than as hoped for. But by very definition it was bound to be different. And for this alone it must inevitably give a different flavor to all his subsequent days and nights.

The drink in his glass was strong beyond all expectation and experience. It swirled and spiraled and burned and then everything ebbed away.

After a while he became aware that he had been sitting in a chair in a public sitting room for some time. As though alerted by his awareness (actually a pathetic fallacy, for no such alert existed), the chair began a slow, off-key, low-key ringing and the seat slid slowly into the chair, obliging him to get up—unless, of course, he wanted to slide to the floor or to insert his creditcard into the slot for another period of uninterrupted reclining pleasure.

He felt just the same as ever.

The thought occurred to him that it might be amusing to go home and see if Fanwell and Elissa were perchance together. But when he opened the door he saw that she and a stranger, not her CPL, were there alone and were about to make love. Except for a brief glance they paid no attention to him but, of course, as the apartment's only chair had been opened out into the bed there was no room for him unless he curled up on the floor—and, as this was already occupied by Elissa's and the stranger's clothes, he could hardly do that. So he closed the door again.

There was something in the mailbox for him. It looked familiar. It was his Timesaver's Policy with the word *Utilized* punched into it. And the date. A note fluttered to the floor.

Apartment will be available to you every other night from now on, it read. It was signed: Raindrop (formerly Elissa).

Every other night—instead of two out of three. The quarter had come to an end and she was free to make whatever new arrangements she pleased. Still, it was decent of her not to have divorced him—then he would have had no apartment at all. He went over to Marchy's apartment but when he slid his card into the slot it slid out again.

Evidently Marchy had finally found someone for her empty third nights.

The only certain thought that occurred to him was that whoever it was it wasn't his wife. And under the circumstances the fact hardly seemed to matter. He headed for a public reclining chair. He might even sleep. Now that he knew what lay beneath his surface personality he had one less thing to wonder about.

ZON

This start of a novel was published in Worlds of If, *May - June 1970. Unfortunately, Avram moved on to other projects and never completed the novel.*

I

When the first thin snows of Winter were being scattered by the whips of the wind Thiobud, called Rooster, mounted on a rough but serviceable pony, made his way northeast across the iron-hard and frozen mud. He was heading for the well-guarded burroughs of the Scopus Valley, where, he had heard, there was an unmanned woman. And he hoped to make a parley about her. A thin pole rode in the leather lancesocket with a white strip of rag tied to its top, and his pockets were conspicuously turned inside out. All this was, of course, no proof that he had no weapons concealed on or about him but it did for ceremony. And if anyone did start any trouble and it turned out that Rooster had, say, a knife hid under his clothes, well, it would serve anybody right. A gaunt, big-mouthed dog loped along more or less beside him. It had already run down and ravened two snowhares so far today.

Rooster's eye-stone began to tingle on its thong against his skin. Someone not too far away was looking at him. He let his own eyes roam but didn't turn his head. Let them look. Even if he were to ride buff-bare they could none of them see inside his head. The dog lifted its horrid muzzle and growled and he growled back at it. They went on.

Two men in a turfy peered out of the peep-holes. Throwstones clinked in their pockets. At the first sound of the pony hooves they had crawled over to peep out, expectant little noises rising in throats and mouths. Now one of them began to swear.

"Chip-eating son of a lesbo Zon—"

"Huh? What? Whuh yuh mean?"

"A whiterag. Cow cunny!"

The other squinted through red cracked eyelids. The disappointment was like a sharp pain. He breathed hard.

He said, "Uh, whuh, we c' take m anyway, uh. Huh?"

"Look how cocky he rides, the cow cunny," muttered the first. "Elbows out—son of a Zon! Muss really think he is a somebody—Maybe is—" He turned a scornful look on his companion. "We c' take m, uh? We juss bonk m withs a bonk stone, easy 's bonking uh chickenbird, uh. *And* the dog. *And* the pony. Nen what? Naa naa. Someone like that muss have protection. So juss when we finish eatin' the pony, down they come, 'Kilt our bruth, didja?' Nex' thing ya know—well, ya *know*, doncha? Uh-uh. I don't want no sharpstick hammered up my sphinc. Nup."

Already the figures were dwindling. Too far away for a successful take. The second man sighed and slobbered a little.

"Besides," he said, "anybody with poke enough to go out whiteragging, uh, mays got uh witch overlookin for m. Person c' fall apart, inch by inch, uh, uuhhh!" His filthy body shuddered in a convulsion not caused by the temperature but he made out it was, crawled away from the peephole. "Gunna throw uh-nuther chip on the red-eye," he muttered. "Gettin cunny cold in this cunny turfy."

Slowly, either from cold or reluctance, his bruth moved, too.

"Son of a Zon—see how cocky he sat on that Zon cunny ponny?"

They blew on the small dung fire and coughed in the bitter smoke. Then they spread out their tattered hands to warm.

◆ ◆ ◆

Wolf Hill and the level circle which was Wolf Hill Pond. Strangers Pass. Buffalo Head. And then Three Rock Brook —nobody, nothing there now but a person didn't tarry without good reason. Bow Gaze, also called River Bow Gaze, and far down below the mist made by the smokes of the many burroughs. A rich and interesting country but not the country, not the burroughs for which Rooster was heading now. And would reach—if he didn't get pulled down by wild dogs or wild men or civil men who just might have what seemed to them good reasons for not respecting a white rag —if he weren't gored by a bull of some sort, crushed by a deadfall, didn't ride into a stakes-pit, get caught in a witch-lace.

Wolf Hill, Wolf Hill Pond, Strangers Pass, Buffalo Head, Three Rock Brook, River Bow Gaze. So far, so good. No landmarks missed. The next one should be Poison Bones Flat, a good place not to go barefoot and requiring a sharp eye and a wide circuit on behalf of the pony. And after that—

He dropped *after that* from the top of his mind and began to think about *right now*, as soon as he saw over the next big rise. The dog didn't so much growl as grunt. And the pony nickered. Rooster counted five other—no—six other ponies. He wasn't able to say just how many people but one of them was a child. That was a good sign—a child. So were the travoys. No one went out venturing (a smooth word for a rough scene), no one went out raiding with children or travoys. He didn't yet know if he wanted to company with them—or if they'd let him, for that matter—even if they were going his way. They wouldn't, couldn't go very fast. Still, never mind, it was time to rest a while, they'd built a fire and—who knows—he might learn something. There—they'd seen him. Some were standing up, pointing.

He raised both his arms and the pole. Not increasing his

pace in the least he guided his mount with his knees down the other side of the rise.

It was the child whose voice split the cold and the silence with a tiny puff of breath.

"White rag," the child said. "A whiteragger!"

And, although the grown ones must have noted that by then, somehow the child's naming it seemed to make the fact certain. They did not, to be sure, unstring their bows but they lowered them, spoke sharply to their dogs. About twenty feet away the newcomer stopped. For a moment they looked at each other. The newcomer saw three men in red-dyed sheepskins, a woman mostly wrapped in an enormous mantle of dark wool, and the child, whose clothes had evidently been made out of the scraps of its elders' clothes. All were of dark skin and eyes, with here and there a lock of black hair hanging loose. And all were still unsatisfied. They saw a young man in leather, the hood of his jacket almost down to his eyes, naturally ruddy face nipped still ruddier by cold and wind.

The woman muttered into her mantle and one of the men said, "Dismount and make your dog bide there." The dog raised a leg against a hummock but showed no disposition to move closer after being bidden. "What do they call you?" the spokesman asked suspiciously.

"Call me Rooster—though I have a birth-name and a father's-name, too. Tell me, then, can I come up?"

A short hesitation.

"Come up."

They slipped their hands inside his clothes, found no weapons. Then they touched his hands with cold iron, to show if he were a witch; and with a silver ring, to see if he were a bloodsapper. And then, since he neither flinched nor cried out nor shrank back, they put a pinch of powdered sign-bark on his tongue and gave him water and watched his throat to be sure he swallowed. It was not savory, to be sure, but he had swallowed worse sign-powder in his life and thanked his witch (if he had one) that none of any of it had been poison—also a hazard of coming up to strangers.

"All clear, saltmaster?"

"All clear, Rooster. Sit by the fire."

"I will sit by the fire...Just a bit late for travoys, isn't it?" He inclined his head towards the wood-framed drag-alongs, cargoes lashed in place.

"The mud is all safe-frozen. Snow's not deep enough for sleds. We'll make our winter camp all right. Have a hunk of our salt. It's good—well made, clean." And the fire was welcome and he, feeling its heat on his face, pulled his hood back. "Rooster, uh? Well, I see why. Never saw a red cresty before." They all gaped—and the child jumped and set its hands to clapping so that the shell anklets rattled and clinked —at the sight of his head, polled to the skin, save for the roach or comb of red hair riding like a crest from brow to nape.

And then the stocky saltmaster spoke a word or two in a low voice, and the staring stopped. "Yes, huh, good salt—uh —trading's been good, too, this season—huh—"

The bulky woman had secured her child and now swiveled slowly around to face the guest.

"Why you whiteragging?" she asked, in a soft, husky voice. "Hunting a loster? Doing a punish?"

The soft comb and curl of wavy red hair ruffled as he shook his head.

"I've got places to go—I don't want to stop for troubles— Scopus Valley is the next place I'm going to—"

The younger of the two other men looked at him, teeth showing in his lower jaw.

"Heading for Scopus? Don't want trouble? Why, that's a Zon burrough, Roosty, didn't you know that? That's the biggest Zon burrough there is in all round uh these parts. You won't gets through The Notch, thems women, thems Zons, ull kill y'. Thems'll cutcher dippus off—"

Rooster shrugged. The saltmaster shook his head.

"No, for the white rag. The rule. Zons keep to all the rule. Nobody keep to all the rule the way Zons do—"

And: "That's right, Cler—"

"True as salt, Cler—"

"Never mind trying to scares him, Cler—" the others said.

Except the saltmaster, who said, "Yes, Cler, maybe you be scare for yourself, uh? Suppose *we* muss go to Scopus before to winter camp? So, salt, we send *you* in first, Cler—"

Cler shook his head so vigorously that most of his lank black hair escaped from under his cap.

"Not me," he said, as the others laughed (not Rooster, though). "I aints a going even near any Zon burrough! Send her, send Bets—"

"You could carry the white rag, you know, Cler," another man said. "Never mind the pole—juss tie it onto your dippus, Cler—"

But Cler, it was clear, white rag or not, wasn't going.

When the laughter ebbed the stout saltmaster said, "Wells, now I don't know. 'Send Bets…' suppose Bets gets to like it there and don't come back?"

More laughter. And Bets gave her husband a hearty cuff and called him, "Dirty fat man—" said she was too old and, besides, had gotten into *other* bad habits.

"Seems pretty good habits to me," her husband said serenely. Then, more serious, "But we have heard, Roosty, that the old Zon Ladyking of Scopus burroughs—what be her name?—it's a story about that it's her death-time—or was—"

"What? Dead?"

Rooster's head snapped up. His eyes left the embers. He forgot the smell from the fat stone caldron sitting in their midst. He met the eyes of the saltmaster, who, with thumb and forefinger, was rubbing a fold of his wattled chin. It was not Rooster alone who was hoping to learn something from this encounter—the older man's black eyes were sharp and keen.

"Dead? I didn't say 'dead,'" this one corrected him. "Not long ago at all we'd hears a story it was her death-time. Mays be she's dead, mays be she'd gets better, all; maybe she's still the same. Perhap you'll learn the truth before we, for we only mays be going there, to Scopus-Zon…But you say you do go there—'the next place—' uh?"

Fire or not, it was cold—the wind rustled and whimpered in the dry snow and blew gusts of it against the guest's naked head. He pulled his hood over and used the excusable action to avoid his host's eyes. No tentpegs could drive into that frozen soil and, had it been the saltmakers' intention to erect one of their yurtlike portable huts, they would already have at least begun it. So—clearly, after eating, they would be moving on again. So—two questions. Where would they be moving? And would he want to move with them?

"Nothing special in the pot," the saltmaster murmured— Rooster felt the undiminished tingling of the eye-stone—"a something of everything. No feast. But good. You share our fire. So. Share our food."

A long moment passed, so long that Rooster, half wondering why he had not answered, became aware that no one was waiting for his answer; became totally aware that half his attention had for most of the long moment been on something else. The continual yip-yap of the dogs had ceased, the hobbled ponies had turned and lifted their heads, the clitter-clatter of the child's shells was silent, the wind itself had gone quite dead. And in the silence and out of the silence came a sound of hooves, not slow, not fast— deliberate. Not the hooves of a horse or a pony, familiar as the sound of human breath, nor the wild, shy hooves of deer, the dumpy ones of swine. Not elk or moose—heavier than bison. Did bison feet ever go at that pace? It was the combination of unfamiliar sound with familiar beat—it was that, yet it was something else. A scent, an odor, heavy and sharp, filtered through the still air. The muscles of the dogs moved but no limb stirred.

They had not been aware, intent in their fire-warmed hollow, of a gathering mist outside and around—and perhaps might not have become aware of it the very instant of their looking and straining towards the odd, approaching sound, its direction at last determined—had not at that moment the source of the sound itself appeared. Half-obscured in the mist, on the spine of the rise, crossing laterally upon it, a figure curiously caped and cowled in strange garments. A figure riding on a strange beast, a huge beast, with great head slung low and great horns outspread. A figure girt about with unfamiliar or at least certainly undistinguishable gear and objects.

The figure moved along in the mist, rider and mount—the two moved through the mist. And the mist moved with the two.

Long, long, the Rooster sat by the dying fire. Or it seemed long. In point of fact it could not, he realized, have been, for the fire was fed stick by stick and chip by chip. The fire was empty, the stone pot was gone from it. No doubt the stout wife was about to dish out the food—it would be welcome. He stretched. By salt! How cold and stiff he was.

With a laugh that caught in his chest he said as he turned to his hosts, "I feel as though I had been under a—"

Under a spell...

The words hung unspoken in the brittle air. He did not speak them because there was no need for him to complete the utterance, no one to address it to. Twenty feet away his pony stood and looked at him in silence.

And they two—and the embers in the fire—were the only living things remaining there in the hollow at the bottom of the rise.

All the others were gone. His dog, too.

II

Morgan kept making mention of the cold, the cold. The furnaces were heated red-hot, then white-hot, and two stout servers (where one had done before) danced up and down on the box-bellows, forcing blasts of hot air into the pipes. Sweat in runnels ran down their heavy faces and their heavy flesh jogged and jounced. Others, hurrying by, perspired, too —though not as much by far—in the unaccustomed heat. Usually, at this time of year, the passageways were tolerable enough with only very small fires.

Two guards, furs slung over their arms, limbs and bosoms bare, stopped another whom they knew.

"The king—"

"She has asked for fruit—let me go—" and she sped on by.

Natural body warmth from all those in the vast bedroom would have served to warm it—it was stifling. Anxiety was on every face—still, much as those already there desired to remain, a sense of fairness and the rule constrained them to depart after a while and let others take their place. The rich and glossy furniture, except for one table on each side of the low bed, had been stacked against the wall. No one knew when Morgan's hair had begun to gray, all knew that she dyed it—it framed on all sides in huge jetty folds the sunken face on the pillows. For moments now the face had been still. Someone on each side maintained a gentle finger on the pulse vein in each withered wrist. Some of those watching watched no longer steadily the sunken, unmoving face— instead, their eyes flickered constantly to the single finger so gently held to each wrist. The room was silent. The face grimaced. A single sigh filled the room.

"The hen—the hen—"

"Yes, Father Mother!"

"—the hen—the hen—"

"Yes, Father Mother!"

The cracked, strained voice mumbled, muttered, dribbled nonsense—it was all the same. She spoke. King Morgan spoke. Therefore she still lived.

"Witches—witches—witches—"

"Yes, Father Mother!"

Hands waved, gestured frantically. The witches—in their glistening blacks slashed with glistening scarlet—surged forward like a black-and-scarlet wave.

The wave ebbed.

"—the hen—the hen—"

"Yes, Father Mother!"

Here and there was weeping. Someone old enough to remember the Zon King when she was not yet Zon King but Morgan alone—young and vital, full of figure, having many lovers—so someone wept. Someone young enough never to have remembered Morgan as other than the source of strength and power and the rule, Morgan, King of the Scopus Zons, Father Mother, sexless strong—so someone wept.

"—the hen—the hen—"

"Yes, Father Mother!"

For a moment the old voice gobbled. It fell silent. The fingers stayed on the wrists. Then the wrists tore away, the withered figure sat bolt up in the bed, tore at the prime and priceless furs, at the butterfly silks. The glossy hair fell like a curtain across the seamed and riven face, was torn aside by the clawlike hands.

"I cannot breathe! I cannot breathe! Fire—fire—I am on fire! You're boiling me alive—alive—"

And, indeed, the gray-pale face had gone dull-red. Hands gestured, waved frantically. Messengers sped from the room, fled down the corridors, signaled impassionedly to the sweating servers atop the huge bellows-boxes. The sudden appearance of the clamoring, gesticulating figures below served chiefly to throw them out of rhythm. They rolled their eyes, could hear nothing, understood nothing, misunderstood enough to think that this relay, as the others, was come to urge them to pump more swiftly. And so, leaving off the incessant jogging from leg to leg, one side to the other, the two monstrous figures, breasts sweating black against coarse dun robes, took firm hold of the support bars before them and began to jump up and down, alternately, to force more air and hence more heat—

—figures began to climb the spiderweb of ladders up to them—

—voices shouted to rake out the furnaces, to douse them down with water—

—shouting, the loudest, about to risk the fearful heat to alert the stokers, was Captain Rack, hot, angry, disheveled—

—laying upon Rack's arm a hand so cool that it commanded instant attention was—

"Memissary! Madame Sir! Yes, what—"

Rack followed back and to the side and to, if not precisely greater silence, certainly to less clamor and noise, the Memissary from the Hodus burroughs—tall, serene, slender, this one, rumored to be in direct line for the kingship of her own Zons, the treble-row necklace of walrus ivory, insigne of her rank, heavy upon her white shoulders.

"Madame Sir, yes?"

"Captain, with or without the steam which your plan must produce, 'twill be hours before the chamber of the Morgan King can cool."

This was so obvious that Rack could at first but gape. Then she bowed. "What does the Memissary say to do, then?"

"Obtain a fitting litter and place the King upon it and remove her to a farther and a cooler place."

Again—obvious. Again—unthought of. Captain Rack placed her hands upon her breasts, bowed twice and, mouth already open for further shouting, turned to run back.

But then She of Hodus once more placed her cool hand upon Rack's hot arm.

"To walk means safer speed at present. I shall accompany you. You will meanwhile be composing yourself."

One after the other the clear, crisp truths. Rack was, among captains, only one captain. Accompanied by the tall, imposing, hieratical figure of the Memissary, Rack saw all in that frenzied throng make way. And, as she composed herself, thus she began to think: it was the death-time of Morgan Father Mother, Zon King of Scopus; did she die today, tomorrow, a soonly death must come. Then what? However smooth the transference of power, things would change, would change for all things. Hence—would change for Captain Rack.

Nothing could prevent it.

She might advance. She might stay as she was. She might find herself descending into unsought obscurity. She might be informed (bland words for Exile) that, "The roster was to be reduced," handed presents, told to return to her natal burroughs. After twenty years! To be flung into the dung-pit of the world of men!

Or...

Rack had never been so close and for so long to the Memissary. Each step they took together, deliberate pace more arresting than the swiftest race, was a step up the stairs of prestige for Captain Rack. Not necessary to hint that they two had been lovers—best (by far) to give no such hint at all. Always, some would believe it. Might it be true, yet? Rack all but trembled. Common sense told her that official and urgent business only coupled them now and that, this business over, they might never—probably never— meet again. Still—it was not certain. One might dream, hope. And more—every Zon burrough had its "private people," its "friends," its "well-disposed" in every other Zon burrough. Rack was showing the She of Hodus that she could compose herself, was dependable. Surely, when it came time to take thought of such matters, She of Hodus could hardly fail to think of Captain Rack. What, after all, could be more natural than that such a high-groomed Zon would want at least one stalwart soldier-type for a close companion?

Indeed, so full was her mind of such thoughts that it was with a mental stumbling of surprise that Rack found the two of them at the chamber of Lady King Morgan, whose death-time had not yet passed. Still the Zon folk ascended and descended from all levels to have their last audience, still they would linger and still their code of honor made them regularly give way for others—for others, were they new-fledged Grade One Initiates or stooped and aging retired Captains-at-arms—on the double, thus, they made way for Rack and the Hodus-Memissary. Fans now waved over King Morgan as she rolled restlessly on her bed, still muttering gibberish, each mutter still evoking its respectful chorus.

"—the cockerel—the cockerel—"

"Yes, Father Mother."

"—cockerel—cockerel—"

"Yes, Father Mother."

"Yes, Father Mother."

"*Yes, Father Mother!*"

III

His birth-name was Thiobud—his father's-name, Phiniad. He remembered his natal burroughs little but that little distinctly—swarms of children crawling in and out of hidey-holes they must have been allowed (in contradiction to all the safety principles of the rule) to grub out for themselves, so small were they—noise by day and noise by night—often hunger. And then one day, riding on his father's shoulders in a place without walls and the roof so high he had no word for it—his earliest memory of the world outside.

Recollection of the Orth burrough began abruptly. Instead of curling up anywhere on a filthy floor one slept in a particular place on a clean skin spread on a pile of clean hay. It smelled sweet—the previous floor had not. Perhaps it was saying so to his father that brought from Phiniad, not given much to words, the comment: *By learning new things we learn old ones, too.* There were fewer children at Orth, far fewer. They dug no tunnels of their own. They were not suffered to stale or ease where they pleased like puppy dogs and were fairly frequently washed. More than this was not exacted of him at first. Later on he and several other children of an age were taken in one group and conducted around the main landmarks of the burrough—with the customary smack across the behind to fix each one the more firmly upon their minds—from the fishponds to the loomrooms (as the saying went). He thought that Orth was a very fine sort of burrough, indeed. And, indeed, he still thought so.

Not long after that Orth underwent its first siege during his stay there. A mixed rabble of turfies (as the homeless, the outlawed, the ragged wanderers were called, after the sod huts in which they lived for lack of burroughs) stuffed up the smoke holes in hopes of suffocating the inhabitants. Who, instead of suffering themselves to be quietly stifled, retreated to lower levels and thence to outside by exits unknown to the turfies and caught the besiegers by surprise—and were themselves caught by surprise.

Seemingly forever over the upper land at an even space which did not vary between them by a hand-span and at an even pace which hesitated not for fear and increased not for zeal and which was perhaps most terrifying of all (that relentless, steady step) came band after band of armed Zons. Their arrows began their murderous songs against the turfies while the archers were still well out of stones' throw. The longaxes finished the job. Only the turfy women were spared—that is, only those of the women who had wit or willingness to tear open their tatters and, by baring their breasts, reveal both their sex and their preference for capture over death.

Not all had been willing.

The Zons had not, of course, come for the purpose of assisting the Orth folk, just as they had not (this time, at any rate) come to attack them. They had not even been on one of their periodic campaigns against the turfies. Long later he had heard that this group of bands had joined with others, and then all of them with others yet—tales of an army of Zons marching westward into the horizon, of great battles somewhere afar off, of witchbirds (buzzards, some called them) covering the multitudes of dead—dead women who had fought more fiercely than men, preferring always the embrace of death to that of men, the caress of bloody black wings to the caress of men.

Always.

Not long after that his father took him to what (he later realized) was in effect a Council of the Elders. He had already seen most of them here and there and one by one, white-haired and white-bearded men in soft white robes—not till then had he seen them all together. In part it was much as though he were visiting any other group of older people— they said he was a fine boy, laid their hands on his head and wished him well, asked him if he liked it there more than in his natal burrough, beamed and chuckled at his emphatic *Yes!* In other part, however, he was aware of a difference.

In the Council cell light filtered from the light-well through panes of translucent shell upon the Elders, some of them so old indeed that their very flesh seemed translucent. And their thin old hands seemed to rest upon his head far longer than usual. He was asked questions other old people never asked him—and some of them dealt with things which were, and some of them dealt with things which were not but might be. And what, he was asked, would he do in such and such an instance? Or under this or that circumstance?

Finally one of them handed him a strip of skin. "Can you read?" he asked.

"Yes, my Elder, I am able to read."

The boy flipped the skin strip over and quickly ran his fingers over the tiny bosses and almost at once a look of ludicrous outrage came over his face.

He cried out, "This is—this is wrong!"

Several of the old men chuckled. One laughed outright. A few smiled. One gazed at the boy intently and without change of expression. And one gazed off as though into infinite space, his head never ceasing its incessant nodding, as though in continuous agreement.

The particular Elder who had given him the strip of skin asked, "Why is it wrong?"

"I don't know why—I know how. Listen, it says, *Thiobud the son of Panerad the son of Phiniad*—and so on. But it is my father who is Phiniad—"

And the old man said, "True enough—but this does not make the record wrong. It refers to Thiobud, who was your father's father and whose father was Panerad the son of an earlier Phiniad. But these things you will learn in time. In time you will learn more than all of us here together have yet learned."

The boy's face, showing surprise at first, then keen attention, was turned full upon the Elder, whose eyes now held his. His red hair seemed the sole spot of color in that underground chamber, all shadows and greys and dim whites. His youth was the sole source of freshness in the Council cell, among the old, old men and their collective weariness, the smell of dust and age and the ancient furnishings.

Demeran, Chief of the Elders (he died soon afterward), said, "No man's life can ever be altogether his own— but yours will and must be less your own than is usual. Prepare yourself for this. When you next see something you particularly desire and may have, deny yourself it. When you next are about to do something you particularly desire to do and may do, deny yourself the pleasure of doing it. Cultivate this habit by day and by night, for it will provide you with excellent training and habits of discipline and self-denial, excellent habits for all men—but most excellent for you."

Demeran said, "You have seen the turfies. Their freedom from the burrough rule and from the need to subordinate and to submit they have purchased at the price of thirst, nakedness, animality, outlawry, incessant hunger, and early death."

Said Demeran, "You have seen the Zons. Wealth and military power they have obtained but they have obtained it by the sacrifice of natural love and natural softness and by the carefully and artificially cultivated hatred of half of humankind."

And he said, "You have seen life in your natal burroughs, whither your father went during a time needed to resolve certain personal uncertainties—and you will have observed and remembered that where there is no constraint there is no cleanliness, where there is no cleanliness there is no order there is no amenity."

His thin old voice had grown stronger and all his fellow sages nodded at his words. There were many more words before he paused in sheer fatigue and sipped at a tiny mug of milk and water. The words seemed to hang in the air, heavy as thoughts—the shadows were gathering in the declining day and it seemed to Thiobud that the shadows were the old man's words and were heavy with heavy thoughts and that they were presently to gather around him.

In another moment he might have shuddered or shrunk away, perhaps even turned and fled—but that other moment never came. Someone lit a lamp and he became aware of the familiar evening (also afternoon, also morning) cramp of hunger in his belly. That the evening meal be postponed in Orth was as unthinkable as that any other essential and scheduled routine be postponed. Therefore the gathering must soon terminate—therefore he could endure waiting until it did. As sure enough soon it did. The old one still gathering his wool from infinite distance and nodding, nodding, nodding, said (as they bowed and were dismissed, father and son). "Be sure, Phiniad, he is one."

Over the stewbowls the harmless halfwit who was permitted to eat with the boys said to him, "Ha, they got you now."

Thiobud said, "What?"

"They got you now."

"What?"

The man-boy indicated the direction of the Council cell— then all thought of it left his face and he slyly stole someone's chunk of bread—something which he did so adroitly and with face subsequently so innocent and immobile that even the victim could not stay angry at him.

"What do you mean, they got me now?"'

But the other merely dipped his crumb and crust into the stew and sucked and munched and gave no sign of either hearing the question or understanding it.

Eveningdole was good—it was food, good food and all boys had healthy appetites. They ate with good will, talked in good voice to each other, laughed, chattered, made plans for tomorrow, passed bowls for seconds to the table captain. And he—Thiobud did the same. But all the time like a wreath revolving and showing the same vines and ferns and flowers, like a wreath revolving over the head of a seated bridewoman, so did words seem to revolve as though visible and seen, the same ones over and over again.

You will learn more than all of us together. Be sure, Phiniad, that he is one. They got you now.

Over and over, around and around. Again and again.

Why would he be learning more than all of the Elders together? He was one what? Who had got him?

The meal went on as before, all things went on as before, but he knew without knowing why that nothing was nor would ever be again quite as before. And, like a wreath upon horsehair threads, like a wreath at a wedding-feast, the endless chain of words revolved and revolved and slowly slowly spun around...

You will learn more than all of us Be sure that he is one They got you now You will learn more than all of us Be sure that he is one They got you now

Around and around and around.

IV

He saw the first of the white-limed boulders from a very far off. Scopus—or at least early sign of it. The sign signified, as all well knew, *Be exceedingly sure that you approach only on what we would consider appropriate business.* All through the whole of the next day he passed such rocks at regular intervals, passed as well fields and pastures, these outer ones all empty at this season of the year. The night he spent in a clean and empty house where, probably, herders lodged. It was spotless and held stacks of fuel but no food—he would scarcely have ventured to help himself to any in any case. A man coming unbidden into Zon country—and when was a man ever bidden to enter Zon country—had to be very careful indeed. He looked around to see if there were any reading-tapes but there were none, not even so much as an empty spindle set. Cautious, the Zons.

It was halfway through the next morning that he saw the first guardpost house, a small triangular structure. He had no doubt that there were ample burroughs beneath— perhaps, even from here, underground ways led all the way to the main settlement, supplied along the way with light and air through cunningly hidden shafts: indeed, rumor even endowed such ways with water in the form of diverted springs.

Two of the guards were already outside. Had they simply sharper eyes than he? Had the underground rooms served as echo chambers, giving warning of his pony's hooves? Or was there some Zon magic at work? Having no answers, Thiobud merely shrugged, glanced to see that the white rag was still a-dangle from the pole resting its butt end in the lance socket and rode on—but before he came within arrow range he tied the pole to the harness and raised both his hands, guiding his mount with his knees.

He had never seen Zons this close before. He asked himself: apart from the neat and trim lines of their winter furs, in exactly what way did they differ from others? A wooden gong made from a slit and hollowed log hung from a tripod and the guard standing by it with beater raised was unmistakably a woman. The one in the doorway, whose bow and nocked arrow followed him as he approached, might have been a boy. Any female curves either might have had were lost in the concealing furs. Friendship on their faces would have surprised him; its absence did not. Neither was fear there, nor alarm, nor hatred—chiefly a certain cool caution. But besides and beyond any expression familiar to him he saw on both their faces a common expression which was not. He could not as yet define it, more than to say in his mind that it was strange, that they both had it, this look—that they were both Zons—and so his mind said, *It is the Zon look*...Well. He had heard. Now he saw. And if he were careful and if luck were with him and if he "had a good witch," he would likely see before very long a number of other things of which he had until now only heard.

And if he were careless or luck were not with him or he "had a bad witch" he might find himself at the bottom of a very deep and very dark pit with several Zon arrows in between his ribs and at least one in his heart.

The guards at First Post had not precisely welcomed him, but he had not expected them to. He was the fly and they the spider, he entered at his own risk and he knew at least in general terms the perils of the web. In fact, he thought, with a sudden smile quirking a corner of his mouth, that sounded like a not-bad title for a minor epic, to be recited in meter to the accompaniment of one or two strings and a small hand-drum: *The Perils of the Web*...A gust of wind came whistling down the valley, froze his grin. He tugged his hood tighter about his face. Greater risks or not, he would they had allowed him to go by the burrough-ways.

No—welcomed he had not been—but the rule was that a whiteragger was entitled to pass and, as the stocky old saltmaster (where had they all vanished to—and how fast —and why?) had pointed out, Zons kept to the rule. No doubt they had helped make it, too. Certainly it benefited them as well, being as they were so far outside the general order of things with their manless society, to help create and maintain an order above all local orders, above even the general order of things. For it was the rule alone and only the rule which enabled them on their periodic rounds to ride up, whiteragging, to any burrough, to engage in that curious spectacle in which their well-trained ponies would rhythmically stamp the ground above the burroughs —an unmistakable signal—and to proclaim to the multitude of never-friendly faces that they were there to accept any recruits...any prisoners...any children for "adoption or education"...any...so long as they were female.

Never a pleasant scene. Often: howls, hoots, jeers.

But the rule was the rule.

And sometimes they did not ride away unaccompanied.

Now Thiobud (the son of Phiniad the son of Thiobud son of Panerad son of Phiniad and so on and on) was himself benefiting. The guards had not cared for his use of the term *freeling*—a good thing to have realized, a piece of information he would keep in mind and pass along for the future—and certainly they would have cared even less for *an unmanned woman*, archaic phrase in any case and ludicrously inapplicable to one raised from childhood by the Zons. So he was obliged to explain that what he meant, exactly, was: *A woman who had been raised among the Zons from childhood but who had not yet taken the Zon-pledge and so was hence able to leave if she so desired.*

The proper term, he soon learned, was "a foster-guest."

Callers such as he did not come often. That was apparent. But something else was apparent, too—it was in the air, it was evident in certain hesitancies, certain glances. And he had no idea what it was or even might be. They had signaled on ahead by gong-beats, which of course conveyed nothing to him, and he had been allowed to ride on. Several guardposts later it had begun to snow and he was beginning to fear that he might perhaps miss his turn-in (or its guards miss him) and ride by it—which brought up not only the risk of freezing to death but the probably greater risk of his being shot at when he appeared in an area where he was not supposed to be...small use a white rag against the white blinding blanket of the snow.

But he did not miss it. The ground was rising now and he was on the lookout. He saw the great stone gates and he saw the guardpost house and the by now familiar gong and tripod (house and gong and tripod all three much larger than those of the outposts)—but he saw no one on guard.

He waited long but the cold overcame his caution—or, rather, under those towering crags, of all Scopus landmarks the best known, and in that snow and wind the cold provided a caution of its own. So he called out his coming and rode up to the post house.

Lamps had been lit and a brick box with a metal door radiated heat but no one was within.

Quite a while he stayed there. Then he heard his pony pawing the ground. Then the wind changed its direction and he realized that the noise he had (without especially considering it) assumed to be the wind was only in part the wind. And was in part—

What?

He sighed, shook his head, went out, brought his beast under the eaves of the house and poured grain into the small basket for it. Then he took up his pole and the small bit of cloth to which he trusted his life—and he went on through the great stone gate.

The Upper Entrance to Scopus burroughs was marked by a huge triple arch carved out of living rock. The spaces enclosed within the outlines of the treble curves were crowded with bas-reliefs and statues illustrative of the histories of the first three kings but statues and reliefs alike were clotted with snow. Beneath the pediment a vast door for each arch had long ago been cut into the rock—or, precisely, the lineaments of vast doors. The doors were for the most part false—rock faces did not swing upon rock hinges—but the lowermost panels were true doors and, as Thiobud came trudging through the road, he saw these doors were swung open wide. The interior blazed with light. A huge tent was in process of being erected and at least a full thousand Zons in every state of dress and undress swarmed around. Some raced up with poles, others heaved upon ropes, some swept from the holes socketed in the ground the snow that clogged them—others kneeled and scooped it out with bare hands, snow falling upon their bare shoulders. Others, while parts of the huge pavilion still sagged and billowed, came tottering forward with rugs and carpets which at once were unrolled. Others staggered beneath the weight of furniture. He saw at least fifty of them bringing in braziers, saw the braziers' red eyes winking and blinking in the uncertain wind.

No one seemed to see him at all.

And now another mass seemed not so much to exit from the huge gaping mouth of the Upper Entrance as to eddy about in it, now forward, now slightly backward, now slightly to one side, a bit forward—and, as the last section of the huge tent reared upright and settled slightly, its rich red and purple folds brightening the darkening day, this new mass of people passed slowly forward and out of the gates and into the pavilion and was hidden from his sight.

A sight so strange this was that Thiobud, observing in open-mouthed astonishment, could hardly be sure of what was happening. But he saw that some, at least, of those emergent had been carrying something upon their shoulders. He thought it looked like a sort of bed—did he also have a glimpse of black hair rolling and tossing in a brief gust of wind? Of a gray face moving from side to side?

The wind of a fierce sudden blew back his hood and his hand moved automatically to restore it—did the gray face (if such it was) turn in his direction? Did a tiny hand fling itself toward him? Did not his eye-stone briefly tingle?

It had all happened in so brief a time that he could be sure of none of it. He saw the gold embroidered tent flaps sink slowly downward. He saw all but one of the doors of the Upper Entrance swing shut.

And stood as alone as before, unknowing what to do.

The motives of one chosen as Zonvizier are notoriously mixed. On the one hand there is the immediate access to great power and prestige via the office of Second Servant of the Burroughs—the First Servant, of course, being the King herself. On the other hand there is the instant realization that whoso has ever held the office of Second Servant may never aspire to hold that of First—and, for that matter, may never even be certain of continuing to hold that of second.

Zon kings never retire and never resign and are never (but never, never) deposed. Zonviziers, on the other hand, hold office solely by the pleasure of the supreme officeholder. And this pleasure is often such by conventional designation alone. In burroughs (not, of course, in Scopus burroughs) where intrigue rather than industry, the arts, affections, or any other emotion or combination of emotions holds sway, it is not unknown for a potential troublemaker to occupy the Second Seat for a very brief time indeed. In the morning the would-be disturber of the scene is called before the First Seat and handed the symbolic Shield of Office—in the evening the Zonvizier hands it back to the Father Mother King. Who hands it back to her. Except that in such cases there comes an evening when the Father Mother King does not hand it back.

"Go and rest," says the First Servant to the Second.

And: "Yes, Father Mother—" says the now-without-office.

To others she says, "Father Mother has been pleased to allow me to rest."

And they reply—if they truly are her friends—"How fortunate you are. Burdens chafe and heavy burdens usually chafe heavily."

Except that sometimes, instead of letting their eyes fall or sighing sympathetically or offering a love-gesture, they say, "Well, that didn't last long, did it? Didn't I tell you that you should (or should not) have done thus and so? Ah, but no, you would not listen—no, not you. Well. Ah!"

She then knows that these are not her true friends and never were but of course it is too late. Those who hold no power can bestow none and so by the brief bestowal of glory the possibility of their ever holding the greatest of glories is forever removed.

But King Morgan had never felt the need to use such tactics —quite the opposite. It was said, though never of course in the presence of a Zonvizier, that Morgan felt it would be unwise in the extreme ever to appoint to the Second Seat anyone who either aspired to the First or who was capable of filling it.

"I govern while I live," was the precise way she put it. "And after I cease to live I shall cease at all to govern."

In other words, she would take no steps to disqualify

as her successor any who might otherwise be qualified to succeed her. In some measure, therefore, the aura of the zonviziership was dimmed and for over a generation it had been held by a succession of nonentities. The present occupant was a Captain Krug (between the captaincy and the viziership there were no active ranks), massive, stolid, more than somewhat dim in personality. Captain Krug, as captain, had gone by the rule and by the direction of her superiors. Zonvizier Krug, as Zonvizier, did the same.

Whenever possible.

At present, however, the Zonvizier scarcely knew what was possible and what was not. A king did not die every day and Krug, who was in middle-age, scarcely remembered the death of the last one. She had certainly not taken Zonvows at the time and so had been obliged to do nothing but weep and follow the prescribed mourning. No doubt the rule had something to say but the knowledge of it had dimmed, ebbed, since then. No doubt there were a few aged Zons about who might remember something.

But not only could the Second Servant not ask the First, "What must I do in this—the matter of your dying?"

Even if the Morgan King were all sharp of mind the Second Servant could not have brought her tongue to say it. She could not bring her tongue to state that it was indeed fell death and not illness alone that stalked the burroughs of the Valley of Scopus. She had an all but fully formed belief that, were she to ask in what manner she should act about the king's death or dying the pace of dying might immediately increase.

Not knowing what to do the Zonvizier did nothing or did whatever the loudest voice suggested she do—assuming it was not against the rule. The face of Captain Rack was just a face to the Zonvizier—but it was the face of a captain and, hence, the face of one entitled to suggest things in a loud voice. The Hodus Memissary was in the same category —no, in a higher one, for the Zonvizier herself had invested the Madame Sir with the customary and honorary rank of captain of captains, which in theory at least placed her below only the Zonvizier. There was nothing, to be sure, in the rule or any other customary usage about erecting the King's Pavilion in the winter—but there had been a few occasions when it had been erected only because Father Mother Morgan had felt unwell and not for the more usual purposes of ceremony.

Captain Rack spoke loudly—the Memissary smiled her cool and enigmatic smile, the Zonvizier—half-distracted with grief and confusion—gave the orders.

Someone was to be sent for—the King had mentioned...

The King had mentioned! The vizier's middle-aged mind, numbed with sorrow and indecision, seized upon this single point. It meant doing at last something one knew that Morgan King had wanted done. The zonvizierial fingers were snapped. Equerries sprang to the zonvizierial side. Heads were bowed respectfully.

"Let the Second Seat say—"

The Second Seat said, "Let the young person Tintinna be at once brought here—that is, not here—we are all going above in order that Father Mother escape this overheat. The Great Pavilion—escort her there at once—at once—at once—"

The Memissary smiled.

Captain Rack did not.

Thiobud thought that the snow-laden winds, grown tired of their amorphous writhings, had taken on shapes and forms. In a moment, though, he realized that the forms were those of people. They spoke to him, gestured, laid their fingers on the sleeves of his jacket. Their faces and their eyes were red—and somehow he judged that this was not from cold. He had for some while prior to this been not aware of the cold. It was the all-encompassing element, it had conquered and transformed the air, had in fact become the air and one usually takes the air for granted. Now, suddenly, he was again aware of the cold and aware of his weariness —he bent his head submissively and began to follow the shapes.

But they had stopped.

For one long second they gazed at him. The nighest one gently (it seemed gently) put up her long, thin, gauntleted hand and pulled down his hood. He had hardly been aware it had slipped. And then, together, they went at a quick pace to the great tent. For a brief moment in the waning day the flurry of snow halted and a thin effusion of the ruddy light of sunset made the purple covering seem somewhat crimson. Then this all vanished. The shadows on the snow were blue and the great pavilion itself turned black.

Those standing on guard just inside the entrance, furs opened and displaying habits of black adorned with gold-broidered work, gave low exclamations of astonishment as the others entered.

"Then there *was* a person—'outside,'" one of them said wonderingly. "Just as Father Mother said—"

"Just as she said. And—"

But one of his guides shook her head, as though to cut off further comment. She placed her hand upon his sleeve and drew him along through the throng of turning heads and opening mouths, through the sudden drop in the low-pitched hum of conversation, through the deepening silence. Incredible, incredible—a swarm of people and all of them women! And all of them—ah, well—all of them had the Zon look. How old did they have to be before they took the oath or pledge? Nor was it that they all looked at him with hate, though hate was there—at least on some faces—it wasn't even that he was a man, rare though men must be in any Zon burrough or encampment. It was simply the look.

"Father Mother, here is he."

The black hair (dyed, it must be dyed), the old, gray,

sunken face, the incredibly rich coverlets and furs, of the woman lying there on what in that brief glimpse he had believed might be a bed. It was doing duty as one now, resting at bed height off the floor; actually it was a sort of litter or palanquin. Had she, whoever she was, actually seen him there outside as they bore her in? The lids fluttered up from the sunken eyes, huge and gray and glazed, barely focused, barely aware of anything any longer. The shrunken lips seemed to struggle, uncertain as to whether to permit or restrain the tongue which at last emerged, then retreated.

What was it she was saying?

"—the cockerel, the cockerel—"

Someone said, "Yes, Father Mother!"

Someone else with a light touch took hold of the hood of his jacket and pulled it back and down. He could feel, as he always felt, the roach of red hair rising as it was released from the pressure of the hood. And he felt—was aware of— the throng's reaction even before he heard it gasp.

"—the cockerel," moaned, mumbled the very old woman.

"Yes, Father Mother," the crowd said, sighed and echoed.

There was a stir not from the far edge of the old woman's litter and a clump or cluster which till then had been an undifferentiated part of the throng now seemed to part from it. Once again he felt something for which he could find no words, as though (and now he seemed to have a clearer image of it) as though something soft and velvet-webby was moving inside his mind, stroking his brain. At once, abruptly, it ceased to be pleasant—a sensation like vertigo hit him hard. Dressed in black robes of wide cut, slashed with scarlet, black-peaked bonnets from head to shoulders and scarlet beneath—it might have been ten women, it may have been twenty—moved, swayed, looked at him, threw up their hands in a sinuous gesture which seemed to run through them like a wave. He pushed back against the ugly, dull feeling—it vanished.

Someone in his ear said, very low, "The witches—"

Now these women set up a keening and repeated one sound three times.

"Oh—"

"Woe—"

"No—"

Uneasy was the throng.

A voice said, "Silence!"

A voice said, "As Father Mother wishes."

A voice said, "Your beloved Morgan King—"

Not quite had each voice spoken together with each other voice. He glanced away from the mass of witch women while the voices still sounded, superimposing their own notes upon the other ones. He saw the sullen, blocklike face he did not know was that of Captain Rack. He saw the sturdy and bewildered face he did not know was that of the Zonvizier —saw the long and gracious and cryptically smiling face he did not know was that of the Memissary. He saw, too, a fourth face, a younger face, felt a stir of something more than merely interest. It was not alone that this was the youngest face, certainly, in all this crowded pavilion, not alone that it was by no means an uncomely face—something more stroked softly across his mind.

It was the only face there that did not have the Zon-look. And the absence of it was as unmistakable as its presence.

V

He had not realized how grateful he had been of the warmth until once more he was out in the cold. Now it was the snow and the outside again and altogether the wrong time of day—night? But another pony was trotting along beside his and someone else sat the second pony. A third one with no rider but a deal of gear was coming along behind. It had all been so easy. It had perhaps been too easy. There had hardly been a parley at all. He had thought of what he would say and no one had asked him to say anything. He had thought there would be great hostility toward him and it had not been directed toward him at all. He had thought to initiate a talk about a woman, no doubt to return again to continue it, to see her, to consider, to return perhaps a third time—perhaps not to return ever. But it had not happened at all like that. And here he was, riding through the darkness and the snow with the woman. He corrected his thoughts: With *a* woman. How could he possibly, in such a brief course of time, know.

Something shrilled in his ears. Without thinking he flinched away from it, found himself hanging over his mount's neck. What in witchbane was it? It was she, the girl or woman, he scarcely knew—it was a whistle she had in her mouth, on a lanyard. An odd white whistle of a sort he'd never seen before and she blew those horrid shrills upon it— but why?

When she had to cover her own ears?

No, she was not muffling her ears. She was cupping them, not trying to muffle the sound but to amplify it. He fell behind her and at once realized something as odd as all the rest of it—he could see her cheeks puffed out as she blew upon that devilish little pipe but he could no longer hear it. Perhaps it had clogged? No—in that instant she veered her pony around and came abreast of him without ceasing to blow and the instant they drew level he once again heard it and he cried out.

At once she stopped. Stopped the whistle, stopped the pony.

"I am sorry," she said. Her voice was the same here as it had been back there, not that he had heard much of what she said, not that she had said much—mostly farewells and thanks. Certainly something of the Zon speech was in her voice—but something was in it which was not. There seemed a faint drawling trace of the speech of a burrough he could almost identify—unimportant, that, now. "But it was necessary. We go this way now. Please?"

He muttered, "Of course—you know that we must soon take shelter?" She nodded. "What is that? Zon witch-magic?"

She seemed to consider how to explain it, then said, "I am trying to find my bearings here in the snow and the dark. The snow distorts the echoes but I think we are going the right way now. Do you know my name?" she asked. "It is Tintinna.'

"And mine is Thiobud. They call me—it is very strange—no, I suppose not so very. Well, they call me Rooster."

"The cockerel," she said. "Yes, it is the same thing, I suppose. Mother spoke of that before she saw you tonight, did you know that? She has been speaking of that for a few days now. 'The cockerel and the hen.'"

Mainly he had shelter in mind. Vaguely he did not relish the notion of viewing their relationship (whatever it was or was not to be) on the simple level of the poultry coop. He peered through the formless dark, could see nothing. She had blown her mad whistle so that she could listen to the echoes. Like a bat.

Abruptly she said, "No, it wasn't that, it's—oh, a new child is always called a 'chick.' But it was just that I was sort of Mother's pet and she called me her hen—that's all. And," she said, still softly, yet firmly, "there was nothing of *that* between us—or any of them—or else it's not likely they'd have sent me off so simply, so soon. Not that I haven't been ready to go for a while now. But you mustn't take anything for granted."

They were on windswept land now. The hooves rang hard and loud on the rock-hard ground. And the way was up.

He said, "I did not think—" and paused, uncertain of how he should word it.

"If not now, later. It would be inevitable—that you at least think about it. Zon is Zon, after all. But I am not Zon. Still —" and a sound in the darkness made his heart warm toward her, for he knew that she was laughing there in the darkness of the winter night—with a stranger. "Still," she said again, "Zon is Zon. Up to the last minute. That old Memissary, the one in the brown robes with the huge ivory necklace—you know, she didn't want me to go. I don't know why—not love, I'm sure of that. But poor Rack—she thought it was. Oh, her poor face! That was why she kept practically shouting in the poor old Zonvizier's ear, *Father Mother wants them away*—And, well, who knows what the poor old thing really wants? A prophecy? Rack made it out to be one. Still, even if Morgan had prophesied your coming, even if she did foresee our being together, who knows that she wanted it so? The witches didn't like your reek at all, did they? Hold on!"

There was a scan of ice and the ponies slipped and slithered, then righted themselves. Then there was a wall upon the right, then one upon the left. Then—echo, echo, echo—suddenly Tintinna let out a whoop and the echoes rolled and multiplied and he knew that they were inside a burrough.

And still the death-watch continued. Extra braziers were brought and, swiftly, deftly, blankets were held up to them to be warmed. Deftly, swiftly the ones on the Zon King's bed were rolled halfway off and fresh ones rolled halfway, then all the way. The Second Servant snored in her chair and most of the former watchers had retired to their own cells for rest. Some, however, had rolled into their furs and lay upon the rugs—now and then walking and rising and watching, sometimes silently, sometimes murmuring to others, usually returning to the rugs for further slumber.

The Memissary had made some concession to her own weariness. She sat upon a stool and her heavy necklace reposed upon her lap where her fingers told the tusks over and over again, as though she were reading a tape. She faced the crouching clusters of witches, a sunken, sullen huddle of black and red.

"Great is the strength of the Morgan King," she said.

After their customary usage they answered her in turn.

"Ah, Mem—her strength is great but—"

"—the truth is, although great strength—"

"—is in her yet, yet her strength is not—"

"—great at all. Ah, nay, Mem, for—"

"—it is our strength which sustains it, as—"

"—one sustains a fire by blowing on it but—"

"—for this fire, Mem, ah, there—is no—"

"—more fuel, ah—"

"*No*—" They rocked their heads.

"*Oh*—" They waved their hands.

"*Woe*—" They sobbed and wailed.

"Nor for much longer—can we thus sustain—our Kingly Lady dear—it is only that we hope—she may yet return her mind—and reveal to all—or at least, at least—to us, to us —who shall next ascend—ascend, ascend—who shall next ascend—the Primest Place—the First Seat—but we fear, we fear—we fear, we fear—not here alone—not here alone—" They chanted and they wailed, swaying from side to side, lolling their heads and rolling their eyes.

The upraised hand of the Memissary was long and slender. She lowered two fingers, placed her thumb on one. The chanting stopped. With dull and reddened eyes they looked at the hand, wetted their cracked lips, breathed noisily through their nostrils. The hand sank once more into the Memissary's lap, once more her other hand caressed the sea-morse tusks.

The Mem had no need to raise her voice.

"I know what it is you fear. I fear it as well. My own witches have warned me—us—that is, the wise ones of my own burrough. Besides, there have been signs. Dreams. Waking warnings—"

The witches sighed and the witches groaned. They had the witch-puffed lips—they had the witch-puffed eyelids, and their hands were puffy with witch-puffed flesh that gave off the witch-bitter reek. Small need then, if identification were desired, for silk-smooth black and the inner lining of blood-slick red.

Their faces were turned full on the Memissary and all their mouths were opened but she flinched not at all from the witch-stale rancor of their witch-stench breath.

"Wise women, wise ones, sisters sage, something trembles in the stillness of night, something whispers in the silence of the stars, something very ancient desires not to be discerned while it struggles to be born anew."

"Oh—no—woe. What may we do?"

The delegate bent her long and comely neck. The witches slithered closer and raised their heads, open-mouthed. An observer might have thought, had she or he been accustomed to think in terms so unhuman, that here was a cobra feeding frogs.

"Listen," she said and her voice was cool and her voice was low and her eyes glittered and the breath hung thin and pale upon the thick, stale air. "Listen, my lovelies and my loves—ah—*listen!*"

Presently the quality of echo altered and almost at that instant the lead pony stopped. At once he heard her dismounting and then making the little muttering noises a woman uses when she searches for something, the location of which she feels she knows absolutely and which she somehow cannot find. A grunt succeeded these homey sounds and then there appeared in the darkness a dim glow that spurted into a ragged blaze of light against which he shielded his eyes. The light settled into the symmetrical flame of a torch blazing evenly where there is no breeze. She was holding it out to him and, he having taken it, she reached her hand into a kind of press or cabinet carved into the wall and took out another torch. It blazed up in her hand.

After seconds, during which he blinked, he asked, "How

did that happen? The torch catching fire just like that?"

"It did not really. That's a photon pile. You don't understand me? and if I said *stasis, non-stasis, space, time, energy, matter, technology*—would you understand me? No, not even in Orth. Well, so I made it light by Zon witch-magic."

It seemed that this explanation quite satisfied her. It had to do for him and, for the moment, he left it so and began to divide his attention between his new surroundings and his new companion. Here, it seemed, was a very old type of burrough indeed, for the echoes had indicated their entrance had been by the customary corridors and now they were entering what was obviously a natural cave or cavern. Such types had eventually fallen into desuetude; they were felt to imply a lack of craftsmanship and sophistication—also, they were felt not to feel snug.

As for the girl—

He swung about on his seat, the torch flaring somewhat from his sudden movement. He saw, close by the compartment where the lights had been stored, a door slowly closing. But it was impossible, both by virtue of the insufficient light and its flickering and by the distance, for him to say if or not it was being closed by whom.

Or what.

He felt wonder. He was aware that he ought to feel fear but was by no means certain that he did.

Things had been calculated rather to a nicety in these corridors, for scarcely had the torches begun to flutter and blink and give less and less light than they came to another place where torches were stored; it was well before this second issue was exhausted that they reached what was evidently their destination for the balance of the night. She looked up at his drawn-out sigh of sheer wonder, smiled faintly and dismounted. If one could imagine such a thing as a vast stone house set squarely upon the top of another such, a third upon the second and a fourth and fifth and sixth resting upon each other, then imagination would supply the likeliness of what he saw before them. All was made—evidently—not by piling stones upon stones but by carving this incredible series of pseudostructures from the face of the living rock of the cavern.

It had not been too long since others had last visited this place, for the bin of broken sweetpods from which she filled the ponies' feed baskets smelled merely faintly musty, the pods were not moldy at all. The animals gave two somewhat dubious sniffs of inquiry and set to eating. Water for them ebbed from a cut in the wall into shallow troughs, overflowed into a channel which crossed the floor and vanished into darkness. Tintinna unloaded and unsaddled her mount and he, having followed her example, helped with the pack beast, the torches reposing in brackets behind which the soot of centuries (and perhaps centuries ago) had stained the walls.

From one of her pouches she withdrew a long lanyard of finely braided colored leathers on which was a single, slender piece of metal. This she dipped into the water and then slipped it into the keyhole of the door.

"A curious kind of key," he said, "which has neither any wards or any notches—"

All her answer was, "Indeed it is."

She found lamps that flicked magically into light with a smoother and smaller illumination than the torches and set them on trays and he took one of the trays and followed her. Presently a series of rooms were illuminated, all furnished with everything not merely needful but desirable, from the mats under the rugs to the hangings on the walls, chairs, tables, divans, couches, cushions. There was food, too, in abundance, and wines and cordials in bottles which sparkled their various colors in the lamplight.

"The last time I was here," she said, "was with Mother. We ate together—here, at this table. I set it, just as I did tonight. And now—strange—I had never heard of you until a few hours ago and I know nothing about you except your name and burrough and descent—Mother—I suppose—will never eat again."

They sipped at something dark and clear and red that tasted sweet and left a crisp, tart aftereffect upon the tongue.

"Were you fond of her?"

She considered her glass and his question. "I was fond of her," she said. "But not very. Now you—"

"What?"

"That is what I ask. 'What?' I have never lain with any man and I don't know if I shall with you. I don't know, even, if that's your purpose. Certainly it is not your only purpose. You have not made the long journey from Orth and at this time of year just to get a woman. And I'm sure you hadn't come with tales of trade and barter and tales of tribute and this and that just to get a woman who had had an education. Orth, I am sure, does not lack for learning. Nor does Orth need to make alliances on such a basis. It's well you came, you know. I made no objection to going."

He passed his hand along his crest and, holding out his glass, "I noticed," he said. He held the glass and squinted through it toward a lamp. Here was richness indeed! Merely a casual meal and no great ceremony—fine liqueurs, and no candles of smelly tallow, softening as they burned but lamps that burned magically without smoke.

"A Zon burrough is never at its best when the Zon King dies. There's always a question of succession and the more one is assured that 'here there is no question' the more one may be certain that a question there is or will be indeed. And for one such as me, partly outsider and partly—well—let us say that my position was anomalous—"

Recollection of those swarming, stalwart, grim-faced females made him wince. If such was the way they were while their king still lived he could imagine—rather, he did not care to imagine—what they might be like when she was dead and a new one not yet on the throne. Or, if one preferred, on the First Seat. And yet it was certain that it was only because he had come at that time and no other that this fortuitous concourse of events had taken place. Fortuitous? Or was it that he had a good witch? If he had, well, certainly she was not among that flock of sullen harpies who had moaned and crooned their distaste, their displeasure and their distrust of him.

"Yes, your position now, I can see—would be anomalous. But what was your position before?"

She looked at him steadily and thoughtfully. "I think that what you mean is, not what was my position just before Mother—before the Morgan King fell ill, but what was it, basically, all along? That is, what was the reason for my being in the burroughs of the Scopus Zon? You do mean—Yes...

"Well," she sighed faintly, "that takes us back to my own mother, my blood-mother, I mean—and *that*—I hope you are patient—takes us back to my grandfather. My maternal grandfather. He was a person of some importance among the northern sea-burroughs. There were intrigues. Threats of insurrections, invasions, oh, the usual ugly scenes. And, being a prudent as well as an important person, he sent my mother—she was only a child—over to Scopus with a considerable present. She was to be educated but she was under no circumstances to be allowed to take the Zon-vows until she had voluntarily returned to her natal place and lived there one year. If, after that time, she voluntarily returned to Scopus or went to any other Zon place—well, then she could do as she pleased.

"Grandfather evidently acted just in time. The whole of the northern sea-burroughs went into turmoil almost right after that and he was killed. Things settled down and were still quiet when she—when my blood-mother returned. I have a notion that she didn't intend to stay more than that year—but she met my father and he was really made to order for her purposes in fact, meeting him must have shown her what her purposes really were."

Her purposes were to find the way to power, take power,

hold power. And here was a charming and widely popular man on the road to legitimate power which he did not particularly desire and which he was certainly and basically too weak to hold for long after he had it. He wanted whatever attracted him at any moment and what attracted him the moment he saw the newly arrived and long-away young woman was she. Calymon was his name, Poridel was hers—the wedding was famous for years afterward. Accession to office followed not long after. Calymon soon tired of it but Poridel did not. Therefore Calymon continued to hold office and, through him, so did Poridel.

"He hadn't really known how you stayed in office," his daughter said. "He thought it was done the same way you entered office. He thought it was because the people liked you and he thought they liked you because you were likable. But she knew better. You can't imagine how useful the Zon training had been for her. She spun webs of intrigue around the other intriguers while they were still laboriously spinning single threads. There wasn't anything she wouldn't do—in fact, there was scarcely anything she didn't do. And he found out. And it killed him."

The final blow was the discovery of his wife's connection with Arteman, a younger and more vigorous version of himself. And, while Calymon lay with his face turned to the wall of his chamber, Arteman was inducted as his successor. Then Calymon covered his face and died. Difficulties? Not because of that—but difficulties certainly. Certainly Poridel wanted power, but she wanted other things as well. Arteman, for example. Arteman was much like Calymon, but Tintinna was Calymon's daughter—she was not Arteman's.

"I was thirteen. She found us together. He was holding me around the waist and I was hitting him and he was laughing...Oh, witches! Her face—"

Thiobud said, "And so she did the same thing her father had done. Sent you to Scopus. To protect you."

The quiet mask of her face vanished. "To protect me?" she

cried, incredulous. "She would have dropped me over a cliff if it could have been done without notice. But, as it couldn't, she sent me to Scopus. And there I was. It's been five years."

"But I don't see—I mean, surely if you were to return now, after five years, wouldn't he—that is—"

A faint smile twisted its way across her face and was in a moment gone. "You mean, she will be five years less desirable and I will be five years more? Don't think she wasn't able to see that. But her hope was that I would, if you follow me, get so Zon that even if I returned and even if Arteman played at me again I'd repulse him, not from fright as before, but as I'd repulse any man. So she hoped.

"Nice, isn't it?"

He grimaced and then, as she got up and reached for a lamp, resolution, if not conviction, snapped up his head. She stood very still, her fingers just touching the lamp, having caught the slight movement. She looked at him intently and without expression.

"Neither do I know," he said, "if your old Mother King was a true prophet. And may never know. But I need not see every spoke to surmise a wheel. Listen, Tintinna, I had come to Zon to make a parley about you, although I didn't know that you were you. I feel now, indeed, that you are woman enough for any man, as I do feel myself man enough for any woman. But there is far more than that and this more either affects us both together or not at all and never. Will you resolve now to come with me, unharmed and unpressed, to Orth Burrough, and there hear and listen and there decide?"

She handed him the lamp. He took it with one hand and took her hand with the other and he blew out the lamp. She took shelter in his cloak. She laughed. She kissed him. And, trusting, with a stranger, slept. Thiobud, dreaming, brought her safely home.

BASILEIKON: SUMMER

Originally published in Quark 4, *eds. Samuel Delany and Marilyn Hacker (Paperback Library, 1971).*

Dear Uncle Wiggly,
   My wife has a large vagina and a short temper. Is there some connection, and if so, what?
                                   (signed) Puzzled in Pleasantville.

Dear Puzzled in Pleasantville,
   Sonny, the ancient Romans had a word for it. *Ars longa, vita brevis.* Set 'em up in the next alley.

                                   Hartford (Conn.) *Courant*

Albertus Fidelus had carefully climbed down the six floors from his one and one/third room apartment on 108th Street. Care was perhaps not required, but he thought that if he practiced it going down he might remember it going up. Time was when he had galloped up as easily as he had galloped down. But that time was a long time ago. It was ten cats ago. Time was when all the faces he encountered going up and down had been Irish faces and their eyes hadn't met his eyes, they were sure that with him being an artist he was committing mortal sins with every young woman who came to his place. Now the faces were Spanish Caribbean faces and their eyes met his eyes and kept on going. They couldn't care less what he did with any young girl in his place, but Albertus Fidelus's hair was snow white now and he would have to strain to think when the last young girl had been there. The hall smelled of criolla rice and beans now instead of cabbage.

   Albertus Fidelus was going to the health food store for

brewer's yeast and wheat germ and fertilized eggs. He was not, not going to the art supply store; he had enough art supplies, staples, he had no money for new art supplies now. He didn't know when he would. It was a genuine surprise to him, finding himself in front of the art supply store. Well...Well, there was no harm in *looking?* was there. Spizzerinctum, no!—And there in the window a new red, it was *the* new red which he had seen in his dreams and which he had been longing for ever since, the way he so often uselessly longed for the things of his dreams: the warm friendships which vanished with the full blast Spanish radio programs at day-up, the beautiful, beautiful worlds with their Maxfield Parrish blues—and then with, also, the beautiful, beautiful red. It was (he had known at once) an acrylic red, it had to be. But there was no such red, acrylic or otherwise, look though he had, all over town; hopeless as his now discontinued looks and quests for the friends of Dreamland.

Only now the red existed. It *was* acrylic, too! He had been wrong to despair. Albertus Fidelus, blue eyes gleaming, forgetful of how little money lay between him and hunger, cheeks pink and a bit aquiver, Albertus Fidelus believed on the God of His fathers and he thanked Him for the new red, and he pushed open the door and entered.

Dear Uncle Wiggly,

My girlfriend insists I rub coldcream on my cock before we capitulate together. What's this for?

Polish John

Dear Polish John,

For the foreskin you love to touch.

Indianapolis (Ind.) *Star*

Mrs. Lopez threw open her kitchen window and tossed her garbage out. Doing the same thing at the same time was Mrs. Gonsalez. They shouted companionable greetings to each other and settled down for a nice heart-to-heart talk at the top of their lungs. The back yard was undivided and ran the full length of the block and was a foot deep in garbage. It was a rat ranch. Now and then one of the residents wondered why it was that garbage did not simply vanish the way it did in Puerto Rico when you tossed it away. Vaguely aware of there being no pigs here and of something being wrong with the sun here, too.—"Look at them fucken pigs," the landlord said. "I ain't gunna clean it up fa them. I done it once, I done it twice, henceforth they can do it thumselves." The children were not even vaguely aware of anything amiss. Their backyard was rich in found objects, and they were keen, appreciative amateurs of its wildlife. The health inspectors never even knew it existed.

Cockatoo, ergo sun.
—The Enclitics of Euphrastus

Grover Wayne dried between his toes and thought of new reasons for hating his father.

Zimbabwe Kunalinga strolled out softly in his new dashiki, half-hoping for bad looks. He was the Commandant of the Army of Africa. Soon enough everybody would know this. Arms and money would pour in from Ghana and Cuba and the Black Men of Asia and the Army of Africa (Zimbabwe Kunalinga, Commandant) would take over the West Side and ride up and down Columbus and Amsterdam and Broadway in his command car and he would listen to the: sudden shrieks of laughter, ear piercers, mind shatterers, axes, knives, destroyers of the dream, three young black sisters from the school down the street LOOK *at a black spook* collapsing in each other's arms shaken by laughter, whoops and shrieks. So let them scream and more when Zimbabwe Kunalinga (slave name Hulber Rudolph) swept the streets and slew and took possession.

Carola Cane sat looking out her front window on the ground floor on 110th Street, feeling vaguely sad. She hoped that somebody *nice* would come along that she could be nice to, somebody with a problem that she could solve, not too big a problem, nobody with cancer for example. But maybe some person who had come out with only 15¢ to buy a cup of coffee and had lost it and then Carola would hand the person a cup of coffee through the window and the person would bless her and they would both feel good. Carola Cane was really a very *nice* person, if only more people would realize. Her husband, for example, now suppose her husband would come in right now this very minute, would he give her an opportunity (at the moment she couldn't think of one) to be her *nice* self to him? No! he would point out the sinkful of dishes, every single dish they owned was in that sink and had been for—well, last night supper was on paper plates. In fact, Carola realized, with a sinking heart and feeling more concretely sad, in fact there wasn't even a single clean cup to give the coffee in to that poor person who had lost its 15¢. "Oh what a commentary on our human condition!" Carola whispered to herself, and ceased to fight against the inexorability of emotion.

Dear Uncle Wiggly,
    Nem szeptet fraszbam a hucsikucsikicsiku kel yoyvad egyen plotz.

Magyar Ember

Dear Magyar Ember,
    So why the Hell don't you go *back* to Hungary?
Reese River *Reveille* and Austin (Nev.) *Sun*

All of these and many more, like fractured mosaics of many-colored glass, were lying around waiting for someone to concentrate on and put them not merely toGETHer again, but to create out of them things of utility and pleasaunce and as it were bauté: namely me. Would you like to name me? Do all those epithets and kennings tremble on your lips. There was the soft flesh of onions rolls *in memory of me* and the sweetysalty flakes of kippered carp *in memory of me* there was the morning cup of blackroast coffee and chicory with the tablespoon of overproof rum *in memory of me*, mory glory and there was smoke a joint in memory of me, no more italics, goddamn guinea bastards anyway. What do I see? in absolutely unauthentic kantioid cloth *kanti kanti kanti* and hatefilled red eyes and funky armpits like incense for the REally what I mean *Black* Mass, bloodbrother. Mephitic Mephisto, smasher of winebottles, jimmier of carwindows, threshingfloor of Menelik have mercy on us and save us from systematic thought. Not kanti but kantioid, and like a torque that purple keloid from ear to ear, stigmata, and that vast shallow boneless nose spreading like a subcontinent from ear to ear. Long ears. Wars of Easter Islands. Big Endians. Blefescu. *Kanti Kanti Kanti Kanti Kan.*

I say to him, he has the hatelook ready to swivle at me, I say SHANTI. AVANTI say I. I say ASHANTI. And I say SHALOM. faint flicks and flickers disturb the face of the black buddha. But he sees no pattern. Shalom no Salaam yes, and nemmine the bloody frothy waters at Ujiji, the trails of bones and bloods to the big funky super slavemarket in Zanzibar, the branch offices at Djeddah, Dar-es-why there it COMES again: —Salam. Slalom.

AVANTI! SHANTI! ASHANTI! SHALOM!

Dear Uncle Wiggly,
    Does Macy's tell Gimbels?

                    (signed) Curious (Green)

Dear Curious (Green),
    Does Gimbels tell *me*?

                    —Der (N.Y.) *Morgen Dzhyornal*

Ultima Thule, Ultima Thule, Ultima, Ultima, Ultimate Thule. Last night I saw an orfut of J. Sender Peabody, in some bushes by the side of a rural road, over a ditch or culvert, you might say, something of the sort: you know how it is with orfuts, "What's in a name," if you know Peabody you'd know it was in his orfut, covered with grillwork, and two or three tiny pin-points of light inside of it; hard to describe, but it was his orfut. It was him. And, you know, long as I known him, I never knew he had that kind of pull. An old-fashioned kind of kidney machine, big *big* sons of bitches, I mean, it never occurred to anyone, try an keep something like that secret. How could ja? I mean, a person was glad enough just a get a use one when he need id it. Like, I was ta this party over on ee upper East Side, anna hostess goes around tellin everybody, Please it's a funny thing a ask anybodyy but please don't use the toilet any mawn you hafta. Because I diddin ree lize at tanight izza night the man downstairs gets a use the kidney machine. An he needs alla the wawta he can get. Six thousan dollars one athem big ole kidney machines costs. But then alla this talk about telapawTAtion. Who inna Hell can unnastan alla them big words? You remember Pillsbury's Best? The big flar company? Use a be, if enough people senn it kew pons, enough kew pons from alla them Pillsbury Flar producks, I fgget jus how many, anyway, the flar company would donate the use a one them big kidney machines f as long azza guy need id it. Funny kine a deal, I mean, ain it? I mean, y senn in kew pons fa free sample a this, aw a set a that. But, sennin in kew pons tuh save a humean bean's *life*?

Well, ennay come up with this telaPAWTAtion. It was suppose a move human beans through space. Aw cahgo. Both. An nenn it turns out, it don' work. An nenn it turns out, it DOES work, only *not* like they thawt it would be*fawww*. Annatz when ee orfuts come in. One pahta it is attachtta ya own body, anny otha paht of it is Jesus Christ knows where.

An so alla them wace produx thattid killya in nee ole days, they get telapwaded from ya kidney aw whevva id is, via the means of these orfuts, and simply dumped in some I suppose sanitary manner out in the wild or the boondocs. Only not entirely deep in the wilderness because the orfuts have to be serviced. Now why they should look in their own funny way just so close to whoevr's orfut it is, this I can't say. But, I tell you, Science is certainly a wonderful thing, and this one doesn't know when he's well off until he sees the other one's troubles.

Dear Uncle Wiggly,

One day when Orville P. Upshur was my agent, and it was a hot summer day, I was in the elevator swabbing myself and wishing I could get something cooler than corduroys, going up to his office in the elevator, and the only other person in it was this pop-eyed little jig who was carrying one of those things that the manuscript messengers use to carry manuscripts. I guessed he was carrying MSS to Orville from a delivery service or returning them from a publisher. I admired his crisp cool threads, and thought no more about it. We both went into Orville's office and he came out and he said Hi to the guy and to me, and he introduced us. And the small black-man was, well, let's call him Jacobo Gaintestes. Instant flash. Author of book, DOWN AT GIEPETTO'S HOUSE. Mygord a real live orthur one whose book was reviewed in the genuflect three times THE NEW YORK HERALD TRIBUNE BOOK REVIEW SECTION, and I said "Oh!" and I could feel my face doing things it didn't usually. And I said, "Oh, how do you do!" And he, well, he sort of slid a nicturating membrane over those pop eyes and he sort of slid the thinnest, coldest, faintest, quickest, fuck-you-est smiles over his face that I ever saw before or sine sice since. And although I had planned to discuss this and that and a few other things with Orville it was obvious to me that he really preferred to discuss them with Jacobo Gaintestes.

I knew my place. I left. Still slightly dazzled. Still feeling the coolth of those crisp summer threads of his. Feeling, like GEE! CRIMINENTLIES! my agent has clients whose books were reviewed in THE NEW YORK HERALD TRIBUNE BOOK REVIEW SECTION (SUNDAY)! And hardly thinking of the meaning of that snakeshit smile.

Orville moved on up in the world and into much posher orifices. What time I waited without the porter's lodge so to speak, and I skip you not still keeping the faith bay-be that everthing Orville had said to me, big tall Orville had said to me, I can get you assignments, I will sell your books; well, and so it was true TRUE; there I was waiting and had sent in muh name and waited and waited, it always seemed to be summer and I always seemed to be broke; in walked Jacobo Gaintestes and a retinue of several blacks and tans and whites and trailed indifferently past me and the receptionist and just no bullshit about plese tell Mr. Upshur I am here please: IN they went and stayed and bloody well stayed and me slowly counting my pennies like rosary beads and wondering why for the entire six months I had been in Mexico expecting the usual at least for God's sake TRICKle of income via my agent Orville Upshur—not one single *sale?* And not one single *check?* And not one single not one single not even one single I don't mean only one single I mean not one single letter or reply had come in six mothering months in deep deep Mexico from mine agent. So here I was waiting to ask what happen and by and by—what took me so long? —still sitting patiently and still knowing my place and out came Jacobo Gaintestes and his black studs and his white studs and his white chicks and his agent Orville Upshur seeing him to the door, the door beyond the door. And his eye meeting mine, but no smile, just a sort of look, and I knew and he knew, and I beat the procession to the door and I went away and I stayed away. And I never came back.

Dear Uncle Wiggly,

There is a young woman who sometimes comes to bed with me and she wants me to kiss her boobs and suck her boobs and lip her boobs and scratch her boobs and caress and squeeze and otherwise play with her boobs, and all this is okay with me but I like to get laid too. You have no ida what a struggle I have to break loose so to speak in order to accomplish this reasonable and moderate desire, viz. getting laid too. And while I am getting laid I do do my best to resume and contune and caress her boobs and lip and suck and scratch and squeeze and dandle and fondle her boobs as well as one can, and also to continue for a while afterwards, but eventually I get tired and discontinue gradually feeling up her boobs and mouthing her boobs and playing patty-cake with her boobs. Then she gets REAL ANGRY and she says, Oh why are you men always so weak and impatient? What do you have to say about all this?

YOUNG MAN FROM KENT

Dear Young Man From Kent,
   Tough titty.

—*Christian Science Monitor.*

Standing in the park abaft the ass-end of the Largest Unfinished Gothic Cathedral in New York, looking eastward down into the Secret City, seeing its thousand thousand smokes, the great rookery, and considering how the smattered pieces are to be fitten together to create the Countenance of the Pantocrator, with Holy Wisdom in her seven-pillard house to His right and She in Whom He Dwelt to His left: and thinking how uncomprehending the darkness, how uncleft and uncloven by a single golden track.

"The German Emperor has not disturbed the peace of Europe," wrote G.K. Chesterton, "and he never will: because the German Emperor is a Poet"; he wrote that in 1911.

Albertus Fidelus slowly climbed the first two stories, the thought of the new red, *the* new red, the beautiful acrylic red, flowering in his heart alongside the lovely Maxfield Parrish blues of Dreamland and the lovely heartwarmingly lovely friends and friendships of Dreamland. Then he began to go faster and faster until he was galloping again, just as though he was still a fresh kid from the Shredded Wheat Heartland of the Midwest, and Daddy Bill his first cat, long wept over, still alive. And then the small astonished dark faces alerted by the unfamiliar heavy sounds. And remembering, slowing down, no, not feeling that sick warning feeling: just thinking about it, stopped in good time, forget it. Forget the lies, the falsehoods, disappointments, friends remembered not, paints manufactured not, art directors interested not: only— *here* we are! Spizzerinctim, let a fellow catch his breath, the key, no, no one broke in this time: someday, though. Someday for sure. Can't stay home all time.

Food forgotten, friends actual and potential forgotten, all forgotten by the bright clear acrylic Red of Heaven, Albertus Fidelus began to paint the glorious landscape of the world of reality, Carola Cane slumped closer and closer to her windowsill and felt a chill certainty that no opportunity was going to occur for her to be nice to someone in a nice way, Zimbabwe Kunalinga came along the sidewalk as one who walks over hecatombs of oxen and faithless servantmaidens, Mrs. Lopez and Mrs. Gonzales discuss in High C at 78 rpm if they should or should not have their tubes tied, Grover Wayne remembered all the wicked things his father had neglectfully done to him, Mrs. Peabody painted her mouth orange and sketched in high brown eyebrows, bialystokers in memory of me, egg baygels and water baygels in memory of me, hamentaschen in memory of me, Manischewitz Dry Concord in memory of me, Mogen David Grape Wine in memory of me, Levy's Jewish Rye in memory of me, a ball of malt in memory of me, Carstairs and Seven-Up in memory of me, Grover Wayne walked along the sidewalk remembering how his father would never let him take driving lessons or drink coffee, anticipating how he could, Grover Wayne could, at least he had enough money for a cup of coffee and his father wasn't here to tell him with an awful look that he had already told him that he couldn't, Grover gratefully patted his pocket to feel the 15¢ change and didn't feel it and stopped to pat and feel and search and his face fell and his mouth drooped and a woman at a windowsill looked at him and slowly lifted her head and slowly leaned over and out and opened her mouth to speak to him. Drink this in memory of me.

HOW MY GRANDMOTHER CAME AROUND THE HORN TO CALIFORNIA

Originally published in The Suspicious Humanist, *Spring 1971. It offers a glimpse into Avram's family history.*

The names of Memel, Courland, and Livonia have all vanished from the maps of the Baltic and its circumjacent coasts. The name of Riga, however, is still there—or was, last time I looked. From that city my paternal grandmother took no material souvenirs, only a few confused memories. "In Riga we had Swedish Rights," she used to say. By which, I have since gathered, she meant that some vestiges of the conquests of King Gustavus Adolphus interposed themselves between the inhabitants and their subsequent sovereigns, the Czars of Russia.

Sometime during the 1870s, my great-grandfather, Moses Rudeitsky, or Ruditsky, perhaps finding Swedish Rights an insufficient interposition, moved himself and his family to Rotterdam. "He had a chemical factory there," my grandmother said. What he had, actually, he had a place where cow bones were boiled down to make fertilizer. He was either a pioneer in organics or a pioneer in pollution, take your pick. The burgomasters of Rotterdam took theirs, which was the latter point of view; and they closed the place down. Great-grandfather took an apoplexy, leaving my great-grandmother a widow. And several children. She opened a small kosher grocery, saved her money, and, as the older children grew old enough, sent them off to America, The Golden Province.

First to go was my Great-uncle Sam, who went off to mine gold (naturally). When it came my grandmother's turn, he wrote and sent her an address in San Francisco, where she was to enquire after him under his New World identity as "Rudy from Sonoma County." I have no idea what he actually *did* in Sonoma County. Maybe he mined gold.

Booth Tarkington, in "The Magnificent Ambersons," describing how housewives would hail horse-car conductors from their windows and say, "Wait for me," and get waited for—Booth Tarkington said, "In those days everything took longer, and so naturally everyone had more time." After arriving in New York, my grandmother wrote to her mother of her safe arrival, and said that she was going to proceed to California by train, as planned..."as soon as I hear from you." She heard, and soon—for those days, soon—but not what she expected to hear.

The news of the early elevated railroads had reached Europe, but great-grandmother had evidently not gotten a very clear picture. Her letter was brief: "I have just learned (she wrote) that in America the trains run over the tops of the houses. Houses are not built to carry such strains and accidents are inevitable. On no account proceed to California by train, but continue on by ship, do you hear?" My grandmother, then sixteen, heard and obeyed.

There was then no Panama Canal, and the ship went down the coast of North America, down the coast of South America (at Rio, the bumboats came out with fresh fruit and vegetables), around the Horn, up the coast of South America, and up the coast of *North* America...

She arrived safely in San Francisco, paid her half-dollar head tax, and went to the address her brother had supplied. But, alas, nothing was known of him there. Well! This was a pretty pickle to be in, sixteen years old, not a word of English, how is it that she was not waylaid by dacoits and dragged off to be a slavey in an opium den, or something? I'll tell you how. Granny may not have known English, but she knew the "English" alphabet, and she simply walked along reading shop signs until she came to one with a Jewish name.

In she went. "Do you know my brother, Rudy from Sonoma County?" "Rudy from Sonoma County? Oh, he moved to Daly City..."

In fact, not only had he *moved* there, he had gotten a job on the street-car line running thence and thither. "Gold mining may be all very glamorous," he may have reasoned. "But does it represent Security? Obviously it does not. Whereas on the other hand, there will always be a San Francisco and there will always be a Daly City, and as long as there is a San Francisco and a Daly City, people will always want to go from one of them to the other one of them..." He went from one of them to the other one of them, with a ding-dong-ding, driving the streetcar for fifty years. And the passage of time has failed to prove his reasoning wrong.

My grandmother was followed on the long road from Rotterdam by Great-uncle Abe—who avenged the Martyrs of the Inquisition by serving in the Spanish-American War— and Great-aunt Dora, who almost became a centenarian— and eventually, by my great-grandmother herself, with the two younger children—destined to become Great-uncle Dave —he who ran for County Judge on the Bull Moose ticket in 1916, a bad year for the Bull Moose ticket, and got 11 votes and was known the rest of his life as Judge Rudy; and Great-aunt Ettie, who believed in reincarnation and sensible diet and wore bikinis well into her seventies.

But I get ahead of my story. My great-grandmother, on arriving in New York and having had perhaps enough of the life on the ocean waves, immediately proceeded to check out the railroads. She was informed that the elevated tracks only went as far as the East Bronx. Thus reassured, she bought one full, and two half-fare tickets to San Francisco. Sure enough, the Union Pacific failed to go over the top of a single house.

LOUPS—GAROUS

This verse was originally published in The Magazine of Fantasy & Science Fiction, *August 1971.*

It was late when I arrived at Dr Glosspan's office.
Overhead, the replenished moon
Rode high, spending itself
Upon the acquiescent earth.
He was none too pleased to see me. Indeed,
As he explained, under the glare of the framed
vellum and the framed sheepskin,
He had agreed to do so only to explain again
How impossible it was
For him to take me as a patient—
His work-load was already so heavy,
Dr Glosspan said. I seized his cold, reluctant hands
And poured out my plaints and pleas.
I told him how I was tortured by dreadful dreams
Of running, naked, on all fours
Swiftly, fleetly, through the endless woods and
fields—
And all the rest of it—the chase, the quarry, the
hazard, and the blood.
Oh, the blood! Oh, the blood!
Scarcely had I begun to realize
That the hand I held had a hairy palm, when
Dr Glosspan groaned.
We watched each others' faces push out to muzzles
And our teeth grow long and white and sharp
And hair grow thick and grey on all our changing

limbs.
Together we slipped from alien clothes and,
Laughing, laughing, howling, growling, we leaped
Through the open window
To run forever through the endless woods and
fields
Beneath the festering fullness of the moon:
The chase, the hazard, the quarry, and the blood.
Oh, the blood! Oh, the blood!

HOW COULD HE DO IT?

Originally published in Ellery Queen's Mystery Magazine, *January 1972.*

B ob and Peggy Morrison both say they like things to be in order, but they mean different things by this. Take the shirts.

Peg comes into the bedroom and there is her husband taking the shirts out of the dresser drawer and rearranging them. First shirt, collar flush against the side of the drawer. Second shirt on top of first, but collar at the other end. Third shirt, collar same as first—and so on.

"Why are you doing that?" Peggy asks.

No answer. Fourth shirt, fifth shirt—

"Why are you *doing* that?" Peg, plump, and worried about her plumpness. Bob, neither fat nor lean nor concerned with fatness or leanness.

"This is the way I like them," he answers. "This way they —well, the other way the pile gets higher at the end where all the collars are and—" He is about to say, "and the top ones slide down and it looks disorderly." But Peggy interrupts him, speaking loudly and firmly over his words.

"Isn't that the silliest thing you ever heard of?" And soon they have the saw going back and forth again, push-pull, shove-tug.

Peggy is determined to root out the reason for Bob's obsession with the topography of the shirt pile. "You are acting like a compulsive," she says.

"Never mind," Bob says, closing the drawer. "Since you can't remember to do it, okay, then I'll do it myself." He moves to leave the bedroom.

"No, Bob," Peg says quietly. But with determination. "We've got to settle this. I want you to verbalize the situation."

Bob considers this, blinks a few times, then translates: "You mean you want me to tell you why I like the shirts head to toe, sort of? I told you. When all the collars are at one end —"

But Peg shakes her head rapidly. "No," she says. "No. *No.* That's an oversimplification. Who *used* to arrange your shirts that way?"

He starts to smile, breaks off the smile, frowns. Then his face settles into lines of utter surprise; his mouth opens, he looks at her, then looks quickly away.

Triumph rises in Peggy's heart. "Oh, now we're *getting* somewhere!" she exclaims. "It was your mother, wasn't it? Wasn't it?"

Bob's smile returns. He laughs. His mother never piled any shirts in her life, he says. Bob and his father had to bring them to the Chinese laundry themselves. But the smile ebbs away and once again he gives Peggy that quick look; then as quickly he looks away again.

She pursues the question. Then who was it? Who?

In a low voice Bob says, "Cathy. I forgot all about it, but it's true, she used to—"

The triumph flees from Peg's heart, the heart gives a really terrible thump. "Who?" Her voice is low. "Cathy? Who's Cathy?"

Unhappily Bob says, "Well. I used to live with her. I was just a kid. She was even younger."

Silence. Then Peggy says, "Well, thanks for letting me know. I mean, thanks for letting me know *now.*"

This irritates him. "Well, for Pete's sake, I was twenty-six years old when we got married," he explodes. "You didn't expect me to be a virgin, did you?"

"Oh, I don't care about *that*," says Peg. (But she does, she does!) "I mean—not telling me! Didn't I have a right—I don't understand how you—"

Bob makes an impatient gesture and once more starts to leave. Peg reaches out and takes his sleeve. "Where is she now? Cathy, I mean?"

Bob stands still, not looking at her. Then Peggy asks him a question about Cathy, an intimate question which she cannot restrain. How did Cathy compare to her? she asks. In lovemaking. Bob makes a throaty noise and Peg flinches. "All right, I'm sorry. But at least you can tell me where she is now. Is she here, in town? Do I know her? I mean, know her by sight?"

Rapidly Peggy considers if she knows any women, any young women, named Cathy. She cannot think of one and is relieved.

"I mean—am I likely to run into her when I go shopping? Does *she* know about *me*? And—"

Bob turns and this time looks right at her. "She's dead."

"*Cathy*?" Peggy wonders if he can hear the relief in her voice, the relief she is ashamed to feel. Then she decides she doesn't care. Hot, frenzied images rise to her mind. Trying to dismiss them, she constructs a sudden notion that Cathy died tragically. An auto accident? Childbirth? Suppose the child is still living? Will Bob expect Peggy to adopt it? No, no, that would be too much.

Peg decides to drop the whole subject and never again refer to it, and she asks, "How did she die, Bob?"

And Bob says, very casually, "I killed her."

He leans against the wall.

"A rotten joke," says Peg.

"I was just a kid. We were boozing. She said something to me and I slapped her and she bit my hand and I lost my temper. I was lucky, I guess. I got only five years and I only served three."

Inside her head Peggy laughs hysterically. He killed a woman and he says, *I lost my temper*—as if he just—as if he only—

"I don't understand you," she says. She feels very cold. "How can you stand there so calmly and tell me you killed your mistress? How could you do such a thing?" Her voice gets louder. "I don't understand how you could *do* such a thing."

Bob merely shrugs. "I was only a kid, I tell you. She kept— Ah, but what's the difference? I paid my debt to society, didn't I?"

Even more than she is appalled by the knowledge that the man she has been living with, loving with, has had a mistress and has killed her and is an ex-convict, even more than that, Peggy is appalled by the brutal and archaic phrase.

"Paid your *debt*? Oh, my God! Bob—listen—the three years you were—away—did you get any *help*? Did you get any *therapy*?"

It takes Bob a few seconds to realize what she means. "No," he says, "I just worked in the print shop. But—"

"I just don't understand how—"

"Listen, Peg, let's forget it, huh? I'm sorry it's come up. We'll forget about it. Put it out of your mind and don't let it bother you. She wasn't worth it."

He smiles and scans her face for reassurance. Which she cannot give.

"'Forget it?' I don't understand how you can say that. How can I *forget* it?" Her voice rises. "How could you do a thing like that? I don't understand! I don't understand! How could you —"

"Peggy!"

But Peggy cannot stop. She screams and screams at him. "How could you do it? How could you *do* it?"

Bob slaps her face and she, as if rehearsed, seizes his hand and sinks her teeth into it, and his face grows red and dark and then, and only then, as his fingers close around her throat and the room swims and vanishes, she understands how he could do it.

ROOKIE COP

Originally published in Ellery Queen's Mystery Magazine, *July 1972.*

T hree of them were running ahead and two were running behind. People running aren't that common on the streets of New York, but anyway it was really the woman who first caught my eye. Everything about her said "rich suburbanite who doesn't have to worry about looking like the latest fashion"—everything, that is, except her mouth. It was a nice-looking mouth, but it didn't go with the rest of her.

For example, it didn't go with her sensible low-heel shoes, without which she certainly wouldn't have been able to run at that speed. And then—not to make too much of my eye for detail, though that's good, it has to be in my business—the fact is, I would have kept on looking anyway. And so would you if you saw two men and a woman running fast, and right behind them two other men running—one of them a cop and the other one yelling, "Stop thief!"

So I decided to follow and see what would happen.

It was the young cop's scene, so I took my time.

He had them braced, palms up and flat against a wall, by the time I caught up. The fellow who'd been yelling "Stop thief!" was standing back and wiping his face. He looked like a middle-aged businessman, which is what he turned out to be. The young cop half turned his head to look at me, and I could see that not only was his face blank, his mind had evidently gone blank, too.

I opened my hand and showed him the shield, and right

away his face changed and started waking up again.

"Boy, am I glad to see you!" he said.

"Leary, Third Precinct," I said. "All right, move along now," I snapped to the rubbernecks. Maybe it doesn't take much to collect a crowd in New York, but it usually doesn't take much to break one up, either. Because they've seen it all.

"You're new," I said to the cop.

"My first day."

It showed. More than the new uniform, his first day out of rookie costume showed. He clearly couldn't remember what to do next. I gave a little sigh and showed him. First I frisked all three, taking just a little extra time with the woman. A pleasure. She even said, "Oh, please." I almost looked around for the movie cameras. Then I said to the young cop, "Okay. Now you'd better handcuff them together."

Which he did. Not exactly deftly—"No, the two men together," I had to tell him.

The woman said, "Oh, thank you," and even started to walk away; maybe she thought it was my first day, too. I said, "Get back there," and she did, but trying out a look on me. Real anguish, tears in the eyes—but that mouth just didn't fit. It was the mouth of a woman who had been around. All the way around.

Next I gave "Stop thief!" some attention. "Who're you?" I asked.

He stopped wiping his face and jumped. Then he said, "The jewelry store—corner of Eighty-third—Brody's the name. They *come* in, the three of them *come* in and say, 'Let's see some bracelets.' *No*—he and she come in, the other one was already—"

This could go on forever. I said, "Let's have your card, Mr. Brody...Okay. We'll get in touch with you when we—"

"Yes! Yes! I better get right back, just my son is there and he don't—"

A gentle shove to Mr. Brody and off he went. Not relieved, just went. Who knows if by the time he got back, maybe the store had really been robbed or maybe the son had taken off and gone to California to be a hippie or something.

"All right, officer, now let's see who they are." And now let's see if his mind had started working again the way it should.

It had. He got their wallets and opened them and looked and then handed them to me. Not a word out of either; they were already calling their lawyers in their minds. The woman started leaning against me a little, but I gave her a gentle shove, too. Then I looked at the names on the cards. As you might expect, there were quite a few names *and* cards, credit and otherwise. And not just cards and credit, either.

I shrugged. "No one I know. Not that it matters. Okay, I'll go phone for a wagon. What's your name, officer?"

"Boberick, sir."

Then I looked at the woman. "My day off. No cuffs with me. No bracelets for the lady? Okay, lady. Let's go." I took hold of her elbow. Then I turned back to the new cop.

"And don't worry about this, Boberick. Everyone's got to have a first time, right?"

A little bit ashamed, a whole lot relieved, and a great big grin. "Right. Yes, sir. And thanks a lot."

"Let's go, lady," I said again. And off we went.

I was right about her, too. She'd been around all right. All around. It was thanks to her that those two in the handcuffs had all those high-denomination bills in their wallets. All that I'd had in *my* wallet was that shield I'd picked up a while back. Lots of ideas, that woman. Lots of fun, too. After she and I finish with Sun Valley I think we'll move on to Lake Tahoe.

Or maybe Acapulco. Plenty of suckers. All around.

AMPHORA

Originally published in Men and Malice, *ed. Dean Dickensheet (Doubleday, 1973).*

The octopus who hunted in the shallows off Capo Tortuga sped after the crab, and would have caught it, too. But the huge shadow from overhead distracted it for a second, and the crab scuttled away. Even so, the octopus might still have caught it, sunk its horny beak through the shell into the soft flesh, and made its meal, but it did not care to leave—as close pursuit would require —the area which was its own peculiar territory. Bound by something having the force of instinct, it never went very far from its den, which it had barricaded against intruders. The great shadow passed on—whatever creature cast it evidently posed no immediate danger. The octopus continued its prowl.

The man bent to the oars was young, sun-dark and sinewy. The woman was merely sunburned, and not so young. A smear of white salve or ointment had been laid upon her nose, but it was melting, and revealed the angry red skin beneath. "I still don't know why you need me," she said, tilting her enormous straw hat farther over her face.

"Well, gee, Gladys, you do so know," the man said. Sweat and oil beaded his skin, ran in rivulets between the banks of muscles on his chest and back.

"You could find it without me if you really wanted to," she muttered. The gaunt escarpment of Capo Tortuga loomed to their left. To their right was Africa, stretching huge and dry and hot all the way from Spanish Sahara to the Red Sea. Ahead was the yacht which had been chartered in Villa Cisneros, an ancient wooden hulk powered by a primeval diesel engine.

"That's not the only reason."

She affected not to hear him. "My stomach is acting up again," she said. "And my head feels like it's going to split wide open. And no sugar and almost no coffee left. Boy—"

He started to look over his shoulder, gave it up. "Is it far?" he asked.

She glared at him. Then her look softened. "No," she said. "No, Eddy, it's not far at all."

The oars creaked, the water burbled around their blades, the sun beat down. "Gee," Eddy said, "some fresh meat would sure taste good."

Conversation between T.J. Nothrup of Sweetwater, Oklahoma, and Luigi di Benedictus of Lugano, Switzerland, had not gone very smoothly at first. Not that there was any element of hostility between them, far from it. But Mr. Nothrup wanted to talk only of his archaeological theories ("Facts, I call them. Not theories, but facts!"), and Sr. di Benedictus wanted to talk only of his amphibious house-car ("A new innovating principle in self-cooling, self-lubricating engines—revolutionary!")

"They'll tell you that no white man ever came this way by sea until the Portuguese," declared Mr. Nothrup.

"How foolish to believe that because of aeronautical progress no new systems of surface transportation are needed," Sr. di Benedictus argued.

"They'll tell you that the Greeks never got past Spain. Haw!"

"Is one to maintain that no market can exist for such an

improved mechanism? Absurd!"

Sr. di Benedictus was engaged in proving the practicality of his car and engine by circumambulating Africa in it. He was a plump, pale little man with thick eyeglasses. Disturbed political conditions did not disturb him, he bore the passport of a neutral nation. Hazardous geographical conditions— from swamps to deserts, mountains to rivers—he merely welcomed as tests of his equipment. He had constructed his vehicle in his spare time as inspector for a sewing-machine company, from which job he had taken a year's absence to make his grand tour.

Mr. Nothrup listened to him, finally, in patient silence, not especially paying attention to anything the Swiss man said. As soon as the machinist finished, Nothrup said, "Well, it certainly is a lucky thing for you that you came along in your tin lizzie right at this minute, because you're going to be on hand for what I mean the biggest breakthrough in archaeology in just years, my friend, just years."

"Ah, you are an archaeologist. I thought from the accounts of you given me in Villa Cisneros that you were a petroleum explorer. Need I point out to you how exceedingly useful, mightn't I say indispensable, my house-car and engine should be to the pursuit of either activity."

They stood out in the burning sun in the middle of Nothrup's camp on the shore of the bay formed by Capo Tortuga, and neither one paid any attention to the heat, the sand, or the barren wastes and blinding sea. The captain of the chartered boat sat in the shade of the cooktent drinking hot bottled beer, watching his one-man crew (who also acted as cook) play dominoes with the local headman. As the cook-mate made up his own rules and the headman simply cheated, the game was not without interest. Of the three natives who had shown up for work today—sometimes none appeared, sometimes the whole tribe—one sat cross-legged looking at the pictures in a tattered and greasy Spanish comic book, and the others took turns searching one another's hair for lice.

"You are absolutely right and I will buy up a whole fleet of them soon's you get the bugs ironed out, as they say, and after I am finished on this project here," Mr. Nothrup said. "By profession, yes, I am an oilman, I have what they call wildcatted all over the world, and also worked on a contract basis, not that I'm so engaged here, because the Spaniard gover'ment wouldn't give me a license, not that I particularly wanted one, just thought I'd keep my eye open for likely oil terrain whiles I'm here, and in fact I believe that so-called captain you see setting on his duff over there and poisoning his system is a spy to make sure I don't prospect or more likely to see if I do, *where* I do. But I'll sure surprise them when I come back with proof, with *proof*, I tell you, Professor Benedict, that the ancient Greeks came exploring and trafficking in this whole area before the time of Alexander the Great.

"And I'm the man who can do it, too…"

The operative word for Thomas Jefferson Nothrup was *thin*. He was thin in frame, had a thin and leathery face, wore spectacles with thin gold rims, and spoke in a thin voice like the creaking of a locust on a hot Oklahoma night.

Had Professor Benedict ever heard of Henry Sleeman? inquired Mr. Nothrup. The Swiss man explained that he was *ingierno*, not *professore*, and what, please, was the name of— Ah, ahah, yes, the gentleman who discovered Troy, assuredly, Heinrich Schliemann. Well, Mr. Nothrup was what you might call a modern-day equivalent of that same fellow. That same fellow made his own pile in wholesale groceries, but his heart, his heart was in archaeology. They claimed that Troy was a fairy story, didn't they? You just bet they did! Wouldn't give old Hank Sleeman the time of day, let alone a single penny to finance his expeditions with. But he showed them. He showed them *good*. Went off and found Troy on his own, just full-up with golden treasures and everything. And they laughed on the other side of their faces then.

You just bet they did!

It all began quite some years back, when T.J. Nothrup was prospecting in the jungles of Nicaragua, just himself and his wife and a native crew. Gladys came with him wherever he went, sharing his hard times as well as the good: he believed in that, believed that a wife's place was at her husband's side, and so did she. It was at that time, observing all those Aztec ruins in Nicaragua, and comparing them with his own historical readings that T.J. Nothrup made the important discovery that the clue to the whole business was right there —Atlantis, the Phoenicians, the Incas, Etruscans, and the Lost Tribes of Israel.

"That's where the bug bit me," Mr. Nothrup said, with a thin smile. "Up 'til that time, alls I'd really thought about seriously was oil and money. History and archaeology and the mystery of human origins, they were just mere diversions, pastimes. But—no more! After what I found out there, I couldn't eat, I couldn't sleep, 'til I'd demonstrated my numerous theories and proved them beyond shadow of a doubt."

Engineer di Benedictus blinked a bit, cast a reassuring glance on his house-car, a structure the size of an American school bus, but mounted on wheels so huge, and slung so low, that the rims reached almost to the roof. He turned his look back to his host. "And you have proved them?" he asked.

"Why, certainly, I have," Nothrup said, surprised. "Don't you fellows there in Switzerland consult your own university libraries? I published three books, illustrated with numerous photographs and maps, had them printed up for me in Tulsa, and sent copies to learned societies and universities throughout the world, as well as prominent independent thinkers in many different countries. What a correspondence that started! I more or less have devoted meself to the subject ever since, and that's what brought me here all the way to Spanish Sahara and Capo Tortuga, just a mere hop, skip, and a jump from the Mauretanian border..."

"That," he said, "and the amphora…"

"This isn't my idea of the way you ought to conduct a scientific expedition," Eddy said, grunting, as he helped Gladys Nothrup up from the rowboat to the wallowing old yacht. "When T.J. sold me that bill of goods I thought it would be like in the movies, with native boys to do all the hard work. Native boys! Why, those natives, you know that, honey, half of 'um are *grand*fathers, for gosh sakes! And they ain't even black, like I thought they'd be, and they never wash —not that I'm any better, 'salt-water soap'—old T.J. and his damn salt-water soap!"

Gladys looked distastefully around the littered, peeling deck.

"Where could it be?" she murmured. "Where could it be?"

"How about a kiss?" Eddy asked, taking her in his arms and hugging her, pulling her off her feet till his lean and muscular back arched.

"Ohmigod, Eddy, my *sun*burn!" She pulled away from him. "Not until you find it," she said coyly.

The young man scowled. "How come if I'm assistant leader of this expedition that I got to do all the dirty work?" he demanded. "Sifting all that sand dirt, like we were going to make mudpies or something? He never told me I'd have to do stuff like that. And what did we find, after all that dirty work, a wonder I didn't get killed by sunstroke? A half-a-dozen old brass cartridges, and a camel bell and a broken teakettle, that's what, and that's all."

The woman bent over, grimacing, and tugging at her blouse where it bit into her sunburned neck, and rummaged in a heap of clothing. She had started shaking each item out and poking into pockets when a roach-like insect the size of a mouse hit the dirty deck with a plop and went scuttling rapidly away. Gladys screamed, dropped the clothing, and jumped backward.

"You can't tell me that the ancient Greeks used cartridges," Eddy said, stepping indifferently on the bug with a noise that fetched another scream from Gladys. He scraped off his shoe. "The ancient Greeks didn't use teakettles, and they didn't go riding around on any camels, either. I know *that* much." He put out his chin and gazed defiantly at the shore, addressing his absent employer. "As for the Lost Continent of Atlantis, that all those ancient Greeks were supposed to have been trading with along here in the olden days, well, Mr. Tom J. Nothrup and all your old sweet talk that sucked me into coming along on this trip. I think your Lost Continent of Atlantis was a fake. Just like you are a fake."

Gladys, who had been staging a little war dance on the heap of clothes designed to drive out any further lurking giant water bugs, said, as she picked up a shirt and prodded around in it, "He wasn't any fake when he used to be just a plain old oilman. He could smell oil a mile under the ground. He made plenty of money, too, let me tell you, Eddy. All over the U.S.A. All over Central America. Why the Hell else do you think I let him drag me around with him? I had malaria, I had two miscarriages, my insides are ruined forever, it'll be a miracle if I don't really have cancer of the skin from all the terrible beating my skin's taken from the sun all these years, like that Spic doctor I sneaked away to see in Villa Whatever-it-is hinted in no uncertain terms. Would he let me stay at home even once back in Sweetwater? Would he consent to a decent divorce and maintenance like a gentleman should? Ha, ha, ha, I'm laughing, that lousy old son of a bitch. Where *is* it? It *has* to be here, I looked all over back at the camp, and in his clothes when he was sleeping; so it just has to be *here*. I stuck with him because he made *money*, honey, and I figured that sooner or later he would either drop dead or retire. Eddy, please, help me look, dear."

Eddy felt rapidly through the clothes, kicked them aside. "Maybe in the cabin," he said. "Let's go look in the cabin. I still don't know what we really need it for, I could break the rack open. It wouldn't be hard." He flexed his muscles.

She looked at him, admiringly, then, taking hold of the upper part of one arm, walked toward the cabin with him. "Yes, but honey, I know you could, that's not the point. Suppose he came back, suppose, I don't know what I'm saying, this heat, this sun and all these years…and notices the rack is busted? No, dear, my idea is the best." It was at first a little cooler in the cabin, but the hot and close air soon asserted itself. Boxes and cases and valises and loose items of gear and clothing lay all around. "He made plenty of money, Eddy. Before he got this bee in his bonnet. Expeditions and printing books, which he gives away by the thousands, and chartering boats…It's going, Eddy. It's going, going, going, and it's not coming in. The ancient Greeks aren't going to bring in any money."

Eddy tried a wooden locker, pulled it open with a jerk that splintered the rotten wood. A khaki bush jacket hung on the hook, and he rummaged around in it. "How much you say is left, about?" he asked.

Gladys settled down on the grimy bunk. She looked old and ill. "Oh, I don't have to say, 'about,'" she said. "I know exactly, and only too well. There's sixteen thousand dollars left, is all. And this old tub is eating up its own value, just about, every day he keeps it here, so he can go scooting up and down the coast looking for ruins with his binoculars. He can eat up that sixteen thousand dollars real soon, and then what? And then what, Eddy? Hmmm? Tell me."

He replaced the bush jacket. From the pocket of his shorts he took a pack of cigarettes and a lighter. After a moment, and a puff of smoke, he said, "Well, I can tell you this much. The boat's got to go back to port in a couple of days for fuel. And unless the great Mr. T.J. Nothrup has found buried Greek treasure by then, well, I ain't going to stick around. Bye, bye birdie, and I guess I never will get my picture in the *National Geographic.*"

A frightened look came over her face, gave way almost at once to one of determination. She got up, wincing. "Let's be systematic. I'll go through the cabin, you go through the hold. But look *carefully*. He won't be gone forever with that crazy Swede or Eyetalian or whatever he is, with the funny wagon...Eddy. Eddy? I couldn't stand it, all by myself, with him again, Eddy..."

After directing his wife and assistant to "kind of keep an eye on things," Mr. Nothrup had climbed into Sr. di Benedictus's vehicle to go for a ride. He considered that it was for the purpose of giving the inventor a chance to look at some promising ruins near the border; the inventor considered that it was for the purpose of demonstrating the functions of the machine itself: both men were content.

Quite far from that were the two Americans left in camp. The Spaniards had lapsed into a siesta, the tribesmen were making motions with a pick, pickax, and a shovel. Partly visible in the side of a hill were stone fragments which might have been a wall or a foundation; Nothrup had informed them to stop work when they had cleared down to within a foot of the remains. At their present rate of progress he might have remained away a week without reaching it.

"Well," said Gladys.

"Well, what?"

"You know what."

Eddy shrugged. Then he said, "I guess some fresh meat would taste good, at that, huh?"

"*I* am certainly tired of rice and beans and that canned camel or whatever is in those dirty old cans he paid a king's ransom for. Give Ali a rifle and let him go shoot a gazelle or a deer, like he said he could."

The young man got up with determination, then looked around, helplessly. "He ain't even here," he observed.

"He's here. He'll come out if we call him, from where he's been hiding, now that T.J.'s gone. He doesn't want T.J. to see him. His feelings are hurt. What did T.J. want to go and hit him for, just because he kept begging him to let him borrow the rifle and go shoot game?"

Eddy scowled. "It's a good thing he never hit *me*. Couple times I thought he was going to, but he thought better of it. I might just as easily hit *him*, old's he is, if he talks that ugly way to me anymore."

She shook her head, urgent and anxious. "No, Eddy. Absolutely not. We'll just do what you said to do yesterday, when we were talking about it. We'll give Ali the rifle to let him shoot game."

And he nodded his head. Their eyes met and dropped. Their understanding was perfect. Ali was the best marksman, the best hunter, in the tribe, but he had—somehow—lost his gun, could not afford to buy another. He was proud, sullen, keen, smouldering, eager; he was in these last few days above all and quite obviously revengeful. The border of Mauretania, a nation which had no particular reason to be zealous on behalf of Spanish justice, lay not very far away; on the other side dwelt the other moiety of the tribe: friends and brothers, refuge.

Eddy and Gladys knew that whatever game Ali might bring down, his first shot would not be for gazelle.

The windows of the house-car were of tinted glass, as its inventor pointed out. "Observe, also, how smooth the ride—eh? Because of unusually broad tires, adapted from aeroplane tires. Excellent for the sand, equally so for the mud and marsh."

"Tell you what brought me here," said the other. "I was heading for Guinea, the French had pulled out, bag and baggage, and I said to myself, 'Why should the Russians get to take over everything there? Now, an experienced and independent oilman, a geologist and engineer even if largely self-trained at both, a man like yourself, T.J., with no ax to grind, now why shouldn't you come to some sort of agreement with the Guinea gover'ment about doing some oil scouting and development for them?' So I took off, but the air transport situation was in some bit of confusion and I wound up in Liberia, and that was as far as I could get at and for the moment. Since there was nothing doing just then via air, figured I'd make my way by land, either cut through the bush to Guinea directly from Liberia, or head all the way along the coast by way of Sierra Leone. I come to a place called Robertstown and lo and behold, what did I see but this woman carrying a load of water on her head. Now, Mr. Benedict, you may question what was so odd or unusual about that, don't they carry things like that all the time? Correct, they do. But whereas the other women were using old gasoline cans for the purpose, this little old gal was using an amphora."

His host spun the wheel to avoid a depression, turned proudly to mark the reaction to the ease which the large vehicle took the wheel; perceived that something had been said which required comment, found that he had none to make, said, "Pardon?"

"An amphora, Mr. Benedict! An...ancient...Greek... amphora! One of those classical-type pottery jugs with a taper to the sides and two handles and a wide mouth. Well, wide, I say 'wide,' matter of comparison some are wider than others. You could of knocked me over with a feather!"

"Oh, so. Very interesting. In Sierra Leone, I will pass, of course, through—"

Robertstown was not in Sierra Leone at all, not for one minute; it was in Liberia. "Now, maybe Hanno the Carthaginian has passed that way, was my first thought. Or— *maybe the ancient Greeks their very selves!* Seeking the Garden of the Hesperides, for after all what were the so-called Golden

Apples but your citrus fruits, or maybe even trading with the Lost Continent of Atlantis. Proof! Proof positive! I like to of snatched that jug off the poor woman's head. Where'd she get it, I wanted to know. Where'd she get it? Well, at first she only giggled and tried to give me that Boss-no-no-savvy business, but I got me out a silver dollar and she savvy'd soon enough, let *me* tell you!"

The woman's story was that the amphora had come from the Spanish island of Fernando Póo, in the Bight of Biafra, where many Liberians had used to go to work on the cocoa plantations. The woman was a morganatic wife of a local man, a Mr. Tolliver, and with the latter's assistance they were able to establish the very spot of origin of the amphora on Fernando Póo, the garden of Mrs. Widow Colonel Alvarez.

"Took me a while before I could get passage for Fernando Póo, it cost me plenty, too, but that widow lady was as friendly and helpful as she could be—touched with the tar brush, my personal opinion, but be that as it may..."

Colonel Alvarez's widow recalled the urn quite well, but could say of its past only that her late husband had had it with him when he was transferred from the mainland colony then known as Rio de Oro, but now called Spanish Sahara.

So Mr. Nothrup saw there was nothing to it but head for the Spanish Sahara, or, at first, more particularly its capital of Villa Cisneros. No one there had ever seen or heard of any amphora; no one recognized the photographs he had made of it. Colonel Alvarez was remembered as Major Alvarez, and it was further recollected that he had often visited in the line of duty the district near the former French and present Mauretanian border.

"Oh, yes...Now, the hydraulic principle which—"

"So here we are!" T.J. Nothrup sailed triumphantly, unheedingly, over the hydraulic principle. "I'm going to stay here and excavate if it costs me every penny I've got, and before I'm through, the name of T.J. Nothrup will go down in history along with that of Bayard and Sleeman and St.

Vincent and Rawlinson and Ignatius Donnelly. If I could find just one amphora, Dr. Benedict! Just a single one! Tell you what, let's stop here, or we'll be across the border before you know it, let's stop here and I'll get out my old binoculars and we'll scout around for those ruins. Too bad my work near the shore has prevented giving more attention—but, who knows, the shore may of shifted since those days."

The bare and lifeless sands stretched all around.

Eddy emerged from the hold dirty, annoyed, and sweatier than ever. He wiped his face on his forearm, smearing both, and looked at the waters of the Bayo Tortuga. "Swim would sure be nice, right now," he said. A noise from the cabin distracted him, and he turned, scowling. There was a confused sound, and then Gladys came running out.

"I found it!" she screamed, her burned face almost scarlet in excitement. "Look! Look! The key to the gun rack!" She waved her hand in front of her as she ran forward to meet him, and something glittered and sparkled in it...something which glittered and sparkled in the air, arching from her impetuous fingers over the side of the boat as she watched, her mouth open, her expression almost ludicrous in its shock. Without hesitating and almost before the key hit the water, Eddy had leaped to the railing, poised, and dived after it.

The key glittered and turned all the way down, fish of many colors regarded his slim, intruding form with mouths as round as Gladys's had been; he was almost quick enough to have caught it as deftly as the diving boys of many ports catch coins flung into the water for that purpose by tourists.

But not quite quick enough.

Still, he marked the descent of the key, saw it vanish into an opening on the floor of the bay. Sea fronds waved, and a school of tiny fish fled in tiny terror. Eddy reached for the hole into which the key had vanished, missed it, touched something, something which moved at his touch, and the hole moved with it. The weedy surface, encrusted with shells, rocked a bit, exposing an undersurface as pink as old brick. It was a jar, a vase; he recognized the shape, to his mild surprise—a recognition which barely penetrated his mind—it was an amphora. He would bring it up with him, fish out the key. He tugged, the amphora rocked again, but, wedged as it was between rock and rock, it could not be pulled loose.

He felt the first familiar press of air surging for release, thrust his hand in, groping for the key. The amphora was full of small stones, or so it felt, but finally his fingers closed on the key, and he pulled out his hand. But not all the way out. The stones had settled around his wrist, pulled up with it, fitting between it and the mouth of the urn, narrower by far than the body of the urn. Was he to be caught like the monkey with a fistful of nuts, in the story? Not damned likely. He released the key. He tugged again. And again.

The house-car came careening down the slope toward shore, sand spurting from beneath its great wheels. Inside there reigned a degree of excitement which had penetrated the single-track mind of even the usually calm Swiss engineer.

"I'll make it worth your while!" Mr. Nothrup said, for the tenth or eleventh time. "I'll charter you and your big old tank, I'll give you a thousand dollars a week, agreed?"

"Agreed, agreed," said di Benedictus. "And very probably I am able to raise some Swiss capital to match the American capital you speak of, as you suggest. But I must ask you—" And he asked him for the tenth time: "Are you sure? Are you quite sure?"

"Of course I'm sure! Hot diggetty! Won't Gladys and the young fellow be tickled when they hear! I haven't done right by that girl, Professor, and I admit it—dragging her all over Hell and Creation; she lost two little babies, did you know that, sir? I figured we'd make our pile and settle down and have more, safe at home, but—I'll buy her—no! I'll build her— the biggest damned house in Sweetwater, Oklahoma. As for that young fellow, he isn't so bright he'll ever set the world on fire, but I kind of taken a liking to him, and I'll give him a cut of this, my word is my bond, I'll make him rich before I'm through, if I've talked rough to him on occasion, why, it was only for his own good, and—"

"But the Mauretanians. Will they agree?"

"Will they *agree*? Will a bear scratch in the woods? You bet your belt buckle they'll agree! Why shouldn't they? Look what they save—the whole costs, enormous, of a search— look what they get: infinite riches! Make their own deal! A new nation, starting from nothing, why *shouldn't* they agree? I won't ask for much, just five percent; Gulbenkian asked for just five percent and the King of Persia made him a lord and he died worth scores of millions, sir! scores of millions! Where are they? Where's Gladys? Where's the young fellow? Hey, look there, Doctor, out at the yacht, the rowboat's tied up at it. I see Gladys. Wonder what they went out there for? Don't matter. I'll send up a smoke signal or something, bring them ashore."

A pale, faint blush suffused the full cheeks of the Swiss inventor. He smiled, a slow, proud smile. "It is not necessary to devise a smoke signal to bring them ashore. You have forgotten that the di Benedictus improved hydraulic house-car is also amphibious. *Hollo!* Watch. Watch, watch—"

The ponderous vehicle moved with deliberate speed down the crest to the beach. Its master pulled switches, gears, levers. The car rolled down to the water, entered the water, breasted the water, rode upon the water. "*We* go to *them!*" cried the Swiss.

"I'll be darned," said Mr. Nothrup. "I'll be damned."

His new associate giggled. "So," he observed, "you think no

more of ancient Greeks and Grecian urns...eh?"

Mr. Nothrup's mouth opened, first to surprise, then to laughter. "No," he said, "no, I don't...didn't...don't...I tell you, Doc, the moment I spied that absolutely gi-gan-tic dome in my binoculars, I thought no more about that whole history business than I did about a grain of sand! Why, I wouldn't trade my chances of five percent of what's under it for every single Greek amphora that ever was! Don't expect there ever were any around here, anyway. But I know what there is!"

"But are you *sure*?"

The boat grew nearer, grew larger. Gladys sat on the deck. "Of *course* I'm sure, how many times do I—look: in order to find oil, you got to find sandstone or limestone, because the oil has accumulated under it and *remained* under it. Now, when I spotted that gigantic surface structure over across the border, when I saw that perfectly enormous surface structure indicating that underneath there just has to be what we call a ground rising or a doming, elevation for elevation as near as I could see and feature for feature i-dent-i-cal with the same thing I spotted that time in Tishomingo, Texas, the one that had the whole Sam Houston Pool underneath it, and not only that but it was practically a recapitulation of what I checked out over the Balboa Pool which I personally discovered myself in Central America, to say nothing of Montana and California and—but, Lordy, I've been running on and on and I don't want to bore you—"

"No, no," the Swiss said earnestly. "You do not bore me. Go on. Go on. Go on."

Sunlight glittered off the water, and off of Mr. Nothrup's spectacles. "Won't Gladys be surprised?" he cried. "Won't she just probably go out of her *mind*?"

Once again a shadow passed overhead, a huge shadow, larger than before, though not so huge as the great shadow, seaward, itself. As always, the shadow passed on. No danger. The octopus, which had darted away at its approach, returned to what it had been doing. It had been investigating something untoward, at its lair. Uncertain, disquieted, it darted back and forth, coming nearer each time. It had taken pains, in its own way, to make the lair safe from intruders, bringing small rocks in its arms and settling and arranging them inside so as to leave room for itself, but nothing else. Now an intruder had come, was still there, completely blocking the entrance. Its eyes stared at the octopus, its mouth was open. Gradually, the octopus approached, touched, assured itself that there was no danger. The entrance had to be reopened. But not immediately. Satisfied, the octopus lifted its horny beak and began to feed.

THE MAD SNIPER

Originally published in Ellery Queen's Mystery Magazine, *January 1973.*

For two years the road through the valley had been in the making, and it had killed a man for each year. The first had been a construction employee whose piece of heavy equipment had toppled over on him. The second had defied the world to remove him from the house where he'd lived for 50 years—a traditional bit of Americana, complete with shotgun, rockingchair vigil, and photographers; but the old man had died of a heart attack before the deputies could lob in their first teargas shells.

But now, as Joe Gunnarson drove along the almost-finished road in the earliest dusk, he thought very little of the road and its history. There would be plenty of time for that. Time to reflect how the road would take him straight from home to work and straight back again, without delays at traffic lights, railroad crossings, or repairs—the old road was always being repaired, it had seemed. Time to reflect on who had lived where, but didn't any more because the new road ran right through the old homesites. And time to compare the disadvantage that he had to leave his car at the foot of the hill and climb up to his house with the advantage that on the old road he could park almost in his front yard.

Right now Joe Gunnarson was thinking about his troubles. The first was his little son, Jody, who had been sick when Joe left home this morning and who was almost certain to be sick when he got back: a pale, whining sort of child, who had inherited his face from his father but not, it seemed, his father's health. It was too bad he hadn't got his mother's looks instead of her metabolism. For Ella was trouble Number Two.

"Oh, leave me alone, Joe," she would say. "Bad enough I could hardly drag myself out of bed this morning"—retreating from Joe's comforting touch—"but the kid was crying the whole damned day. And as if *that* wasn't enough, your rotten brother—"

Was trouble Number Three. All his troubles were people, and the same ones all the time. Joe had a good job, his own health was vigorous. If only his wife and child were in better shape. If only his wife and brother got along together. Because Keith and Ella were at each another all the time, it seemed. Ideally Keith should be living somewhere else. But that was out of the question: he had no job, claimed (and it sounded reasonable) that he couldn't get one because, who knows?—he might be drafted.

So Keith slept late—which annoyed Ella; he sloped around the county in his old car that Joe had financed—which burned Ella up; and he came home as it pleased him, to eat big meals, for which, of course, he never paid—which enraged Ella.

"Let me alone, Joe. I said *NO!* Are you deaf? Do you know what that brother of yours said to me today?"

Joe sighed and the valley and hills grew darker and it was only with abrupt care that he kept from ramming into a car which had stopped on the road.

"My lord!" the man who belonged to the car kept saying. "My lord, I was shot at! Someone shot at me! Oh, my lord!" He was an ordinary man, middle-aged, in rumpled work clothes, and he had a Southwestern accent.

"Why would ennabodda wawnta do that to me? My lord, I was just drivin' aloeng and *peeng!*—there come that ol' bullet

—right through *here*"—he put his finger through the hole
—"an' hit right *here*—see that ol' dint? An' I heard it rattle
around but now I cain't find it. Expect it might of fell out
when I opened the door. Say, do you have a flashlight?"

Joe didn't. "Listen, what makes you sure it was a bullet?
Couldn't it've been, say, a pebble that some car kicked up
passing the other way?" Joe suggested.

The other man looked at him with an outraged expression
that the shooting (if that was what it was) had failed to
produce. *"Pebble?* Why, that wasn't no—now, you look here!
No, never mind, you git aloeng about your own business. *I'm*
goin' a drive in and *ree*port this to the Shurf. *Pebble! Oh,* my
lord!"

Joe Gunnarson parked his car at the foot of the hill behind
the house and climbed up the narrow path. Keith was lying
on the floor in the living room, watching television. Ella
poked at a pot on the stove, as if with intent to maim. Jody
squatted in the doorway between the living room and the
kitchen, sniffling.

"Funny thing happened as I was coming along the new
part of the road," Joe said.

Keith said, "Ha, ha," his voice level, his face blank.

"You see, Joe? You see what I mean? That's how he is, only
worse, the whole day long—fresh," moaned Ella. And little
Jody kept reaching his hands for the piece of candy his father
had brought "for after supper" until finally he spilled his
milk. Joe pushed him back firmly and Jody began to cry.

"What do you want from the kid?" Keith asked. "He's
hardly two years old. Get off his back, will you?" The little
boy glared at his father. Joe sighed. After a minute he praised
the supper (lying like a rug), but Ella just made an impatient
noise. He went to bed early, but when he got up afterward,
Keith was still on the living-room floor, smoking, watching

the Late Late Show. And Ella, it turned out, was still in no better mood. Joe sighed again and went back to sleep.

Gunnarson worked for the J. F. Guernsey Corporation, an outfit which prepared and packaged dried fruit and dehydrated vegetables for manufacturers of other food products. It was a fairly small outfit—there were only four foremen, and Joe was one of them. In the row of big barnlike buildings Joe was happy and felt more at home than in his own house, though he didn't like to face that fact and pushed the thought away whenever it occurred to him.

"Funny thing happened to me last night when I was driving along the new part of the road," he said to the other foremen as they changed into their working clothes.

"Funny thing happened," he confided to the waitress at the lunchroom. It wasn't till he finished telling it to old Mr. Guernsey himself that a little voice between his ears said: Say, you're getting a lot of use out of this little incident. His face twisted as he had to admit it was true, and all he could think of in defense was to ask himself: Well, what else is there to talk about? They don't want to hear about my troubles. But it bothered him, so instead he started a conversation with the boss about cars.

"I see you got a last year's Chevy, just the same as mine, Mr. Guernsey," he said. "They sure get dusty—cars, I mean, about this time of year, and the whole road not all fixed yet. Why don't you get Manuel to give it a good cleanup?"

The old man pursed his mouth. "I *could* tell you that when I want your advice I'll ask for it," he began.

"Aw, now I—"

"But I know you mean well, Joe. So I'll just put it like this: at my age and in my position I can afford not to give a damn."

"Okay, Mr. G., I only—"

"If I want to spit on the floor, I spit on the floor. If I want to go without a tie, I go without a tie. And if I want to let my car get dusty, why, I *let* it get dusty."

"Okay, Mr. G., you're a hunderd percent right. Sorry I—"

"And now let's see the new onions that just came in." Mr. Guernsey closed the subject.

It wasn't till the day's work was finished that Joe gave another thought to the previous day's incident. It was in the shower that Bob La Motta, another foreman, mentioned it. Over the splashing and stomping and raucous yelling and singing Bob called over, "Hey, Joe! This old guy you were telling us about? Claim he had a *bullet* shot through his car and you claim, no, it was a pebble?"

Squeezing water out of his eyes, Joe yelled back, "I didn't say it *was* a pebble, I—"

"'O Roe-za rosa Sanantone!'"

Gesturing to Bob that he couldn't hear what he was saying because of the noise, Joe finished his shower, dried, and dressed. La Motta came over and said, "So you were wrong, Joe. The deputies, they say it *was* a bullet."

Joe said that deputies had been known to be wrong before. Bob nodded sagely. *He* knew that. "But it happened again today. Lady from the city. Just driving along and— wham! Right through both back windows—a *bullet!* You can't mistake a bullethole in glass."

That was the second one.

The next day there were three more.

For the next two days the deputies scouted the hills to see who was—or who could be—sniping at cars on the road below. The answer as to who it could be was that it could be anybody. There were miles of road and many more miles of hills. But as to who actually was doing the sniping, they learned nothing.

For those two days and for two days after that nothing happened. And on the day after *that* someone fired six bullets into four different automobiles up and down the valley.

"Who in hell could be doing a thing like that?" Joe

wondered aloud.

Ella had a prompt reply. "Some bum," she said. "The woods are full of them. They think the world owes them a living."

Keith swore. "Oh, get off my *back*, will ya?" he demanded.

"You going to let him talk to me like that?" Ella asked shrilly. And the battle was on again. Joe felt he'd had enough of it and made up his mind to ask Mr. Guernsey to find Keith a job even if it was uncertain how long he'd be able to hold it before he was drafted. No matter how low the pay, Joe would insist that his brother accept the job.

At least it would get him out of the house, give Ella a rest from quarreling with her brother-in-law, and let her pay more attention to the little boy. It would be nice to hear the kid laugh for a change instead of crying or whining. It was almost funny the way the same expression—pettish, annoyed, aggrieved—seemed to be on the faces of both uncle and nephew so much of the time, exaggerating the family resemblance between them.

"I think he must be a crackpot," Joe said, deliberately ignoring what had just passed between his wife and his brother. And the next day he wasn't surprised to see that the newspapers seemed to agree. Even the city newspapers had given it a three-column headline: *Who Is the Mad Sniper of the Valley?*

There were two uniformed deputies in the lunchroom one day during the week and Joe brought the matter up, asking them what they thought.

A thin sad-looking deputy said he thought maybe the papers were right. "Guy'd hafta be outa his mind to do a thing like that," he said. "He coulda killed somebody! I think it must be like they say, some poor fella like this here Mad Bomber back East that time, he figures he's got a kind of a grievance, and his mind snapped. Or maybe he was cracked all the time, only it took a nincident a some sort to bring it out inny open. If he'd only write a *note!* A *letter!* Then we could trap him like the Mad—"

The waitress pointed out that Jack the Ripper wrote enough notes to paper the walls at Scotland Yard, but they still never caught him. But the thin sad deputy said, "Yeah, well, but that was *years* ago, before the First World's War. Today—"

However, the other deputy, a heavier man with a small steady smile on his ruddy face, he didn't agree with his colleague or the papers.

"You want *my* opinion," he said, offering it without waiting to hear if it was wanted or not, "it's some punk kid. Nobuddy's doing it for revenge. If they was good enough ta hit the doggone ottamobiles, they'd be a good enough shot to of *killed* somebuddy by now. Right? No, it's some punk kid doing it for thrills, *my* opinion. Like playin' 'Chicken' with these hotrods. Prob'ly tryinna see how close they can git to hittin' the driver or the passenger without ackshly doin' it. Punk kids," he said, not stopping smiling. "Too soft onn'm. Otta bring back the wippin' post. Otta have one a them big ol' leather belts with brass studs in it. Git some a these punk kids," he said, smiling, "strip 'm down, an' git some blood out of 'm. Make 'm scream. Otta—"

But the waitress said he would make her scream in a minute, so would he please stoppit? And the deputy, his smile neither larger nor smaller, said, "Why, sure."

Joe was about to ask Mr. Guernsey, after lunch, about a job for Keith, but the old man started talking first, and what was his theory? The same as the thin deputy's. Only Mr. G. had carried it a step further.

"Wouldn't be a bit surprised," he said, pinker than usual with the power of his idea, "but what it could be somebody who was kicked off his land when they put the new road through. Lot of people weren't a bit happy about that, you remember, Joe? Of course, in a way—now, don't get me wrong—but in a way you can't blame some of them. I'm not condoning violence, you understand. And we did need the new road—"

"We sure did," Joe said. "Before, I never knew if I was going to be late for work or not unless I started real early; or *when* I was going to get home. But now it's just like clockwork. Oh. Excuse me, Mr. G."

After a second the old man went on to say, "But it wasn't really fair the way they paid for it. They figured that every house of such-and-such a size is worth so much money. And that's all they'd *pay*. Didn't matter what improvements you'd put into the house—new paint, carpentry, plumbing, while your neighbor was letting his own place run down. No, same price for the both of you. So maybe somebody figured he was cheated and he got to brooding and now he's taking it out on just anyone who uses the new road."

Joe nodded slowly. "I wouldn't be surprised. You think you ought to tell the sheriff so maybe he could check up on everybody whose property was condemned for the new road?"

Old Mr. Guernsey's eyes and mouth grew o-shaped at the thought. "Do you suppose I really should, Joe?"

Joe's slow nod continued. "Well, I hate to be the cause of getting somebody into trouble, but—case like this? Yes. I really think so, uh huh."

And so he forgot all about asking about a job for Keith.

The next morning he got to work to find the place all excited, and the sheriff's officers' cars in the yard. "Burglary," Bob La Motta told him. "Broke into the office and smashed the cashbox, rifled the desks, stole a couple of typewriters and a radio and an adding machine and I don't know what else."

They heard old Mr. G. saying to the deputies loudly and sort of upset, "Of *course* I have ideas who did it. You really want to hear them or you going to give me the brush-off the way you did yesterday when I told you my ideas about the Mad Sniper?"

At this Joe immediately quit hanging around and summoned his men to work. If the boss had followed his advice and the result was that the boss was only embarrassed and made to look like a fool—why, then Joe didn't want to call any more attention to himself than he had to. He fell to on the peach-drying detail. Too bad, and it still seemed like a sound idea. However—

However, the solution to the burglary didn't take the sheriff's deputies very long, and this tended to diminish somewhat the value of the ex-homeowner's revenge theory in Joe's mind.

Not long before lunch, Manuel, the porter, buzzed up to the second floor on which the sulfur rooms were located and came over to Joe and his crew, very excited. "They caught 'im! The burglar! And you'll never guess who it was. Go ahead, guess."

"Miss Ponsonby?" someone offered, raising a laugh. Miss Ponsonby, who still wore a shirtwaist with a watch pinned to it, had been with the outfit as long as its founder, and was a model of all possible rectitude.

"No!" said Manuel disgustedly. "What're you, crazy? Miss Ponsonby! No—well, you wouldn't guess, so I'll tell you. It was Ray!"

This was certainly a surprise. Ray, the bookkeeper, a quiet young man who lived with his mother and played the organ in church. It was almost as unbelievable as if it had been Miss Ponsonby.

Manuel, his round face lit up by his news, explained. It seemed that Ray had been stealing money from the firm "all along." Why? No one knew exactly—at least, Manuel didn't know exactly—although several ribald and rather unlikely explanations were put forward by Joe's crew. The boss had caught him and had made him sign a confession.

He said to Ray, "I haven't made up my mind yet what I'll do."

The matter, not unnaturally, had preyed on Ray's mind,

and he finally made up *his* mind what to do: steal the signed confession, quit his job, and deny everything he had admitted about his original crime.

Glancing into the sulfur room to see how the peaches were drying, Joe half asked and half suggested, "So he figured that while he was at it he might as well take the typewriters, the radio, and the other stuff."

But, according to Manuel, this wasn't just the way it was. "Ray said he figgered like this: If all he stole was the dockiment, they'd right away know who it was, see. So he figgered like this: If I steal alotta *other* stuff, they'll think it was a *real* burglary and so they won't suspeck *me*. See? He figgered like this—"

However poor Ray had figured, it threw his employer off the trail only long enough for him to discover the missing confession—which was, after all, an item most unlikely for any "real burglar" to have bothered with. And Mr. G. told his suspicion to the deputies, who (this time) listened. And Ray, jerked back into the *real* real world as soon as the uniforms confronted him, admitted All. He was now down at the jail, and so was the boss.

"He gunna press charges?"

"He say he hasn't made up his mind what to do yet."

Mr. Guernsey was reported to have remained in doubt all afternoon, and then decided it was his duty to discuss the matter with Ray's mother. Just a few minutes before quitting time he took off in his dusty car and headed down the valley for the home shared by Ray and his mother.

In the shower Bob La Motta asked Joe if he heard the latest about the Mad Sniper. "Whoever's car gits hit with a silver bullet is intitled to a free ticket to a vampire movie!"

Joe's mind was full of thoughts as he drove home in the thickening blue dusk. So once again he almost missed observing a car by the side of the road—only this time someone was waving a flashlight. And this time he knew whose car it was.

"Keep moving, buddy, just keep on—I said, keep moving!"

"But that's my boss's car, Mr. Guernsey's, isn't it? He all right?"

The light was flashed in his eyes and stayed in his eyes. Joe, even before shading them, had recognized the voice of the heavy deputy and could imagine the smile. Then the light went back to the road.

"No, he ain't all right. He's dead. One a them bullets got 'im. You work for 'm, huh? What's *your* name?" He talked right on through Joe's cry of shock. A siren sounded. Another sheriff's car, light blinking rapidly and redly, came speeding down the road.

The old man lay fallen forward. Joe couldn't see his face. He felt this was just as well. "Bound to happen," said the thin sad deputy. "Sooner or later, you keep shooting at cars, you bound to kill somebody."

An idea sprang fully formed into Joe's mind, and without realizing, he began to think it out, aloud. "Suppose it wasn't an accident," he said. "Suppose a man wanted to kill a particular person, but he wasn't in a hurry. Suppose he wanted to cover his tracks in advance. Couldn't he start shooting at cars, not to hit anybody, but just to get across the idea that somebody—a maniac, maybe—was shooting at random? And then, when he *did* kill the man he wanted to, maybe then everybody *would* think it was an accident. Isn't that possible?"

No one made an answer. "But who," Joe cried, feeling genuine grief at the old man's death, unaware that he was asking the traditional, almost the ritual question—"Who would want to kill old Mr. Guernsey?"

In the headlights he could now see the half smile on the heavy deputy's face. "Not that sissy who was stealing from him, that's for sure," the officer said. "Besides, he's in jail. *You* worked for him—the old man have a girl friend on the side?"

Angrily Joe snapped, "He's a married man!"—then the sense of tense hit him—*was* a married man. Old Mrs. Guernsey, sweet and slow and childless—and tears formed in Joe's eyes.

The red-faced deputy snorted. "He's a married man! Buddy, you otta git wise! What's that gotta do with the Grand Army? Well, never mind, we'll find out. You better git movin'. We don't want no traffic block here. Come on, *come* on—"

Joe drove off. By and by he stopped seeing the road, except through a mist, half of grief, half of anger. He parked at the foot of the hill, knowing it was done clumsily, but not caring. He floundered his way up the path and threw open the door, aware that tears were running down his cheeks.

Ella and Keith were there, as usual, and he didn't know which one cried out first at seeing him come in, weeping. He felt half ashamed at feeling gratified that they were both so obviously upset at seeing him that way. They love me after all, he thought, moving forward and trying to smile at them to show he was really all right. Despite what they act like most of the time, they really love me.

It was a quick thought. It was replaced almost at once by another. What is the rifle doing in the kitchen where the baby can get at it? he was about to say. But then Keith got up, running, and he heard Ella scream at him, "You said he was dead! You said he was dead!"

And Joe looked at his wife's face and he looked at his brother's face and he understood what she meant and he understood everything that had happened and had been happening for quite some time.

But he didn't stand still as the understanding hit him. He moved, moved quickly, beating both Keith and Ella to the rifle, which was quite the worst piece of luck Keith and Ella had ever had.

IF YOU CAN'T BEAT THEM

Originally titled "An Apple for the Teacher," this story was published in Ellery Queen's Mystery Magazine *as "If You Can't Beat Them" in August 1975.*

Where the highland jungles of the Andean Republic begin an almost imperceptible slope toward those of the United Amazonian States, the tiny *poblacion* of Homero Roldran stands as a last outpost of civilization. The town is less than a hundred years old, and its name commemorates a national poet minor even in his own nation. The massy stone structures of the lowlands and the western highlands, built in colonial times by impressed Indian labor, are missing here; everything is made of wood.

The few streets of the town, beyond the unpaved plaza, show uneven rows of thatched houses; however, the buildings around the plaza itself are decently roofed with corrugated iron. There is the Municipal Palace, the Police Station, the Post Office, the Customs House, and the chapel where once a month a tired priest arrives to say mass; and there is the one fairly large store, the two smaller stores, and the three *cantinas* which sell only raw rum, loose cigarettes, home-rolled cigars, kerosene, and *centavito* candies.

In one room on the upper floor of the large store building, with a magnificent view of the Greater Homero Roldran area plus several hundred kilometers of mountains, lives Billy Bob Blake, the resident American Aid Corpsman. His work is mainly with farmers, and the farms begin behind the plaza.

"You see," he says to a friend, "I have a cow in my backyard." A second later he adds, "You hear her?" Billy Bob

Blake is tall, dark, and handsome; but fortune tellers never told him anything about Homero Roldran.

"To tell you the truth, Billy," the friend says, "I already smelled her. Coming in." The friend is fair and chunky and is named, euphoniously, Eugene Levene. Gene and Billy Bob were classmates at the Aid Corps School back in Maryland, and Gene is spending one day of a four-day vacation visiting Billy Bob. The other three days are spent coming from and going back to Puerto Lombroso, where he is teaching the use of small cooperatively-owned canning machines. "Smells better than fish," Gene says.

The aged bus which, groaning and grinding, brought Gene up to Homero Roldran from the end of the railroad line included a chunk of ice in its cargo, so the two friends are enjoying drinks of rum mixed with bottled cola, faintly cool. Such drinks in Homero Roldran usually range between tepid and hot. Gene hopes, aloud, that none of the water from the melted ice got into the bottled mixer. "I don't want to get the runs again," he says.

"I already got them," Billy Bob says.

Gene, who has been looking closely at his friend, asks, "So —is that what's got you down? Why don't you take some —I brought along some—" and he reaches toward his small carry-all.

Billy Bob's gesture stops him. "I'm taking some. It helps—I haven't got 'em bad. No, that's not what's got me down."

"Spill me the beans," Gene invites him sympathetically. "Conceal nothing. The girl back home who's been keeping herself pure for you, has she run away with a linoleum salesman? Tell Uncle Gene. He was born under a lucky star, he knows all, advises all, cures all crossed conditions."

Thus encouraged, Billy Bob lets it all out. He had hoped—

For one thing, he had hoped to encourage the malnourished Indian farmers to grow more than just corn and chili. He'd explained and exhorted the virtues of growing upland rice, for example; it is rich in minerals, and for the surplus there'd be a good market. And black beans, so rich in protein.

He had urged the Indians at least to plant their corn in contours along the hillsides, and not in rows going straight up and down the slopes, the soil of which washes away in the rains. Useless urgings, vain hopes and efforts. And he'd demonstrated, also in vain, how to construct sanitary outhouses.

"No wonder they're half starved and sickly," he says.

He had hoped to set up a small cooperative to handle the sale of the wild produce gathered in the bush. "But they just go right on doing things in the same bad old way," he concludes mournfully.

Gene says judiciously, "Well—"

There is a knock on the door. Billy Bob calls, "*Pasé!*" and in comes what to an alien eye might seem to be a prematurely aged child but is actually a full grown Indian man in clean but tattered pajamalike cottons. The newcomer takes off a large worn sombrero, presses it to his bosom, and bows.

"Don Esteban," Billy Bob says, "this is my good friend Don Eugenio."

"For to serve Your Grace," Don Esteban murmurs. Billy Bob asks questions, Don Esteban answers. Often he does not, except with a sigh or a shake of his head. After a while he bows again and says, "With permission."

Again Billy says, "*Pasé*," and when the Indian is gone he says to Gene, "Well, there you are. He's the only one who respects me. I dunno why the others don't even respect me, but they don't. I do my best trying to help make a better life for them, but they don't even respect my efforts. And yet they respect Don Lucifero."

Gene gulps his drink and sets down the glass. "Say, who *is* this dude? His name kept popping up in your conversation with Don Esteban."

Billy Bob gestures out the window to the infinity of mountains and jungle bush. "His real name is Niceforo—

Niceforo Lopez—but everybody calls him Don Lucifero. I guess not to his face, though. He buys nearly all the bush produce, and he pays pennies or he pays in rum. *When* he pays. They all hate him and they're all afraid of him. How he exploits them! He takes their women. He scoffs at modern methods. Mean-looking, big old fellow with a scar next to his nose where someone cut him with a machete. Too bad that —oh, well, can't blame *him*. Blame myself. Fought in a war I didn't believe in, tried to make up for it by joining the Aid Corps and coming down here, and—"

Gene says, "You can't just tell people this and that. It doesn't even help to *show* them, unless they trust you. You call it respect, I call it trust. Face it, we're foreigners. Aliens. Might as well be men from Mars.

"Why should they believe us? Why *should* they trust us? The *only* way to do it is to join in with them. In doing the big important things *they* do. Whatever they happen to be. They didn't trust *me* at first, in Puerto Lombroso. Didn't invite me to do anything, so I invited myself. When they saw I could haul in a fishnet, they figured, well, maybe this dude *does* know something. The first wedding I went to, had to invite myself. Now *they* invite *me!*"

Billy Bob sighed. "These Indians here aren't really Christians. Aren't even Catholics. Pagan savages is what they really are, although I don't like to say that."

Gene shrugs. "Listen," he says, "if life hands you a lemon, make lemonade. Must be *something* important they do that you could join in on. If they dance in their breechclouts in the full of the moon, well, strip down to your breechclout and dance with them!"

"Haven't got a breechclout."

"Well, *get* one!"

Thus, talking, they drink a lot of rum and cola. Gene stays the night and leaves on the bus early next morning, repeating his advice.

◆ ◆ ◆

Directing the activities of the American Aid Corps in the Andean Republic is Wiley H. Smith, Ph.D. in Agricultural Sociology, who visits Billy Bob Blake in remote Homero Roldran three times a year. He has already visited twice and departed each time with a sigh and a silent shake of the head.

But on his next visit he views things differently. "I see you got them raising rice and black beans as well, Blake," Dr. Smith says.

"Yes, sir."

"Very good. Taught them contour planting for their corn, too."

"Yes, sir."

"*Very* good." Dr. Smith has a long solemn face, a bald head, and a grizzled chest. They swing into the plaza. "I am particularly pleased with your success in setting up this little co-op for the collection and sale of bush produce—wild wax and honey, raffia, hides, gum, and so on. Why shouldn't they get the most for their labor and their goods?"

"Oh, yes, right, sir."

They turn up the stairs to Billy Bob Blake's room over the store. "And what I find most unusual, and most commendable, you have even persuaded them to build sanitary privies."

"Yes, sir. Let me take your hat, sir."

"Thanks, don't bother, I'll hang it up myself." Dr. Smith opens the door of the closet, gives a slight start, and chuckles. "Ahah, almost fooled me for a moment! One of those simulated shrunken heads, I see—make 'em out of deer hide or something nowadays for the tourist trade."

Dr. Smith hangs up his hat, gives one more look before closing the door, and turns to accept the rum drink Billy Bob is holding out. "Very realistic. Even got a scar alongside the nose. Ha, ha!"

"Ha, ha!" echoes Billy Bob. "Yes, *sir*!"

CARAVAN TO ILLIEL

Originally published in Flashing Swords! #3: Warriors and Wizards, *ed. Lin Carter (Dell, 1976).*

Corydon, the son of Corydon, sat upon the wharf at sea-girt, wyvern-haunted Styr, moodily contemplating his empty belt, which lay loose and uncoiled between his feet, where he had thrown it in a fit of anger and despair.

Black and slick was the belt from long usage, for he had gotten it when his first beard was growing, a decade ago; but any glance more than the hastiest would have told a thing or two about that belt. Left front, for one, it drooped, and there were marks upon the leather. To the right was a thong, and this, where it emerged from the serpent knot (the men of Styr know well the art of tying the serpent knot), showed a tag end exposing the original color of the skin. One did not need the seven-year apprenticeship of the augur or the divine madness of the oracle to read these several signs and tell their meaning. The thong had once held a purse, and from the purse Corydon had been wont to pluck the piece of silver and the piece of gold which, thrice a year—once, on the Kalends of March, and once, upon the Gules of August (and both were set times according to immemorial custom), and once, on any day which might be demanded, though demanded thus but once a year—Corydon, as it might be of any man not of the Co-Kings' Guard, had to pay for the privilege of wearing a sword within one league of the Land Wall of the City of Styr.

The purse had been made from the scrotum of an aurochs,

and was the Great Gift given him by that same Spellwoman of Scythia with whom Corydon (who was well made and by no means ill to look upon) had spent a twelvemonth in dalliance. Scythia is full far from Styr, and the journey thence and thither is both perilous and long; but Corydon had not begrudged the time. Not any of it. The purse was more than merely commodious, for it produced two pieces of silver and one piece of gold each and every month for the mere thrusting for them—a gesture which the Spellwoman had perhaps had in mind when she had wrought and sorceled it for him, saying (as she placed it in his hands) with her invariable faint smile, "When this thou see, remember me." And he had said he would; and of course, so he did.

Not one day more than one week earlier, Corydon, strolling with his proud swordsman's walk down the great Middle Way which bisects Styr at an angle determined by Geat the Geomancer the day of the city's foundation— Corydon, walking in all his manhood down the very middle of the great Middle Way, had heard the blowing of the conch horns by the Co-Kings' Guard, had seen their patrols tapping swordsmen with their scarlet wands, had reached with a slight show of amusement and a slight show of boredom for his purse, had found the purse gone and but the tag end of the purse thong where the cutpurse had cut it (and a curse upon his mother's navel and may wild goats soon void their stale upon his new-dug grave), had swift as rage and swifter than thought clapped hand to his sword as he spun about...

Soft and gentle the tap-tap of the scarlet wand.

As useless, argument, here, as argument before the face of the Wizard of Death.

"*Take that one's sword.*"

Resistance was met (when resistance was met at all) with an end not merely unspeakably painful but unspeakably demeaning and obscene.

The peace was kept in Styr by a high price.

But the peace was kept, in Styr.

◆ ◆ ◆

Corydon had no mind to play such games as slinking round with a mock hilt in an empty scabbard; his sword was gone; very well, let it be visibly gone. Nor did any voice mock at him, as voices sometimes did at some in such straits, usually from behind the elaborately latticed windows of the old stone houses of Styr; had any dared do so, he might well have, leaping, ripped out the wooden lattice and...

There was, after all, no tax on having hands in Styr.

He might, for much less than a piece of silver and a piece of gold, have bought the cutpurse's name in one of the shabby and stinking wine shops which clustered in Styr Old Town, near the Port, like flies about a dead dog (though Styr Port was not dead; dead cities there were—and are—but Styr was not yet one of them). He might have bought the name for a stiver or a groat. Of course, he had neither stiver nor groat any more. Any more than he had the purse which held them.

The sea was the color of his green-gray eyes and here and there small boats and rowing barges plied to and from the great tar-black hulls of the cargo vessels moored out in the channel: yonder gallipot held ware of terra cotta, from huge amphorae to tiny votive lamplets; the narrow sailing craft beyond her (as the breeze even disclosed) was laden lightly with unguent of nard stored in flaçons made of the small horns of yearling goats, each one costing the price of a Scyth slave; no cargo less precious would make it worth while to send so slight a craft so far. Beyond these twain ships stood at anchor a vast sea-mother of a ship, a sort of sea-sow, with piglet boats nuzzling all alongside of her and receiving, sack by sack by sack by sack, the cargo of grain: millet and wheat and barley and spelt. Rice and rye and pan.

Fisher boats slid down the channel, in from the Islae of the Reef; rust-colored sails slipped up, slipped down; skiffs like scrannel dogs made for each one in turn, eager to snap up cargo of tunny and eel and squid for the fishmongers, searching fishwives even now standing on the middle mole and clamoring for the cargo.

Warships, men-o'-war, there were of course none here; they had their stand in the Arsenal Port, clear beyond the Point and out of sight.

Pomegranate rinds, chaff, husks, bobbets of clush and clutter, floated on the sluggish waters of the in-port, struggled half-sunk beneath the sullen swell. Corydon half-felt that he might as well be in among it, amongst the muckle muck and the port trash. Should he offer to cut bait and haul nets for a supper of fish-bones-and-heads chowder?—he who had worn a sword proudly down the very middle of the great Middle Way? Bend his back as a grain porter? Sign aboard the potters' boat as a landsman, for a landsman's keep, making his sign in the soft wax of the master's tablet?

None of these made much eagerness within him. True, he did feel some slight stir of interest when he observed the knife-narrow lines of the nard ship; but this was—all such were—manned by foreign crews indeed: men with golden skin and loops of jet in their ear lobes, slightly built folk with arm muscles like wire rope, speaking a sing-song speech which no one even made show to understand, and clad in light tunics bordered with colored thread in odd design. They gave no sensible man cause for affront, save that they sold much and bought little, often departing with iron rock for ballast. And certainly they took on no hands here in Styr to haul their odd-shaped sails.

Corydon sighed, half-rose, sank down again upon the rock bench, worn smooth by centuries of sitters; gazed along the line of mossy wharf. That way lay the Arsenal Port; there he might try to see if he was wanted. The leechcraftsmen for the war vessels would strip him bare as a slave for sale, examine him as the copers examined trading horses, grip him in his private places and bid him cough; did he pass the probe, they would shave his head and body and send him off to the Islae of the Sands, and there keep him for long and long, the while he trained and trained; and of this schoolery in weapons and in warcraft and of its bleak severity, he had heard much—but not much which was pleasant.

He leaped off and up and spun around, but even before the motion was complete he had swallowed his annoyance; for he had seen that the tap-tap on his shoulder had—again—again—come from a scarlet wand.

Holding it was Euphrastes, a Warder of the Co-Kings' Guards.

"Ah, Corydon. Shall we stroll a ways together, then?" asked Euphrastes. He was a Styri of the Styri, and the folk of Styr are ever dulce of speech.

"Certainly, if it would please the Warder Euphrastes." Corydon the father had come as a lad from the Land of Bulls, but Corydon the son was bound to show no less smooth a manner for all of that. "A bit of a stroll, only a saunter, as it were," said Euphrastes lightly. Nevertheless it was he who chose the way and the direction, which was underneath the arches of the wax warehouse and thither to the Lesser West Way—which might lead anywhere.

"You are certainly a man, Corydon, and not merely a man-sized boy of a man's years. It has been observed that you have borne this recent change in fortune and in circumstance with a man's patience, not tossing down begged-for cups in wineshops whilst making moans and threats. Such is the law of Styr, and men must make their way under law; else we be but as the Wrynecks, who have their dank homes in the holes of the rocks. Many hundred years of observation had shown the Municipal Fathers that two things were sure: one, that neither the House of Gilead nor the House of Harth would yield aught in their claims for the kingship; second, that a man with money but no sword was safer than a man with a sword but no money—for if I be but cheated today I am still alive tomorrow, the god permitting, but if I am slain today I am still slain tomorrow. Therefore the Municipal

Fathers, which same be called Philosophers"—Euphrastes was sometimes prolix; but much must be forgiven one who holds office as a Warder of the Guards—"enacted two great and good laws: one, that Harth and Gilead alike should wear a crown and sit upon adjacent thrones, the elder of the twain being but first among equals; and, two, that a man who lacks money should also lack a sword, at least within one league of the Land Wall. These laws having been at once recognized and accepted by a universal acclamation"—here Euphrastes bowed slightly to a passing matron whose face was modestly draped in an absolutely transparent gauze—"the great city Styr has ever since been quite free of all civil disorders soever; is it not so, Corydon?"

"Who would deny it?" asked Corydon, rhetorically, elliptically, and (to tell the truth) just a trifle glumly, he being after all overyoung to make a philosopher.

Still, still (Euphrastes bought a pair of posies from a flower woman, and he and his companion held one each to their noses as, with brows politely raised, they continued their stroll past the fish market)—still, it was more or less as the Warder said. A century of intermittent civil turmoil had been ended, more or less, by the institution of a co-kingship. And the Sword Law, almost heartbreaking though it could be, did at any rate serve to keep Styr free from broils and battles such as were so often found in other cities which had no such law.

"Sometimes," Euphrastes commented, as they strolled past the Arcade of the Scribes, whence arose a forever murmur like the buzzing of bees as letters were dictated and contracts indited, "sometimes it is unwisdom which unswords a man. Sometimes it is a swift stroke of fortune, or if you will"—he waved his hand indulgently—"misfortune. We know that you, Corydon, had neither drunk your money nor gambled it on dice stones; nor did you wastrel it upon whores male or female, nor dispose of it by fomenting rebellions. Nay.

"It was a stroke of fortune, a gesture from the Omnipotent

Infinite, which caused your purse thong to come in contact with a sharp object or other. Elder men," he said smoothly, without emphasis, "often tend to store the most of their moneys in a sunken jar, and upon the tile under which the jar be sunk to sit their oldest, ugliest, and fattest female relative—that is, such moneys as be not invested into house properties, farmlands, ships, horses, cattles, and so on—But I would not offend you by discoursing upon economy; vulgar subject." He gave a sigh, a grunt.

"But younger men prefer to keep their fortunes upon their frames. This often is futile. And often it is otherwise. Wisdom inexpressible and kindness not to be priced have caused those in whose hands the god has given the governance of Styr to allow unto everyone who has lost the Sword Right one full week of indulgency thereafter." He smacked his lips and sucked in his breath, and slightly he shook his head at the thought of such benevolence.

Other cities, other potencies, might suspicion that a man deprived of his sword could in one week plot mischiefs to recover it, or precisely, the money to recover it. But not Styr.

Corydon stifled a slight sigh. He had recognized the flower seller. That is to say, he had known her very well at one time. That is, he had wound up all the business he had to wind up by saying goodbye to her. Sometimes she sold posies, sometimes she sold peaches, sometimes she sold pomegranates—she sold whatever was in season— and sometimes (often) she sold another commodity which almost always was in season—save, of course, for a very few days each month.

"...and so, Corydon, your week's indulgency being up almost to the very moment, I could not deny myself the sentimental pleasure of a final stroll with you, ere you depart. Do not think ill of other cities and their citizens, Corydon. However brute and barbarous the ways of them will seem, be tolerant. And you will, of course, and I am certain I need not say," said Euphrastes, "upon finding out—

as I do fear you must and will—that *their* laws may lack the essential clause forbidding anyone so exiled from returning in less than a year under penalties the most strict, stringent, and unsuspendable, do not sneer at them for their weakness. Conceal your smile. Make the best of it. Fare thee well, Corydon son of Corydon. May the sun ne'er afflict thee, and may no jackals gnaw thy bones. Watch your feet."

This last caution was perhaps less poetic or pious than immediately relevant, for they had come to a place both narrow and confined, where steaming piles of excrement lay thick upon the ground: *videlicet* the Eastern Excise Gate, whence all caravans and traffickers of any sort had need depart the City of Styr.

Corydon had had his chances to depart by sea, and had passed those chances by. Now he must needs depart by land. So the Municipal Fathers had decreed, and so the Co-Kings, via their Guard Officers, were obliged to enforce. From somewhere out of sight came great sobs and cries of anguish, grief, and pain. Corydon shivered, though the air was mild (in fact, confined in the narthex of the Eastern Excise Gate, it was stifling). Was some poor wight who had returned untimely in defiance of the benign law even now being impaled by bankrupts?

The cries ceased abruptly. Out from the Chamber of the Excise, with a shrug and a movement of his eyebrows, tall, gaunt, sandy-haired, and stooping, strode the merchant Abélaphon, retying his purse strings. Catching sight of Euphrastes, he cried, "Another such payment of export tax, and I, too, shall join the ranks of the bankrupt and be obliged to defile myself and my seed unto the fifth generation by impaling recusants; filthy task! The god!—what cruel law!"

He stopped short as he made this plaint; the man coming behind him almost walked into him—almost, not quite— the man walked around him. Holding a bundle wrapped in scarlet cloths and bound with tapes of crimson and sealed with sundry seals.

Abélaphon blinked his watery-blue eyes. "Aha, aha, my new rear guardsman! Well. Seems a likely fellow. That last lunatic you assigned me—Well, well. The cheese is old, forget it. What is your name, fellow? Corydon? To be sure. Well, Corydon, your share is to be one-twelfth of one-twelfth of one portion, and this caravan has been divided into eleven adventures consisting each in one hundred and thirty-five portions. Deductions are to be made at the customary rates for all beasts and baggage lost, blood geld for human lives, and you are obliged to vow for the safekeeping of our caravan an offering of one spoonful of frankincense and one-half spoonful of myrrh to be burned upon an altar to be chosen by consensus in the city of our destination—forget not that 'tis but the tiny incense spoon and not some ghastly great porridge spoon; an uncommonly generous arrangement, by my foreskin."

Corydon cast his eyes along the caravan. It was too long for its cargo to be composed of baled sacks of precious stones—and in any event, one could not eat precious stones, did the wells give out on route and the commissary beasts be lost. On the other hand, Abélaphon was a merchant of repute, and hence the cargo would not consist of dogs' dung bound for some distant tanneries. "I tell thee what, Merchant-Master," he said, "do but add a reckoning of one silver piece for every five beasts which arrive safe and sound at the city of our destination, barring sales upon the way, and we can leave thy foreskin out of it."

Abélaphon, on hearing this, appeared to choke upon a large piece of one of his lungs, but in a moment events proved it to be merely a phlegm, which he hawked behind a heap of ordures. "Aha, aha," he said, having wiped his mouth upon his saffron sleeve, "this fellow is no mere brute bully boy, he hath a sense of humor and a keen nose for commerce. Well. So. So be it. A silver piece for every ten beasts arriving safe and sound, and we will leave my foreskin out of it. At my time of life 'tis left out of almost everything. HO!"

At this, all the caravan's men afoot, each after the other, cried also "HO!" the while that all the caravan's men then mounted simultaneously cried "HEH!" The cries rattled off the walls and echoed through the gate, and, the sound of them dying away, Corydon heard Abélaphon murmur, "...on with it, ere the moon pass into Pisces, a pretty kettle of fish," as he swung himself onto his sumpter mare.

The caravan filed out through the Eastern Excise Gate, beast after beast: gelding and stallion and cob, mule and jackass and mare, camels and oxen and colts; here a dog and there a dog, and a fawn-colored bitch of the hunting breed, someone's pet by her sleek looks and bright-brassed collar; fat old merchantmen with patient eyes and new, young merchant adventurers with eager face; shaven priests and bearded passengers (they wore no beards in Styr) and stubble-faced guards. One of the guards, a dark man though no Afric for all that he rode an ox in Afric style, with an old slash across his nose, gave Corydon a friendly grin and, leaning toward him, said in passing, "Aware of the white mule with mooneye, mate, for she doth avenge herself her sterility with an evil bite and an even eviler kick. HEH!"

And so, to these traditional cries and sounds (bells, bits, a pair of petty drums, a flute) the caravan defiled out the gate (it had already defiled the courtyard and the street) and into the Yonder Road.

Corydon followed after.

He did not look back.

A tall, white-limed stone marked the league. The caravan did not entirely or exactly stop: it slowed. The priests offered incense and a victim. The excise man offered over the bundle wrapped and taped and sealed. Corydon swiftly broke the seals and ripped off tapes and swathings. Almost his hand trembled in his eagerness to hold his sword in his hand again; it had been his for full five years and he would have known it for his in the blackness of a moon-dark night: short and heavy and broad, forged in Dammaseq, and the hilt bound in dogfish hide—this was not it! All the woes of the week smote him now at once. This scrannel strangeling, what was this!

"*This is not my sword!*" he cried.

"It is now," said the Styri, turning his head round and heading back toward the city. He did not look back, either.

The caravan crawled along the sun-white hills like a millipede. Six pair of legs detached themselves from the aft part of the body and waited for six pair of legs at the end to come abreast. Corydon had perforce attached the sword to his belt and was sadly and sourly reflecting on how unnatural it felt there. His long legs dangled on each side of the short and sturdy black cob he had picked in preference to the warned-off white mule, although 'twas certain as the sea was salt that mules rode better in any but the shorter laps. As for riding oxen, he had never learned the art.

"Ahoy, mate, why so long in the chin?" inquired Slashed Nose, falling in beside him. "Look what I got to trade," he said eagerly, not waiting answer, but holding up a string of torc-stones. "What do 'e think I'll get for these?" he asked, suddenly anxious. Despite his sorrows, Corydon, who had a keen eye for a good stone, was moved to look.

"These are raw," he said at once, "and must be cured." He wondered the man had not known that—as, clearly, he had not; the scar across his nose darkened, and his mouth went down in the corners. One would not have wished to be his jeweler at that moment.

After an ugly breath or two, his face still red, he asked, "But they can *be* cured—?"

"Oh yes." Somewhere ahead, far, far ahead, a sudden brief

twinkle of light, a day spark, was gone.

The ox-rider woofed his relief, became suddenly cheerful again. "The god be with you, mate! But, say tell, what was *your* complaint?"

Corydon wordlessly removed his sword and handed it over, belt and all (the belt, at least, was the same belt).

"Well! As my name is Didius the son of Memnon...uh..." He ran a practiced hand over the equipage. The wooden sheath was fairly new, the upside had barely weathered; the downside, however, had evidently slapped long and often against a none-too-clean thigh, well anointed with some sort of grease. Didius raised it to his nose. "Butter," he muttered, "but not Scyth butter. By your leave," and swift he drew the sword. The blade was longer and more slender than the broad, short swords of the Coast. The hilt was also wood, unbound with anything to afford either a better look or a better grip. Didius tapped the hilt with a finger. "Magpies set in that tree," he said. The hornbeam was, by preference, named as seldom as possible. Now Didius turned his attention to the blade. Grunted.

At once, gloom swallowed by interest, Corydon moved his head so swiftly that his mane of brown curls rose and fell back. "What do you see?" he demanded.

Didius' finger this time did not touch anything, merely the thick nail hovered over what one might have taken for mere scratches.

"Smithy marks?"

"No mate—say, what's your name, mate? Corydon?—No, Corydon. These are sooth signs. Seen them before, I have, though I forget exactly where. Or when. Odd work, this sword. What's about it?" And so Corydon told him what was about it. The caravan wound over and around the bosom of the hill. Far behind, the sea glinted at them. A gray smudge which was Styr fell out of sight. Half, Corydon wondered when he would see it again. Half, he did not care (he told himself) if he ever saw it again.

Didius returned the sword. He seemed pensive.

"Well, well," Corydon said, "I suppose I must make the most of it. However, as the excise man gave it to me and I gave him no copper in return, I am afraid that it has already cut our friendship."

Didius snorted. "That's right, mate. The right spirit. We've got a long journey ahead of us yet, and will need all the laughs we can find."

"Why do you ride an ox, Didius?"

"I'll tell you why. An ox rides easy. And when you've fastened your arse to the saddle as often as I have on longies like this one, you'll want the easiest ride you can muster. Not the best-looking. Not the fastest—because a caravan moves at the speed of its slowest member. The easiest." His nostrils splayed out and he took in a deep breath. The wind was away from them, they did not smell the strong smell of the caffle itself, just the haze of dust which still hung in the air despite the breeze. And the smell of the trampled grass. The herbs off and down in the bosky. "And as to why I ride this particular ox—Juno is her name, she's really a freemartin—why, it's because she's got such a cunning muzzle on her, such a clever nose, as you might not believe as yet. Right just before now, I saw her lifting her head and giving a snuffle. *I* can't say what it was. *You* can't say what it was. But by and by and sooner or later, we'll both know what it was...Let's scout round a little bit, hey?"

They scouted around a little bit, swords slapping thighs, signal horns bouncing on chests. Never a sign of stranger, beast, or man did they see. Nor that night, in their first encampment. Nor the next morning.

Till noon.

That must have been the brief flash, the winkle-twinkle of light, Corydon thought, seen yesterday. *And* what the ox scented. The man had driven his lance into the ground—one would have thought, with his last bit of strength, had one not wondered how, in that state, he could have had any strength at all—and had somehow, somehow, gotten his helmet atop the butt end of the lance. Yesterday the flash of the helmet in the sun had been too distant and brief; today it had drawn a rider off the trail to investigate. He had come back full soon, full grim, had spoken in tones low and swift to the caffle master. Whose head had snapped back in an instant. Abélaphon had then beckoned to three men, of whom Didius was one and Corydon another. And the five of them—Didius, this once, on a borrowed horse—saw what there was to see.

The dead man's horse was still nearby, but it was a mercy to dispatch it, and dispatch it they did—Abélaphon thoughtfully sending the butcher back to take the better parts later.

"Tartar arrows, you see," said the outrider.

"Closed the Zud-vel Pass, that means," said Didius.

The others said little more, but Corydon was able to put it all together. They had been preceded on this route by another, smaller caravan three days before, heading for the same destination, the City of Illiel. Strong suggestions that they all wait and make up but one caffle had been rejected: three days gained on the greater party—and perhaps no word to the effect that the greater party was but three days behind, only—meant an edge on the market, sales at higher prices, purchases at lower. This was not unusual. It was, as it turned out in this case, unwise.

Fatally unwise.

The Tartars seldom came as far as the Zud-vel Pass. They never came beyond it. They must have waited till the entire caffle was within the narrow ways of the pass before attacking. Perhaps this was the only man to escape—as far as he had escaped.

Abélaphon, on their return to the main party, at once called a council, in a few words explained what had happened. A middle-aged merchant gave a quick cry of grief. In a moment he had control of his voice. "My brother was with them. We must start at once," he said.

Abélaphon eyed him with compassion. "'Start at once,' ah, Numenyon! Go if you must. At once, if you will. But you, Numenyon. Not 'we.'"

Numenyon did not go.

Fortunately, there was another route open to them for Illiel without their having to turn round; another day and this would not have been so. It was not a good route. It was neither swift nor safe. But it was at any rate for the present possible. And the other route, the one they had intended, the way by way of the Zud-vel Pass, for the present was not.

How long the present would last, no one, of course, could say.

And no one, of course, urged a return to Styr. Caravans might falter, caravans might be lost, taken, pillaged, destroyed. But caravans did not return to their place of origin without having reached their place of destination. Of course, caravans had been lost, taken, pillaged, destroyed in the attempt to reach it. Abélaphon and sundry others could have done so without losing anything more than reputation. Many others dared not do so because the loss of time would have meant the loss of ventured investment: having no wealth save that in their packs, there being no point in trying to resell—at other than a loss—where they had bought, the return and delay would have meant the eating up of their venture. And so, eventually, beggary.

The risk of death and slavery was better. Few of the caffle's men could write; those who could might as well have written *risk* for *caravan*, and saved space. The two amounted to the same. A sage Brython had once observed that being a seafarer was like being in prison with the added danger of being drowned. What might he not have said on caravans, had they such in his own land?

On this, Abélaphon said nothing; what he did say—with a grim look about his mouth and his red-rimmed eyes intent —to Corydon was: "Rear guardsman, this journey thou will earn thy sword..."

◆ ◆ ◆

They had planned, by two days more, to have been on the road into Vast Valley, where the herdsmen come down from the hills and offer fat cheeses, oozing oil and milk, for sale. But Vast Valley was not for them this time, and though there were a few who sighed and swallowed as they thought on the cheeses, likely they bethought them also that cheeses are ill-appreciated by those who lack tongues; or even heads.

Two days more saw them enter, instead, the wide uplands of Arhadamanthia, strewn with gravel and with rocks and stones; here a dour, suspicious race took grudging toll of them in the form of crumbles of slab salt. And that night, as the caravan settled down for the night and the dying glow of the dull, red sun gan to be matched in miniature by the growing glow of the dull, red dung-fires, Corydon became aware of folk gathering on a hill not afar off, and he called this to the attention of Abélaphon.

Who said indifferently, "'Tis nothing," and yawned. And then said, "Well, 'tis something, true. As you have never seen it before. Wait. Watch."

Anon the sun sank and anon the moon rose. And from the summit of the hill arose with it such a howl of outrage and of hate as shocked Corydon, watching and waiting though he had been. The Arhadamanthians cursed the moon, they shook their fists at it, they flung stones at it, and some e'en shot their arrows and cast their lances at it.

"Why, what is this, and what is this?" Corydon asked, almost dismayed.

Didius grunted. "They curse the moon," he said. "It is their religion. Why not? Is it not logic? If there be those that bless the sun, must there not be those who curse the moon?"

Said Corydon, "This is logic chopped fine, indeed. The sun brings benefit. But what harm brings the moon?"

Didius shrugged, flung to the dogs a well-chewed bone,

licked his fingers. "They say the moon leers at them. They say the moon sees their shame, and sneers."

Stones passed the face of the moon like birds. "Yahhh!" cried the Arhadamanthians. "Uch! Uch! Epheu! Yahhh!"

"Full strange," said Corydon. "I marvel at it. Do not you?"

"Sleep not too far from the fires, else you will awaken from the cold," Didius said, spreading his sheepskin. "Sleep not too near the fires, lest you roll into them and burn."

And, though long endured the chorus of shouts and howls, the casting of stones and lances, and the shooting of arrows, Didius said no more words. But now and then he snored.

Next day, as they prepared to part the site, Corydon saw men in brief consult, nodding, turning to their caffle mates next beyond; as a sort of ripple, this went down the line. He waited for it to come to him. As, thus, it did:

"Hence and till the mountains, the word 'gold' is not be spoken. If necessary, refer to it as 'shiny stuff,' or 'yellow.'"

Ever the road wound upward. The rocks were white, almost they hurt his eyes to look on them so white they were. Was it the whiteness of the moon which caused the Arhadamanthians to hate it so, Corydon wondered. Almost he felt he hated the rocks. His eyes twitched, and so did his legs—at any rate, so did his left leg, his left thigh. High and high and higher up was one black rock among the white ones. Damn it! how his thigh did twitch! With an exclamation of annoyance, he lifted the skirt of his tunic to see was anything there—an intrusive insect, mayhap, or some wind-blown bit of...anything—his sword hindered his investigation and he had begun to lift it when he felt, he was sure he felt...could he really have felt it move within its scabbard?

"Do you see yon black rock up there above?"—Didius.

With a grunt of surprise (for he had not seen Didius ride

up), Corydon looked in the direction where he had seen the black rock; it was no longer there, he looked for it in vain, then he did see it: could it have fallen so far behind in so short a space? "Almost it seems to have *moved*," he murmured, perplexed.

"It did move."

"But...it seems to have moved, not down, but across..."

A slight smile flitted across the dark face of Didius. "It did move, not down, but across. No; no one moved it. And there is another one. And over there another one. They are not indeed rocks. Indeed, they are not indeed black, but only seem so from here." And in the face of Corydon's continued incomprehension, Didius, again with the flicker-smile, said, "Those are gryphons."

In his mind, Corydon saw what his eyes—at that remove—could not: *videlicet* a gryphon, one of the Spawn of Gryphus, the fell Hound of Zeus; if not indeed vast as aeons, yet vast enough and part lion and part eagle. He saw the huge wings, the color of thunderstorms—saw the great talons, sharp as scimitars (though much, *much* longer!)—the somber, deep-set, darkling eyes, veiled and hooded behind no less than three transparent membranes: one for that dust and sand be kept without, one for to act as does a globe of water or an enlarging slab of quartz and enhance vision e'en beyond the far horizons, and one for that they might gaze full into the face of the sun itself. Some say the gryphons sleep for centuries and even more endurant sleep. And some say that contrariwise they never sleep at all.

Startled, somedel alarmed and somedel confused, Corydon stammered, "And so—but—what...?"

"They are guarding it. What is theirs to guard and ours to take, if we but dare, which we do not." Corydon had just opened his mouth to say a word when the thick hand of his caffle mate was suddenly covering that mouth. "The shiny stuff," said Didius. "The yellow. Remember? That other name is not to be used, here, now." And he took away his hand.

Corydon thought it best, for the moment anyway, not to resent the gesture; asked, "Why?"

"They take no note of us now. They think we are all but so many beasts. Yet if even one of us but says that other word aloud, the gryphons will hear it and will know that we are men. And the gryphons do hate men full strong; for men have been known before—and I fear me, fools! will be known again—to try and take that." He paused and checked his own speech.

"That shiny stuff. That yellow."

"Yes. And so now to other subjects of talk lest the traitorous tongue does slip."

So they carefully spoke about the mountains and about the moon and about women and about several sundry other subjects.

And they did not speak of gold.

When they first felt the cold breath of the snow of the Heliborean Hills upon their faces, a stir went through the caravan. Corydon, too, looked up: high and towering higher, higher than the white rocks where the gryphons lay guarding their gold, and much, much whiter; he saw the mountains and their immemorial burdens of the snows. For a while afterward the air grew warmer and the way dipped down again. But this was a mere respite. Soon enough the way went up again. That first night, Corydon slept somewhat closer to the fires.

That first night was shorter than other nights, the signal for rising was given three hours earlier—and given by word of mouth in level speech or by shaking sleepers who responded not; but the signal horns were not blown. Twice, Abélaphon went up and down the lines; once, he warned against any loud sounds, and once, he handed out kerchiefs of dark blue gauze. "If you can help it, do not even sneeze!" he warned.

And his younger nephew, a lad on his first caravan journey, was assigned to throw (as it might be) either bits of bread, or stones, to keep even the very dogs from barking.

"I have heard of the blind leading the blind," murmured Corydon, as he submitted to Didius binding the dark gauze round his eyes in the right way. And although he had been prepared for it, he was surprised to observe that he could see well enough through the blue (almost black) gauze of the filmy cloth, but that now the snows dazzled him scarce at all.

"Ah," said Didius with complacent gloom, "and I could tell thee tales galore of some who felt free to let the bandage drop, and of what dread things happened to them, strick blind from the snow glare, wandering off." And, Corydon gesturing that he did not wish to be told, Didius proceeded with relish to tell him.

"Ah," he wound up, "this trip, this journey, and the next—and it may be, at most, the next—is a mere change of scene and of pace for you, my boy...for if you do not find the means and the money to return to Styr and to pay your sword fee again, I be much mistaken...an interval, this life on the open ways of the world is to you a mere interval. As stays in Styr or any other town are to me. But the caravan life is the way of life itself, to us." And, for once, he waxed poetic, as the caffle toiled upward, upward, across and, slowly—so slowly—down again, and still beneath the lowering heights of snow.

The life of a caravan man, Didius said, was somewhat like that of a sailing man; and though both were full risky, at least with a caravan one was spared the ultimate indignity of seasickness. Let those who would, sing of the brave days of old, when men stayed within sight and sound and smell of the hamlet where they were born, eating the grain they wrested from the land day after dull, dull day—and eating little else. What were such men but beasts of graze? The story of civilization was foremost the story of caravans. What else tied together in bonds of freedom and the exchange of niceties the inland cities of the world—but caravans? And what but caravans tied together the inland cities with the cities of the sea? What brought salt to savor the fish and allow it to be dried and preserved? Caravans. What brought preserved fish (and, for that matter, flesh) to feed those who toiled in the barren lands where salt was mined? Caravans. Wine to the perfumeries and perfumes to the wineries, jewelry to the gold washers and gold to the jewelers? Winter wool to the linen spinners and summer linen to the wool shearers? Grain to make bread for the fruit pickers and dried fruit to the grain growers? Caravans, nought but caravans.

"And as for those, whatever their rank, who spend their lives in but one city-state, knowing but the ways and hearing but the ways and thinking only the thoughts of one, only one, just one single place," Didius said, waving his arms and exerting visible effort not to raise his voice, "why, mate, I pity them. I do. I do."

His arguments were persuasive, but he had dressed his morning's victuals strong with garlic (an item also carried by caravan, to savor the food of lands where garlic was not grown); and so Corydon, not desiring to offend by merely turning his head aside, instead turned it—and his mount—full around, with a murmur of "taking a look to the rear."

His short exclamation, his abrupt gesture, brought the speech of Didius abruptly to conclusion.

Several things happened, then, almost at once. Corydon felt his left thigh thump. Didius, low-voiced, said, "They've followed—" For, far behind, but perhaps not all that far behind, along the narrow and winding path defiling beneath and between the crags bowed down by snow, a line of small black dots appeared. Corydon, urgent: "Tartars?" Didius, aghast: "Tartars!" And more, and more, endless line of black dots appearing...

"Go fetch Abélaphon!"

Didius did not waste the moment with words as, "I am senior to you," or, "What should I tell him?" or, "Go fetch him yourself!" or, "Who are you to give orders here?" Didius went.

And neither did Abélaphon give vent to useless spleen or pride on hearing that a mere rear guardsman had summoned the Captain of the Caravan: Abélaphon came at once. Few words were spoke. Attempt of the entire caravan to outrun the pursuing Tartars was certainly vain. To divide the caravan, dividing and combining on such lines as light merchandise, swift mounts, fighting men, precious bales, and all such considerations, could scarcely be done quickly. But, quickly, Corydon spoke his few words.

Abélaphon lifted his red-rimmed eyes—for the moment, he had slipped off the black gauze scarf, the better to squint and peer—and scanned the scene beneath the shelter of one shielding hand. He nodded. They waited, half-holding in their breaths. On and on, behind, but heading forward, the black dots emerged into sight from behind whatever distant mountain spur thrust forth into the curling road. But wee dots they were, yet all knew full well what manner of man each dot was, all could see them as plain and clear as though painted in colored wax and set before their faces. *Tartars!* Tiny black eyes beneath fur caps, scarred cheeks, teeth filed sharp, short sharp spears, wiry and untiring ponies round whose rough necks bounced vile necklaces of babies' skulls.

Another dot emerged, and another, another—

Half, the watchers held their breaths—

And then no more.

And then no more dots came into sight, the end of the pursuing column was in sight, although already the head of it had vanished behind another curve.

Abélaphon cried "HO!"

And without thinking, half the caravan cried "HO!"

And without thinking, half the caravan cried "HEH!"

Abélaphon thrust horn to mouth, filled his quivering cheeks, and blew with all his might. Corydon, Didius, drew their horns and sounded them full strong. Heads turned, astonished. But habit was strong. Up came every horn to every mouth. *Boo-boo. Bee-bee. Baw-baw...*

Silence.

Echoes.

Now see Abélaphon, hood slipped half-off, scant sandy hair aflutter in the chill, chill breeze, galloping up and down the caffle line, whipping at each beast as he passed. Hear Abélaphon, the Captain of the Caravan, as he shouts and screams:

"Tartars! Enemy! Pursuit! Flee! Speed! Death! Life! Oh, hah!"

What shouts and cries, what floggings of mounts! The horses gallop, the mules trot, the asses run, the camels lumber, and the oxen lurch. What sounds of alarm, what sounds urging speed—

What sounds!

The sounds fly up the ragged canyon, where already the sounds of the first HO! and HEH! have flown, where already the sounds of the blasts of the horns had sped: high, high, higher, high into the towering snows. The snows flinch. The snows quiver. Tormented by the staggering sounds, the snows release their hold.

Behind, with undiminished pace, the column of black dots comes on. Above—

With the noise of a thousand thousand battering rams, the snows released from a thousand years in frozen chains, the snows come hurtling, tearing down the mountain sides, pouring over clefts, forcing the other, reluctant snows on ahead of them. Mouths open, men, beasts, lungs strain, feet, hooves, yet no whisper of so great a clamor can be heard above the ear-shattering thunder of the sundered snows.

The white sky is filled with flying masses. Have the heavens fallen? The black dots seem gathered together in one mass. Can the sky have turned solid? What is this, when all Tartars know that the Skygods Themselves have given all the mass of mankind to be the prey of Tartary, as the rabbits and the doves are given to be the prey of hawks?

Afar, amidst the stinging spray, Corydon, looking back

from the saddle of his laboring mule, sees—he thinks—the black mass come apart, half-onward, half-backward. He blinks. There is nothing there but white. Onward and downward slide the rumbling snows. The winds blow their snowy dust over the caravan.

But not more.

"'Twas nicely calculated," Abélaphon says at last. The caravan has halted—part, because it is exhausted; part, because the danger is clearly past. To Didius he says, "'Twas nicely calculated." Abélaphon rides slowly on, murmuring, "A bit more...a bit more...downhill, from now...easy, 'tis easy..." He murmurs them onward.

"Aye," says Didius, patting his pack ox, whose huge sides expand and contract like some giant bellows, "'twas nicely calculated."

For a moment wrath keeps closed Corydon's mouth. Then the knot is unloosed. "Nicely calculated! I should say it was nicely calculated! As to who it was calculated that if we broke silence we would bring down the snows behind us—but not on top of us—why—why—"

Didius turns his swart face upward. "I don't know that I myself would have realized that we had come to that part where the snows are so thin that no avalanche would threaten us," he says. He turns his swart face down again and looks levelly at his indignant companion. Thinly, swiftly, he smiles. Leans over and pats his companion's right leg; says, "No laurel grows in these latitudes, mates. But if dried laurel leaves will do, best see Antorn the herb merchant. Perhaps he can fashion thee a wreath."

And rides on.

Corydon allows the outraged pride to ebb away. After all... After all, it had saved his own life, too. After all, it is all in the day's work. Blankly, he looks at his right leg. Slightly puzzled, as by some other thought which will not come center to his mind, he turns his eyes to his left leg. His left thigh. His sword. Something about his sword. What about his sword?

Damned, skinny, strange sword! It is, after all, *it is not his own sword!*

Slightly sullen, he knees his mount. One half-glance he sends behind him. He then rides on.

As though relaxing not from the danger, passed, of death, but from the simple necessity of having been confined to the narrow way through the Heliborean Hills *(Hills!)*, the caravan for Illiel, on descending onto the highlands next beyond, spread easily out into line more horizontal than vertical. No one, for now, needed tread the dung of the beasts before him. The new spring grass had begun to send its green prickets up through the soil, and Abélaphon did not urge full speed, but let the animals move slowly at a grazing pace. It was but for a day, and if the animals did not know this, be sure Abélaphon did.

Too, if Abélaphon had not praised Corydon to Corydon's face, it seemed certain that he had given the credit for the saving stratagem—of bring down the snows by sound—where it was due; for Corydon found that many a face which had gazed at him with indifference was now turned to his direction in full, friendly approbation. He was invited to sit at more campfires than he could make shift to manage, and asked to dip his cup and spoon into more cook pots than even his healthy, hungry belly could arrange to accommodate. Faces he had only seen now became names, names which he had only heard now became faces. Antorn the herb seller made him free of all the condiments he could want. Haddadyon the perfumer poured soothing scented oil into Corydon's palms and bade him smooth his wind-roughened, cold-nipped face with it. Jarred the jeweler lent him a necklace of great blue beads for the neck of his horse, and to his finger put a ring for which he waved away mention of price; the metal may not have been of the purest, and a close eye might have observed a flaw in the stone, but 'twas but the tiniest of flaws. It had been awhile since Corydon had had a ring. He had once had many of them, a gift from—but that was in another country, and besides—

Besides, he had sold them all, all of them, for the money he had put into the purse from which he had drawn not only bread and meat and wine and oil and lodging, but the piece of silver and the piece of gold with which, thrice a year, he had paid for the right to wear his sword in Styr.

"Stay close to the road when we descend into the lower lands ahead," cautioned Jarred, a man of a certain ugliness, with a warty nose, but no fool for any of that.

"I shall. Say why."

"Why? Why, because the Pygmy Wildmen will shoot arrows at thee if thou dost stray, is why."

"An arrow is a good reason indeed."

Jarred grunted. "They have many such reasons in their cat-skin quivers. Their arrows do be but reed and their bows be scrannel and bent. I know not who taught them to make such ill bows, but I know who did teach them to make the poison in which their shafts be dipt. 'Twas Devil himself, aye, the very Daemon!"—here Jarred went "Tup tup tup" and spat three times. "'Tis a poison boiled from the cast skins of evil-worms, and if one but scratch thee no more than do a tiny berry thorn, ah, my son! thou shalt turn black and swell until thy belly burst!—the while writhing and screaming and biting thine own tongue; epheu!"

"Epheu!"

And so Corydon kept the road, and so—he observed—did they all. Not even the beating of the drums—made (so he was told) of sections of hollow tree trunks—in the nighttime, though it stirred somewhat his blood, not even this could stir him to leave the road. He made his bed there, though ill-comfort was the hard, trodden ground beneath his sheepskin, and to the thrumming of the drums he fell into a sort of sleep.

He was sure he had not fallen full aslumber, and the thump which waked him he took with ill-grace for a summons to rise for his stint at guard; and it made him grumpy, for, a rapid scan of the sky of night informed him, the song-stars had not risen yet—which were to be the sign his watch's hour had come. Yet he had not even begun to rise or to complain when his ears advised him of a soft pad-pad-pad nearabouts. It was lighter than the tread of a man, yet not at all alike the tread of any beast heavy enough to—

It took no more, next instant, for him to draw his sword than for him to draw his breath. Something lightened in the darkness, he saw a pallid figure the size of a child, the thought flashed across his mind, *Ah, shame, to slay a child!* and his sword had met flesh and passed through it.

A low wailing sound, checked at once—

At once someone was at his side.

Someone with a stick of wood barely alight, hastily snatched from a ward fire. Didius.

"Corydon, mate—a bad dream?"

"Stand still. Give me the splint."

Didius handed it to him. Corydon got up upon his sheepskin and, thrusting forth the bit of wood, having blown once upon it, peered into the darkness. "Ahhh…" said Didius softly.

Almost at the foot of the slumber pad and in a small puddle of blood: a severed hand. "Oh, woe," Corydon said. "It *was* a child!"

"No," said Didius. "You have never gotten, and will never get—nor I, nor I—such 'child' as that. 'Twas a Pygmy Wildman, mate—a White Pygmy, as some do call it, although never have I seen nor heard that there be black ones —full grown enough to have slain *thee*. And look"—here Didius thrust into the darkness with his lance and dragged something somewhat closer. Corydon bent the burning stick in the same direction and saw a broken reed with a bit of bone shard bound to one end; and the reed, whereabouts the shard of bone was bound to it, a sticky and oozing greenish-black.

"It would have shot that fatal arrow. You would be dying now, mate—dying the ugliest death and most painful, too, that man can know. Better to be impaled. Better to be flayed."

Corydon swallowed a noisy lump. "Had you not poked me awake," he said. "We are even on the matter of the snows... more than even, for that would have been a swifter and a cleanlier death, and—"

But Didius, withdrawing his lance and leaning on it, looked at him, dark face adancing in the dancing flame, yet all serious for all it danced. "*I* poked thee awake? I never touched thee. I never came nigh nor near."

There was silence. Corydon asked, "You never touched me? It was not you who waked me? But...ah, but surely it *was* you who threw the burning splint to give me light to swing my sword?" Again, dumbly, astonished, Didius shook his head no.

The sound of the tom drums had ceased. The night was still, the air was dead. Nothing stirred in the blackness. Corydon had not slain a child, he did not even know that he had slain a man: *struck*, yes. That the Wildman Pygmy might die of his hurt was a certain possibility. But he had brought his wound upon himself, Corydon had kept the road, had not ventured an ell nor an inch off of it. The land was the land of the Wildmen, the Pygmies. The road through was open to all. And...

"Then what," Corydon asked, half of his friend and half of himself, "what—or who—did strike me awake? And who or what did make that slash of light for me?" He exclaimed upon a sudden thought, dismissed it. "'Tis the wrong time of year for a heat lightning." He bent his brows into a frown of thought. Yet the thought trickled away. He gave a sudden sigh, a shrug.

Didius straightened up, moved his lance. "This is a strange land, mate," he said, his tone almost matter-of-fact this time.

"And several strange things may happen to us before we get us out of it. Finish your sleep, then." He pressed Corydon down upon the sheepskin, moved off. Over his shoulder he called, "And all in the night's work..."

Corydon must have fallen asleep even before his cheek had snuggled the tangled fleece-curls down. He woke to see the song-stars all ashine, rose up and took his watch, pacing between one small fire and another. And so the pale dawn found him.

Presently they came to a land where there was a plain all steaming and smoking; here, with grunts of satisfaction, they stripped off their garments and stooped themselves in pools both warm and hot and washed the muck and dust and dirt of the long roads from bodies and clothes. Corydon, who had much missed the hot baths of Styr, took a particular delight in the lucid waters.

Cleansed and refreshed, they resumed their journey. Now the way led through a forest in which they heard strange, deep, rattling noises, with now and then rude cries which seemed like shouts of menace and alarm. In a wide clearing in the midst of the forest rose up a tall structure of mottled stone, on which seemed to be designs both odd and ugly; but Corydon, coming closer when the caravan paused, saw that they were in truth no designs at all, but only moss and lichens. He watched in wonderment as the sundry of the merchantmen drew forth dried fruits from their bales and baskets, and, placing them in pottery bowls of the cheapest sort (shards of which lay scattered thickly all about), added water to reconstitute a semblance of freshness.

From the surrounding woods arose again the curious sounds of deep and guttural rattling, but now it seemed devoid of menace. And in another moment, they were on their way again; looking backward, Corydon saw dark, stumpy figures swarming from the woods and clustering round about the offered fruits.

He turned, amazed, to Didius, who said, "What, have you never heard of the Tower of the Apes? That is it, and they are them. They will not harm us now. To be sure," he added carelessly, "we could surely beat them off, but their bites do fester and the wounds do stink."

Next day they encountered a country where slimy green thickets grew high as low trees, and from this thicketry came disturbing sounds, although not loud at all: rustles, hisses. And as before, they came to a wide clearing in the threatening bosk, and here arose another, taller structure, all of slippery stone and dripping with an evil ichor.

As before, the caravan paused; as before, various merchants and adventurers opened packs and sacks and set forth low, wide clay vessels. They filled them half with water, as before, though now to the water they added sun-dried curds; and this mixture they beat and whipped with twigs, revolving the leafless ends of the twigs between their palms in the manner somewhat of fen men making fire. The confection of milk complete, with a touch of haste the caravan resumed its way. The place smelt ill.

Again Corydon looked back as they departed; this time he saw no shaggy forms of creatures which had once been men but had sunk from that high status out of slothfulness and sin; instead he saw, as it were, a carpet moving by its own motion from all sides out of the thicketry, black and yellow and brown and green, rippling as it moved, and engulfing the bowls of confected milk.

And Didius said, "That is the Tower of Serpents, and those be all serpents which you see," and Didius said no more.

Next they came to a low and flat and marshy area where King Fever reigned; and here the manner of their marching was clean reversed, for they slept half the day in tents of goats' skins and of woven goats' hair, and they marched the whole of the night enclosed in breeches of leather and high slippers of the same and with gloves which reached high up their arms and were tied at the elbows with laces and with thongs; and their heads were covered with hoods and a bandage of white, transparent gauze across the eyeholes.

"Else," Didius explained, "else the malign mists and vapors are absorbed in through the skin, and fever will inevitably result."

There was no sign or sound of living things throughout that low marshland, save for the *car-rock* and the *wee-dit* of the frogs, and the strumming of some small insects like little flies.

Yet, and despite their full precaution, some of the corrupt airs engendered by rotting grass and slime must have made their way into some several of the men, for six of them came down with fever, and of these, despite the best tisanes of Antorn the herb merchant, three of these died.

Two of them had kinsmen who took charge of all their beasts and gear and wares, but the last of them had not. Abélaphon drew up a short statement of the facts, and several others (reputable merchants, and having signet seals) attested to them, imprinting their sigils in the wax. "Sad it is that he did die, so far from home, and his wares unsold," said Abélaphone, "but by favor of the god he died here, where no king reigns, for full many a king does claim and seize the entire property of alien venturers who die within their suzereignties. Now the Council of the Caravan will see that his things are sold at best price, and the same will be duly delivered to his heirs—minus, of course, the usual charges—and, by immemorial tradition, everyone in the caffle is assessed one-half a piece of silver to be expended on incense for burning to benefit his shade. What, young rear guardsman Corydon, what? You scowl. You do not approve. Why?"

But Corydon, leaning slightly on the shovel with which he had helped dig and fill the new grave, shook his head. "I did not scowl at that, Abélaphon," he said. "I scowled because I miss my own true sword."

Abélaphon threw his head back and his hands out. "Your sword! His sword! Epheu, this is mere finicking. So long as it has temper, swing, heft, and edge, why, what can it matter?"

Corydon looked at him, and then away, gloomily. "It matters much," he said. "One grows accustomed to one's own sword. And...and besides...there is that about this one which mislikes me somewhat. Which mislikes me much," he burst out. And added sullenly, and as sole explanation for what he felt unable to explain, "Besides, the blade is scratched."

Abélaphon's only answer was to swing away his horse and to cry "HO!" And half the caravan at once cried "HO!" and at once the other half cried "HEH!"

The long, winding caffle got under way again. And soon the rude mound of unturfed dirt was left behind.

But to report in detail all the things seen and done—or, for that matter, unseen and undone—on that caravan journey would require much time and parchment; and while some might find it full of interest, there are those who might find it tedious in the extreme.

It has been recounted elsewhere that the walls of the City of Illiel are surrounded by groves of pomegranate trees and that the great gate of the city is wrought out of red bronze, and carved with figures of sea dragons and dragons that have wings. (Alas that all-consuming Time has long since consumed the greatness and the fame of Illiel, from which the river and the inland sea alike have receded, and that the site of the grove of pomegranate trees is heaped high now with drifts of salt and sand; moreover, the dragons which nest in the caves of its ruins are of a sullen humor and given to devouring the sons of men; as to their treatment of the daughters, this is not the place to speak.)

There is still extant a bill of lading, writ upon papyrus from the Canopic Nile (than which there is no papyrus better), commencing *Merchandise Carried Atween Styr and Illiel,* and signed with the seal of Abélaphon; and there is no reason to doubt that it refers to the very caravan in which Corydon the son of Corydon was a rear guardsman; and it includes such items as these:

> *Skins, crocodiles', from Nubia, perfumed*
> *Linen, waxed, from Egypt*
> *Linen, painted, from the Ethiops' land*
> *Chests, carven sycamore wood, of Libya*
> *Sponges, purple, from Tyria*
> *Hangings, blue, of Sydonia*
> *Oil, of the first pressing, scented, Pontus*
> *Oil, of the first pressing, scented, Cappadocia*
> *Unguent of almonds, Greeia*
> *Cups of cold amber, carven, from the North*

To bring such articles as these from Styr to Illiel, the caravan had braved the Tartars and the snows, dared the Wild Pygmies and the Fever King, risked the Tower of the Serpents and the Tower of the Apes.

Surely many caravans each year must have uncorded and unpacked their wares in the great walled market of Illiel, and yet from the rooflike walls many people watched this one now as its men performed the necessary task; and some of the watchers were women, and one of these wore a mask of gilded leather.

And, "I wonder why she does so," Corydon asked of Didius.

"No doubt, poor female, she is deformed of countenance."

"Ah, to be sure. No doubt. Alas." Corydon believed that she

was in other respects of good enough figure, but the sun slanted somewhat into his eye, and he had started to pace a few steps so as to obtain a better view of her; when someone thumped his thigh, he at once looked about to see whom, saw no one—and when he turned his glance again toward the roof of the wall, the figure which he sought was gone. Where she had stood, stood now a gaudy, fat woman all but bursting from a scarlet gown, who, observing Corydon's observation, simpered, smirked, then hid her moon-wide face in her fingers, between which she peeped.

But Corydon did not peep back.

There are men of commerce who are never swift to pay what is due them, and such men never lack reasons, such as: Such a one hath not paid me and so I cannot pay thee, or, At noon of the morrow—knowing full well that by noon of the morrow he will be elsewhere—or this, or that. It may be of a simple hope that, sufficiently delayed, the debtor will simply disappear; or it may be of an equally simple if equally reprehensible reluctance to part with cash. But Abélaphon was not one of them. The money owed Corydon by the caravan, he, as Caravan Captain, promptly paid. And no nonsense of: We have not yet met and talked and calculated; he had the money, he paid it, and in his own good time, he reimbursed himself of it. Would there more such!

Corydon, with money in his purse (and this purse he bound about his naked waist, under his tunic and not outside of it: once robbed, forever cautious), for a first thing, purchased himself a clean sheepskin and a small carpet, and for the smallest coin there was clean straw to spread them on. Next he asked directions to the hot bath and soaked and soaped and scraped off the dust accumulated since the last one. Then he returned to his corner of the caravanserai, and even while the chaffering and trading went on but some several steps away from him, he laid down upon his bed and slept and slept.

It was fairly dusk, and fairly quiet when he awoke...awoke

from odd, strange dreams. His limbs felt lighter, but his head felt numb, and in his mouth was a thick and stale taste. Sitting upright in the hot, still air (the moon being then in the Scorpion), he reflected that he had at that moment no desire to do anything whatsoever. A voice falling then upon his ears, he looked up without interest. A fruit woman set her basket down before him, and speaking softly in a tongue full strange to him, she showed him the red-hulled pomegranates and peeled a quartern of one to show him the moist pips adrip with the sweet blood of Attys, lover of Cybele. He ate it; its tart-sweet taste seemed to clear both mouth and mind, and it bethought him there was after all one thing he did desire to do. He gave her a silver coin and he looked at her. She pouted and gestured that she had no change. He looked at her. She was not young and her body was not slim, but she flashed him a smile which showed white teeth, and then she shrugged and then she laughed. And then she took off her russet ragged dress and hung it up for to curtain the niche, and she joined him on the carpet with a sigh in which there was no sound of sorrow.

The gown and the woman were alike gone when he awoke, and it was the time of the false dawn and the second dew was distilling. The morning star blazed. The air was fresh. All around lay sleeping men and beasts. Afar off sounded chanting and the clash of cymbals, and so Corydon thought he would go and thank the god, or whatever deputy of the god had a temple in Illiel, for granting him a safe journey. So he settled on his footgear and he began his way, idly thinking how here the women wore sandals of feathers and the men wore slippers of snakeskin.

In the temple of the god, priests moved back and forth in robes which were both red and black, and now they turned all one side at one time, and they gleamed red in the temple lamps, and then they turned with one motion to the other side and all was black.

Corydon observed with amazement that each priest was

shod with a feathered sandal on one foot and a snakeskin slipper on the other; he marveled, and he mused at what it meant; and he dismissed the only thought which came to him as being unworthy and unclean. He fixed his thoughts upon the god and breathed some prayer of thankfulness, and then an odd and almost painfully strange thing happened: his sword moved within his scabbard and, as though struggling to escape, distinctly beat upon his thigh three times.

The carpet he was kneeling on was soft and thick and woven in many colors and with many pictures of men and flowers and trees and wolves and wyverns and gryphons and dragons and greeths. Corydon had half-turned and was looking, open-mouthed, at his scabbard when he slightly moved his eye to meet a slight movement on the gorgeous carpet. He saw a foot shod in a feathered sandal and a foot shod in a slipper of snakeskin. A soft voice said something in the sibilant speech of Illiel. Corydon shook his head. And the voice spoke to him next, oddly accented, but fully understandable, in the language of the empery.

"The god is surely very pleased with your worship, comer-from-afar. Gracious be your arrival." The voice ceased. The feet remained.

"Holy one, is this temple the shrine of an oracle?"

There was a slight pause. "It is not usually regarded in that special way," the voice said. Another pause. And the voice said, "Though perhaps that could be arranged..."

Corydon said, "It has already been arranged." He bowed down his head once more; then he got to his feet.

The priest was of no certain age, not young, not old, with a clever face. "We are of the middle way," the priest said calmly. "We serve the god, and we serve the man."

"Lead, lord; thy servant follows," Corydon said.

Down corridors polished smooth by centuries of faithful feet, the priest led him. Through gardens luxuriant with splendid plants and gorgeous trees in flower, across courtyards still and sterile and paved with blanched stone sprinkled with yellow sand smoothed in strange patterns, and through antechambers innumerable, Corydon followed the priest. In one room he saw three dwarfs painting with hot wax upon slabs of scented cedarwood, and in another he saw an ambidexter scribe with a pen in either hand inditing lists of offerings upon two pages held in place by pins of steel with heads of golden amber.

At length the priest brought him to a chapel against the wall of which there stood a bench cushioned with unshorn sheep fells dyed in scarlet grain. "Take your ease, seeker," said the priest, with a gesture, "and I shall presently return." Scarcely had the purple curtain ceased to rustle behind him when it parted again and a young person with the shorn head of a postulant entered with a goblet upon a tray and, kneeling, offered it to Corydon with downcast eyes, and departed silently. The goblet contained pressed juice of pomegranate pips, sweetened with honey syrup from the reed called suchari. Corydon sipped of it. It had been cooled with snow. He waited. He waited.

Slowly a sound commenced, at first as though it were a ringing within his ears alone, but soon swelled louder. Somewhat, it sounded like the echo of a gong—but no gong had been sounded. Somewhat, it resembled the mum of a glass goblet whose wet rim is stroked with a skillful finger —but what glass goblet could there be to produce a sound so strong? The sound mounted higher and stronger and it seemed to come from every wall and from every corner of the chapel room. Corydon, on his feet, fixed his gaze upon the disk whereon was engraved the Eye.

The sound had already begun to ebb away.

A figure stood before him.

A woman's, surely.

Hooded.

Veiled.

Hooded though she was, veiled though she was, priestess

—or oracle—as she surely must be, *at least,* Corydon took a step toward her. He felt within his body as though every one of those particles which philosophers call *atoms* was being separately rubbed, and tingled. Distinctly, he felt every single hair upon his flesh standing upright, yet he felt no fear. He took another step forward. He knew what it was she would say even before, in a voice clear and strong and musical, she said it.

"Wilt thou be my groom?"

His mouth was already opened to answer, his hands had begun to move toward her, under his feet (unshod, since the first corridor) the scarlet rug was like a bed of glowing coals, yet his feet were unburned. And—

And at that moment the sword leaped in its scabbard like a salmon in the spate.

He took a step backward.

'Twas she, now, who took a step forward, and as she was doing so, she reached up her hand, she loosened her veils (he did not count them), she bared her face. Her face was concealed by a mask of gilded leather; he turned and he fled as she lifted the mask.

He looked back once over his shoulder. She was not at all deformed in countenance, she was full lovely, her face was young and strong and clear. Her face—

Corydon did not stop.

Back through the courtyards of sand and stone, back across the gardens of flowering trees, back down the endless corridors, he fled. The statues spoke to him, the images called his name, the pictures smiled at him with her face, the walls murmured, the trees sweetly urged him pause. He must have taken a wrong turning somewhere, he was in a place of dusk and gathering darkness, and the epicene priests moved to interpose themselves before him. He felt again his sword leap, he seized his sword, his sword came out without effort, light flashed and lightened the darkness, the priests shrank away and winced and hissed and babbled softly—

He was outside the temple precincts. He was in the streets of Illiel. Slowly, and much bemused, he found his way to the great walled market, with its sleeping niches and its storerooms and warehouses. A face familiar met his eyes.

Didius.

"Didius," Corydon said slowly, "do you know aught about a woman in yonder temple who is a veiled priestess or an oracle?"

Didius pursed out his mouth and slowly nodded, then he said, "She is more than that, Corydon, mate. She is the Sacred Spouse."

Something flashed within Corydon's mind. "Then who... then who is the spouse of the Sacred Spouse? Who, then, is her groom?"

"Whomsoever she does choose, mate. She chooses, they do tell me, she ever chooses them full young and strong and lusty—and thus she news her own youth, do you see? What though she may take, as it were, a year of life and health from him—and they say that she be in truth old, old, old, in years of life—he will never miss it. For one year he is her consort, he has her to joy in and he may joy in as many other women as he may wish, he lives like a king for one full year.

"And for no more."

"Does he die, then?"

"Mate...he *must* die, then."

Corydon's thoughts, which were many, were broken into abruptly by a clamor from a more recently arrived caravan: agreement had just been reached on a sale. Corydon, looking, saw Abélaphon clasping and swinging hands with a great, red-bearded person.

Didius, following his comrade's eyes, said, "That is the captain-commander of the caffle just down from the North. Mayhap we should wander over that way and see if there be some odd lots and trifles of broken bales which we can buy on our account for trading adventures, as they be called."

There were great packets of ermine and sable furs from

the frozen North and ivory of morses' teeth from the icy and sullen seas, there were hides of aurochs and pelts of wooly wisants, and cakes of wax, and slabbets wrought from the rocks of the great Copper Mountain. The red-beard was saying to Abélaphon, in his singsong and guttural tones (though in the language of the empery), "...for it warns of danger when danger be not merely nigh but approaching and it flashes light in the darkness and the thief—may the god-rot eat his bones!—the thief who's taken it, he ripped off its rich trappings, he sold the hilt cover and the scabbard in two places whereto I traced them and bought them back; but as for my own true sword itself, though far I have seeked it and much have I offered for its return, no, never have I found it; and the best I can do is this short broadsword of shiny Dammaseq work. And my own true sword, it e'en had upon its blade the words *Seek Roryck*—which be me, sirs—encut in mystic rune signs. Would any son of man and woman, be he nobly or be he basely born, return Roryck Runesword to me, ah!—and would I not place my rings of gold upon his fingers and my torque of gold upon his neck and bring him back with me, my new-made brother, so to speak!—to sit beside me on the finest horse, and make him free of half my right and title to the mountains and the meadows of the great north land..."

His voice died away and his eyes went wide, and seeing Corydon advance with unbuckled sword in hand, he unbuckled his own. The two men first changed swords. Then, with eyes to eyes and hands on the other's shoulders, next they twain embraced. And the watchers-on, who had scarcely understood, and had indeed drawn back at first sight of hands to swords, now raised a great cheer.

"Ah, well," said Didius, with a smile and with a shrug, "and 'tis all in the day's work, to be sure...to be sure..."

THE OTHER MAGUS

Originally published in Edges, *eds. Ursula K. Le Guin and Virginia Kidd (Pocket Books; Berkley, 1980).*

Vergil was seated in his Glass Garden on the upper terrace of the Castle of the Egg one morning when he became aware, first, that someone was looking at him and, second, that he had heard no one enter.

That inner awareness which he had so long cultivated now directed him to turn his eyes to the left. There, in between the saplings sent him by the Soldan of Babylone, cuttings from the Tree of the Sun and the Tree of the Moon, was a man with the willow wand of The Order between his hands. "Compeer," said Vergil, "you are thrice welcome." He rose, and gestured his fellow mage to come and sit beside him.

The man did not move. "Canst fly, thou?" he asked.

"I am neither Phaëton nor Icarus."

"Their mistakes need not be made.—Can thee fly, thou? Teach me how!"

"This gift I have not," said Vergil.

"Nay, but I will pay thee for its sale."

Vergil, puzzled, abated not his courtesy. "If I had it, perhaps I would neither offer nor suffer it for sale, Serrah."

The strange eyes of the other stared at him and, it seemed, partly into him. "All gifts are for sale," he said simply. After a moment's silence he made an abrupt gesture, vanished.

Vergil examined the floor. Earth was present, and sand, but no trace of any human feet. "He treads more lightly than I," murmured the Brundisian. With his own wand he inscribed on the sand and loam a circle full large to include whichever ell or inches the Apparition of the Mage had superimposed. Next he took up the lectern and set it down in the midst of the circle. "Be thine eloign never so far, compeer," he said, softly, "but I shall find thee out." He set on top the lectern the codex called *The Oracles of Maro* and gave the movable top a single spin. Then with closed eyes asking, "What mage was this?" he opened the book at random and thrust gently at the page with his own willow rod. And opened his eyes.

The word was *Minos*.

"Strange," he said.

And ordered books brought him.

Long centuries ago a Phoenician vessel had foundered off the Cumaean Sands, and only long later shifts of winds and drifts and tides had exposed first her sundered timbers and then her wrack-choked cargo-hold. The glass had grown iridescent in the passing of time, but perhaps the shock of shipwreck or the pressure of sand centuries endurant, or whatsoever, had snapped the neck of almost every bottle, and shattered the sides of most: only the thicker glass of the bottoms had in every case survived uncracked. And Vergil had used them to build the iridescent walls and roof of the Glass Garden on the Upper Terrace of the Castle of the Egg. Rose spots, violet whorls, green and red and golden marks swirling round his face and hands, rainbows rippled the surface of the books.

"Strange," he said. "I find no mention of any mage named Minos. Could his entry to The Order have been clandestine?"

And later, Clemens, his beard and Poseidonian-heavy locks as thick and curly as ever, but now full white, said to him, "Have you after all found your mage Minos, then? You have! Good. How?"

"By the simplest way. The Oracles spoke anagrammatically. His name in truth is *Simon*."

"Simon," said Clemens, considering. "Simon? Simon Magus? Of Samaria. So." A faintly odd expression crossed his face.

Vergil asked, swiftly, "Do you hear them, too?"

"Hear them?" Clemens asked, cautiously. "Hear what?"

"Echoes..."

Clemens looked at him, slightly puzzled. "Again, your echoes. Of what this time?"

"Oh..." Vergil sighed. "Of books never written in our world. Of parables never told..."

Clemens put his head slightly to one side. Then he shook it. Then he reached for the small flask containing the fifth essence of wine, and its colors glowed and rippled, and he poured himself a few drachms. "No," he said, and sipped. "No," he said, "I cannot say that I do." He ran his tongue over his lips, and swallowed. Then he made a sound in his face. "What I *can* say is that I am afraid that when a Samaritan is bad, he is very, very bad."

Vergil nodded. He seemed faintly abstracted. "No doubt there were times when he, too, was good," he said.

THE APE

Originally published in The Magazine of Fantasy & Science Fiction, *October 1981.*

T he man came into the room and took a step or two towards the desk in the corner. It was high-piled with books and papers. Some of the papers were typed, some were in longhand. Pens, a few of them capped, and pencils in two or three colors, lay on top of the papers. In the background was the sound of water running. "Forgot to jiggle the damned thing again," the man said. He half turned. Then he sighed. "Hell with it," he said, and sat down on the sofa, which made a noise of its own, and he pressed a tab on a device.

Without any prologue his television screen went from blank into chaos and flux, first of a most familiar sort and then of a most unfamiliar sort; next the screen cleared with an extraordinary clarity and showed what was perhaps an animal from a nature show, although the TV schedule, to which the man gave an annoyed glance, indicated none such. And the animal gazed at the man, and the background on the screen was odd and curious and extremely so.

"Too small for a gorilla," the man said. "Too small for a gorilla." He often repeated his own words. "Too big for a, oh, *gib*bon? An orang—uh...uh...not squat enough. Baboon? Nope. A chimp? A...oh, hell, *I* give up, what are you?"

And the creature said, as though it were the most natural thing in the world for such a conversation to take place and it to have the power of speech, "I am that same great old ape which offered its hand to Dr. Faustus. And he refused it." The voice was both high-pitched and husky and only somewhat quavery; its accent was odd but easily understood.

"'Where was *this?*" the man asked. A can of beer sat on the soggy arm of the dingy sofa. And the great old ape told him that "some said" this was in Dr. Faustus's own hall near the University of Wittenberg, but that they lied who said so and that it was instead near the University of Cracow, which he (the great old ape) described, vividly, though whether accurately or otherwise is not for us to say, though we may hazard, as "a sewer of many devils."

"And he refused it," the animal repeated.

The man sighed and considered turning to another channel, but, it happening that there was then available neither a talk-show nor girls in wet T-shirts, forbore. He reached for his can of beer; his can of beer was warm; after a moment he gestured instead towards the papers on his desk. "'*The Dark Ages were really misnomered, being illuminated by the fires of the Spanish inquisitioning.*' You like history? From a student in the second year of college. What kind of a *mark* would you give that one? 'Buy sound common stocks,' my uncle said, when he signed over my trust fund, but, no, *I* had to piss it away on grad school." He sighed. "You are *who?*" he asked. "*What* famous old ape?"

"That same great old ape which offered its hand to Dr. Faustus."

The man cleared his throat. "Who refused it. The prick." He sighed and seemed to think a bit, and said, "Yeah, I sort of remember now, where did I read it, his name or should I say your name…name was Benedick or Dominick or was it or is it Habbakuck…?"

"Some say," said the beast. The beast, whose head had nodded a few times, perhaps in agreement or perhaps from great age, pursued for a moment a flea or a flake of salt sweat, then looked up at the man again, and directly into his eyes. Then it held forth its hand.

"Too heavy on the interdisciplinary studies, trouble with

Faustus," the man uttered. He concentrated on the hand, which was rather near in front of him, and he mumbled the word *Holography.* "Probably in a minute my phone will ring and they'll tell me I was chosen to take part in an experiment. Oh, well, and what the hell. So Dr. Faustus *wouldn't.*" The man sighed again, for he sighed a great deal, and he leaned forward and made a gesture with his own hand towards that of the great old ape, and, actually, their hands did not as it were pass through each other, nor were they impeded by the television screen: their hands met, there was *no* electric-like shock, merely the man felt the warm clasp of flesh and rough pads for a moment, hairs atop and bones inside; then their hands loosened one from the other.

"Oh, well, what the *Hell,*" the man said again. He looked towards the phone and cupped his ear. After a moment he said, "Hmmm. Well, then, *what?*"

Habbakuck or Dominick (or perhaps Benedick) gazed round about the man's room, his teeth chattered a bit, just a bit, perhaps in perplexity, perhaps in displeasure; he said, "I had understood that you were a Doctor in Philosophy at a university, and yet your chamber, for hall I cannot term it, seems furnished neither richly nor in full; on the other hand, neither is it the cell of an anchorite nor an ascetic. Pray explain to me." An instant later he added, "For I am your unfamiliar."

Dr. Mortimer Hepgood (our account has not sought to conceal his name from you; it is that the matter has not come up till now) uttered one of his sighs. "You certainly *are,*" he said. "*Well.* I have this contract with this University. This University in this contract styles and terms me as 'vendor.' Do you get that? Did they used to do that at Cracow or Wurtemburg, pardon me, *Wittenberg?* Not, mind you, as *'scholar,'* no, nor even *'the party of the second part.'* Uh-uh. *'Vendor!' Me;* the guy who delivers the chickenshit for the campus lawn; the man who supplies *laundry*—all of us. *Vendor.* Nice, huh? They do *that* at Cracow?"

"A sewer of many devils…"

"Well, this University, an organ of a Public Entity, as another of its favorite phrases goes, to wit, this *State*, maintains what it calls Maintenance Policy. Maintenance Policy is that I have been issued the full supply of furnishing fitting for a Ph.D. who has neither *Tenure*—which means that I could not be fired out of hand, as I could now—nor whose job is *Tenure-track*. I must apologize for the barbarous locution, '*Tenure-track*,' meaning 'in line to receive *Tenure*,' but such is the vocabulary, or, if you will, the jargon, argot, or cant, currently in use and fashion amongst the Groves of Academe: *hence* the rug of the color called (though maybe not by rug-merchants) landlord-green, whose most tattered and torn portion is concealed beneath the dog-puke-puce sofa, which is actually a fold-away bed—and hence the chairs whose seats are mended with masking tape, the ghastly ghouldscape in the chipped frame, the scrofulous…" He paused. He sighed. The great old ape stayed silent, though now and then it scratched its axillae.

Said Dr. Hepgood, "And I may add that not I nor any other faculty member of this Public Entity-owned University who lacks *Tenure* or *Tenure-track* is permitted to remove or *durst* remove from the premises *any* of these furnished articles or artifacts, and in fact twice in each term I have to sign an inventory which is brought here by a member of an ethnic group formerly underprivileged although possessed of a very *rich* culture of its own and who now bears the title of Assistant Associated Coordinator of Maintenance—where the fuck *was* I?—ah, yes, he comes with a list on a clipboard and, as he puts it, 'is obliged to check and have me sign the inventory according to the appropriate statute.' Of course none of this crap would fetch jack-*shit* at a garage sale…

"— who pays for *your* use of not-quite prime time, may I ask, er, Hucklebuck?"

"'Habbakuck,'" the great old ape corrected him, in an absent-minded tone, as he scratched an axilla. And then asked, "Does this Assistant Associated Coordinator have *Tenure-track?*"

"Oh hell no. He has *Tenure.*"

At this the beast gathered his aged limbs and gave himself a shake. "I have been out of junction with your world a long time. Is your lack of these honors, *Tenure* and *Tenure-track,* due to your having defended with insufficient authorities or inadequate arguments your dissertation before the rectors, proctors, consuls, and adepts of the University's Faculty?"

Dr. Hepgood gave a little laugh. He reached for his can of beer; his can of beer was warm. "Oh, we don't do things that way anymore, Hack. We are required to issue a certain number of publications, Huck, 'Publish or perish,' as the phrase is, and some of them have to be *books,* you know. Which I *have.* But, well, Hank, there is more to it even than *that.* See, at least one of these books *must* have on the back of the dust jacket (the paper cover over the whole book, I mean), on the *back,* of the *dust* jacket, at least one of the books has got to have a picture of the writer, the author, holding a pipe in one hand...

"See?"

Habbakuck the great old ape shuffled his haunches and shifted his rump and muttered, somewhat crossly, "Always in dealing with these learned doctors one is obliged to say to them, 'Define your terms, define your *terms!*' A pipe, a pipe: A measure or container of wine? A tube for blowing vessels of glass? A musical instrument, as it might be, a syrinx or flageolet?"

Dr. Mortimer Hepgood laughed at short length, then explained that by pipe was meant a pipe consisting of a cup or "bowl" situate at approximately right angle to tube and commonly now made of wood but once commonly of clay and in which (in the "bowl") an herb, *tobacco,* was ignited and its fumes inhausted via the tube through the mouth. "Ah," said the great old ape (Dr. Faustus had refused to take his hand). Dr. Mortimer Hepgood laughed another short laugh and enlarged his explanation: that, in addition to such licit pipes there were pipes non-licit in which were enfumed substances even less licit. "Ah," said the great old ape.

"I had wondered much," said he, "*why* writers have to be depicted holding pipes for smoking. Now I believe I see. Dr. Albertus Magnus had one such," said he; "by means of it he enfumed the burning seeds of henbane, a most dangerous substance, his excuse being that it relieved aches in his teeth, to which thesis he cited in defense Pliny the Elder and sundry others; what time he, aforesaid Doctor Albertus Magnus, had finished his infumations he would, were I there, and often I was, gaze upon *me*, and mutter, 'I am, have been, or shall be, in Hell.'" The great old ape Dominick or Benedick or Habbakuck said again the word "Ah!" several times in such rapid succession that it seemed almost he barked. Or, laughed. Then he mused some moments more, his grizzled muzzle held in his hand.

"So, just in case you were wondering," Hepgood said, "how come there are all these goddamn photos on dust-jackets of all these goddamn writers holding *pipes* in their goddamn hands—"

"We were not wondering," said his unfamiliar. Adding, "—about that." Still he sat a while; then spoke. "Thus it is, then, if an adept or scholar of the degree of Doctor has had sundry books emprinted upon and by a press or presses and if at least one of these books (and I doubt not that they are very learned books indeed) bears upon it a coverlet of paper and on the back of this a portrait of said scholar holding in his hand a tobacco-pipe, this author and scholar will then be granted by his Faculty and University these utile honors called *Tenure-track* and/or *Tenure?* So he be not easily cast forth from his employment?"

"Yeah," said Hepgood. "*U*sually.—Otherwise: *no.*"

"And if this is done, then such a one will be granted a greater chamber, even an hall, with seemlier furnitures?"

"Right on, Hab."

"And you wish this done?"

"Oh, you bet your li'l bestial ol' bottom I wish this done. But, well, the *publishers*—"

The great old ape waved the hand which Dr. John Faustus had refused to take. "Then it will be done," he said. "It is being done. *Now.* In effect, retroactively, it has been done."

Silence.

Dr. Hepgood sank somewhat further down into the sunken side of his moldering sofa. "Now just a minute here, uh, *Hunk*," he said. "Anything as dreary as a deal with the Devil would make me a laughing-stock amongst the faculty. And all the born-again students, many of whom are very *large* young men and women holding athletic scholarships, they would at the very least burn me in effigy. And who knows if they would stop there?"

The great old ape, who had begun to show signs of impatience, weariness, annoyance, and fatigue, waited however till Dr. Hepgood was done. Then he said, in the manner of an old-style predicant pleading points of logic with his congregation, "Firstly, I am not the Devil. Secondly, I do not desire your body or your soul, nor did I desire those of Professor John Faustus, D.D.; I desired only to shake hands. For, thirdly, I desire *always* to shake hands. Such is my manner and wont, for I have an affinity to clasp the grasp of high scholars, and who can say or indeed *need* say why I am so inclined? I am an ape (noun) and it is my nature to ape (verb); I see it done and I desire to do it; enough. Fourthly, when the hands were shaken, the deal was maken. *Made.* Struck. Only the details remained to be arranged, *videlicet,* you on your part receive *Tenure-track;* I on my part receive a mention in your book—I have *always* desired mentions in the books of men, and yet it is so difficult and they are so rare!—a mere footnote will do; and, fifthly, has already been done—page 325, the chapter ending high upon the right-hand side with plenty of space for a nice long footnote."

And the great old ape Habbakuck, Dominick, or Benedick,

recited the contents of the footnote in detail, with copious references to incunables in the Vatican, Uppsala, Widener, and other libraries; plus microfiche copies thereof available from Esselte Video, Incorporated, for merely nominal sums in Swiss Francs: there was a knock on the door; the television screen went blank and then began to display a hockey game in West Winnipeg, sans sound.

"Come in," called Hepgood, who could not think of anything else to call.

In came a *very* well-dressed man carrying a clipboard; "Well, here I am again, Dr. Hepgood: Crispus A. Castro, Assistant Associated Coordinator of Maintenance, and, say, I want to congratulate you on your new volume which I happened to see just now in the window of College Books as I was coming by—"

Dr. Hepgood said he thanked him very much. But—

"*Very* nice picture of you, didn't know you smoked a pipe; *well*: reason I'm here ahead of my usual time schedule, Doctor, your Department has informed the Dean of Faculty that your *job's* now become *Tenure-track,* and, as you know, or maybe you didn't, the Tables of Organization for your Department already has its full compliments of *Tenure-track* faculty members, at any rate since the latest cutbacks which will be announced shortly: *So,* since your contract under these circumstances is self-terminating, you having become supernumerary, here I am again, obliged to check the inventory according to the appropriate statute and have you sign it as usual before you move out—this weekend will be okay, won't it?—so let's *see* now: One carpet, Grade D, green: *check.* One sofa, from Old Warehouse, puce: Uh-huh: *check. Two* chairs, superannuated from Dorm Three, repaired: *check...*"

Dr. Hepgood reached for his can of beer. His can of beer was warm.

DEAR FRIEND CHARLENE

Written by Avram Davidson and Grania Davis, this was originally published in The Magazine of Fantasy & Science Fiction, *August 1984.*

Ms. V was a beast again today, and everyone at the office was so worried about Charlene, who operated the sleek word-processing system. She just turned thirty, and a drunk in a big pickup rammed her little Honda on the highway. Need I say more? I needn't.

Janet wanted to leave early so she could visit Charlene at the hospital. We'd all chipped in for a fancy card and a gift, and Janet wanted to avoid downtown rush-hour traffic. Even if fighting it *is* supposed to build character. When Ms. V saw Janet fixing up her desk to go, she swooped on her broomstick. Ms. V is our office manager, and she sure must love Halloween. She wouldn't need a costume to win the prize for beastliness.

"Where do you think you're going?" the V snarled.

"To see Charlene," said Janet softly. "Would you like to sign the card?"

"I've already signed the card," snapped Ms. V. "What time does this office close?" As if she didn't know. Must have a time clock up her innermost sphincter.

"Five," sighed Janet. Janet's kind of pretty.

"And what time is it *now*?" growled Ms. V. Her and her goddamn *word* games.

"Quarter to five, but I thought..."

"You are paid to do accounts, not to *think*," barked Ms. V. As if *she* were paid to bark clichés, and not to manage the office.

"Sorry," said Janet, settling back into her desk. "I'll go later." Ms. V flared her nostrils a bit, then moved off, muttering. What a sweetheart.

Charlene never returned to the office. Never recovered. Just slipped into a coma and died. It hit us hard. She'd worked here nearly seven years, and everyone liked her a lot. Charlene was friendly and competent. Was single. Was a slight, attractive woman with dark blonde hair, married and divorced young. No kids or relatives in the area.

The news hit Janet very hard, and we could all see she'd been drinking heavily during lunch. Janet was small, intense, a wiry brunette. She and Charlene had been very close friends—they were about the same age, both single, and lived in the same neighborhood. They liked to go out for dinners and shows together on the weekend, or for afternoon walks, shopping, lunch. In the summer they went biking and jogging together. Close. Too close? I don't know. Just wondered, seeing how hard it hit Janet. Because I like Janet. I like her a lot.

I liked Charlene a lot.

"We'd better get Janet sobered up before Ms. V sees her," I muttered to Carol, whose desk is nearest mine in the office.

"Let's take her somewhere for coffee, Jack," she murmured. Warm, dark, plump, with a quiet and motherly sense of humor. That's Carol. Janet seemed grateful that someone noticed and cared.

"Where have you three *been*?" demanded Ms. V, when we got back from coffee break a little late.

Before I could say, *Up the cow's ass for a milk shake*, Carol laid her large, friendly hand on Ms. V's shoulder.

"Janet was a little upset, so we went for coffee. I'm sure you understand, Ms. V."

Ms. V wriggled the hand off and ostentatiously sniffed

Janet's breath. "I understand that Janet gets *upset* pretty often lately. Don't think *I* haven't noticed. Anything that reduces efficiency is something I *must* notice. If Janet shows up again, lurching and reeking, well, you can be sure Mr. K will hear about it." And she hustled off, her heinie where her head should have been.

What the hell! This was the first time that Janet's drinking had been noticeable at the office, though we all knew she was a boozer. This was a rough day for her—for *her*? But she wasn't 'lurching or reeking' (vodka doesn't *reek*, for God's sake!), and her work as an accountant was just fine.

What the hell! But life is rarely fair—not out in the real world. So what could I *say*? If I provoked Ms. V, she'd just focus her hostility on me. Because, except for Mr. K, I was the only man in the office. I felt a knot twisting in my stomach as I returned to my desk.

A therapist would have told me to pound a pillow. But the office doesn't *have* any pillows—and I can't afford a therapist. Anyway.

Later that day Mr. K called me into his comfortable wood-and-leather private pen, to tell me with an oily smile that I'd been promoted to Charlene's old job, operating the word-processing system. *Oh,* boy!

See, I took a masters in Icelandic Poetry. That means I'm only employable as a mid-level office worker. At least a masters teaches you to *type*.

Ms. V continued to be a beast, and Janet began showing up at the office, late, after lunch. We knew she was hanging out in a cocktail lounge near our building—the bar on the corner —drinking, hardly eating at all. Sometimes she almost *was* lurching. She made several major errors in the books, and her face grew haggard. Charlene's death had really blown Janet's fuses. Ms. V took over the master accounts herself, saying the company couldn't afford any more mistakes. She was on the warpath, and we were all worried. *And then one day—*

One day, as I was storing some bookkeeping files onto the diskettes, a very spooky thing happened. Suddenly the video display screen went entirely blank. I thought I'd accidentally deleted something, and braced myself for a confrontation with the V. But no matter which controls I tried, the screen remained blank, and the system seemed down.

Then very slowly, almost haltingly, the bright cursor moved across the screen, as letters appeared and shaped themselves into words:

JANET MUST STOP DRINKING OR SHE'LL LOSE HER JOB.

What's *this*?

More: I MISS JANET, TOO, BUT SHE CAN'T DESTROY HERSELF.—YOUR FRIEND CHARLENE

What the hell? My *friend*—Charlene! Was this some kind of rotten hoax? I jerked my head to Carol at the next desk, to come over and look.

"What do you think of *this*?" I asked her as she peered at the screen.

Her reaction was almost the same as my own. "Is this some dirty, rotten joke?" she asked.

"I don't know what *else*. Just doing some routine storage when it suddenly appeared like that."

Her angry scowl gave way to a look of uncertainty. "Maybe Ms. V did it to frighten Janet...Let's just delete it and forget it..."

I typed Y to eliminate the strange line on the screen. The words vanished. The video display screen went blank, and the cursor paused and flickered—then new letters and words formed:

DON'T SEND ME BACK.—YOUR FRIEND CHARLENE

On a whim I typed in, "BACK WHERE?" (return)

BACK WHERE IT IS SO VAST AND LONELY.—CHARLENE

"DO YOU KNOW WHO WE ARE? (Y/N)," is what I typed next.

JACK AND CAROL.

Right—I'm Jack, and the woman at the next desk is Carol—and there's no way a computer could possibly know that.

Carol inhaled sharply with surprise. "What *is* this?" she whispered. *Whimpered*, really.

I typed: "CAN YOU SEE US? (Y/N)."

SEEING NEEDS EYES.—YOUR FRIEND CHARLENE

Oh, I didn't want to think about her eyes when she was alive! Her lovely eyes—

"HOW DO YOU KNOW IT'S US?" is what I typed. "HOW DO YOU KNOW JANET'S BEEN DRINKING? HOW CAN YOU COMMUNICATE?" (return)

I DON'T KNOW. KNOWING NEEDS A MIND.—CHARLENE

"WHERE ARE YOU?" (return)

DON'T KNOW.

"WHAT'S IT LIKE?" (return)

LIKE TV STATIC—EXPANDING ENDLESSLY IN EVERY DIRECTION—SOMETIMES IT CLEARS SO I CAN...

The words on the screen wavered, flickered, disappeared. The video display screen remained dark for a moment, and then the cursor and bookkeeping data reappeared—all in proper order. Good thing, too, for there was Ms. V, the sweetheart, standing alongside my desk. Same stale old scene, but she would play it over. And over.

"What's going on here? You're paid to work, not to stand around and gossip. Well?"

"Carol and I were just going over this bookkeeping file," is what I said. I was in no fit mood for a V tantrum. No. But—

"Carol is no bookkeeper; why should she inspect the books? I recognize time-wasting when I see it. Well?" Ms. V folded her thin, leathery arms over her flat bosom and scowled, deepening the creases in her narrow face. She wore an expensive-looking gray wool suit, and a new-looking gray silk blouse, such as nobody else in the office buys. *So how does she afford those clothes on her salary?* the gals used to ask about Ms. V. Her hair was short, gray, and wispy, and she exuded hostile grayness.

Carol slipped back to her own desk, and I went on entering the bookkeeping data; but I felt weird. Wouldn't you? Sure, it was still the same musty office on the fourth floor of the brick Haskell Building. The walls and carpets were still blah beige. The long row of windows, lined with scruffy potted plants, overlooked the same tasty view of a treeless city street, lined with crud and cars, low commercial buildings and more crud—ah, the romantic city! The fluorescent lighting tubes and dusty white acoustic tiles were overhead as always. The word processor, Cuisinart of the mind, sat on its own walnut-finish desk top in high-tech splendor, while the drawers contained the usual clutter of paper clips, tissues, and scribbled notes. And yet, everything had suddenly changed in a creepy, frightening way—and I didn't *like* it.

I'm a sensible man in my late thirties. Just starting to show some gray at the temples—and hoping it looks distinguished. Divorced, with an ungrateful teenage son. I've worked this job for years, to feed my rotten kid and keep the roof unleaky. I spend my weekdays at the office, and my evenings doing chores, and relaxing with a little TV and a little drink. On the weekends I do more chores. Try to talk to my son and heir. Try to have some small fun.

I'm not religious, maybe reformed agnostic. *I* don't believe in ghosts, reincarnation, or any of that. I don't believe that dead people can communicate with the living...I'm not even sure the living can communicate with each other. Just look around you...I believe that the dead are *dead*. I *know* they are. See?

Well, so how could a computer display messages from Charlene? How could a machine know that we were JACK AND CAROL? It frightened me. And I didn't like it. Not one damn little bit.

A few days later. I was editing some form letters when the text on the screen suddenly vanished. Once again there was the slow, halting movement of the cursor, and the formation of words...

IS JANET STILL DRINKING?—YOUR FRIEND CHARLENE

I quickly typed, "YES, SHE IS." (return)

SHE MUST STOP. YOUR SON'S CAR NEEDS BRAKE WORK. THERE COULD BE AN ACCIDENT.—CHARLENE

Huh? Ann Landers and Her Electronic Motor Repair Manual. What?

"HOW DO YOU KNOW?" (return)

SOMETIMES IT CLEARS AND I CAN...

The screen went blank, and the text of the form letter reappeared.

I told Carol at the next coffee break.

"Are you sure that's what you saw?" She looked uncomfortable.

"Of course, I'm sure! You saw it yourself the other day—"

She looked worried now, as well as uncomfortable, and these emotions obliged her to readjust the neat blue polyester knit suit where it wrapped around her ample behind. "Should we tell Janet?" she asked.

I had doubts. "It might *upset* Janet, make her go on a *binge.*"

"Or it *might* snap her out of it," Carol said. "Charlene is right. Whenever Ms. V thinks Janet's been drinking, she mutters like a teapot about to boil over. Jan easily could be fired."

"So you really think it's Charlene?"

"I don't know what to think, and it's scary!" said Carol. "I wonder if we can...summon...Charlene. Then let Janet see and decide for herself."

We walked nonchalantly back to the word processor. I typed *d* from the menu to "OPEN NEW FILE: CHARLENE."

The computer peeped like a baby chick, and signaled an invalid file name. Then nothing happened. Nothing at all. We were disappointed. But mostly relieved.

I decided to call home. Timmy answered. Nice of him. He probably thought it was some girl, by the way he said, "Oh.

Dad. You." He rallied. Asked, "Uh, what's *happening?*" I rarely make phone calls from work. Ms. V doesn't like personal calls on company time.

"Timmy, how are your brakes?"

"Uh. Y'know. Fine. I guess. Why?"

"Get them checked today."

"Uh. *Why?* Y'know?"

I get no respect. "Because I say so, that's why! Besides. A crazy hunch, they might be bad."

"It costs a wad takin' the car inna shop—just for some crazy hunch—y'know?" Get a *job* and you'll *have* a wad. However—

"I'll pay."

"You *will?* That's radical! Uh—could I get, y'know, a new battery, too? Been having trouble starting on cold mornings." His tone was calculating. Thought I'd gone crazy, but decided to humor the old man. Get what he could *while* he could. Y'know?

Still. My *son.* "Yeah, sure, get the battery. But have those brakes checked first!"

"O.K. Don't hyper-spaz, huh? Paint's chippin', too—looks grody. Could *rilly* use a new paint job, uh, with racing stripes —y'know?" he said, pushing his luck too far.

"Check the brakes! Get the battery. Forget the paint. Take the car. Check. The. Brakes. You hear me? *Right. Now.*"

"Fer sure!"

When I got home that evening, my lanky blond son in his regulation T-shirt, faded jeans, and bumpy complexion, looked up from his snack and TV, and gave me a long, strange gaze. "How didja know about the brakes, Dad?"

"What happened?"

"The mechanic said the seal on the master brake cylinder was leaking and ready to go. The brakes could've failed any time—there could've been a bad accident!"

"Just a crazy hunch," I repeated. Gave him a weak grin.

"You shrewd dude," he said, grinning back. But the grin

wobbled.

I slipped shakily into the cluttered kitchen, with its worn and battered appliances, souvenirs of my ex-wife, Gloria, who went off to find herself. I slipped a package of frozen crud in the toaster oven, and mixed me a drink.

SOMETIMES IT CLEARS—AND I CAN...

That's what the video display screen had said. But how could a computer know my son's brakes were bad—*how*? And why didn't my son do a few chores to show appreciation? Where would Charlene appear next—in the grimy glass door of the toaster oven? On the TV? Maybe Great Aunt Hattie, the spiritualist, will show up on the old Singer while my mother is fixing a seam, saying *"There Is No Sorrow in Summerland"* in white thread!

It was creepy—still, I was grateful. She (or It) might have just saved my son's life. Rotten kid. I resolved that next time, I *would* tell Janet. And I finished my drink.

The following Monday. Everybody had the start-of-the-week blahs, and the weather was chilly and overcast. Janet looked bleary-eyed and hungover, with puffy red blotches on her pretty face. Must have been hitting the bottle all weekend. As soon as I tried to retrieve a file, letters and words began to form on the screen: JANET MUST STOP DRINKING. —YOUR FRIEND CHARLENE

I raced over to Janet's desk. "There's something I got to show you," I said.

"Just a *minute*, I'm right in the middle of these books," she said, irritably.

"This won't wait, Jan. It's important."

She was in one rotten mood. Grumbled, but came to my desk. By the time we got there, the message had partially faded. It read: JANET MUST STOP DRINK...

She snapped, "What's this, a tract from AA?" Furious red

blotches showing in her cheeks. Red threads in her blue eyes.

"No. It's some kind of weird message. From Charlene."

Janet flashed a glare. "*What?*"

"It's true. It's true. Ask Carol."

"That's not funny. That's not nice. If you guys have something personal to say about my drinking, well, just *say* it." A tear welled in one red-threaded eye.

The message was slipping away, slipping away. JANET MUST, was all it read now. Charlene was fading out, and there was no way to call her back or make Janet believe me. She'd think I was on her case about drinking. Just like Ms. V. Oh, hell. Why is life so—

Suddenly the message flashed quickly and clearly back onto the screen in highlighted caps: JANET MUST STOP DRINKING.—YOUR DEAR FRIEND CHARLENE

"What's that all *about?*" Janet whispered.

"*I* don't know," I said. "It only happens occasionally. Claims to be messages from Charlene—from Beyond? I didn't believe it at first, thought it was a hoax. Then it said that my son's *brakes* were bad—and it was *true.* Now it repeats that you must stop drinking or you'll lose your job. And Carol saw it, too."

I could hear Janet swallow. Then she asked, "Can you respond?"

"Well…you can't summon it, but you can type in responses. Sometimes it answers and sometimes it just fades away."

With a painfully tense expression on her face, Janet typed, "IS THIS CHARLENE? (Y/N)."

YES, JANET, IT'S CHARLENE. I MISS YOU.

Janet murmured, "A computer can't do that."

"I know."

Janet typed, "WHERE ARE YOU?" (return)

IT'S SO VAST AND LONELY. IT'S NO PLACE YOU KNOW.

"WHAT DO YOU WANT?" (return)

PLEASE STOP DRINKING. YOU'LL GET SICK. YOU'LL LOSE

YOUR JOB.

Tears puddled in Janet's eyes as the message gradually faded to: PLEASE STOP...

Then Ms. V swooped down to my desk. We'd been so engrossed, we hadn't noticed her watching and preparing to pounce. Like a buzzard waiting for the moose to drop. Moose? Gazelle? Gorilla? Gerbil? Oh, who gives a shit. "What's going *on*?" growled Ms. V.

"Just checking the accounts." Mumble mumble.

"How *dare* you fool around with the accounts! Have the books moved Janet to tears—or is she *upset* again? It happens more and more often, and her work has declined badly. I'm doing *all* the master accounts myself, even though it's not in my job description. I think maybe we'll have a little *chat* with Mr. K this afternoon." Ms. V was flushed with rage. At least maybe that muddy tinge in the gray skin of her face was flush.

"Ah, come on," I began. But she was too trembly-angry to be ah-come-on'd. "As for *you*, Jack, you spend an awful lot of valuable work time hanging around and gossiping with the women. This is a place of business, not a singles bar." She jerked her head around. Sure enough. No ferns. Then she glanced at the screen. "Why have you entered PLEASE STOP...?"

"It was just a sample, to show Janet some functions of the system."

"Maybe the system would function better if you didn't keep bugging it with your *samples*," Ms. V grumbled as she stalked away on her flamingo legs, claws clicking.

Then the message faded entirely. Was instantly replaced by a new one: I LOVE YOU, JANET. STOP DRINKING.— CHARLENE

Tears streaked Janet's cheeks, and she raced to the ladies' room so Ms. V wouldn't see. (I think Ms. V has no bladder.) (I think Ms. V has no vagina either, but I lack all desire to investigate.)

The message faded slowly, the computer functioned normally for the rest of the day, and I managed to get away a little early.

After that the messages came irregularly, and whenever they appeared, I tried to get Janet's and Carol's attention without Ms. V noticing. But now she was watching us closely, and whenever she saw us grouped around the screen, she would fly over on her damn broomstick to spy and curse and hiss. "Playing your fascinating computer games *again*, people? I wish you all found your *work* so fascinating! Plugged into some computerized dating network? Don't think it will do any of you much good." And she leered off. Damn the person. I hoped a maddened aardvark would do sundry sordid things to her.

Charlene seemed to sense when Ms. V was coming, and the message was usually gone before the V could see it. Only sometimes not.

CAROL, SELL RUTHERFORD STOCK.—YOUR DEAR FRIEND CHARLENE

This flashed on the screen one drizzly afternoon. "Wonder how she knows I have Rutherford stock?" asked Carol, with a small, scared smile.

"Same way she knows anything," I said. "Didn't she always like to play around with the stock market? Kept track of company earnings and splits with charts and graphs. Did pretty well, too—I'd pay attention, if I were you."

Suddenly the message faded. Ms. V materialized behind us; all she caught was a glimpse that said: CAROL, SELL RUTH...

"Why in heaven's name has a sophisticated and costly piece of business equipment been programmed to read, 'Carol sell Ruth'?" demanded Ms. V. "And *who*? Is *Ruth*?"

"Just a...a sample," I said, lamely. I knew I'd been using the excuse too often. Guess my days of slick excuses were over.

Oh, boy, though. Didn't she glare at me! "Either this system has bugs, or *you* do, Jack," Ms. V snarled. "We'll have it checked out. *One* of you could be replaced."

After that I was more cautious. Instead of showing Janet and Carol the messages, I just jotted them in a little notebook. Janet missed being able to respond, but she *was* trying hard to watch her drinking. It was a battle for her, but she *tried*. Hard. The messages from Charlene gave her hope. She knew that someone (or something) really *cared*.

Actually, I really cared, too. Had a little crush on Janet for a while. But gotta watch the eleventh commandment: *Thous shalt not screw around at the office*—especially this office.

I finally had to believe it, but I could never really accept it. It was too spooky and extraordinary for a sensible and ordinary person like me. Yet it *was* strangely helpful. Janet *was* drinking much less. And Rutherford *did* go bankrupt, and Carol would have lost a bundle if she hadn't sold out in time. And I could never forget my son's brakes. I couldn't accept it—yet I had to believe it. Was it really Charlene, or some creepy glitch in the system?

After all, the brain gives off electricity, and, well, maybe the *mind* does...Who used to say that? Someone—

Oh.

Charlene.

One morning Mr. K came over to my desk. "Morning, Jack," he smiled. Mr. K always smiles, and Ms. V always frowns. Are they playing good-cop/bad-cop? He gave me that we're-both-*men* upper-arm punch. Son of a bitch.

"Good morning, Mr. K. The weather's improving," I said. Yockle-bobble blurtle-smurf.

"*Oh*, sure. *Got* to. By the way. Ms. V mentioned that you're having, ah, *problems*? With the *word*-processing system?"

"Problems?" Never *heard* the word. What mean, *problems*? "No, no *problems*—none at all."

The oh-but-you-can-tell-*me* look from him. The really-I-am-not-catching-*on* look from me. Onward. "Ms. V says that you and the gals often fiddle around with the keyboard, and that odd, inappropriate phrases sometimes appear on the screen." Gelatinous smirk. Son of a bitch.

I heard my voice say, "No, no, nothing inappropriate!" Heard my own voice grow tense, trying to reassure him. "I was just showing the gals how to operate the system. Those were just *examples*."

"Yes, I *see*," said the K, with his baby-oil smile. "Still, we must avoid any so-called glitches, which could wreck our efficiency for *days*. Hmnymf? Ms. V is usually pret-ty reliable. I'll have the word processor checked out. It's due for regular servicing soon anyway. In the contract, you know." God. What would this mean!

An anxious voice was babbling, "Oh, it's working just *fine*! I'll guarantee that. No reason to send it in yet, no reason at all. That would just interrupt my work flow. It's just fine, Mr. K—be*lieve* me!" K's eyes flickered, like a half-submerged crocodile's.

"*We'll* see," he smiled, and he oozed away from my desk, leaving a strong reptilian musk behind him. Or maybe it was just aftershave.

I felt something close to panic. If they sent the word processor in to be serviced, what would happen to that infinitely delicate, incredibly tenuous connection, never supposed to be in such electronic whizbangs at all...? What would happen? What would happen to...*Charlene*?

That day I ate with Janet and Carol in the little cafeteria on the top floor of our building. Had my usual gourmet lunch, egg salad on whole wheat. Black coffee. Carol was on a cottage cheese diet, as usual. Janet wanted to gain some weight. Had a hot roast beef on rye. I couldn't afford it.

Nobody ate very much.

Out with it, Jack.

"Ms. V told Mr. K the word processor has *bugs*. He wants to send it in to be checked. I tried to tell him it was O.K., but I could see he didn't believe me."

"But what will that do to Charlene?"—Carol.

"Who knows."—Janet. Grimly. "The whole thing is so strange...and delicate. Who knows what'll happen if they mess around with it."

"Oh, I'd miss her!" sighed Carol. "...if anything happened."

"So would I," Janet said, a sad look on her thin, pretty face. "It would be like she died all over again."

"What should we *do*?" Me asking. Answers? They looked dismayed. Shrugged. Power; we had no power. Opinions; sure, we could say things starting with 'In my opinion,' but we had no real voice in office policies or procedures. Nobody asked our opinions. And assertiveness training doesn't help much, that I can see. Mouthing off was/is one of the quickest ways to get yourself canned.

"Terminated," they say nowadays.

We looked at each other helplessly.

"Maybe we should steal it."—Janet. Softly.

"*Steal* it?"—Carol. Loudly. Too loudly.

"Shhh!"—Janet again. Looking around as though for spies. "We *could* steal it. And substitute another identical word processor in its place."

"But they cost ten thousand dollars," said Carol.

"You'd have lost nearly that much if she hadn't warned you about Rutherford," said Janet. "And how much is Jack's son's life worth?" (Don't ask, I thought.) "If we each chip in a third, we could buy a replacement, kidnap, well, uh... kidnap Char*lene*!" Simple. Chip in—as though my own chips contained any spare $3,333.33.

"But how would we get it out of there?" is what I asked. "It's a big piece of equipment. You can't just slip it in your purse like taking a handful of paper clips. And Ms. V always stays on her guard dog duty until everyone else has left."

Janet had evidently thought about it all. "You could hide in the john," said she to me. "On Friday afternoon. And there's that big broom closet where *I* could hide. I'm pretty small. I'd hunch down behind all that junk stored in there. Then, while you both carry the old system down to the freight elevator, I'll disconnect the burglar alarm and unlock the doors from inside, and you bring in the new equipment. It's the *only* way to rescue Char*lene*!"

That's what she said. Wild idea. A crackbrained caper.

I asked, "What if Charlene can find us only here at the office? The Haskell Building might be her main connection, not the computer."

Carol nodded. "We should *ask* her. And—"

"And what if we get caught?" is what I asked. "The building *is* guarded. We wouldn't be invisible, lugging expensive electronic equipment at odd hours. We could go to jail—or lose our *jobs*! I can't afford to lose mine; can you? And try to find another job if you get fired for stealing equipment."

Remorseless logic. They wilted. Sad to see. I was right, of course. Janet wanted to do something wild, like a Grade B action movie. I was being sensible, as usual. Sensible, but... well...helpless.

Charlene knew what was happening. That afternoon these words formed on the screen: INTERFERENCE MIGHT DESTROY THE CONNECTION.—YOUR DEAR FRIEND CHARLENE

"HOW CAN I STOP THEM?" (return) is what I typed.

STOP THEM...was the answer. Then the words faded. So many things fade. Life. Beauty. Hope.

Because, realistically, *how* could I stop—well, *anything*? Oh, sure, I was the only man on the floor, often invoked for that reason to Open Things That Were Stuck, but I was just another piece of office equipment to Ms. V and Mr. K.

The V hung around my desk, lurking. Smirking. She knew I was upset about something. I think she really believed I'd plugged the computer into a secret social network...and in a way I suppose it was true. Charlene alternated between trying to cheer us up and trying to warn us of danger. Whenever Ms. V was gone, message followed message:

DON'T WORRY.

THE VASTNESS IS ELATING.

YOU'RE DOING GREAT, JANET.

IF THEY TOUCH THE SYSTEM, EVERYTHING WILL

CHANGE.

YOUR JOBS ARE SAFE.

STOP THEM.

THEY NEED YOU.

STOP THEM.

And, over and over:—YOUR DEAR FRIEND CHARLENE

It was a bad, very *bad* day when the men came to carry away the word processor to be serviced. Pall bearers. Just before they disconnected the video display screen, I saw it flash—Guess what?—CHARLENE...Then it vanished. Nobody saw it. Nobody knew. All gone.

While the computer was down, Ms. V plugged me into one of our Selectrics. And when the computer came back and was installed again? No Charlene? *No Charlene.* Drive a man to drink.

This all hit me hard. Very hard. I *missed* Charlene. *Me.* A lonesome, mid-life, mid-level office worker. Well, it didn't matter. Hell with it. Didn't matter. Let Ms. V rant all she wanted to. Didn't—

Then, *then.* Right then on that damned drizzly, dreary afternoon, I heard a sudden shriek from Ms. V—followed by a porcine grunt from Mr. K—followed by exclamations of surprise from everyone in the office. As every typewriter in the place—electronic, electric, and the few holdover old manuals, went berserk. *Really* went berserk. Began typing, each one on its own, keys drumming—drumming wildly— and each relentlessly repeating the same phrases; exactly the same phrases:

MS. V IS FUDGING THE BOOKS.

MS. V IS FUDGING THE BOOKS.

CHECK: MASTER ACCOUNTS DATED FEB. 13, MARCH 12.

MS. V IS FUDGING THE BOOKS.

CHECK: MASTER ACCOUNTS MARCH 26, APRIL 12, APRIL 20.

SHAME ON YOU, MS. V.

SHAME ON YOU, MS. V.

—YOUR DEAR FRIEND CHARLENE

A commotion! Ms. V frothed. Mr. K assured her that it was some sort of trick. "...and whosoever is responsible, I'll have their *jobs!*"

Lots of luck, Mr. K! V flapped her bat wings and fainted. K moved off at full speed, grunting, "Have'm checked, have'm checked, have those accounts checked! *Now!*"

Some people clustered around Ms. V. "Omigod, she looks like *death,*" I heard someone moan. Carol maybe. *I* didn't think Ms. V looked like death, I thought death must look like Ms. V.

And others just stared at the office machines, now rapidly clattering out more dates, dates...I just sat where I was, feeling as rotten as I'd felt for months. As aging corporate clone, with a rotten child and a rotten job. One beautiful thing had happened in my life, and it had happened briefly, and it was all over, and it would never happen to me again —and everytime I thought of it was like a knife in me, and I thought about it all the time. *What about me? What about me?* What with the late hour and the commotion, I knew I could slip away easy, not to the bar on the corner, but the bar *around* the corner—

Halfway out of my chair, then on my video display screen there silently flashed these final words: LOVER, I DO REMEMBER. BUT PLEASE, JACK, YOU'VE GOT TO CUT THE DRINKING.—YOUR DEAR FRIEND CHARLENE

Then they carried out Ms. V.

THE HOUSE SURGIS SWORD

Originally published in Amazing Science Fiction Stories, *September 1984.*

S lowly the House came to order, though the dull flop and clatter of chicken-bones and almond-nut-shells falling on the floor continued. When something like silence obtained, one arose at the head of the Housetable.

"I am Surgis Han Househead," he said. "I lead the House to victory, in war; and in peace, I maintain its honor." And sat down.

"I am Surgis Clea Housefemale," said the next to rise. "I am mother among mothers, first among equals, with Surgis Han Househead I share the great Housebed." And sat.

"I am Surgis Nel Housewebber. I lead the spinning and the weaving of the gorgeous fabrics which distinguish the males and females of the House in peace and war from those of other Houses, the equal and the less."

"*There are none greater*," growled the group.

One by one they rose and declared their grouptitles. There was Surgis Carl Housecutler, who kept sharp the knives and spearheads, Harold Househorseman was there, of whom a permitted jest was that his smell announced for him; also present was Delmar Housedogtender, who attended the Housedog on peacetime hunts, and whose further task it was, when so directed, to let slip the leash, meanwhile crying *Havoc!* Also rising and declaring title and duties was Surgis Syl Housespy, whose retirement had been expected for a pair of decades now, though still she thought herself capable: her last duty had been as a kitchenhelp in a certain other House, into whose small beer she regularly poured strong beer: and reported back the intelligence gained from their babble. So no one moved to depose her.

Yet.

One by one the holders of proud titles rose up and declared themselves and their titles and one by one sat their holders down again. Again there was a dull flop and clatter of chicken-bones and of almond-nut-shells on the floor.

"Have all spoken?" asked the justly-proud Surgis Han Househead.

No one rose, but a voice was nonetheless heard, in a low grumble-mutter. "I puts em out boxes and cans for peoples should be able ter trow bomes and shellkas inter," said the growl. "So what happens. Where dey trows um. Onna flaw." This was greeted by a snort or so, a sniff or so, and an abrupt harsh laugh. Or so.

"Oh for pity's sake," said Surgis Clea Housefemale. "Must we have this at every Great Housecouncil Session? Can the person not simply rise and declare, as do all others? Besides," she said, turning her head a bit aside, "the person *smells*..." The person was not the Househorseman: no.

There were demands of *Rise, Rise, Declare.* Slowly from a far corner a figure emerged. "Who rates to shower last?" it asked. "When alla hot wawda is uze dup? An lotsa time: no maw soap left? So how can I—"

But the proudly patient Househead had had enough. "Surgis Cedric Housethrall," said the Househead, "at a proper time and place you may move that a Householder be deposed and you fitted into his or her place instead of your present one. And/or you may challenge Surgis Bully Housechampion to ordeal and combat. But—"

The mutter-mumble said, *Naa...naa...*The Housechampion said nought. The figure in the far corner rose. "Om, uh, Surgis Cedric Housethrall, an I om clean up everybody's crap an crud. Sure. Why not. Oh sure. Who'm I?" The Champion lifted a mailed fist against the light. The sullen slattern figure sat down hastily in the corner once more...A general sigh. A light one.

Then House Surgis got on with its new business, namely the outrageous conduct of the other Houses roundabout. It was well-known that The House had had a bad harvest, and yet no other House had advanced to fill its bread-bins and its rapidly-emptying chicken-coops and nut-baskets; if it were true, as claimed, that other Houses roundabout had had bad harvests, well, was that the fault of House Surgis? Certainly not. It was voted that War be declared, and, though this next was a mere formality, that Surgis Han Househead draw the Speaking Sword.

A mere formality because, after all, who else would draw it? and next, no one had ever heard the Sword speak.

But that was its *name*.

Han Househead arose and gave his cloak a toss and reached out his hand to draw the Sword.

The Sword spoke.

That is to say, it cried out in a shrill voice, "Oh leave me *alone!*"

Surgis Han Househead sat down abruptly. There was, for once, no other sound in the Great Housechamber. No one tossed a chicken-bone, no one cracked an almond-nut-shell. The words echoed in the silence. With a furious gasp, Clea Housefemale suddenly flew from her place and grasped with both hands for the hilt. Again the Sword spoke. "Get *away* from me, you *rotten thing!*" it exclaimed. Clea fell back. But still the House proceeded to do all in order; it was not until Surgis Bully Housechampion was repulsed with the cry, 'All you ever think of is your own pleasure!," the sword somehow striking him a bloody blow about the knuckles, that a stir of unease rippled through the room.

"Thee won't do aught to *me*," said Surgis Carl Housecutler, confidently approaching. "Oftë have I sharpened thee, so," but the Sword, saying shrilly that it was *Tired!*, evaded his grasp.

After a while, praise was tried, blame was tried, the House went through it all, turn by turn, title by title, *twice*: the Sword would not be placated, and, at one point or other, somehow or other seemed to crawl down into its own scabbard and pull it in after it.

"We shall certainly win no war and fill no bread-bin *this* way," said...someone.

"I propose that the one who hasn't tried it yet should *try*. For goodness sake." At once it was obvious who was meant. Though not yet obvious to *him*. And so, finally...someone... said, "Well, never mind Cinderella and never mind the Sword in the Stone: who knows, the very stink of Cedric might turn the trick."

Guffaws.

Mostly nervous ones.

Some of them weaker than others.

Cedric was told what to do, he didn't do it, folk threw chicken-bones and almond-nut-shells at him, he dodged them, then he arose and went to do it. He did it. Well, he sort of did it. That is, he did actually seize hold of the hilt of the Sword. Then, dazed by his own presumption, there he stopped, with his slushy face turned round to face the company, and with his gappy mouth slack-open. And the Sword said, with a sigh in which one could sort of see the simper, "But you are so *rough*..."

Unaccustomed success made Cedric bold.

"*Ah'll* rough yuz!" he said.

"Oh, you might *break* me!"

"*Ah'll* break yuz!"

The Sword jiggled in its scabbard. "Break me! Break me!" it cried.

"Ah'll pound yuz against a great big rock an dint yuz!"

"Oh, dent me! Dent me!"

Then, addressing the Sword rather in the tone of voice he

might have dared use to an apprentice scullion, Surgis Cedric Housethrall said, "Ged owda dere!" The Sword got. Cedric stood alone, with the Speaking Sword sort of palpitating in the dirty hands of him.

The silence was at length broken by Surgis Buford Housebutler's saying he was off at once to heat hot water and prepare vanilla-scented soap and warmed towels. Surgis Bully Housechampion did not throw down his mailed gauntlet. He very politely set it down and placed Cedric's foot on top of it. And Surgis Lulu Househoyden came forward and, not saying a word, caught Cedric's eye and hoisted her hynie.

Surgis Han Househead blubbered and sniffled and spoke of past heroisms: to no avail. Ever since had he performed the duties of Housethrall, much moaning about chicken-bones and almond-nut-shells. But Surgis Cedric Househead went right briskly to the other Houses roundabout, the Speaking Sword in hand and Speaking of the simply unSpeakable things it would *do* if—or if not—followed by the other Surgis Males- and Females-at-arms, as well as the Dog of War (who was really too much a martyr to senile canine colitis to be safely let slip); and, what with one thing and another, not only were the House Surgis bread-bins filled, but something was supplied for the smokehouse, the larder, the buttery, and the stillery-room, as well. Cedric and Lulu kicked not only Han and Clea out of softest and featheriest places in the great Housebed, but Clea out of her role as Housefemale; however, she fills that of Househoyden passing well.

The Sword has not really been heard to Speak again.

But now and then it Snickers.

BODY MAN

Originally published in Isaac Asimov's Science Fiction Magazine, *June 1986.*

The customer pushed his lower lip into his upper lip, shook his head.

"What," said Birnbaum.

"'No warts,' I told you, Birnbaum."

"'No warts,' of course you told me 'no warts.' Who says 'warts'?"

"So why are there warts?"

"What warts, where warts?"

The customer averted his head, pointed. Said: "Look."

Birnbaum looked. He looked the look of one who saw no warts and merely wondered greatly. Then a look of disbelief, then a look of astonishment, then a look of outrage. "I'll kill 'im, I'll kill 'im, that dumb kid assistant! 'No warts,' I told 'im. 'Customer doesn't *care* the present body has warts, customer doesn't want warts on the new body,' I tell 'im; talk to the dumb kid assistant, talk to the wall. Warts." He shook his head from side to side with little stiff jerks. A moment later he said, hopefully, "A, a dermatologist, one—two—three, zzzzzzzz?"

"I wanted a dermatologist, Birnbaum, I'd go to a dermatologist. Eight million, eight hundred thousand—"

"*You're* right, *you're* right. Okay. Okay." He flipped through his order book, smeared back the pages, mumbled. "'Consolidated Factors, two Account Execs,' 'Regular Republican and Democratic District Club, one Politician (attention: Smile), Church of the Former and the Latter

Rains, one Spirit-filled Evangelist, customer will supply own Spirit, eighteen and a half percent discount plus regular ten percent clerical discount...'" His mumbling stopped, he gave a quick look up, said, "Two weeks."

"Two, *weeks?*"

"All right. All right. Next Thursday. Ready by five o'clock, quicker than that it couldn't be done, figure it out, 800,000 a day overhead, one customer gets two discounts, one isn't enough, you could live but they won't let you, you think I lick honey in this rotten business, go train a good body man like he was your own son you live in fear and trembling eventually he'll go open his own place with your own customers some of them loyalty doesn't mean a thing, present company exempted, and if you should dast mention to an assistant untactfully a reprimand: right away: the Union."

"Birnbaum."

"Thank God the Summer is a long way off, comes July, August, the pippick people, 'specialists,' you hear? 'specialists,' they start walking out off of even the little bit of a day's work you ever get from them, 'Not only are the pippicks melting but we are also melting too in this terrible weather where you could pass out in any minute,' the specialists—"

"Biographies I don't want, Birnbaum. Warts I don't want, Birnbaum. Next Friday at what time is none of your business Birnbaum I have a very important appointment, God forbid I should have warts, Birnbaum. You hear." The air was tepid and smelled of elastiform.

"You wouldn't, you wouldn't. Thursday at six o'clock."

"*Five.*"

Birnbaum gave a despairing look around the cluttered workshop, slumped into a weary sigh. "So let be five, I'll go with*out* lunch, who has the heart to eat? Five. Not before."

The young assistant had his own problems, but, "Listen, Bobby," said Birnbaum, "I regard you as my own son almost, what, the nose mixture I didn't confide in you, the formula that Kaplan and Kelley I let them eat their hearts out I didn't give, so when it says on the *blue* slip 'No warts,' so why do you put warts?"

Bobby looked up slowly from his sandwich, mayo drip on his lower lip. "You know what she says to me, Morris? 'All you want is my body, Bobby, maybe you been in that business long enough and maybe we been together too long,' how do you like *that*, how do you *like* that?"

Birnbaum, whose wife had long since ceased to make similar accusations, was, despite business pressures, interested. "*Who* said? Sheila?"

"Who else but Sheila, you think I'm some kind of a philander, I have the soul of a great artist, Morris, I'm no philander; what does she mean, '*all* I want,' as though it was a mere nothing of no consequence: *Maron!* You seen the body on her, Morris?"

"I didn't seen."

"Oh my *God* what a body. '*All*,'" he said, bitterly, biting into his sandwich with savage teeth.

Birnbaum breathed a breath or two, nodded. "Yes, but Bobby, I also was once young, similar stories I could tell you, passion I appreciate completely, at the end of the week when she or any other young lady she demands 'Take me here and take me there or I wouldn't even let you look at it,' and you're reaching into the pockets with both hands and the left foot: so how, so tell me, so explain to me, Bobby, how do you expect you're going to find anything in the pocket, Bobby, if we lose our paying customers because you paying no attention to the *blue* slip where it says, clearly and distinctly, Bobby, 'No warts'?"

Bobby took the last swallow of sandwich, followed it with a long tug at his soft-drink bottle, turned his large and glistening eyes upon his employer, put the bottle down on the spray-tray, asked, "Medium-brown hair slightly receding hairline, 'Reduce obesity by ten pounds' it also says on the *blue* slip?"

Birnbaum, encouraged, nodded and nodded. "The cne, that's the one—"

Bobby burped; said, "Morris, to you I may be just a young kid whose erotic impulses, like, overshadow his importance of economic considerations, but let me tell you, Morris, I love artistic integrity above all things, and believe me, Morris: I don't put warts where they don't belong; okay, okay, I see I still got ten minutes left on my lunch hour, but I'll bring it in on the dolly and I'll take a look at it; don't tell the Union."

The next week passed in the usual grind of occupation; Bobby came to work placidly, disconsolately, frenziedly, haggardly. At five on Thursday afternoon a customer perhaps twenty pounds overweight and with a slightly receding line of medium-brown hair came in with his eyebrows raised, followed Birnbaum's finger, examined the work, examined it carefully, gave several nods of more than merely grudging acceptance, verbally expressed his total satisfaction, and microzapped for the 8,800,000; Bobby came to work on Friday morning sullenly and contentedly; he and his employer toiled together without many words, Consolidated Factors' Account Execs (two) were picked up by a mere menial; the Representative of the Regular Republican and Democratic District Club praised the quality of the crafted smile, and, smiling, sold Birnbaum two tickets for a dance and ball, Birnbaum offered them to Bobby: Bobby, with a quick jerk of his head, declined.

He declined lunch, too, was offered and accepted his check plus a small bonus, and helped get the order finished and ready for the Church of the Former and the Latter Rains' Evangelist a bit ahead of time, thus avoiding an opportunity for the Church's representative to engage in prolonged witnessing; "*Two* discounts," said Birnbaum, shaking his head. "Some have the name, whereas others play the game."

At five Birnbaum began to put things together in order to put things away for the weekend, and to sweep and sort; when he looked up to say a parting word for Bobby, Bobby wasn't there. Shortly before six the front door crashed open and a *gorg*eous young woman entered, screaming. "You bastard, you son of a bitch, my brothers will *kill* you, wait till I tell them," she shouted, some degree of hoarseness hinting that she had been screaming for some while; "Where *are* you, you bastard, you son of a bitch, they'll tear you apart, what you did to *me*," she cried, ignoring Birnbaum's presence, though Birnbaum did not ignore hers; "Where *is* he, where *is* he," demanded the splendid creature.

She beat upon the doors of the finishing room; "Where is *who*?" queried Birnbaum.

"That son of a bitch who *works* here, that rotten bastard, Bobby—"

She raised her foot to kick the door which Birnbaum at once flung open; "He's not *here*, go look, go look, then calm down; my God what did he *do*?"

All the while Birnbaum was inviting her to look, she was looking: no dice; when he asked the question she swung her unflawed face and gorgeous body around and, looking at him, she screamed her answer: *"Warts! Warts! Warts! Warts!"*

LANDSCAPE WITH GIANT BISON

Originally published in Isaac Asimov's Science Fiction Magazine, *September 1986.*

S trictly speaking it was not a trolley car for there was neither overhead wire nor sub-level trench, nor could there have been: car and track were miracle enough. At intervals there was a depot and the controlman, Robert Haas, slid the two ready-to-go-spent batteries out through their port-holes and into the wind-charger, but did not wait till they were recharged. Two more were ready, and slipped in where the others had been. Onward. There had been problems in the Triassic; once a tyrannosaur had charged the wind-vane and there was neither Quixote nor Panza to do anything about that. The blades had not been made to withstand it. Also the earth was not yet firm and the tracks were sometimes rippled and wrenched for miles. Then too the work-crews had not performed well in the Triassic. Astonishing how many had gone mad, with all resultant problems. So the Triassic Line had been reluctantly canceled.

Things went much better in the Pleistocene. Sometimes an entire day might go by without even a mammoth attacking the big red car, and when one sometimes, only rarely, did, the bell usually made it swerve off; if not, the hooter always did so. Robert Haas dinged the bell to attract attention, announced, "Cataract Sixty-seven is our next stop, folks. Cataract Sixty-seven..." Far off in the distance a cloud of dust caught his eye. "I see there may be, just may be, giant bison crossing the track about five miles up ahead. Well, we'll see. If we're held up by them, the candy butcher has sandwiches, root beer, and ginger ale." He fell silent. The passengers being rather tired, there were no questions. A wooly rhino appeared out of nowhere on the right side of the track, its red hide caked with mud and dust, and paced the car for two miles; then it slackened and turned away, was lost to sight.

A cloud of dust? Smoke?

One year the Turghaghulor, a people whom only animal cunning saved from near-idiocy, who by slow drift down the land had come to the embanked track, did not even recognize it as something out of the way of nature: finding a convenient bare-spot, a convenient raised-place, they had laboriously piled wood upon rails and ties alike and blew upon their firesticks...the Turghaghulor cannot kindle fire with either rub-wood or strike-stone...roasted what small game they had caught alive, and what carrion they had managed to wrest from the grasp of larger creatures. No one ever saw a Turghaghu kindle fire and no one ever saw a Turghaghu put fire out; this fire burned for days and it was days before the damage could be repaired. So far as was known those microcephaloi had never yet encountered one of the big red cars moving along the track; had they done so, be sure they might have taken it for a mastodon or the like and tried in their shambling way to lure it into a swamp or off a cliff so they might more easily kill it and eat it.

Wild two-toed horses galloped alongside, picked up speed as the car slowed down a bit, jumped the track just in front, were gone. Immense giraffes with their rocking-horse gait racked along. Hills appeared, black eye holes in them, white threads rising. Robert Haas dinged the bell. "Way back to the right, folks, those are the West Trog Hills' first outcropping, you see that the Frimdhadhulor have observed the steam from Cooky Joe's caboose, so they are sending back their signal to us. So we like to say, anyway, but it's almost certain they are signaling to other Frimdhadhulor up ahead. There's a place before we get to Cataract Sixty-seven that's dedicated to the Mute Trade, the Dumb Trade or Silent Swap. The Car Company traditionally allows us to stop a bit and anyone who wants to set out items of small value can do so; coming back you'll be able to see what the Frimdha have put down next to each item and what they are willing to give for it. We suggest you be content with whatever it is." He did not voice aloud a silent prayer that there be no repetition of the incident in which a cracked cup with bluebells painted on the side had been paired with a very well smoke-dried, very dead old woman.

Robert Haas had a blood brother, a Frimdhadhu. Somewhere. He knew that in the mouth of one of those caves people were holding up babies to see the distant steam-vapor, exposing arm-pits which had never been kissed by razors. Whenever, which was not often, they found a suitable bathing place, the Frims bathed, thus revealing themselves to be White and tow-headed; most of the time, they, too, like the red wooly rhino, had hides caked with mud and dust. A suitable place was not easily come by. It had to be deep enough at least to sit in, and devoid of any alarmingly fast currents: the Frimdhadhulor did not swim.

The Frimdhadhulor did not swim and thought that only critters could swim. *All* such critters they called *Fish*. The immense otters sometimes seen were *Fishdogs*, and there were also *Fishbirds*. Once they saw in the middle of a lake creatures very much like men and women, they had red hair some of them and black hair some of them and were probably an outloping band of the Brunghughulor. The Frimdhadhulor did not, however, refer to them as Brunghughulor; they called them *Fishfolk*. Scores of thousands of years later their descendants spoke of mermaid and merman. Robert Haas heard voices raised just a bit and thinking that perhaps a question had been asked of him turned around. What he saw was no questioning face but a mild ad hoc celebration; a card-game had been unexpectedly won.

Giant ground-sloths ambled slowly along, a cave-bear, unusually far down into the lowlands, reared up to its immense, incredible height, roared defiance at the car; made, fortunately, no move to attack it. The cloud of dust, at last. Sure enough! Giant bison! They had crossed the track, all, all. Well, all but one. A vast old bull-bison, no longer able to get cows for his harem, outcast, ugly, rogue, probably bad teeth and trouble with both grazing and chewing, head bowed, beard almost in the dust; fleece shabby and peely, hump flabby and saggy, horns—ah, those horns!—ah, those horns!

And—right in the middle of the track!—the huge old bull paused and began to piss. Robert Haas slowed, slowed, dinged the bell gently: like a flash the old rearguardsman-bison giant turned and charged straight up the tracks, straight towards the car. With Haas now decision was instant. The car surged forward at increasing speed, the hooter howled, the bull did not exactly give way altogether but he seemed to lurch off center, gigantic head sweeping from side to side seeking to see this new enemy—the bull lurched, slipped, had almost regained himself when the car struck him between the shoulder and the brisket: he went up, he went down, he went over, kicking hugely, lay still. Still, there, there, in the middle of the Pleistocene—

Again, voices, a voice. Louder, closer, it was the winner of the card-game, holding out a hand, not alone his own hand and its five fingers but a handful of cards. Evidently the winning hand in the game just won. "There!" cried the man. "There! There! Look at that! Was that worth coming on this trip for? Eh? Hey? What do *you* say? Oh boy! *Worth* it? What do *you* think? Would *you* kick up your heels? What would *you* do?"

Robert Haas thought he would sigh.

Then he dinged the bell again.

LOUIE AND THE LIBRARY

Originally published in Ellery Queen's Mystery Magazine, *August 1986.*

L ouie's father was the janitor in the shabby-genteel apartment house where Miss Meriwether lived on the third floor in an apartment filled—if not almost overfilled—with memories of an age much richer than our own.

Miss Meriwether was not very much aware of Louie, or, for that matter, very much else—except for the poems of Emily Dickinson, which she read and reread, and her will, which she changed often. However, from time to time noises would ascend even to the third floor, at which times, disturbed, Miss Meriwether would descend to the basement, where in a smaller apartment, equally crowded—though not all with memories—lived the janitor. And she would knock.

"Oh, Mr. Labonna. The noise."

"I'm sorry, lady," Labonna would answer, his dirty, mended eyeglasses clouded with sweat and tears of rage and shame. "My boy, he give me *lodda* trouble—he very bad boy, lady, very bad. I'm sorry, lady." This meant, although Miss Meriwether did not realize it, that Louie had been caught stealing again and that Labonna, whose views were perhaps simplistic, had been beating him up again.

"Oh, dear. Louis. Oh, my." Miss Meriwether produced a dime—a dime!—and extended it in Louie's direction. Louie would slide by his father, grab it, and run like hell. Miss Meriwether's vague and benevolent smile, her departure. Labonna, turning to Mrs. Labonna, who knew three hundred and eighty-one ways to cook noodles, cabbage, and potatoes and not a goddamned thing else, would open wide his arms in a gesture not of love but despair.

This happened often.

Finally, Louie got caught and sent to the reformatory.

Miss Meriwether grew just a trifle tired of Emily Dickinson and concentrated for a while on Sidney Lanier, with occasional dips into Celia Thaxter and—a big step for Miss Meriwether—Edna St. Vincent Millay. She kept on changing her will.

Louie got out of the reformatory.

"Why, Louis. Hello."

"Hello, Miss Marywedder."

"What do you think of doing now, Louis?"

Louie shrugged. "I dunno. I tought maybe I'd loin ta drive a truck."

Miss Meriwether considered. One felt a certain responsibility for the janitor's boy, now almost a young man. The word *truck* did not penetrate. "Louis—have you ever thought of joining the public library?"

"Whuddayamean?" he said suspiciously. She opened her purse, a gesture which he observed apathetically, no longer needing a dime even to slide past his old man's fist—Labonna knew when he was licked.

But it wasn't a dime that came out. It was a small rectangle. At the top were the words MUNICIPAL FREE LIBRARY. In the middle were a series of numbers. On the bottom half it said:

Miriam Meriwether
324 Hamlin Street
City

Louie held it in his hands. It seemed to fascinate him.

"I ain't got one," he said.

"But you can obtain one, Louis."

"Whuddayamean?"

"You do know where the public library is? Catercorner from the high school? Well, all you have to do is go in and apply. And they will issue you one."

He handed it back. "Tanks, Miss Marywedder." She went up the stairs, books under her arm, feeling faintly excited, faintly daring. *Amy Lowell!*

The librarian suppressed a sigh. "May I help you?" she said.

"I wanna liberry card."

"Do you have some identification?"

"Whuddayamean?"

"Do you have a driver's license?"

"I ain't got one."

"A Social Security card?"

"Notchett."

The librarian produced a postal card. "Well, just address this to yourself and we'll mail it. When you receive it, bring it back. That will indicate that you have a residence within the city." Louie had learned a number of things in recent years, whilst away from home, and one of them was how to write his name and address. "As soon as your permanent library card is ready, we'll mail it to you, Mr. Labonna," the librarian said.

"Tanks, lady."

He walked out very slowly, looking all around. He had not really realized that there were this many books in the world.

Meanwhile, although nobody wanted to teach him how to drive a truck, Louie ran errands and did odd jobs and kept his nose clean. Old Labonna, very slightly less discouraged, gave him a few dollars.

"Have you obtained your library card, Louis?"

"Come in taday's mail, Miss Marywedder. Look."

"There. Isn't that fine! Now, Louis, all the treasures of world literature are yours for the mere selecting!"

"Tanks, Miss Marywedder."

He watched her heading down the street, Amy Lowell under one arm, her big hat bobbing and nodding. Then he went up to the third floor. The library card was made out of the best goddamn plastic he had ever seen—it took him hardly any time at all to slide it between door and doorjamb and open the latch. Afterward, he hitchhiked to New Orleans, where, he had been assured by classmates, dwelt the most generous fences in the nation: perhaps a matter of opinion.

Miss Meriwether, who had been finding it increasingly difficult to bend, squat, stoop, or otherwise get the hatbox from under her bed, never noticed a thing. Eventually, her trustees did notice the absence of several pieces of the jewelry mentioned in her will—her wills, that is. There were eleven of them, all different, all unsigned.

As for Labonna, he dropped dead one night while stoking the furnace. His widow returned to her native country, where she moved in with her widowed sister and bought a cow and some pigs. Besides these, she has Social Security, and once a year Louie (who lives in a western state where he owns three trucks) sends her a hundred-dollar bill.

Whenever this happens, the neighbors smack their foreheads with the flats of their hands, cross themselves, and wish that they, too, might move to America, land of opportunity.

MR. AND MRS. PIGGOTT

Originally published in Ellery Queen's Mystery Magazine, *Mid-December 1986.*

L ived in a vine-covered cottage at the bottom of a street lined with two-storey red-brick semidetached houses. All of which had once been The Piggott Estate. In the Old Days. Before The Crash. Had been obliged to take a mortgage on The Property. And then a second mortgage. Unable to meet Their Obligations. Terrible. Terrible. To see the Old Home razed to the ground, green fields vanish under bricks and mortar. Lucky to save the cottage.

"Tell her, 'We don't know how lucky we *are*,'" Mr. Pigott said, waving his hand toward his wife. "Just to have a roof over our heads." He raised his eyebrows and blew out his moustache and nodded his head. A large man. Mr. Piggott's nose was veined like some kinds of marble or cheese. Little tufts of grey hair grew on the bridge of it, on the backs of his fingers, in his ears.

"Well, it certainly is a wonderful thing," their visitor said vaguely. This was Miss Winslow, Registered Nurse, round and pink.

If Mrs. Piggott did not, indeed, know just how lucky she was, it was not from having been insufficiently reminded by Mr. P.

A little white sparrow of a woman. Whatever she had ever possessed of strength and beauty seemed to have vanished —or have been absorbed by her hair, coil after black coil of it, piled up high on her little head. "Yes, Jacob," Mrs. Piggott would say. Or, sometimes, depending on the previous remark, "No, Jacob."

Her lord now pounced upon the visitor's last enunciation. "Wonderful?" he cried, bulging his eyes still farther out, and waving his arms. "Wonderful? See the hall of one's ancestors crushed to rubble? Wonderful?"

Miss Winslow, whom a thousand and one or two such occasions had not taught better, grew agitated. Licked her full lips and shook her head. Leaned forward for emphasis.

"No!" she cried. "Oh, noo! I didn't mean—*not* having your house torn—What I meant was, it was so wonderful that you were able to save this lovely little cottage, and—all that. *That's* what I meant, Mr. Piggott." With a final lick of her lips, she settled back in the chair. Like most in the house it rocked uncertainly, had leaking upholstery and springs which threatened to lunge and assault unwary flesh. But not, of course, Mr. Piggott's chair.

"Say no more about it," he said now, generously. Almost genially, warm from forgiveness. "Misunderstood me. Almost as bad as my idiot wife, ha ha ha."

And Miss Winslow, with a tiny glance darted at her hostess, laughed, too, throwing back her head. All just a little joke of Mr. Piggott's. Jolly Mr. Piggott.

"Well, well. Enough of my own sorrows and trials. Cheated by the world of commerce which I, as a rich man's son, was never familiarized with until as an adult I learned the hard way. Reality. Knowing reality from illusion. My only salvation. Unlike my gooney-bird wife, ha ha ha!" (*Ha ha ha,* from Miss Winslow: else how to admit that one thought a woman might be insulted before one's eyes? No: *Ha ha ha!* Another of Mr. Piggott's little jokes.)

"You, the same," said he now—Mrs. Piggott having silently disappeared into the kitchen—smiling. Miss Winslow cleared her throat inquiringly. Illusion. What she lived by. Pandering to the fools who thought they were sick. First illusion. That medicines could cure them. Second illusion. That Miss Winslow knew anything *about* medicines. Third illusion.

His guest drew back her head, moistened the corners of her mouth in preparation for speech. Had no chance. There were in the whole country how many men who really knew anything about the subject? Would Miss Winslow care to guess? Ten thousand? *One* thousand? One *hundred*? Made a man laugh. How many? Oh, no. Never anything like it. Nothing like it. *Three*, that was how many. One was Professor Schuyler, who had written a book about the medical racket. And what was his reward? Kicked out of his job in one of the biggest universities in the country. The second was a medical doctor with whom Mr. Piggott had once played golf. Before the Crash. Admitted as much. Question put to him point-blank.

"Know as much about it as if you were a trained medical doctor yourself, Mr. Piggott," this man had said. "Impossible to fool you. Truth. Starve to death if I said it publicly," this man, biggest man in the medical profession, had admitted.

"Welll," Miss Winslow began.

Enter, silently, Mrs. Piggott, coils of hair wobbling, bent beneath a heavy tea tray. Thereon: a huge teapot, three huge teacups, three saucers, a tea-caddy, and several rather dry and dusty-looking cookies of the sort which had been peddled through the neighborhood almost a year ago by the local Girl Scouts.

"What have we *here*, gooney-bird?" jovial Piggott demanded. He hazarded a conjecture. "Tea?"

"Yes, Jacob."

Rubbed his hands. "Must feed the inner man in his corporal nature well as his spiritual." Lifted the lid of the ancestral teapot, opened the caddy, spooned in two spoons, far from full. "Leave it to Dumb Dora, black as ink," he said. "Tannic acid: deadly poison. As well drink arsenic. Eh, Dumb Dora?"

Mrs. Piggott's Christian name was Alice. "Yes, Jacob," she said. After a while poured the pale-colored fluid into the cups, adjured by the master of the house not to stint, to pour full measure regardless of possible loss to the rakeoff she skimmed from her housekeeping money.

"No, Jacob."

"What 'No'? Ghosts, I suppose, put money in that empty jar on the top shelf in there. Spooks. Gooney-bird. Idiot. Ha ha."

Faintly, something about "for emergencies." Fainter yet, a something about "giving her little enough for housekeeping." A redness about Piggott's face then, except for the nose, which showed a whiteness about the nostrils. Veins of red and blue and purple standing out. Teeth bared, crooked and yellow, under the dirty moustache. Not a nice sight then, Piggott.

"Delicious cookies." Miss Winslow speaking loudly, thrusting the plate with them toward her host. Glare—at her, at his wife, at the plate—then, chuckling, picked up a cookie, thrust it into his mouth, biting down hard and fierce as if it were his wife's birdlike little bones crunching between his jaws. "Delicious," Miss Winslow's voice sank.

Piggott cried out. Eyes screwed up. Hasty mouthful of weak, warm tea, jagged swallow. "Oh," he moaned. "Mmmmm. Oh."

Suddenly in her familiar element, "Why, what is *wrong*, Mr. Piggott?" Miss Winslow, Registered Nurse, inquired. "Did you break a tooth? I hope—"

"Dry as a bone. Hard as a stone. Idiot. Jackass." Piggott snarling at wife.

"—not."

Bruised a gum, said Piggott, calm, though breathing heavily. Miss Winslow begged him to let her look. Proud, disdainful: no. Just *look*? she pleaded. What would it hurt to —Mr. Piggott bent forward as suddenly as if he were intent on snapping the buttons off the bosom of her tailored jacket with his lemon teeth and pulled his lower lip down between tufted thumb and tufted forefinger.

"Oh, my," said the nurse, dismayed. "Oh-oh-my." *Not* a bruised gum at all. Not at *all*. Mr. Piggott, she said, had Vincent's angina.

Leaned back in his chair, smiling. Sneering? "Illusion," he said. "An illusion of pain: my part. Illusion of disease: your part. Your profession frighten people. Take their money. Fleeced like sheep. Lambs. Eh, jackass? Ha ha."

Meekly, "Yes, Jacob." Faintly, to Miss Winslow, "Catching?"

Oh, highly contagious, she was assured. Became agitated. A glee upon the part of her grisly lord, and laughter. Gooney-bird was afraid of getting sick, he crowed. Idiot was scared her lovely teeth would fall out. Brushed them three times a day, her white teeth. Use dental floss, if someone in the house didn't have sense enough to put his foot down.

"No, really, it is *highly* con*tag*ious. You must keep all your dishes *sep*arate, Mr. Piggott—" Looked down with some dismay on her teacup.

Now quite happy, elated indeed, rubbing his Roquefort nose with two tufted fingers, Piggott absently thrust the other bit of the cookie into his mouth, again cried out with pain—illusory or not as that may be. Miss Winslow followed up Mrs. Piggott's weak-voiced plea of, "Take something, Jacob," with an offer to procure him a preparation for the cure of Vincent's angina. But to no avail. Take foreign substances into your body, man would have to be even more of a fool than some people took him for. And subsided thenafter into sullen silence, lower lip and cheek and moustache moving as questing tongue explored the tender areas.

Miss Winslow left after a little while.

"Why do you go back if he's so terrible?" Winslow's old friend from nursing school, Stromeyer from OB (Winslow being in Out-Patients), asked her. Oh, well, Winslow explained with a shrug, who else would the poor little thing ever get to see if she (Winslow) stayed away? Besides—such a lovely little cottage. Besides (unspoken), who else would the Out-Patients nurse get to talk to on her day off? Stromeyer having, firstly, a different day off and, secondly, a family. The other nurses, well, all the young ones ever thought about was *men*, and what did she want with the others? Bunch of old maids, poor things!

"How is your mouth today, Mr. Piggott?" she asked. Not caring to risk a repetition of the arid and adamantine cookies, she had made bold to bring along some nice cream-cake: it looked so tempting, she explained, handing over the bakery-box, that she just hadn't the will-power to resist. Would they forgive her?

Didn't fool Mr. Piggott for a minute. "Oh, our humble fare is no longer good enough for you?" he charged. "Impossible with us to compete with the dainties served up to the hospital staff. Note: I say 'staff.' Patients something else altogether." He took a piece of cream-cake and thrust it into his mouth and chewed it. And chewed it. And chewed it. And —

—caught Miss Winslow's eye. She looked away at once, too late. "Food-bolting: digging your grave with your teeth. Secret of good health? Fletcherizing. Chew each mouthful a hundred times. Don't believe it? Bad as my imbecile wife, ha ha ha. Only way to eat. Masticate every mouthful, soon be the picture of good health."

Mr. Piggott did not look the picture of good health, looked yellowed and sick. Fell silent a moment as Miss Winslow continued to pick at her piece of cake with her fingers, sneak a glance at Mrs. Piggott. Mrs. Piggott looked none too well, either. Under her eyes were blue smudges which might have been caused by lack of sleep, on her cheek a blue smudge which couldn't possibly have been.

Piggott's voice, next heard, sounded unlike his usual self-assured, ride-over-all one. "Been having such illusions of pain and illness," he muttered. "Nausea—"

"Oh, that's too *bad*," Miss Winslow said, professional and concerned. "Your mouth—"

The old Piggott returned with a roar. "Nothing to do with my mouth! Said it was an illusion!"

Miss Winslow was very sorry, but it was no illusion. She guessed she knew Vincent's angina when she saw it. She was very sorry to have to disagree with her host in his very own house, but trench mouth was something she had been familiar with since her earliest days in training, and there was no doubt about it.

"Your *mouth*," she said, "must be in *agony* by now."

Piggott, moaning, plagued by idiot women (he said). Piggott once again drawing down his lower lip, then lifting his upper one, thrusting out his tongue, exposing the lining of his cheeks. Piggott, seeing her astonished face, triumphant. Well? Look like it's in agony? Eh?

Miss Winslow shook her head. "Why, it's almost *gone*," she said, wonder-struck. "What have you been taking for it?"

Taking? Piggott? Foreign substances into his body? Nothing at all was what he'd been taking. Fletcherizing was the answer. Chewed his food until it was in proper shape to be digested and washed his liquids around in his mouth until all the enzymes were absorbed.

"I never saw anything like it," she marveled.

Piggott's look of triumph vanished. Bent over, moaning. Came up green. "You—are—*sick*," said Miss Winslow. "*I* am going to call a doctor."

"Slam the door in his face. Quacks. Nurses, too. Think I'm blind, you and them and my wife. Ahh—" Came convulsively to his feet, left the room at a trot. Could be heard in the bathroom, retching.

Silence. Miss Winslow, shocked by his illness, vexed by his words, dismayed by the look of utter malignancy cast after him by his wife (what *was* that bruise on her face? poor little thing), began to babble.

"Well, I never in my entire professional career saw such a remarkable recovery from a case of Vincent's. Vincent's is a *very* troublesome thing to get rid of. Peroxide, of course, well, peroxide *does* help, but the *best* thing, the *best* thing, Mrs. Piggott, is arsphenamin. Arsphenamin, I don't suppose you've heard of it, it's made from arsenic, they paint the mouth with it—" Her voice trailed away.

Oh, how suddenly little Mrs. Piggott's eyes left the hallway onto which the bathroom opened! Oh, what a look there was in her eyes! As if she hated Miss Winslow, too, not just Mr. Piggott! Mr. Piggott—Suddenly, suddenly and all the little bits of pieces fell into place: Mr. Piggott's yellowed face, his nausea, his Fletcherizing, constant chewing of every bit of food, round and round in his mouth, each mouthful of solid or liquid round and round, against cheeks and tongue and insides of lips, and the odd blue bruise on Mrs. Piggott's cheek.

"Mrs. Piggott," she breathed. "Oh. Oh, Mrs. Piggott!"

Mr. Piggott was still to be heard vomiting and groaning as his guest found her feet and fled from the lovely little vine-covered cottage and into the street.

She had to tell someone, of course, and so she told Stromeyer. Stromeyer told Dr. Callanan and he spoke to Dr. Brosy, the police surgeon. Mrs. Piggott, all things considered, drew a very light sentence. She could, in fact, have gotten out on parole in a couple of years or so, but she refused to apply. For one thing, she explained (her lovely long hair short and grey), she'd have to say she was sorry, and she *wasn't*. And for another thing, while prison had its drawbacks, having to live with Mr. Piggott wasn't one of them. It was just as well that she hadn't succeeded in killing him, since it was all found out, but since it was up to her she thought she'd just stay right where she was.

Yes, Jacob.

WITNESS

Originally published in Night Cry, *Winter 1986.*

T he man in the booth was cradling the phone between ear and shoulder and looking into a newspaper. He looked like the sort of man who would have picked up the paper, perhaps without paying for it first, and was now phoning about a job. In other words, like anybody. Nobody.

A woman answered and spoke a number instead of a name. She repeated it. He said, "Ah, I'm calling about the ad? In today's paper?"

She said, "What ad is that?"

"It said to call this number."

"Do you have the ad with you? Could you read it to me please?"

The man sighed. He gave the paper a shake and a snap. "Witnesses to accident at Elm and Harriet Saturday noon, please call 324-4457. Is this the number all right?"

The woman said, "Yes, sir, this is the right number. We are very pleased that you have called. Now, um, could you give me *your* name and address, and your own telephone number?"

The man in the phone booth dropped the newspaper and shook his head. "Hello? Hello, sir?"

"*Oh.* Ah, *no.* Anyway, not yet. Why do you wanna know?"

"Well sir. So that we can get in *touch* with you."

"Yeah? Well, you're in touch with me *now.* So—"

There was a brief pause. She asked, "Could you describe the accident, please? Sometimes, you see, people call us but they are confused, and they describe some *other* incident, so—"

He thought this over. Then he said, slowly, "I get it. This is a lawyer's office. Isn't it. Sure. This is a *law* firm. And you handle lots of accident cases. Right?"

They didn't exactly squabble. But he didn't get a direct answer. He asked, why should he tell her anything? She said, because a good citizen—He asked her not to give him that. And after a few more words, the woman said she would put it to him *this* way. Let him describe what he saw. And then they could take the next step. After all, what did he have to lose? Did he see what she meant?

For a minute he simply stood and breathed. Then he scratched his head. "Okay, I guess. Listen. I was coming down Elm. And I seen, I saw this red Jag coming like real *fast*? And in the same second, I s—I saw this guy step off the curb. Evidently *he* didn't see *nothing*. And before I could, like, say a word. *Bam!* So I didn't say—I was, like, in *shock*? Do you know what I mean?" She said, oh, she could *imagine*. And she asked him if he could describe the victim and the driver.

The man twisted his face. He seemed to be in deep thought. He said, "What's in it for me?"

"Nothing," she said at once. "If that's what you tell us. If you tell us nothing, nobody *gets* nothing."

He breathed deeply. Then he said, "Listen. The uh, *victim*? He was what I'd call like, a middle-aged man? Dark-complected? He was wearing what I'd call, ah, fancy-type Western clothes. And the driver? A big guy. Real heavy. Big. Grey-haired. Sports clothes. He got out of the car, well, no, he *didn't* get out, he only stopped and he *started* to get out. Then —huh?—ah, he was wearing this green sports—Ahah. Ahah. Now ya *believe* me, hah?"

"Now I believe you," she said. "Now I'll ask you—I have to ask you to wait just a second until I get Mister—until I get somebody else on the phone." He grunted. Asked her to make it snappy.

It was perhaps closer to a minute. The voice was smooth and confident. "I understand, sir, that you witnessed the tragic accident on Saturday? And are you willing to testify on behalf of the unfortunate victim, or, rather I should say, his family. Good. Good. Now won't you supply us with just a few —"

At this point the voice of the operator broke in demanding money. It was quickly paid. Then the man said, "You got that, Counsellor? Deposit money. How much ya gunna deposit with me?"

"Why, sir."

"Never mind. Never mind, 'Why sir.' You got a lotta witnesses? Then you don't need *me*. You ain't *got* no other witnesses? Then you need me plenty. Suppose you get a judgment for a million. What's it worth to—"

The smooth confident voice said that, "Speaking absolutely unofficially," a small, a very small amount might be forthcoming for, say, unofficial expenses. The man in the phone booth wipes his face with his free sleeve. "I can get you two hundred dollars this afternoon, on that basis."

"Two *hundred*. I want ten *thousand*."

"Ah, my dear man. Who knows how long it might stretch out. Or what a jury might say. Or what settlement might be reached. Whereas. Twenty nice tens in a manila envelope. This afternoon. Hm?"

The man in the phone booth said, okay: this afternoon. But no two *hundred*. "Two *thousand*. Or the hell with the poor victim and his poor family. Huh?"

There was a sigh. "You drive a hard bargain. Where'll we meet?"

After hanging up the phone the man walked quickly up the block. Then he looked at a large clock of an old-fashioned store. Then he slowed his pace. For a while he seemed to be walking aimlessly. Various emotions played on his face. Then he began walking briskly. Block after block. Eventually he made a turn. A long alley intersected the block. Someone was there, holding a manila envelope.

"This about the auto accident?"

"Yeah. Here. Count it."

"Don't *worry*. I'm *gunna*." As he was opening it a heavy-set man with grey hair, and wearing a green sports shirt, stepped very lightly up behind him and shot him twice behind the left ear. The other person stooped and picked up the manila envelope. They walked out of the alley rather quickly and, stepping into a red Jaguar which pulled up just then, were driven immediately away.

ADDRICT

Written by Avram Davidson and Grania Davis, this was originally published in The Magazine of Fantasy & Science Fiction, *January 1987. You can learn more on* The Avram Davidson Universe *podcast,* https://www.buzzsprout.com/1310005/6707275.

Here's S. Claus on Santa's new modelry, one-person, one-photon-unit skimmer. Well, it *was* new…when the twenty-first century was new. Well, it *works*, doesn't it? Even though my hands are shaking so much.

It's Christmas Eve, year 2020, but I don't *care*—don't care about ho ho humbug and deck the halls-balls. Only one thing I care about—same thing I care about every day of the year. And every night, too. Price is up—keeps *going* up. Every day the costry is higher, and my dealer just laughs when I complain. "So strike the habit," she says. But I *can't* strike the habitry. *She* knows it. *I* know. It.

Everyone knows it. My mangley family and their loving lectures. "Try. Just *try* to go without it for one day," my everlovring used to say. "If you can manage for one day, you can strike it."

Yeah. Sure. How cold is *your* turkey?

But I never got through even one day without getting the jitters and shakes so bad I just had to have it.

I must have it.

And my mangle-mouth bossry: "We've tried to be lenient and understanding, as the Sympathy Law requires, but you just aren't carrying your own psychic weight around here.

Better smarten out."

Better thisry, better thatry.

Hard to carry your own psychic weight when you're shaking and twitching, can't think or concentrate. Can't think about anything except *getting* it...*getting* it...needing it...*needing* it...*so. Bad.* I used to be an outstanding empathetic, spousery, model employee—until the craving got so bad.

It's *like* that when you're snared. People can honey-talk you and paraempathry you and try to persuade you to quit, but deepry downry you don't give a cram about *any* of them... everlovring...bossry...mother...best friend...affinitry....They mean nothing compared to *it. Itry. Gotta* have it—*now.*

—Sell my share in a Moon Condo, if I had one to sell. Oh, there's plenty of ways to get it. Don't *need* a job-bob, don't *need* family, friends, paraempathry, share in a Moon Condo. *Zucks*, just need some *bucks.* A big wadry of bucks, mintage, *cooky.* Price goes up every day, but I don't care. I'll cut the cooky somehow. Sell my bod-hod. Gongle something. *Lift* something. Getting *good* at lifting. Only snagged once, invoked the Sympathy Law. Nothing on the record; getting *good* at lifting. Well...was. Hard when your hands shake-snake. Can still drive the skimmer, though; never touch the ground.

Tonight? *Easy.* Christmas *Eve.* All those packages of costly new merch so nicely wrapped in color-spang and sitting around oh so visibly. Around the gaily decorated tree-bee. Just skim around the right poshry neighborhood dressed in my Santa suit, and my Santa beard and my Santa bag. *Bag-hag.* Just slip inside an unlocked door or gongle open a window that's hidden from the street. Just climb over a force-fence, gongle open a lockry. Getting better at this all the time *ho* ho ho; tricks of the trade-raid. Tricks of the trade. Never carry a gunry, ho ho *no!* Penalty too *stiff* now. Instant death, what could be stiffer? Knife will do if someone bothers me. If there's trouble.

But I'm not after trouble-bubble. After something else. I just *need* it—*soon*.

A poshry house where nobody's home? That's easy. Tonight. *E*veryone has skimmed off to church, or parties, or family dinner-spinner. Plenty of houses empty tonight—and they all have those big green *trees*—surrounded by unopened, unused, ex*pen*sive things. *Salable* thing-wings.

I went to church when I was younger, before I got snared. *I* went to parties and family dinners. *E*mpathy! Now I go to church only to lift the collection, sly-fly. Or get a free meal. Family and friends don't invite *me* anymore. Don't like to see me twitching and shaking and visibly craving itry.

Fence said he'd be around all night. Right. This is a *big night. Zucks,* all those empty *house*s! All that valuable new *merch,* color-spang-wrapped *merch*andise sitting around those *trees.*

Gonna make a *good* haul tonight. Gonna carry off a bunch of lootry in my Santa bag. Gonna sell it fast to my mangley fence. He'll cheat me as usual, but I don't care, I'll have so much stuffry. Jewelry, maybe. Photon-unitry, microcomputers, maybe. Real wool sweaters (getting rare-bear); portable 3-D video, silverware, maybe. I'll have *e*verything. Fence will sure peel off a wadry of bucks, mucho cooky, and then I'll hustle-bustle right over to my sweet *deal*er—

"It's *Christ*mas!" is what I'll say. "Ho ho *ho*! Gift me with a free sample, dealy-feely!"

Oh, she'll gripe, she'll snaggle, but she'll give. Hands will stop shaking, then. I'll feel so much better. I'll *bar*gain with her over price-nice. Tonight is an easy night, she'll be feeling goodry. *E*mpathy. Me in my Santa suit...I'll buy *big*. Maybe enough to last till New Year. *Zucks!*

But—

Gotta be *care*ful. Can't get *caught*, get caught in one of those big richry houses. Can't get caught with my lootry, they'll *take* it—leave me with nothing—nothing but shaking hands.

Can't ever get caught.

This neighborhood looks plush. Looks poshry. Plenty of rich mangle-heads live here. *Lotsa* good stuff around *their* trees. Think I'll try *this* big house-mouse. No skimmers hanging in the skimway. Lights are dim. Just enough so the house looks occupied—not to *me, I* can't be fooled. Done this too many times. *This* house is *empty.* People skimmed off to church or a family din-din party. Fa la la la and silent night to *you,* folks, whoever you are—you're about to help a poor addrict with shaking hands and a big need-feed.

House all decorated for the holidays—strings of lights and a big wreath. *Real* holly. Jolly. Almost as rare as real wool, costs a wad for that stuff nowadays. *Rich* folks. Deserve to treat themselves right, all that cooky. *Presents!* Maybe jewelry, silverware, mini-video, photon-units, *all* kinds of goodies. Now I'm going to redistribute the wealthry a bit. Modern Robin Hood, taking from the rich and giving to the poor mangle-heads—*me.* I'm the poor mangle-head with shaking hands. Gotta have it—*soon.*

Little window at ground level back here on side. Lightweight glom-locks on these things. Easy to gongle it open and crawl inside. *No* sign of a zeeper alarm. O.K. now, just push a little harder, a lit-tle—'kay. Snapped-zapped. Window yielding easy. Easy, baby, easy. *In*side.

Nice house. Real richry. Good furniture, big 3-D video. Just skim around a little. Just check out the drawers, the closets, other likely hidey places for cashry or jewelry or silver. Then hit the presents—stacks of them around a big tree-bee, a *real* one, all decorated with silver icicles and angels. My mother used to put angels on our tree—but I haven't seen *her* in *years.* Cheers. Not since she found out who'd been robbing her. And *why.* And—empathy. Forget.

Oh. What's *that?* A noise. Probably just a cat-rat, or I'm getting spooky. (*Soon,* baby, *soon.*) Sounds like footsteps. Am I imagining things? Withdrawal hallucinations? Oh, God, it's an old lady! A frail, wrinkled little old lady with thin white hair and a quarter-unit walker and a frilly nightgown, maybe the last one in the *world*. Reminds me of my—

Why aren't you at *church,* you old witch-bitch! Why aren't you at the big family dinner? Don't you like parties and eggnogry, hey, oldbitch-witch? What are you *doing* out here in the living room? If you were too sick for church or party or dinner, then aren't you too sick to be wandering around the house by yourself—especially nowadays when there's so many prowlers about, the mangley gonglers. Go back to your *room,* old-bitch! *I*'ll stay out. *I* won't bother you. Did you hear a noise? It wasn't me. It wasn't a burglar in a Santa suit with shaking hands. It was only a cat-rat. You don't *have* a cat? Well, maybe it *was* a burglar, but what can *you* do, with your thin white hair and deep wrinkles, your frilly nightgown and your quarter-unit walker? I could snap you in *two* oldbitch-witch. I could *gongle* you! Go back to your *room!*

Zots, she *sees* me. Can I calm her down with a ho ho ho routine? No. She's starting to scream-dream. Thin, hysterical, *use*less screams. Heading for the vidi-phone. What to *do?* The copy—the fence—the dealer-feeler.

Oldbitch put that *phone* down! Put...it...*down*....See, I've got a knife-life...my hands are shaking...Put it *down*. Stop *screaming.* You sound like my—

Now she's stopped. She's down on the floor. She'll be quiet soon. Should have kept your *mouth* shut, oldbitch. Should've stayed away from that vidi-phone. You've had a long life— and a comfry one, too—*look* at all this plushry furniture, big 3-D video, all these unopened packages of color-spang-wrapped merch. Were gonna die soon anyway. Why bother to live if you can't even go to church or the big family dinner-spinner on Christmas Eve?

Stop shaking, hands. Stop *shaking*. Gonna pour myself a drink-think—expensive? You bet; *scotch*. Plenty deary in this year 2020, like real wool, real holly, real—Merry Christmas, oldbitch. Can't stay too *long*. Sorry.

Quick; find some jewelry, find some silvery, find some

micro-appliances. Open these packages, open this merch, take the *good* stuff, the stuff I can sell to my fence.

—A purse. Must be the old lady's purse. Money out of her wallet. I.D./Credit, can always get bucks for I.D./Credits, even hers, so old-mold. Take her gold cross and chain, too. (Got to *have it…soon!*) Heavy. *Real* gold, no snytha-chem.

Zucks!

What *else* have we got? Hey, here's the jewelry box with pearls and gold chains, rings and opal earrings, *lots* of nice stuff-puff. Good taste. Fine people here. *Fine.* Mine.

Presents. Wow, holo-camera, for *me?* Oh, thank you, Santa! A real wool sweater? They're so expensive now! And this jade bracelet? For *me?* Whee. No. For my fence. Gotta hurry. Gotta —

Soon, baby, *soon.* Hands'll stop shaking, *soon.*

Hurry. Dining room. Sniff around. In the sideboard; what? The family silvery, is what. Sterling. Good taste? The *best!*

Just toss it all into my Santa bag. Adjust my Santa beard. Hey, this could be lotsa *fun!* Well…coulda *been.* If oldbitch hadn't gotten in my way. If my hands weren't *shaking* so. If I didn't need *it* so much. Well. *Out* the window. Bye, folks. Jokes. Thanks for everything…and…Merry Christmas!

Just walk down the streetry in my Santa coat and my Santa beard, with my Santa sack bulging with gifts for my fence? Oh—yeah—but for *me,* too. Here's my skimmer. Oldry but goodry. Onto the metro and away we *go.* Ho. A big fat haul, undetected, and I'm feeling *good* now. Pow. Gonna unload all this rich stuff. Gonna collect my wad from my fence. Gonna rush right over to my dealer for some Christmas *cheer.* Hear? Gonna feel *fine.*

(*Soon,* baby. *Soon.*)

—Kinda rundown neighborhood. Fence doesn't live in such a poshry house as the poor oldbitch. Gotta be more careful around here. Lotta tough types-hypes. Keep my fingers on my knifery. Feels so cool and reassuring in my sweaty fingers. So—What is it?

Oh, God, it's a setup. An unmarked copskimmer! Staking out my fence's old shack; his living low doesn't fool *them*! Waiting for a bit of business to show up! They found me. They're after me. Gotta *run*-fun. Gotta *hide!*

No, baby. Stay cool-cruel. Just skim along at legal speed, skim around the block. No one will suspect ho ho old Santa, heading home to delight his family. 'Kay. Go, go, *go*—So.

Stay cool. Don't shake so hard. They following? Not a sign. Didn't even *see* me. Didn't even *notice.* Calm down now. No shakery. What to *do?* Ah. A*h!* Unload the stuffry on my dealer-feeler! Sometimes she'll take merch instead of cash. This is costry stuffry. Holo-camera, silvery, jade bracelet, microcomputer, pearls, gold chain and cross from old—won't mention that part-heart. Dealy will give me a mangley price; always *does*—but gotta un*load* this stuff. Gotta get it *soon.*

Used to be legal long ago-so. Yeah, used to be able to buy it openly. Still more-or-less legal in some countries, I heard. Not *here.* Not any *more*-sore. Cracking down *heavy.* Growing. Selling. Using. Stiff sentences now. Pow. They say it's bad—but it's worse if you can't get *it.*

Heavy robo-sensor border patrols confiscating huge amounts from attempted smuggles. Shouldn't snag the poor smugglers, should give them a medal. They're doing a public service-nervous, supplying poor addicts like me. Shouldn't put them in *jail*-wail. *They* take it...and probably use it themselves. Drives the prices up and *up.* Used to be legal. Long ago. (*Soon,* baby. *Soon!*)

Almost there. Fence and dealer not very far apart. Here's her house, and there's no cops-bops, no cop cars. The lights are on, and I hear music—she's home-poem!

"Hey, dealy! Look at me It's *Santa* bringing lots of good *presents* for you. Take it all. *Yours.* Merry Christmas! Just let me have a decent stashry of it. My hands are shaking so *bad* I can't *stop*-pop.

"What, dealy? My fence? Cops' stakeout, so—No, nobody followed. I got *such* a good haul! (Never mind oldbitch bleeding on the rug-bug, not a word of that.) Lotsa nice Christmas toys I knew you'd love. Jade bracelet, silvery, holo-camera, pearls, microcomputer, real wool sweater. *Good stuff-puff. Ex*pen*sive. Mostly brand-new, never used. You can get a wad for it. Could wait, sell it myself, but kind of in a *hurry.* Hands shaking—*You* know. Feel *gongled. You* know— you've had the shakes-snakes. Hey, how about a free sample, dealy? It's *Christmas*—so how about some Christmas *cheer?*

"No, hey? Down to business, hey? Well, *look* at what I brought you. Just give me a decent stashry and you can have it *all. Look!* Opal earrings, holo-camera, microcomputer, real wool sweater. O.K., cute? Cutery? (Hands shaking so *bad-*sad, gotta have it *soon…)*

"*One?* That's all you'll give me is one? Cutery, look, I brought you so much good stuff; worth at least *five-*jive. Camera, computer, sweater, bracelet, silver, gold chain, cross. Look. *Look* at all this stuff, worth at least five, maybe six, seven—

"Things are tightry now, huh? Can't let me have more than *two?* That's your final offer? Well, O.K., baby. I'm flexible. I understand *Zucks!* (I *need* it now!) Maybe next time you'll gift me some samples, but I'll take two now. Pow.

(*Soon.* Hands'll stop—)

"You know it used to be legal. Long ago. Sure, when I was younger you could buy it in any supermarket—what's *taking* you so long?—Then they said it wasn't healthry, but I never could strike the habitry. So guess I'm hooked-cooked. Ah…. *Here*—

"*My two jars of instrant coffree!*"

"Gotta cup-pup?"

MOUNTAINEERS ARE ALWAYS FREE

Originally published in The Magazine of Fantasy & Science Fiction, *October 1987.*

Old Raynal Smith had been mechanic of the No. Two Tipple for over twenty years and had seen his eldest son die from catching one on his back when the ceiling fell in Tunnel Six off the Andy Johnson Shaft, and his second son blown up when they let the dynamite set too long at Level Two, Wilson Shaft; the third one, time the cage just *dropped,* Black Tuesday, had a thighbone drave through his right eye socket. So they say. But you couldn't hardly tell from the way he was holding his youngest son's right shoulder. "He says it were a baby one," said Old Ray.

Young Doctor watched hydrogen peroxide bubbling in Little Ray's leg and grunted, "Whyne the hell don't you boys keep *away* from—"

"Well, he don't know, rightly, whure he *was,*" the old man apologized. "We hain't buried none back thur sence *I* was a baw, them wooden markers is all fell down, and *ain't* hardly none o' them old Free Will Babtiss People still *'live,* hardly, an' they too *ol* to take ceer o' the place!"

"Place ought to be *marked!*"

The boy, noting the rise in the doctor's voice, began to howl right dolefully. His father kneaded the shoulder more intensely as the doctor sloshed hot water and liquid green soap. "Well, now, Baw, hit was only a young 'un, way you tell, reckon hit dent like bitin' you any moren you liked bein' *bet!*"

"Why'd 'ee do it, then?" demanded the boy, speaking words for the first time.

"They'd never *believe* this back at the university if I were to tell them, which I sure as hell won't!" Young Doc tugged at the hard-pulled homemade leather bootlaces, and the boy howled some more.

Old Ray was mighty patient. "Cuz hit were only a *young* 'un, Baw, hit were sceered, jist as *you* was—" He stopped, and his face and neck moved convulsively as Young Doctor reached for the scalpel. "Oh, sir, *cain*'t you *save* it, *please?* We air pore folks, but—"

The doctor slashed the laces and pulled the boot off the dirty, smeary leg and foot, then dropped the scalpel in the basin and picked up a clean sponge with a hemostat and swabbed at the mingled blood and dirt and cedar-smelling green soap and peroxide; all the while he went on speaking, "'Save it'?—why, that's up to you, but it doesn't look to me that it'd stand up to another cobbling."

Old Raynal's face and hand went slack. His mouth hung. Then he said, "You mean...the *boot?*"

"Sure the boot, what the hell you think I mean?" Slosh, scrub; the boy howled. "They'd never be*lieve*—*look* at...look at those *teeth* marks, *oh* my—"

"*Whut'd* I *thenk* you?—I thought you meant the *foot!* The *laig!*"

At mention of foot and leg, the boy screamed and jerked and struggled to rise; his daddy, though it was not very convenient for him to do so, fetched him a good punch the side of the head: blood spurted. Little Ray subsided, nose bleeding. He moaned a bit.

Young Doctor had been there a year, so he was not terribly shocked, but he was new enough to be angry. "What the hell'd you *hit* 'em for, Smith?"

The day was full of bad surprises for Old Ray, and still they came on: half a day's pay as good as lost; only living boy-child bit by a Parson John, if only a baby one; he, the boy's daddy, just now feeling worse than if a daughter had been caught whoring (boy a *cripple? bet*ter dead), and now *this*—

"—clean it out real good, give him a tetanus shot against lockjaw, lucky no reports the Parson John carries rabies—say, Sonny, instead of just crying, why don't you *tell* me *what*—"

Young Doc's eyes did not see that Smith's face had already gone red and mean. He jerked his boy up so that the wet leg slid out of the doctor's hands, then slammed him down again. "You don't tell 'eem *nothin'*, Baw! You hear me? As for you, why I reckon the company pays your wages same as mine, I hit 'em to make 'em *mind,* is why! We ain't *clean* enough for ya? You city people thenk you own the yarth, but you don't own the folks in Cobb Cove, hyurr, and you don't own Raynal Smith!" He struck his son again. "Git that boot awn, you *hurr* muh?" The boot was scarcely on when he left at the double, dragging the boy. Boy didn't utter sound. The young doctor knew that the boy might get poulticed with cobwebs and cow shit and might recover and might not, and that nobody would be*lieve* it at the university that the boy had been bitten by a young ghoul, were he to tell it. And that he would not.

VERGIL AND THE CAGED BIRD

Avram Davidson's The Phoenix and the Mirror *(1969) introduced the magus Vergil, in whose world the medieval scholastic beliefs about the nature of things are true. Here is an episode from his life, originally published in* Amazing Stories, *January 1987.*

Assuming each letter to have its own numerical value, which is after all to assume the obvious, as every schoolchild does well know—assuming each letter to have its own numerical value, the word *crowd* does not add up to the word *true.* Or *truth.* Scan them. Let A = 1, and so C (for *crowd*) equals 3; take it thence. Vergil had taken the presence of the crowd for granted. He had not summoned it and scarcely could he have prevented it from gathering. And yet. There stood he and there stood the one whom he must question and around them stood the crowd and around the crowd stood the buildings of the center of the city of Naples, some of them standing from its foundation, plaster peeling and stucco scumbling by the knife and brush of time and the rubbings of many bodies, breaking it down to show the rough rude stones of the founding day.

"Whence comest thou?" asked Vergil, speaking, not as one having authority, but speaking, simply, as might one to another. And yet almost he dissembled. And though the man he addressed might have merely shrugged on by, instead he paused. He stood a moment silent, in one hand a cage with a bird in it. The bird was caged and the bird did not struggle;

still, it did seem that this was not a cage-bird type of fowl.

"High 'Pulia," said the man who held the cage.

Vergil was doubtful. Vergil *seemed* doubtful; nevertheless, he *was*. The crowd was varied as are most crowds, therein lie their savors. A session of senators, a tiring (as one might say) of tailors—whatever—would lack the same savor. There near-bye was a fowl-sharper, next and by no means as acute-looking an aging produce-broker. Vergil stood so the man with the cage could not civilly brush past him; Vergil turned to the former, one Cocko, not his real name and perhaps he did no longer know what was, perhaps he *need* no longer know: what use to him now agnomen, cognomen? *Cocko!* Good enough for all days, nowadays. The man was short and stocky and his face square and well-lined with grooves of self-satisfaction. Cocko could supply a lawful capon fattened for the cook-spit better than any; also he could, did he desire, fix any pigeon-race; he did not desire. Any longer. Rare birds he could cozen and catch—Vergil spoke to him.

"Well, Squire Cocko, and what bird be that in cage?"

The man's face changed, he pursed his lips and moved them a bit, not as the old produce-broker, whose aged chops moved incessantly: Cocko moved his own lips *now*. As if he liked the taste of something. Such as the word *Squire*. "Ah, whoa, Master Magen," he said, touching his new white-woven-hat, "tez a farty—that is," hastily, "in our cant, ah whoa. In *yours*, me Master Magen, tez a pheasayant." A pheasant it was indeed which the man, an Asian of some sort, Lydian, Cappadocian, Phrygian, Pontian, perhaps, had in the withy-cage. A fairly new-fangled bird. So.

"Squire, so: right you are." Why should no one else ever have called 'Cocko,' *Squire?* 'Twas harmless...and he *liked* it. The Asian liked it all not, but yet he moved not away. It was just as well. Just as well. A woman at the well let water run into her jug, a one which sang a bittle as the air went out. Now and then the novelty was in the fashion. Now and then it was out. Now and then a woman at a well might find herself giving water to some lord not tired as such, or to the steward of one far-off. For the most part the woman merely toiled, however, and did she find the few short notes of music a relief from toil, 'twas pity she might not always find such a jug for a new one when the old one broke. For, lords, stewards, music, not: the old one always broke.

"Squire, so, right you are, and tell me, can your art extend to causing the fayobirdy," here Cocko and a few others laughed, and neither they nor Vergil paused to explain why, "to extrude the contents of his crop without hurting him?"

But here Vergil over-mastered himself, and a slight cloud settled on the fowler's face. At once the fellow at his side, whom one would have thought till then a porter between porting jobs, forgetting a perfectly-planned schema to play ould Cocko's shill in a moment, burst out, "Ee magen squab, 'Meck ya cree meck ta fay-flowely, push his yock belay outchen un?" In an instant Cocko had the bird out of the cage, his fellow peaceably but effectively blocking the Asian's protesting arm: a slight movement, and there, lo! *how* the crowd laughed: there inside the crown of the fowl-fooler's own new hat lay the contents of the pheasant's crop.

The old broker-dealer spoke up, chawing the while. "Olive mash," said he, having given the mass in the hat a glance.

No more than a glance.

Vergil said nought.

No one said aught.

Then someone, by looks a tenant-farmer out of tenantry, said, slowly, "Why...they bain't moshin oliva yet. Nay. Nay."

The old produce-man gummed away. "Olive mash," said he.

He suspected nothing, expected nothing, was privy to nothing: he knew what he knew and said what he knew. Vergil asked—of no one in particular—"Where be they mashing olives now? Does any know?"

Any knew. In the Senate perhaps might not any know, or in a lodge of taylors or of tylers, no: in the crowd: yes..."Why, nerezt they bringen in oliva now, why me lard sor, it S'uth S'cilia. Be." The statement was repeated, pronounced correct. The crowd pressed close. The Asian, and it was surely one of Little Asia, that droop-cap, that bone-stiff nose, blue eyes, blue beads, and red-shoulder cape, surely added up to no other provenance than Little Asia, had said a thing they now knew was not so. *Why?* They asked this aloud. Then they asked it loud.

Little recked the Little Asian, but a little he did reck; an ass-cart piled high with parsnips rattled by and as soon as the trundle-sound ceased, eagerly the man said, nervously, "My lor's, my sers, masters, may I swear it by my nose and ears, I ben not in Sickillia South for this time twellev year..."

And Vergil said, with a nod, "He speaks the truth." A sigh from the Asian. Who would move on. No one moved away. Many a sigh. Then—"But then you have been now...where?" The Asian now displayed a tongue. The tongue caressed lips. The lips parted.

"Oy hearn whut hay tall," said old Cocko, having casually assumed, probably for mere practice, one of the many accents at his gift. The woman had filled her jug, began away, observed the crowd, became one of it; a Tartar she was: a slave, to say. "Oy hearn hay tall hay ben at High 'Pulia. Nay, so? Way oll hearn. Nay, nah?"

The crowd affirmed. The Asian stole a swift glance. The crowd pressed closer. "I don't believe," Vergil said, "that in High Apulia they are gathering olives in yet, alone crushing the fruit for the presses. But may hap so? May hap an early—"

The Asian seized hold of Vergil's hands. "I swear by what chee ask, I ben not—"

Vergil said, "They say that twice a year the caged quail beats its head against the cage; at other times is still. Well. I've said I know you spoke the truth, for far more than a half-a-year have you not been in Southern Sicily. True. Twelve years? True. But it may be...mayn't it be?...that the bird has been?"

The crowd stopped buzzing, began to look at each other and at the bird and from the bird to the Asian and from the Asian to the Magus Vergil and then at each other and in the silence from half-way up the street was heard the voice of a mendicant street-narrator, half-blind or all-blind, *"And the King of Cappadocia he sayeth, Galatia shall be mine, he sayeth, sayeth the King of Cappadocia, and he skarpens the skythes upon the hubs of his cherriot wagons for to rip the Galatianses to p'ices, skarpens he, and the King of the Galatianses he gatherers his wise men to set for a council, saying, Och, wisha, what shall I be doing to portect my wee ones? is saying the King of,"* but this account, if one might term it such, had been crawling its way along the length of Little Asia, Larger Asia, AEgypt, Lybya the Less, Lybya the More, Syrtis Major, Bauboo-al-zing, and places it were valueless to compute, without anyone ever learning anything of detail, let alone of value, as to what decision was come to by the Galatians, a people not known widely for coming to decisions: and old Cocko asked, "The bird, ser?"

"Yes. Of what, for instance, Squire, does the fayobirdy smell?"

Cocko said, "O' millet-meal," he sniffed the bill and plumage, "of old bread, of arjoram-yerb, like unto un were going to stuff un for a bankette," but instantly the fowler dropped the jape, something struggled to pass between the plumage of the pheasant, glints of red amidst the brown, red almost purple it were fanciable, and the old man's nose; '—of arjoram-yerb such as grow, such as *grow*," excitement caused his voice to grow high as actually he himself was actually calculating and reckoning; "as *grow*, arjoram-yerb, in Sitchly Squatch, *this bird ben there!*"

The crowd cheered, then, puzzled, began to growl and move; Vergil drew the Asian closer, for safe-keeping, by his side: the man came. Marjoram did indeed grow by the marge of the Sicilian Sea, on land too cut up for the great wheat crops to flourish: and what had this to do with this and that? Why was the great sage who housed himself in

Naples to do with kitchen-herbs and caged birds, had he not a cook or cooks? and why troubled he to act as judge in a minor crowd-quarrel which, in truth to speak, he had largely himself begun? In truth to speak? In truth he could not have well said. It was not quite his nose, it was something more subtle, it was something pertaining to a fifth element, neither wind nor fire nor earth nor water, not any known of the humours: something on seeing the man with the caged bird, had said: *Pause*. And said, *Question*. And here he was, backed into a corner between a fountain of waters and a tiny temple frequented perhaps once a year by those who lacked even lares and penates, very slightly uneasily hoping he had not easily begun something which—

Nothing sublime. Merely ridiculous. Cocko's nose had never been lovely. It was reddled now, its nares opened wider than usual. "Smowk!" crowed old Squire Cocko. "Ee smal of smowk!"

And then Vergil asked, Where had there been of late some great fire? Such news was already getting around and right then the news gat *all* around: "The Toe! The Toe, Master! Ser Mage, they say—"

Bit by bit it was, after a manner, calculated. The bird was either loose when the fire started, or the bird was let loose? to save its life? had the bird somehow *gotten* loose, "lured back" *how*? had the bird been in High Apulia, *no*, it could not have flown thence to Southern Sicily and there have eaten the mash from the olive vats, thence to have flown back again; *yes* it could have flown across the Messinian Straits, *how* had it been recaptured? For surely there was reason and there were reasons why the Asian had behaved...

When women are of a crowd they are never of a crowd as are men; in the sudden silence she never noticed, the Tartar slave-girl poured water into a tiny cup and offered it to the pheasant and when it had drunk she murmured, "Oh thou such a pretty bird," and pouting out her pale-pink-coral lips, kissed it, so. Suddenly a man stood there, and no bird more.

The slave-girl did not scream, old Squire Cocko it was who screamed. The crowd gazed, stunned. The Little Asian was the color of glazier's ash. "Welcome, lordly ser, and who are you, that we might greet you well? I am called Vergil, of the Mages."

The tall man in the purple-red-brown sea-smelling robe said, "Woman, thou art free. Go, Asian, never again are we to see thee, alive, lest the bowyer bring ye 'tis-well-known-what. Magus, may one have some wine, there is a bitter taste in my mouth like that of olive mash, I know not why." He gave an abrupt shake of his head. "Citizens and subjects of Galatia, *I am the King of Cappadocia and*—Stay! *What place is this?*"

KNOX'S 'NGA

Originally published in Weird Tales *293, Winter 1988/89.*

Belle Abernathy was not Grandmother Welles's favorite grandchild, in fact, GW had said semi-publicly more than once that Belle looked "like a plucked chicken," and that, although perhaps Belle could not help being skinny, she needn't show it off like that. These criticisms were heard no more after the skinny chickenny Belle had whispered in Grand's ear the Dreadful News; another grandchild, Lou Anne, who had married Robert Owens in A Lovely Church Wedding following upon a mere Civil Ceremony of vague circumstance, and was now expecting a *child*? Well, Belle *hated* to have to say it, but the birth was a mere five months after the church wedding, and as for the civil wedding, there had been no civil wedding.

"They were just shacked up, that's all," Belle said brutally.

Well, figure it out. Although in her very heart of hearts Grand would have been able to forgive, had they come to her and confessed—*had* they? No. Tried to pull the wool over her eyes. Country going to damnation. Her own grandchild. Hippies. Probably smoked hish-hash, or whatever it was called.

So, to the Quarterly Dinner at the old Welles house, *who* were not invited?

Well, *well*: what to do. Bob Owens didn't care. Lou didn't care much. Lou's mother cared. Lots.

"Only one thing *to* do," Lou said. "Baby must be named 'Philander Knox'."

"'Must'?" asked Bob. "Is 'Must' a word to be used to

fathers?" Just the sort of thing he would have said. Dry sense of humor. Quiet man, and, well, *small*. To tell the truth. Shacking up hadn't really been his idea. Like more than a mere few men of nowadays he had come home one day to find that the lady who held the extra key had moved in, and that they were now, well, *no*, not shacking *up*, did one shack *down*? But certainly, a fact: living together. "Why, 'Philander Knox'?"

The women exchanged looks. "An ancestor," they said.

"Well, yes, understandable. But surely there are others. Why not, ah, 'Welles'? Welles Owens, sounds classy. No like? Too many sibilants?" They shook their heads. "Oh, Zz not a sibilant? Oh—"

His wife now pronounced his name in a manner which gave it a sound of having several syllables and a warning to shut his mouth.

"Welles, well, Welles is my mother-in-law's married name. Just as it's *mine*. But Philander Knox was a cabinet member, oh, TR and Taft—"

"Ancestors?"

Getting near the knuckle, Owens. Want a knuckle sandwich, Owens? Want to be accused of implicit misogyny, Owens? Whose enormous phallus rapted and rupted this virginal little girl, three inches your taller and three years your elder? Owens. Shut the funk up and lis-sen.

Philander Knox had held cabinet positions. He was a distant cousin of Grandmother Welles's grandmother. True, there had been a Welles who'd been in Lincoln's cabinet but those were different Welleses. Spelled the same? Philander Chase Knox, Secretary of the Whatever It Was. *Nobody* anymore knew who he was. But Grand *thought* they did! And if The Baby were to be named Philander Knox Owens, people were bound to ask How, Come? Enter Ye Dowager Mrs. Welles, with a muscle in her bustle, and Able to Explain.

Well, there are those who say that God is a Woman and this might explain why the baby *was* a boy, *was* named Philander

Knox, *did* reduce Old Great-Grandmother to a puddle of pink flesh and Instant Reconciliation.

Belle Abernathy shrank even further into her plucked chickenanity and was never heard from, almost, again.

The baby was called The Baby as long as was reasonable, and then a bit more. The Baby began to walk, lurch, stagger, teeter, totter, "Come to Great-Grandmother, Knox. Come to Grand," said Guess Who; "Knox."

"Knox" came. Totter, teeter, stagger, lurch, walk. Collapse. "*There*, see he knows who he is and he knows who I am," said the Dragon Lady.

The three Owenses are at home. "Knox," said Bob.

His firstborn shows no sign. "I *know*," says Lou.

"We *could* call him 'Philander'."

"No, we *could*-n't!"

Bob bares all, did his wife think there was no gamey secret she did not know? Hah! "I had a great-aunt named Rectalyna," says he. Lou screams. No he *did*-n't! Oh yeah, yes he did. She was long ago and far back on the Coonass and Peckerwood sides of the family, gummed snuff and thought shit was a household word. Her most famous, well, only well-known, wehhell only *known* utterance, was, "The government is going to punish this nation because poor Mr. Bryan is dead," came to the attention of H.L. Mencken, who said Hot *diggetty*! and made a note and on finding out the woman's name said, "Hot *diggetty*, poor old Jehovah, woohoo, Rectalina with a long *i*? Oh with a *y*. Godfrey Daniel!" and it appeared in some preliminary work on *The American Language* but got cut out of the regular editions. "So my sweet, compared to Rectalyna, I guess we can live with Knox, hey we could call him '*Phil*'!"

It was all in vain. No, they couldn't. He simply was too young and a baby to be a Phil.

They took to calling him My Son. Where's My Son. Come here My Son.

Grand of course, well, what do you think. Grand liked a

ride in the country but Grand did not like to drive. Once there had been a chauffeur, or, as he was called in the highly democratic Welles house, a driver. McDowd. McDowd, returning to An*trim* for a visit, had been convicted of an uncommonly brutal murder and jerked to Jesus in no time at all. A*n*yway. Grand dearly loved to be called for and driven around with her descendants, whom she would treat to ice-cream cones and Coca-Cola and suggest they drop into country sales and so on and afterwards she would slip something into Bob Owens's hand. He *said* that at first he thought it was a Merry Widow (Lou: A *what*?) a French letter (Lou: a WHAT?) *Oh* Hell. But it was a twenty dollar bill, folded small and thick.

"Oh look there. *What* does the *sign*-y say, Knox? Read it for Grand. It says, Ya-a-r-d Sale. *Yard* sale. Oh Bob do you think we—"

Bob plays it up. Milk-buckets? He asks. If Grand wants a nice bucket he Bob has a friend who can make them a good price for a dozen. Soon the old lady has passed from *pshaw* and *the idea* into giggles, and there they are, Rumplemayer's or whatever the name of the place was, the worn inhabitata of three generations, cut for sale, nary a tear. "What, those old pie-an-o rolls," says Mrs. Rumplemayer, "Oh they blonged to my older sister she had infantile pralysis and my folks got her the player pie-an-o but then she got like pralysis of the brain so nobody had no more use for them, why she died years ago, how much the tag says? Three dollars? Shucks. Why you just take 'em all for two."

Knox is a little bit testy. He does not exactly reject Grand, would he *dare*, all those gravel road bonds, but he doesn't want his parents to move away, either. "He wants his bottle," Grand remarks.

"Want must be his master," Lou says. She read that somewhere.

"*I* always—"

"You had Colored Emma."

Well. True. Mrs. Welles the Elder *did* have, or *had* had Colored Emma. It may be thought that the adjective was here used as a title. But it was really used to distinguish her from Dutch Emma, a foreigner, who was dumb enough to do the heavy dirt work in spite of being in a house with a N----r in it.

"Well," said Grand, deliberately quirking the corners of her mouth, "I can see that Bob wants to get over and look at the *books*," you *rogue,* you, Bob. *Books.* "So let Mamma and Grand take one each of Knox's hands and we'll go for a little walk-y of our own, did you see any old dress patterns, Lou-lou, dear?"

Philander Knox Owens was not a year and a half, quite. His hair was light silky brown, his skin was a pinkish-brown showing white-*white* inside the elbows and behind the knees, and his eyes were hazel. Sometimes he strode along, sometimes he dawdled, sometimes he swung, now he began to grizzle and mizzle and whimper the syllable, "Da..." The old woman wanted to console him and wanted to carry him but neither was allowed. Suddenly he was leaning against a pile of things For Sale and he put out his arms around it and he said, distinctly, the syllable, "'*Nga.*"[1] A bit harder to interpret than *Da.*

Afterwards Lou said that her grandmother had paid for it. Later Grand said she had done so because Lou said, Oh, he might as well have it. All minor parts in the eternal game of trying to assign blame in order that the decrees of the fates might somehow be recalled and reissued. Changed.

Well, Grand *did* find some old dress patterns. Lou had gotten a *damn* fine bargain on the player piano rolls, *sure* Bob found not only books but some excellent early paperbacks at an excellent two-bits each. "And Knox has his taxidermical item." said Bob, feeling good for all of them. "Was it a bargain My Son? Is that what happens with my loose change? What has it got in its pocketses? What in the Hell *IS* this thang?" Just then old Mrs. Welles espied a store which sold what to her was a Sunday afternoon special/staple. "Oh what kinds of ice-cream do they have?" And the choice between them caused the other things to be forgotten.

Knox, a.k.a. My Son, who has begun—with weaning—to be rather querulous of nights, sleeps like slugged. Satisfaction changes in Lou's bosom to something like alarm, "Oh I was going to take it away and have it dry-cleaned or *washed* or something." She gets up, returns soonly. My Son, a.k.a. Knox, is wrapped all around it. In the morning.

In the morning everybody feels just fine. Everybody has had a good night's sleep. Mom and Dad have by the way had more than just sleep, being undisturbed throughout every inch and sigh of sweet dalliance, but it melted sweetly into sleep, so—same thing. Argal, instead of the day's being Rotten Monday it is Marvelous Monday. Followed by Tremendous Tuesday, Wonderful Wednesday... well, wonderful until about half-way through din-din with My Son ("Knox") in his *hi*chair, zumbling and drooling...but *eating*, mind you: *eating*...hear Louie give a frightful scream, worthy of the discovery that one has on the wrong nail polish—

The Kid seems mildly interested, rewards the scream with the word, "'Nga!"

The Dad has no such thing to say. Gapes. Why is his wife screaming, why waving her hands and why writhing? He would know these answers? *Would* he? Tough. The Mom has become aware of something very urgent, it requires her to get out of the breakfast nook, *fast!* Her figure is still, a year and a half after childbirth, thicker than it was when she was a junior in high school: *good*, though.

Good.

But she cannot simply slip out from behind the bar. The too, too solid flesh refuses to melt. Why doesn't her husband realize that she, *needs*, to get *out*? Why doesn't she just tell him? A dumb question. Her mouth is still full, that's why.

"My God, Lou-lou, what's the *matter*?"

The dumb son of a bitch; finally she, with upturned face

and look of agony, Belinda going down for the third time in the whirlpool, sucks in her gut, slides under the immovable and comes up the other side; see Knox give a gurgle of delight, cry, "'Nga, 'Nga," and throw up his tiny arms. What is that which falls to the floor, p'tah-*thud*, upon which Louis all but throws herself: "*Here* it is! I don't know, maybe some kind of irradiation would be best to get rid of all those germs, no: I'm going to throw it out." Her march towards the neat-and-clean plastic-bag-lined garbage cans in The Back is arrested.

Knox is screaming. Face red as not before, ever. Arms waving wildly. Drool, slaver, howl. And before his Da can seize hold and turn him upside down to dislodge the tessaract or *what* is it, Knox finds enough breath to scream, clearly as clear can be, "'*Nga!* '*Nga!* '*Nga!*"—glottal stops and all.

How is it that, already, so soon? At once they understand?

"It's his security blanket! He wants it!"

"He wants it! It's his security blanket!"

Knox the Kid, with a strangled *sob*, takes the thing in his arms and buries his face in its surface. There are no more screams.

"After all," says Lou, "he's had it all night Sunday night, all day Monday morning, all day Monday afternoon, all night Monday night," Bob nods and nods and when she concludes with "...all day Wednesday afternoon," Bob says: "And his dick didn't drop off, either." They nod solemnly. Lou says, "*A*, it's got to be *wash*ed, I'm an American *moth*er, you see how my teeth are clenched? And B, what the Hell *is* it?"

Debating *A* reminds them of old middle-aged Dr. Horn whose word of wisdom was, "No miracle drug has ever equalled the miracle of warm, soapy water." A solution of such is made, a clean sponge by Du Pont is broken out of wrapping, and, very, very cautiously and while Knox grasps one side in a deathgrip, his mother slowly soaps it. What is *it*?

Well, really, it is not a blanket. But what—? Well, it is about half the size of a rather small cheap kiddy blanket. It is rather thinner than a cushion and it is stuffed with something. The top half is a sort of fur and the bottom half is a sort of hide, a very soft leather, rather like chamois. "Some home-made combo comforter and stuffed animal," says Bob.

"Yes. There's...sort of...the head...see, the ah, *nose*? and oh look the eyes." Really, no, there are no eyes. But suppose at one time there to have been eyes? the eyes say of glass to have been firmly tied on? and some other child to have tugged... tugged...tugged...night after night, year after year...The "eyes" had long ago vanished. But there were two, well, sort of, ver-y small protuberances. Where the "eyes" had been. "Are those *legs*? Here? Here?"

Bob has a different idea. It was never intended to be a real animal stuffed toy. It had no existence in zoology, any more than the Country Dutch *Distelfink* had in ornithology. "*We* see eyes and ah arms and legs because we expect to see 'um, old Hans Yost or gee whatever, he or rather she, Tanta Tessa Hoo-Hah, merely cut and sewed in a sort of dream-state. No eyes, no arms, no legs, no tail."

"No nose, no...No *dirt*...well, hardly *any*...well, how do you *like* that!" The Rumplemayers, or whoever, whatever, where the, ah, 'Nga, well, ah, they'd seemed pretty *clean*...? But no, says Lou. "Even if they'd cleaned it just before they sold it, and it didn't feel damp, you know, well, what, uh, *Knox*, has been getting on it, milk, cereal, smudgy tears, snot, the *floor*, the *yard*—Where's it all gone to?"

A thoughtful silence. Then Bob makes a show of pounding hand in fist, silently, pronounces the curious word, "Coatimundi."

"Co—?"

"Coatimundi. An article I read somewhere. This animal, kind of like a raccoon? Has the gift of sort of, well, *it* doesn't, no. Pelt. Its pelt does. Sort of self-cleans itself. Article I—"

The dictionary confirmed the existence of such an animal but did not say anything about its supposedly self-polishing pelt. *Be that as it may.* Lou lost her fears of the what-was-it's having picked up God knows what disease(s). The Kid, "Knox," was allowed to have his kidly way with it. They were seldom seen apart henceforth.

Nothing is perfect, however, not even the love of a boy for his 'Nga; Bob came home from work one evening to find, instead of a cocktail shaker already shaken and a plate of snacks, his wife close-lipped and flushed. Even the Bobs of this world, the little men nobody looks at twice, have their moments of supernal wisdom. Bob repaired to the bar cabinet and, ignoring the staple six o'clock specials, martini, gibson, manhattan, made something sticky and bright-colored and sweet: *sure* he knew that Lou-lou loved it; why didn't he make it more often, then? Ha. He replenished her glass before she had finished it; by and by she began to soften.

"Well, in a word—or two—Clemmi and his Mommi came across the street to visit and while we were talking, Clemmi tried to hijack 'Nga." She tilted, drained her glass, set it down, he poured, she sipped. "Little prick," she murmured, her hair soft and ringletty as she tilted her head and smiled half a smile. "Served *him, right.*" ("What happened?") "Knox bit him. Well bit him or *clawed* him. Kid was sure bleeding. Clemmi's Mommi took off to put a tourniquet on his scalp, the proverbial scalp wound, and I've been waiting ever since for the cops to come and take Your Son away. The pricks." She drained the last of her Pink Ma*goon*[2] and sat smiling while Bob made supper. For a change.

By and by Clemmi's Poppi came across the street. One could not say he accused. One could not say he apologized. He said that small children were both by nature aggressive and territorial. Poppi's real name was Ferenc, rhymed with Terence, and he did something at the local college/university, whose residential exclaves were everywhere. Bob Owens broke out the one and only bottle with a green tax stamp on it. Partly because of a *small* desire to make amends. Furthermore he had noticed of educated foreigners that while they may not like the government, the economy, the educational system, in the USA, they are all without exception in like with US bonded 100% whiskey. As why *not?*

After only one drink, lo, a knocking at the door, it was not O'Reilly, it was not a Raven, it was a Dr. Nudge, a *paisan* of Poppi who, having called across the street, had been directed thence to hither. Dr. Nudge raised no objection to a draft from God's bonded warehouses. He and Ferenc exchanged a few words in their own, perhaps, language. Ferenc said, "Dr. Nudge is a world's great authority on pelage." He pronounced it to rhyme with *dressage, pe-läzh.* And, anticipating the Owenses' next question, Dr. N. himself said, "Pelage, or you would say *pel*-lij, or sometimes called *pile*, is in two words, hair or wool. Hair *and* wool. Pelage."

Immediately Lou said, "What do you know about the skin or fur of the coatimundi?"

"Well—"

"One on the couch where My Son is snoozing. Take a sight. In fact," she wrinkled her nose, "take a sniff." There was indeed in the room what Our British Cousins call a Pong. It struck Bob suddenly that he had smelled the smell before...

Nudge cast a swift, surprised look at the couch. Immediately he said, "No." Then his nostrils twitched. They were large, Lou noted, and rather hairy. Both she and Bob had also sipped of that which had lain hid six years in the cave, and both were a bit quick to resent Nudge's quick denial. "Why *No?*" was their common cry. Mouth pursed in a manner not meet between guest and host, the authority rose and went towards the couch, "It is *No* because coatimundi —" wee little Knox shifted and his 'Nga shifted with him and whatever the odor was just *rolled* across the room. Nudge stopped. Nudge's nose flared, froze. Nudge's face went sick. We have all heard, read, seen cartoons of people's hair standing on edge: Nudge had but a ring of bristles: they now bristled. He gasped. He put out his hands. He staggered.

He looked at Ferenc. Ferenc whispered something. Nudge whispered something back. Ferenc said, "Yoy..." Something passed between them. A glint. A...surely not a *knife*? Owens was heaving himself upward and outward and Nudgeward when there was a smaller but quicker convulsion on the couch. He was not able to figure out what had been doing by whom to whom to which or what to whom or whence whither widdershins, and Nudge screamed. Fell back. Something else fell, a pair of small scissors of slightly odd, doubtless foreign design. Blood on it. Blood on the couch, rug, blood on Nudge's hand, face—

Ferenc, Clemmi's Poppi, screams, stands there stooping to Lou and Bob Owens, hands clawed. "I will report to police, you are butcher people, *mord*, you are murder people, you try killing my *kis* child, you shall be punish—" Ferenc turns and flees, a hoarse breath not a scream comes and goes with him. But now watch Nudge!

In a way, Nudge is admirable. In a corner, a far corner, is, a, the vacuum cleaner. On a small end table a day-old newspaper. Nudge walks backward like Shem and Japheth in the tent of Noah. Nudge stoops, spreads paper, slowly without taking his eyes from the couch (what's there? "*Knox*" is there, rhythmically rocking himself and crooning, "'Nga...'Nga...'Nga..." He is cradled in the odd fur, the odd hide, the—) Nudge unscrews the dust-bag from the vacuum and takes out the inner paper sack and wraps it in the newspaper. A sudden stare into their faces. Nudge is gone. *Do* the police come? Do these perhaps justifiably nervous foreigners actually report—?

"What do *you* think?"

Lou perhaps answers the question, perhaps not. "I figured it out. First he wanted to cut some of the hair off the 'Nga. It defended itself. See? So he figured that there has to be some of its hair taken up from the floor into the vacuum-cleaner bag. Eh? And he, one of the world's greater authorities on pelage, he is going to find out what, kind, of *hair*, it is!"

"Is My Son a monster?"

"You know he's not!"

"Yes…Is My Son in danger from that…from 'Nga?"

"Oh, you know he's not!"

The Ferenc family moves, suddenly. Nudge does not return. The Kid is, equally suddenly, two. How old is 'Nga?

"Knox" is three—

"Knox" is four—

Great-Grandmother Welles dies. Sure enough about the will; no tricks there. Now they can change the boy's name. Hank! Buster! Dale! Chris!—No they can't. Somehow.

"Knox" is five and sitting in the crutch of a tree with Guess. Has nobody caught on outside his family? Ha Ha Ha *Ho*! Half the boys at that end of town have said to the other half, say and say in turn, "Nobuddy knows whut it really is but he keeps it tame." They have of course given up mentioning anything of it to Mumma and Daddy. Philander Knox Owens is a rather odd boy, just slightly odd, certainly immature, that was what one of the savants over from Europe, having wangled stuff out of Nudge, said. "In a way he is of course perceptibly less mature than his compeers. One must attribute this to his having to do less to establish his own position." We are skipping the accent. The accents. "On the other hand his position is one of a certain sophistication."

Q. Why 'Nga? What does it mean? A. It may be the first syllable uttered by primal pre-Man, it is uttered very far back in the throat.

Q. What is 'Nga? A. We may say only that the same type of hair or fur is found in the Caspian Cave, along with scattered pollen, dried flowers, two braided gold-wire torques studded with eleven pieces of amber, and bones not all of which have been positively identified.

Please identify them tentatively. A. (A gentle academic smile.)

Conversation: Q. Knox, who is 'Nga? A. My friend. Q. What is 'Nga? A. Just…'Nga. Q. Where did he come from? A.

Nowhere…Perhaps as unstimulated by this as the Owenses are by the "bones not all of which, etc.," the savants go back to Europe; by and by comes a folder of reports, all wrapped in white linen and cold as the clay. They are in English and while it is only necessary to know Latin to understand that English, a knowledge of all four languages spoken in Switzerland helps a lot.

Local talk: Well, I don't say one thing proves another. I say that's the tree you always see that boy and last week I seen eyes, I seen bur-nin eyes, a-up in that tree. Boys' eyes don't burn. Y'all know.

Lou doesn't tell anyone of the night the old rogue runaway shepherd dog called Timber came prowling round the Owens home. Oh God what noises followed next. She heard something die real soon and all night long she heard something being eaten real slow. In the morning…what? A forensic lab might find out…something. Who tells them? No one. Here.

Philander Knox Owens is five. Sometimes his mother sighs, silently, Whoever took my little boy please give him back! My poor Mowgli with his own cub-mate not of this world! One of the people called oddly enough, Developers, ruptures part of an ancient swamp and pathways dry up and reveal themselves. Lou Owens, followed by, very languidly, "Knox," walks slowly along one such path. There are brakes of wild cane. There is a cave, she cannot quite find a dry way yet to go into it, but she can see it down there in the thicketry. She can smell it, oh *God* it is rank, like the jock-strap of an elephantseal, like the foreskin of a moose and the groins of a muskox and the pizzle of an Arctic wolf: that cave. Nothing like it could she have ever imagined to exist. Like the armpits of an orang-utan. And yet and yet…

Doesn't she know that awful scent?—or something rather like it?

Doesn't she know what sort of scent it is?—She does, doesn't she?

The flat wind falls, the awful stench ebbs. But within the cave, *what* is that? Is it? it surely is! no how can it be? here they *come*. "Has 'Nga been with you all this time?" Slow nod. A yawn. Well, and if so, *what* had she seen in the cave? What had she smelled in the cave? And, oh dear God what is she smelling now from the cave? Philander Knox Owens, what hast thou in thy bosom? What is it which seems to creep up his arm? To, almost, stand? that not-blanket, un-toy, nul-rug. *Does* it, so to speak, poise? *Point*? A flash. It is not there! Where is it? She sees it rush past her through the thick grass, hears a shocked cry, "'Nga!" hears the canes crashing, sees the reunion at the mouth of the cave, observes them fade from the mouth...to what epithalamion?

The boy leans against his mother, whimpering, "'Nga...'Nga..."

Far away, and yet not so far away, the voices of boys, one can almost hear...one hears..."Philly, hey Philly! C'mon Philly we got a ball Philly..."

The most extraordinary change comes over the child. He jumps up and down and claps his hands together. His face gleams. He shouts, "Heyyy! Yeay!! A ball, a ball, a—" In an instant he is running, running far from her, crying, "Give us the ball, give us the ball, give us the ball,..."

Philly.

Of course.

NOTHING LIKE A CLEAN WEAPON

Originally published in Weird Tales *293, Winter 1988/89.*

That's what Grandpa used to say, and he said it often. "—how it was with the Apaches," he'd say; "fire a few rounds[3] and then they'd run off. Couldn't stay to fight, because they didn't keep their rifles clean. Guess maybe it would've taken 'em too long to clean'm." And Grandpa, who'd been twenty years in the *old* army, would tell another story, too: "Heard this rifle go *crack*," he'd say. "I smelled black powder, could *see* it, too. Knew right away that it wasn't no American fire, because by that time we was using smokeless, y'see. So I knew it was the Spaniard. *First* thing, I checked my rifle, t'see if it was *clean*. Because there's nothing like a clean weapon." And so on. Real often.

Joe Baines, grandson of Grandpa, was incessantly and obsessively intent on becoming a war veteran. Maybe people hadn't thought much of Joe Baines before the war, but boy they'd change their minds when he came back! How he had envied Pop and Uncle Mike their World War stories, Grandpa his tales of the Indian and Spanish-American Wars; barely he could remember Great-grandfather Muller and his accounts of actions and inactions of the Civil War of the Rebellion Between the States. Three generations of stories beginning, "There was this girl—" or, "There was this trooper—" "—this sergeant—" and sometimes, "There was this horse—." And, "The Top," or, "The Gunney—" "he says to me, 'Remember this: *nothing* like a clean weapon!'" Not knowing when he'd be coming back, though quite certain he'd *be* back, Joe Baines had cleaned and re-cleaned his old deer rifle, wrapped it up, and put it and the cartridges away down cellar. And went off to start to become a war veteran. Killed or wounded? He really couldn't picture being dead...wounded? like maybe a broken arm? Nothing wrong with being a war veteran who'd been wounded; like to see anybody giving him the cold shoulder after *that*!

Farewell to Mom and Velma. Mom even turned her radio off—well, she'd turned it *down*.

Boy, nobody would ever make fun of Joe Baines, *War Veteran*!

To Joe, a war was an immense opportunity for a man to amass story-material for a life-time. From the day of his induction he began collecting his experiences, rolling them over and over and over in his mind until they became properly and smoothly tellable tales ("Doing push-ups in the snow" took a while: but it came out okay). But *the* great source of stories (and those not fit to tell at home could be very well-told at Schuster's Bar and at Leo's Tavern), the *great* source of stories would be, of course when at last The Government sent the 24th R. T. and D. overseas, and Joe Baines with it. Then Joe would begin to come into his own, and treasure up lots and lots of stories beginning, as it might be, "There was this French girl—" "There was this Kraut—" Well...you fill 'em in...

A store of war stories would stand a man in good stead no matter what: marriage, death, divorce, depression, good times, bad times, the kids listening (sure, Joe and Velma would have kids; her folks wouldn't make that tight-mouthed look no more when Joe Baines, *War Veteran*, came proudly back), the old men for once and ever, forever treating him as an equal. "Then I seen this mortar-shell comin' down and I heard it whistlin' as it come down, and—" Details, details. Just you wait till The Government sent the old R. T. and D. overseas; meanwhile, not that he *liked* all that KP and

Latrine Duty, damn Noncom; needn't tell about it...

Set for life, Joe Baines set for life. "Oh I pray for all you GI's," Velma wrote. Mom? "Oh I don't have no time for that," Mom'd say, looking up from her radio. But Velma's photo was on Joe Baines's locker door. Velma—

And then The Government had made a terrible, terrible mistake. It had never sent the 24th R. T. and D. overseas. At all. Nor Joe Baines.

Coming back after Discharge in '46 and seeing the already no longer new signs on the small old neighborhood houses, WELCOME HOME JACK, WELCOME HOME ROCCO: on the old Baines house: nothing. Mom of course would have had no time for that. Mom. Her radio programs.

Oh well. Can't have everything.

"Mom, I'm *back*, Mom!"

"I just *warshed* that floor," said Mom.

"Have you seen Velma today Mom?"

Mom patting her hair and looking somewhere else, "Well, you know I wrote you she got married."

"*Mom!*"

Velma's faithlessness and Mom's lie: together like a blow on the head. He kicked his duffle bag into a corner and walked out. Feet automatically found their way to Schuster's Saloon: some of the same sour, puckered, beery old men still there, still there, dimming old faces turning towards him; did he hear a mutter of One a them dumb Baineses...? pretend he didn't hear it. Slowly a rusty voice, "You just git out?"

"Yeah."

Maybe he shouldn't have come here; too late now. Now would come the inevitable two questions. He awaited them with a tightness in his chest. Knew he would hear them the rest of his life if he even ever started to tell a war veteran story: Push-ups in the snow, oh shucks! The same voice, with another rusty voice right behind it: "*Git overseas? See any action?*" Joe faintly knew that others in his shoes might say that war was not a spectator sport, that troops in action depended on all the military machinery and men behind them and hence not in action. But those others, they were not Joe Baines. Out with it.

"Uh...*no*."

Slow faces turned slowly away. A whispered question, an unwhispered reply, "Hell, let him buy his own drinks!" Middle-aged Schuster nevertheless filling a glass of whiskey for him, *This one is on the House*. And the last one that ever would be, Joe Baines well knew. He paid for the next four or five himself. And drank them by himself.

A man might as well be dead. Better have died, to have died for his country; no chance, though. Would have, sure; but no chance. More or less unnoticed, Joe had gone away. Already unremembered, he had come back. Come back to what? Might as well be. Might as well. Three years of his life, five glasses of whiskey. Well, one more for the road.

Down cellar, ammo right where he'd put it, deer rifle right where he'd left it. Check it out. Give it one more going over. Velma first. Velma's husband next. Then—Mom, too? Mom too. Then the old bastards at Schuster's: the raw wartime saying, "Screw 'em all but six, and save them for pall-bearers." There'd after all be others who'd remember about Joe Baines; save *six*? Hell no.

But a pity Joe Baines himself wouldn't be around to hear all the stories. Oh well. Can't have everything.

Nothing like a clean weapon.

BENNY AND GEORGE

Originally published as a "Postcard Story," #4, Surplus Wyvern Press, 1989.

There were gaps in their educations.

Benny didn't know his local post office worked a night shift, broke in the back door, was caught before he could get any money orders.

George, returning from a tour of the rural agriculture of our friendly neighbor nation to the south, was asked by the U.S. Immigration, "Let's see your papers." He dreamily pulled out a packet of a variety good for rolling your own. Immigration gave Customs the high sign. What was found under the floorboards was not Bull Durham.

Benny and George, who had not met before they became roommates, both agreed that bad luck alone was responsible for misfortune.

Their host at the time, the Federal Government, endeavored to rehabilitate Benny and George through an industrial training course. Perhaps a firm of manufacturers willing to employ men trained to the use of machinery at least twenty years obsolete might have found their services useful.

But Benny and George did not think so.

And they concluded that the best thing to do after they got out was to rob a bank.

Just one bank.

"The First National Bank of Portland," Benny said. "I know it inside out. I use to be the janitor there. Me!" He gave a scornful laugh. George echoed it with a scornful snicker.

They agreed that, as they had different things in mind in regard to what each would do with his share of the take, there was no point in discussing that; so instead they spent time discussing the robbery itself.

They didn't spend much time discussing it because it was all so simple. Benny, who knew the bank inside out, was to commit the actual robbery. George, who prided himself on his driving, was to be waiting outside in the getaway car. He was due to be released a month before Benny. They set the time and the date.

Benny did in fact know the First National Bank of Portland inside out and in fact did indeed rob, but failed to find George outside. Whilst engaged in looking for him he sprinted more or less right into the arms of a Maine State Police Officer who, although off duty, still and all persisted in a closer examination of the situation.

George, sitting in the getaway car outside the First National Bank of Portland, observed a comely young woman passing by, on the instant leaned out and suggested that they meet for sociable purposes that very night. The young woman, offended by the terms in which he couched his invitation, promptly continued passing on by until she found a policeman.

George was still in the car waiting for Benny to come out of the bank when the policeman came up and said, "You're under arrest."

George, all outraged innocence, said, "What for?"

The policeman told him what for.

George, astonished, cried, "That ain't against the law!"

"It is in Portland, Oregon," the policeman said.

CONVERSATIONAL TALES OF THE WANLAND
Number One: Of Sundry Tribes

Originally published in Pulphouse *#3, 1989.*

EDITOR NOTES: Admirable Davidson, recuperating from health, in perambulating Gondwanaland, the justly-legend-haunting Wanland, *was canny enough to capture from an adventurer in merchantry (though in all modesty also amateur ethnologue) by means of "tap-casette" [technical term] several conversations not free from information and anecdote. In the time suspiciously small available to one from cares of commerce and industry (27 uterine aunts, also many issue), I have agreed to "edit" these recension from audible strib. An end to misunderstanding and abuse! It is not for me to disparage the jealousy of my competitors. "Whoso has even licked his lip by the light of my sheep-tail-fat, he may be a friend." So it is written. Subside. Examine. I demand no more.–Editor M.E.*

◆ ◆ ◆

M r. Eshmadai Patapata, General Goods of Wide Variety, Godown 33, The New Market, Rahkráh. Show this page to obtain incredible discount on any Good, old or new. Also social introduction. (Demons not.)

◆ ◆ ◆

Mysir, your interest is admirable; who can say indeed why no one is permitted with a woman of the Pikhir when she sheds light to a child young? For one thing, the Pikhri Womans are so full of strength and gust always, often one does not even know when such-a-one is gravid! Only now and then, when she returns with issue, does one even realize that she has absented. It would not be good custom to enquire, "Such-a-one, Wherefore goest thou to absent?" And, then, too, you are an educated, each people has its own habitudes, and so it is, as our wise man ("The Uncles," we call such) say thus: "Is it not so?"

Indeed. Accept. Mysir is interested in beautiful zinc-filigree? Of this I know a something, it is not for me to diminish the esteem of my compeers. Momentarily mysir is not, so. Yes. "Accept," says the proverb; "do not look too closely at the sleeping shoat." A marvelous metaphor. You agree? You agree! Excellent. Sweet? A comfit of anhydrous treacle and mess-nut? Oh, I am honored. Yes...we have many metaphors. You also? And in your heritage are there also similes? So. Impressive. "Like the many thorns upon the bush which impede, nay, rend, the traveller's road"...road...? oh, "*robe*." I am unwittedly droll. And what say you? Mysir has a question? But ask! The ifrits send visitors, therefor be bland to them; your dog has eaten the gristle of my gazelle, and the dust of your feet enriched my close-stool; ask.

Ah, no, mysir, the Dhoomjee in each region are of two moieties, not more, never. In Rahkráh, for a paradigm, the Tlotl, or upper moiety, repair cellars, dig tunnels and water-courses, clean wells (needless to say that no *new* wells are ever dug; to do so would be unthinkable, water is too scarce), and excavate pits for storing garong; no Gondwandi meal is considered complete without these nourishing yam-mush dried globules, well aged; foreigners donot consume them, alas. The lower Dhoomjee moiety, or K'nomr, clean cess-pools.

It is obvious, therefore, is it not, what is implied by

the terms Inflected and Uninflected Dhoomjee? The Tlotl
employ all 76 inflexions; the K'nomr employ none whatever.
The Tlotls' speech is declared on all excellent authority to
be incomparably beautiful, and their poetry is famous. The
dialect of the K'nomr is very easy to understand as the
prattle of babes. A depth, to them, is a depth, simply. You see.
Second Assistant Commissioner Goole, a young man with a
brilliant future, requiring to have his well cleaned, went and
spoke with Paramount KA. Somehow or other, S.A.C. Goole
became persuaded that Paramount KA had nowhere to keep
his nose-tobacco, and gave him, slightly relunctancy, a silver
pocket-box with a design appearing from his old school
tie. Paramount KA, mistaking this for a miniature garong-
chest, replied that—alas—his maiden-aunt's housekeeper
was unavailable for concubinage (it being a lunar leap-year
with five Gungles in the fifth month), and offered the S.A.C.
thirteen castrated yemp-colts as Bhoo, or Consolation.

Mysir is interested in quality souvenir? No? Plastic
gumboot? Nay, but I digress grossly. Or "I grossly digress"?
Thank you, mysir. Chew. Chew.

S.A.C. Goole went off and easily engaged a K'nomr and his
step-nephew to clean his well.

When this became mysteriously known, the High Priests,
all both of them, ceremoniously extinguished the fire in the
Old Market Place by an act well-known to be considered
infamous by the Shaheen, the Dubie, and the Gotes. Among
others. Trade and Commerce ceased in Gondwanaland for
eight days and several (Old Style, true, including dusks and
cockcrows, but quite enough, thank you; are the living to go
hungry for the sake of the dead?). Ah, me. Eh? Oh.

No, mysir, I have been unable to discern what
subsequently became of Second A.C. Goole.

Should it seem to you, then, mysir, that a Dhoomjee is
speaking unclearly, beware. Should it seem to you that a
Dhoomjee is speaking clearly, beware even more.

In the Wanland are many paradoxes. Paradoces? Mysir

flinches; you see, we *know*; *we*, *know*! Permit me a small rictus.

The Gotes, who are breeders of guinea-pigs and -fowl, are regarded as unclean by the Shaheen, the Dubie, and the Inflected Dhoomjee, or Tlotl; needless to say by higher tribes or castes, ha *ha*. The Uninflected Dhoomjee, or K'nomr, eat for meat the dead donkeys of the Gotes. The Kullah, whom you may see at the outskirts of towns ingeniously pretend manufacturing of shoe-belts, actually make sustenance by supplying male and female cotqueans to the K'nomr; they say that bones and hooves of ungulates provide an excellent soup, "yuk-yuk" they call it, which means "Sap of Vitality."

The Kullah are sometimes very vivid, despite their simple ways.

Mysir is perhaps interested in natural ammonia supplies, tribal preference adjustments being easily arranged by one who—Another time? Excellent! A more comfit of anhydrous treacle and mess-nut, with, should one wish, a noggin of yemp-milk? Ah, mysir is abstemious. Admirably quality. So say the Uncles.

Have I spoke of the Kullah? I have. Well, and. One does not willingly speak of them over-often. So, next, the Difdook.

The Difdook, with scarcely an exception, may be spoken to only by the Kullah, who engage them from time to time for sorceries. Many ridiculous and superstitious stories are told about the Difdook, who have, apparently, no other patrimony; despised as they may be though, by the Agricultural and Pastoral-Commercial Tribes, it is not at all correct to describe them as Outcasts or "ostracized," as has been done by Mr. M.P. Marchmain, you know of such? Of course *not*, who does? An obscure and baloney person and English Man, author of the so-called *Gondwanaland and Her Peoples: Ancient and Modern*. We spit upon this silly book. P'too. As is well-understood to everyone who knows and loves of our ancient and modern country-land with its exquisite production of filigreed-zincwork and rich stores of natural ammonia [Pause], the Difdook may (indeed, if I am allowed pawky, *must*) associate also most freely with the Buraf, whom they employ for purposes of odd-job. Enough!

The Pikhir, or growers of wheats, barleys, and nutritious hemps, delight to share with high guests rich beefs and swines and muttons, all cooked most enticely; I speak with, I hope, a becoming modesty, when I describe of them as being at the highest caste: the point does not allow of disputation: indeed would be non-ethical to consider. The Nanbar, subtly famous for cattle-breeding and baking of a marvelous scented stiffbread—pride is one thing, justice is another, and it is to be admitted that the Nanbar rank only slightly below the Pikhir—I myself had a great-cousin by marriage who was, so I have heard, a Nanbar of birth; she brought a large dowry, excellent woman, I was never allowed to see her.

The Pikhri and Nanbri peoples both, ah, mysir! What vast quantities of powdered dung do we burn upon the occasions of faring well to our deceaséd ones. Phenomenal! But great is grief, even Dhoomjee (both moieties), the Gotes, the Shaheen and Kullah, who practise crematings; when they themselves are in mourning, do not disdain to offer their best glass beads for strangers to tread up. They eat hedgehog and poultrys, I see the fire has gone out and it is not permitted actually to spit. So. Thus.

The Kullah merely sulk.

The Burafs expose their passed-ons to the wolfs of the gullies. They are outside the circle. It is not known what they eat. But who cares.

Eh, mysir asks what? Ah. Who indeed can say. On that point one can shed no light.

No one has ever seen a dead Difdook.

DOWN BY THE DEPOT

Originally published in Ellery Queen's Mystery Magazine,
August 1989.

Bob Mills told me this story.

He met someone, let us call him Stanley Slade, as they both were about to belly up to the refreshment counter of a certain bat-cave. Although Bob didn't know Stan very well, he knew him well enough to ask, "How come your face is, ahm, kind of bunged up? Did you fall?"

Stan repeated the last word in a peculiar tone. Then he said, "Yeah—from grace."

"How's that, Stan?"

Stan for a second or so did not answer. Then he said, "Are you buying the bourbon?"

"Sure."

"Then I'll tell you. As soon as it comes." When it came, Stan drank it in a gulp, rather unlike his usual placid sipping manner, and yet, despite what he'd said, he remained silent. A second signal given, a second drink having appeared, Stan tossed it down as quickly as the first. And after a bit more silence, he began to talk—slowly, and with interruptions, and with many sighs and broken breaths.

Although the commuter feeder-line train Stanley Slade rode had been allowed to decay almost to a streak of rust by a venal state railroad board, several trains a day still ran —or rattled—some by day, some by night. The handwriting was on the wall for the midnight train, yet it, too, still plied its tired, sullen way between the bigger station, where Stan changed for the city train, and the two small depots beyond the one where he got on in the morning and got off in the evening.

In Stan's boyhood, there had been great plans for the region around the depot, some way from the village proper. What remained of the forest primeval had been lumbered off, the few old houses and the one old shack store torn down, and the view improved by a billboard prophesying development. The Depression and changing population patterns had put paid to these plans, and the ravaged area had tangled up into second-growth thicket. College education, military service, manhood, marriage, and employment had all combined to move Stan Slade into the city. Divorce, alimony, and the death of his aged Uncle Tim had moved him back to the old family home almost a mile from the depot—a distance he always walked, except when the vilest weather obliged him to use a cab.

By now there was only one, and it no longer met the late-night trains.

If Stan took the early train after work, he played a game of cards—on a board supplied by a veteran conductor who kept the change—with three other men he never saw anywhere else and likely wouldn't have recognized if he had—probably vice versa, too, as Stanley was of no outstanding appearance. He very seldom went to the village any more, and was very seldom recognized, even dimly, when he did.

There was no longer a Mrs. Slade to be vexed if Stan were "delayed at the office," but this evening he *had* been delayed at the office. He took the late (though not the late, late) train, he had had no game of cards, he had not even thought to get a newspaper. The train was dirty, the lights were dim, and he fell into a rather listless state, devoid even of revery.

The train drew away from the stop almost as soon as he had left it, lumbered away under the bridge at the far side of the depot, and, with a despondent hoot, was gone. Stanley, without even raising his eyes, began to tread the all too familiar sidewalk, which had for decades been fulfilling President Hoover's prophecy about the grass.

Suddenly he felt a blow on his head. An arm encircled his throat and, speechless, shocked, and dazed, he was dragged off into the thickets that crowded close upon the cracked and riven pavement.

He was aware of a harsh and heavy breath laboring close to his left ear. A shove sent him crashing to the ground, then came another punishing blow as he raised his head. Resisting no longer, in dull and painful astonishment, he was aware of his clothes being stripped from his body.

Feet crashed off through the underbrush and he was left alone. His attempt, by and by, to get up was not successful, but as he fell again he was aware that he still had on his underwear—and with this as his comfort, he sank down into the coarse and painful twigs and the dim, dim light from outside the long-locked depot seemed to fall entirely away. Next he felt cold. Next he felt nothing.

When at last he did come to himself, he felt quite sickened and unable to think much about his situation, but he did somehow know that he must rise slowly, and in stages. He was on his painful knees when he heard a voice from no very great distance, and in the otherwise deep silence he perceived the sound of footfalls on the paved bridge over the railroad tracks. Collecting his few fragments of strength, he lurched forward and burst out of the thicket, confronting a teenaged girl who, at once ceasing her low and off-tune crooning of a popular tune, gave voice to a scream the like of which he had never before heard even on a television horror show—and, still screaming, she fled like a deer back the way she had come.

Looking after her, Stan happened to look at his hands: and saw blood. He sank to the sidewalk in a crouch.

He had no way of knowing how much time had passed before he heard, this time from some distance, the faint— but increasingly less faint—sound of a police-car siren. There was no other way to go. Back he fled into the thicket.

If indeed he wasn't following a faint track or path he somehow remembered from his boyhood, the feeble thought that he was gave him a measure of comfort—otherwise he might have screamed himself. In school he had been taught that a policeman was your best friend and he had never had any trouble with the police in his life, but what chance would he have—an older man clad only in his underwear— against the fear and trembling of a terrified young girl? The taint would never leave his name or person, he was sure of almost nothing but he was sure of that. He felt his feet give way and himself sliding sideways and down, coming almost instantly to a soft stop. He was in the cellar-hole of one of the little old houses so long ago demolished to make way for the development which never came. He crouched against the leaf mold and the drifted dust and prayed that no tradition of this might be in the minds of the policemen.

The siren drew near, then ceased. He knew the car had stopped. The policemen didn't beat the bushes—he could not make out their words, but he could make out their voices, and they didn't sound excited. After a while they went away. Stan, in the safety of his hiding place, hoped that they thought no monster was on the prowl and that only the baseless panic of a young person, too young to be out alone, anyway, was the sole cause of the alarm. He also hoped that they had not gone for reinforcements or bloodhounds.

These thoughts helped liberate his mind to consider for the first time what might have been the cause of the attack upon himself. Robbery? Then why had all his outer garments been wrested off him? A hasty grope informed him that although he still had on his socks, his shoes had been taken. Finding no answer as to causes—no who, no why—he reflected on what he had better do next. And reflection told him that he had better make his way to the sidewalk again, walk a long block, turn off onto another long block, rap on the door of a house he knew was there, tell his story, and ask for the help that only a human being in sore trouble and deep distress has the right to ask of another fellow human.

The house was neither large nor old nor new. Stan had half hoped someone would answer his ring fairly soon, and so let his turmoil cease, and half hoped it would take a while, so that he might think of something immediately reassuring.

The door, in fact, was opened almost at once. One might say that it was flung open. The middle-aged man who had opened it took a look at Stan, cried, "*Oh, my God!*" and slammed it shut again. Stan, on the doorstep, heard a nervous voice say a word or two and heard the man half cry, "Will you get away from the phone, damn it? *I don't want to get involved!*"

Stan, as he moved rapidly off again into the cold and darkness, for the first time blessed the attitude of non-involvement.

Crouching in the thickets near the depot once again, Stan sent up a plea for help to the silent stars. Just supposing he risked the police seeing him thus—even supposing the girl were to say, "Well, no, actually he didn't *do* anything at all, I just got scared and ran"—he had with him no ID, no money, no housekeys, no one in the village he could think of to speak up for him. How would the police know he wasn't a vagrant? Should he resign himself to spending the night in jail and in the morning try to call his employers to send someone all the distance from the city with good words and cash for bail? No, no—not to be thought of. Even if they did it, it would be the end of his job. His career. Perhaps his life.

I can always smash the back window to get into my house, Stan thought. Wash off the dirt and the blood. I need my *clothes*, Stan thought. I need my size ten shoes, my size eighteen shirt. I need my size forty pants. I need my broad-shouldered suitcoat. If I had them all, I could walk home without fear, Stan thought.

As he crouched unthinkingly almost in the position of one about to start a footrace, something ooping and bumping and dimly lit slid into the stop by the depot: the never-taken-by-Stan, entirely-forgotten-by-Stan, soon-to-be-abolished midnight train. As might have been expected, very soon it slid out again. The first passenger, clumping briskly along, was very large. The second passenger, coming not so briskly, was a skinny little runt. The third passenger, strolling slowly and alone, *he* was just right.

EVENTS WHICH TOOK PLACE A DAY BEFORE OTHER EVENTS

Originally published in Isaac Asimov's Science Fiction Magazine, *September 1989.*

T he principal prisoner in the principal prison paused in his recital of complaints to consider a particularly interesting thought which had only that moment, like the sullen roll of heat lightning, flashed across his mind. He at once broke into a laugh at the droll notion. "Oh yes, ah yes," he agreed, speech confirming thought. "Oh, certainly there must be people who would consider me insane. There are certainly people who consider me criminal: else why am I *here*?!" And he chuckled again. "Well, well," he reproved himself slightly, "one must continue with one's work. Duty calls." Once again he raised his voice.

"If you call yourselves citizens," he cried, his mouth close to the bars of the tiny window, "then consider that citizenship has duties as well as privileges. Arise! Rise up! Erase the infamy! Strike off the fetters which a society, itself more cruel and corrupt than any mere one of its elements can possibly be, has in effect bound around my hands and feet—and also around yours!—Haven't I been saying this for years?"

Again his thoughts were interrupted.

Without having realized it, he had been standing on the one and only genuine hollow spot in his cell. At one time, a pipe, constituting part of the primitive sanitary arrangements (which had been replaced some years back by the present and almost equally primitive and certainly totally unsatisfactory arrangements—imagine! for one of his refinement and breeding—ah well—) had run to somewhere: an unknown distance away. The masons, themselves convicts brought here from a less distinguished prison for less distinguished prisoners, had satisfied themselves (and the warden) with ripping up the part of the old pipe immediately near the surface of the cell's floor, and covering the hole with a tile. From beneath this tile now came a faint but at once perceived rattling, part sound, part tremor: familiar, and only at the moment unwelcome.

"Do not go away," the prisoner shouted. "I shall return to continue explaining to you the wickedness, and indeed, the futility, of all of society's notions of punishment...." He turned away, with but a faint sigh, and, *"Noblesse oblige,"* he said, grunting as he got down on his hands and knees and pried at the tile. He had begun to pick at the mortar before it had dried; *why,* he had not at first exactly known—or, rather, he had pretended to himself that he had not. But of course, actually, his mind, so infinitely superior to the minds of other men, had always considered the possibility, indeed, the likelihood, that the old pipe might also have served some other cell, lower down in the vast prison structure.

Prison structure vast and cruel, as though a type, one in fact might say an *archetype*, of the government and the society which erected it and maintained it still: still! in an age supposedly enlightened. "It is myself!" he called down the hollow space. "What is it that you want, you damned philosopher?"

Long practice alone had trained the two, incapable of speaking to each other face to face, to make out each other's voices despite the distortions caused by the odd area and space those voices had to traverse.

"My aching bones have gradually begun to ache just a

little less," the echoing voice of the philosopher came rolling up through the long, narrow passageway, no larger around than a man's arm, "so it must be noon, with the sun at its strongest...I can see only the usual dimness, but my bones... Well, as you usually are kind enough to talk to me at noon and you did not signal, I was afraid that you were ill: so I rattled to attract attention. You do not sound as always. I hope you have not been ill, then?"

"You do right to hope so," the principal and most distinguished prisoner said. "Suppose I should die? Beside the immense loss to a mankind deprived by my death of the message implicit in my teachings and my practice, the loss to yourself would be even greater. *If possible*. To whom would you speak if the cell up here were empty?"

The fretful philosopher, whose knowledge had failed to endow him with wisdom, asked, "Why didn't you signal to me at noon? What were you up to? Some other crazy scheme?"

"If my crazy schemes were only admitted to be the paradigms they are, would humanity be in its present unhappy situation? The question is rhetorical, and requires no response.—What was I doing? I was addressing the mob. The mobs, to be exact."

A sound somewhat like coughing came up the old drainway.

After a moment, the voice asked, "*What* mobs?"

"The mobs which even now surround our prison. And I have been preaching to them at the top of my voice the important principles of freedom and of liberty, which have no greater advocate than I, and that '*Do what thou wilt* shall be the whole of the law.'"

The philosopher—the fellow had a *name*, but what did it matter?—the philosopher said, "There is no mob. There are certainly no mobs. You have been shouting yourself hoarse, useless and unheard. No one will listen, for no one stops to try; no one can see your face from so far below, and no one could even hear your voice, anyway..."

He did not indeed say the very words, *You are mad*, but the belief in them was in the sceptical tones. "I must beg you to excuse me if I seem to differ from your own undoubtedly well-founded opinions, nevertheless: I am in a better position to judge than you are." The distinguished principal prisoner spoke only with the gentlest of sarcasm (being, basically, the most gentle of men: but one who knew his own nature: and how few know theirs?). "The fact is, however, that immense throngs are gathered around the prison to hear what I have to tell them: How it is absurd to call one line of conduct *cruelty*, and to punish it. How human beings are what they are because they *are* that way, and cannot change, and that our entire and so-called system of justice is at best an immense farce. That one's nature is formed by forces both inside and outside of ourselves and incomparably stronger than we ourselves are. And that society's 'justifiable constraint,' so-called, is an atrocity as atrocious as any atrocity so designated by the laws, be they social or criminal. And that is why I have been addressing the crowds. *And that is why they listen.*" And at this moment, as if overwhelmed by the importance of the task, he scrambled to his feet and shuffled to the tiny, barred window.

"I recognize you all as my brothers!" he screamed. "I embrace you equally! Would that I were as free as you are and that you were all as free as I am! But how is it that you remain passive, so passive? Why do you all simply stand around, or move and moil to no purpose? You must fall to arms! Form your battalions! Stain the thresholds with the impure blood of the enemy! Liberty!" he screamed. He shouted, and he waved his free hand.

"*Liberty!*"

Then he fell back from the window, exhausted. And then once again, on hands and on knees, he called down the drainway, "Did you hear? Did you hear, you philosopher fellow?"

"Part of it I certainly heard," the dim and wasted voice declared. "What irony that only the voice of a criminal and lunatic solaces my solitude apart from my own thoughts, and that my only hope is that I may die in this living grave before you do. What! Do you still imagine that mobs of people have gathered, and are suffered to remain gathered, to listen to you? To hear your beliefs, which would be humorous if they were not so grotesque—the idea that *you* may do as you wish, to others, but that others may do nothing to prevent it, to *you*?"

The most distinguished prisoner smiled a small, tight little smile, almost a grimace. "You call them 'grotesque'? *I* do not call them grotesque at all. To me they seem as clear as the limpid waters of a forest pool. And I will tell you, sir—"

What he told him, having hastily inclined his head towards the thick, thick door of the cell, was, "Hsst! Be quiet. Someone is coming—"

He had barely time to scramble to his feet and shove the tile back into place before the horrid grating noise of the hinges sounded. The door creaked open. A small group of people was there. Some remained in the corridor outside, darkness of the inner prison dimlight relieved by lamps and torches. And some, headed by the warden of the prison, came swiftly into the cell. By the warden's side was the assistant warden, two guards, and a lackey. In the warden's hand was a pistol. Aimed.

"I must ask you, sir," the warden said, restraining himself with an effort which left his normally red face almost white, "to be prepared to leave here at once for another place of confinement. Do not, I beg of you, attempt to offer a resistance.—So. So that," he gestured to an artifact near the tiny window (the lackey had begun to place, with much haste, the prisoner's few belongings into a portmanteau), "*that* is the means whereby you have been making yourself and your inflammatory cries so audible to the mob?" He was about to say more, but pressed his lips, gestured towards the door of the cell.

The distinguished principal prisoner bowed his head politely. "Yes, it is. It may be described as a sort of auditory device which I have made from a wine-funnel and a piece of the piping from my most unsatisfactory sanitary arrangements.—As for 'offering a resistance,' pshaw! *Noblesse oblige*. Lead. I follow."

They led him through long and almost endless corridors and down long and almost endless stairs, down into an immense courtyard. There the vehicle waited. The assistant warden went in first, then one of the guards, the prisoner followed, the governor came next, the other guard got in last. The guards sat facing them. A gate opened, the vehicle moved out. It was a side gate, the throng was not at its thickest there, and it seemed as though it were one of those odd moments in time when—the clock perhaps at twenty minutes after the hour—everyone had fallen, for a second, silent. The crowd opened automatically to let them through.

Just then the prisoner sprang up and thrust his head out the vehicle's partially-opened windows, thrusting the heavy curtain aside. "*To arms!*" he cried. "*Arise! Rebel! Revolt! Save me! I am—*"

The guards lunged, seized, struggled with him, pulled him, still struggling, down back into his seat.

The warden cried, "*Faster! Faster!*"

The postilion spurred the horses, the carriage lurched rapidly forward. The warden had his pistol again at the distinguished prisoner's head, the assistant warden's hand sought to cover the distinguished prisoner's mouth. But the distinguished, the principal prisoner, of the principal prison, screamed, turning his furious face from side to side, evading the hand that sought to silence him. And one more time he shouted, before they muffled him silent and had passed through the still uncertain thronging mob. "I am he who has been so cruelly, so unjustly imprisoned!" he cried out. "Liberty! Equality! Fraternity! *Down with the Bastille! I am the*

Marquis de Sade!"

HISTORICAL NOTE

It is a fact that the Marquis de Sade was, for just what reasons you might think, imprisoned in the Bastille at one time. During the revolutionary fervor, mobs did gather round this fortress and prison, and he did, by just the means described, address them: although his words may not be exactly known. The warden (or "governor") of the Bastille did remove him, and "at pistol point," to another prison. The date of this removal was July 13, 1789. The Bastille, as is well-known, "fell" the next day—not alone because of the patriotic or revolutionary fervor of the mob, but because the Swiss guards defending the place surrendered under a promise of absolute safety. They were then disarmed, and, to a man, killed.

—A.D.

WAITING FOR WILLIE

Originally published in Isaac Asimov's Science Fiction Magazine, *October 1989.*

When she returned her mother asked, "Did you catch a sight of him? Will you just give him a chance?"

"He's hiding under the porch—yes! I 'caught a sight of him!'—crying, because he didn't win a prize. I'll give him a chance, I'll wait half an hour and so I'll still give him a chance —"

Her mother murmured, "Don't be too hard on him, Dee. He's only twelve."

"'Hard on him,' oh that's very funny. Well, what about *me*? *I'm* only twelve! What am I supposed to say to my *friends*! Willie! I didn't pick him out on purpose, his name just came out of the darned old bowl."

"Well, that's the way it always *is*." Her mother found a thread to snip.

Dee stamped her foot. "Darned old prize. Boys care about that, girls don't care about *that!*" She made a face, exclaimed, "*Ohhh!*"

Her mother sighed. "—if you'd just go and *talk* to him, quietly and friendly—"

"Well, I *won't*! Stupid Willie. Sissy! Now I'll have to wait six months, and all my friends—"

Mom said, if he only knew it, Dee was the best prize. Dee said, scornfully, well, he didn't know it and at this rate he never would. "Might as well pour out that lemonade and throw away that cake." But her mother of course did neither.

In came Buddy. "All dolled up, Sis, say, you look great, say, where's your beau, what's his name, Willie?"

Dee, who'd smiled at the compliment, scowled. "Why do you boys always have to have your old contest *now*?"

Buddy seemed a little surprised. "Well, gee, that's when it's supposed to be. Where's what's his—Willie?" His fingers edged towards the iced cake but withdrew after a warning headshake from his mother.

"Hiding under the porch? Crying? Because he didn't win a prize?"

"Hey, that's dumb. Want me to talk to him?"

"Oh, Buddy," said Mom. "If you only *would*."

But Sis called out a long defiant ascending "*Nooo!*"

Buddy was perhaps easily surprised. "But suppose he goes into the river?"

Dee ("Sis") shrugged her pretty shoulders petulantly. "Well, suppose he *does*? Then his dumb genes won't be in the pool anymore."

Her brother shrugged, said, "Okay, hey," and went out via the side door where there was no porch.

Sis continued to suffer. "Dumb old beau," she said. "Crying because he's afraid his *thing* isn't big enough. Big enough for *what*? *I* ought to be the judge of that, not a bunch of smelly boys! Oh just my rotten luck on my First Time to have to craw some kid blond wimp out of the bowl!"

Her mother sighed. "Yes, I *know*. I'm sorry." There was a sound from outside and a little below, scuffling, sobbing, then feet running. "There he *goes*," said Mom. "Sure enough. Towards the river." She sighed again. "Well, you'll just have to wait the six months, then."

Dee stood up. "Might as well take these darned frills off, and—oh, Mom! You worked so hard to make them—"

"Mothers only want their children to be happy, dear. *I'm* sorry!" She put a piece of waxed paper over the cake to keep the flies off.

HAVE YOU TRIED GUMMIES

Originally published in 2AM Magazine, *August 1990.*

At a centrally-located table in The Caravan a group of its regular men-customers sat talking about Art Cooper, the bartender. He had some notion of this, but it did not greatly interest him. The Caravan had no hard liquor license so he was never bothered by requests for fancy drinks. You could have light beer or dark beer or white wine or red wine and you could have it by glass, mug, or pitcher. And if these simple staples did not satisfy, you could go elsewhere. Monk Mollins, the owner, said that he preferred things simple. He never fixed anything unless he had to and he never painted anything at all. Still, The Caravan was crowded every night. Art Cooper occasionally wondered why.

A young woman with grossly over-painted eyes, otherwise unobjectionable and intact, sat down at the bar and leaned across it. Art said, "Yes?"

She smiled. "Do you have a faintly sweet white wine?" she asked. "Something like a—?"

"No," said Art. "The red wine is sweet. The sweet wine is red. The white wine is dry. That's it." He moved down to the beer hose and began to fill a pitcher. When he moved back the young woman leaned across the bar again and looked at him with undiminished friendliness.

"There, you *see?*" one of the men at the centrally-located table said to one of the others. "That's the sixth one tonight. Can *you* explain it? What has he got? It isn't looks, it isn't charm, it isn't conversation or personality, or *what* is it?"

"It beats me, but I see what you mean," somebody else said. "They just come over to him and all but climb over the bar to get at him—Here—Look at *this*."

This was a young man of the sort whom women, in speaking to each other ask Did you ever see such a beautiful man? "Our drinks came, Jane," he said. Jane, when he repeated this, looked at him. She blinked. Then she recognized him. "Oh. Uh...Yes.—All right," she said. They went to their table and sat down. She fidgeted a while. Then changed her chair. She listened, or she seemed to listen, to her escort. Now and then she nodded.

But her eyes looked past him to the bar.

"Yes," said the man at the centrally-located table. "And that's the way it goes on all the time. Does he have some sort of an irresistible odor that only women can detect? Because— you see it for yourself: when they first come in and sit down they don't pay any more attention to him than they do to the God damn wall. And then all of a sudden they can't let him alone. So *you* tell *me*. What—"

But nobody could tell him what it was, whatever it was, that Art Cooper had.

Art Cooper hadn't always had it.

Sometimes, if a young man is shy, his shyness is noticeable. Sometimes his shyness constitutes an attraction. But Art's difficulty was that he wasn't shy enough to be attractively shy, and so it was usually mistaken for mere dullness. When a young woman has sighed a certain sigh and looked at her watch or reached for her purse then it almost never makes any difference what the young man says —assuming that he has pushed himself to the point at last of saying something—whether it is, "Let's go to my place" or "Can you spend the night?" or "Let's make love." Or similar variations on an age-old theme.

Sometimes a shy young man thinks that if he had his own car or his own place, then things would be easier. Usually they become easier—but a block is a block, and as long as the block lasts things are never easy. Sometimes, of course, words are not necessary. Circumstances sometimes ask their own questions and supply their own answers. And if a young man is shy without being attractively shy then creating or even assisting the circumstances can be as difficult as giving voice to the words.

And sometimes, of course, women do not wait nor require to be approached, sometimes women do the approaching or the creation or the setting up of the situation and the circumstances. Sometimes. But not so often, not nearly so often, at all, as some young men (let us mention sophomores and sailors) like to try to lead their friends to believe. Oh dear me no.

Which is of course a shame. Particularly if a young man is shy.

Precisely what it was which caused Dirk Peterson to throw up his job as bartender at The Caravan, Art Cooper never learned. And throw it up he literally did—that is, he threw up his bar towel high into the air. The gesture caught the eye of Monk Mollins as he sat in his corner table, fluffing his vast beard and pontificating on politics. "Hey, Monk," Dirk called. "I'm quitting!" Monk said nothing, but Dirk walked towards the end of the bar.

"What, now?" cried Monk.

"Yup. Now." He walked around the end of the bar and towards the door.

Monk, still only half-believing, rose half-up from his chair. "But you've got money coming to you!" he yelled.

"I don't *want* it!" said Dirk, who kept on walking. From

his failure to suggest anything which Monk might do with the money it did seem that no animosity had caused the decision. His face wore the calm, pleased expression of one who was simply doing what he wanted to do, and he walked out the door and never came back.

And so Art Cooper became bartender and Monk, much relieved, was able to resume his seat at the corner table and the duties he considered proper to the owner, that is, fluffing his vast beard and pontificating on politics. Art found that the job was not onerous and the pay adequate, but he did not find that he was less shy. Sometimes there were even tips, though not often, and usually left by those who didn't know any better: for example, by the little group of older people who came in one night and ordered wine and tasted it and shuddered and ordered beer and spent the rest of their time there discussing singing commercials of the '30s—a subject which Art dimly thought might have been "in," but he didn't keep up with such things.

"And how about *this* one?" a man with thinning hair asked, began to sing:

"Who's that little chatterbox?
The one with pretty auburn locks—"

One of the group's women clutched her purse, got the key to the lady's room, and headed for it, joining in the line, "*Arf! That's Sandy!*"

Art, at a signal, refilled a pitcher of red wine for a semi-regular customer whose name he didn't know.

"Little Orphan Annie?" said the red wine customer, as Art set the pitcher down.

"What?"

"Little Orphan Annie, a kiddy's program which your great-grandparents listened to on their crystal sets by the dim and flaring lamps of whale-oil...The one that babe was just now singing on her way to the john. Her second trip. Every babe that comes here makes at least three trips to the john per evening, but I suppose you've noticed that yourself."

"Oh, yeah," said Art, who hadn't. And added, seriously, "I suppose that's because of the small size of their female bladders."

The red wine drinkard dismissed this with a bad word, and said something about the small size of their female something else. "Ha ha," said Art, who could think of nothing else to say, and who naturally promptly began to think of no other subject but that one.

"At *least* three trips. Three at a *mini*mum. The first one always within the first five minutes after arrival."

The Little Orphan Annie woman waved the key at Art, and, when he came to get it, said, "If the city provides this place with free water, by all means continue not to fix the toilet," rejoined her group, which had gone through the theme songs of The Happiness Boys (*"That's our hap-hap-hap-hap-happi-nesss..."*), and Eddie Cantor (*"I love to spend...this hou-ur with you..."*) had by now begun on Bob Baxter, the Real American Boy. Art considered the woman's words, then, with a sigh, took up the key and headed headwards. It was the first time that night, but it was not the first time. Monk *never* fixed *any*thing. The group was in full cry.

"Won't you tryy Gummies?
Just the best gum-drops you ate!
Won't you tryy Gummies?
Bob Baxter thinks they are great!"

In for once quickly conquering his shyness and asking for the bartender's job, Art had had in mind not merely employment but increased opportunity among young ladies. But red wine and white, light beer and dark, glass or mug or pitcher, served as nicely as he knew to the nicest girls he saw, had not served to work the miracle. He sighed, turned the key in the door, shyly slipped into the ladies' room and locked it behind him. It was a moment's work to fix the toilet, an ancient floating ball job whose rubber suction cup or plug had gotten stuck on its copper rod again. He extricated the rod, guided the plug home, watched the water rise in the storage tank. His foot moved on something. An eyebrow pencil. He picked it up, set it down on the sink where the owner might find it later, and his eyes noted a new graffito. This one for a change had nothing to do with politics or lesbianism. In bold strokes well-worthy of emancipated womanhood someone had written, *Jack Jacobs is the best lay in town!*

Art considered this tribute to a well-known swordsman who seldom came to The Caravan. "They don't write those things about me," he muttered. And then the flashing question: *Why not?* and in one swift moment he took up the eyebrow pencil and wrote underneath the tribute to Jack Jacobs, *Yes, but have you tried the bartender here?,* pocketed the pencil and let himself out. He almost ran back to the bar. The group was still engaged in vocal timebinding.

"They're chewy and gooey,
And too sweet to beat—
Bob Baxter just loves them,
Oh boy! What a treat!"

"A mug of beer please," someone said.

"Light or dark?" he asked.

That had been some months ago. Tonight he observed incuriously the gaze of the girl with the too much eye makeup, who, from the table of the beautiful young man, was still gazing at him, Art. He had his eye on a small, slightly plump blonde who was wearing no eye makeup at all. *She* had already been to the ladies' room *twice.* And by and by she drifted barwards and over a glass of white wine opened a conversation which, as Art had with utter confidence known it would, eventually reached the point of her asking him, "What are you doing when you get off work?"

At the centrally-located table one of the men said to another, "Well, there you are, he's clicked for tonight. That cute little pussytail is parked there safe and sound till closing time. And guess who *she* is going home with?"

"Not with me," his friend said, with a sigh.

"Not with me *or* you. Damn it. Damn it. What is it with that guy? It isn't looks. It isn't charm. What is it? What is it? What is it?"

MR. ROB'T E. HOSKINS

Originally published in The Magazine of Fantasy & Science Fiction, *November 1990.*

D id Bertha Schwamm *have* to act the way she did when Hoskins asked her for a date at the movies? After all, *who* was Bertha Schwamm? The fact that she knew real well that most people didn't think she was Hoskins's superior didn't mean that she was ready to accept herself as his equal; if people just sort of looked down at him, well, maybe she would have taken him up on it anyway. And after that, who can say?

However. It was as if the people there at Armstrong's had taken a vote and agreed that Hoskins was someone you could always poke fun at. *Should* always poke fun at. Like he deserved it. And Bertha, well, she joined in the fun. After that, of course, there was no way she could think of him as a friend, let alone as a, like, suitor. So there it is. Even then it might not have been so bad. Suppose Bertha had said, in a sincere but civil way, "Thank you, really. But my mother being always sick and all, well, I just don't go out much without her. But thanks."

Suppose she had said that? Would it have hurt? Do you think that Hoskins would have pushed the matter, saying, "Well, let's all three of us go out, then"? That's not likely. Likelier, he would have mumbled something civil, and gone away. And never bothered to return with another invite. But no, that's not what Bertha did. She just, oh, laughed in his face.

What was so *funny* about Hoskins? Well, O.K., he *looked*

funny, pop-eyes and little chin. But gee, other people looked funnier. *Was* it really the breast pocket always full of pens and pencils? Because even though he carefully explained that each one was used for a different purpose, still, they all laughed and made fun of him. He explained that he wrote purchase orders with one pen and sale slips with another, and this third one was for interoffice communications, and then this one he used for personal notes and letters, and so on...In a way, it *did* seem sensible; all he had to do was look at a piece of paper even upside down and a few feet away, and he knew what it was for, because of the pen strokes. Every one different. And it kept him from wearing his favorites out too fast.

But Patty Birch, she snickered and mimicked him. "Interoffice communi*ca*tion," she said, snickering. And then somebody else snickered. And so everyone understood: Bob Hoskins was somebody to make fun of. Bye-bye, Bob Hoskins.

And then there was what Mr. Armstrong Senior called "the intrusive *R*." Why did Hoskins have to put in the letter *R* where it wasn't supposed to be—why, that is a question. Because his spelling was usually no better than anybody's, and better than some's. Well, his sister, she said when he was a child, he used to leave the *R out* of some words; and his teacher, who'd never been married, and she had to take it all out on her students, she nagged him and nagged him. You know: *Look at me when I'm talking to you!*, and, *Do you hear me?*, and, *Well, what is wrong with this word?* In those days, boys didn't graduate from their diapers into long pants, and I can just see poor Bob Hoskins in his knickers, mumbling, *No R,* and the teacher saying, *Well, put it* in, *Robert.*

Of course he still had no idea of *why* it should be in, and the teacher, she was too busy pushing her control onto him to take the time and sound the word out for him. So, a long time, even, after all that was behind him, when he was, like, tired or, oh, upset and, om, confused, why, without his even giving it a thought, in would creep that letter, where it didn't be*long*.

twenty dozen srafety pins

it might be. Or, it might be

two boxes dry-cell barteries

Mr. Armstrong Senior, who blustered and sometimes raised his voice, but was really very nice at heart, sighed once, and said, "The intrusive *R*, that is poor Bob Hoskins's King Charles's head." Which goes to show that Mr. Armstrong was *a very well educated man*!

But as for Hoskins himself, and Bertha Schwamm, Patty Birch, and Ellen Kelly, and the others there in the office: never mind some King Whozis's Head. That was just more proof that Hoskins was not a person you took seriously. And if Patty Birch, if that was the conclusion she came to about you? Too...*bad*.

Usually.

Skidgell the janitor.

Well, Skidgell *drank*. Who could blame him? Somebody came across him once doing something at his broom closet, and it had nothing to do with the brooms or the mops and buckets. Skidgell was keeping his *bottle* of *booze* there. To tell the truth, there was something else wrong with Skidgell. Something he was born with. Well, his mother— her name was Mayme White—knew Ella Steale real good, and Ella Steale was a first cousin of Francis X. Reilly, you know? The assistant commissioner? And *he* was very close in politics with Alphonsus Brody, the state chairman of— well, you get the picture. And when Mayme White went to Francis X. Reilly and said, "Francy, what am I gonna do about poor Jacky?," well, Francy Reilly said, "Leave it to me, Mayme; I'll speak to Mr. Brody." Mr. Brody must of spoken to Mr. Armstrong Senior, and Skidgell went to work as the janitor's helper at Armstrong's, and he stayed there, pushing his broom and lugging his pails and mops and lurching and staggering from whatever name they give it that he was born with. But mind you, he earned his own living. In those days they didn't give you no charity work. Any charity check. They give you a *job*. And that was *that*. And that was ten or twelve votes that Brody never had to worry about.

Anyway. Patty Birch. Oh, *that* one. So when Skidgell came lurching and staggering across the main office the day after, Patty—oh, that brazen one; still, you got to hand it to her, *she*. Is not *afraid*. Of *any*one. Well, she put her arm up with her hand near her mouth, and she said *hic*. She said it like this: *hic*. And everybody snickered. Like, *every*body. And Skidgell made this *ter*rible face at her, and he lifted his hand like he was going to *hit* her. And she turned her face away and sort of cleared her throat with this high-pitched sound, and she went back to her typewriting, and she never bothered *him* no more. Anymore.

Anyway. Anyway, so when Hoskins asked Bertha Schwamm to go out with him to the movies, what Bertha did was make a real funny face and turn her face to Patty and Ellen, and she made a noise like steam coming out of the radiator or something. And of course they put their hands across their mouths, and they rolled their eyes, and it was like they had all they could do to keep from busting out laughing.

Hoskins went away walking backward—oh, it was the funniest thing. Oh, what looks he give them. Gave them. After that he pretended like nothing had happened. But I bet you he brooded. And, oh, about his big adventure!

Once upon a time, it seems Hoskins, he did try to do something more than just try to work for Armstrong Wholesalers. Quite an adventure story. Hoskins's aunt, she died and left him two thousand dollars. So what did Hoskins do? He quit his job! Wrote Old Man Armstrong a letter. *Owning to new circumstances, I hereby tender my resignation effectrive immediately. Yours truly.* And it came out that he read in a newspaper that because of some war between the warlords over in China, there was likely to be a big shortage of hog bristles that they make paintbrushes out of. And he right away got on this steamship, and he went to this place called Tientsin. It's in China. And keeping just enough money for his traveling expenses, he bought hog bristles till they were coming out of his ears. And he came right back to sell them and make a bundle of boodle; in other words, a fortune. So *he* thought. Hoskins! Would you believe it!

I guess he thought that he was the only person who read that newspaper and got the same idea. Well, you bet that other people must of read that paper and got that same idea. Little did he know that by the time Robert E. Hoskins got to Tientsin, China, those others, they had bought up all the good bristles cheap. And by the time he got his junky stuff back to America, nobody was interested in what *he* had to offer. Benny Kowalsky said, "Well, I'll be pickled in dill. I often heard of people taking a slow boat to China, but Robert E. Hoskins is the only man I ever knew who actually done it. And by heck, it was *too* slow!"

So Hoskins came back to Armstrong's with his tail between his legs, and back he came, and he begged could he have his old job back. The Armstrong family, you can say what you like, they have kind hearts; and, ah, sure, they gave him his old job back. "Let this henceforth be forgotten from amongst us," says Old Man Armstrong in that high-fangled way of his. "Forgotten," haw haw. Every now and then again, somebody with a straight face, they would say, they would say something like this, "Say, I bet you someone could make a killing buying bristles in Tientsin for paintbrushes."

Hoskins with his pop eyes popping out, and lifting his head so he looked even more chinless than usual, Hoskins would never exactly let on what really happened to him; he just pulled this long, serious face, and he'd say, "A lotta people, they lost a lotta money in Tientsin merchandise."

That's all. That's all he ever said; he didn't bellyache about it. Just, well, *he* lost a lot of money; well, it was a lot of money for *him*. Boy, they pulled his tail plenty about this— say, Patty Birch would ask him, "Why don't you take Bertha Schwamm out to dinner at the Van Horn Inn; you can afford it: you made a lot of money speculating in rice or something in China. Show her a good time; that's what a girl likes. Then she'll respect you." And Bertha would make that noise like steam, and snicker and roll around in her chair. She had a lot to roll, come right down to it.

By and by, Hoskins got wise, and he stopped explaining that all he had was his salary. He said this pretty loud once, and Old Man Armstrong, he stormed out of his office and shouted, "Don't you *like* your salary, Hoskins?" Hoskins didn't know where to crawl and hide. By and by, he got wise that they were pulling tricks on him. All sorts of tricks. Phone calls that he should meet a blonde-haired lady, who, she really had admired him; meet her by the clock at the Railroad Depot at eight that night. Riding by at 10:00 P.M., people would see that he was still waiting. Maybe he'd still *be* waiting, except that Patty asked him the next day, "Meet any cute blondes lately, Bob?"

Skidgell, a little later, asked, "What's Mr. Hoskins doin' in the corner by the furnace with his face to the wall and his fists, like, clenched?"

As for all the times someone would steal one of his pens and pretend they didn't, well, who counts? You'd think they were made of gold! And, anyway, they'd put it back when he wasn't looking. Usually. All kinds of funny tricks they pulled on him, because he was a fellow that couldn't take a ribbing: well, too bad, if you can't be a good sport.

But, like I say, eventually he caught wise. First Patty Birch had an anonymous telephone call in the middle of the night. He must of finally caught wise. This disguised voice, well, it must of been disguised, because she didn't recognize it; he probably put a hankie over the mouthpiece like you see in the movies. Patty, she'd never say what the exact words were. "Oh, I dassn't," she'd say. "It was too immoral and threatening." And next, the next one, that was Bertha Schwamm. Her old mother, she never *did* learn to speak English real good, but she'd bundle up in fifty-seven layers of clothes and go downstairs when she'd hear it ring, ring, because she was sure that her brother in Pennsylvania was dead in the coal mines: she figured why else would anyone want to call her at one in the morning? And she'd yell and yell, "*Who? Who?*" and "*What you say?*" And Bertha would come down and push her away and ask who is it? And then she said it was, oh, just the most terrible threats and vile language. And this same anonymous voice, he also called up Ellen Kelly and did the same thing. Did I say Patty Birch, too? And this one and that one.

The telephone company and the police, they said they had *no* way of telling.

And after a while Mr. Armstrong called Hoskins into his office and stormed at him. But Hoskins denied it all. Of course, the whole thing pretty soon got on everybody's nerves. Who looked worse, the girls or Hoskins? That would be real hard to say. And...complaints? Accusations? Oh boy —And then all of a sudden, who came in but his old-maid sister who kept house for him, and she had this real funny, high-pitched voice that goes right through you. And she says, "I just want you all to know that I had the phone company come and take the phone out of my house, and I hope you're all very happy!"

But the calls, they kept *coming*.

The police, they asked down at Mayer's Pool Hall, and they asked at the Busy Bee and at the Depot. And everywhere the people said, No, they never saw Hoskins use the phone at night or even not at night. And that was all the public phones there was, because in them days there was no phone booth on every corner. Those days.

Now get this. What he'd been doing, he must of shinnied

down out of his window so his sister couldn't hear him leave the house, and then probably he must of sneaked over to Fisherville and used one of the phones *there*. Can you *imagine*? I mean, that's a good five miles over to Fisherville. And then another five *back*! Know how it all came out?

The night of that big blizzard, when this whole part of the state, it was snowbound for three whole days? Well, the blizzard must have caught Hoskins on the way *back* from Fisherville; he must of got there first, because all the girls, they say, *sure*, they got one of those terrible phone calls that night. Well, I don't know if you remember the old Holzapple house? On the old Post Road? Closed for years after Old Lady Holzapple died. Well, guess he had to stop by the time he got there. Get in out of the storm. And it seems like some tramp, they don't know who, *he* was holed up there, too. And somehow they got a fire started. Well, nobody had fixed the old chimney in *years*, and while the two of them were asleep, the house caught fire. We could see it blaze from here, and they could see it blaze from Fisherville, but of course no fire engine could get there. The whole place burned down. And in the ruins—

Well, my father told me they identified Hoskins's body by the *teeth*, well, anyway, by one tooth. Old Dr. Stoltfus the dentist, he had died by then, and his records must have been thrown away. But Hoskins's sister, she remembered that he had a gold filling in a side tooth, and sure enough...

Well, after that there were no more calls with those terrible threats. But then, why did Ellen Kelly disap*pear*? And who killed poor Bertha Schwamm? Patty Birch, she never came out of her house after that, and she must have put a hundred locks and chains on her door. Do you believe that the dead *walk*? No, there was never a clue; well, just this one letter from Philadelphia. Do *you* know anybody in Philadelphia? *Nobody* knows anybody in Philadelphia. It was, like they say, anonymous. And it was typewritten. And all it said, it said, oh yeah, real short; it said, "A lot of people were pretty cruel to Mr. Rob't E. Hoskins when he was alive, but they are very sorry now that he is dread."

What do you make of *that*?

SEEOMANCER

Originally published in Isaac Asimov's Science Fiction Magazine, *February 1990.*

L ater it turned out that Francis really did never drink coffee. They had been sitting there, near the Museum, for hardly a minute, just time enough to give their orders. Then this *man* leaned up to the table. "I'm a seeomancer," he said to Annie. Startled and surprised, she was, and was she somehow disappointed too? "I'm a seeomancer," he said, "I see things, mancing." He observed the effect. He took pride in it, he had staked his claim among the ages. "You are Lena's child," he said next. He leaned back, looked at Annie, Shelli, Francis; the man was *very* content. "I see it, I see it. Harry helped raise you when he lived with Lena on 23rd." Came shock, then came a wave of love. Love! "But I was a tiny little child," Annie said. She remembered, past memory, even. *Had* she called him Harry?—or was it Daddy? They were in what Shelli had named The Absolutely Honest Little Greek Restaurant. It wasn't famous or fancy, but it was nice, anyway; and at last they were meeting Francis. Francis was handsome, really, in an odd sort of sleek way: Hungarian, maybe, Annie had thought. Or Argentinian—not that she *knew*—The hamburgers were almost not quite hamburgers, greaseless, must have been from really lean beef, the grillman had hardly bothered to pat them into shape, they still bore the mark where his clean fingers had torn them out of the mass. Francis showed them his restoration of the Himyaritic text, with his own lettering. It was, in a second, absolutely impressive. "It's better than

Ventris," she said on the impulse, meaning it, though barely she remembered reading about Ventris in her cousin's archaeology book at twelve—those odd, *odd* signs!—Francis sat straight, and looked at her, certain in himself of his knowledge, science, craft. "Well," he said, calculating, "it's as *good* as Ventris, I think. And your...we're both good artists." It was clear that this time he had not meant himself and Ventris. "But that's apples and oranges," Annie cried. "Still... thank you." Shelli meanwhile had been eating, not entirely without sounds, and now she made another sound, sub-speech, announcing, as she waved her free hand for emphasis, that she would say something once she swallowed; *then* the man across the table spoke: the seeomancer: and Francis watched, eyes turning from him to Annie. Later, much later, Shelli was to ask, "Is that really true about Louie—" "—Harry—" "—Harry—he helped raise you? Your mom's boyfriend, then, or what?" But Francis did not have to ask that. He asked, "What do you see, mancing, for us?" The man—had he *known* Harry? no use to ask Lena, her face, first surprised, would turn sullen; she would slam things around, with not a word. "For us, for all of us?" asked Francis—the man considered. "For her, little Annie, I see two books like this," he measured with his hands the size and shape of the *Sketches*. "One already I seen. Now I just now seen another, just the same size. For you, mister, also I seen books: seven books, mister, not very thick, but very deep." Francis went a deep red. "But that's *true*. I have five—no, six, counting the—*six* more notebooks. And I was, I *am*, sure that The Press will publish them as fascicles too—oh, this is *marvelous*, this is like living in the age of Homer...well, not *Homer*," he said. "Well, say some centuries later.—*Marvelous!* you've seen what *is*, without full form, but, it, will, *be*." Francis sat back, his rather large flushed mouth a bit open. And of course, at once, Shelli had to move in; and of course, she missed the point, and held out one hand, palm up, stained a bit with condiments (the restaurant had not served the grilled ground beef on buns, but on slices of crusty bread…"Rather a nice touch, wouldn't you agree?"—Annie. But Shelli, intent on mustard and ketchup, hadn't answered). "What do you see about *me*, about *me*?"—Shelli now. The man ignored the upturned palm. "I seen the baby," he said, "the one dead. I see another baby, this one lives, but not with you. No more men I see, not the Black one, not the White. Only ladies I see in my mancing: the Black *and* White." Shelli's face slackened, began to tremble. "But *that's* not nice," she said, "that's not nice at *all!*" She put one hand, with the ketchupy fingers, over her face, pushed, flung back the chair, and ran off, awkward and flapping. "Shel-li," Annie called after her. Shelli swung the other hand, up, down, didn't stop, was gone. "She done it herself," the man said. He turned a bit. "So Lena is okay, and she thinks she'll go back, hey?" No one had talked about it, not here. "She ain't happy here, no of course not, and she won't be happy *there,* either. With the other sister, trouble." He nodded his absolute certainty. And Francis said, "But this is *great*, this is *wonderful!* Seeomancer. *Sir.* What else do you see, mancing?" The man liked the *Sir.* He shared the proud look with them. "Else I see? I see you thinking sell the house for money to dig the hill in that country, what they called 'the happy,' but is not happy no more. Men with guns I see there, also I see the hill empty." He put his hands flat down on the table. No longer flushed, "Arabia *Felix?*" said Francis, almost to himself. "Tel Omar is empty? Then I won't —you're sure?—of course you're sure. Then I better not sell the house. I won't sell it. Then…" his voice ebbed away. "I see, mancing, but already you know: the two of you. Sometimes the other, she comes a little bit to visit in the house." In a low, assured voice, "But of course," Francis said. He and Annie looked at each other; too soon, quite yet, for even smiles. The man got up. "Mister, I know, here the men don't kiss." Annie moved her arms awkwardly about him, and then the man went away. The waiter came over. Francis stirred. "The man paid," said the waiter. "He paid before you come in. Seventeen seventy-eight, you got two coffees coming." "Two *coffees*?" Francis asked. "Oh, I never drink coffee." The waiter's face became very slightly troubled, his lower lip very slightly pouted, he consulted an order pad. *"One* coffee, I mean. Lady, you like Greek coffee?" Annie said, "I love it."

UNFORCED ENTRY

Originally published in 2AM Magazine, *August 1990.*

A lthough no one and nothing was behind it, the aged tabby prowled along the fire-escape as though heading a procession: stiff, deft, dignified, it became flatter as well and passed between the lowered window and the window-sill. Was gone.

The well-known choreographer, Walter Wilson, told the police that he was baffled. "I would have thought that my guard-dog would have torn him to pieces, for one thing." A low insistent growl came from the door behind which the guard-dog was now confined. "Furthermore, I don't see how any normal human being could have gotten through that narrow an opening. And as you *see*, there is *no* sign that the window was *forced*."

The new cop asked, "Happened before, you say?"

"Yes. Yes it happened before. This block is robbed at least once a month. Happened to me about six months ago and now it's my turn *again*: where were the police I'd like to know."

The older cop sighed a bitter, defeated sigh. "If nobody in this whole condo didn't notice anything while the offense was being committed, how come the police who are patrolling the streets in their squad cars are supposed to notice anything?"

Wilson grimaced. "Well, I just hope that nobody says 'cat-burglar' again. You know as well as I that this type of crime is almost invariably committed by some hulking seven-footer with a set of master keys who can walk off with a tv under each arm, so don't insult me by the suggestion. Besides, cat-burglars went out along with flagpole sitters and barbers who would *shave* you."

The older cop said, with only moderate sarcasm, "Urright, we'll call it, uh, 'Same type of crime. Unforced entry.' Urright?"

Elsewhere.

Al, of Al's Cameras and Fine Used Articles, counted out bills. Al stopped. Al sighed. Al's customer began to sob. Al counted out more. "So that's it," he said, almost desperately. "I'm sorry for you in your trouble, lady, that's *all*, honest to—" She swept up the bills, muttered blessings in a broken voice, was gone. Al sighed again.

In came Cooney. "Whutsa matta wit *chew*, Al?" he asked. Al wiped his nose. "Ah, them little old ladies. Whutta they gunna do when they got nuthin maw t'sell?"

Cooney denied knowing. "Gotta nutha *list* faw ya, Al," said Cooney.

Al cleared his throat, scanned the police-form. "Na," he said. "Na. Na." He paused. Then shook his head violently. "Na, na...What's the list *of*?"

Cooney shrugged. "'Cat-burglar,' they say. Who the hell knows. Okay, keep your copy. Seeing ya."

The worn, very worn, name-plate read *Schofield/Clark*. Ella Schofield had not always been heavy and sad. On the wall hung a yellowing class photo and in the center of the figures clad in gym clothes (as gym clothes then were) was a pyramid of lithe, lively young bodies. Which was Schofield? Which was Clark? "I'd like to see the mayor do it," Ella muttered to herself. "I'd like to see the governor do it. I'd like to see the president do—"

In came another woman, rosy-cheeked, as old as Ella, but an excellent example of the phrase "little old lady" not always being a figure of speech. A middle-aged sheltie jumped up and pranced. "Did Betty miss me?" the newcomer asked, bending down and picking it up. "Did you, did you? Oh, I met such a nice gentleman dog tonight, he smelled you on me I think, do you smell him on me, Betty, Betty?" The sheltie evidently did, continued sniffing after being set down. "'Like to see them all do' what, Ella?" She rummaged in her shopping bags. Offered a paper.

Ella glanced at the copy of yesterday's news, put it aside. "Do *what*? Why—live on $213 a month. Is what. I'd like to see —why, oh, where did you—why, *bread*!—why, where did it all —oh! French sourdough bread! Italian cheese! Sweet butter! Oh, do I smell coffee? Wine! Fresh-sliced ham? Oh and the *lovely* fruit! Oh the cream and oh the fish! Oh you've done it again! But how? But how?"

Her room-mate shrugged, with the gesture of a ballerina tossed Ella a rose. With infinite coquettishness, she thrust one behind her own ear, put a tiny hand on a tiny hip, strutted; winked prodigiously. "Entertaining sailors," she chuckled. Opened the fresh-roast coffee and began to measure.

Old Ella Schofield's large mouth opened in feigned shock. But she couldn't maintain the pose. Laughter tugged at her wrinkled jowls. "Oh, Kitty Clark, *you* are a *scream!*" she exclaimed. "Oh, Kitty, Kitty, Kitty!"

Kitty, seeing that just a little cream had spilled, licked it up with her little tongue.

LEG

Originally published in Isaac Asimov's Science Fiction Magazine, *July 1991.*

B ennet Fink was an official of the Gratuities Bureau. The Gratuities Bureau did not have any employees. It had *officials.* Some people who didn't know any better referred to the moneys distributed by the Gratuities Bureau as *Pensions.*

Widespread ignorance.

"You got to make them know that every penny they get is a *Gratuity,*" said Pogue.

Bennet Fink was a Number 23–b/level official at the Over-All Civic Functions Department, of which the Gratuities Bureau was a part. Peter D. Pogue was a Number 23–a/. Difference? Slight.

But perceptible. To Fink now spoke Pogue, in between heavy breaths: and every time Pogue let his breath out, Fink held his own in. Poem by Herrick? Later. To Fink now Pogue, saying, "Whuddaya got?"

Fink: "Skeeley, Gertrude Clara. Widow's Gratuity, $237 per mensual unit. File Number 11–75–763–e/e 13/7. Subject's stepdaughter succumbed of lawful causations. Subject, Skeeley G.C. eckt eckt, claiming to be 'Cleaning Out Apartment,' actually removed and extromitted therunfrom a certain quantity of previously used aluminium cannage materials and was observed to of (a) taken them to a recycling establishment and (b) subsequently was observed to of drunk a semicontrolled substance of which labbatory analysis determined to be gin and ginger ale, obtained at a licensed location idennified as Birdy's Big Time Bar and Famous French Dip O Juice."

Promptly, Pogue: "Concealment of Vassets. Fixed Agency Policy, she had a right to of reported said Dassets and/or their liquidation to the Agency for subtraction offa her Gratuity. She didn't? Automatic Estopment of Gratuity. But Subject may file a Nappeal." A slight flicker in Pogue's eye, a slight flicker in Fink's. *They* knew that the Appeal Form stated, *File Number, which must appear on Appeal, is the number directly to the right of subject's name on Notice of Estopment*; whereas those numbers were for this purpose meaningless, the actual File Number appearing on the line *above* the Subject's name on said Notice. This might take the Subject months, years, to find out; meanwhile little recked the Taxpayer how much moneys the Agency was saving him. Her.

Bennet Fink said, "Right. What else of we got?"

"Else we got...We got a Suspected Malingerer. Ambrose, Rich-ard Leo-nard, File Number, blabbady blabbady. Myeah. Subject Suspected Malingerer in receipt of a Gratuity of $302 per mensual unit on grounds of he hasn't got no left leg. Ampa*tee*." They silently regarded the photographs and X-rays, unlovely abject objects, of Ambrose Richard Leonard: sure enough: no left leg indicated. A sudden thought occurred to Pogue. "Say! A cup la more a these, you'll of made your Quarterly Quota!" of which the first rule was to deny the existence of such a quota; "—whereas Gratuities has reason to believe that Subject is ackshally wearing a Prosthetic Device, to wit a nartificial lim*b*." Few people were as meticulous as Pogue, who always pronounced the final *b*. "Said artificial lim*b* being for left lower extremity. See whutchaget. Take three bucks from petty cash. Onnyaway."

Bennet Fink said, "Right, Chief." This was not, actually, Pogue's title. But. Did he like it? He *loved* it.

Bennet Fink easily found his landmarks. On the north, a privately owned blood bank. On the south, an empty premises still with its old sign, The Cask of A Montilado.

Premisee and sign-painter, between them they couldn't have spelled shit with two *tees*. But who cared.

And in between these points was one identified by a neon sign (itself perhaps worthy of being in the Smithsonian, next to Lindbergh's areoplane) as Conni Place. Maybe a letter and an apostrophe had dropped out. Maybe's Conni's Mom couldn't spell, either. Listen. Hurts *you*? Just as Fink was about to enter, he with some alarm restrained his foot, thinking that he saw a dead body lying on an old blanket; but on realizing that it was really a zonked-out drinkard of the People called Native Americans by journalpersons—a puzzling poser: what, then, are all the rest of us, also born here?—he slouched firmly forward. Bennet Fink's standards were not exacting. The word which formed in his mind was *sleazy*. Conni, if indeed there was a Conni and the word was not an adjective in an alien tongue, was not in evidence. At all. What was in evidence, at all, was a jukebox. But it was silent. Maybe someone had whammed it one with a good solid crutch as part of a non-funded program in musical appreciation, or maybe nobody had a spare two bits. There was, however, continuously, a Sound; it seemed composed of syllables, sibilants, glottal stops, and surds, with now and then a labial or fricative. But it made no sense to Bennet Fink, and, he suspected, it may have made no sense to anyone else in the place. If, on the other hand, it *was* making no sense to the bartender, it was also making no difference to him. He turned slowly from something he was doing in the cash register, maybe treating quarters with nail-polish so as to distinguish The House's quarters as they passed in, through, and from the jukebox; only maybe not; "If you find an honest bartender," said "Prince" Michael Romanoff, that great authority, "breed him"; and slowly faced Bennet Fink with a face which had, conceivably, not moved in a long time.

"Diet beverage," said Fink. After a moment, the bartender's stance not having altered, Fink produced some coins and set them on the crudded bar. Presently part of a previously opened bottle of, presumably, diet beverage, was poured into a not very large glass, and the rest returned to the space beneath the bar. Perhaps it was put there for the brownies. No ice was forthcoming, but then, none had been requested. Of a sudden, prompted by some stimulus not apparent to Bennet Fink, the bartender shouted a number of words, one of which was *you*, and two others of which were *shut up*. "When asked his opinion of Welsh Nationalism," it has been said of Dylan Thomas, "he replied in three words, two of which were 'Welsh Nationalism.'" Poets are not commonly so succinct. There was certainly no sign of any nationalism in Conni's, nor any sign of its ever having been patronized at any time in any way or to any extent by people who might possibly buy drinks for poets or who could for that matter, *read*. For Christ's sake. But the Sound ceased.

In a jar half-filled with mirky liquid behind the bar in between a small collection (say, two or three) of allegedly smoked sausage (thin ones) and a rack exhibiting several items sacked like potato chips or hard candies but perhaps sold for prevention of disease only, there floated an ovoid something which, thought Bennet Fink, was probably an egg: he didn't see what else it could conceivably be. And, having been made very suddenly aware by the cessation of the Sound that something had probably caused it, he now looked around and asked, "What *was* that?"

"Make like you're gunna buy it a beer," said the bartender, "and yull see." He gave perhaps a respiration and a half, added, "Er a glassa wine. Er a box a Sterno. Ya gimpy *son* of a bitch," he concluded, entirely without emotion.

As this insult scarcely fitted Fink, perhaps one of the few which wouldn't, he twisted around to see whom it might. In a booth farther back in the barroom, not so much seated as propped, a stained figure was fumbling with a stained finger around what was probably a glass. Probably a stained glass, too. Bennet pretended an uncertain identification.

"That's not old Bob Baker?" he asked.

"Yeah. 'That's not old Bob Baker,'" said the barkeep in what might have been intended for sarcasm. "Nye suppose that's not old Dick Ambrose, either. He's always in this soor. Piss inna beer glass an see if he don't drink it. Er any other kine of a glass."

"Dick Ambrose," said Fink, carefully. He got off the barstool —it had, very long ago, been mended: either because it had even longer ago been slashed, or because the bartender had had some extra tape which he hadn't known what to do with; his job was perhaps not the most interesting way to pass the time. "Dick Ambrose," Bennet Fink said, sliding into the seat opposite the stained figure. Who was, literally, stained, as well as very, very dirty. Someone had smeared his face with what were probably coal-tar derivatives, whether from Montpelier or elsewhere; perhaps it had been done by a medical intern at what are significantly called "teaching hospitals" or is it "learning hospitals." Medical interns do not learn off of the rich; the snobby things. Or perhaps by an interior decorator trying out new color schemes.

"Dick Ambrose," said Fink, for the third time.

An eye like a barely poached egg trembled. "Hey buy me a beer," said perhaps-Dick-Ambrose. He rather resembled the face in the photo attached to the file in The Office. But he didn't look as good. "Buy me a beer," said the voice. It sounded more like the unharmonious Sound than not. "Hey buy me a beer, hey buy me a red port, a white port, a muscatel, a balla malt. Hey buy me a nale, a shotta rum, a jigger a gin, a, num, a, ah...ah...ngong, ah...ah...ahh...ahnn..." The voice shot up the scale somewhat. The eye still trembled: the mouth, badly chapped about the lips, and so oddly stained and rather broken, still made its plaint, or whatever it was that it had been making. But, like a tape-recorder set at somehow the wrong speed, it made no further sense whatsoever.

Bennet Fink gave a gesture which, he had long ago learned, meant "Money Over Here," to any bartender within the jurisdiction of the International Postal Union. And...just in case...he fished out a dollar bill and showed it somewhat.

A full glass appeared on the table. Ambrose slowly sank down to it and began to suckle. "Ya coulda filled it in the terlet and he woulda drink it," the bartender said. "I seenum all in this soor, I seenum all, an I never seen nothing like it. Paint-tinner, tawpeda fule, heeltaps like from anybody's heel, the spiders outa the glasses atta leper-colony: showum, he'll drinkum. Ya gimpy *son* of a bitch." He pulled the dollar and went away.

Why old Ambrose's gait particularly bothered the man, Bennet Fink had no idea. However. To business. "How's your *leg*, Dick?" he asked. For, although a scratched-looking cane was propped in the corner against the scummy wall, crane his neck as he would, Fink could perceive no empty pants-leg. *Cane.* Not crutch. But with that type people, Fink realized, you could never tell.

Ambrose, having sipped up the miniscus and being no longer in as much danger of spilling any of his drink, now lifted it with a tremorous paw. Drank. Drank. Then, a moment later, and rather tentatively, he began "Ahnnh..." But Bennet had not risked an entire dollar from the Publick Funds merely to listen to an extended phoneme. "How's your *leg*, Dick," he asked.

"We *come* offa the beach-head," said Ambrose, as one who had already set time and place, and, continues, thence, the tale; "We *come* offa the beach-head and there's this *Nam*bu in a declevity," and he made a spasmodic sound, as might a child playing a war-game.

Bennet Fink, however, had not come all this way to listen to what might easily become an account seeking sympathy. He secured the half-empty glass and hauled at it. "How's, your, *leg*. Dick?"

"Well, *you* know," said Dick, suddenly. "It ain't like it was the old one. I gotta, like, take it real easy when I walk. And dit ain't got no, now, *toes*." Never could tell, you couldn't: just when for a change they start talking half-way rational, along comes something way out of left field. *No toes.* And was there ever an artificial leg which *had?* Toes?

"Where'd you get it, Dick?" Dick suddenly moved and grabbed the glass back before Bennet Fink could make a move. Boy! Had to watch them every single minute. He made, again, the signal which would have brought a drink even in Tannu Tuva or the Land of Uz; this time he took hold of it himself and even though he did set it down on the table, he did not let go. "Where'd, you, *get*, the, *leg*, Dick?" Not that it made a basic difference, from some eleemosynary agency, probably...almost certainly...where else? Not from Sears via Dick's little piggy bank...but the info would round out the file. Wind it up, too. Bennet Fink, however, had to find out, had to consider the at least possible, that Ambrose had bought it; stranger things had come to pass. In any event, it, The Leg, was an Asset, wasn't it? Betcher life. And Ambrose hadn't Declared it, and if he were to Declare it, it—being an Asset—would have to be liquidated and the moneys deducted from the Gratuity. And so—

"Gimme the drink," said Ambrose, with a look which was to *cunning* what the steps of an aged and arthritic ballerina are to *dancing.* "An I'll letch a look attit." His manner, Bennet thought, fleetingly, was that of a free-lance geek. Life hands you a lemon, make—

"Here," said Fink, sliding it over the crusted table-top.

Ambrose grasped the glass with one hand, and, sliding part of himself out from under, began to hoist up his pants-leg with another. It had clearly been a long time since any of these had been clean. Ambrose had tentatively begun the drone, but broke it off. "The, om, whatchacallit, the, like, *scar*..." He dropped the theme, the leg of his trousers, the conversation—but not the glass—and began to suck. But Bennet Fink had seen what there was to see. It was not, actually, a scar. It was simply (*simply?*) a line around the leg. A heavy, deep-looking, and irregular line. What color was it? The line itself seemed to have no color. The flesh was of one dirty tint above it. And the flesh was of quite another dirty tint below it. The sores, both above it and beneath it, added a touch of versimilitude—"Gaw head," Ambrose invited, with another grab at his own garment. "*Tutchitt.*" Bennet Fink did not *want* to touch it; he had never seen anything like it in his life. And he did not believe that anyone else had, either.

But now there was a stir and a noise at the door. Had someone come in? Two someones had come in. "Is *this* the place?" a voice asked. At once adding, "Oh, I don't *believe* it!"

Another, and a younger, voice said, "This is the place, Professor. I reckernize the place, all right."

"Oh, I don't *believe* it! My God! My—"

"And that's the one I was telling you about," and at this the younger man gestured. Fink was aware of having previously seen neither one of them; ergo, the young man could only mean Ambrose. Who now very slightly rolled up his eyes and finished, with a long susurration, his drink.

"He couldn't have consumed twenty-seven ounces of absolute alcohol at more or less one gulp and still be—"

"Professor? Honest, we diddin mean to! We mixed them all up, and—It was just a joke, y'know? One of those jokes that kind of got out of hand?" Perhaps thinking of the joke made the young man break into a guffaw, but he immediately broke out of it. "Professor, you aren't going to flunk me, are you, Professor? I gotta get a C for the Bio course, or they won't let me *play* this term, gee, I'm sorry, Pro—"

"But he *could*n't have just drunk it all! I mean, Jesus Christ, boy! *My life's work?* You gave it to some dirty old drunk, and —"

Here the nameless bartender, whom nobody had addressed, leaned his elbows on his bar, and said, "Whaddaya mean, 'Couldn't'? I mean, I been working in this soor for five years now, and *I.* Never seen nothing *like* it. Put it in frunn of um. He'll drink it."

The professor ran frantic fingers through his sparse grey hair. "But my God, man! Drink 27 ounces of alcohol absolutus containing dye-stained tissue-samples from the regenerated tail-stumps of 536 insectivorous lizards? He *drank*—"

"—me a red port, a white port, a nimported vodka, a dmestic vodka, a rye, a burbun, a muscatel, a schnapps, a tokay," continued old Dick Ambrose, who had been intoning his list of drunkards' friends all the while. But who listened?

Fink was at The Office at the usual time. Pogue, his (slightly but definitely) superior, asked, "Whuddaya got?"

Bennet Fink said, "Ambrose, Richard Leonard. File Number 12–423–781 f/f 6."

Pogue stirred the file with a finger like the leg of some medium-sized mungiverous bird. He breathed. "Lemme see, now." Breath. Breath. *Lungs, when he sits downe to eat,/ His breath doth flie-blow all the meat*—Herrick. "Mmm. Ambrose...Myeah. Suspicion of concealing Gassets, to wit, one artificial leg...Myeah. Whuddija get?"

Fink said, "Nothing to it."

Pogue breathed a couple of times. "Ohwell," he said. "Ya can't winnem all."

THE DAY THEY ALL
CAME BACK

Originally published in The Magazine of Fantasy & Science Fiction, *June 1991.*

Mrs. Julia Dennison had put in a rather hard afternoon, canvassing for the League of Women Voters. She felt that until tomorrow she never wanted to hear another word about The Issues; what she wanted to do was go straight to the sunken fireplace in her living room, sink down on the step, pour herself a premixed (she had mixed it herself) martini from the thermos, and just sit there and sip it and welcome and be welcomed by Tawney, her cockapoo dog. A fresh breeze alerted Julia to the fact that the french windows were open, which should have been shut; and where was Tawney? She next saw *Them*—whoever *They* were—and *They* were squatting on the step by the sunken fireplace, chewing and eating something grilled, and it did smell good. Besides the grilled smell, there was another smell—had Tawney disgraced herself? All this passed like a flash through Mrs. Dennison's mind; next she realized that *They*—whoever *They* were—were all dirty and all mother-naked, and that, lying carelessly as a dropped glove, turned almost inside out and all bloody, was a skin with a flash of tawny hair showing at one end; and then she fainted dead away.

Helga had long had her First Papers, and not long to go before she got her Second Papers. It was a nice job she had with the Johnsons, and a nice room in town. Money she sent home, and she had already bought herself a small automobile, a color TV set, and a Polaroid camera. She was still muttering angrily when the Johnsons returned. "What you think," she burst out at once; "what I saw, a kangaroo eating the hice-plans; I take he'm a picture and I hit he'm mee't mine purse. He go avay porty queak. Look, see." Mr. Johnson, who had made nothing of all this, took the offered snapshot, described it to his wife as she put her things away. "This is the house, all right," he agreed. "Cocktail, Johnson?" asked Mrs. J. "No, thanks, dear...and this is the ice plant, all right...out-of-focus again, Helga!—Yes, dear, I will have that cocktail after all." She brought it to him. "You sound funny, Johnson," she said. Don't tell me there really *was* a kangaroo? Where would it come from? There's your drinky, dear." He thanked her. "No, it's not a kangaroo, dear. As you say, where would it come from? The Neighborhood's going to hell." He downed the drink in two gulps. "It's a duck-billed dinosaur, dear—Dividend?"

Major Watson had put some of his own money into returfing the green, and it was quite a shock to him, all the damage the red wooley mammoths did before fleeing into the swamp half a mile off, where, once all that weird *noise* was traced, there was still a strong, rank odor in the air, but—as, twenty-seven minutes after everything began, it invariably proved—no bodies, living or dead, of any intruders were found. "And the goddamned Eastern Liberal Establishment wants to disarm us," the major concluded. "You *saw* what I did with my elephant guns; you *all* saw it. Well, where're the *bodies*; tell me *that?* Not even a head to mount; so much for your *ecology.* I'll be fine in a minute."

Mr. Etuala Ntabe, famous voice as melodious as ever, said in his interview at the airport, "No, no, nothing to do with it, I tell you, nothing at all to do with it. I appreciate everything your splendid chaps have done, trying to get me the role of General Lee in the television series; it is simply that I have decided to resume my very well received lectures on the Lake Poets at Nyamanyama University College. Besides the point that those other events—well, they simply do not occur in my country; they simply do *not*. Government does not allow it; General *Mwasa* does not allow it. I tell you it had a head large as *six* crocodiles. Is that my plane they are announcing? Must run."

...But all of this was of little use to Mrs. Pritchard when, about to enter the motel inside of which was waiting for her a man considerably younger than Dr. Pritchard, she was taken instead by a tyrannosaur.

The 193 daring smash-and-grab raids attributed to the notorious Baby Bandit Couple diverted public and private attention the following week.

IN BRASS VALLEY

Originally published in Amazing Stories, *February 1992.*

"**M**azatlán," I said, "has buzzards the way gringo cities have pigeons."

"But Mazatlán is *great* in October!" said Mr. Bucktoo.

"But I prefer Brass Valley, then. So. Nope, but *nope*." Short way with dissenters.

"Sister Josepha says she wishes she could find him, and maybe find out where he *got* it, because maybe he's got more." So Robby said.

"But why 'Brass' Valley?" asked Mr. Bucktoo, shifting ground. His name wasn't, of course, Mr. Bucktoo, neither was it a nickname referring to his teeth. His name was Tim Brown; *now* do you get it? And was it worth the effort?

"Probably a million years old, but looks almost new."—Rob.

"I'd be afraid to eat here, but the coffee's good." Probably Yar. Might as well be Yar.

"And why *not* Brass?" That was me.

In writing down an alleged transcript of conversation, it is customary to have it follow a straight progression. "Like a railroad apartment: in the front door and out the back." Supposedly this furthers the story line; if it doesn't further the story line, throw it out. Any teacher of creative writing (which is, of course, totally unteachable) will tell you. Well, almost any. Actual conversation, however, is often idle and meandering: an attempt to ignore this just leads us back to those earlier fictions supposedly being told around a campfire while the faceless company manfully smokes its pipes; after a few opening lines one speaker gets the floor and begins to tell his story ("Curious you should say that. Rather reminds me of something which happened to me once on the Upper Slumgullion, don't know if you chaps know the UpSlum...") and then the story unfolds, page after page and paragraph after paragraph, each paragraph naturally beginning with a fresh set of quotation marks—because it is, after all, a transcription of some one person speaking. Very grammatical. And very tedious.

Most conversations, if real (always excepting those very real conversations beginning, "Wanna come down to The Station with us so we can talk about it?"—and just what if one doesn't wanna? Ho *ho*) are *idle* conversations, and jump around from person to person and subject to subject. Plant a tape recorder sometime, unknown to the tapees, and then listen to the replay. (And please, will someone, anyone, tell me what "unbeknownst" conveys, which "unknown" does not?)

"Why does Sister Josepha want more, when she can't read the one she's got?"

"No, the coffee *isn't* bad. Food isn't bad, either, when you come right down to it."

"I'm not *going* to come right down to it. I have my pride. Eat in a place which says it serves *Put Rost*?"

"Snob. Fred just cooks better than he spells, is all."

Sister Josepha said that if she had more of it, instead of only a page of it, it would Pique People's Interest. How much it would really pique the interest of people in Brass Valley (where Sister Josepha was librarian of the small college) to have, oh, seventy pages, instead of only one page, of a Coptic Gospel, was not hard to say. Hardly at all. But Sister J. was an optimist (it is true that she couldn't identify even the single page, but she had the smarts to send a xerox copy to the library at a Jesuit, or No Fooling Around, university downstate); also she wanted very much to encourage donations to her own library, the ones she usually got being along the lines of *Life of the Blessed Aloysius McGonnigal*, *by Rev. Peter O'Praty, P. P.* ("It belonged to Grandma, Sister, not that she was ever much for reading. It must be *very old*, Sister, look: *Roman numerals!*" Sister Josepha could read Roman numerals, even though the donor couldn't, but was kind-hearted, and never bothered to say that 1922 was not very old.)

"According to the booklet they printed up for the Centennial, it was named after some pioneer called Colonel Joseph Brash, and somebody got the spelling wrong."

Nothing was likelier, of course, than that somebody would get the, or any other, spelling wrong; what the Centennial pamphlet didn't say was that one of the pioneers who could and did write had mentioned...once...*that old scant-soap Joe Brash and other trash*, plus...once...*Joe Brash warned agin about selling his Bad Whiskey to Indjians*...Colonels then, of course, were as common as chicken pox.

"Hey, I was sitting in the dentist's office once and he came in and handed me half a page of a newspaper."

"Who did?"

"The guy."

"Same guy?"

"Yeah."

Someone said he *still* thought they should've dragged the G. B. B. again. Someone else said, "Dick Bayrish is not in Great Brass Bay."

"So where *is* he, then?" A shrug.

"Coptic newspaper?"

"No, local newspaper." Sometimes Mr. Bucktoo showed a sense of humor, and sometimes he didn't. "And then he hung around like he was expecting something and I said, 'What's this for?' and he made a funny noise and went away."

"Maybe that wasn't a funny noise, maybe that was Coptic."

Another turn on the platen. "What you don't realize, Yar, is that a cheap place to eat, like this, with good cheap coffee, is an amenity. So are the other few cheap restaurants here in

Brass Valley town. Unless you *like* paying seventy-five cents plus tax for coffee with a plastic hostess. Or twenty bucks for supper."

Yar then cited us his perhaps favorite line of philosophy. "'As through life you go / Whatever be your goal / Keep your eye upon the donut / And not upon the hole.'—Isn't that better than Plato?"

"Plato. Him and his pansy kings."

Yar's great question remained unanswered, and an oral list was gradually made of the town's amenities, including several really *good* restaurants, a *large* public library, the pleasant old campus of St. Anne's College, several good bars even not counting the two good jazz bars, four bookstores (what if one of them did also sell incense?), a first-rate second-hand clothing store, a couple of stationery stores offering something besides computer paper, a real good marine supplies place that didn't charge you an eye and a leg for a grommet ("Hey, don't you mean 'an arm and a leg'?" "No, I mean an—").

Pat, previously silent save for coffee-slurping sounds, busted out laughing. Robby said, "It's got more amenities than the capital of the State of—"

Mr. Bucktoo again wanted to talk about selling or trading one of his time-share deals, but no takers.

"Plus it's got The Place." At this, heads were nodded. "*The Place*" was what most people called an externally rather bleak-looking building which covered more ground than it seemed to, had a rather long official name, and employed all of us then at the table in Fred's. Fred's was one of the, say, inexpensive eating-places with good coffee. Local people of the kind who go often to Katmandu and keep an apartment in Martaban, serious older hippies with serious older trust accounts—the ones who casually describe gross piles of organic rot and filth heaped up around the houses of the once-nomadic Glopp People and also casually tell you that although they don't like eating hunted meat, eat what the once-nomadic Glopp People hunted because the Glopp were really beautiful people, man, and they were cne with the spirits of the earth. Man.—these who write books, *How the Picturesque Ethnic Natives Loved Us.* Y'know?—these people had eventually decided that The Place, though either partially or entirely government- and university-fundǝd, posed no pronto problems to being One with the spirits of the earth; and therefore left it (The Place) alone; and got on with going after the ass of a local official who allegedly wasn't good to guppies. Man. Next to *Fred's* was *Clem's*, another amenity: in the front of its pool-hall cold soft drinks wǝre sold, also magazines not exclusively confined to the do-it-yourself-RCV-culture. Next to *Clem's* was an old-established family bakery whose bread, however thinly sliced, bore no resemblance to blotting-paper: *God!* it smelled good! And just around the corner from the old-established etc., several of the smaller private label Valley wineries maintained an outlet store, and encouraged casual sipping. There were lots of trees, and the river, as it curled through town, was only partly canalized on its way to Little and Great Brass Bays. Where Dick Bayrish probably was not—where *was* he? Ah.

Though sometimes I found I needed other stimulation, still, I am sorry for a State Capital or other city where amenities of these sorts do not abound. Or, anyway, exist. Though sometimes a person did look for other diversions. "What are you laughing about, Pat?" someone asked, for the conversation had not really paused while I was thinking these long and deep, deep thoughts.

"What's the connection with that Copital whaddayacallit?"

"Cop*tic*. Well, I heard that he handed it to the guy at the window inside the union hiring hall. Huh? Oh...the Teamsters Union, I guess...the Warehousemen's?...and *he* finally gave it to Sister Josepha."

Pat finally had finished his laugh. "Must be the same guy," he said. "The bishop, you know I live next door to a bishop?

Bishop Olson. Said that a man came into his office and handed him a beat-up-looking paper. And by the time they had figured out what it was, hey, he was gone!" And Pat began to laugh again. Figured out it was *what*? It was a lab report. An old one. For a Wasserman test. And, no, Bishop Olson hadn't mentioned any name. Maybe there wasn't any name: *old*.

Not only was there the caff called *Fred's*, there really was a Fred, it was Fred who called it a caff, Fred was an Englishman; furthermore, Fred was just then present, as why not. And had overheard. As—

Fred asked if this wasn't the funny old bloke? (Bloke, that's what he called him; evidently a word in actual use; makes you think, doesn't it?) Asked, What funny old bloke? Fred said that there was a funny old bloke who'd been going around town handing things to people. What'd he hand you, Fred? Two dollars in food stamps. Yar said he thought they weren't supposed to be used for restaurant meals. No, said Fred, they weren't. But as the old bloke didn't exactly look like a caPITalist (Fred's exact word, a caPITalist), so, he, Fred, had given him a bag of sandwiches. *Dirty* clothes, looked like he'd been rolling about in the sand.

"Suppose he can't help it," said Fred, "but I wasn't too keen on his hanging round here, so I sort of gestured [hard g; to each his own] him to follow and I handed them to him at the door. Funny old bloke." And, ah, what had Fred done with the food stamps? "Used them to buy *food*, of course. Yes, *mahm*!" He moved away to wait on a customer. In this transcription I have refrained from doing anything cute about the absence or intrusion of the letter *h*, because Fred was really very nice, and never once complained about our taking up table space for (mostly) little more than coffee at his cafe (or caff).

Couldn't help what? one may well ask, but those familiar with the appearance of the funny old bloke at once explained to those not, that he looked *odd*, perhaps belonged to another race than those generally visible around Brass Valley (Q.

Which ones *were*? A. All of them; well, all most of them, most all of the other ones, that is.) and/or was probably down on his luck. Way down. As well as being dingy. "And besides all that," said Robby, "he just looks, well, damned *odd*."

After a musing moment (yes, yes; the kettle itself does not boil; *okay*?) Yar said, "Behaves damned odd, too, evidently."

But Pat (I think it was Pat) said that didn't figure at all. "It seems to me," said Pat, "that this guy is maybe a bit mixed up, but he at the bottom of his mind has the notion that if he hands the right papers to the right person at the right place, then he will get the right something. Like, to eat. Which he *will*. But he doesn't always manage to make all the connections."

A hot wind, but not very hot, with some faint scents of grapes and hay, blew through the open doors. There was no more old railroad, but there were still some old railroad men, and one of them sat down at the counter and said, "The pot roast, Fred. I could," the casey jones informed the world, "eat Fred's pot roast all day long and every day." Yar murmured, "A survivor from the age of faith."

"Well, but where *is* Dick Bayrish?"

"Probably on Mission Street, with a jar of muscatel as big as his head."

"—Dick *Bay*rish? Naa."

"—okay, then: Dick Whittington—"

To Pat I said, "Don't you call that 'behaving damned odd'?"

Just then the telephone rang. There is no long arm of coincidence involved, the telephone when it rings is ringing *some*time, and now and then that time happens to be "just then" time. Fred answered it, it was after all his telephone, and after we heard him say, "Fred's Caff," after a moment, we did not hear him say as I once did hear him say after saying that, "Well, fook you, too!"; we heard him say, "I'll ask, Doctor." And he looked over at us. "Is Doctor Patterson or Doctor Nelson or Doctor Knight or Doctor Brown or any of you gentlemen here? It's Doctor Jefferson." Fred always had a high respect for those of us who worked at The Place, and always called us each *Doctor*, which we weren't each, or all. And he had just named every one of us.

It didn't seem to matter which one of us answered; Pat was nearest. "Patterson here," we heard him say. Then, "Uh-huh, uh-huh…He *did*?" For a second Pat said nothing. Then he said, "Jesus Christ." Then he hung up and came back, more slowly than he went, and sat down, and had a gulp of coffee. "It's that same *son* of a bitch that we were talking about. The fluke who goes around handing out *funny* papers."

"It *was*—? Well…what did he hand Jefferson?"

"A birth certificate."

Stir of interest. Several people asked, almost together, well, where's he *from*? "Oh, it isn't his own birth certificate," said Pat. "It's Dick Bayrish's."

Maybe I ought to have explained about this, earlier. Shuckins.

Dick's first wife came with two ready-made children, girls, Toni and Tini. Their *names*. None of us were ever sure what their onlie begetter's name had been called, he was a vanished man, she had vanished him, told him that she and the children "had the right to a new life in which he had no part or place." So, "naturally, Dick adopted them." Law of Nature and of Nature's God. Dick was once dopey enough to say (I heard him), "When we have children—" See her eyes open wide. *Wide*. She had but *no* idea what he could mean. "'When'?" she said. "'When'? We *have* children." You will have noticed the use of only the pronoun, so far. At an earlier stage in human development Mrs. pre-Bayrish was called Caroline: fine. Then she became Caro*lin*, *Carolyn*, *Carolynn*, Kar—you think I am making this up? No. Hold on. She next became aware that, on a certain level of society, girls of Old Family were being given last names as first names, just as boys had been for centuries. Their turn now. Carter Smith, she. Harper Hopkins, she. Hopkins Carter, she. I am not totally sure that her maiden name had been Kraemer, but I doubt if that had been her first husband's. Somehow, I doubt it. And so anyway, she became Kraemer Bayrish. Very suddenly Dick was supposed to have divined it, as he was supposed to have divined the other changes: and he hadn't. Didn't. Singing telegrams, you ever hear of screaming telephones? Can you imagine waking up not knowing the name of your own mate? And God help you if you called her today by her name of yesterday: telephoned screams all day long. No use at The Place for whoever answered the phone to say that Dr. Bayrish couldn't take the call at that very moment, because the call would be repeated every moment on the moment until he could. And did.

Very well, Dick was a dolt. But a harmless dolt. How did a simple soul like his ever get into such a pickle? Mathematically, Dick may have been a genius; socially, he was a moron, and no maybe. While I don't suggest that he had had no woman prior to "Kraemer," I suggest that he hadn't had many. And then.

And then it became obvious that she had found, shall we say, a man with a bigger dick than Dick's? Obvious to everyone save Dick, that is. God save Poor Dick. Hershey Bars and all…he never smoked nor drank. Reveling and Carousing to him was a tablespoon of (gag, brack) Manischewitz Red.

"Where *did* he say he was trying to go?" Yar asked Mr. Bucktoo, at Fred's.

"Must've told you almost a thousand times."

"Tell me again. Maybe this'll be the thousandth blow that splits the rock."

That day had been a day of many, many telephoned screams. The proper form of her latest name was just a straw in the wind, mighty strong winds were blowing, and the winds were full of straw: why was it supposed to comfort *her* that her husband was a mathematical genius? If it weren't for *him*, if he hadn't been a bastard and a son of a bitch, *she* would have been a mathematical genius...an opera star...the head of an advertising agency.

Whose fault was it that she wasn't? Whose fault was it that the world did not discern her teeming talents, that she had two small children whom she had decided not to want? It could not have been her fault, because nothing *was:* therefore it was Dick's.

Then, who knows why, a lull. And Bucktoo had come across Dick, not at his usual desk, but at his carrel in the library. At The Place? Of course. "Perhaps it's merely supposititious," said Dick, as though they had been a while in conversation.

And *that's* when he said that mysterious thing? "Yeah"? Well, *would* one mind repeating it? The usual—well, usual with Dick—swathe or swale of Hershey Bar wrappers on and under the table; well, it beat chewing pig-tail plug, hell yes. Only maybe not. "Attempts to reach the perhaps entirely theoretical fourth planet of Orion's Dog, via gamma-grade kineportation"; wouldn't *you* call *that* mysterious? I certainly would.

One agreed? More coffee, please, Fred?

Pat: "Well, what's with the little girls?"

"One of them was eating flaky paint. And the other one was eating her own hair. Maybe they miss Dick."

Sad silence. Broken by, "Dick may have had a nervous breakdown." Yes, and maybe Daniel Boone was antisocial. Thanks, Fred. *Anyway,* Dick had disappeared. The Place had enough pull ("clout," it's called now) to persuade Brass Valley to have the Little Bay dragged. No Dick.

Mr. Bucktoo asked, "And what the hell *is* Coptic? anyway."

As it hadn't happened that I had had a lot to say, I said this: "A late form of ancient Egyptian speech and writing, both heavily influenced by Alexandrian Greek. So Father Flynn wrote to Sister Josepha. And he also sent a transliteration, and the same text in Latin."

Someone said, "Whenever things got tense, he lit out for a library."

Again, silence. "Sister Josepha lets you read her mail?"

With dignity, I: "Sister Josepha was kind enough to xerox Father's letter and enclosure. She said she thought it might pique my interest." I reached it out of my pocket. Mr. Bucktoo said, Sister Josepha and her xerox; when he was a boy the Sisters never used anything more complex than a yardstick. Which they used to whack hell out of him for eating apples during catechism class. In the back row.

Yar said he had absolutely no sympathy with him. "If there's anything I hold in contempt, it's one of your furtive apple-eaters. Shame on you. Bordering on heresy and schism."

Bucktoo said something vulgar. To *Yar*. To *me*, he said, "And you just happen to have the letter with you?" Heavy on sarcasm.

"All right, then, it's a talisman. A talisperson. The *old* one wore out. Barodi a Soldan. Hoyts *you*?"

They peered at the paper...the papers...one can't say that they peered at them very intently. Yar "read" a pretended version of the transliterated text, something like this: "Yah-yah gombo bubastis luxor memnon logos, osiris ain't *got* it, *p'tah*." Pat, amused (anyone who would write that, "An amused Pat," with its implication of several amused Pats as well as several unamused ones, should be condemned to unscramble pied type in hell), asked that he next do the Latin. But Yar said that he preferred to leave the Latin in the decent obscurity of a learned language. And Robby said, "He probably ripped it off from a library."

Asked (I asked) why did he say *that*? Robby replied that the guy ["The, ah, *bloke*?" "The, ah, bloke. Yes."], well, because he gave that impression. Too many years close confinement with the Dewey Decimal System had addled his eggs... Maybe...

I picked up the copy of the Coptic transliteration, and, for some reason, was moved to read it aloud. And, for some reason, they listened.

"Evol ghar sa khoun evol ken piheet ente piromi shavi evol enje nimokmek ethoou nipornia nichiouwe no khotaib nimetnoik.

"Nimetchiengons nimetpethoou nimetdolos nisaoaf nival ethoou nijeoua ouchisi enheet oumetatkati.

"Ny teerou ethoou evneyou evol sakhoun ouoh sesof empiromi."

Silence. "Sounds impressive. Odd, mind you. But impressive. More."

"More."

"If you want more, you'll have to have it in Latin. Okay?" They said, okay. So I read on.

"Ab intus enim, de corde hominum malae cogitationes procedunt, adulteria, fornicationes, homocidia.

"Furta, avaritiae, nequitae, dolus, impudicitiae, oculus malus, blasphemia, superbia, stultitia.

"Omnia haec mala ab intus procedunt et communicant hominem."

Silence. Someone muttered, "Which nobody can deny." I wished that I had studied Latin longer and more recently: still...still...slowly something of it kept seeping in on me... but...what...

Mr. Bucktoo gave a start, a jerk of his head. "Here he *comes*," he said. In came the nut...fluke...bloke...guy...weary, fatigued, confused, dogged, and several other attributes I couldn't quite put my finger on. Was he heading for me? Immemorial cry: *Why me*? Answer: Why *not* me? Somehow I very much wanted not to have to have this, too. So I turned my head and began babbling. "Not Mazatlán!" I said. "They eat goat's-head roasted with the horns on, and tripe and hominy soup for breakfast!"

Didn't take much to turn him on. "Well, if nobody wants to buy my time-share in Mazatlán, how about my one in Alexandria? I'm just over-bought, y'see. Alexandria is *great* in April!"

But the goop not only headed towards me, he circled me, never taking his eyes off me. I got up. Why? Why not? He came around and faced me at fairly close range. It seemed important to me to do what I next did. Which was to open my wallet and remove an old color photo of self and D. Bayrish, side by side. The odd fellow peered, blinked, made sundry sounds, said words. Moved by too many half-exposures to too much second-rate cinema, novels of the same rank, who knows what else—so I held my hands out, palms up. The bloke dropped something very crumpled into them. It did not take long to identify the items as the inner and outer wrappings of a very common brand of chocolate bar. But by that time the alien had disappeared entirely: I had a hunch: never to return. And, just after that, the phone rang. Again.

"I can't *talk* now, Kray—"

And her voice in my ear, weeping and screaming, "It's not Kray! It's Rā, with the macron—as if you don't know, you son of a bitch, you bastard, as if you don't know!"

My turn now.

THE MAN WHO WAS MADE OF MONEY

Originally published in Borderlands *3, ed. Thomas F. Monteleone (Borderlands Press, 1993).*

Beth and Joe Braidel (accent on the last syllable) hadn't even moved into their new home when old Mr. Goodworth came to see it. She said, "And how do you like our ranch house?" And instead of a decent, "it's very nice," at the least or words of praise which any civilized person would feel were only proper, the old man had to ask, "And where are the cattle?" Oh, of course Beth smiled, but she really could have killed him; however, as she told herself, she didn't have to live with Harry Goodworth. Let him look around and make his remarks, in a few minutes he would go away and write up the policy, that was all he was there for, and there wouldn't be any nonsense about his calling every week to collect the money the way he was still doing for that piddling little life insurance that Joe's parents were still paying for. No thank you, none of that for Beth, the new place was far enough away from the old neighborhood and besides, with this kind of policy you only paid once a year. Twice?

It was a lovely house, a beautiful house—

Beth could have done without old Harry Goodworth altogether, not only in regard to the insurance on the new house, but the one on Joe's life, which had been taken out years ago. Who needs Goodworth, she had argued back then. Maybe the old man knew that and that was why...? No. That's just the way he always was. Well. One of these days.

A yellow face like that, he wouldn't be around much longer. And the policy could be transferred, couldn't it? To someone who could really be of use to Joe in business...so. She wasn't having any more of old Goodworth or of Joe's parents, or, for that matter, of her own parents, than she could help. It was her house and it was going to be furnished her way. And this was where real loyalty came in. Never mind what it all cost. A woman has a right to have nice things in her house, isn't that right?

When we say that Beth Braidel didn't want too much to do with her own parents, that isn't to say that she didn't want anything to do with them. As soon as the house was ready to show people, one of the first she showed it to was her mother. Wall-to-wall carpeting in every room, every appliance the human heart could want, serving-for-ten of everything, original modern art on the walls—

"Well, did your little girl do all right for herself?" asked Beth, in her funny way.

And Beth's mother, nodding, and with that typical little dry smile that only Beth's mother can do so well if she wants to (and God help you if she doesn't!), said, "Not...bad. Not bad at all. See what you can do if you handle the husband right?"

Meanwhile, and far more important for the moment, were her two closest friends. Her two closest friends.

It was perhaps just a little bit unfortunate, their both having the same first name, thus requiring them to be referred to by their last ones as well, Joan Raisen and Joan Kaye. If everyone had gone along with the simple little idea which Beth had thought of, namely calling one "Joan" and the other one "Joanie," but some people for some reason seemed unable to grasp this concept, even their husbands, for example, so there was nothing to be done about that: And after Joe Braidel had said, I know...I know, very apologetically, he gave every indication of having learned his lesson...

Keeping up with the Joanses!

Some sense of humor.

After all, why does a woman want a nice home? For herself? Hardly worth the worry and aggravation. For her husband? Does the average man, left to himself and his own devices, even know? He doesn't know. Food, a comfortable old chair, a couch and a bed and a television set—enough for him. As for children, too ridiculous to consider that and that was a bridge she didn't even intend to come to, let alone cross, for a goodly period of time, if at all.

No.

A woman wants a nice home for the same reason she wants a nice husband, because what else is there to compensate her for everything she gives up when she gets married and everything she has to put up with after she gets married? She wants a home and a husband that she can show her friends and family without being ashamed. And to say that "a woman's place is in the home," to interpret that as meaning that her place is only in her home, is disgusting. But after all, where does the average woman have a better chance to display what she is really made of and what she really is, except in her own home? Beth's little cousin Kippy, now just take Beth's little cousin Kippy. Two children in two rooms and a filthy so-called artiste's studio, and in what a neighborhood! And when does she ever get out with her stupid artist husband, and then where do they go? A museum, a gallery! And yet she says she's happy!

Whereas a successful woman, a woman who has a lovely home, a woman who has time and leisure and means to go where she pleases when she pleases, a woman who has the latest of everything, such a woman can, so to speak, open her home to the whole world in complete confidence that nobody can turn up a nose and nobody can look down on her and/or pity her. Such a woman need bear no resentment for the past regarding if she were perhaps treated unfairly by a parent or if an older or younger sibling had favourite status. Such a woman can look her aunt, let us say, in the eye and she doesn't have to say such words as, "your marvelous Vicki that you were always boasting off: Does she have two dishwashers? Three freezers? A floor-level wine-cellar? Stereo, with speakers and controls in every room? Ten complete servings of imported tableware? The very latest subscription copies of French and British magazines? Not just a few copies you bought six months ago and six months from now the same ones will still be there staring you in the face, but the latest!" Such a woman doesn't have to say things to her aunt. Her aunt has eyes. Her aunt is not a complete fool. Neither is her mother, and not her school friends and not their mothers, aunts, sisters, and so on and so on.

Such a woman is a success!

And success can only be matched against other successes.

It had always seemed that Joe Braidel had appreciated it. If you have a lovely home, if you have a lovely wife, if she has jewelry, if you have two decent cars and a station wagon, and if you have enough insurance, well, what more can a man ask for or expect?

Suppose he had a wife who insisted on going out to work and he could never be sure that she was really in her office and not in a little apartment with her so-called employer, instead of taking care of her lovely home or enjoying some well-earned leisure with a woman friend or two.

After all, Beth never for a moment forgot what her duties were. And neither did she demean herself by forgetting what her husband's duties were. And a lovely home and everything that it entails has to be kept up, doesn't it?

But a man feels he has to grumble. He has to? All right, let him grumble.

"Why do you need a new station wagon, now?" grumbles Joe.

"I need a new station wagon? All the groceries I buy for myself I could carry on a scooter. You want to do the shopping?" is how Beth puts it to him, pithily.

Of course the new wagon has more room in it than the old one, but that's not the point, the point is that it's a new one. What man wants his wife to drive around an old heap of junk already over two years old?

"And the insurance is due next month, too," Joe concludes. This is supposed to be Beth's fault. As though Beth had demanded that he arrange quarterly payments, let him pay it annually like the fire and burglary insurance, or semi-annually, whichever is the most convenient for him, as she points out. And he talks about her clothes! A man can wear a suit from one year's end to another, as long as he remembers to have it cleaned and pressed regularly, but that's just not the way women's clothes are. And that goes for every kind of clothes, from underwear to fur, as well as accessories, wouldn't you agree? Of course!

"No, I don't want you to make your panties out of flour bags" says Joe, "but what in the hell do all these bills have to do with wearing underwear made out of—?"

"I'm sorry about the bills, Joe," she says contritely, and points out that if he put more money in her account she could pay cash.

And sometimes it is necessary for her to tell him not to raise his voice to her. You just don't let them get away with it, that's all. If they say no you have to keep after them until they say yes, and if they try to get away then you stand in the doorway or you follow them into the bedroom. "Everybody in the neighborhood will hear you," says Joe.

"Everybody in the neighborhood will hear me? Then everybody in the neighborhood will hear me," says Beth, letting him know what his own words sound like. "If everybody in the neighborhood will hear me—"

Joe holds his head in his hands, because men love these little dramatic tricks, and pretends to groan and moan and then he says, "All right, all right, oh my God—Yes! Yes!" He opens his mouth again but is forestalled in his intended underhanded tricks by his long-suffering wife who quickly reminds him that everybody in the neighborhood will hear him, if he doesn't stop his shouting, and this never fails to shut him up.

"Just like a child," says Joan Raisen.

"They are just like children," agrees Joan Kaye.

And they caution one another.

"Never make a man jealous," they say, "there are better ways."

It is agreed that if there are no children, and there are as yet no children, then mention of more insurance should always be made casually. It is agreed that insurance is very important. And they squabble politely over the tab, and whose turn to pay it.

Beth is feeling so much better. Such afternoons are, after all, a form of therapy, wouldn't you agree? And how would Joe like to have to pay those kind of bills? So, Beth is sorry to deny her friends the pleasure, but insists that it is her treat. "My Aunt Simma," she just remarks in passing, before they part, "who is in many ways really an awful old woman, always used to say, 'Better insurance without a husband than a husband without insurance.'"

Her friends, nodding solemnly with raised eyebrows and lower lips tucked under, digest this...and then assure her, that, Yes, well, it is an awful thing to say, but...still...you know...

Beth has almost forgiven Joe by the time she gets home.

However, Beth is not the morbid type, and rather than let her mind dwell on such subjects, decides that Joe deserves a good break, something nice: something really, really nice. So she trades in her old car and buys an imported sportscar for him. Since the day she had her friends over for the special viewing on the then new house, Beth has never felt so happy. She anticipates the look on Joe's face…

But the look on Joe's face is not at all what she anticipated. Joe, in short, proves to be a real bastard and a son of a bitch about her lovely present for him. And he insists on holding some kind of senate hearing about it. How he can't use it for his work. How they already have two cars. How even if they sell one, what will it bring? As though Beth is supposed to be a goddamn blue book; how is she supposed to know how much it will bring? And how this and how that, and so all the pleasure she anticipated in driving the lovely little sports car is gone, it is just gone, and she breaks into tears. And he is still a son of a bitch! Not until Beth has completely lost control of herself and sprawls on the ground weeping in anguish does Joe decide that this time he has gone too far.

Joe looks at her and evidently he reads her mind through her face. She raises her head and touches her hair. "Oh, now, don't bring up that bull about sewing your underwear out of flour sacks," he says, with sadly misplaced humor. "Just try to remember that I'm not made of money—" Beth says nothing, she just looks at him. "Well, am I?" he asks.

No one could stand it, and Beth's iron control breaks down and she all but screams at him, "Yes! Yes! Yes, you are—you have to be! Somebody has to be! Who else should be? Me? Me?" And she clenches her fists and her jaws clench, and she says, beside herself, "You have to be made of money!"

Well, for a wonder! Joe does not carry on anymore: now that the facts of life have been laid before him, so to speak, all he says is, "So I have to be made of money…" And then he goes and takes some pill or capsules with milk and goes off to bed. And Beth—

And here comes the funny part. You have never heard anything as weird as this in all your life. Because after he drops off to sleep, or maybe before, it doesn't make any difference, Beth has this absolutely fantastic and incredible dream! She dreams that suddenly she is wide awake and some sort of little glow of light is in the room, not electricity and not moonlight, but enough to see by very clearly, and she goes and looks at Joe's bed and he is there, yes, but very, very different. In fact, in this dream there is this huge and enormous mass of money in the bed and it is shaped just like Joe! Joe is actually made of money. So in this dream Beth immediately gets up and tiptoes over and slips several bills off the pile where his stomach was, so to speak, thinking to herself, "Well...he weighs too much anyway." She giggles and opens a drawer in her dressing-table and slips two bills clearly identified as $500 each and one $1000 bill into a little purse she had there and closes it up and giggles to herself again and gets back into bed and goes to sleep.

Have you ever heard of such a thing? No, of course not, and neither has anyone else.

Next morning Joe seemed kind of tired and, not grouchy, just sort of, oh, slumpy. Hardly gave her a civil word! Maybe he hadn't slept well, if so, that's his problem, she didn't write those prescriptions. And yet Beth had this crazy sort of idea in her mind that Joe actually had been awake and had seen her take the money and put it in her purse and that after she went to sleep he got up and took it out and—oh, she couldn't imagine the rest of it. It was a crazy idea, but the more she thought of it the more she resented it: after all, it was her money. So what right did he have? And the more she thought about it, the more she resented it. Which is what effect a selfish husband can have upon even the most unselfish of wives.

Finally, as Joe was getting ready to leave, she simply informed him, "Joe, you won't forget to make a deposit in the bank, in my account?"

Give him credit, he didn't complain, he didn't raise his eyes, he just said, "How much?" and she said the first figure which popped into her mind, which was "two thousand" and he nodded. Which was very nice so she went over and gave him a kiss and a hug and of course he at once started getting ideas and of course Beth knew how to handle him and gave him a little pat and sent him off to work. So that was that and that was alright.

Well, two thousand dollars, to a child that is all the money in the world, but, after all, to an adult used to a moderate but respectable standard of living, what is two thousand dollars? Two thousand dollars is nothing. It would have been a perfect day if Beth hadn't taken pains to add up the cost of the few absolutely essential little accessories which it had been necessary to purchase for the sports car, and thus observed that the two thousand dollars was barely adequate to cover her expenditures. This is what is meant by maturity, a child imagines that two thousand dollars will last forever and is angry if it doesn't, but to a mature person the matter is otherwise.

Nevertheless this matter must have rested on Beth's mind because she had exactly the same sort of dream again; but whereas before in the funny dream Joe had been lying on his side, now he was lying on his back. His pajamas seemed made out of paper money and his legs and arms sticking out seemed made out of checks and it seemed as though his hands and feet were made out of gold coins, and his head too, except that his hair was money orders and his nails were silver coins. It sounds crazy but it was really the most realistic thing imaginable! Like—here's a tiny little detail which stuck in Beth's mind, just for an example—as she tiptoed over and in her dream stood looking down at Joe it seemed as though one of his eyes was just a little bit open the way it sometimes is with a person, even though he's asleep, and it seemed as though the eyeball was gleaming under the eye-lid. Actually, of course it was only an edge of a silver coin shining underneath a gold coin—but so real!

Well, it was all so silly that Beth, in her dream, could hardly help laughing but, thinking to herself that "business is business," she helped herself quickly to some money, only this time she observed what she was doing in greater particulars and this time she took $5000. She wondered, where should she put it this time, and the thought occurred to her, why not put it in the toes of one of the new shoes in her closet? And she glanced at Joe while she was crouching by the closet, but his pajama-top just kept on rising and falling just as if it was really a man breathing and not a pile of money in the shape of a man. Then she went back to bed and fell asleep.

Sure enough, next morning the shoes weren't in their usual neat lines but do you think that any money was in them? Not on your life! Beth had this idea again, just seemed to feel it; he'd been awake the entire time and looking at her and after she had fallen asleep he'd gotten up and taken the money! Oh, she was burned up! But...after all...what could she do? Face him with the facts? He'd deny it, of course he would; who was it who said, "If you find an honest man, breed him?" Some joke. So she took the only sensible action, she thought, Well, Beth, so you have a $5000 line of credit with your husband, so to speak, and she restricted her next credit purchases to that amount, and not for any inducement could she have been persuaded to exceed that sum.

And despite Joe's sneaky behavior in taking her money, let it be said to his credit that Joe did not complain about these bills, he merely paid them all in full for the new things, the envy of all her friends and family; not only because it was no more than right, but because it was his duty. The wife keeps the house and the husband pays for it. That is what is meant by equality.

◆ ◆ ◆

Anyway to avoid repetition, this same scene or variations on this or similar scenes, continued. Why Joe Braidel had to play this silly little game, Beth could not imagine; why he didn't simply say, I understand that there is an inflation, that I am married to a polished and sophisticated woman used to a certain standard of living which must on no account and under no circumstances be diminished. So therefore I am raising your allowance and increasing the household money, I am doubling and tripling both of them—why Joe did not simply say and do this, who indeed can tell? He didn't have the money? He did have the money, if he didn't have the money could Beth have spent it? But there you are, men are just like children, so immature, they have to play these games all the time in order to bolster their infantile egos. So Beth simply shrugged. If Joe wanted to play these foolish games in the world of dreams, well, go ahead. Some wives would have made scenes, but that is not Beth's way, another reason why she is so widely admired and envied.

Which is more than can be said for some people.

After Beth realized that her pent-up talents for creativity were now to have freer play and that Joe wasn't going to make silly fusses, well, for one thing, she had the entire house redecorated. To show how inconsiderate some people are, who showed up then but Joe's parents, sneaking and peeping nosily asking how much it was all going to cost and other matters none of their damned business. And then had the nerve to ask if she didn't think that Joe wasn't spending too much money.

"No, I certainly do not," was Beth's crisp answer.

And she let them know that she was not the kind of wife who interfered with her husband's desires.

However, the matter preyed upon her mind to such an extent that as soon as the redecorating was finished and completed, she simply had to yield to her fatigue, and went to the Bahamas for a month.

Upon her return, of course, needless to say that Joe was

overjoyed having her back, he was really very sweet. But once the novelty had worn off, who could say where things would be? In fact, so little had Joe gained in maturity, no sooner had he fallen asleep and was dead to the world, when Beth observed that once again she was indulging herself in the selfsame dream fantasy as before, once again she was imagining that he had turned into a big pile of money. Though one or two signs indicated that things were not quite as before. Although the outlines of this so called "body" in the bed were Joe's outlines, and the "body," in fact the corpus delectus, was composed of such things as treasury notes, government bonds, federal reserve notes, checks, money orders, and silver and gold coins; yet the pile was of lesser bulk. So Beth merely extracted the money needed to cover accumulated bills and perhaps an equal amount, or maybe even just a bit more to stay on the safe-side, as a contingency. And she put it all in the upper left-hand drawer of her vanity.

Feeling much, much better after this, and feeling fully able to cope with the problems of every day existence, she had now to face the fact that one reason why her husband seemed so restless and at the same time listless at home was that it still contained almost all of the same old junk which had come with them when they'd moved, more or less. So regardless of the toll which such exertions had always taken, Beth fearlessly began to tackle this next problem. Who could deny, therefore, that many of the obsolete items anyway, did not fit in with the house's brave new decor. The old order must change, or something like that.

But Joe's new attitude struck her like a thunderbolt, to wit; he informed her that he'd been advised on medical grounds to stop work, leave home, and to enter a small private hospital for what was obliquely termed "observation"! He added, as though it mattered, that his parents agreed. His parents! His mother, he meant! No wonder Joe was showing the strain.

But Beth had to steel herself on these points, though her

heart ached, because it would not only have been unfair to her, it would have been unfair to him. Imagine what a thing it would be if she had allowed a man of his age to begin yielding to his mother, for heaven's sake! A man's duty wasn't to his mother, was it? Of course not, ask any psychologist; a man's duty, first, last, and foremost, is to his wife. After all, was it for herself that Beth wanted new furniture and so on? Don't be ridiculous. But the fact is that she wanted it and so it was his duty to provide the wherewithal. When a wife wants something she has a right to have it, a man assumes this responsibility at marriage. It is his duty to care for his wife in all things and, if not, then that's his fault, and if it's his fault, then obviously it's not her fault.

And another thing, suppose Joe were to play this game of his about turning into a pile of money at night, right there in the hospital. How would it look to the doctors and the nurses? How? To have his ego destroyed in this manner by strangers? And therefore she couldn't consent. Why should strangers be plucking and pulling at him while he was in that condition? It would be simple robbery, because who could check up on them?

No!

"I didn't marry a man who's in the hospital," she reminds him. "I want a husband who's here at home when I need him," she says. "All the doctors want is your money; who owns that small private hospital? The doctors," she says, no longer able to control her emotions and, unlike her usual self, talking in a somewhat loud voice. "I'm the one who should be in the hospital, I'm the one who has the worry and the concern and aggravation. Sickness is for old men and I didn't marry an old man!" Sometimes it's necessary to be blunt. Sometimes you just have to tell them about it and hammer it home. "You'd better wake up before it's too late," Beth reminds him, aghast to realize that she is practically shouting—

—but, after all, it's not her fault—

And what does Joe do then? Sit there with tears crawling

down his face! How weak he is, she thinks, how weak he is. Beth is obliged to take control and for his own good make him admit she is right and he is wrong. "Yes," he says. "Yes, yes...yes..." And she gets him up to bed and brings him his medicine and brings him warm milk and she tucks him in and sits on the edge of the bed until she is ready to drop and finally he falls asleep. After all, what is a wife for?

However, Beth was gaining in maturity and ceasing to engage in projecting infantile fantasies. She was still dreaming that when asleep Joe turned to a pile of money, only with her decreased interest in the game, it was really not a pile any longer, it was just an outline on the bed. One layer of paper money and underneath were make-believe bones of gold coins. Beth stood there very thoughtfully. Just suppose that Joe did something unwise, such as spending the night somewhere else at a time when he was still under this delusion? This far-out possibility continued to prey upon her awareness, and it seemed that her entire life was just one worry after another. It wasn't fair, it wasn't fair.

So Beth, with a sigh she was unable to conceal, gathered all the money from the bed, every single bit of it, and she put it in her safety-box. However, at the last minute, with a shrug and a slight smile, because no one has a keener sense of humor than Beth, she withheld the tiniest coin, a two-dollar gold piece no bigger than a fingernail, and put it back on the bed. And then, unable to keep her eyes open any longer, she yawned and stretched...but no one was there to appreciate her exhaustion.

And so there you are. People talk so easily about tragedy and heart-ache, but do they even know what the words mean? Joan Raisen can tell you that people don't even know what they are talking about, and so can Joan Kaye. Between themselves they speak in whispers, they think that Beth can't hear them, but she hears them all right, even though she is under very heavy sedation, because it is a thing of the past that a woman should be expected to go through an ordeal of this sort without the protecting miracles of modern scientific medicine. Although she hears what they are whispering, nevertheless she doesn't mind, it doesn't matter. The only thing that matters is that she get through this very difficult period without breaking down. They are protecting her, she doesn't need to see other people at a time like this; what good would it do Beth? —old Mrs. Braidel, with her screaming and carrying on, as though she didn't have other children, and even grandchildren, and what is so much more important, she still has her own husband.

And not only her, the mother-in-law, but this horrible old man, Harry Goodworth, and an insurance-man is supposed to be a comfort to you at a time like this. But do you call this a comfort, the way he kept sneering and intimidating as though it was in some way Beth's fault that her husband was a mere shadow of himself, mere skin and bones so to speak, when he passed away?—as though it were Beth's fault somehow that it turned out that Joe had been milking his business and taking everything out of it and putting nothing back into it and how he had borrowed, borrowed, borrowed on the business and on the house and on the insurance policies and who knows for what? Who knows for what? Whether he was gambling or whether he was keeping a woman or whether he was taking drugs—until who knows what would be left for Beth if she hadn't been able to put aside a little something, and if she didn't have her jewelry and her this and that and a few other things? No.

No. Nobody needs old Goodworth hanging around and slandering the living and the dead. However, Beth is after all a young woman, she still has her good looks and her good friends, and they will look out for her. They will see to it that she has a good lawyer, and if Joe's family thinks for cne moment—

—but her friends don't want to raise their voices—Beth will find someone else. There are lots of good men who go along thinking that they will never get married but you would be surprised, a young widow with no children hanging around her neck—well, well, time enough to discuss that afterwards. As for Joe, who would have thought of it, so deceitful, so irresponsible and after everything she did for him...well, no doubt he had his purpose to fulfil in the world before he left it; that's what the greatest philosophers all say and we have to believe them.

GEORGE'S SHIRT

Originally published in Asimov's Science Fiction, *April 1995.*

Toward the end of day the animal-watcher's wife, whose name was Peggy, stood at the door of their pre-fab watching for the animal-watcher, whose name was George. The day was quite dim, later than usual, when, almost alarmed, she saw the white flash of George's shirt. She waved gaily and turned inside to light the lamps and do needless things—the needed things had all *been* done, really —to make the table ready for dinner. In the early days of their marriage in a city where everything was available, they lived in determined trendy squalor, eating on the floor; here, here, where Jungle and Savanna met, she lit candles on the dinner-table.

Dusk twilight and the gloaming, it was in fact later than he usually returned from his daily watch over the Rock Monkeys in the Zuli Woods. Then: as usual: quite without announcement, there he was. She never saw him emerge, but always suddenly he was there. She could make out almost nothing at this distance in this dim, but as he waved to her (she waved back) there was the flash of his white shirt. *White?* nay, but he would have it so. He said it was absolutely absurd to suppose that the Rockies were not perfectly aware that there was an alien crittur close nearby them and a khaki shirt made no matter at all. Across the intervening savanna, the equivalent of, say, several blocks, there was a low declivity or depression; it and the high grass enough to hide his figure after he stepped out of the Zuli Woods, a section of the great Malangwa Forest. Always at that first flash she waved, she seldom caught the wave back, nam port, this was the high point of the day...well...the second-highest...the evening meal.

To an extent, meals were planned a long while ahead: meals containing things they had brought with them—canned, dried, or fittable and keepable in the small kerosene-powered refrigerator. A pleasant note of novelty and freshness was added by what came with the fortnightly Cessna or the monthly Land Rover. Sometimes either one might bring a fresh fish or a fresh piece of meat, sometimes fruit for dessert or salad greens. And sometimes George had brought back something—a small plum-like thing several times—a chunky succulent once. "The Rockies were eating this," he'd said each time. "So it's got to be good." The "plum" was very nice: they decided to leave the greens to the Rock Monkeys. Who, after all, were why they themselves were here—

Who was at the door now?

As they embraced she said into his ear, "The figure entering the door was wearing a tussore silk suit and a solar topee. It was that of Hartley Vandergould, the man she loved." Well, that was the basic sentence, a part of her own family tradition since she and her older sister had read it together, howling with laughter, in a really shitty old cheap romance-novel which had belonged to Aunt Ednah (better not forget the *h*). Poor old Ednah had been a clandestine reader of these cheap romance-novels; she treated them as though they were pornographic; they poured from the closets when, after her death, the poor old lady's room was Cleaned Out. (Also in the back of one of the closets, buried in a box, was a slim folder made to look like a book: what it contained were six photographs showing—from various angles—a naked young man in, how shall we put this, upstanding good health. By the worn state of the pseudo-book's binding, and by the total absence of dust on that box alone of Closet Stuff, it was adduced that Aunt Ednah had looked into it very very often; poor old Ednah). That was the basic, or original, sentence; Peggy often used variations, "The figure entering the door *was* wearing a pickelhaube helmet and sky-blue golf-knickers. It was that of Bernardo O'Schimmelpfennig—" or, "The figure entering the door was wearing a racoon-skin coat and an Eton Boater—"

"Had a busy day at the office, dear?" that was one of his contributions (it, the pre-fab, actually was her "office") to The Canon. They weren't rich, but they had lots of fun.

Lots.

And...*Question*: Who *washed* those white shirts? *Answer*: All clothes were jointly washed, jointly rinsed, jointly wrenched dry, and also jointly hanged up on the line. Hoyts *you?* (how's your joint?)

The grant for this four-month period of Rock Monkey-watching had come from the C.D. Bridges Foundation for Primate Ethology (*no n*); old Cecil Davies Bridges it was who first set a watch over the primates, sending Glady Senlac to peer down upon the Gibbon (later, the Gorilla); Emma Anderson to go and spy on the Lemur; Enid Grool to observe *Tuan* Orang Utan; and Doctor Alys Elwyn to overlook, first, the Langur, then the Chimpanzee—and God help any biped who forgot the *Doctor*. It is seen that all of these were women; old C.D. said that he was sure that women would *bond* (his word) more easily with the wild primates than men would. Women were gentler, said old C.D. They were less likely to disturb the Alpha Male (his phrase) by their mere presence. Their voices were softer and less disturbing (C.D. had perhaps never heard the voice of a woman scorned? Perhaps he never *had*, it being unlikely that he had ever scorned one; so one had heard)...and here old C.D. (smiled) (smirked) (leered) [*one*]...also, said he, they *smelled* better. Said he. Some said that Cecil Davies Bridges, primate ethology's Grand Old

Man, was a Dirty Old Man; some, that he knew more than he was saying; but the point was mooted and the voice was muted by that sudden, violent, and still mysterious death in the tent hard upon the borders of the bush in the upper Utenanguo. The Foundation had offered the Rock Monkey grant to Peggy no sooner had the Old Man been buried a hundred yards from the site of the tent, buried much deeper than any quasi-urban grave—for—for more than once had he quoted Kipling's poem—

> *After the burial parties leave*
> *And the baffled kites have fled;*
> *The wise hyaenas come out at eve*
> *To take account of our dead.*

—had he some unvoiced fear, doughty old Cecil? else why had he even whilst alive selected the very stones (very large stones) to be piled between coffin and grave-mound? eh?

> *How he died and why he died*
> *Troubles them not a whit,*
> *They snout the bushes and stones aside*
> *And dig till they come to it*

But Cecil Davies Bridges had taken account of *them*, and by now, baffled, they must long since have given up any hope for *his* old bones.

No sooner had the Old Man been buried, then, than a faction in the Foundation had come out for George. And not Peggy. But he and she persuaded a joint grant out of the Trustees.

"They are, yes, equally qualified," said the Trustees, at length equally agreed. Whittaker said so. Szabo said so, too.

And, at last in *situ*, she revealed a painfully kept secret. "I didn't either *wrench my ankle*," she said, showing him the swollen joint. "You aren't either ever *too young to have arthritis*. 'See a doctor at once,' poo. Is the sight of one therapeutic? Time for all that later. This opportunity won't occur again...or it won't if we give it up now." She gave the foot an annoyed jiggle and at once at once she yelped. "Oh, George," she moaned, "I can't trudge, I can't crouch or squat or kneel or fold my legs. *You* take the notes. *I'll* write them up."

"Equally important," said George, stroking her arm. Was he being gallant? No. Just truthful. For far more than mere transcription was involved. Repetitions must be made sense of, patterns recognized, effects adduced from causes. Initiation separated from cycle. Hypothesis. Demonstration, well, you couldn't exactly always get the Rock Monkey or any other animal to *demonstrate*. Oh, sure, you could leave a lady-finger or a fig-newton out on a rock, and the Rock Monkeys would demonstrate that they would find lady-fingers or fig-newtons edible. But for this, one did not cross miles and miles (leagues and *leagues?*) of golden grass suddenly and very fast. The savanna had lost more and more of its green and gained more and more of its golden, before the heat had reached major shimmer, and long before everything bowed before the rain and the wind, they would have taken down the pre-fab, packed neatly, buried and burned neatly, and gone. Gone by Land Rover, gone by lorry, gone by Cessna. *Gone.*

Would the Rocksters long before then have gotten quite, quite used to George and his white shirt? "One must hope," said George. "The court is certainly entitled to hope," he said. And would the monks, the monks, notice his absence and wonder or even pine, and if so, so for how long? "¿Queen sabu," George said. George said, "¿Queen sabu?"

"Dinnah!" he says, rubbing his mitts. If one had a vision of the two of them dining off wart-hog or even bush-beef, nyamas, which either one had shot somewhere roundabout with a rifle or shotgun or even for that matter an arbalest or arquebus; well...no. The last of the Fresh Vetch, carefully saved, was, well-oiled, in a bowl; so was the last of the Hobbled Eggs, so was the 1st of the pinocchio-cans, well anyway its contents. Mr. Ramchand of the shop of that name in the District Capital was very nice and did his best to brighten the corner where they were, with fresh-baked bread when it fit in with this shedjul or with that; he saved them special jars of chutney made by his sister-in-law's sister down in Durban, and if, rarely, there was a rump-steak from a rump which had not perished of acute senility: that, too. Koejavels in stroep, that, too. And if a can of the exceedingly scarce anchovy came slipping up over the horizon, Mr. Ramchand (in secret they called him *Little Mr. Ramchand*) would whip out of the shop and bag it with his slipper. But however willing and able he might be, his command of Italian was not copious; who cared. If the price of cans of anchovies for the salads depended on Peggy and George calling them pinocchios, well why the hell *not*.

Now and then, until evidently they went out of season, the sweet little fruit they called rock-plums, for dessert; now and then some so-called *pudding* or *custard* or *flan*, confected out of a package and by means of reconstituted milk and purified water. Louisa, a highly educated colleague who was English or anyway *Manx*, Louisa professed in civilized places to look down on such *sweets*, was *sweet* qauite U? as being both middle class and having no flavour. But Peggy and George being American/Canadian, didn't have to worry about the class structure or the class struggle, they really looked upon the desserts as camp, Sotch Fon. Whir-whir with the egg-beater. Rattle. Splush. Not *a* sweet. *Sweet*. Num.

Speaking of Louisa, Peggy [recalling conversation]: "...and she wanted to know why all the way up here to watch the Rocksters in the Zuli Woods, when the ones in the Tenguato North were nearer? why that's just it I told her—*white man if you touch that last pinocchio you* **die**—I told her that's just it, it's *too* near, here we'll split that, the Tenguato, it's a relict population, maybe it's too inbred and its behavior patterns affected, maybe they're affected by the nearnesses, don't you see—"

"*Right—okay, and you can have the heel of the last egg, then.*"

So they, Peggy and George, chose the Zuli and its Rock Monkeys and hoped they'd be more numerous, healthier, unaffected, and so on. Not made goosey and afraid of people, afraid even of harmless animal watchers, not made fearful of George and Peggy because of hunters and trappers and poachers...phoTOGraphers!

Full five years later it was still a scandal a group of Continental European magazine photographers had deliberately spooked a troop of Rock Monkeys in the Tenguato North in order to snap them in living motion as they fled, their grey eminences despoiled by terror and alarm. The Secret Tradition had it that, one night after these rogues had returned to Uru, the U Ten North capital-town, and laxly spread their story; the Secret Tradition had it that all the primatology people then in Uru (well...all the *men*) had gathered after midnight and solemnly and successively pissed into the gas tank of the scoundrel photographers' safari wagon: thus causing them to blow their budget on repairs, miss the targeted issue of the (spit) mag, fail to get their respective next assignment: and serve them all bloody well right. Nyaa.

"*That*'s what I wrote her," Peggy concluded. And at once began another story.

Would observing the Monkey People without of course disturbing them, *would* it help the Human People understand themselves? understand love, hate, communality, commensality, quarreling, sharing, *not* sharing, crime, punishment, the passion between the sexes, child-rearing, rivalry...? The primate ethologists sure hoped it would. One must hope, said they. Cain and Abel, War and Peace? Entitled to try, said they. They said, nothing to lose...

Tomorrow was Sunday, *did* Peggy and George read the Bible? Sometimes they did, but never in relation to its being Sunday. Read the Bible on the Lord's Day? Alas no they *didn't*. Why not. *Not enough about monkeys in it*, George answered the single missionary who, unsolicitate, asked them about it. Slightly surprised, said he, "The Bible doesn't mention monkeys. The Bible mentions *apes*." *Well there you are*, said George. Made no sense? no it *did*n't. Bless you.

"Say, Sunday tomorrow. Wash day." They used a cleaned-out oil-drum cut lengthwise, water by bucket from the spring, and a plumber's helper and a long pole. They washed George's white shirts and his skivvies, and they washed what Peggy called her Dainty Underthings: the same sort of skivvies as George wore. What if I wore a bra? he asked, for answer she grabbed his crotch. Not *too* hard.

"Fine. Say, can we have something to eat afterward with garlic?"

"Great. Hey *two* good reasons to make love *tonight!*"

Having a decent respect for the English language they did not say, *Have sex*. Too bad about those who do, probably name their sons *Darren* and their daughters *Misti*. Whither goes The Language? down, down, down. Male gender. Female child. Common hangperson. *Down*.

Making love by the moonlight which poured through the gauze curtain of the window in the small pre-fab, Peggy saw...Peggy thought she saw...influence, she told herself later, of her puritan grandmother, who could only copulate behind a locked door in an otherwise empty house... something at the window. She gave an involuntary small sound and a start of surprise or alarm. George must have thought it (if he thought then at all) thought it a part of the passion, not only never stopped, never paused. In a moment, she had also forgotten.

◆ ◆ ◆

"Hey," said George one night, reaching for a British pickle: "hey, who is it said, 'Imitation is the sincerest form of flattery'? Is it Oscar Wilde?" he bit into the cowcumber.

She waited for him to mutter, as he always did, Too much vinegar and no discernable garlic at all, before answering, "It usually is."

He pointed to her whilst turning face to someone not there, Stage Left, "Say, not *bad*. Worthy of *him*." The smile vanished off his face and the rest of the morsel stayed unchewed.

Their eyes met. He broke contact, brought it back again, turned his head for the tea-pot. Coffee for breakfast: for supper, tea. *U*sually. But there had been some miscalculation of supplies, and, oh, what the hell *diff*erence did it make? "If you talk," said she, level-voiced, "I will listen." Actually, the meal was Sunday Lunch, and a coin had been tossed: what to drink. Actually, what Maugham called, *that delightful meal which in Borneo is called brunch*, when he was not forgetfully calling it, *that delightful meal which in Malaya is called brunch*. Old fart. Insisting almost to the end that he wrote for hours every morning, did he *burn* twenty years' worth of writings? if not, then what had he *written?* mash-notes to sailors, probably. One single slim late flower in an empty jam-jar on the table, George had brought it back with him. The figure now coming through the door with a flower between his teeth—

"Something in the woods is watching me," George now said. Very quietly. Finished his mouthful. Poured tea. Drank.

Tick. Tock. Grandmother had always liked a very audible clock. "It is like another person in the room," said she. Tock, Tick. "What could be watching you, George?"

"Nothing," he said. "Tea too strong." Added hot water from the thermos. Took a slice of bread and applied some New Zealand butter, the NZ butter had been dehydrated if that was the word, and could not be fried; could be smeared, though. All this while she had not asked a question, neither by voice nor face: he always preferred it that way. "Of course nothing could be watching me in the woods. Nevertheless, I *think* something *is*. I think, therefore I am." He looked straight at her, raised his eyebrows. Turned back to the food, atop the New Zealand butter put Australian jam. Slightly gesturing to the canned corned beef (Nigeria), he said, "A veritable Commonwealth meal, ah the British mustard."

"Stay home tomorrow, George."

"Old Man Coleman...the Mustard King?...said that he made his millions not out of the mustard that the people ate, but—"

"Stay home tomorrow, George. Be sick, or fake the notes."

"...but out of the mustard the people left on their plates; I have never faked a day off sick and I have never faked a single note and I never will. Never so weary a river but winds somewhere safe to sea; put on a record. How about Nilson, *Nobody* Cares *About the* Rail*roads* Any *more*—"

While she was putting on the record, of a sudden didn't she glance in the mirror, there he was looking hard at the calendar. There were, she knew, full three weeks before they were to break bivouac. Such is our human lack of accommodation to the immutability of time that often and often we try to mute it. Mu*tate* it? look at the calendar oft and long enough, and who knows? maybe the Pope or Parliament would have fiddled with it again, this time maybe giving everybody a couple of weeks more instead of less; is there something wrong with the arithmetic of the concept? *oh* well. Nilson's mellow melancholy voice sang about the railroads, but, like just about all of the mourners for the old trains sang nothing about the stale air, the tepid water with flecks of soot, the ugly surly trainmen, the dirt dirt dirt...

Not until supper did she ask, why the question about imitation being the sincerest form of flattery. He sat up very abruptly and hissed in his breath. "It's a coarse, gross, totally stupid anecdote, I'm *not* glad you asked, but it is a reasonable question, so—I had to squat...who or where is it,

Even Caesar squats to cuck...?" but here she couldn't help him, sure only that it wasn't Oscar Wilde; "...and as always I dug a hole, right? and afterward I covered it up...as always...I even remembered that on the spur of the moment I kicked up a little divot, a hunk of turf, and planted it on top with a bawdy jovial comment. This was to the right of my pitch. *Okay*. That was *Thurs*day. As I came along on *Fri*day, just before I got in sight of my pitch, ah, well, somehow I thought there was just a slight scuffle in the bush. Very *slight*. And just the slightest wavering in the shrubbery. So. I set up my gear...as usual... and, ah, well, an impulse...nothing more....Just a few feet off the path, uh, to the left of my pitch—"

"To the *left*—"

"To the left—there was a hole...some...some entity," how slowly he pronounced that word: not *someone...something... some entity*...had dug a hole (George said, speaking very slowly), "Not dug it as well. *No* boy, nowhere near as well. But. Had. Dug. A hole. Dug it for the same purpose—"

Very quickly: How did he *know?*

Very slowly: Had. Used. It. For. The. Same. Purpose. *And* (pause)—

"Had missed it. Missed the hole, I mean.—*I* know what you're going to ask. 'Could it have been me? Couldn't I have forgotten?' Answer: No. I couldn't have. One thing, no tee pee. Another," and he gave her another reason; it was, as he had forewarned, coarse, gross. It was, also, entirely convincing. Unasked, he reviewed other possibilities; dismissed them. It was not the spoor, the scat, of the rock-monkeys. Nor of the colobus nor the vervet. Chimpanzees? had either of them ever seen or even heard of any in the region? No. Gorilla? None in any direction for hundreds of miles. A silence. She next asked, "Baboon?"

Quickly, "This is not baboon country."

A longer silence. "Now...this may seem silly...but could it be a rogue?"

A rogue baboon? All the way over here? What did one

know of such? Was there ever such? "When you've dismissed the impossible," George said, "what remains, however improbable, must be the truth. Or something like that, *Hound of the—*" He did not finish, ended on a questioning tone. *Some*where in Sherlock Holmes, she murmured. And then, as she pushed over to him, with a you-finish-it gesture, the remains of the can of corned beef hash, and he shook his head a short shake and pushed it away; then, thus engaged with just about the most unmysterious object in the world, a can of corned beef *hash*, for God's sake!, almost simultaneously they exclaimed, "What remains?"

And then they stared at one another.

Next day, "I'm coming with you today, George—"

"No you're *not!*"

"I'm coming *with*—"

As she came forward, reaching for her pack (he had of course observed it before), just then, then, just then, her traitor body let both hip and thigh go *Ohh!* and she half-turned to the support of the chair; he was there in a moment, helped her sit. She wept. Not very deeply, it is true, but she did weep. "Stay here today, George," she begged, "I am sick. I need you. Take today off," and she pleaded, she pleaded; he nothing her heeded. He was all Resolution. The horse bucks you off? Mount it and ride again. You fall down? Don't just lie there: get up. She watched the flash of the white shirt, then she watched for the flash of the white shirt, then she held a good thought for the white shirt, and for George, who wore it.

They reappeared at the usual hour, George and the shirt, vanished as usual; inside she made all ready as usual. "The figure coming through the door," she said, hugging him, hugging him, "and wearing a flower-pot hat and a rose between his teeth, was that of Sebastian Wigglebottom, the man she loved…" Hugged him. Hugged him.

And what happened *that* day in the woods? Oh nothing said he. George. "Probably I am suffering merely from a sort of subscutaneous dissatisfaction with myself or my career, only nor*mahl*, maybe not so much dissatisfaction as uncertainty, only to be expected as a passing phase in a man on the brink of his thirty-fourth year, wouldn't you agree? I mean, next year I'll be thirty-*five*. And you know what *that* means. The oldtime peoples had it figured out. If the days of our years are three-score and ten, equals seventy, then half-way there, eye-ee thirty-five, why that's middle age, Don't it figure? And who knows what then?"

At once, reflexively, as though goosed, Peggy said, "And then you meet Dante in the woods, and he leads you down through hell!" So soon as she had said it, see him blink furiously, his face fall, his jaw tremble. At once he caught control of himself: at *once*—

At once she literally laid her head upon his breast, said she was *sorry*. She was *sorry* she'd said that. Oh George. What does a man do, when a woman lays her head upon his breast? He embraces her, no? And says, Why never mind. "Why never mind, she-person. *That* would be all right. Nothing wrong with *that*. So now it's clear. Sometime after I turn thirty-five I will write my epic opus. George's *Commedia. The Monkeyana*. Say, what's for supper? I love you madly," he added, quickly.

Supper? For supper was tinned tongue, a product of Botswana. Hamming it up, Botswana *East*, says Peg. Oh that's great, says he. If there is one thing he can't stand, it's tinned tongue from Botswana *West*. "And let me mix up some exotic Coleman's Mustard in the wee mustard pottle." Sitting at meat, he commends the jelly in the tin. Eats. Silently. Of a sudden asks, "Say. Where is that folder of the Old Man's stuff?"

"In the red box," Peggy gestures. "Why?"

"Tell you by and by." He gets up and places the dirtied meat plates in the dish-pan. Sits. *She* gets up, dishes out the dessert. Koejawels in Stroep? Guayabas in Almimbar? Guavas in Syrup? Something like that. "Time for another rayroe record," says George. "You ready for another rayroe record? How about Lowell Moore singing *Ten Years Ago on a Cold Dark Night...?*" The stickyfruit is savored, juicydrop by juicydrop. *The judge said, Son, have you an alibi? If you were somewhere else, then you don't have to die. But I said not a word, though it cost my life. For I had been in the arms, of my best friend's wife...*Although what that all had to do with the handbrake, the high-ball, and the journalbox-lunch, scholars have yet to determine.

Dishes washed, dishes put away. Ready on the right, ready on the left. The nocturnal insects are courting in the noct. The red box with the odd, that is, the not-really-required-for-the-project notes, is gotten out. "Wasn't there a pale-yellow folder? I thought there was a pale-yellow—"

"The Old Man's stuff? Yes...there was...*here* it is..."

There it was. The Project no longer uses pale-yellow folders, (a) Dr. A. Stewart Kydd, successor-pro-tem, didn't *like* the pale yellow folder, for doubtless sound reasons known (only) to Dr. A. Stewart Kydd; (b) the firm which mfged them in, of all places, Water*loo*/Ont (no period), of a sudden raised its prices. "*There* you go." Said George, Sundry, mostly, xeroxes. Xeroces? Some photographs. Some (ancient, crumbly) photo*stat*, the half-way state, white on black: a *great* way to go blind: some ineffable effing son of a bitch was too cheap to pay the extra cent to rephotostat them and make them black on white. "Yes, my children," Peggy murmured, "There was Life before the Xerox and the Canon-copier. And that was why scholars and authors were called *ink*-stained wretches," and she pointed to a smudge in the corner of a page of old Cecil Bridges' sprawling hand-written notes, even before the ball-point pen. 'Twas he who'd given them the name of Rock Monkeys, before that they'd been known as Hagenbocker's Lesser Grey Macaque. Or something. Peg always says that George made that up.

"What do you make of this?" *this* is some white scrawls on a solid black background.

"Not much to make of. It's the GOM's, for sure"; *Grand Old Man* pronounced as one word, rhymes with Prom. "Just a Rocky. Gom wasn't really much of an artist, but it's a Rocky for sure, what else? A guenon? A proboscis? A macaque?—wasn't really much of an…gave *this* one a slight touch of personality, though, didn't he? Would you buy a second-hand peanut from this monkey?—just a Rocky, from down there in the Tenguato. Eh?"

Not so sure: George. And why not? Wellll…something about the proportion. Proportions. Suppose you saw a sketch of kitty and a tiger, without any markings on either, couldn't you tell which was which? Even with nothing to measure by, you'd note a difference between the proportions. Wouldn't you? eh? *Sure.* And then the record was turned over, and Lowell Moore sang to them about *The Wabash Cannonball.* George put the things back in the pale-yellow folder. Reluctantly? Maybe so. Maybe so.

The next day went as most days. She wrote up the notes… did she scan them extra-carefully? was she trying to read between the lines? in his observation that "Boris," the Alpha Male of Group A, during the time that the so-called *monkey-fruits* were at their prime, spent more than twice as much time eating without relieving himself than otherwise, did George mean to report anything except the observed facts themselves? and what about this, *this?* "Does the presence of Rocky hair at more than half the usual distance from the ground indicate that at times the Rocky will stand on its toes and extend body very much higher in order to use tree as scratching-post: *why?*" and was there something in the very principal physical body of that note which…And here, feeling for one thing very silly and for another like someone imitating an old-fashioned actor imitating William Gillette as Sherlock Holmes, here she did actually get out the large magnifying-glass and examine the paper of the notes. *Imitating...Imitating...imitation...!* hadn't George said something, well, asked something about that not so long ago? yes...George had...

The notes had been done in pencil, why not, even the best of inks might unavoidably prove to blur from a drop of unexpected sweat or leftover raindrop or lizard-piss. Pencil, also: easier to erase. Look there, *there*: certainly the paper roughened by an eraser...an erasure...what had been erased? Hold the paper at an *angle*, that inner voice, sharp as any shrew's, commanded her, commanded Peggy. So she did. The sunlight, sharp itself in a way that no Temperate sunlight ever is, very clearly exposed the lines of impression in the fibers of the paper, Dick Tracy would love it. She had never trained as an Investigator of Questioned Documents, but—well—she *had*. Trained. To look carefully at usual and unusual. And her conclusion was she would shave some of the point of that very soft lead pencil which she so much liked and he so much didn't, preferring the hard lead by far; would shave it carefully and sort of shake the black dust around on the paper of the notebook, and...and...

Rocky-like hair so high up, why? WHY?

What had his instant thought been, that it was not Rocky hair but only (*Only!*) "Rocky-like," and if so WHY?

Deceit came suddenly very naturally.

Deceit, she didn't mean deceit, she meant sneakiness.

They, George and Peg, Peggy and George, changed their shirts at least once a day. And George's shirt of yesterday was in the cardboard box in the corner; where would he have *put* the suspect bit of hair, in which *pocket*?

Of course he hadn't left the entire tuft there; where he'd hidden it and under what code-name was another well-to-be-asked question, but. *Here* it was, the softer and almost off-white outer hairs, just two were left; and the coarser and darker underhairs, just two were left; the combination giving a sort of a silvery color if you wanted to be romantic: sort of grey if you didn't. Exactly two of the underhairs. Left behind clinging to the interior of the pocket, always by some universal law dating back to the looms of the Pharaohs and the Kenites, always somehow rougher than the outside of any pocket: just four hairs clutched and left behind. Coarser? They were all coarser? Kitty and the tiger. "Pile," such study was called. Such a subject was called "Pile." Pile was not much emphasized, they were ethologists and not zoölogists, weren't they? Study of Pile was important in matters of classification, but they were not (Peggy and George) taxonomists—old Kinsey was a taxonomist, had been a great authority on the classification of the gall-wasp before sliding slowly over to the consideration of the hot hump and thrust of human sexuality—what had made her think of *him?* of *that?* of "Murder and sex and other dreadful things," Grandmother had said once, fretfully summing up the content of the daily newspapers; and, at the same time, summing up Grandmother, or—rather—Grandmother's mind. Peggy and George were not taxonomists. NO.

Peggy and George were ethologists (no *n* for God's sake! "No mask? *No mask?*" no…no *n* in mask), they studied animal behavior; the way Physiologus had studied viper behavior? no, for old Phys had studied books: the Viper as Succubus. Incubus. Ick. She put the four unfair hairs back in the pocket and the shirt back in the box which served as soiled linen hamper. What is like is not exactly so. Not so? Maybe so.

She carefully washed her hands and carefully, not at all like Queen Victoria, sat down in her own camp-chair; there was a letter, what about it? A letter from Natalie, never to be in a rush to read a letter from Natalie, usually telling you more about penguins than you wanted to know, and so a letter from Natalie was usually set aside. Hypothetical postcard with the Mouth of the Zaire on its front: *Dear Natalie, Your letter was eaten by an aardvark* (aardvarks in

Zaire? nam port. change the thought), *and so, alas—*

The letter had her rubrico or cartouche, Assistant Nathan cartographed or at least cursived just above the heavily engraved words *THE MUSEUM OF NATURAL PHILOSOPHY*; it meant merely that Nat was an assistant (oldspeak: secretary) to some Third Associate Curator of Stuff, but it gave, inexorably, the notion that somewhere in the mazy bowels of Old Nat Phiz there was a Chief-Nathan and a Vice-Nathan and a row of Assistant-Nathans, of which Natalie Winifred Nathan was naturally first among equals in the ranks. The Old Nat Phiz, is there anyone capable of reading those words who has never heard of The Museum of Natural Philosophy? *natural philosophy* in the old sense of *physical science*: at a meeting already many years ago a new Director had said, perhaps too briskly, "We are going to have to change the *name* of this museum!" and an old Trustee had snapped, perhaps too brusquely, "Then you are going to have to change the method of financing the Director's pay, you might try peddling peanuts in the lobby next to the picture post cards —" Name had stayed, of course.

Of *course.*

When you are trying desperately to think of Something Else, a letter from Natalie is all kinds of a godsend.

And, in this case, the source of all kinds of welcome possibilities and conjectures. Peggy read it twice in grim purpose, set it aside, baked her never-failed-to-be-appreciated Grandma cookies, using the last of this and the last of that, including the sweet butter and the vanilla extract and the mango juice and Peggy's energy, resolve, and self-control. Then she read the letter once again and then a fourth and last time (for then) with growing hope lightening heart and mind.

The gloaming came and as it gloamed she stood in the doorway and she watched and she waited and then there came as always the flash of George's shirt as he waved, emerging from the brim and brink of the Zuli Woods; he vanished into The Dip as always, and, as always, she went and did This. That. The other thing. Table setting. Candles. Flower in the jar? Still fresh, well, fresh enough.

"The figure coming through the door wearing a sable pelisse and with a corncob stuck up the funnyhole was that of Herasim Efremovitch Cock*adood*ledo, the man she loved," as they embraced. It was a long embrace, and, even as she rejoiced in it, she felt with dismay the rigid muscles of his back and the tenseness of his hold and grasp. "What—" she began, stopped.

Like a character in some non-Academy-level movie, he wrenched the whiskey bottle from its station, poured far *far* too much of it into a glass, and drank most of it far too fast. "The life of man," he exclaimed, half he gasped, then finished it.

Several times that afternoon had she rehearsed how she'd open the subject, the newest subject. I've *read* Natalie's letter, was to have been one way. *Guess* what Natalie writes: another.

"Felt it watching me again," George said. Sank with one abrupt sinkage into his chair; hear the frame protest. Reached for the whiskey, shook his head; not much left. "Hey, the gin," he said. "Tonic? Some. Ice?" But please don't dawdle. "*Watch*ing me again." The gin went down almost as fast as the whiskey. "No, no more," he said. She hadn't asked. "Not yet," he said. "*Christ*," he said. His favorite bamboo back-scratcher? Snapped it—once, twice. "Why are you still standing *up*?" His face, turned full toward her, was defiantly blank: brows high, mouth tight, eyes wide. She sat. Gazed.

"Watched me this morning when I was taking off my shoe to get a pebble out. Could I turn? No.—Watched me this afternoon while I was taking off my shirt to catch a breeze. Could I go after him? No. And then...*that*!" almost he lunged out of his chair, the wind from the gesture as he swept his hand toward the flower in the jar caused a swerve and flicker to the candles: "Throw it *out*!"

No time to ask *Why?* with the squeeze on the word which indicates the asker knows damned well *Why?* No time and no purpose.

He had found the flower's mate lying directly in his path just a few feet from his pitch. Neatly, well, almost neatly, broken off. Know what that means? Did Peggy know what that *means?* Did Peggy ever ever see or hear an account of a Rocky or any known ape or monkey plucking a flower as a flower? A chimpanzee might pluck a stalk happening to have a flower on it, might pluck it in order to strip the leaves *and* flower off it so as to stick the bare stalk into a hole to probe for ants which it (chimp) would then lick off: but this stalk had everything on it, it was a stalk of the same flowering plant which he (George) had broken off to bring home.

"Not even any of the Nationals around the Zuli," *Nationals*, that was newspeak: *Natives* one would have said in former times; "Not even any of the Nationals around the Zuli Woods would even think of plucking a flowering stalk, just isn't part of their culture."

"Well, why—"

He didn't even try to suggest why. "Watched me while I stopped to take off my shoe and shake it and watched me while I stooped to put it on again, and went away and later on came back and watched me while I stood up to take my shirt off and then I know it went away I felt it go away and then just as I started to put the shirt back on I felt it watching me again—Hey. Maybe I'd better eat a meal, huh? Sorry for all this, huh?"

Useless to describe all the faces made while he was eating or all the attempts he made not to make any faces: when he was, as he often was, awkward, Peg did hear a voice, a level voice, almost in the very holes of her ears, *Sit closer to the table*, it said. *Use both hands*, it said. *Taste it before you add salt*, said the calm voice. It was the voice of Grandmother, dead thirteen years and yet speaking out of the midst of Peggy's girlhood in the same sane, calm, level voice with which, handing Peggy a copy, a copy of Marjorie May's Twelfth Birthday, courtesy of Kotex and its makers, she had said—

But now, oh so certainly, Peggy could not remember *what* the immensely good woman had said. That time.

"Natalie Nathan wrote that the Old Nat Phiz had finally gotten the Sandler Bequest straightened out and they are getting ready to consider the first award and Whittaker, Natalie says that Whittaker? wants to interpret that *One or more qualified candidates?* you know that line in the Bequest, she says that Whittaker wants to interpret it as a husband-and-wife team; and she says that Szabo is more or less agreeable and she says, Natalie I don't mean Szabo, says, So why don't you and I apply for it?"

Either George read her mind at one jump ahead or he saw through her mood like glass; "I've never left the work of a grant unfinished and I—"

"All the Rock-Monkeys in the *world* aren't worth—"

At length, at long length, after the high words, the tense ones, the near-shouts and quasi-cries have died down and the weepers have ceased to form on the guttering candles, it is agreed that an informal approach will be made about the Sandler Bequest and that they will. They *will*. Stick it *out*. As if nothing had happened. Was happening. Out of the way. There remained, after all, how many days? Odd how all at once neither one wanted to count the days left: damned odd. No taint as to Quitter would lie upon either of them. Peggy's arthritis? Developed during their stay here at Zuli, too bad, sure, but The Field was not essentially exclusive to the career, careers, of very experienced ethologists: particularly not if they had behind them the unquestionably grand éclat of the Sandler Bequest. The thing was not to draw attention to possible flaws, weaknesses, by any actions (or inactions) at all.

Hold fast, George and Peg. Peggy and George? Hold fast. Many a guid mon and woman had heard things which go boomp i' the nicht. Talk about it later, hey? Now—? For now

—? Stiff upper lip.

Stiff lower one, too.

The next day out?

Okay.

Day after?

Okay.

"There was the curious incident of the thermos bottle in the woods, though," George said.

"The—?"

"Must've neglected to tighten it real tightly. Or maybe hadn't poured the hot stuff into it here, soon as it hotted up. Too cool, I thought, when I poured. There. So: Poured it back. Made a little fire. Heated it hot enough in the old canteen cup. Drank it down with a toast to The Queen—"

"God bless her!"

And he said the cookies were great, too!

Of course Grandmother had never had any mango juice to add.

And every two weeks it somehow or other always happened that everyone would be going somewhere else and Grandmother would be alone in the house.

Except, of course, for Grandfather.

His flashing gesture as usual there where the woods left off, and all her little detailing-attended-to: but a swift wisdom made her at once aware that even time must have a stop and there are seasons for omitting even the most well-beloved of nonsense. So all she said, as they embraced, was, "The figure coming through the door was that of George... the man she loved..."

"He's back." Was all he said. George said only, "He's back." Not *it* or any other locution. *He*. Is back.

"You felt...him...watching...?"

"*Oh* yeah. *Oh* yeah. Not only that. Not only that. Remember

I told you how the stuff in the thermos had gotten cold? Yesterday? And I'd built a fire. Yes, well, it was just as small a fire as I could manage. I heaped up dry grass and twigs between two stones, didn't even need three. Came back there to my pitch today?" His voice this time didn't even rise by a note. "Oh, what did I do with the fire? Pissed it out.—Came back today. What. A few feet from the left of the pitch were two stones. And they weren't even set up evenly. But more-or-less piled up in between them was a pile of grass and sticks. Hap. Hazard. But there it was."

"George...oh..."

That was not all. A few feet from the *right* of the place where George pitched his non-existent tent as the base for his non-bird-watching, guess *what?* "Two *more* stones. Not that they matched. And...in between them?...Another pile of grass and sticks. And, oh I don't say Wherever I looked, because believe me that somehow I didn't care to wander around looking: must have been easily half a dozen of them. Stones. Sticks. Grass."

Silence. Silence. He didn't even go for the whiskey or the gin. *She* did. Made drinks for both of them. Stiff ones too.

"Cause and effect," George said. Sipped. Then drank deeply.

"You think he's figured it out?"

"*Oh* sure. 't's obvious. Of course he hasn't gotten it *all* figured out. Hasn't got it figured all out yet. Not yet. As yet, he can't make fire. But he's figured out that fire can be made." Neither he to her nor she to him, the next question: What next?

"Well," she said, by and by, "at least now you know it's really not your imagination—"

"Do I?"

Slowly Peg began a very token packing. Would only be a very few days. Then on the same day the Land Rover, the lorry, the Cessna would arrive. Everything they were taking away would be packed. Everything else would be buried. Or burned, burned completely and scientifically, so that after the next rains no unsightly shambles would remain. House would be gone as well as pitch. And the places where they had been would know them no more. George watched as she moved, in her symbolic movements, and he said nothing. Did he seem relieved? He seemed to be thinking. "Unless," he said, after a long while, "unless I'm recapitulating my own anthropology...or something..."

Everything in his pack was calculated down to the last pennyweight, and she did not want to disorient him even by that much. She diminished the provisions just slightly enough to allow for a few cookies. And it seemed that that was all.

At the door, he said, "There's always somewhat of a let-down when you break bivouac. Anyone who's ever soldiered can tell you that. That's natural. But no camp lasts forever. So don't fret." A few words, sounds of love, and he was gone.

On this today she could not concentrate on reading, even reading, his notes. Time for that. Time for that. She began again to work on the packing. Slowly. Slowly. No camp lasts forever. That was a good thing to remember. Truisms became truisms because they were true. And so the day passed. And the end of the day approached. She hoped it had been not a bad day. Whatever the meaning of it all. By and by she went to the door and stood there, enjoying the sounds and scents of declining day. By and by she saw the setting sun flash on George's shirt. Sighing with relief (for it *did* seem a little later than usual) she turned and went inside. Did her doings. Waited. A bit longer than...he must be tired. Or why was he dragging his foot like that? *Why*—She turned abruptly.

The figure coming through the door was wearing George's shirt, and one of George's shoes. But it was not George.

SACRIFICE

Originally published in The Magazine of Fantasy & Science Fiction, *February 1996.*

T hey started to gather at six o'clock. Sonya, who always got there first, at once went into the kitchen and made coffee, so there was a hot cup ready for Slauson's elderly cousin Willis when she arrived with the cakes and cookies. Ava came by and by and of course told them that she wanted nothing to eat or drink, but she was already contentedly eating and drinking when Arno drove up with, "my dears, *the* most succulent roast turkey (already sliced) which I have ever *made* and *you*. Have ever *tasted!*— and *where* is our dear old Slauson, may I ask," he demanded, setting down the vast plate.

"Where should he be?" asked Heimberger, striding in with wine and whiskey and filling the place with his vast bulk. "Upstairs, inserting semicolons in this year's epic opus: can a publisher sell semicolons? I have probably lost a thousand dollars for his every semicolon over the past twenty years! But I still have faith." His huge hairy fingers reached out and captured a glazed turkey-wing.

So they were all there when Farmer came in, pretending to shield his eyes and scout around. "And where is this year's or shall I say this month's Slauson's new friend? Hello Heimberger, Sonya, Ava, Arno, Willis...This time I drove five hundred miles to the reading, so it better be good, although," he lowered his voice, "I'm afraid it won't."

Willis, her voice by now almost quavering, so old she was, "Oh shame on you, Farmer. Shame on you."

"If he didn't waste *his* time and your *money*, Willie, on those so-called new friends of his," Ava began.

Arno didn't wait for her to finish. "Well, Slauson *will* just want to live in a house by the side of the *road* and be a friend to man and woman. They leech *onto* him, they *drain* him, they are *off*, one never *sees* them again, and then poor *Slauson* tries to *write*. And *tries* aannd *tries*..." He sighed, said, "A *teeny* taste of that cake, Willis. *Oh*. OH. *It*, is, so, *goood*! Willis, where do you *buy*—"

Slauson came in just at that moment.

"Are you all right, dear?" asked Ada. "You seem a trifle—"

"It is nothing," said Slauson. "I was in the cellar burying a body."

"Of your dead past, no doubt?"

Everybody chuckled empathetically and when the chuckles had quite died away Slauson cleared his throat and began to read.

He read for half an hour. He read for an hour. He read for an hour and a half. No one coughed. No one lit a cigarette. No one did anything connected with water. Slauson read for one hour and fifty-seven minutes. When he had done, the silence still went on.

Then Sonya began to scream and when the scream was understood to be *"Bravo!"* others joined her. Willie clapped her splayed arthritic paws. Ava kissed him repeatedly. Arno murmured passionate impossible murmurs in his ears; and Heimberger, mustache wet with tears, could only mutter, brokenly, "...morrow...contract...advance... greatest...escalator clause third hundred thousand..."

Finally Farmer's dry, critic's voice, slightly husky now, was heard to say, "—worth *any* sacrifice: For having written *that*, an entire life is not too much to have given!"

Hear, hear! they all cried, Willis thumping her cane on the floor.

Hear, hear!

VERGIL AND THE DUKOS: HIC INCLUSUS VITAM PERDIT
or, *The Imitations of the King*

Avram Davidson expert Gregory Feeley calls this Vergil Magus story an important one. You can learn more on The Avram Davidson Universe *podcast, Season 3, Episode 1, (https:// avramdavidsonuniverse.buzzsprout.com/). Originally published in* Asimov's Science Fiction, *September 1997.*

Sicharbus the Sidonian, on business in Néápoly, called upon his old friend-in-fire, now the Mage Vergil. And having talked of this and that and eaten many a snail and more than one mess of garlic and semsamum-seed querned a-moil in its own oil and dipped in with crusty Calabrian bread, they fell to talk of a few lesser things than the price of purple and the cost of calamus and coin-of-gold. For...*does gold buy silver? or does silver buy gold?*...to this question not all the sages of the Midland Sea can come to a conclusion; those who would cannot compound with those who would not; *Up* goes the one end of the quiver-plank. And *down* goes the tother: so. So see now Sicharbus, his yellow face assuming a serious look, and now hear Sicharbus make a sound as he nums his bread and dipping so as to make it known he intends to talk so soon as he does swallow; let none assume to speak until he is done.

The scene is the upper room at the seaward side, the

topmost floor in the house on the Street of the Horse-Jewelers. The view of the Voe of Naples is vast. Surely the guest means to speak of it to the host, surely the host has himself contrived it and thus deserves acclaim. Or else, like any Phoenician, this one in a moment may well speak of dye-stuff. And of dye. The price set aside, some words alike to, "Ayond the Gates of Gades, where the gryphons gyre—"

"Where do you *get* all these little pots of paints, frater mine? eh?"

Vergil spreads his dexter hand upon his bosom. *He?* Pots of paint, and little ones at that? Vergil wears a light shirt of *vinewool* distained with mallow-pink, that shade between madder and pourpre.

Says Sicharbus, he means *doors*. In his own country, in *his* country, doors are never painted. *What?* paint cedar-wood? "*Cedar*-wood to paint? In all the worlds beside the Great Sea, the Interterrains Sea, no wood like unto cedar-wood! Of course: *no*! Why would paint? For beauty? For comely? Cedar is by far the lovelier than paint. As for it should last, we don't daub it with painteries, we rubs upon it with wax. With a pure wax unfiltered from the best of bees, we rubs it, the cedars. But in the Greekly Lands, if Magna or Minora, cedar, much, they do not have. What have they? Oak, a some. Pine, such a much! And pine, though soft to cut, is quick to weather. *Much* preservation needs. All the bees in the Grecian, not sufficient wax could make. A natural thing: The Hellenes, the Achaeans also called—the Folk of the Oak, as make the Acorns—are lovers of paint. Paint they their marble, paint they their wood, all very bright—the Dans, also they are so-called—*Fear the Dans*, who it was it said that?" Vergil owned having heard it, did not know who had said it.

"In Grecia the doors are painted so brightly, your eyes they might put out with dazzle. But. *But.* From three-horned Sicilya past Néapoly north-ward even unto Romatown: what we see upon the doors? Here a bit of reddle paint, there a splotch of blue, somewhere else someone has a bit of green so he smears it as thin as it were tissue of gold. Always just a small of paint, always spread it thin, thin, so very very thin..."

Sicharbus quaffed a quaff of beer from the wooden quaff bound about with silvern bands, rolled his eyes above the rim to Vergil, put the drink down. "*Why*?" he demanded, "Why? Poverties? shortages? meannesses?"

Vergil laughed, slightly embarrassed. He had been obliged to acknowledge that what the Sidonian had said was true. But *why* the South Italian mode of smearing a muchness of a variety of cheap paints on doors, and of smearing it so very thin that it could have been of no use much in preserving the wood against the wear of weather and of time, at then he was not able to say. Only now did he know. Only now!

"Where is the ceremony being held this year, my don, my dan?"

"In the starry chamber, my ser proctor. Have not been there?"

Vergil paused, showed thought. "Yes. Once. My first time. I am sure I couldn't find my way there again. Someone was with me, who? you?"

Belladuc the Rhetor had been coaching Vergil in the Encantation, shook his head the *No.* "Was not me then. Cannot be me now. My sorrow. Seek the third right corridor from the atrium where they keep the waterjars, pursue it as far as the doors are green, go a left three doors, then through the red door, and—"

So then Vergil understood. The doors of Sicily and all Italy the South had been colored as a form of code for those who could not read. The doing once done had continued of itself, and by now most often had nothing to do with what purpose of which room behind where the door. Ah, well. As a Patrician he was in the pool of those liable for selection as proctors. More: he was a Doctor in Sorcery. And being in Rome, his name was drawn for proctorship at the Encantation of the Dukos. It would take place in the starry chamber. Behind the red door. The ceremony had twice before included him, and although he had been a somewhat touched, the one taking place today would touch him a deal more.

A good deal more.

The word was *dokos* in the Greek, but almost everyone in the Latin World pronounced it *dukos*; there was something said by subtle grammarians about *o* and *u* being sister-sounds, but—Vergil neither knew nor much he cared. What he did know was that among the *dukoi* at today's ceremony, one was that of Phillip of Assyria, whom Vergil had known, unlike any of the other and earlier ones Imitated.

Had known well.

And the other *dukos* had been Imitated from his friend Quintus, the inimitable and well-beloved *Quint*. Inimitable? But...he had *been* imitated. He *had* been. Both Phillip and Quint were dead...but their dukoi lived on. A conversation heard in the Collonades of Hercules, the sun slatting in between the pillars:

"...*Septimus...what?*"

"...made a *dukos*."

"It is death to make a *dukos*."

"Perhaps that is why he is dead. *He* is dead. But the *dukos* is still alive."

Phillip the Assyrian. A swart, saturnine fellow. Keen of mind. No one knew better than Phillip the art of making wine-presses, olive-presses, larger mills, water-wheels, mining-drills...war-engines and siege machines: 'twas these two last which (it was said...in the Herculian Collonnade... Apollo's Court...by the Steps of Woe...that enclave in the Aemilian Wall...at all places in Yellow Rome, in fact, where folk stopped to garrulize and gossip—"What say you, my ser? Nay, but merely we exchange information. Nay, but we just

—")...In Phillip's native hills and mountains rich in raisins, quince, pistuquim-nuts; so one had said to Vergil, oft was Phillip heard to laugh, head a-thrown back, teeth a-gleam: in Rome? Vergil had never even seen him smile. 'Twas his great gift and skill at making and even alone conjecturing making, siege machines and other engines of war, which had brought Phillip beyond the gates of death. *Far beyond the gates of death, dan Vergil*—! And Vergil had bent the corners of his lips a bittle. Just *Beyond,* was quite sufficient. Was it that the King of Alpha had feared Phillip would prepare sapping-devices for the benefit of his bitter, his most bitter enemy, the King of Beta? Had it been true that Count Gamma, a Sovereign and no merely Titular Count, had hired of Phillip a set of ballistas that would have caused the walls of the castello of Baron Delta to flake like so much pastry...but then had not paid for them, promising payment out of future booty— What! Do you doubt that your engines will work? Doubting, then, deserve no payment; get thee gone at once!—*Did* Delta suspect that, with purses of many coins of gold, Phillip might turn his hand and coat and, after all, return to Gamma—?

Intrigue has no limits. In such intrigues even a *dukos* of the Assyrian would well fit in. Silently Vergil sighed. "The atrium where they keep the waterjars," where *was* it? This place was an enormous rabbit-warren, really, one needed a warrener as guide; and Quint?

Phillip, however often seen, met, conversed with, scanned scrolls together, even—once or twice—worked upon a work together; Phillip after all was an acquaintance. Quintus was a friend.

Quintus was a friend from earliest days and years in Rome, Quintus with his bad eyes that never got better and perhaps because Quint could not refrain from eating the prescribed ointments instead of applying them to the insides of his eyelids ("Because the salves smelled and *tasted* so good!"), Quint who languished for the purling brooks when in the purlieus of Yellow Rome and languished for the roiling streets and quickstep scenes of the Capital of the World when in the leafy quiets of the rural scenes. Who much rather roses than gold. *Pecunia non det*; and rather nuzzle the armpits of the ugliest of women than press his nose to the fairest flowers in the rosebeds of Paestum "the double-blossoming"; who had first put himself out to help the very youngest of aspirant-sages when new in Rome from Brundusy? Quint. And who had adventured his own life on the open sea to save Vergil's, though any true Roman detesting said sea as violating the laws of nature by unstable and infirm composition? Quint; Quintus, Quinto, tied to him by a thousand hundred cords, and even one single thread would have sufficed: *He was my closest friend and I did love him.* Why had *he* died? and who had wanted to counterfeit a likeness and semblance of him and the way he moved and spoke and somewhat smiled, the merry look that hardly could it be resisted and the unmerry look that could never ever be resisted at all; who? Whose weekly letters, when they were apart were the joys of Vergil's weeks; and whose daily discourse when they saw one another day by day were the joys of Vergil's days? *Whose* mere glance told Vergil more than half a great chamberful of books in the Great Museum of Alexandertown? Quint's.

And now yet Quint was dead, surely he left no *larva*, no evil shade, behind him; surely to his *lar*, his goodly shade, one might offer grains of spelt and myrrh; why should some shambling and unclean reflection of a creature be suffered and endured to lurch up and down the Roman roads in Quint's own likeness, reproaching his death by its own life? *Not* to be allowed. Not.

This damned building ought not to be allowed, either. It was certainly not intended to have been builded as a labyrinth but the effect was certainly that. Formerly it had been a fortress, everyone knew that. Rounded so that enemies might have no corners behind which to hide or sneak, full of semi-secret passages even below ground-level, so that weapons, munitions, and stores might be kept in case of civil commotion or of siege; the colossal structure even had its own flora: a muckle of many plants that one saw nowhere else; and legends murmured that they had first come hither in bales of fodder and of feed for cavalry and cattle. Indeed, legend, not with this content, pushed back the origin of the enormous and baffling building even farther, said that it had been built as an amphitheater and that the strange plants had come thither as feeds for the wild beasts —And now? In the filthy corridors, pomegranate rinds and stones of jujube-fruits, peelings of the orangë, bitter-sweet.

"Are you here to do The Imitations of the King?" someone half-snarled half-barked at him, he knew that face with its unkempt beard and more than half-mad eyes: *Guido Porc* the man was called, a licensed warlock and an astrologue with an only semi-licet practique in sorcery: nigromanty pure (or impure!) some did not hesitate to say.

"No, I am here to do The Encantations of the *Dukos*—" but the man had with a further snarl passed on without pausing for to listen: thus he did. To put anyone off balance however slightly, to cause anyone an embarrassment however small, such things he regarded ('twould seem) as great victories, *Guido Porc*. So named, said some, for his swinish habits, his manner like a boar caught pissing; others said for his Brute, the porpentine, or Spiney Pig: motto, *Touch me not save with care*. Vergil strongly desired to touch him not forever. And —*What*? What was this, all a-scribble and a-scrawl, taking up line after line on the scrabbled, scumbled wall, skipping many a place where the plaistering had flaked and fallen off— what was *this*—?

HIC INCLUSUS VITAM PERDIT
THE ONE SHUT UP HERE LOSES LIFE.

He had not seen it on either of his two earlier visits, perhaps he'd been careless, perhaps it was put up since.

There was indeed a representation of the labyrinth, to call
it a *mural* would be to describe it higher than it...to call
it a *sketch* would be to call it by less than...It was rough.
Irregular. Vigorous. Unmistakable. And, unlike the average
representation, it had not one "center" but also two: unlike
most picturations it showed not alone the Minotaur, but his
twin brother, the Tauromine: not just the man with the head
of a bull, but the bull with the head of a man. Had those
twain ever met outside the womb? was the instant thought
in Vergil's mind, but he did not follow it—*follow it*—follow
it whither?—through the maze of the labyrinth? and within,
within, there walked the seus, Theseus, Theseus, sword in
one hand. And in the other he held the thread supplied him
as his guide by the Princess, and there stood *she*, outside the
maze.

> *Hic quem Creaticus edit*
> *Daedalus est Laberinthus*
> *de quo nullus vadere*
> *quivit qui fuit intus*
> *ni Theseus gratis Adrianae*
> *stamine intus**
> This that Cretan Daidalos
> brings forth is the Labyrinth
> from which nobody is able to
> walk out who once has been in
> except Theseus thanks to Ariadne
> with a thread inside.
>   —tr. Reno W. Odlin

The inscription was a little less crude than the art; not
much. Its purpose who could know. In so many cases a
graffito was merely a copy. An imitation. And perhaps even
this, atypical among the graffiti though it was, was, even so,
an imitation; perhaps of an original seen in perhaps Delphos.
Athens. On one of many of the gates of Many-Gated Thebes.

Or even in Candia, the *Crete* (so some scholars said) of Magno Homero, Father of Geography and Alchemy. One never knew with a graffito. Vergil had once been told by the occymist Clemens that he Clemens had spent an entire day on his side with a wax tablet and a dim and flaring lamp a-copying long lists of the Kings of the Etruscans, alleged to be encoded forms (as well as historical catalogues) of the engrediants for a certain philosophical experiment; only to find with increasing feeling: astonished, outrageoused, and aghast: that dynasty listed the names of *Cluny*, *Lupo*, and *Blungjum*, all well-known local Roman professional loafers—"To *think*!" cried Clemens, blowing out his vast moustachios, "of the waste of labor on *their* part, let along on *mine*, mine, MINE!" And, he demanded, "For what purpose, did they this? For a —what? For a *jape*—?" Clemens's mind could much conceive, but a jape, not.

And now the tufa of the corridor walls were no longer the black or grey or brown soft stone of the outer parts of the immense building or of those with some illumination from the much-encroached-upon atrium, second- and third-hand light as it were: but now the walls were made of orange tufa, as though by this brighter hue to make the dun less dim. And, as though some unwilling awareness that, *this will not do...this will not do...*every too many paces was a torch lisping in its socket. And by the light of one such he saw, far down the hall, a group entering a room with...indeed...prophetic Sicharbus...a reddled door. Should Vergil have hastened his steps? For why? None had any other pressing task that could compare to any pressing task that *he* might have; and he had none. The ceremony could not commence until he were there. For whose benefit indeed, any haste or hurry? *Slowly hasten*, had said the Emperor Julius II, he so fond of nibbling on stale bread, hard cheese, little fishes; had not hesitated to slay his own babe brother, no possible claimant for a throne at any future time to leave. Slowly hastened Vergil.

The Room was several rooms away from any direct shafts

of light and had a few several stands of many lamps, well-trimmed. The room had light-blue walls, the blue toned down with grey, door and framing were dull black. The ceiling was somewhat domed—concaved somewhat— and covered in darker blue and painted thickly with stars of a king's yellow, tending slightly toward a pale green: each yellow-green star with seven rays (the childish nature of the Guaramantes was nowhere better shown than by their simple belief that a star has but six rays! they have naturally made little or no progress in astrospection) and each star having the countenance of a saint: Jupiter St. Pluvius with tears running down for the sorrows of mankind and womanflesh, St. Thor Barbarossa giver of thunder and lightning the both essential for omens, Odin St. Cyclopes with one eye in the center of his brow, Thrice-great Hermes St. Mercury the messenger of good tidings, Saintly King Poseidon who rules the Realm Sea—all, and more, looked on, looked down, and it seemed that each face changed expression: cheeks moving, eyes widening or narrowing, mouths opening, closing, pursing. Rather larger than the other stars and formed in a triangulum:

Melcarth

Memnon   Minrod

All twinkled, scowled, frowned, leered. None smiled.

Vergil and the magistrates exchanged salutes. It was not indeed laid down in the Pandects of Numa that any court session must begin with the judge clearing his throat, nevertheless almost always it did. The proceedings proceeded. Witnesses' ears were touched. Doctor Procopiax, the Chief of the Physicians, forth came and testified as to what a *dukos* was, he pronouncing it *dokos*; that the making of a *dokos* (droned old Procopiax) or *simulacrum* required sperm, spittle, flesh, skin, phlegm, at the least ane strand of hair and ane cutting of the nails of finger or/and toe

—all these of the person intended to simulate or imitate—
that the manner in which these elements were acquired did
not affect the enterprise, that although at least one drop of
the blood had must need be that of the original *mannus,*
but that after that the main quantity of gore need only be
of any hot-blooded beast (of bird would not do), of bullock
was most commonly of use affected and that said gore must
be of approximate the weight of the mannus *ipso;* and that
this (drone drone) and this that (moan moan). *After* which
more or less Dr. Procopiax chanted or at least sang-song,
that the *primus,* the so-called Significant Tissue, rested nine
months in a sealed container at the warmth between that
of a man's rectum (if the speaker were of a modest not to
put it prudish nature, he might say, of a man's oxter)[4] and
that of a woman's privy orifice ("the which," averred the
Dr. Procopiax, "is well-known to be the hotter and in time
of emergency a source of publix fire"). This heat might be
supplied by some fired-chamber akin to the incubatoria of
the Ægyptians, but it must be kept steadily hot. *Or*, and
most commonly, it might be—the place of warmth used
—simply in the depths of a dung-heap, whose steady and
unvarying heat was commonly known to ripen cheese and,
less commonly, to be of avail in many alchemical procedures.

At the latter point of discourse Dr. Procopiax rather
abruptly stopped, there was at least a whisper in the lane
that a warning was issued to him, did he not, a bag might be
slipped over his head. "Having exstablished the nature of a
dokos," said he, it seemed a good reluctantly; "we now move
on to the matter of the evidence." Came forth witness who
testified that the *dukoi* were in the likenesses of one Phillip
of Assyria, "a subject of the Petty King of Courdistan the
same being a confœderate and ally of the Roman Emperor
and Empery; and of one Quinto Horatio Flacso, a Citizen of
Rome—[Vergil being Proctor in this case could not testify
of any knowledge known to him, *Not even under an inferior
title*, as now and then rarely the Emperor did]—I say, 'of one

Quinto Flacso a citizen of Rome, sometimes called "Horry,"""
thrimble thramble penis puffpaste Oh get *On* with it,
Thundering Jove! thou droning dunce! perhaps by reducing
emotional cases to the level of a bloody bore The Roman Law
meant to prevent the spread of litigation, "sometimes called
Quint," and here Vergil's head stopped its nod-nod-nodding
for that day and several.

Today was the day before the Lustrum, the quincennial
lustration, and all were in a hurry to get on with matters, the
two cases therefor being tried as one. Witnesses came forth
and pledged that may they be flayed and pegged if they had
not seen and heard the very likeness of Phillip the Assyrian
discussing the manufacture of that kind of catapult called an
isadoreion and at a time when the genuine said Phillip the
Assyrian was registering in Muro Luccano as being a member
of a pilgrimage to the Shrine of Fingers-Mercurius the Prince
of Thieves and Craftsmen. Came forth witness who swore
the very same and frightful oaths and deposed that they had
seen the semblance of a certain man they knew as Master
Quinto leaving from an apothecaries' shop with a small
pottle of a well-known eye-ointment and then in a litter gone
to the home of a Roman Matron the name of whom was not
to be mentioned by accord of the court and for the peace of
Rome. Nor allowed query, Did he impregnate her? ahem and
yet that very day videlixet the day before and so the
testimony dragged on. Many exempla could no doubt have
been give. Septimus the fabricator of the *dukoi* had been
questioned and had even displayed the means and the
instruments of his fabrications. He had of course been
tortured to get this cooperation and the fact of his next
having shown the officials the details of his crime was
merely another proof, no proof more being needed, of the
stern and salutory effects of the torture. But then something
unspeakably vile had happened. It had been intended that
Septimus should of course be burned alive. By secret bribery
he had gat two of the examining officials to connive at his

suicide, disguised as an accidence. The truth must out, and very shortly afterward the two malefactors themselves had been, first, tortured, and then burned. Above their screams the judges and all the crowd of spectators had recited the last line of every judicial procedure: *Rome has spoken, the matter is now concluded.* At that point most of the crowd left, the games being about to start. Only a handful of boys and their pedagogues remained, the boys being obliged to get the lesson of obedience thoroughly into their small bodies as well as being punished by not seeing the herd of monoceroids attacked by slaves mounted on ponies and armed with short lances. Several of the boys sniffled and wailed at the strict punishment for having neglected their lessons, but most bore it with a stoical attention boding well for their futures.

And as well stayed some minor criminals pleased to see the judgment of those who had formerly judged them. *There is a wheel turning in the world,* Quinto Flacso had often said.

And, "*Conceive!*" he'd also said at least once, "of a world crawling with *dukoi!*" and had shuddered.

The *dukos*-Phillip was staring with a deep intent upon the chamber's floor, just so had Vergil often seen the veridical-Phillip often stare upon some pattern scratched in sand. The false Phillip next raised his head, and, half, Vergil expected to hear him say, as so often the true one had, "Eh! Messer Vergil! Let us go off and discuss the matter further over cakes and wine. Eh? Messer Vergil?" Up came false Phillip's head, but his eyes slid past Vergil's as though Vergil had not been there. What a broil of intrigue and small war the life of this *dukos* had for at the last two years been! Enough, the report went, for two real lifetimes.

The *dukos*-Quint? It...he...he?...out of some vat slime and stenk with feculent blood no *he* could have come! *It* had been facing the wall with the blank face of the sleepwalker. Of some sudden second its eyes met Vergil's...creature's eyes as bloodshotten as the real Quint's oft had been...the idiot blankness left the face. Something moved upon the mouth, the gaze fell, the gaze half-rose, fell again the gaze. Some bad movement in Vergil's belly. Something caught his collions and bade them crawl. A shudder went quickly through the proctor's hair.

"Rome has spoken," the magistrates said, less raggedly than one might have assumed considering how unfashionable any voiced unison was among the judiciary. That such "sounded false," was all their explanation. Some few of them were not past giving what might pass for verisimilitude by clearing their throats, hawking phlegms, and other nasty acts "...now concluded," the magistrates said, no drop in voice indicating that, indeed, this was their very last set of words. Without any formula the stage and play passed to the proctor. Vergil was his name.

He took from its place in his doeskin budget a narrow case or quiver made of white eel-skin. The case itself was sometimes used to flog the sons of Patricians not yet old enough to wear the virile toga, for the white eel, said long ago the Senate, was not an animal: therefor its skin for such an use was lawful: not so, the black. Why? Who knows why? Rome had spoken, the matter was now concluded. Vergil drew forth the slender verge of mountain-ash wood, very old it was. Quite worn.

"*Dukos and simulacrum,*" he the proctor began reciting (to read this rite was not lawful)—

"*I, Vergil Marius Mago, as Proctor in Nullification of Sorcery, exsolve and absolve thee of all rule and regula imposed by your fabricator*"; the elder of the two simulacra, the Phillip-*dukos*, stood there, slumped, of a sudden looking very weary; "and in the name of the Senate and the Populus of Rome, I offer thee the choice offered to the innocent and the inculpable: wouldst will instanta to leave all toil and pain, returning unto quiet and to dust? or wouldst rather will become the Servitor of said Senate and Populus of Rome, assuming and subsuming all rule and regula thereof? Choose now, *now* choose: *Now*—"

Said the *Dukos*-Phillip, hands clasped before, head low, "I choose to will instanta for quiet and for dust."

With but the tip of the ashwood verge, Vergil Proctor touched the *dukos* so lightly on the crown of its head. "Fecit," said Vergil. A look of utmost gratification and of peace, something like that of a man in the instant of sexual surge and release, slipped instanta over the countenance of the *Dukos*-Phillip; in the same second its whole form sank inward and outward into its robe with a sound of a susurration and a moment the garment fluttered with the inflow of an ashy matter, then lay still upon the floor.

A moment's silence they gave the demise. Vergil then turned to the other. A curious small movement moved the lips of the Quinto-*dukos*; had Vergil not seen such a motion before? "*Dukos* and Simulacrum," he said. "As Proctor in Nullification of Sorcery, I exsolve and absolve thee of all rule and regula imposed by your fabricator"; *fabricator*, was that same Septimus who had kept his kip a-nigh the Steps of Woe where certain malefactors sat with the heads of animals—cow, swine, dog—a-top the shortened necks, they sat propped up holding their own severed heads in their own laps and a piece of rotten fruit clenched in teeth; "and in the names of the Senate and the Populus of Rome, I offer thee the choice offered to the innocent and the inculpable; wouldst will instanta to leave all toil and pain, returning unto quiet and to dust? or wouldst rather become the Servitor of said Senate and Populus of Rome, assuming and subsuming all rule and regula thereof? Choose now, *now* choose: *Now*—"

In that single second of silence there came again into Vergil's ears the question of the bristly lout called Guido Porc. There was a Great Mystic Doing done by the Emperor as Roman Roy and done but once a year and its ins and outs and complex pacings were more than he could do...sometimes... Sometimes he practiced on a simulated practice-ground... elsewhere...so as not to be seen by the general. A wise king, his temper controlled beneath his feet, would practice often (Averroës: every day). A weaker one would put it often off... and who might protest, "Your Splendor has said *Tomorrow* for many days now?" Now and then Rumor's many tongues reported that someone of the Emperor's build with a well-made mask of the Emperor's face performed the involved and stately steps in his place; if the crops failed the next year, were the Senate and the Temples struck by lightning, if a fleet sank on a day of no storm in waters where no shoals...were not the Immortal Saints of Rome justly vexed? Eventually the ceremony underwent a change...Someone went ahead of The King, The Emperor, The Roy, slowly pacing the steps... The Emperor, The King, close behind: imitated.

'Twas in the nature of things that the initiatory steps did not count, though copied. Only the imitation counted. Hence a phrase, The Imitations of the King. The King was not imitated. The King was imitating.

In the infinite swiftness of memory, Vergil now recalled discussing it with Quint once. Quint was being poor that year. They were drinking wine, Quint had poured, Vergil was sniffing and sipping, and...pausing, asked, quizzically, "Falernian?" "No," said Quint, "I can't afford Falernian now. It's just common wine, weak and thin, but I had it poured into the cask of the last Falernian vintage. So something of the scent and flavor of Old Falernian it has. Enough to make me remember older and happier days..."

Vergil still pausing now upon the question and the echo of his Answer *Now* still sounding in the ears, said the *Simulacrum*-Quint, simply, "SQPR." Senate and populus of Rome. Said Simulacrum-Quint. A well-familiar-voice. Vergil moved and touched the simulacre with the slender wooden wand, not—this time—upon the crown of the head, but on the right hand. The right hand for an instant blanched and blenched, its slight tan replaced by pallor, how black the much thin hair there. Then it flushed the dull color of deep madder, that right hand of counterfeit-Quint turned a dark dull red as of madder out of Maddergant or Maddergaunt, that Great Red She-Island that bleeds monthly into the Circumambient World-Stream, on one side the Afric Ocean and on the tother side the vast blue Indoo Sea; island eyket called Cernautis, Red Heber, Biltis-island, Island of the Rufous Ahyab, Roque-land; others. Thrawn, scrannel voice from out the night, *Sailing down the Courses of Azania...Come one...*

The proctor gestured and the thing with its tell-tale hand gan move out, soldiers alongside it, its stance now absolutely the slight slouch of the obedient slave. Vergil saw the eyes move toward him but before glances could meet, turn away. A life of perhaps no great toil or pain lay ahead of it. Perhaps. Clerk in a warehouse of the Fisc, tutor to some public ward. Perhaps, though, there lay ahead a life of stooping beneath sacks of flour or grain in the stifling air of a State mill. Or in a Storehouse of the Gabelle, arms and legs and mouth and eyelids red, raw, crusted, scabby, stacking slabs of salt. Condemned thus by his madder-hand: *He can never pass as man more*, Vergil thought, *not with that madder-hand; never.* So ran Vergil's thought, ran right after that one, this one: *He could wear gloves. He might fee a physician for a concealing skin-paint. Perhaps find employ as a dyer.*

The *Dukos and Simulacrum* reached the black-framed door, the Soldiery were old and tired and indifferent and did not push him on; commenced to pass beneath the lintel, slightly turned his head a bit. Vergil had not stopped looking. This time, briefly, briefly, their eyes did meet. *Hic inclusus Vitam Perdit.* The one shut up here loses life. *Ni Theseus gratis Adriane stamine intus.* Except Theseus thanks to Ariadne with a thread inside. What? *What?* But *how* escape, to do these things? was Vergil's question. Pseudo-Quinto, with a slight compression of his lips, turned again his head, seemed somehow to have given a slight nod, satisfied. And *I would help*, is how, was Vergil's answer. Not-quite-Quint passed through the door.

Rome has spoken, the matter is concluded.

Is it, then?

In another and more common version of the eternally familiar labyrinthal line, *the thread held by Ariadne.* The proctor had three names. None of them was Ariadne. But it was he who held the thread.

BLUNT

For this story, we have the good graces of Henry Wessells to thank. Henry maintains an Avram Davidson newsletter (check out www.avramdavidson.org for more information), and he has been assembling a bibliography of Avram's work. During the course of his investigations, he discovered a manuscript entitled The Corpsmen, *an unfinished novel from the mid-1950s that was Avram's first sustained attempt at a novel. The book consists of a series of loosely connected character sketches about members of the WWII Naval Medical Corps stationed in Mullet Bay, Florida, and one such sketch stands up well as a complete story. This story was originally published in* The Magazine of Fantasy & Science Fiction, *October/November 1998.*

He had the usual mountain boyhood in one of those mountainous counties below the Mason-Dixon line—differing from most other such counties only in being one of the few that regularly voted Republican—where there was not much schooling; but somewhere in the course of what schooling there was, Huey P. Blunt read a piece about yellow fever and the Panama Canal and how one was conquered so the other could be built, and he decided to be an Army doctor. Someone (in after years he tried to remember who first told him, but so many people had agreed and repeated it and everyone took it for granted it was correct) told him that the way to do it was to enlist soon's he was old enough and work his way up. Blunt wasn't talkative and he was six months in the Army before anyone there knew of his plans, and before he learned what they were worth. What they were worth officially, that is. He made them worth something, after all, by an illegal conversion of knowledge. He listened, he watched, he read, he worked; and he learned much. The Army Medical Corps taught him more than it planned to. Blunt had deft hands and a good memory.

After his enlistment expired he went back to the hills, to his home country. There was a very old man practicing medicine there, his name was Elnathan Wisonant, and he had never been to college either, having picked up all his knowledge of medicine as apprentice to his father, a "doctor" of similar status. At one time there were many practitioners of that kind around—it would not be accurate or fair to call them quacks—they represented an older tradition in native medicine than the A.M.A.—they supplied the only care available at a time when medical schools were few, and not too well thought of, either. Gradually they became extinct. For the last forty years of his career old Wisonant had been protected by a state law that exempted all those in the trade at the time the law was passed from having to meet the qualifications required thereafter. Blunt became his assistant, which meant that he very shortly took over most of the hard work while old Wisonant sat by watching and advising, and speaking ill of "college doctors."

"Horse-leeches," he called them; "bumshavers, quacksalvers, peddlers of snake oil and pink aspirin.

"A trust, a vile and contemptible monopoly, a guild of grave robbers aping their betters among the natural philosophers," he would snarl.

One morning the old phlebotomist was found on the floor of his office, white beard pointing to the ceiling. Although urged by the hill people to carry on and the hell with them city doctors and their laws, Blunt declined. Roads were coming into the hills, and automobiles. The day the old man was buried from the little church of the Foot-Washing Baptists, Blunt was approached by the only representative of Big Business in the county, the manager of a lumbering outfit that was winding up operations, there being no forests left worth ravaging.

"We can use you out in ——," he said, naming a western state.

"You know I haven't got a license," Blunt said. The lumberman's reply was brief and obscene.

"Can you set a broken leg? That's what counts," he continued.

On the advice of the lumberman Blunt went out to the western state and told the company's hiring agent that he was a former medical student whom lack of finances had forced out of school. His story, enriched with details from the gossip of the Army doctors, sounded reasonable; but the company was not too particular. Few doctors were available for the rough life of the logging camp, and the supply of those whom liquor, malpractice, or conviction for criminal abortion made available was rather short at the time. He spent several years in the woods before he moved on.

Once, he bought an interest in a small town drug store, chiefly to improve his knowledge of pharmacy. He was not a businessman, and when his partner took to tapping both the till and the *spiritus frumenti*, Blunt did not wait for the end, but just walked out. There are agencies that never advertise, as their business, though needful, is illegal. Through one of them Blunt became *le docteur* on a sisal plantation in Haiti; he added, to the professional journals to which he subscribed, one on tropical medicine.

All that he did, he did with seriousness and sincerity, and as much capability as was possible under the circumstances —which was a great deal more than the medical monopolists could have afforded to admit, if they had ever known about him. They never did, of course, because he went to places that never saw them.

Unlike the woman of Valor, who (we are assured on the best authority), Laugheth at the Time to Come, Blunt never even thought about it. He was in British Honduras when the European war broke out, but paid it little attention until the invasion of Denmark and Norway by a people who might have eventually become civilized, had the British in the early part of the previous century not prevented the French from continuing to civilize them. Something stirred in the heart of Huey P. Blunt as he read the accounts of the armed parachutists dropping from the troubled sky. He went back to the United States and enlisted in the Navy.

So there was Blunt at thirty-odd: big, balding, not very talkative, not much booklearning, no licenses, but a lot of practical experience for a Pharmacist's Mate, First Class. His advancement in rating was indefinitely postponed because he lacked the requisite six months duty at sea or overseas required of chief petty officers in "non-specialized" ratings. By the Byzantine logic of the Navy, a Pharmacist's Mate, 1/c—who had to know First Aid, Minor Surgery, Anaesthesia, Materia Medica, Anatomy, Physiology, Nursing, Hospital Administration, Embalming, and so on—was not considered a specialist; while Physical Culture instructors, whose only duty and only qualification was the ability to direct mass push-ups, *were* so considered, and were rated CPOs *en bloc*. In the ordinary course of an ordinary tour of duty in the Hospital Corps a Ph.M. 1/c would have been certain to get sea duty, and thus, a rating as Chief.

But Blunt's very competence undid him. He knew too much.

"I can't spare you, sorry," Dr. West told him each time he put in for sea duty.

"Long's they know he kin do ever detail here and do it better than enna bodda else, Ol' Huey goin stay here"—Tester to Pawson.

"Ol' Huey's a mighty good man," Pawson said, but neither the "Ol' Huey" or "the mighty good man" indicated affection. No one liked Blunt, no one *dis*liked Blunt, no one told any stories about Blunt; there were none to tell. Blunt had no personality. He was not a character. He had no existence apart from his rank—which he did not abuse—and his skill—

which, by its greatness, baffled and discouraged speculation. If orders came in for a Ph.M. 1/c to be shipped out, the SMO saw to it that another one was shipped. Once Blunt, on leave, went to Washington, and pulled strings, but Dr. West, when he saw Blunt's name on the orders, pulled more strings; and was authorized to make a substitution. The other First Class Mate was older than Blunt, he was married and had two children, but he knew incomparably less and he was lazy and inefficient; and for these failings was destined to die while splashing his trembling and middle-aged legs through the lukewarm waters of a tropical beachhead.

But before that happened, Blunt had fallen in love.

Wilma Swanson's family belonged to one of the several colonies of Yankees settled in Cataline. Besides the usual superannuated railroad men and retired wholesale plumbing dealers, besides the seekers after more sunshine and health, there was a group drawn to Cataline by the presence of a small denominational college that Had a Good Name. At one time it had been Southern terminus for the Chatauqua Circuit. Retired clergymen, retired schoolteachers and principals, even retired deans and presidents of other denominational colleges (small), had settled in Cataline so as to take advantage of its advantages.

Mrs. Swanson said that Cataline had *everything*.

"There's this lovely old town and those beautiful oak trees and Spanish moss. And the lovely flowers, all the year round. There's Mullet Bay, and the St. George River, and the ocean— lovely swimming and fishing and boating and water games. There's Vallance Beach just a short ride away, and Seminole Springs. There's this lovely little college and the intellectual atmosphere it creates here. There are some lovely people who winter here—call them Snowbirds, if you will, but I say that some of them are just lovely. As for the year-round people, well, you just won't find a lovelier community; that's all. And the Colored People are simply lovable. That's why I say that Cataline has everything."

Mr. Swanson backed her up in all this, but since he had Investments locally, naturally, he saw things from another point of view as well.

"There's your naval stores," Mr. Swanson said; "your turpentine and rosin. There's your citrus fruit. There's your lumber. There's your real estate. And I must add," he added, "last but not by any means least, there's your Sunshine and your Clean, Fresh Air."

Wilma had gone to Cataline College and graduated. She had majored in Domestic Science, that being what the aptitude test had suggested for her.

Somehow, no young man from a lovely family had ever offered to provide Wilma with the domesticity. Mr. Snyder, to be sure. Mr. Snyder, a fine Christian gentleman, had once hinted to Mr. & Mrs. Swanson that...but then, Mr. Snyder was getting on in years, he had low blood pressure and a married daughter...No. Wilma could do better than Mr. Snyder, lovely man though he was. There was no hurry. Mrs. Swanson had been much older than Wilma when *she* married *Mr. Swanson*. Wilma was a lovely cook and had such a warm personality, and, really, when she took off her glasses, you could see that she had lovely gray eyes. Only she seldom took them off because she couldn't see very well without them. So Wilma stayed at home. Then, when the war started, she had so much wanted to Do Something, and it was really very fortunate in its way that Miss Olauson, who was Dr. Wondermaker's nurse, had joined the Army. Of course, Wilma wasn't really a nurse, but she had her Red Cross card in first aid, she made even the most nervous patients feel at ease; and besides, there just weren't any nurses available for Dr. Wondermaker. But Wilma learned very quickly and Mrs. Wondermaker said she really didn't know *what* Doctor would do without her, because she (Mrs. Wondermaker) simply had her hands full with the children.

And there was no end to the shock of the Swanson family when Dr. Wondermaker tried to kiss Wilma one day, in his office. Of course, she couldn't stay after that. Dr. Wondermaker insisted it was all a misunderstanding, he regarded Wilma almost as one of his own daughters; but of course, she couldn't stay after that. Fortunately, in addition to the Domestic Science courses at Cataline College, Wilma had studied typing. She couldn't take dictation, but she could type; she had typed all of Dr. Wondermaker's records for him. Wilma got a job in the office of the Dispensary at the Naval Air Station. Mrs. Swanson said that some of the sailor boys were really just lovely, if you got to know them, came from very fine families, really. Besides, Chief Shillitoe worked in that office, and he was a very fine man, really lovely...

At first only Ribacheck showed any interest in the new office girl. The nurses responded to her very openly expressed admiration for nurses, but only Ribacheck (at first) showed any interest in her as a *woman*. Ribacheck belonged notoriously to the Lowest Common Denominator school of venery, and was therefore interested in *all* women *as* women. The other Corpsmen claimed to find a lack of niceness in this. Ribacheck's taste, they said, was All in His Mouth. Of course, Wilma was very polite to all the men, and when Ribacheck smiled at her, she smiled back. In fact, as his smiles grew warmer, she allowed herself to look into his record book in the files. She had never heard of Poynkers Mills, New Jersey, listed as his home town. And, heavens! she couldn't even pronounce his mother's first name. Lutherans were all right, although not perhaps quite so much as Methodists or Presbyterians, but what on earth could a Slovak Lutheran be? Growing more and more dubious, she noted that Ribacheck had once been operated on for a varicocele. Later on she looked up the word in the little Gould's medical dictionary in the office. She blushed, even though the definition was far from explicit enough. Would a varicocele...? Or wouldn't it...? There was, of course, no one she could ask. After that Ribacheck smiled in vain.

And then, one day, Blunt came into the office. Wilma didn't

realize it, because she had taken off her glasses to clean them; but she was looking up when he came in, and smiling in his direction. She really *had* lovely gray eyes. After that Blunt came in the office rather often. He was exceedingly shy with women, and found it difficult to talk small talk with them until he knew them well, but Wilma was a bit shy herself.

Blunt, in short, began to court her. Before long, they had an understanding. Mrs. Swanson said that he was really a very lovely person. So quiet, she said. And really, an astonishing knowledge of medicine. After all, a First Class Pharmacist's Mate was almost the same as a civilian doctor, wouldn't you say? Mr. Swanson said that he was one of your steady young fellows. Seemed to know quite a bit about your lumber, too, Mr. Swanson said. Everything was going so smoothly that Blunt overcame his uncertainty as to the propriety of the invitation, and asked Wilma, while they were walking one afternoon near the bungalow he rented in Cataline, if she would care to just look the place over. She said she would.

"I hired the place already furnished," Huey said, leading the way. "Some of the things are real pretty," he said, waving his arm at large. Wilma looked at the pink cloth lampshades with beaded fringes, the heavy red portieres hanging from wooden rings.

"Mmm-hmm," she murmured.

"But this house, like every house, it needs a Woman's Touch," he said. Wilma's heavy cheeks turned a deeper pink.

"Oh, a house *does*, it *does*!" she said fervently.

Huey stopped in front of a closed door. He stood with the key in his hand and half turned to face her.

"Now I'm going to show you something that I haven't ever showed another person here before. You're the very first, Wilma." Her face burned. She looked at the faded and threadbare carpet. She heard the key in the lock and the click of the light switch, and followed his feet inside. She had to take off her glasses and wipe her eyes.

"...and a woman who has, besides, a Scientific

Background…"

Putting back her glasses, she saw opposite her a shelf with a row of little bottles, each one containing something like a dried mushroom, only not quite…With a slight frown of puzzlement she read the neatly typed labels.

Redund.Prep., Cumberback, Alonso T., Steward's Mate 1/c
Redund.Prep., Williamson, Jno., Officer's Cook, 3/c

Lost in pride, Blunt fell silent and looked at his collection. Row after row, shelf after shelf, of bottles and jars, lined the large closet. In cold glass wombs that would forever preserve but never nurture them, floated homunculi, in every stage of development up to the sixth month—after that they were always claimed, though burial (Blunt thought) was a foolish waste. Nobody ever asked for an appendix; there must have been over a hundred of them. There were tonsils, tumors, fingers, a few ears, a whole foot, several eyes. Swaying gently in response to distant vibration was something like a bunch of grapes, labeled *Youlihan, Bette Lou*. A shy smile on his lips, Huey reached out and touched with a gentle finger a bottle containing a twelve-foot tapeworm (*Le Maistre, Cleophile*). He rested his hand affectionately on a mason jar that held a scalp of chestnut colored hair. He cleared his throat.

"I don't suppose that there's another collection such as this in the whole country, in private hands," he said, in his high, flat voice. "I was hoping…" He took out a handkerchief, spat onto a corner of it, and rubbed at a speck on a bottle with a rather faded-looking testicle in it.

"I was hoping that after we were married, after that, then I was hoping that you and me could sort of catalogue it all, together, Wilma…

"Wilma?"

He walked rapidly through the bungalow with long strides.

"*Wilma?*"

But Wilma was already on the bus, bound, not for her home, but for the Station. She rode in tight-mouthed containment until the Nurses Quarters, where she allowed herself to be helped off in a state of convulsive hysteria. After being drenched with aromatic spirits of ammonia, and after weeping her dress and those of the nurses tending her into quasi-transparency, she retreated with cold compresses to a darkened room. The nurses, who were fond of her, had watched, like everyone else at Sick Bay, the slow progress of the courtship. It was certainly not to be thought that Blunt, of all people, had made improper advances; they thought that he must have jilted the poor girl; they pressed sympathetically for Details. They got them, and the account of Wilma's Terrible Experiences strained through sobs and hiccups, spread almost at once to Sick Bay; and thence, to the Navy at large, gathering details at every step...

(Pawson, for example, reported to Tester that "Ol' Huey got a closet full o' pickled collions, an' a two-headed baby in a jar o' formaldehyde!")

"But what *I* want to know," said Doctor Wallop, "*is* she marrying him, or—?"

Miss Stuart said, "According to her, Not If He's the Very Last Man on Earth."

"'She does not regard herself, nor yet wish to be regarded, in that bony light,'" Dr. Wallop murmured, sneaking his hand onto Miss Stuart's kneecap. Miss Stuart giggled.

Dr. Slide confided to Sam McIntyre that he'd been on the point of suggesting to That Crazy Fool to join the Brethren, but not anymore.

A Bo's'n's Mate named Blascovitch got roaring drunk and hammered at the door of the bungalow one night, demanding his appendix back.

Church and State, appealed to by Mr. Swanson To Do Something, declined to do anything. Chaplain Meyers, with a far-off look in his eye, said something about Samson in the

Old Dispensation having made a similar collection. Chief of Police Elsworth Smith didn't know of any law against it.

Blunt himself, vexed at the whole affair, put in for sea duty once more, and Dr. West once more refused to approve. Blunt, he patiently repeated, was Much Too Valuable a Man. Wilma, of course, couldn't stay on after that. It seemed that Huey was doomed once more to wander lonely as a cloud: but instead, he came into his own, at last, as a fully rounded "character"; a fabulous personality who was known to and talked about by everyone on the Station. In a matter of days he became famous in Naval aviation installations all along the coast and in bases in Cuba, the Bahamas, and the West Indies. Eventually his fame became a legend, as it spread in widening circles, until he lost his name and entered mythology. The closet became part of it, too.

"This old Pay Clerk," any sailor you care to name might be saying in a bull session, "was supposed to pay off the whole Ship's Company of this battle wagon in dry dock. Only whiles he was coming aboard he kind of stumbled and the whole suitcase full of money fell open. Well, they pumped that dry dock what I mean *dry*, but they never could find only a *part* of the money. Course, he drew a Court and they retired him, but, funny thing, long about six months later he opened up the biggest damn bar and grill in Honolulu. And everybody was real surprised because he never had the reputation of being a saver. It just goes to show, you never know."

"Reminds me," someone else was sure to say, sooner or later, "of this old Chief Pharmacist's Mate, he—"

"Oh, yeah! Y' mean the one who—"

"Hey, *you* wanna tell this story?...Well, like I was saying...

"And his wife," the story wound up, "she took off an' never come back; and they say that she never *would* open another closet door again unless someone else was in the room!...It just goes to show."

But by that time Blunt had been obliged to hire Harold, the Sick Bay porter, as part-time houseman, because no Colored woman in Cataline would enter his bungalow—and indeed, they fled the streets for blocks around when he walked or drove through town.

No one knew when he had started the collection. It may have begun in some mountain cabin filled with screams, or it may not. It could have been prompted by a curiosity that thought to answer mystery by amassing matter; or by a personal idiosyncrasy of no greater depth than one that brings some men to collect stamps, old silver buttons, or used trolley car transfers. Certainly, to Blunt, each item was in its way an *objet d'art*. And certainly he must have been doing it for years without being—oh, not "caught" or "detected" or "discovered": these words imply wrongdoing, and Blunt came as near to anger as anyone ever saw him, when he defended himself.

"People like you," he said to Miss Sweeting, who was trying, in her tortuous way, to express Shock; "People like you Impede the March of Science."

VERGIL MAGUS: KING WITHOUT COUNTRY

Written by Avram Davidson and Michael Swanwick. Although he never met Avram in person, Michael Swanwick has always been a great admirer of his work. When the estate asked him to complete one of Avram's unfinished stories, he was happy to do so. "Davidson was one of the great prose stylists of science fiction, and it was no easy task emulating him. As I wrote, I could feel Avram's ghost standing grumpily at my shoulder, making disapproving noises whenever I got it wrong. He had left clues throughout the text, however, pointing the way to the story's resolution, and I am confident not only that 'Vergil Magus: King Without Country' ends the way he intended, but that I have correctly identified and solved each and every clue he planted." This story was originally published in Asimov's Science Fiction, *July 1998. If you want to listen to more of Michael Swanwick discussing Avram, you can do so on* The Avram Davidson Universe *podcast at* https:// avramdavidsonuniverse.buzzsprout.com/.

Emericho, Count Mar, Master of the Ceremonies to the Emperor. Oria, Countess Mar, Wife to the Master of the Ceremonies to the Emperor. Count Mar came from a very high and noble family indeed, and was indeed the last of his line. There had indeed been one sole cousin, an heir to the shrunken meadows and the crumbling chastel and to the very many honors, privileges, and titles. And when he had in fact died in battle against distant barbarians so barbarous and so distant that even Count Mar as a historian of war had never even heard of them (*Turks*, they were called. They were called *Turks*. And it was assumed that now that the Sub-commander of a Legion the Knight and Patriarch Ser Audulen Mar had given his life to defeat them, that they had slunk back into the wild wastes from which they had come, and would never again be heard of. Whence? That heartland of Asia More, Bactria Extra Oxum or some such syllables and babblement. *Turks!*), Count Mar had set up an altar and burned balsamum and myrrh. Himself the August Caesar had attended, as well as members of the Old Aristocracy. Which excluded those ennobled during the last seven reigns, or, rather, their descendents...unless said descendents were also descended from the *Old* Aristocracy. And everyone remarked how straight and erect had been Emericho Mar, the Count Mar, the Master of the Ceremonies at the Imperial Court, at the Court Imperial.

No one knew that afterward, all the servants sent away except that one servitor as old as the Count Mar and in fact his bastard brother by a gardening-maid, no one knew that the Emperor's Master of Ceremonies had put his face upon his arms and wept aloud: not because of an especial fondness for the Sub-commander Ser Audulen Mar, whom he had never seen, nor had he ever seen his Father: but because the ancient and noble House of Mar had all but come to an end. The contents of the chastel might he leave as he would, but the chastel itself and the meadows at which grazed a flock of grizzled sheep of a race seen nowhere else, these would in no great time become escheat to the Crown Imperial, and the Emperor might do with them as he would.

House Mar: no more.

Vergil wiped the blood from the blade of his dagger, and set it aside. Carefully, he splayed the dove's intestines and read the signs: Audacibus annue coeptis. *Be favorable to bold*

beginnings.

He laughed and clapped his hands. The portents, horoscopes and auspices all agreed. This would be a marvelous day for the great work.

Which visible display of cheer should have spread quickly through the workshop major. Odd that it did not. There were a dozen workmen employed in various aspects of the Great Labor and though every man set to his task with a will, they exchanged many a nervous and even dark glance. They were all on edge. They would turn hastily away at his approach, as if there were something about his clothes or his appearance or his shadow that displeased them. Yet so good was their discipline that no one did speak a word to him. Not so much as boo.

None except the Chinese wizard Ma.

Ma came trotting up to him and with puppyish eagerness, said, "Great sir, stop. You are being superstition. Consider the sky. Consider the winds. Consider all life. Instead of kill birds, you must throw coins, separate yarrow stalks, consult *Book of*—" And then stopped, chagrined, because the tome whose divinatory authority he was about to (and, it might be added, far from the first time) call upon was not in his immediate possession. It had been some time, indeed, since he had last seen it. He was beginning to think he had left it behind. In his study. In Tai-Ting.

"Rest assured, my young colleague," Vergil said, "that Roman science is quite advanced in the area of Prediction. Why don't you go help out Oria in the workshop minor?" He was feeling particularly tolerant today. The signs were as good as he'd ever seen them. With such omens, absolutely nothing could possibly go wrong.

Also, as a scholar himself, he understood the pain of misplacing a book.

But Ma only shook his head pityingly, and thrust his hands each up the opposite sleeve of his tunic. When he was in such a mood there was nothing to do but ignore him.

The Chinese wizard had come to Vergil, as so many things did, as a gift. Technically speaking, he was a gift to the Emperor from the Great Cham the Son of Heaven, Conqueror of Hind, Tibet, Java Major and Minor (any day now, the deed was as good as done), Benevolent and Absolute Sovereign of the Middle Lands, aka Cathay, Qara-Khita, Greater Meng-tse, Serica, the Land of Silk, et cetera and cetera, amen. Who had heard distant reports of his beloved cousin's glory and so sent, along with his compliments, a caravan of presents, including jugglers, carvers-of-ivory-balls, tigers, elephants, book-printing machines and mechanics to operate them, blackpowderers, kitemakers, fireworks artisans, and the odd inconvenient lateral heir to the throne itself, to say nothing of robes of hyacinth-purple silk, bolts of fine scarlet cloth, sandalwood casks of emeralds y-carven with Zodiacal ideograms, hempen sacks of peppercorns from Malabar and Tellicherry, cinnamon from Ceylon, brocades from the Isle of Lanka and dragon's blood from Serendip, oh really the entire catalog is too tedious for recital. Let it be said: Munificent.

So the caravan set out for Rome. Past the Great Wall. Past the Gobi Desert. Over the cold Pamirs. Past the frozen and lofty Himalayas. Over the Oxus and the Jaxartes Rivers. Under the shadow of the Great Stone Tower. Across the waters of the Caspian Sea, heavy with sturgeon and epsom salts. Along the winter coasts of the Black Sea. Over the bars and shallows of the Indus with its ship-killing tides. Through the burning waters of the Erythraean Sea. Skirting first the crocodile-ridden lands of Gog and Magog, and then the hashish-beautiful lands of the Old Man of the Mountains and so to Babylon and past the ruined stump of Babel's tower and then Byzantium and...well, it was a long trip.

At the end of which Ma, with his thousand-drawered pothecary chest, was the sole survivor to prostrate himself before the throne and offer the Chinese Emperor's fondest compliments to his cousin, the King in Rome.

The King in Rome.

Caught ye that? as the Emperor would say. King in Rome, which was as good as to imply nowhere *outside* of Rome. It was a calculated insult. No sooner were the fatal words out of the politically innocent (to say nothing of pig-ignorant) Chinese wizard's mouth, than the court generals bristled and clapped hands to swords, ancestral memories of martial glory kicking up dust in their ancient skulls, and prepared for the clarion call to a senseless decade or two of yet another ruinous land-war in Asia.

But Good King Festus, as the denizens of the war-foddering classes were wont to call him, when they thought of him at all, which was—let's be honest—not all that often, Festus as we began to say, had an original and straightforward mind. He knew how to make trouble disappear with a word. "No, no, dear child," he said with a dismissive flick of the fingers. "I am the King *of* Rome. You want the King *in* Rome, which would be..." He consulted with an advisor. "Vergil. King Vergil, on the Street of Mages. Down the via and second left, you can't miss it."

And so the bewildered but ever-loyal-to-his-Emperor's-command little wizard had come trotting down the yellow brick streets of Rome and into Vergil's life.

"It's going to explode!" the bellows-boy screamed.

The apparatus was a combination of pelican and sublimatory. Which is to say that the furnace had an iron bar running transversely through it just below the thick glass pelican (thus regulating temperature) and a perforated disk above that that held the glass vessel in place and vented the hot gases from the furnace. The pelican had two looping necks that returned the distillate to its residue for redistillation. Which process—called cohobation—might recur some five hundred times before a state of absolute purification was achieved.

Cohobation. An unlovely word. And yet...

An emerald through cohobation might improve its water threefold, though it were cheaper to simply buy a finer stone.

A base metal such as lead could, through cohobation, be improved into gold at a cost not *many* times greater than the value of the gold.

A certain Tincture through cohobation could be so clarified as to extend life—and in perfect health! no sibylline ironies *here!*—for so long as to be...well, indefinite. And no price was too great for that.

If one succeeded.

If the apparatus did not explode and kill everyone in the laboratory first.

The prevention of which catastrophe lay not in spells, talismans, and the employment of minor demons, but in regulation, constancy, a discerning eye. Watchfulness! While his laboratorians labored in silence, Vergil stood unblinking (those who mistook the sorcerer's stare for aught other than simple and absolute attentiveness, who indeed found it downright *spooky*, were simply misinformed) and motionless. He held in his mind and at the tip of his tongue a cantrip for the regulation of the heat. Apprentice smiths extended long spoons (called "devil-suppers") into the flames, each spoon containing a liquid that would bubble, steam, or sublime at a different known temperature. So that when a gust of wind coming through the laboratory door caused the flames to rise and hotten, Vergil was ready.

He spoke a certain Word.

With a *whoosh*, the flames leaped toward the ceiling beams. White-hot they were, far hotter than could be explained by any natural process. Hot almost as that Red Man whom Vergil had confronted (and fought; and defeated) in the deserts of Lybia. Insanely hot. Magically hot.

"It's going to explode!" the bellows-boy screamed.

All stood frozen with horror.

Save Ma, who stepped forward and calmly poured a sack of

salt over the flames.

With appropriate sputterings and smokings and belchings of stinks, the flames subsided. "What a mess!" exclaimed Petronius, his blacksmith-general. "What a damnable mess."

Vergil, though outwardly composed, was disposed to agree. His contrivances, to say nothing of his cantrips, had been of the best—he was sure of that—and the auspices had been perfect. Yet it was his application of a spell to regulate the heat which had caused the flames to flare up so alarmingly. Which spell he had successfully applied an hundred times. Why had this happened?

What could possibly have gone wrong?

How?

The Emperor had given no thought to what he would do with the escheats of House Mar, as, well, why should he? Grizzled sheep, shrunken meadows, stone-cankered chastel, *pah!*, more trouble to rid oneself of than worth the getting (at least if one were as rich as—but who was?—his most August and Imperial self). But he had given a somedel thought as to what he would do with the Count Mar.

There was indeed an Empress, she came not to Court. Never? Indeed, never. She had been a camp-follower when the Sovereign, then a soldier of the line, took it into his head to marry her. She made a good-enough wife for those days, but those days were far off; the ways of court were not the ways of Petronella, Empress of all the Roman World, known generally as Aunt Pet to the hordes of nephews, nieces, ancient uncles, aged aunts, scraggy sisters, be-bent-over brothers, scrannel cousins, and all the rest of them over whom she was Empress; giving orders, handing out favors, throwing largesses of cheap coins and cheaper sweets: it pleased them, it delighted her, there she stayed, in her town of origin, received she allowances, came she never up to

Rome.

Or any else where the Emperor might be encamped.

Save that once a year or so they did meet, both incognito, at a small farmhouse in the Libertiex of Etruscany. Conversation might go rather like this:

"Hast everything tha needs, Petsy?"

"Yes, Festus. Mother has tooken it into her head, she must have a closed litter, such a nonsense; 'What's thee wants ith such a thing,' I have asked her. 'Wants to crawl into it to scratch me tits, it's not befitten for the Emprey's mamm-in-law to do it fore the world!'" The Empress guffawed, showing missing teeth and present stumps.

"I'll have it sent. Does any bother thee?"

"Nay. They dasn't. Do they feed Us well at Court?"

"Too well. But there. Such is the nature of the camp. Hast any petitions or positions wanted or pointments made?"

The Empress stretched towards a basket, failed, quite, to reach it. Was the Empress...*fat*...? Foolish question. Members of the August House are never *fat*. But sometimes they are large and comely. The Emperor fetched the basket up himself. "I've made some lists." *Had some made, I being ignorant of book*, went without saying.

"I'll bineby have a look. What's this, thy puppy dog?"

"I must always have one such. Going away, is thee, Festy?"

"Aye. Here's some Roman sauce and sausage for thee. If tha but somedel needs, send a word. If any durst vex thee, squat and cuck upon them. *Vale*, then." A brief embrace. Nothing more. Would be false.

Oria emerged from the lesser workshop, glass mask yet in her be-gloved hand. The mask was a protection against the caustics and mordants employed in alchemy, such as might threaten her perfect and most *valuable* complexion.

Setting the mask carelessly aside, she rushed into the

workshop major, past the bellows-boy cursing and slapping at spark burns on his arms, to clutch Vergil's hands and peer anxiously up into his eyes.

"Countess," he said.

She dimpled with pleasure, as she always did when someone of quality had the courtesy to employ her proper and supposed title. Her face aglow with excitement, eyes large. A beautiful, beautiful woman was Oria.

Vacuous as three days in Gaul, but beauteous nonetheless.

What wanted she with Vergil? What did any attractive young woman with political entanglements—a dozen such he turned away from his door in a week—desire?

Aphrodisiacs.

Aphrodisiacs and fertility drugs.

Yet here was the curious fact that those who most required a love philtre were they who could least afford that knowledge be made public. It was the potion which dared not speak its name. As well ask for extract of pennyroyal to undo an unseemly swelling in the stomach! 'Twould get out.

No more did a mage of serious aspirations desire a reputation of being willing to provide such potions. There were spirits to conjure up and demons to put down. Discoveries to be made and most dire secrets to be kept. Who had the time? Life was short, alas. Life was short.

All of which led to the fastidious young Oria, with such connections as would compel cooperation from anybody, even a King Without Country, prenticing herself three mornings of the week as a pharmecary-in-training. Solely for the love of learning, to be sure. Oh, la! How she did swoon to distill and compound.

And Vergil, who was a compassionate man, had set her to learn the basics of distilling perfumes from the liqueurs of flowers and compounding ochres and vermilion for the ornamentation of the skin. She would tire of the sport, soon enough. 'Twere cruelty not to let her get from it something she'd value.

Oh, and by the bye: *don't* teach her to prepare any poisons.

Oria gaped about the shambled laboratory, blinking most prettily and simultaneously pretending not to notice the admiring glances of the workmen. It was an act of great social dexterity, one that not just *every* girl could have managed. "Who was your friend?" Oria asked, and then, "Why did he leave so suddenly?"

Ma gestured helpfully toward the door. "He go that way," he said eagerly. "Down street." Misunderstanding, as usual, the question.

"Friend?" Vergil asked blankly.

"The Black Man. Who *was* he?"

Thus far, then: the Empress. Every day for a break-the-fast she had a specially baked white bread with honey, until her twenty-fifth year she had never even *tast*ed white bread. Every day for a nonetide muncheon they brought her a fresh-made sausage of kid's flesh and veal with an abundance of onions, leeks, and garlic; she ate it boiled, with a sauce of must of yellow wine and sharp yellow spice-seed ground fine: fennel often as well. And for her supper every night they gave her a fine dish of pullets and capons and cockles also boiled, with the broth: more onions, more garlic, and carrots and parsley and weed of dill. Petronella was greatly fond of this broth and drank it loudly with frequent eructations. The fowls she pulled apart and fed bits of to her preternaturally old crone Mother and gave out larger hunks and chunks to her kin—*Eat this fine wingy, Auntie Ara. Ah, what a tender pi'ce it be, a grace upon thy pudenda, niecey mine! A num a num! That's what it's here for...let me pull thee off this bump of arse, so, ope thy gob*—Also His Imperial Majesty by Verteu of the Coinage Right each month had her sent five vast leathern baggs a-full of specially minted stiverkins with her own picture on one side for those who couldnae read the motto *Petronella Empratrix.* These she scattered day by day, grinning and chuckling: for this had she humped her hucklebones to many a grizzled decurion before the Festus had come to take her in marriage, for this had she brakked the ice on a muckle mountain pools and washed the Legions' filthy clothes. For this she had marched with cracked and bleeding toes many marches on far frontiers, weaving counter-spells against the frightful fearful witcheries of the Petchenegs and the Galicians and the Picts, the Sassenags and Scotes; rolled along the great wrought-iron kettle when the very ass-of-burden had perished with the cold in Northern Dace a-nigh the savage Geats, and therein had she cooked the Soldiery their stolen grain and stewed their plundered porks.

Her present life as Empress of a rude valley full of ruder peasant-kin? She loved it. She a-grudged The Festus nought. The Roman King, the Roman Roy, the King over all the Kings, His Splendor the Selected Emperor of all the Roman World? Nought. She begrudged him nought.

The Black Man. Just who the devil—and *what*—was he?

Everybody tried to talk at once. Luckily, they all had the same story to tell:

The Black Man had walked all morning in Vergil's shadow unseen. Unseen by Vergil himself, that is. Everybody else had seen him just fine, thank you, and had assumed that Vergil was equally aware of his presence, and was eager to describe this negative-apparition:

He was tall, to begin with, taller than Vergil himself, who was not a short man, by a head at least. Nay, two heads. Naw yourself, but one. Didn't blink. Had a harsh and scornful look. A look of command. Command—who'd obey such as *he*? Run's more like it. African in origin, no doubt about that, consider his features, and yet like no African anyone had ever seen. Was black too.

Blacker than an Aethiope.

Blacker than an alembic's bottom.

Black.

What did he in Vergil's shadow? Well, he gestured thus and so. Arms wide. Fingers a-wiggle. Most particularly had he gestured thus when Vergil cast his ill-fated cantrip. The gestures that were made—but perhaps they were not accurately reproduced; "to lie like an eye-witness" being a phrase of most ancient lineage—were like nothing Vergil had ever encountered. He had made his gestures and then retreated to the doorway, to watch their results. Had left shortly after Ma poured salt on the flames. Was now gone. Where, no man knew.

"Emericho Count Mar."

"Roy over all the Roys, I hear but to obey."

They were in the Great Red Room in the New Palace. A sage-femme had once said that red was good again the measles. None had changed it syne. "The Archiver, ah, the *Great* Archiver, he tells me that at least five generations of your line, that Line of Mar, descended so he says from the gens of th'Emperor Marius, at least five have served this Imperial Court and Seat. Saith well? Saith well. All know that none but the House of Mar knows best the Ceremonies and the Manners. We wish Count Mar to understand quite well that there is a certain Lady very close to the Imperial Heart whom We should wish to see at Court. She be of good sound yeoman stock, you know, Count Mar, a widow-woman, her late vir was a captain of tens in the Sylvan Legion that fought valiantly in the Second War of…"

It was a work of vanity for the Roman Roy to tell Count Mar what War the Sylvan Legion had fought in valiantly, Count Mar already knew; Count Mar knew all such things.

All such things of import. And Count Mar knew well exactly what his Sire and Ser imported, the Emperor imported now that he would that a someone of rank should marry this a-said Lady so very close to the Imperial Heart, and by so doing give title and status to her, in fait the Roy's chief concubine. For, without someone of such rank did so, she might no more appear at Court than the laundress, be the laundress never so close to said Imperial Heart. Certes that no young man might do, for a young man might easily allow his veins to carry him away with a notion that literally he was a husband to the Lady, and to attempt and insist upon the fact. And this would not do, it would not do. And for sure that no one of recent creation of nobility would serve, for such had so very odd notions of their stature, the very newness of their station being such as to make them sensitive about it.

But someone of Emericho Mar's age and Emericho Mar's antiquity of title? Such a one would ken full well that 'twas an honor to be the Crown Lady and, hence, in mere title the husband and the vir de jure of the Crown Lady: an honor. Others? Let others prate that *Antiquity means decadence*, and *Let no baron be a bawd to the Bed Royale*. Mar was indifferent to such things. What held Rome together? The Roman Roy, held it. The Emperor was the sole fount of honor to the Empery, and therefor so—And the Emperor Festus, that same Festus, spoke very keenly to the Count Mar's ear when he murmured, "There are certain folk at Court descended from creations of the last three reigns who might look upon this with scorn..."

"...*canaille*..." muttered Count Mar. Rabble, what had *they* to be scornful about: contractors grown rich selling musty meats and rotten grain to the Governance-at-War, parvenus from Over-the-Seas whose origins might be (and therefore were) unspeakably low; the get of rich lawyers, sons of successful engineers (by definition: common as tufa), painted pimps, and tax-farmers; foreigners using tainted fortunes (foreign? by meaning: tainted) to buy their titles:

Count Mar regarded the New Nobility as he might the throng about a bawdy house. "...*canaille*..." What did *they* have to be scornful about? Furthermore did he know for a fact that some of them had got their feet in the stirrups of the Order of Knights by charms and cantrips and by witchery and guile unspeakably vile, their women being poisoners and abortionists and contrivers at assignation. Scarcely did such so-called nobility know how to adjust a toga. Eh? The Emperor? Clean a different thing, the Emperor was selected by seven kings (some said: seventeen: sage folk split no hairs), and by the process of Selection became Roy, became Royal. *Numinous.*

Strapping the sword about his waist—the *inconvenient* sword that was almost as much a nuisance as the young Chinese pothecary was, for he was obligated to wear it will-he, nill-he wherever he went these days, his badge of office, the sword with no name—Vergil set out to find the Black Man.

It was on the face of it no easy task to find a single man among the swarming millions of Rome. Yet even in eternal and eternally jaded Rome a man seven feet tall, darker than any Aetheopian, and unblinking—such a man is noticed. And, for a copper or two, remembered.

The trail of small coinage led Vergil first to a poor neighborhood, and then to a yet-poorer tenement house. Three cabbage-smelling flights up, there was a door. He hammered on its frame. A silence. The creak of feet on old floorboards. The door opened.

Skin black as obsidian. Eyes unblinking as a snake's. "I am in the presence of an inferior," he said to the air. "But *how* inferior is he? Does he have such standing among his barbarous upstart race as to allow him admittance to my domicile without shame to me?"

Seeing his bearing, the palpable hauteur that hung about the man, the sneer that had not been achieved in less than thirty generations, Vergil knew the man for Aristocracy in his own land. Nor New Aristocracy, nor *Old* Aristocracy either. Old, *Old* Aristocracy. Older than the founding of Rome. Older than the rise of the Greeks or the Abyssinians before them. Older, perhaps, than the Flood.

Old.

Suppressing a quite inappropriate urge to bow, Vergil drew himself up and called upon his titles. "I hight Vergil Marius Mago, Bail to the Vicus of Ravenna, Captain of the Communality, Ser Messenger to the Doge of Naples and to the Vicar Imperial of the South, Co-Keeper of the Golden Clicket to the Golden Lock, Titular Count of Calabria, Titular Prince of Palermo, High Baron of High Barbary, Min Dan in Danland, Roman Knight and Patrician of the Romans, Magister of the Mountains with Ambulatory Jurisdiction..." Suchlike worldly tokens did not Vergil himself impress; nor, he saw, was the Black Man moved by them as well. Feeling absurdly like a small child reciting his accomplishments before a visiting adult dignitary, he cut short the list of his civic (for he did not of course mention any of the ranks he held in The Order of Sages and Mages; such were forbidden) honors. "King Without Country."

The Black Man moved aside to let him in.

There was a feel in the room...of power...indecipherable, though. It came from the Black Man himself, but was like nothing Vergil had ever felt. Intuited. Experienced. Vergil well knew the feel and smell and even color of magic. This was nothing like.

This was something before which sorcery was a weak and strutting upstart. This was its negation and perfect opposite.

"I am stranded upon your sterile shore," the Black Man

said. "Without family or friend or wealth. As for family, I am the last of my kind, and as for friends..." He shrugged. "But before I die, I would return to my homeland. Gold will buy my way south to Nilus Meroë and Ophir, and from there to Farther Africa, where memory of Good King Boris may yet endure, and then through Equinox to lands whose names need not be defiled by your ears. So: gold I must have. My talents have been engaged by one who thinks his lineage sufficient. It is not. Yet the one behind the one behind that one I may without disgrace serve."

"Sir, I quite understand. As the poet said, it is enough to have perished once. Let us not compound poverty with disgrace. Yet your activities..." he sought the neutral word, "*inconvenience* me. Surely you can see how they would?" No response from that face. Might's well be carved of obsidian. Or, more aptly, black granite, like certain monumental visages that Vergil had seen in Aegypt of that conqueror Dynasty that had swept down from the South like wolves upon the...well, not lambs, exactly. And yet..."Let me propose a solution. I have money. It flows to me effortless, these days; 'tis not my doing, but fate alone and my lack of desire for such; were I to bar my doors and windows 'gainst it, 'twould smash them down in its eagerness to reach me. Allow me to share some small fraction of my good fortune with you. Say...twice what your sponsor offers? No names required! Only allow me the honor of paying for your peaceable passage home."

For a long moment, silence.

Finally, "How came you to be King Without Country? Is it —" the Black Man hesitated—"an *old* title?"

When Vergil was done explaining, the Black Man looked thoughtful. "It is not a hereditary position, then?"

"No."

"I had thought—well." The Black Man stood. "I am afraid you must leave now, sir. I can do nought to help you."

With greatest courtesy, he showed Vergil to the door.

◆ ◆ ◆

Count Mar led the lady in question to the Nuptial Throne and by himself placed upon her fair hair the matron's saffron veil and drew it down upon her brow: Oria, her name.

As for whatso gifts the Crown and Throne might make available in the Fisc to the order of the Count Mar, the Count Mar was largely indifferent. Now and then he drew upon them to erect monuments to sundry foreparents not yet memorialized, including that famous Roman matron Julia, the *Conjux Carissima*, who had died fighting side by side with her vir, Audan, against the Samnites near Néápoly. Every now and then, using a small chauldron filled with Earth of Delphos and a brazier of burning laurel leaves, Count Mar would summon up the shades of his ancestors: and look on them at battle for the Roman altars and the Roman hearts.

However, less and less, lately.

The third day of the third week of each month (barring the Summers' heats) had usually...well...often...seen Count and Countess Mar together, not so much at Chastel Mar— though there, too—she savoring, even slightly, the pretense of being in fact as well as in law a Lady of Title with her titled husband in their titled fortress; he savoring, even...and thus and thus...the fancy of having a real wife. He *had* had one. Once. Long ago. She was dead. The child too. But as for the most of the hours of the third day of the third week of each month they had showed each other off where the Roman World could see. Reclined together as they were borne in one litter. Sat side by side in the same carriage rolling and rocking ponderously but elegantly (one did not think of *comfort* in those slow, clumsy vehicles: one thought of *show*. Paint. Gilt. Escutcheons. Heavy well-kempt horses with scarlet harness; heavy well-kempt horsemen in scarlet livery) down some suburban road. Worshipping together. Paying visits.

But for a full six months now: less. In fact: seldom.

And the old count's concern and increasing vexation about this seemed to fit in with his vexation and increasing concern in the matter of the King Without Country. Vergil by name.

By name Vergil.

King Without a Country.

Which King returned to his workshop to find it empty. Those hired specific to the day's work had been, of course, released. But Petronius, his blacksmith-general, who should have been repairing the damage and then awaiting his further instructions was also gone, along with—what was more ominous—all five of his sons.

The Chinese wizard Ma entered the workshop, face stiff with disapproval. "I warn. I say, you are like wine-skin that bulge with wine. Full of own thoughts and ideas. If you not empty yourself, I say, how you expect me to teach you? Hah? But they no listen."

"Where?" Vergil asked, with a premonitory chill. "Where did they go?"

Smiths are all sorcerers. Repeat: all. Consider Vulcan, consider Hephaestus, consider Daedalus, consider Weyland of Gaul...the list could be extended indefinitely. Or, if not sorcerers, then alchemists, which is to say privy to the exoteric if not the esoteric secrets of Guildery. Which, combined with the formidable musculature resultant from a regular fourteen hours per day at forge and anvil relieved by frequent leathern tankards of cooling buttermilk, inevitably combined to convince all the breed of their own invincibility.

When such strong, knowing, and confident men were *loyal* as well...'Twas a formula for disaster. In their self-certitude, they would feel for their Master a combination of protectiveness and condescension. They would think it proper to follow him to a dangerous confrontation, from a distance to be sure!, and wait nearby with their hammers and amulets to see its outcome. And when their Master swept by the alley in which they lurked, dark-browed and clearly defeated in his purpose...why, then, they would bethink themselves to take matters into their own brawny and capable hands.

So reasoned Vergil Magus as he ran through the piss-yellow streets of Rome, the nameless sword slapping against his side with every running stride, the Chinese magician squeaking and scurrying in his wake. Back the way he had come. Into the slums. To the tenement where the Black Man dwelt.

He turned a corner and stopped, aghast. Before him stood Petronius, smith-gen. and artisan...burning, aflame, sooty flakes rising from the crisped horror of his body. And his five sons as well. They all six burned like candles fallen into the fireplace coals.

It was too late to help any of them. Yet still, Vergil tried. He did try. Moving widdershins, he called up his salamandaric powers, learnt in the Phoenicia of Sidon and not in the Phoenicia of Tyre (Tyre, burned to rock and ashes; Sidon, yet standing), and attempted to quench the flames.

With such lore had he defeated Phoenix himself. Yet now did the flames respond most disobediently, leaping toward the sky, hottening, burning whiter than angels...until, fuel gone, they dwindled, guttered and died.

Leaving nothing behind but greasy stains on the brick street.

Beyond where Petronius and his sons had been stood the Black Man, unblinking. Their eyes met and Vergil's mind filled with words. He had heard others, both human and *not*, speak within the sanctuary of his skull before. This was not like that. Rather, it was as if every word in his head, other than these, had temporarily been erased.

You were shown hospitality. And betrayed it.

Vergil Magus stumbled away, numb with horror.

A here and a there and of a not infrequent time, the presence of a king was requisite; even the times of the republics had known the Kings of the Sacrifices. Kingdom after kingdom had been added to the Empery, was it not so? So it was. An empery was by definition a foederation of kingdoms and of kings. Not so? So. And so it was not alone natural, it was necessary, that kings of kingdoms, roys of royaumes, should participate in certain matters of empery, that empery being as it were a kingdom of kings. The Council to Confirm the Accession of Territory. The Council to Advise on the Sending of Envoys into the OEconomion and Beyond. Council to Supply the Tars and Spars for the Fleet. Council to Authorize Debasement of Common Currency. And so on. And on, so. Now on the one hand a king might well agree that action on this matter or on that ought not occur saunce consent of kings, still, not always did a king wish to leave his own kingdom. *Dost tha see*? as Festus Imperator et Rex used to ask. Suppose a needed council required the presence of a set of kings. Perhaps to authorize (or not) the inclusion of another kingdom yet. Might the King of Cappadoce not feel affairs at home steady enough for him to leave. Perhaps the three Kings of Gaul did not trust one another at the time. Possibly the King of Aspania was in sooth sick. And yet a quorum was needed. Suppose said quorum of kings required another king more? what to do...what to do...? And then as well. Imagine that a king from outside the Empery arrived as visitor and guest, what more pleasant that, on route to be received by the Emperor said King (of Cush, let one say) said foreign king be first received by a king of the Empery? Agreed: 'twould be pleasant, good for good relations—*Thrice welcome, Scion of Memnon, Melcarth's Heir.*

—but suppose there *was* no King of the Empery to receive him?—

Eh?

What then?

Often the Emperor might wish to take council of someone higher than a mere councilor. A consul? one of the (always) two Consuls of Rome, of which by now the Emperor was always one? This would not always, for various reasons, do. Hence the Emperor Ptolemy, but three reigns ago, finding himself in need of a King in Rome when no Kings *were* in Rome, took hold of The Patrician Ser Appius Appian, and crowned him King. "King over *what*?...Your Imperial Majesty?..." "All in good time, there. Presently. Come forth thou, then, King Appius Appian, and sit at my side in a royal seat." The need, whatever it was, being by and by over: so what then? See now Ptolemy showing that what wit he had was not a false byword: a Document of Full Appointment of Appius Appian to be King Without Country.

King Without Country!

A master stroke.

Every right and pleasure and duty that any other King had (outside his own country), so had the King Without Country. Any office that any other King could hold (outside his own country), so could be held or holden by the King Without Country. And...but...here came the kernel within the nut...however...*no one who had ever held the Office of King Without Country could ever hold the Office of Emperor*. At one stroke just about any cause for jealousy among any of the Seven (or Seventeen) (not less than Seven) (not more than Seventeen) Selectoral Kings was removed. Why be jealous of some fellow in distant Rome? Why fear any plotting, what might he plot about? *The King Without Country could never be selected Emperor*. He might resign. He might be appointed and crowned another time or another hundred times: never might he, in royal office or in out, be selected Emperor.

And even, mark this, many ones said to many other ones, should an Emperor suspect that such a one, a clever fellow, capable, popular, charming, might possibly even if not now take steps to become Emperor e'en though not a King (in within the letter of the Iron Laws, some man not a King might be selected to the Seat Imperial)—that such a one might someday intrigue...might plot...take up arms...plan...connive...this or that...someone alas not politic to kill...Well! A solution was always at hand. Kneel, thou loyal subject dan Fulano. We crown thee King Without Country. Rise, Fulano King.

As for income, income must follow. Income might follow out of the condescension of the Imperial Hand. And...even if the Hand Imperial be stayed a bit just then...there was always this: A purse of such and such at every Ides or Kalends. To be paid out of the Salt Gabelle. For salt was not *very* difficult to procure. Salt was an Imperial Monopoly. *Byword: the Roman Roy doth eat no salt.* Meaning: The Hand Imperial received all the income from the Salt Gabelle. And gave it all away. The astronomer Such-a-One had discovered a new star? named it after the Emperor? or the Empress? A purse of six gold solids. From the Salt. The salt. Byword: *The Roman Fisc is full of salt.* Somewhere there was said to be a tribe, a sect, a sept, which designedly did eat no salt. So 'twas said, and, 'twas said, always their teeth fell out and their finger- and toe-nails, too. Nay, but each soul it must eat salt. There was always plenty salt. The tax itself? A trifle. A few stivers to the sack. The sack was large. Even if the Emperor was not lavish in assigning fiefs and such, still, never lacked for money in his purse, Whosoever: King Without Country. Nom.

When you have led through the Court Ceremonies a maritime magnate almost like a bear save that he had braided nostril-hair and broke wind with every ponderous step, then a well-mannered wizard was perhaps an acceptable relief. The Mage Vergil was more than civil to the Master of the Ceremonies. The Master of the Ceremonies was never more than civil to anyone.

Except to his wife.

When he was with her.

◆ ◆ ◆

Vergil sat alone by lantern-light, closeted with books. He was alone. Save for Ma, of course. Who was (politely, admittedly, oh, invariably politely) hectoring him again. He must learn *fang-shwee*, path of dragons, paint a circle on the wall, place a mirror before the door so that any goblins entering would see their reflections and flee, direct a stream *just so* through the courtyard. All in the name of harmony and balance. It was easy enough to ignore, though every now and then a sentence would pop up out of the murmurous flow and astound:

"Must drink own urine every morning. Then never get sick."

A less charming way to start the day Vergil could not imagine. Scowling, he concentrated on his grimoires, grammaryes, and tomes of discouraged lore (it would be centuries before anybody would be so foolishly selfless as to actively *forbid* such useful learnings). And here, now, before him, what was this? A rarely employed technique labeled *Magica Alba*. White Magic. A magic of blizzards and milk, presumably, of lilies and ivory and goose down. Yes. With rising excitement, he began to read.

Yet even as his mind sought to fix itself upon the words, they wavered on the page, growing fluid in outline. Moistly the ink pulled itself up and off the parchment and formed into globs like quicksilver that rolled off the book and plashed from the slanted top of the reading table.

Leaving him with ink-blackened floor and a manuscript book of virgin parchment.

With a groan, Vergil raised his hands to the heavens (indeed, the roof was in the way; yet his intent was clear) and cried, "Where...*how* can I learn the secret of the Black Man's power?"

"That easy," said Ma. "I tell you."

Was Count Mar surprised when the Emperor Festus made Vergil Magus his King Without Country? No one ever knew if Count Mar ever was surprised. If he thought (others thought) (some others thought) that a background as the adopted son of a former servant to a company of wandering astrologers turned farmer was scarcely an aristocratic one, the Count Mar said not so. Said the Count Mar, at the point The King Without Country kneels upon his left knee: so. The King Without Country now arises. So. Let here at this point The King Without Country kneel upon his right knee, bow his head once...twice...thrice...so.

Such, the conversations between Vergil King Without Country and Count Mar. The Master of the Ceremonies and the Roy Saunce Royaume. In fact, the neither of them gave a much thought about the other one of them. And then one day—

But wait. *Earlier.*

For full six months now, more and more seldom were the gaunt old he and the buxom young she seen together. When last had they dined at the high table in the Chastel at which nom else dining had been there for decades? Long. It beseemed the aged Count. Seldom were he and wife seen together? Seldom *were* together. More and more as the auld conde sat in the cold library in his chilly chastel unrolling the rent rolls of a hundred years before, looked down upon by gesturing posturing sword-brandishing members of the Line of the House in their dusty likenesses and limnings, or making notations for the tenth time about the Journal of his Grandser's campaign against the Kingdom of Carsus —or some such prideful and utterly vain antiquarianizing— more and more often did he realize it was and was only on the said third day, The Third Day, when his chamberman brought him a message and an elaborately carved and adorned case containing straw-padded covered dishes: "My Lord the Count, my ser and sire. My Lady the Countess much regrets that her work at Court with the Empress's Silk Woman [Attiring Woman] [Embroidery Woman] must needs alas prevent my Lady the Countess," babble...babble... babble..."and send herewith a disk of one brace of partridges farced with liver of lark and almondbread," babble...

...babble...

...babble...

...babble...

Suddenly.

(What? when the Empress, never coming to Court, had no use of silk, embroidery, or attire soever! of a surety the things were for the use of the Countess, sole; what then?)

Suddenly there entered vision of a scene small thought of at the time. Vergil King passing through the Hall at Court wearing his trews of white samite and a broidered tabard, looped round with ropes of wire of gold the scabbard of a sword that only a King might wear at Court, passing in a quiet and full-seemly pace; should pass at angle before him and at once kneel and quickly kiss his hand, *who*? Oria, the Countess Mar. So. Of course she needs kneel and kiss the royal hand, the hand of any roy, cum royaume or saunce royaume. It was seemly that the king would at once half-bow and raise her. A word of grace between them. She passed on her way. He passed on his. A thing of nought.

And now this day, The Third Day of the Third Week of the Month, what? She was not to be here. Thus, what. Kissed the hand of the King Without Country. Was not to be here to be one sole day with her vir, her own husband. Was at Court, was perhaps even now a-kissing the hand of—*Lightning-bolt*: Why should not Count Mar, of his ancient House and Line, why should *he* not be, have been, *King Without Country*? There came to his mind: reply? nom. Count Mar's pride was high and deep. It was also very narrow. High and narrow. Narrow and deep. And thus he sat alone at his table, suddenly full of bitterness. And brooding sullen, ancient pride.

Sat he there long? None marked the time. In tumbling seeds of sand, selected by some long-dead sandifer for the hour-glass, perhaps not long at all. He sat. His chamberman stood. Usually Count Mar would flick his fingers at the courtly kickshaws, the chamberman would then serve a tepid polenta with cheap cheese, take away the dainty victuals and eat them with his family (his family would rather have had the common, coarse feeds to which they were accustomed, but the chamberman considered it a stiver saved and carefully dropped a stiver in his savings-pot; someday he thus hoped to buy a milch-goat for his thrall-mother, growing too old for chewing even turnips, even grain). (Even common-folk have feelings, some philosophes know it not, eheu.) Usually, then, indeed, always, disturbed in his reflections on family pride, senile hunger satisfied and sated with traditional porridge or such loblolly, the Count's habits inclined him rise and go to Court.

To duty.

To duty.

For—family dead...or...all save one...and he half-dead—what remained?

Duty remained. Duty. Duty. Therein the real glory of the Line of the house of Mar of the gens of Marius Marcus, not sword and spear and brave death in battle, not for them alone, but in this: Duty. Duty. And if duty took the form of one who had usurped a place that should by rights have been and be his own? That scrawn stirk of the outlands? son of really who knows whom? Called "Marius" too, was he? All the more, then! Some day the stirk would stumble. The knacker would have already made sharp the knife.

◆ ◆ ◆

So Vergil listened while Ma explained a totally new (to him) system of divination.

Passivity seemed to be the key. Where conventional forms of foreseeing the future all tried to impose order on the universe, this divination demanded nothing, imposed nothing, expected nothing. All the world, Ma explained, was flux and flow (well; even the Greeks knew *that*; could not step in the same river twice; nor even once; perhaps there was not even a river; but that was digression), and if one could but discern the direction of this flow...well, then one would ken whither it goest. Eh? By the reading of small, random, and chaotic events, the greater could be discerned. Once explained, it was orthodoxy itself.

It was worth a try, anyway.

Ma went into a frenzy of activity, removing dark yerbs from his chest of many drawers, boiling water, preparing a suffusion. At last he proffered a cup of dark liquid to Vergil. "Now. You drink down most way to bottom. Not all way. Stop here. Most important, you stop here. Not later." Ma drew an imaginary line four-fifths of the way down to the bottom.

Vergil bethought him of the many visionary potions he had imbibed in his researches, and their attendant side-effects. Vomiting, diarrhea, headaches, to begin with, and progressing quickly to bleeding from the nostrils, mucous discharge from the anus, rashes laced with boils, incontinence, simultaneous loss of hair and balance, spontaneous generation of worms within the flesh...The more primitive the culture, it seemed, the greater the discomfort attendant upon discovering so simple a thing as the future. "Wouldn't it be simpler to just pour it off?" he asked.

"Drink."

He took a sip. The dark liquid was bitter and astringent.

He shuddered and with suppressed loathing drank the rest, down to the prescribed line. Then he handed the cup to Ma.

Holding the cup in his left hand, Ma swirled the liquid three times around and then with a snap of the wrist inverted the cup onto the table. When he removed it, the wet *chai* leaves had formed a pattern.

Both men leaned low over the leaves.

"What does it say?" Vergil asked.

"What? Hey? Seneschal—what?" The seneschal was a-most as old as his courtly master. "My sire and ser, my dan the Count. A visitor. His Honor the Varlet to the Vavaseur of Idalia."

A varlet to a vavaseur was so low on the List of Honor as barely to be there at all. But be there he was. Be *here* he was. Who the devil *was* he? Who the devil was *he*?

Duty. Duty. Duty.

"The Varlet to the Vavaseur of Idalia will munch with me."

A gust of sudden sigh. "I am so unworthy—"

"True," said the Count Mar. In the air, hanging, *Nevertheless*, unbespoke. The chamberman set the trestle-table. The visitor got one of the partridges and the Count addressed himself to his nutmeal mush. The chamberman and the other partridge withdrew. (The extra-ancient Mother-thrall might mumble the almondbread dressing with loud *Ooos* of delight, or she perhaps would spet it out with even louder *phoophs*. One never knew. Life was full of change and interest even for a serf.) The Count, meanwhile, completely forgot that he even *had* a visitor; his pale-blue eyes slightly milky, even a thin film upon them like that upon a lightly basted egg, and rimmed with red, veined and weined with red, looked upon an older scene: a Chastel mar filled with noble men-at-arms, the Old Count's Father, the Older Count, in armor and full prime and pride of life, and

—But such scenes with or without the assistance of Delphic earth and burning smoking laurel-leaves, such scenes no longer served. Even as a prisoner will sate and cloy his womanless life with masturbatory fantasies, so for long and long the Count Mar had sated and cloyed his warless life with fantasies of war. After many a winter the prisoner's fantasies cease to have any individual particularity, merge into one single flattened-out omnifantasy, and cease to be of an avail: so the bellic fantasies of the Old Count Mar.

In his heart he cried *War! War!* but there was no war.

"The bosom is full of thorns—"

What? *What?* What strange buffoon was this, ill-shaved, ill-washed, in dusty integuments, hypocrisy overlaying him like a membrane thin: but clearly visible; *who?* Instantly recognized, the worn-down badges of a varlet...authorized to fly the narrowest of bannerets...and of a vavaseur...the lowest rank of an hereditary honor...*the serf of a thrall, a scullion's vassal*, instanta formed the scornful thought... but which vavaseur? which yerb upon that dirt and sweat-stained broidered badge, *which?*—second knowledge to the old courtier: *Idalia*. Produce: Thyme.

"The bosom is full of thorns to observe how this wittold warlock The King Without Country—"

Count Mar was full awake now, "'The King Without Country,' *what*—?"

Doggedly the shabbykins repeated his stupid formula, *that the bosom was full of thorns*, "to observe how this wittold warlock The King Without Country behaves, to the total and intire dishonoring of the lordly Count Mar, Reverenced and Worshipful Master of the Ceremonies—"

The so-pale-blue of the ancient eyes deepened. The yellowed face tightened. Even the untrimmed white hairs in the nostrils bristled. The whole figure of the classical and insulted figure was at once full of life—

—of rage—

—like a hungry wolf who lights upon a scent—upon a

spoor—

"And so? the Varlet to the Vavaseur of Idalia? *eh*? EH?"

The visitor let his eyes roll around the room, proved it empty save for he and host. Eyes a-gleam like a beastling's in the night; he bent forward, unbrushed brow-hairs, untrimmed cheekbones, ears, unwashed body—reek! sharp! pungent! careless of all—

"There is come from the crypto-court of the unacknowledged heir to Boris King of Africa, of Farther Africa, Count Mar," he whispered as he leaned; "a one with a singular specialty of craft. *He performs sorceries upon sorcerers!*" Triumphant, the man sat back. Smacked the table softly with his palms.

Count Mar smacked his own palms upon it, pushed himself up. His mouth dropped open. And, "*War!*" he cried.

He cried, "*War!*"

War! War! War! War!"

Fumbled in his pouchet. Withdrew a whetstone. And next drew forth a knife.

The Black Man stood in the middle of the Street of Mages, waiting for Vergil. Had this been difficult to arrange? It had *not*. Though the Black Man had abandoned his tenement lair ("Skipped out, and good riddance," said his landlord, spitting for luck on a floor that had patently endured more than its share of such treatment), Vergil had simply sent criers throughout Rome crying a challenge to the Black Man to meet in the Street of Mages at noon. It was a challenge he knew would not be refused.

A challenge to fight a wizard's duel.

The Black Man, as had been said, stood waiting. In the crowd to his back, hopping excitedly from foot to foot, waving scrawny fists, shouting deprecations (and yet nobody save Vergil paid him any attention; might's well be one of the hundreds at a chariot race for all the attention he got; and Vergil paid him little enough) was Mar of House Mar. He was tired of being a spectator. He had come to smell blood.

Not that blood had much of a smell *per se*. Which fact Count Mar knew. He was a historian of war. It was in a metaphoric sense that he desired the smell.

There were thousands of onlookers, for the criers had gone everywhere. The buildings bulged with spectators. The roofs overflowed. Many had brought with them lunches. In front of the workshop behind Vergil all his faithful workmen, even those whom he had not seen in years, stood shoulder to shoulder in their best smocks, displaying solidarity with their sorcerous Magister. Everyone who could talk his way in was there, Oria and Ma as well.

The two mages strode toward each other until they were close enough to spit upon one another, were either undignified enough (they were not) to do so.

The Black Man raised his arms.

Vergil drew his sword. The sword with no name.

It was no easy thing for a sword to avoid acquisition of a name. The least trait or incident would suffice. Dost whistle when swung in the air? Deathsminstrel. Born in the forges of Caliburnus? Excaliburn. Left it leaning on the outside of the tavern on the sunniest day of the year and came out not more than three drinks later to find it all a-rust? Stormbringer.

Vergil had overseen the forging of the blade himself, the work done by a blacksmith mute from birth, and when one of the apprentices had cried out on its emergence from the cooling bath (it was a stock sales technique; *let the mark leave happy* being a byword of greatmost antiquity), "Ah! 'Tis a very—" "wonder" he was about to say, or "marvel," and there 'twould've been, Wonderblade or Wizard's Marvelment, when the magus's fist in the hollow of his stomach had cut short the thought.

"Thank you," the mage had said. "I'll take it."

It was important that this be a sword without a name,

for if Vergil were to occasionally find himself wearing such a thing during his researches (in a situation, say, where his professional and pseudoregal duties coincided), why then, it were wisest that the blade were alchemically neutral. There was magical power in names. And in this sword, none.

Vergil swung up the explicitly un-magical sword. The Black Man flung his arms out to either side, fingers wriggling like snakes, to turn his magics against him. For what use had a magus of a sword? Well, a hundred actually. All of them powerfully magical. None of which involved a straightforward stab into his enemy's chest.

Blood gushed.

"Oh," said the Black Man.

He fell forward.

Dead.

In the stunned silence, Vergil turned to Count Mar, who stood suddenly exposed by the fall of his champion. The old count did not return his look with any great enthusiasm. "You," said the magus, sternly. "Lord Mar. What earthly reason do you have for this unprovoked attack upon me?"

"I...well...of course..." The Count flapped a hand toward his Countess, his wife, Oria. "The...ah...the insult...to the honor...of...my wife?" he ended weakly.

"For jealousy?" Oria said. "You tried to kill King Vergil for *me*?" She ran forward and flung her arms about the neck of Emericho, Count Mar, Master of Ceremonies to the Court, her husband. "Oh, 'Rico!" she squealed. "You *darling* man!" And to his absolute befuddlement, kissed him then and there.

She was a girl who knew which side her bed was buttered on, was Oria.

So there it was: Hero triumphant, villain dead in the dust, and now the clinch: the two lovers reunited. And if one were a trifle old for the role, well. One can't have everything. To a man and women, the bystanders cheered, whistled, stamped, and threw their caps in the air. They might not know exactly what had just happened. But they knew a good story when they saw it.

Count Mar then set his wife, Oria, Countess Mar, to one side and, with the astonishing assurance of the Old Aristocracy, took Vergil's arm and led him aside. "This is a touch embarrassing, old boy, but I'm certain you in your professional capacity as a wizard and negromancer will of course...well, to put it bluntly, one finds oneself in need of a yerb or potion, something that will—as the saying goes—put some lead in the old stylus.

"For a friend, you understand," he added quickly. "Not for one's self."

A King Without Country had many responsibilities, as many, indeed, as the Emperor in his wisdom might choose to heap upon his shoulders. Withal, he could not levy taxes, nor raise troops. Neither could he set policy nor declare war. He had not the powers of High nor Low justice, could practice neither infangthief upon criminal villeins, nor outfangthief upon suspicious-looking vagabonds, could not condemn a felon, nor imprison a traitor, nor e'en so much as *fine* a citizen, be the rascal never so annoying to endure. He could not aspire to the office of Emperor.

What advantage then, when all is said and done, hath a King?

Ans.: A King may forgive.

"I have," Vergil admitted, "just the thing."

Of a night not many months after, Vergil met with a certain Lady, incognito, at a small farmhouse in the Libertiex of Etruscany. The Lady was accompanied by her aged crone of a mother and a ragged varlet with emblems of the Vavaseur of Idalia whom Vergil did not recognize, for he had never before laid eyes upon the man. Vergil was accompanied only by his unshakable Chinese wizard. "So she's tupped-up, is she?" said the Lady, when he was done his tale, wiping tears of laughter from the corners of her eyes.

"Most gracious Imperial Maj—" he began.

"Call me Aunt Pet," she said. "They all does."

"Aunt Pet. Yes, she is. Pregnant."

Her eyes narrowed. "Ye're not gawna try nor conwince me it were *Mar's* doing? I'se not so provincial as all *that*! I don't care how much lead thee puts in an eighty-year-old stylus, t'ain't gwinter write no such nonsense."

"No, Maj—Aunt Pet. The child is the work of your husband, the Emperor."

She wheezed with laughter, and slapped her thigh thunderously. "Well, b'ain't that just like him! As ready to rut as a goat! I remember a time when—"

Patiently, Vergil endured a ribald tale the single repetition of which in the Eternal City would be worth his head and the pole upon which it would be stuck. Standards were different out here in the country, of course. Then he said:

"Aunt Pet, I would there were peace between us."

"Why, lor bless you, why shouldn't there be?"

"You convinced Count Mar to hire the Black Man to kill me. I thought you might have had some reason."

Aunt Pet blushed.

"Mummsy," she said gently, "why don't you go with that nice Chinee-man, the Babylonian or whatever. Have him show you how to fix up someat magical from his little boxy-thingie, eh?"

Then, when the reverenced hag had dragged young Ma off to the kitchen, she lowered her voice confidentially.

"It's me mother. The Imperatrix-Mum. *Her*." She gestured with a nod of her head. "She enjoys a spot of court intrigue, so we keeps a few spies, traitors, assassins, and so on, on the payroll. Just so she can keep a hand in—it means so much to her, old dear!" She lowered her voice. "They none of them does any *real* spyin'. Just sits in Rome on the expense account, boozin an whorin an guzzlin an makin up lies to send home." Then, raising her voice, "All save for one wha's too *dim* to understand that when it's raining soup, ye holds out yer skirt."

She glared at the varlet who shivered and hunkered further down into himself.

To break the tension, Vergil said, "One more question. Just who is the Vavaseur of Idalia?"

She clucked her tongue. "Why, bless you, sweets, *I* is! It's a hobby I has. I collects titles. Big ones, little ones. I has one of each by now, I reckon. I don't fancy it costs dear Festus nothing."

Which pretty much wound up everything Vergil had come to ask. It would be impolite, though, to leave so abruptly. Also dangerous. The lady was still the Empress, and it was night, and there were (doubtless) wolves. So Vergil stayed, and talked, and listened. It was surprisingly pleasant to deal solely with inconsequalia for a change. Even a King (even One Without Country) can enjoy a touch of gossip.

After a time they began to speculate on the sex of the Emperor's forthcoming bastard. Not that it mattered to the Emperor, he had dozens of the things, one more was simply one more, and rumor had it he was growing tired of Oria (and why else would she have arranged for the child otherwise?) anyway. But for Lord Mar, who yearned for the continuation of House Mar *by whatever means necessary*, as the saying goes (nor would it be the first time the blood of the Old Aristocracy had been thus refreshed by intercession of the Emperor), and for Oria, who had gone through so much to acquire an heir, it made an enormous difference whether she whelped a boy who could inherit the name *and estates* of Mar, or a girl, who could not.

"An she were here," said Petronella, "I could tell by looking in her een. They always shows there, boy or girl."

A shiver went up Vergil's spine, for occulomancy was an old witch's trick, and he remembered stories he had heard about the Empress's past. Weaving...how was it the revered sage of Terra Incognita Occidentalis had phrased it, a passing reference in a long conversation through a brass tube that had occurred years after the man's ostensible death?..."weaving counter-spells against the witcheries of the Petchenegs and Scotes..." *Some*thing like that.

And with that the last piece of the puzzle fell into place.

The Black Man had refused his offer of money because his pedigree was insufficiently old. Whose, then, *could* he respect? Not Count Mar, who was (by the Black Man's standards) something of an upstart.

Some titles, however, were older than Rome. Older than civilization. Older than anything that can be named.

He cast a sharper look at the creature he had at first taken for some mongrel breed of lap-puppy and now recognized to be no such thing. No such animal as this was existed. On this world, anyway. Such creatures existed on the physical plane only as familiars.

Quickly, Vergil slid from his stool onto a single knee. "Eldest," he whispered, and then a word of homage in a tongue that not a dozen men alive could speak.

"Hush," Petronella said sharply. "Sit back down, thee. Have a hazzlenut. Festy sent me a bushel just last calends. Should be some not rotted yet."

This line of conversation was interrupted by the abrupt reappearance of Ma. He carried a cup of the same steaming suffusion with which he had earlier unraveled the knot of knowing that had so bound Vergil. He thrust it at Aunt Pet.

"You wish to know about child," he said. "Drink."

Horrified, Vergil reached to stop the royal hand. But it went, instead, to a nearby honey-pot (it was the honey of thyme, not clover-honey or wildflower-honey; there was in

Idalia no lack of thyme), there to dip a spoon and stir, once, twice, thrice, and up. A golden glob of sweet and amber-brown honey came up with it, and descended into the drink. Her majesty stirred, set aside the spoon, tasted.

"Nowt half bad," she decided. "Might go nice with a touch of cream."

The Chinese wizard waited until the cup was near-done. Then he took it back, and before Aunt Pet's shrewd eyes gone suddenly gullible, swirled the liquid in the cup around and around. In which instant Vergil saw, with an intuitive occulomantic leap of his own, that among the next basket of trinkets and favors to be begged of the Emp. Festus IV, would be one requesting the custodianship of a certain young outland magician.

With a crisp turn of his wrist, Ma snapped the cup down onto the table. He lifted it away.

They all of them, even including the Varlet to the V. of I., leaned low over the leaves. Such is the miracle of a child's birth that, though it happens every day a thousand thousand times over, interest in it never dims. The wonder is ever-green.

The Chinese wizard spread his hands in joy. "A boy," he said. "A boy!"

KINDLY HOLD OUT YOUR RIGHT INDEX FINGER

Avram made a second draft revision of a section of Dragons in the Trees, *his travel journal to Belize. "Kindly Hold Out Your Right Index Finger" was likely written in the late 1960s and was published in* The New York Review of Science Fiction, *June 2000.*

T he packet-boat *British Queen* was standing down the Bay of Honduras, having left Belize City the day before and not due into Punta Gorda Town for quite a while yet. To port lay the great green mass of the MesoAmerican mainland. To starboard with good eyesight you could make out the long white line which marked The Second Largest Barrier Reef in The World, at this particular point certainly twelve miles away. Twelve? Let us bargain... say *ten*, will you settle for *ten*? Okay...we were perhaps two miles offshore, and *on* shore, buried in the jungle (here called The Bush), lay Golden Home, the long-abandoned and long-buried Confederate colony: quite another story. As I stood a-staring, a man sharing that part of the railing with me turned and said, with gesture, "This caye," he pronounced it *cye*...kai?...rhymes with *high*..."just ahead of us, sir? Florentine Caye. I was school-*mah*ster there two years. A very productive island, grows oh*ranges*, lemons, coconuts, pears," the so-called *alligator* pears of my boyhood, long since transmogrified into *avocadoes* in our northern speech; "— pears, governor *plums*, bishop mango, hairy mango—"

This cornucopial catalogue was just then interrupted by

a rather ordinary-looking Cauc, who, ignoring me, came up to the other man and, rather abruptly, *I* thought, asked, "Are you by chance a member of the Black Carib Tribe?"

"Lorenzo Zabada, sir, is my name, and I *am* a member of the Carib people," answered the schoolmaster, very civilly; he had, I noticed, not quite repeated the phrasing of the question asked.

"Kindly hold out your right index finger...*oh!*" It had evidently just occurred to the newcomer that perhaps some sort of explanation was or at any rate might be considered a desideratum; he went on to say, "I am Doctor Collins P. Wilbraham of the Biological Anthropology Program at the University of the Miskatonic—" "Very pleased to meet you, Doctor," said Mr. Zabada; "I hope we'll be no more strangers." Dr. Wilbraham ignored that hope (I found it charming; and still do); "—and my purpose here is to obtain scientific evidence on the question, 'Are the Black Caribs really Amerindian, basically? or are they, basically, really African?' Kindly—"

Florentine Caye came nearer, dead ahead of us, while Master Zabada said that he could answer the Doctor's question. "We are Carib Indians, sir. Oh, I suppose we may," in a slightly indulgent tone, "*may* have Black generation in us, perhaps, as you say in your own nation, 'Maybe the bull jumped the fence'...*some* bulls...but—"

"In order to demonstrate the matter in terms of scientific accuracy, I shall require 543 random blood samples, would you kindly just hold out your right index finger?" How very suddenly there was some sort of *kit* in Doctor Wilbraham's own hand. Schoolmaster Zabada affected not to see it. "—but we are certainly Carib Indians, some other American professor, I think a Professor Thompson? from The Pennsylvania University? Has written a book on the subject and demonstrates evidence that our language is the very same Carib Language as written down by the olden-time French and Spanish explorers and that our culture in all respects—"

"...require merely 543 random blood samplings; would you kindly hold out your right index finger and..."

Master Zabada said that he was just going to "take" his luncheon, and, repeating the ever-so-pleasant national hope of his country, that we would be no more strangers, simply vanished away.

Florentine Caye, although I could identify none of them save the gracefully-bending coconut palm, certainly was crowded with trees, and we seemed quite certain to run smack dab into the middle of them. Although aware that the packet-boat made this same run twice a week, God *Willing* said the pious placards, still I was just a bit nervous: but not Dr. Wilbraham. "I can't under*stand* it," he said, slightly shaking his head. "They just won't cooperate. Why not? Aren't they *interested* in their own basic identity?" Things (I suggested) were seldom simple, and this was evidently not one of them. Were the Belizean Caribs indeed simply the descendants of a blending which had occurred centuries before, when runaway slaves from various places made their ways by stolen boats to the island of St. Vincent's, where the Carib Indians still held out against colonialism? The Caribs themselves certainly were, or had been, themselves invaders, coming early in the 1400s from the South American mainland and conquering the Arawack Indians (who in an earlier age had displaced or subdued the Taino Indians there before *them*), killing the men and marrying the women. So said one account; in another were African warriors on fleets of war-rafts, swept up by storms and ocean currents and making unchosen landfalls on mountainous St. Vincent's Island...

The common lore said that on that small island during a century and a half or so, two processes were going on. The Caribs (said the common lore) assimilated the Negroes. Culturally. And the Negroes (said the common lore) assimilated the Caribs. Physically. These Africans (said the common lore) not having a single tongue or nor a single culture adopted the language and the culture which obtained amongst the Carib Indians on St. Vincent's. Good relations, bad relations, with Caucasians—Spanish, French, British— was an up-and-down thing: sometimes peace, sometimes war. Mostly the islanders just cultivated their cassava and their coconuts, caught and cooked their fish. But then, at a date in the 1790s, all agreed, the Caribs had made One Big Mistake.

They had backed the French.

Against the British.

And lost.

The result was not massacre, but exile. Almost en masse the Caribs left St. Vincent's in their little boats, made their way across the Spanish Main, were now found (many) in the Republic of Honduras. And (many more) ironically once again under the British Crown in what was still called, when I was there, British Honduras: now Belize. Unvexed. Always they lived near the water; in tiny "plantations" the women *cultivated*—the exact word used, people did not *grow* or *farm* they cultivated—the cassava and the coconut and other traditional crops—bananas, plantains, chocho a.k.a. chayote, yams, and sweet potato—and the men went out and fished... very often in dugouts whose designs had not changed since the Stone Age.

"The men come back late in the morning with their catch," one of them said to me, "and the women come back from their plantations and prepare luncheon. Of what? Well...usually...cassava bread or grated cassava worked up into a sort of starchy pudding called *fufu* or *hu*DUT...plus fish cooked in coconut milk." His eyes gleamed as he named these yum-yum goodies. I waited a moment. "And after luncheon...the women go back to their plantations again." I waited another moment. "And what," I asked, "do the men do after lunch?" He looked at me with a very slight surprise. "*Nothing*," he said. And once a White Belizean said to me, "I would trust the Caribs with my life, I would trust them with my silver and my gold. *But,*" he summed up, "I would not trust them with my coconuts." It may be, may have been, there might be such a thought that, just as the Masai are said to believe that God meant all the cattle in the world to belong to the Masai and therefore what others would consider cattle-rustling is nothing but the Masai reclaiming what is rightfully theirs: perhaps...just so...perhaps *some* Caribs, anyway, may have believed that all the coconuts in Belize really belonged to them by Divine Right. And worse than that, certainly, I never heard said of them.

But how did one, off-hand, tell the Black Caribs from the Black Creoles or Baymen, who had (as some of them anyway so often said) Been There First; how? Every National (i.e. citizen) assured curious foreigners that it was Easy. "If they have Spaniard names, sir, supposed to be Caribs," for Spanish priests had converted them and given them Christian, i.e. Spanish names. "—unless, well, of course, sometimes if have Spaniard names, be *Span*iard," said one National, helpfully. And, observing me Slightly Perplex (the final syllable of the past tense has vanished from Belizean English as much as, for example, in ice*d* cream from U.S. English), he turned and asked a fellow National, "What that other name they cahl 'Panya?"

"Mulatto?"

"No...not Mulatto. 'Nother name, begin with *M*. Ah. *Mestizo.*"

Things are seldom simple, and this—

Of course, one did not always *know* a person's name at first, na true? For my own part, I can now state, after few years' stay, that...it seemed to *me*...Caribs' eyes were (often) rounder...their hair (often) had a looser curl...their women tied their kerchiefs differently...And...often...and, in fact, very often...very, very often...one heard them speaking their own language. That it was Amerindian, I was prepared to believe on faith. But had I been told that it was African,

I would have had no knowledge to deny it. Though...of course...there were loan-words. Scene in a shop. Two elder women buying victuals.

First elder Carib woman: Anka tanka lanka *pigtaili*?
Second elder Carib woman: Lanka tanka anka *pigsnoutu*.
Loan-words.

But, as for Doctor Wilbraham...

I hesitate to say that he had no interest in the Carib language or in their general culture or ethnic diet. If he did not understand their absolute passion for fish, cassava, coconut...well...neither did I...

I *am* prepared to swear that the packet boat *British Queen* did not swerve as it came head on towards Florentine Caye. The only other possibility, since we did not crash, is that Florentine Caye swerved. Doctor Wilbraham did not appear to notice. "It isn't as if I were asking a lot," he confided. "All I want is one drop of blood. Which I will proceed to test and classify. And, after taking 543 random blood samples, if I find that the [blank] type predominates, then we will know that, basically, the Caribs are an African people. And if we find that the [blink] type predominates, well, then we will know that the Caribs are, basically—"

"Amerindian," I said.

He looked at me in gratified surprise. "*Yeeesss!*" said he.

I say *blank* and *blink* because I simply don't remember the other names. In *my* day blood-typing was simple. One was A or B or O. Unless one was AB...was it?...or was that the name of an Irish poet? Slowly the dedicated doctor made his way around the deck of the small packet-boat (I see many trucks which are bigger), calmly explaining his scientific mission, and asking people if they would kindly hold out their right index fingers. But they kindly did not do so. Not even hardly ever. They did not precisely reply, "Head belong Caucasian roll along deck"; the Caribs are a very civil people. And when, by and by, we drew to a slow halt perhaps a half a mile off the shore of the village of Dumphries (should you be surprised at a Scottish name in those tropical parts, it is true that, alone in Queen Victoria's dominions Beyond the Seas, British Honduras once had *two* religious establishments: the Church of England...*and* the Church of Scotland...although only briefly) a long...as it looked to me...dugout canoe pulled up alongside, Doctor Wilbraham was assisted down into it, many strong black arms plied their paddles, and a song —evidently composed on the spot—was sung (I was given to understand) about a White*mahn* who was harmlessly addled by too much sun and wanted people to do something laughable and absurd, that is, to hold up their right index fingers for no discernable reason whatsoever.

After that last sight of him I must reconstruct his story out of second-hand third-hand reports. Evidently even before reaching shore Dr. Wilbraham had become greatly discouraged and was convinced that no Caribs at all had any genuine interest in his scientific mission. And in this he was, I suspect, absolutely right. Dumphries was not at all the logging town it had been, what time many Scots had lived there. But it lay along a major traditional trade-route and all the bush-trails and paths converged on its shore. Boatmen with nets and strings of fish, women with food and firewood (and even axes on their heads) passed in front of his small house during most of the daylight hours. After a while none of them even tried to understand Dr. Wilbraham's tired croak as he sat on the porch. Dumphries had a few shops. It had two churches and a half a dozen small bars of the sort called "liquor booths." Plus a police constable and ex oficio postmaster who was trained in first aid. "Government" (*no* definite article) tried to attract medical practitioners there with offers of exemption from income tax. But none were attracted, at least not enough to have stayed.

One day towards the end of his first week (and evidently it had been a very looong week) as he sat on the front porch perhaps dreaming hematological dreams, he saw a man trudging up the dusty path. "Doc-tor Abraham?" the man inquired.

"*Wil*braham."

"Doc-tor *Wil*-bra-ham...I have ter-ri-ble headache. Aspirin not help me. Bush-medicine not help me. Doc-tor...Doc-tor *Wil*braham...may-be *you* can help me...?"

Doctor Wilbraham looked at him with tired and sun-dazzled eyes. "Kindly hold out your right index finger," he said.

The man's name, I think, was Luis Barrios. He later told his story in the shops to the vendors and the vendees of *pigtaili* and *pigsnoutu*. He told his story in the liquor booth over the glasses of watered low-proof rum. He told his story in the churches, and he told his story in *front* of the churches as well. To the fishermen cutting the spiky snout off the sawfish and the hunter-turned-butcher as he disjointed the almost-purple flesh of the tapir (called in the country the mountain-*coe* [cow]) he told it, and indeed he told it to everybody whom he encountered at whatever task and (particularly if it were afternoon-hour) at no task at all. Everybody knew Luis. And everybody knew about his mysterious and long-lasting and treatment-defying ache of the head.

"What did he do for you, mahn, Luis?"

"He took from my finger wan lee drop of blood. *And at once I felt myself cured.*"

"And what he did charge you, Luis, mahn?"

Luis looked at his questioner with very great intensity. "I will eat your arse with sahlt if he did charge me *anything*. Not one shilling. Not one cent. There are medicine doc-tors? There are bush doc-tors? There are snake doc-tors? This man, he is *ah blood doc-tor!*"

"And you now have no pain ah-tahl?"

"None. None. I tell you: none ah-tahl: Enta wenta penta *miraculousu!*"

His listeners crossed themselves. They hastened away. They told others. I hesitate to confirm that the drums beat all night long. I cannot attest that the church-bells rang out long and loud. And, on the other hand, neither can I deny it: for I was not there! I can merely assure you that my informants assured *me* that the next day there was not alone a line of people waiting to see Dr. Wilbraham, but that there was a *long* line of people waiting to see Dr. Wilbraham…the wonderful, miraculous, magical, charge-no-money, utterly efficacious blood-doctor.

And the next day. And the next. And the…

"He just take one tiny drop of blood, you see. He put it ona piece of glass…"

"…tinka tanka tonka *piece-of-glassi*…"

"…tonka tanka tinka *bahd-bloodu*…"

Doctor Wilbraham, not least of all his attractions, as I have said, charged no fee. But he had, my confidants confided in me, all the fish, cassava, and coconut he could have wanted to eat. Cooked crab. Mango, "pears," governor plums, bananas, plantains. Rice? Beans? Rice and beans? *Lots* of rice and beans.

Rice and beans with *pigtaili*.

Rice and beans with *pigsnoutu*.

This was all some time ago. And by now, I am quite sure and certain, it has been scientifically determined if the Caribs are, basically, Amerindian. Or if, basically, the Carib are African. Far be it from me to speak one word more on the subject. I am content to let Dr. Collins P. Wilbraham at the Biological Anthropology Project, University of the Miskatonic, tell us in his own words.

And, whatever they are, I hope we will all be no more strangers.

THE WAILING OF THE GAULISH DEAD

A huge thanks must be made to Henry Wessells who published this story in The Nutmeg Point District Mail *in 2013 in the* Publications of the Avram Davidson Society: Number Four. *The story was written in 1981 and is part of* The Adventures of Unhistory.

> *There is a place where Gaul*
> *stretches her furthermost shore*
> *spread out before the waves of*
> *Ocean...*
>
> > *There is heard*
> > *the mournful weeping of the*
> > *spirits of the dead...*

A question long disputed: the portrait of Justinian and Theodora (especially of Theodora!), the literary portrait, that is, as drawn up like an indictment in the *Anecdotes* (or *Secret History*) of Procopius: is it a fair portrait? Is it in any way even an accurate portrait? Can this portrait, by Procopius the Attorney, be termed a portrait at all? rather than a caricature?—this question has not yet been answered. Perhaps it never will be. Perhaps it cannot be. And yet behind it, like a face behind a mask, exists another question yet: *were the Anecdotes of Procopius by Procopius?* At all?

I cannot say.

But I believe that I can say—as though it depends

at all on me to say!—that it is scarcely doubted but Procopius, the Christian writer of Caesaria in what is now Israel, Procopius later of Byzantium...Constantinople...New Rome...was indeed the author of *De Bello Gothico*, the book about the Gothic Wars. Surely no one doubts that Claudius Claudianus, called Claudian, was really the author of *In Rufinum*, the tirade against Rufinus. The Byzantines were great conceptualists, but the conception that there might exist such a thing as freedom of speech or pen would have caused them the utmost damned astonishment. Such punishments as being blinded in both eyes and scourged whilst dragged at a camel's tail prior to burning alive might be inflicted on those who offended whoever was in power. Hence, if we read in Claudian's *Against Rufinus* a series of vitriolic sneers about that Imperial official, and know that the book was published while Claudian was still alive, it is clear that Rufinus was not; and it is clear from the fact that Procopius, however he died (and we do not know, really, exactly how or when he died), had not died of being tortured, that the book by him which accused Theodora of performing other acrobatics than those in the public circus —it is understandable that the book had certainly not been published while either Procopius or the Empress Theodora was alive: hence its name of *Anecdota*, or *unpublished*. Hence its translated title as *Secret History*, for the present common English usage of "anecdote" we owe to Doctor Johnson. A long time later. About 1300 hundred years later, to be, if not precise, approximate.

But so much for the *Anecdota*. As for the *De Bello Gothico*— Let me go back a bit.

Whilst yet collating data for a series of novels, *Vergil Magus*, which I am writing about the *legendary*, as distinct from the *historical* Vergil, there occurred to me the following notion: since there were in the ancient times seven structures generally known as the Seven Wonders of the World, might there not have been a number—say, seven —of equally wonderful things which were, however, not structures? Herodotus, for instance, refers to "the gathering-place of the rhinoceros, in the region called Agysimbia," and one learns with curious interest that the Greek word here rendered *gathering-place* in other contexts refers to the assembling of citizens of the Hellenic city-states to vote at their polling-places (Citizen: "Say, I don't know your name, but as I can't write, I'd like you to scratch the name of Aristides on this here pot-shard [*ostracon*] so I can put it in the voting-urn, as I want him ostracized for six years, sent off into exile." Second Citizen [Actually Aristides himself]: "Why, sir, has Aristides injured you in any way?" First Citizen: "No, he hasn't, but I'm just tired of hearing him called 'Aristides the Just'!" Aristides, "with a rueful smile," obliges. And goes off to exile.); the notion of the ponderous pachyderms assembling and gathering, snout to snout and horn to horn and side by armored side for the purpose of perhaps choosing leaders or perhaps ostracizing leaders; or perhaps deciding on a migration to greener pastures...or whatever...why, such a notion is, I think, wonderful indeed.

And then as I pondered this general thought further, another phrase came into my mind, I knew not whence, "The Wailing for the Gaulish Dead," and I wrote it down in my notebook—only to find, rather to my surprise, that I had actually written, The Wailing *of* the Gaulish Dead. I corrected it. Some while passed, and again there occurred to me as one of the (as I had come to call them) Seven Great Mysteries,[5] again there occurred to me the phrase, *The Wailing For the Gaulish Dead*; again I wrote it down, and again I discovered that what I had actually written was *The Wailing of the Gaulish Dead*! Now, there is certainly a difference, an immense difference...and I decided to let the second phrase stand, believing that something was trying to tell me something. Nowadays an awareness of the informational tendencies of the unconscious or the subconscious or the subliminal mind (that which lurks beneath the *limen*, beneath the threshold) is so common that we no longer believe such odd and sudden thoughts to be purely mystical revelations. We no longer believe, do we? that physical revelations occur in dreams? And yet we well know the story of how the great chemist, Kekulé, whilst dozing in a horse-cab, suddenly saw what which—when he awoke—he recognized as the discovery of the benzene ring.

The wailing of the Gaulish dead, however, unlike the benzene ring, is not subject to laboratory analysis; something had been, perhaps, revealed to me: *what did it mean?* I had no idea. Something was certainly missing from this revelation. I would wait. I would wait for the rest of it. I would simply wait and see. By and by I encountered, alas I no longer know where (what one fails to note is often as wonderful as what one fails not to note, and no one can note, as no one can remember, every single encounter or thought), a reference to a phrase in Claudian—who was Claudian? Not exactly a household word, eh? Claudian was a poet, a Latin poet, one of the last pagan poets of Rome, one of the last poets of New Rome, Constantinople, to write in Latin. After him, the deluge: the Christian religion and the Greek language.

But what has a poet writing in Constantinople, the furthermost point of Europe in the *east*, to do with the Gauls, a people whom we know chiefly as having inhabited what is now France, more-or-less (if one discounts islands) the furthermost point of Europe in the *west*? (—and if someone wishes to point out a point in Portugal as being actually further west, let him—or her—) I could be picky, and say that the Gauls *had* lived in the Eastern Roman, or Byzantine, Empire...even more to the east than Constantinople, in—in fact—Asia; in Asia Minor...but actually those were a cousin-folk, fellow-Celts, whom we know as Galatians. And besides:

Claudian makes it very clear that her is referring to *Gaul*. In the *West*.

> *Est locus extremum pandit qua* Gallia *litus Oceani praetentud aquis...*

> There is a place where Gaul stretches her furthermost shore spread out before the waves of Ocean: 'tis there that Ulysses is said to have called up the silent ghosts with a libation of blood. There is heard the mournful weeping of the spirits of the dead as they flit by with faint sound of wings, and the inhabitants see the pale ghosts pass and the shades of the dead.[6]

Well, this was *it*. Wasn't it. Obviously the peninsula of Brittany. True the word *wailing* does not precisely appear in the translation of Maurice Platnauer, but surely *mournful weeping* is close enough. Very well, this is it; is this all? By no means. The *it* continued to build up, bit by bit, for years—for more than ten years—I don't think I have it all quite yet. *I do not seek, I find. And, when I do not find, I seek.* We all have such experiences. Sometimes that which is sought for comes forth, as though obedient, at once. Sometimes it seems to hide from us, "...now reveals, now discloses...," and some transient thought or key word must be waited for, before the chamber may be unlocked. I have to consider the possibility that the original phrase may have had its origins in *The Ancient Explorers*, by Messrs. Cary and Warmington (Penguin Books, 1963), which I had read some years before the phrase occurred to me...which I had certainly read, and *perhaps* read some years *before* the phrase occurred to me. Here it is:

> "[Claudian says that] the home of the dead was located at the Western extremity of Gaul, whence the sounds of their wailings was born across to

Britain."

Britain, mind you. Not *Brittany*. Let us see. Claudian, as I have said earlier, was (in this text, *The First Book Against Rufinus*) denouncing the praetorian prefect of that name, by then safely murdered—safely for Claudian, that is—of whom the poet says, just before the verse bearing on the title of this Adventure, that "all the wickedness that is ours in common is his alone." And, since very little in the way of legal principles favoring "the liberty of the subject" were then on the statute-books, Claudian prefers less to denounce Rufinus for unconstitutional behavior than to take out his, Claudian's, poetic license and lambaste the deceased with the full force of metaphor and mythology.

After having evoked the long-dead and legendary kings Numa and Minos, Claudian then introduces the goddess Megaera, one of the three Furies, who, having "gathered together her dress with the black serpent that girdled her," and this and that, "then plied her swift wind o'er sluggish Tartarus."[7] Allow me to quote again the lines which follow, and to continue with the as yet unquoted lines which follow *them.*

"Sluggish Tartatus," that is, Hell—

> ...plied her swift wings o'er sluggish Tartarus. There is a place where Gaul stretches her furthermost shore spread out before the waves of Ocean: 'tis there that Ulysses is said to have called up the silent ghosts with a libation of blood. There is heard the mournful weeping of the spirits of the dead [no longer "silent," note] as they flit by with faint sound of wings, and the inhabitants see the pale ghosts pass and the shades of the dead. 'Twas from here the goddess leapt forth, dimmed the sun's fair beams and clave the sky with horrid howlings. Britain [*Britannia*] felt the deadly sounds,

the noise shook the country of the Senones, Tethys stayed her tide, and Rhine let fall his urn and shrank his stream. Thereupon...she enters the walls of Elusa...

Hmm. The Senones. "Their territory lay some sixty miles S.E. of Paris," says Platnauer. Tethys was Ocean's wife. And Elusa was Rufinus's home-town, "in the Department of Gens," in, are you surprised? Gaul. Well. What are we to make of this? It seems of *me* that it was *not* "the mournful weeping" of the ghosts which reached Britannia, but the "horrid howlings" of the serpent-girdled goddess which did. Her entry into Elusa, "in the guise of an old man," was just so much allegorical gizmadoo: but if the rest is not a metaphor for the effects of an earthquake or something very much like it, then, well, Claudian has out-done his efforts. Platnauer says that "...as a poet Claudian is not always despicable"; so let us leave it at that.

As I suppose one does not always have the dates of the rise and fall of Rufinus at one's fingertips, it may be useful to learn from this same source that "The date of the composition of Claudian's...'In Rufinium' is certainly to be placed within the years of 395-397"; what about Procopius? Here is the recent Encyclopedia Britannica; it says that he "was born...probably between 490 and 507"; and never mind why—but this certainly plays hob with any notion that Claudian and Procopius were contemporaries...and perhaps exchanged stories on the Constantinopolitan cocktail-circuit. But...in this context what *about* Procopius? Why have I dragged him in by his Byzantine buskins? Because Procopius is on record as reporting the following fascinating little item:

"Procopius de bell Goth. 4, 20 (ed. Bonn. 2, 567), speaking of the island of Brittia, imparts a legend which he had often heard from the lips of the inhabitants. They imagine that the souls of the dead are *transported to that island*. On the coast of the continent there dwell under Frankish sovereignty, but hitherto exempt from all taxation, fishers and farmers whose duty it is to *ferry the souls over.* This duty they take in turn. Those to whom it falls on any night, go to bed at dusk; at midnight they hear a knocking at their door, and muffled voices calling. Immediately they rise, go to the shore, and there see *empty* boats, not their own but strange ones, they go on board and seize the oars. When the boat is under way they perceive that she is *laden choke-full* [i.e. chock-full], with her gunwales hardly a finger's breadth above water. Yet they see no one, and in an hour's time they touch land, which one of their own craft would take a day and a night to do.[8] Arrived in Brittia, the boat speedily unloads, and becomes so light that she only dips her keel in the wave. Neither on the voyage nor at landing do they see any one, but they hear a voice loudly asking each one his name and country. Women that have crossed give their husbands' names.

"Procopius' Brittia lies no farther than 200 stadia (25 miles) from the mainland, between Britannia and Thule, opposite the Rhine mouth, and three nations live in it, Angles, Frisians and Britons. By Britannia he means the NW. coast of Gaul, one end of which is still called Bretagne, but in the 6th century the name included the subsequent Norman and Flemish-Frisian country up to the mouths of Scheldt and Rhine; his Brittia is Great Britain, his Thule Scandinavia.

"Whereabouts the passage was made, whether along the whole of the Gallic coast, I leave undetermined"—and so, for the moment, do I—but who is the "I" whom I am quoting? It is Jakob Ludwig Karl Grimm (1785-1863), who, with his brother, Wilhelm Karl Grimm (1786-1859), gave us the famous fairy tales—but it is not from their joint work that I have quoted, but from the *Teutonic Mythology* in four volumes, first called to my attention by Mr. Ed M. Clinton, and which Jakob Grimm alone produced: more from Jakob later.

So. Claudian and Procopius. Claudian says that on or off

the westernmost coast of Gaul the souls of the dead may be heard "mournfully weeping," and Procopius says that they are transported thence by boat; Claudian, in re their transportation or anyway movement, says only that they are "flitting"; Procopius does not have them making any sound but a muffled one, and that of loudly calling and answering the roll. If Claudian does not precisely say that their wailing may be heard in Britain, certainly he reports that, somehow, in this connection, certain quite loud noises were heard there. Procopius places his Brittia not far from Britannia and the mouth of the Rhine; Claudian says that at the time of the "horrid howlings" the Rhine "let fall his urn and shrank his stream." We observe both the similarities of their accounts, and we note the differences as well.

Confused geography, spook-stories...nothing more?

Maybe. Only maybe not.

If I were to sum up the principle purpose of these Adventures in Unhistory, I would say that it is to investigate certain old myths and legends to see what truths, if any, may lie behind them.

And, yet once again, I quote Charles Fort (or whomever Charles Fort may have been quoting), "One measures a circle beginning anywhere."

Time and again I have found that "even when I do not seek, I find"—*serendipity*, this may be called, it being understood that what one finds is found while seeking something else—not always, alas, but often, often, often: once one has determined to find something out, it will find itself out for you. Often. To invent an example, suppose that you have become interested in butterflies as articles of human clothing. You may find information under *butterflies*, you may find it under *clothing*; then again, you may not. The matter may be half-abandoned, half-forgotten...

for a while. And then, without a thought in the world as regards butterflies as articles of human clothing, casually you begin a book about—say—Virginia Woolf. And there, on pages 27 and 28, you find yourself reading—as it might be —that Virginia Woolf's eccentric cousin Algernon Stephen as a young man spent a year in Fantaanago, a country in the Central Indies, where to his astonishment he found the natives adorning their clothing with the wings of gorgeous butterflies. In one of his frequent letters home he wrote...

And so on.

I repeat: this example is fictitious.

The following is not.

In the Fall of 1981 I thought that I already had enough information on the subject of The Wailing of the Gaulish Dead, and that I had only to assemble it all (not a simple task, for it was scattered [as are so many of my papers] in places hundreds of miles apart) and then set myself to the writing of it. It was however necessary to wait a month more before I would be able to journey in search of part of my data. The matter then sank from the surface of my mind, and so one day I encountered and began to read, purely for pleasure, a book by the Anglo-Canadian author Geoffrey Ashe, whose *King Arthur's Avalon* (1957) I had read a few years earlier with pleasure, and from which I had made extracts and abstracts in connection with my *Vergil Magus* work (mentioned very early in this Adventure): this second book is *LAND TO THE WEST/St. Brendan's Voyage to America/A Search For Irish and Other Pre-Viking Discoveries of America* (Viking [!] Press, New York, 1962).

To be as brief as is possible in writing of such a subject, I had for long years known of the so-called Voyages of St. Brendan, whom it might be unfair to term an Irish Sindbad... what St. Brendan himself might have written (if he wrote, himself) of his alleged voyages by sea in the course of which many strange sights were said to have been seen, it is not now possible with certainty to say. Dr. Ashe, however, says much which makes sense...if not certainty. And it was when I read the lines on p. 30, "Druidical reincarnations persisted as a theme of romance, tumuli became fairy hills with strange occupants, *haunting presences brooded over islands and across waters generally*[9]..." that it occurred to me that Dr. Ashe's researches might serve as a paradigm of my own—nothing more, of course, as St. Brendan's times were much later than those of Claudian, or even of Procopius. Here and there something might be quoted from *Land to the West* exemplary of *The Wailing of the Gaulish Dead*. And so I determined to note at least some of these as possible quotations for this Adventure.

...*haunting presences brooded over islands and across water generally*. Might it not be said that among such haunting presences were those of the Gaulish Dead, wailing across the waters of their exile? I thought so, and began to make note of such passages as this (p. 42), on the immram or immrama, a type of old Hibernian[10] tale:

"An Irish trait which has been called the desire to 'penetrate the unknown and make the unseen world actual' produced a crop of adventure yarns dealing with quests in alien regions best defined as Otherworlds. These Celtic Otherworlds were variously conceived, sometimes as abodes of the dead, sometimes as homes of gods and fairy-folk. A carefree aristocratic Elysium quite like its Greek counterpart was pictured under many names, and sometimes located in the ocean: such was Tir-nan-Og [lit. 'Land of Youth']. In a romance probably written by a monk of Bangor the Celtic god Bran, transformed into a more or less human hero, was made to visit a place of this kind, and his fame helped to inspire a series of voyage-romances describing tours among imaginary western islands—quests, in a sense, likewise, but with a shift of emphasis."

Well! *This* was promising, was it not? Was, then, this my "Wailing of the Gaulish Dead" perhaps a fragment of some such voyage-romance? Could its entire lineaments be rediscovered, this in mind? Who knows? Read on. Read on.

"Oral transmission being in any case customary in dark-age Ireland, and the evidence being so much in favor of a developed and conscientious artistry, the mere absence of early documentation is not in itself decidedly adverse. Because the tale was only set down at a certain date, it was not necessarily invented then; and experience shows that the historical lore of a rooted, pre-literate, story-telling people should not be brushed aside.

"As Freeman wisely said in another connection, a legend may not be a record of facts, but the existence of the legend is itself a fact, and requires explanation" (p. 49). Well-put. Onward.

And now see Ashe cite from the equally Celtic *Voyage of Bran* as (perhaps) a cognate to the Voyage of St. Brendan: The "companions see twenty-nine wonderful islands and a few incidental wonders between. Sometimes putting ashore, sometimes not, they visit an island swarming with huge ants"; here one is reminded of the gold-delving ants whose griffin-guarded gold was thefted by the greedy, canny one-eyed Arimaspeans in the Adventure, *The Secret of Hyperborea*; "an island of terraces and bright-colored birds; a sandy island with a monster guarding the beach"; shadows of Talus, the metal man whom the Argonauts found guarding the coast of Crete; "a flat island where a demonic horse-race is going on; an island with an empty palace; an island with a ridge all round it and giant apple-tree in the centre; an island with animals that devour each other; an island with a circling wall and a monster rushing madly along it; a large beautiful island which is hot to the touch and inhabited by red-hot swine; and an island with a palace and a magical cat, which destroys one of the foster-brothers. Then—"

But perhaps enough (pp. 57, 58). In our "Gaulish Dead,"

as set down in the first, brief quotation from Claudian, as the epigraph to this Adventure, and which I believe to be the basic text, all this madly Celticly colorful Irish blarney is absent...lost...and only a few sad elements remain. But is it so? Perhaps nothing at all has been "lost" from the account of the dead and wailing Gauls—nothing, that is, but the truth behind it—perhaps, instead, this brief matter is not a remnant but a source. Perhaps. Perhaps? Well, let us see.

Ashe again (pp. 61, 62): "Behind all immrama, written and oral, was clearly that ancient dream of an Otherworld Quest. It was not peculiar to Irish mythology, but the Irish imagination with its interpenetrating planes of reality, its persistent striving to localize and actualize the unseen"— ah, indeed! it is the site of the wailing Gaulish dead, all but unseen though not unheard, which we are indeed *striving to localize and actualize!*—"pursued the vision of an attainable fairyland with a special ardour. The aristocratic Elysium, where favored heroes feasted and sang with immortals, was placed variously here and there, and divided and reduplicated. But it was identified in particular with a marvelous western island, or with a group of such islands: Tir-nan-Og and Tir-nam-Beo, Mag Mon and Mag Mell, where the climate was forever warm," O Hyperborea, Hyperborea O! "and the soul forever untroubled."—True, the souls of the Gaulish Dead, with their wailing and their mournful weeping, do not seem at all *that* untroubled, but—"Long before the *Voyage of Bran* was written, Celtic myths must have been telling of men who had to seek out some Otherwordly place, under a hill or across water, for some such purpose as obtaining a cure or fetching a treasure. For these missions the potentialities of the Atlantic Island motif were especially alluring, and it was through the use of it that story-tellers drew the whole medley of oceanic themes into their repertoire: speculation about the range of the curragh [or coracle, the bull-hide Celtic boat] and the secret regions of the west, phantasmal sunset visions, lore concerning the old gods, yarns spun by fanciful fisherman, reminiscences of the sea-roving monks and island-hermits," later on, remember those island-hermits! "Immram literature resulted from the importation of all these things (the Ocean-mythos, as it were) into the Otherworld Quest. But a shift of interest ensued; the Otherworld goal itself faded into a problematical haze, and adventure by sea became a subject in its own right."

—And, it may well be, a far better subject: but one which we cannot follow now and here.

St. Brendan, then, "looks westward, and with miraculously strengthened eyes he glimpses the land across the ocean...he calls his monks together. They build three great curraghs equipped with sails and oars, each capable of carrying thirty, and set off across the perilous Atlantic, 'over the loud-voiced waves of the rough-crested sea, and over the billows of the greenish tide, and over the abysses of the wonderful, terrible, relentless ocean'...(p. 64)[11]

"Somewhere," says Ashe of Brendan (p. 66), "somewhere in the background, at however many removes, is a realization of maritime fact and an insistent murmur of the actual... Somewhere behind the mist and spray loom the figures of real voyagers reporting real experiences." As with our own briefer accounts? Let us see. Let us see.

Q. As for the immrama, these "Irish voyage stories," how do we know that they aren't merely entirely Irish blarney-stories?

A. One examines them as one would any other stories, in terms of their times, their contents, and their methods. And while much of what is said of old Castle Blarney is, a word, "blarney," the existence of the castle itself is no blarney. It is a fact.

For a coherent and sustained account of the Voyages of St. Brendan, one will have to look elsewhere than to this Adventure—to Dr. Ashe's book and to other books—what will be found of that here are only samples—however, not random samples. See here: "...they turned back towards the island of Sheep and sailed along the coast for three days. [Nearby] they sighted another island [Herm?] across another sound to the west. [More of this later.]...this island, in fact, was called the Paradise of Birds. One of them spoke and told Brendan that they were spirits in disguise—intermediate spirits neither angel nor devil—and that they flew abroad and saluted God on holy days." Do you see? You don't see? Then let me digress.

A very early Patriarch of Moscow had a parrot which he taught to say, "*Hospodi pomilui,*" Lord have mercy on us, a phrase frequent in the Liturgy of the Russian Orthodox Church. The bird escaped one day and a peasant, seeing the gorgeous creature, tried to capture it; the parrot, startled, flew up into a tree and squawked, "*Hospodi pomilui!*" The peasant fell on his knees in the snow, snatched off his cap, crossed himself, and cried, "Forgive me, forgive me! I thought Your Reverence was a bird!"

"Brendan's doubtfully historic visitor ['Barinthus'] has been equated," says Ashe, "with St. Barrind...A preternaturally swift crossing, such as he recounts, is an ancient legendary theme. Odysseus returns to Ithaca from the land of the Phæcians between dawn and dusk. Procopius, a Byzantine contemporary of Brendan, refers to Celtic accounts of the ferrying of the souls of the dead from Gaul to Britain; the nocturnal voyage, he says, is accomplished in a single hour, whereas the normal time of transit from the same point is a night and a day." Hm, very interesting... *what?*...hold on! In my mind, as I was reading this, I was already italicizing *a preternaturally swift crossing*, when I was brought up short and sharply by the totally unexpected words, *Procopius, a Byzantine contemporary of Brendan.* What was this? Surely Brendan had lived several hundred years later? [check all this] Ah, but no, he hadn't. I had somehow misfiled my information. The literary account The Voyages was written several hundred years *after* the voyages themselves—but the two men were themselves and indeed contemporaries. Shock was succeeded by another emotion; I felt like someone who, thumping a vending machine in hopes of recovering a recalcitrant dime, is instead rewarded with a shower of quarters: for Dr. Ashe's analysis of an historical voyage, far from providing merely a paradigm for my very own attempts at analyzing a mythical one, now proved to be set on the very same sea-track—even though I was "merely" interested in St. Brendan and Dr. Ashe was "merely" interested in Procopius (he does not mention Claudian). Once again, magic had moved in.

Dr. Ashe says, and says well, "The mind is governed by the laws of its context; and who can say through what customary symbolism, what conditioned apparatus of riddling imagery, the men of the past really saw their world? When a Hebrew writer relates a miracle or an Irish writer relates a marvel, what are they trying to convey? If one could get inside them and recover the key to their unintentional cryptograms, perhaps a book like the [*Voyages*] would be neither far-fetched nor obscure at all. One lacks resources." Indeed. In order to make this Adventure well, I should really explore the entire Gallic coast, as well as its circumjacent islands; ask

> *Ye islands and ye highlands,*
> *O say, what ha'e ye seen?*

But I lack resources. Therefore my explorations must be limited to books, and within those limits one does the best one can.

Among the books which I had explored in the course, the long course, of the *Vergil Magus* researches, is *The Ignorance of Certainty*, by Ashley Montagu and Edward Darling (Harper and Row, 1970); they say, "The adventure [of Jonah and the 'whale'] is seen as one of those journeys across the Styx or into the Land of the Dead such as Ulysses and other humans took: a period of stress and torment, of trial and agony. King Arthur is full of instances in the Grail sequence, and compare Beowulf and the Nordic sagas of Asgard." Well, not right now, I think; but, Ulysses? Recall that *There is a place where Gaul stretches her furthermost shore spread out before the waves of Ocean: 'tis there that Ulysses is said to have called up the silent ghosts*...I have, in other and earlier Adventures quoted from a marvelous book, *The Coasts of Illusion*, by Clark B. Firestone, subtitled *A Study of Travel Tales* (Harper, 1924); many a pickle makes a mickle, let me quote again. "The tides were the breath of the living earth, Solinus thought." However unscientific this may be, compare it to the explanation of the tides offered by some old-time Canadian Indians: "A large man on the beach of the ocean gets up and sits down twice a day. [...] The Gauls," however, "endowed them with life," but evidently the Gauls thought that life malevolent, "for they attacked them with weapons"! And, perhaps, also tormented them with gongs? Well, as Firestone sums it up, "A voyage to those strangely peopled countries of the world's yesterdays would be a voyage among the bays, gulfs, and promontories of the human mind in the states of dream."

Though even dreams may have geography. "Sea and sky," says Firestone, "had their part in the drama of life. To the Celt the voice of the waves carried warning of sympathy or prophecy. The ninth wave was larger than those before it. It was thought that no man or animal beside the Gallic Sea died with a rising tide." If they died with an ebb-tide, would it not be reasonable to assume that the souls would go "out" in the direction of the tide?

"What happened to old So-and-So?"

"Caught a bullet. Went west."

Where does the sun set?

But perhaps by now we ought to cite the certain texts of Homer pertaining to this incident, and not take a knowledge, or even a memory of them for granted. They begin in Book X and continue into book XI. Let us remember that the *Odyssey* was written in Greek, whereas the *In Rufimum* was written in Latin, and that he whom Claudian called Ulysses is here of course called Odysseus. He and his shipmates are still on the island of the sorceress Circe (who had changed them into swine, and then back to men again), somewhere in or near the central Mediterranean. Circe speaks:

> "'Royal son of Laertes, Odysseys of the nimble wits,' the goddess answered me, 'I am not going to keep you in my house against your wishes. But before I can send you home you have to make a journey of a very different kind, and find your way to the halls of Hades and Persephone the Dead, to consult the soul of Teiresias, the blind Theban prophet, whose understanding even death had not impaired. For dead though he is, Persephone has left to him, and him alone, a mind to reason with. *The rest are mere shadows flitting to and fro.*[12]

> "'...Set up your mast, spread the white sail and sit down in the ship. The North Wind will blow her on her way; and when she has brought you across the River of Ocean, you will come to a wild coast and to Persephone's Grove, where the tall poplars grow and the willows that so quickly shed their seeds. Beach your boat there by Ocean's swirling stream and march on into Hades' Kingdom of Decay. There the River of Flaming fire and the River of Lamentation, which is a branch of the Waters of Styx, unite around a pinnacle of rock to pour their thundering streams into Acheron. This is the spot...'"

(This is the translation of E.V. Rieu, Penguin, 1962). Circe further directs Odysseus to dig a trench and make to the dead offerings of, in turn, honey and milk, sweet wine, water, and barley, and two sheep; followed by "prayers to the helpless ghosts of the dead." Odysseus obeys; and in no more than a day and part of a night, reaches

> "...the deep-flowing River of Ocean and the frontiers of the world, where the fog-bound Cimmerians live in the City of Perpetual Mist. When the bright Sun climbs the sky and puts the stars to flight, no ray from him can penetrate to them, nor can he see them as he drops from heaven and sinks once more to earth. For dreadful Night has spread her mantle over the heads of that unhappy folk."

Thus, the famous "Cimmerian darkness"; what was it? "Fog" and "mist" seem to present no problems, and perhaps the mantle of "dreadful Night" is a report of the long Arctic or even sub-Arctic winter. The ancient Greeks considered Homer as the pre-eminent geographer, but Homer was not singing under oath. The Atlantic is not famous for the constant clarity of its weather, and anywhere north of southern Portugal might have offered mist and fog for long enough to have seemed perpetual to a traveler from Greece, where the air does indeed seem to sparkle.

Very well, Odysseus offered the honey, milk, wine, water, and white barley to "the glorious fellowship of the dead"; then he took a young ram and a black ewe and "cut their throats over the trench so that the dark blood poured in. And now the souls of the dead...came swarming up...[and] as they *fluttered to and fro*...there came *a moaning that was horrible to hear*. Panic drained the blood from my cheeks." Somewhat later he heard his mother's spirit tell him that, "once the life-force has departed from our white bones...the soul slips away like a dream and *flutters on the air*." And, at the last, "the tribes of the dead came up and gathered round me in their tens of thousands, *raising their eerie cry*.[13] Sheer panic turned me pale...I made off quickly to my ship," and who indeed could blame him? The ship set off while it was still night, and

> "From the flowing waters of the River of Ocean my ship passed into the wide places of the open sea, and so reached Aeaea, the Island of the Rising Sun, where tender Dawn has her home and her dancing-lawns,"

supposed to have been somewhere on the eastern coast of the Black Sea, "where we fell into a sound sleep that lasted till daybreak."

Well, here is "a preternaturally swift voyage" indeed! From the Atlantic to the Euxine in only a part of a night; and so much for the geography of the great geographer, he could never cut the mustard at Rand McNally.

Nevertheless, we have learned a great deal. The notion that the land of the dead lies on or near a *coast*, and that the spirits of the dead engage in a great deal of flitting and fluttering and make a great deal of scary noises, first enters *literature* with Homer; Claudian long later locates this place in western Gaul, Procopius sets *his* scene in *northern* Gaul, perhaps the present Belgium or Holland, vis á vis Britain.

I refer again, as elsewhere in these Adventures, to Monsieur Maurice Bessy's *Pictorial History of Magic and the Supernatural* (Spring Books, U.K., 1968), and again I caution that M. Bessy seems much given to stating as facts things which may be exclusively the opinions of M. Bessy, though perhaps his is a very educated opinion. He says of the Eleusinian Mysteries that "the initiate...must know how to subdue the sea, symbol of genesis, for which reason he learned to pilot a shop at sea (*symbol of the transport of souls into the beyond*)." Italics mine. *Bon voyage.*

Geography. Again. Ashe. Again. Citing Homer on the visit

of one Odysseus, a.k.a. Ulysses, "to the frontiers of the world, where the fog-bound Cimmerians," generally thought to have been a Celtic people, "live in the City of Perpetual Mist," asks—Ashe asks—where the Cimmerians and their perpetual mists may really be? Answers, "if they are anywhere, they are surely in the British Isles. [...] The passage in which the Byzantine Procopius, Brendan's contemporary, reports with many particulars how the souls of the dead are imagined in north-east Gaul to be ferried over to Britain," again we see this perplexing and confusing matter of *Brittia* versus *Britannia*, "might be excusably ascribed to the persistence or recrudescence of ancestral belief" (p. 166). *Might be.* But...might there not be other, nearer, and less mythical explanations? I think...I think there might be.

Well, and just in case you are becoming just the faintest degree bored with what Ashe calls "...the Celtic fantasies of Otherworld Quests by water, and island adventures..." (p.283)—I myself am not—let me take you somewhat away from said scene, for a while anyway. First to Italy, and then to Scandinavia. Marcel Brion informs us in his *Pompeii and Herculaneum* (trans. by John Rosenberg, Crown Publishers, 1960), that a "bas-relief decorating the outside of the funeral monument to Munatius Faustus has...exited the curiosity of archaeologists," and not of archaeologists alone. The relief shows a ship, with crew and sails. Something is going on. Is the ship coming in to port? Is the ship leaving port? Is the ship caught in a storm at sea? Does it refer to some particular incident in the life of Munatius Faustus, whoever Munatius Faustus was?—perhaps representing, perhaps a vow he had made if granted a safe voyage—better than offering a hecatomb of elephants, as one opulent Roman was said to have done for a similar purpose. M. Brion concedes the possibility of this. But he suggests that the scene may have represented a purely religious matter: with ocean as a symbol of death, and the ship as a symbol of salvation. Not of Christian salvation, to be sure, for

Christianity was then a small and persecuted sect and the scene shows not one specific Christian symbol—no cross, no fish—but nonetheless, salvation. From death. It may be so. I do not know. But for the ship and funerals and intimations of immortality, let us choose (there are many sources from which to choose) another pagan notion, that of ship burial, as discussed succinctly in an article, "The Vikings," by Howard LaFay, in the *National Geographic Magazine* for January 1973: just one line: "A great man or a great lady merited a fully-fitted ship as a sepulcher; slaughtered horses, hounds, and slaves accompanied the dead on that final voyage. Lesser men would be buried with boats. Those of no resources would, at the least, have graves covered by stones, arranged in the outline of a boat."

Well, this certainly fits finely into the tall story reported by Procopius...doesn't it? Was the notion of the souls of the dead being ferried from this world to another based upon the ship burial of the Teutonic great based upon the notion of the souls of the dead being ferried from this world to another?—for such a notion we find all across the old world: a coin for Charon, the ferryman of the Styx, said the ancient Greeks; at the furthermost off-shore point of Asia the Japanese added some ghastly, ghostly details: the old ferryman had an old wife, and whoever ghost had not money for the fare, such a one she stripped quite bare, and hung up the clothes on the dead trees which bordered the river of hell. "Strange fruit," indeed.

By the time of Procopius, say about ?500 to ?562 of the Christian Era, the Teutons were, as the Romans had been before them, pushing and pressing hard upon the Celts, and so successfully that the Celts' very languages, which were once spoken from Asia throughout Europe (northern Italy, Austria, France, Belgium, Spain, the British Isles) are now spoken—where they are still spoken at all—only on the Highlands and the Islands of the misty Atlantic: northern Scotland, the Hebrides, Wild Wales, western Ireland...and of course, Brittany, once called Armorica, their very last tonguehold in what was once called Gaul. The account of Procopius speaks of the Angles and the Frisians as already living in Britain along with the Britons. So the myths of the Teutons and the myths of the Celts were already blending.

So—did actual ships or boats ever be sent off to sea with the bodies of the dead upon them? Even if not, those outside the Norse world might well have imagined this to be done, thus contributing to the legend as told by Procopius. Burial involving ships or boats is likely to have been an important element in this matter of The Wailing of the Gaulish Dead.

And so—what else?

Enter Professor L.C. Wimberly, whose learned *Folklore In the English and Scottish Ballads* surely does not fall within a certain category designated by my compeer Poul Anderson, who once said in print, "To be sure, much of Avram's arcane knowledge comes from books, but they are often books whose contents are known only to God, the author, and Avram Davidson"—for, whoever first published Wimberly in 1928 (my notes have lacunae), it was certainly re-published in 1965, by Dover Books, of New York; and Dover Books, despite a somewhat noticeable tendency to publish books already in the public domain, surely publish for a much wider audience than me alone: onward.

"The custom of boat burial...implied the belief that one must cross the sea in order to reach the country of the spirits." Does it? Need it? May it not have implied a sensible belief that arable land in coastal Scandinavia was too hard come-by to use any much of it for burial ground? Or...or, and/or...may it not imply that at one time a dead man's boat became as taboo as a dead man's Hogan is among Navaho today? If so, might as well place him in it and send it out to sea...would have no luck fishing with it, anyway...To imply either, however, might not much advance our Adventure, so let us, therefore accept Professor Wimberly's implication, and proceed...proceed, for instance, to his quotation from

Thomas Rymer, who "...*saw neither sun nor moon, / But heard the roaring of the sea*" (p. 121).

Wimberly says, just as though I were not trying to prove the opposite, "The ballad geography of spiritland is decidedly puzzling if one thinks of fixing a specific locality from the Otherworld of traditional song"—*Hm!* Is it possible that there was once a song, now lost, about The Wailing of the Gaulish Dead?—and that our prose accounts derive from it? It may be so. I do not know. "He who would map out this sphere of souls, fairies, and demons is confronted on every hand with only fragmentary descriptions. Moreover, these descriptions are likely to represent not a single faith but to give evidence of the rival claims of various beliefs. Some confusion arises, for example, from a frequent merging of Christian and pre-Christian ideas. Is the abode of the departed, or the land of elves and demons, associated with the forest; is it on a hill or mountain; is it subterranean, submarine, *over the sea, or on an island*?"—italics mine. Again. Remember them, later on.

Remember, too, that Claudian connects the Wailing of the Gaulish Dead with *horrid howlings*; remember that Thomas Rymer heard the *roaring of the sea*. The sea is like to roar alike in any quarter of the world? Still, let me take you away from all this and to a place where it may roar a deal differently. Or was once wont to roar so. I have no recent reports. My source is the well-known *Periplus of the Erythraean Sea*, said to have been written by some old sea-dog sometime during the reign of Nero, when attention was paid to the performing arts a deal more than in most previous or subsequent reigns or administrations; and yet there are those who say that N. was such a disagreeable man—well, enough of this nonsense— the passage coming up ahead, I have in my notes not once but twice: once from the U.S. edition of *The Periplus* (Longmans, Green, 1912) and once from good old Cary and Warmington in their *The Ancient Explorers*. I'd copiously annotated C. & W. before finding out that one entire signature was missing; this prevented my turning in my copy for a new one, and I have yet to read it in full. But: *Periplus*:

"For so great are the forces of the uprush of the sea at this time of the new moon, especially the flood-tide at night, that as soon as a putting-in begins when the open water is calm, at once there is carried to the ears of those at the river's mouth a noise heard afar off like the shouting of an armed camp, and after a while the sea itself rushes over the shoals with a roar." The scene was the northwestern coast of India. Rather far from Gaul. What is the connection? I should state it to be, *strange sounds heard at sea.* Speaking like a land-lubber, one might term them to be *horrid howlings.* Am I reaching far too far, and far out? Is it not possible, though, that some equally natural phenomenon might have produced that weird sound heard off the northwestern coast of Europe? If so, then why is it not heard *now*?

Perhaps because whatever produced it, if anything did produce it, *is no longer there.* Perhaps there was once a similar phenomenon, noise-producing shoals, a tidal bore, remember Claudian's "goddess," who caused the Ocean to halt its tides, and the Rhine its flow? which I suggested might have been the results of an (otherwise unreported) earthquake? or sea-quake (if one might use the word…say, a submarine quake)…after which, *perhaps*, the sound was never heard again. Or, to invent (cry alleged to have been uttered by Jules Verne upon first reading H.G. Wells: "*Il invente!*"), perhaps the sound of the "dead" was produced by the wind moaning through a cave opened at both sides—a tunnel, that would be? so let be a tunnel—perhaps the tunnel has since caved in. The subject is a very general and open one, so select your own hypothetical natural phenomenon; any number can play.

—And what do we know about the home life of Procopius?

Well, really, nothing. Evidently he reserved his gossip columns for the high and the mighty. Perhaps the real source of his grievance against the Empress Theodora was that she had been an actress at an earlier stage of her career, and, even earlier, when she as in fact a child, had helped her parents care for the bears which performed in the arena. I am afraid that Procopius was a snob, as well as a bureaucrat and a writer, and no doubt uttered many a mutter that "the Byzantine, or Eastern Roman, Empire, is going to hell in a fruit-basket"—whereas, as a matter of fact, it was to be about another 900-odd years (some of them very odd years indeed) before the forces of the ultimate enemy breached the great walls of Constantinople, and Mohammed the Conqueror rode his horse, red to the knees with blood, down the nave of the great Cathedral of the Holy Wisdom. There was certainly some wisdom in the exclamation of the cathedral's builder, that same Emperor Justinian, "Solomon, I have surpassed you!" for the Temple of Solomon is no longer, while the Cathedral of Justinian still survives (though now a museum).

Justinian's (not immediate) predecessor, Constantine, selected the city named for himself to be the New Rome and imperial capital because it was in a way the cross-roads of the world; only some slight bodies of water dividing Europe from Asia there. The climate is not always genial, fierce blizzards sweep down upon it out of the immense land-mass of the great continent to the east, but the same waters still teem with life...or did: pollution is now said to be severe. Is it still so, then, that "dolphins migrate" past it, "going from the Mediterranean northward in the seas of the Hellespont and the Marmara"? I do not know, the statement is quoted from Messrs. Devine and Clark, authors of *The Dolphin Smile* (Macmillan, 1967). The dolphins "remain for a while in the Black Sea and then return to their starting point. They fight in herds against the bonito or thon [tuna]."

The subject of the migrations of animals, fish, birds, and other creatures is a rich and fascinating one. Also to be seen in those waters: "Scarcely a minute passes but flocks of aquatic birds, resembling swallows, may be observed flying in a lengthened train from one sea to the other. As they are never known to rest, they are called Halcyons, and...damned souls...They are superstitiously regarded by all...skimming along the coasts in lines of many hundreds...because of their restless habits and somber plumage Moslems believe them to be tenanted by the souls of the condemned." Procopius must have seen them, as well; let us follow this train, or trail, for a bit. (This last citation, by the way, is from *The Folklore of Birds: An Enquiry into the Origin and Distribution of Some Magico-Religious Traditions*, by E.A. Armstrong [Houghton Mifflin, 1959], p. 214. I have quoted from this book to, I hope, good effect, in an earlier Adventure, as to the alleged enmity between eagles and dragons. Assuming, as I assumed, the dragon in the long run to be the crocodile, the allegation seemed based on sound observation indeed.)

Ever heard of the Gabriel Hounds? Don't look for them at your local kennel club; they are certainly to be associated with the Wild Hunt, that clamor in the air at night said to be the passing-by overhead of the pagan gods and goddesses. I don't know if any precise number has ever been assigned to the Gabriel Hounds, but Wordsworth wrote

> *He the seven birds hath seen that never part,*
> *Seen the Seven Whistlers of their nightly rounds*

Others imply that this could not be, for The Whistlers and Their Kin are "said to be six birds in search of another. When they find him it will be the end of the world." Not surprisingly, they are also said to be death omens. And we are also now back in western Europe. While you weren't looking. So let us pick up the trail of Procopius again, pausing to consider for a moment or so a couple of members of the highwellborn Blücher family; *for those who do not care for this sort of thing, there is always the cinema and the detective novel.*

Few fancies are so outrageous and *outré* as that entertained in the last days of his old age by General Blücher, conqueror (with Wellington) of Bonaparte at Waterloo: he firmly believed, and often repeated, that he was "pregnant with an elephant, and by a British soldier..." By comparison, his nephew, Prince Blücher, seems hardly eccentric at all in his own desire to raise wallabies in Europe, well, *why not*, not just any old where in Europe, mind you: only on the island of Herm, one of those Channel Islands of which we hear that there "the Queen of England reigns as Duke of Normandy"— and if I hear it again, I'll *scream.*—Oh, *hi*, Duke. Hi, Ricky— Why are you becoming so restless? *I have a* purpose *in writing all this!*

Now, right after telling us about Procopius, who, in the latter's capacity of war correspondent and news reporter, revealed that the souls of the dead are, with muffled voices and, I would suppose, muffled oars as well (*Natty British Boatman*: Damn you, you've broken my oar! *Nasty British Bargeman*: Oh I 'ave, 'ave I? Well, speaking of oars, 'ow's yer sister?—*I'm* sorry—), ferried from somewhere or the Gallic coast to or from Britain, Brittia, Britannia; right after this, old Jakob Grimm goes on to impart a further piece of intelligence. "...near Raz, at the farthest point of Armorica [Brittany, its Gaulish name]...we find a [place called the] bay of souls (baie des âmes, boé ann anavo). On the R[iver] Treguier in Bretagne [Brittany, Armorica]...it is said to be the custom to this day, to convey the dead to the churchyard *in a boat*, over a small arm of the sea called *passage de l'enfer* [Hell's passage], instead of taking the shorter way by land; besides, the people all over Armorica [Brittany] believe that souls at the moment of parting repair to the pastor of Braspar, whose dog escorts them to Britain..." (p. 833)

And, elsewhere, Grimm says, "The popular opinion of Greece also regarded the soul as a winged being...not bird, but *butterfly*, which is even more apt, for the insect is developed out of the chrysalis, as the soul is out of the body; hence [psyche] is also the word for butterfly...We shall come across these butterflies again as will o' the wisps (ziebold, vezha), and in the Chap. on Witches as elvish beings..."

Butterfly, eh. Well, that is a pretty (if a pretty innocent) concept; certainly it would account well for Homer's *flitting to and fro, fluttered to and fro,* and *flutters on the air*; as well as Claudian's *flit by*: there are however one or two difficulties, for instance one: nobody has ever heard a butterfly utter a *moaning that was terrible to hear*, or raise *an eerie cry*. If butterflies have ever engaged in *mournful weeping*, the fact has not been reported to me; and as for Lepidoptera issuing forth *horrid howls*, forget it. Back to Grimm.

There is a notion stirring somewhere here which will not lie still, a notion of an island, perhaps Homer's "rocky pinnacle," an island in a sea or ocean, with a reputation both religious and weird: the great island of Britain will not fit, it is too large. Grimm refers to an "island [which] took the name of hêlegland," that is, holy land, "Helgoland, which it bears to this day; here also the evangelists," that is, the early Christian missionaries, "were careful to conserve, in the interests of Christianity, the sense of sacredness already attached to the site," i.e., in pagan times (p. 230). Helgoland, in the North Sea, came under the rule of Great Britain in the early 19th century; in the late 19th century the British traded it to the Germans for, would you believe it, Zanzibar. The Germans preferred Helgoland because of the ties of blood and history binding them to its inhabitants—whom they packed off somewhere else, and turned its once-sacred soil into a mass of gun-emplacements. It had the hell bombed out of it in W.W. II, and is now *a bird sanctuary*. Grimm says that there are "similar names, often confounded with it," and next turns his attention to Scandinavia; I turn mine...somewhere else.

Now, considering the origins of the words Hel or Hell, old Jakob Karl Ludwig G. notes, (p. 315) "In the south of Holland, where the Meuse falls into the sea, is a place called

Helvoetsluis. I do not know if any forms in old documents confirm the idea contained in the name, of Hell-foot [*Helvoet*], foot of Hell. The Romans have a Helium here..." It is a commonplace of geography that, for one, names are duplicated (and sometimes more: twenty-four *Philadelphias* in the ancient world!); for another, names move around. Sometimes names are abbreviated, distorted; for *Helium*, try *Helm.* You've tried it and you don't like it? Try Herm. Herm. The l/r shift, or r/l shift, is almost universal. Grimm (p. 1388) quotes, "'to make believe our Lord is called *Herm.*'" I suggest this indicated some lingering memory of some holiness attached to the word. However backwardly.

Herm. Never mind Prince Blücher and his goddamned wallabies; consider this brief summary: "Herm is somewhat less than 3 miles distant from Guernsey...at present comprises about 400 acres of land, [and] was in early times the abode of monks."—Or, in other words, *herm*its. And Guernsey, one of the Channel Islands of Great Britain, is [35] miles west of France. Or Gaul...

Grimm, p. 802: "The O[ld] Saxons at first, while their own hellia [remember Helium?] still sounded too heathenish, preferred to take from the Latin Bible *infern*, gen. *Infernes...* and even shortened it down to *fern*..." As examples of consonantal shifts, try Spanish *h*idalgo and Portuguese *f*idalgo, try Hebrew Abra*m* and Spanish Abra*n*. H/f, f/h, m/ n...Fern=Herm. Eh?

Well, well, I hear you whispering, "why nothing is easier than mere tinkerings with words and letters; and what could be hellish about a mere 400 acre islet whose climate is bland enough to breed wallabies?" But tut. In the beginning hel or hell meant *bright*, with anyway an implication of holy. It was where the good old heathens went, in the good old heathen days. They *went west*, my dears, because the bright *sun* goes *west*, and then the sun *dies*, don't you see. And the furthermost west is an island off the coast of furthermost Gaul. Is there a "rocky pinnacle" on Herm? How the hell do *I* know. Pay my fare, and I'll go look.

You still won't have Herm as a site for the Wailing of the Gaulish Dead. Some of you are hard to please; have *this*:

> ...darkness had come...We were supping and talking when a horrible rasping cry rang out... It came thrice—in long-drawn blood-curdling succession. Between each wail there was an audible but ghostly indrawing of breath...wild mocking cry...a frightful tell...elusive wail...sobbing wail... wild notes...

Makes you quit shuffling *your* feet, eh? Stick around. And have *this*:

> ...a bedlam of weird screaming. There seemed at first no intelligence in that wild howling—it was the crying of insane spirits wandering without aim and restrain over the rough rocks...Indeed I cannot now describe that noise...Silent except after dark... a babel of varying sounds, some harsh, some soft and crooning...screamed more and more often... wild screams...a half-strangled shout...a half-strangled cry...Shrill yodeling...bellowed...

That's all you're going to get for now. And, no, none of it is from H.P. Lovecraft, either.

Lord Clark reports this. A well-known Continental orchestra conductor is being interviewed in England. "You say that in between rehearsals, you *read*, Dr. Pfiddledick. *What* do you read?" "Oh, Shakespeare, sometimes Goethe." "Yes, but, surely, Dr. Pfiddledick, you must sometimes read purely for relaxation; what do you read *then*?" "Oh, then I read Nietzsche."

If you, too, then you may be disappointed. I am about to

read you from Rabelais.

These passages are from J.M. Cohen's (Penguin, 1955) translation of *The Histories of Gargantua and Pantagruel*.

I'm sure that island will be just another Sark or Herm, which are islands that I saw once between Brittany and England. (p. 592)

The nearer we came, the louder we heard this jangling, and it seemed likely to us that it might be Dodone with its kettles, or the Portico of the Seven Echoes in Olympia, or perhaps the perpetual humming of the Colossus which stands above Memnon's tomb at Thebes in Egypt, or the clanging that was heard of old around a certain tomb on the island of Lipara, one of the Aeolian group. But the topography did not agree with these suppositions. (p. 607)

He showed me the island's chief features, and told us that it had originally been inhabited by the Siticines or Dirge-singers. However, by Nature's ordinance, by which everything changes, they had been turned into birds. (p. 609)

Hereupon I received a full account of all that Atteius Capito, Pollux, Marcellus, Aulus Gellius, Atheneus, Suidas, Ammonius, and others, had written about the Siticinnists; and we had not difficulty giving credence to the transformations of Nyctimine, Procne, Itys, Alcyone, Antigone, Tereus, and others. We raised no doubts either concerning the children of Matabrunem who were changed into swans, or the Pallene, in Thrace, who were suddenly transformed into birds after bathing nine times in the Tritonic lake. (p. 609)

Well! And what are we to make of all *this*? Of any of this? Nothing? Anything? Something? Is good old Father Rabelais, M.D., merely funning us? Merely taking the mickey out of a certain type of scholarship? In a large part, yes, of course he is. But not entirely. The figure and journeys of Don Quixote are fictitious. The same as to Homer in re Odysseus and his Odyssey. And, I think it is safe to say, the same about this series of quotations from *Gargantua and Pantagruel*. There is no sense in trying to make sense of all of it; can we make sense of any of it? Let us see what elements they contain which might apply to our present Adventure. *Sark, Herm, Islands, Brittany, England, Strange Sounds, Tomb, Dirges Sung, Metamorphosis into Birds*, and *Transformations connected with Water*. I don't mean to say, or even imply, that Rabelais is here trying to tell us anything about The Wailing of the Gaulish Dead, but I do mean to imply that there may have remained in France as late as the time of Rabelais (the 1500s) some memories of traditions which may have preserved fragments of accounts originally connected with the matter of that wailing.

Hold on now (you say). When did we see any mention of *Metamorphosis into Birds*? Pray indulge me, sir or madame (I reply), I am about to let you see mention of it now and here, for...says Firestone..."In many places the tradition lingers that migratory birds become men when in other lands." May we turn this over? It now reads, "In many places the tradition lingers that men become migratory birds when in other lands." Including the land of the dead? *Especially* the land of the dead! In a previous Adventure in Unhistory, *The Boy Who Cried Werewolf* (1982), I have gone deeply enough, I hope, into the matter of metamorphosis, metempsychosis, shape-shifting, skin-turning, and lycanthropy, and transformation that I may be excused from going into it all over again here; and if you will accept as a *given* that it was, for that matter *is*, widely believed that human beings alive or dead become or enter into birds, then we can get on with it.—On with what? Why...birds.[14]

Peter Matthiessen says, in his *The Wind Birds* (Viking, N.Y., 1973), as to the marvelous direction-finding ability of birds, "in regard to such a mystery, the exact scientists must do much better than they have done in the way of rigorous explanation if the rest of us, the awe-struck individuals who still glimpse fine strange happenings through the screen of words and facts, are not to continue calling mystery by its proper name."

There is certainly some mystery about the Scilly Isles, which lie off the coast of Cornwall, whose Gaelic-related language died out at the end of the 1700s; the Prince of Wales is also Duke of Cornwall (and also, among other things, Baron Renfrew and Lords of the Isles), in which capacity he receives some rather odd revenues—besides, of course, *cash*: "Tenants used to pay rent in a number of ways: roses, a grain of wheat, pepper, a greyhound, a pair of silver spurs, as well as money. Scilly Isles rent was three hundred puffins, decreased to fifty during the reign of Henry VI." I am glad to have learned this, for otherwise my knowledge of Henry VI would be an absolute minus. My source is *The Queen's Year*, by Andrew Duncan (Doubleday, 1970). The real mystery is, of course, *are* the Scilly Islands the Cassiterides or Iles of Tin, spoken of not only as a trading outpost of the Phoenicians but also as the home of "men in black robes, dressed as the Furies," and alleged to have been Druids? The Druids were of course spread throughout the Celtic world. But their capital or headquarters was in Gaul. —Remember Gaul?

Puffins, eh? And what were *they* valued for? Surely they are not peculiar to the Scilly Isles? Off the coast of Madeira (a Portuguese province lying in the Atlantic nearer to Europe and Africa than the Azores) lie the Desertas; they are truly "desert," for they have no water. Rupert Croft-Cooke writes in his *Madeira* (Putnam, 1961), "For many years the shearwater, whose delightful Latin name is *puffinus puffinus*, yielded valuable down, but the bird is now protected, for the fishermen needed its guidance. 'The eye of the fisherman' it has been called, since it swarms over the small fish where tunny feed"—thus of course disclosing, sans radar, where the tunny (tuna) are. And this brings up more than one provocative thought. Remember those "herds" of dolphin fighting with the "thon," or tuna, in the Bosporus? Remember, too, those flocks of birds, ceaselessly patrolling the Bosporus, and said by the people to be the souls of the damned?—those birds which Procopius could perhaps hardly have helped seeing? But...puffins in Byzantium?

"Look to the puffin, thou sluggard," I murmured to myself...and consulted an ornithological friend, who informed me that "a lot of puffins are called, commonly, '*shearwaters.*'" Well, one thing leads to another, and, under the kindly advice of Dr. William Elwell, who made me free of sundry books, I looked to the *Audubon Guide* of the National Audubon Society (Country Life Press/Doubleday, ed. of 1953). It seems that *all* shearwaters belong to the genus *Puffinus*; that the family *Alcidae* includes auks, murres, and puffins; and that the family *Procellariidae* includes fulmars and shearwaters. So. *The Field Guide to the Birds of Britain and Europe* (alleged headline in British newspaper: Fog Over Channel, Continent Isolated) divulges even more, via its authors or editors, Messrs. R.T. Peterson, Guy Mountfort, and P.A.D. Hollam; and its publishers, Riverside Press, 1967; to *wit*: the Eastern Mediterranean race of shearwater, or *puffinus puffinus yelkouan* (would *I* kid with *you*?), ranges through Corsica, Italy, the southern Adriatic, northern Greece, and the eastern coast of Turkey—and yet another race, the Common or Manx shearwater, *puffinus puffinus puffinus* (would *I* kid—?), is found flitting, or one might say fluttering, or shall we simply say, flying, as well as, ha ha, breeding, from southern Iceland through the Faroes and Shetlands and northern Scotland, through England and

Ireland, and at the extreme, or furthermost western tip, of Brittany: in other words, *Gaul*.

Well, you may ask, and what *of* it? Was Homer a bird-watcher? Was Claudian? Procopius? What does it matter if shearwaters *were* found in both Gaul and Byzantium, and places in between, as well as further north? Well, I have to inform you that the first paragraph quoted on page 26, the one beginning *darkness had come*, is taken from T.A. Coward's *Bird Haunts and Nature Memories*; and that the paragraph right after it, the one beginning *a bedlam of weird screaming*, is from R.M. Lockley's book *The Shearwaters* (London, J.M. Dent, 1943). Go back and re-read them. Need I tell you that both refer to the cries and calls, the sounds, the noise, of the shearwaters? I shall now proceed to tell you even more, from...practically...all around the world. George C. Munro, in his *Birds of Hawaii* (Bridgeway Press, 1966) reveals that the wedge-tailed shearwater nests in "burrows...Its cry is a series of groans, snores and *wails* [italics mine], with an intensely weird effect when a large number of birds are performing." He says that "During the mating, hatching and nurturing of the young large numbers come in to the breeding islands from the sea from early dusk till midnight. Numbers leave at daybreak..." Of the Christmas Island shearwater, "Large numbers came to the island in the evenings and filled the air with their groans." Newell's shearwater: "...uttering its eery cry 'ao'" (Odysseus: "The tribes of the dead came up and gathered round me in their tens of thousands, raising their eerie cry.") Newell's shearwater "came only at long intervals and *was thought an omen of death by the natives*." [Italics mine.]

From the *Audubon Guides: All the Birds of Eastern and Central North America*, by Richard H. Pough (Doubleday, 1953): Sooty shearwater. "Voice: A squawk or cackle. On breeding grounds it is very noisy, uttering many *weird*, guttural, choking sounds." Nest: "[...] in an underground chamber lined with plant material at the end of a 3- or 4-

foot burrow..." The Common or Manx shearwater. Habits: "Breeding colonies are generally in grass-covered areas on small coastal islands...Voice: A babel of guttural, half-strangled clucking or cooing notes, *heard only at night*..." Nest: Underground. The Dusky or Audubon's shearwater: "About the breeding areas at night they are noisy, uttering *mournful*, cat-like mews"; (Claudian: "There is heard the *mournful* weeping of the spirits of the dead.") and "plaintive, liquid, twittering notes." The Great or Greater Shearwater. "When fighting over food or frightened, the birds utter peculiar grunting and *wailing* sounds." Nest: In a burrow. Cinereous or Cory's shearwater. "Voice: On breeding grounds all through the night the birds utter harsh, guttural *wails*... Nest: In burrows...or in crevices and holes in rock."

More. From Richard ffrench's *Guide to the Birds of Trinidad and Tobago* (Livingstone, 1973). Audubon's or Dusky-backed; Dusky; "Diablotin" shearwater. "Voice: a *weird* caterwauling, heard at the breeding grounds *at night*. [...] Nesting [...] usually in a burrow."

—And, returning once again to Peterson, Mountfort, and Hollom: Cory's shearwater is "Nocturnal at breeding grounds...Voice: On breeding grounds, a long *wailing* note... Breeds socially in crevices among rocks on islands."

And yet one more.

> It took us till dark to get the camp set up and functioning properly. As the green twilight faded and the sky turned velvety black, awash with stars, as if at a given signal there arose the most extraordinary noise from the bowels of the earth. It started softly, almost tunefully, a sound like a distant pack of wolves, *howling mournfully* [Claudian: "mournful weeping"] across some remote, snowbound landscape. Then, as more and more voices joined the chorus, it became a gigantic, mad mess in some Bedlamite cathedral. [Lockley:

"On dark nights in March," in Britain, "the calls increase in frequency until what we called 'bedlam' nights occur."] You could hear the lunatic cries of the priests and the wild responses... [Lockley: "...the crying of insane spirits..."] This lasted for about half an hour, the sounds rising and falling, the ground throbbing with the noise, and then, as suddenly as if the earth had burst open and released all the damned souls from some Gustave Doré subterranean hell, out of the holes concealed by the green meadows, mewing and honking and moaning, the baby shearwaters burst forth. They appeared in hundreds, as if newly-arisen from the grave...providing such a cacophony of sound that we could scarcely hear each other speak. [...] This lasted till dawn.

This last took place on Round Island, Mauritius, in the western Indian Ocean. It is a vivid and a striking testimonial, coming as it does from the opposite hemisphere, many thousands of miles away: the writer is Gerald Durrell, in his book *Golden Bats and Pink Pigeons: A Journey to the Flora and Fauna of a Unique Island* (Simon and Schuster, 1977). I have transcribed these descriptions of the cries and habits of the shearwaters as I have found them, for it seems that the testimony of many observers confirms that there is certainly a certain common quality to the cries and calls of the shearwater, regardless of which shearwater, or where it may be found...If it may be found...more of that, later. It is interesting that not a single one of the literary naturalists who I have cited has made a single reference, not one in any of the books from which I've quoted, to The Wailing of the Gaulish Dead! Am I indeed the first to have put all of this together? It has taken me a very long time, I can assure you. I wish I knew if the shearwater *does* nest in any of the Channel Islands. Perhaps Gerald Durrell might know, for he directs the excellent work of the Jersey Wild Life Preservation Trust in the Channel Island of that name, only [26] miles from the C.I. of Guernsey, which is itself a bare three miles from Herm. And so, again, back to Herm.

Herm. We have here *Some Lovely Islands*, by Leslie Thomas (Coward-McCann, 1968), and Mr. Thomas has here...well, let's see. "The northern nose of Herm used to be called Les Hommes...but to most...it has become...the Common... It was here that the ancients buried their dead." Well, you say, and what of it?—had to bury them *some*where; *dead*, you know. Just wait. "—buried their dead, and their tufty burrows sit aptly amid the mounds...Thousands of people were buried on Herm, and, since the island up to the 18th century was all but barren, it seems logical that tribes from the other [Channel] Islands and from France must have used it as a depository for the dead, leaving a solemn few of their people ashore to see that the graves were tended or whatever they did to graves in those lost days.

"It seems that the name Herm is some form of Rima, the word the Romans gave to the island...meaning open and barren." Doesn't fit *my* explanation of the name, does it? Oh, well. However. Not so fast. *It seems logical that tribes from the other islands and from France*...Well, it doesn't seem logical to *every*body; I wrote to Mr. John Christopher, author of *No Blade of Grass* and other well-known novels, who lived for many years on Guernsey; and Mr. Christopher was kind enough to reply: "...it is just possible that people from *Guernsey* may have ferried their dead over there. (It's three miles of choppy sea, and the project would need to be well-motivated.) I find it just about impossible to believe, however, that bodies were brought from the French coast, which is only discernible as a faint smudge on very good days. The distances in those regions are greater than people think." So.

Hm. Well, perhaps ecological conditions on Herm have changed, perhaps it didn't used to be so barren as later and had a larger population; perhaps it used to be a part of Guernsey, perhaps Guernsey (and Herm) used to be part of the mainland. And how ancient is "ancient"? Isn't there a reference...somewhere...that the burials are Neolithic? Doesn't "barrows" imply a much higher degree of antiquity than merely early classical times? Besides...really, it would only be necessary for knowledge of old burials on Herm to have passed to the mainland for the legend to grow.

And grow, and...*On the other hand*. "Well-motivated," well, *here*'s an interesting motivation, and from Mr. Thomas again, though this time he is speaking of the Scilly Islands.

> ...they float...when they lie in the sun's westering path, more like optical illusions, mirages, than a certain reality...the appearance...is of one island; which has a justice in it, since in remote antiquity all the larger islands except St. Agnes very probably were conjoined. At Land's End [Cornwall] you already stand on territory haunted by much earlier mankind. Their menhirs and quoits and stone lines brood...even today the Scillies can in certain lights...re-become the Hesperidean Islands of the Blest; Avalon, Lyonesse, Glasinnis, the Land of the Shades; regain all the labels that countless centuries of Celtic folklore and myth have attached to them. Adam and Eve braved the sea, probably as long as four thousand years ago. Their burial places are scattered all over the present islands, and so densely in places that one suspects the Scillies must have been the ultimate Forest Lawn of megalithic Britain, though interment there would not have been an ambition of only the dying. The spirits of the dead could not cross water, and

the living may well have cherished that thirty-mile *cordon sanitaire* between themselves and their ancestors.

And that's another explanation.

Here's another, and one that comes close, very close, to my own in all but geography; its source is, again, Armstrong's *Folklore of Birds*. "So many superstitions about bird-human transformations are concerned with birds whose voices have a human quality that the most plausible explanation of the Birds of Diomedes is that the legend of their earlier existence in human form arose through seafarers landing near the breeding colony being impressed by the moaning, wailing and squalling underground noises on an island over which shearwaters flitted restlessly in the dusk. It may be that the *Isole dei Triniti* were regarded as haunted by human spirits long before the reputed landing of Diomedes and his companions." And goes on to emphasize "the impression made on people by the calling of [birds] arriving on dark nights from their northern breeding grounds," which, their arrival being unseen and their breeding taking place underground, may have been in effect invisible—small wonder that, being far from inaudible, they were regarded as "souls...death omens..."

Mr. Robin Mead does not refer to any of this in his up-to-date and fairly matter-of-fact *The Channel Islands* (Batsford, 1979); although he does say that Herm seems to have a "fairytale atmosphere"; more to our point he adds to what Mr. Thomas says. "The twin hills of Le petit Monceau and Le grand Monceau form the southern boundary of the Common, and their lower slopes were once a Neolithic burial ground. Indeed, the entire northern part of the island is of considerable archaeological and historical interest, for there are numerous cromlechs and stone circles [the remote source of Homer's "rocky pinnacle"?] there and bones and pottery fragments dating back to prehistoric times have been unearthed. It is thought that this part of Herm may once have been a burial ground not only for people from neighbouring Guernsey, but also from the coast of Normandy [adjacent to Brittany]. Major Wood's charming wife, Jenny, a sensible yet sensitive woman, says that the Commons has a strangely haunted air, as if great emotions have been aroused there at some time which still linger to charge the atmosphere. Mrs. Wood is not alone in feeling this, for many visitors to the island have gone away with a similar impression of the Common."

Professor Wimberly asked, of "*The ballad geography of spiritland...the abode of the departed...is it over the sea, or on an island?*" And we might ask, if the latter, over which sea? or on what island? Blind Homer harped of burning Troy, but of not burning Troy alone. Somewhere in the restricted, eastern Mediterranean world which was his—the mainland of Greece, the isles of Greece, Ionian and Adriatic and Ægæan, Asia Minor to the east and Italy to the west—there came, and there come, a kind of shearwater whose nocturnal cries from out beneath the burrowed ground sounded so eerie and so plaintive in their hundreds and their thousands, that they were thought to be the despairing ululations of the dead. The magic of Homer's harp transferred all this further to the west—where as it happens (and, did Homer know it to be so? perhaps...perhaps), another kind of shearwater also nests in the hollowed rock and earth, also shrieking and moaning. Well more than a thousand years after Homer, the paler talent of the poet Claudian took up the theme; through him we know the site was thought to be that peninsula of Brittany, once Gaul, outthrust into the remote Atlantic. I have suggested, as others have suggested, that it might be the Channel Island of Herm...although the later legend of Procopius seems to remove it rather north somewhat...others yet suggest, perhaps the Scilly Isles. All, all, are, or were once, part of the widespread, mist-shrouded, bird-haunted Celt-lands: the Gaels and Gauls and Gallicians, where the Welsh whose name for themselves is Cymri may have been thought to have lived in Cimmerian darkness amidst a perpetual mist. Somewhere thereabouts, then,

> *There is a place where Gaul*
> *stretches her furthermost shore*
> *spread out before the waves of*
> *Ocean...*

>   *There is heard*
> *the mournful weeping of the*
> *spirits of the dead...*

But enough. I wish to close this Adventure of The Wailing of the Gaulish Dead with another paragraph from Peter Matthiessen; he refers in fact not to the shearwaters but to other birds, traditionally, of omen: the curlew. And the golden plover.

> Both birds were known as harbingers of death, and in the sense that they are birds of passage, that in the wild melodies of their calls, in the breath of vast distance and bare regions that attend them, we sense intimations of our own mortality, there is justice in the legend. Yet it is not the death sign that the curlews bring, but only the memory of life, of a high beauty passing swiftly, as the curlew passes, leaving us in solitude of an empty beach, with summer gone, and a wind blowing.

...there is justice in the legend.

ENDNOTES

[1]With the **ng** as in singing.

[2]One jigger of kirsch, one jigger of maraschino, one jigger of vodka, *lots* of cream, top off with club soda, and shake, stir, jostle, or bump. *Deadly.* The Greeks had a word for it, but preferred hemlock.

[3]Told me by Sgt. Jack Jones WWI based on something told him by his father, a veteran of the Indian Wars.

[4]Though these warmths are not of the same degree exact, as **The Matter** doth aver.

[5]Let me emphasize that I do not here use mystery in a religious sense.

[6]*Claudian, with an English Translation by Maurice Platnauer*, Vol. I. William Heinemann, 1963.

[7]Look up in a *good* Classical dictionary.

[8]Could this mean that it is a day and a night from Gaul to Guernsey but only an hour (with good wind and weather) from Guernsey to Herm?

[9]Italics mine.

[10]¿Hibernia=Herm...? via *Ierne.*

[11][compare lines from Sindbad..."we...sailed athwart the dashing sea swollen with clashing billows..." (Burton)].

[12]Italics mine.

[13]Italics mine.

[14]Here is one reference out of possible thousands: "*Absence and Recall of the Soul* [...] There is a German belief that the soul escapes from a sleeper's mouth in the form of... a little bird." (*The Golden Bough* by J.G. Frazer, Macmillan, 1960).

ABOUT THE AUTHOR

Avram Davidson (1923 – 1993)

Avram Davidson (1923 – 1993) was born in New York in 1923 and was active in SF fandom from his teens. He is remembered as a writer of fantasy fiction, science fiction, and crime fiction, as well as many stories that defy easy categorization. Among his SF and Fantasy awards are two Hugos, two World Fantasy Awards, and a World Fantasy Life Achievement award; he also won a Queen's Award and an Edgar Award in the mystery genre. Although best known for his writing, Davidson also edited *The Magazine of Fantasy and Science Fiction* from 1962 to 1964. He died in 1993.

ALSO BY AVRAM DAVIDSON

Vergil Magus
The Phoenix and the Mirror (1969)
Vergil in Averno (1986)
The Scarlet Fig: Or Slowly Through a Land of Stone (2005)

Kar-Chee
Rogue Dragon (1965)
The Kar-Chee Reign (1966)

Peregrine
Peregrine: Primus (1971)
Peregrine: Secundus (1981)
Peregrine Parentus and Other Tales (with Ethan Davidson) (2016)

Other Novels
Joyleg (with Ward Moore) (1962)
Mutiny in Space (1964)
Rork! (1965)
Masters of the Maze (1965)
Clash of the Star-Kings (1966)
The Enemy of My Enemy (1966)
The Island Under the Earth (1969)
Ursus of Ultima Thule (1973)
Marco Polo and the Sleeping Beauty (with Grania Davis) (1987)
The Boss in the Wall: A Treatise on the House Devil (with Grania Davis) (1998)

Beer! Beer! Beer! (2021)

Collections
Or All the Seas with Oysters (1962)
Crimes & Chaos (1962)
What Strange Stars and Skies (1965)
Strange Seas and Shores (1971)
The Enquiries of Doctor Eszterhazy (1975)
The Redward Edward Papers (1978)
The Best of Avram Davidson (1979)
Avram Davidson: Collected Fantasies (1982)
The Adventures of Doctor Eszterhazy (1990)
Adventures in Unhistory: Conjectures on the Factual Foundations of Several Ancient Legends (1993)
The Avram Davidson Treasury (1998)
The Investigations of Avram Davidson (1999)
Everybody Has Somebody in Heaven (2000)
The Other Nineteenth Century (2001)
Limekiller! (2003)
AD 100 – Volumes I & II (2023)

Coming Soon
Dragons in the Trees
Dear Annie Vandergale

www.ingramcontent.com/pod-product-compliance
Lightning Source LLC
Chambersburg PA
CBHW030742030726
47497CB00001B/101